Books by
Kim Harrison

PALE DEMON
BLACK MAGIC SANCTION
WHITE WITCH, BLACK CURSE
THE OUTLAW DEMON WAILS
FOR A FEW DEMONS MORE
A FISTFUL OF CHARMS
EVERY WHICH WAY BUT DEAD
THE GOOD, THE BAD, AND THE UNDEAD
DEAD WITCH WALKING

White Witch, Black Curse

KIM HARRISON

HARPER

An Imprint of HarperCollinsPublishers

HARPER Voyager

An Imprint of HarperCollins*Publishers*
10 East 53rd Street
New York, New York 10022–5299

Copyright © 2009 by Kim Harrison
Excerpt from *Black Magic Sanction* copyright © 2010 by Kim Harrison
Author photo by Kate Thornton
Cover art by Larry Rostant
ISBN 978–0–06–113802–7
www.harpervoyagerbooks.com

First Harper Voyager mass market printing: March 2011
First Eos mass market printing: December 2009
First Eos hardcover printing: March 2009

Harper Voyager and Ↄ® is a registered trademark of HCP LLC.

Printed in the U.S.A.

10 9 8 7 6 5 4

To the guy who finishes my sentences
and gets my jokes. Even the lame ones.

Acknowledgments

I'd like to thank my editor, Diana Gill. The more I know, the harder her job looks. And my agent, Richard Curtis, my knight in shining armor.

White Witch, Black Curse

One

The bloody handprint was gone, wiped from Kisten's window but not from my memory, and it ticked me off that someone had cleaned it, as if they were trying to steal what little recollection I retained about the night he'd died. The anger was misplaced fear if I was honest with myself. But I wasn't. Most days it was better that way.

Stifling a shiver from the December chill that had taken the abandoned cruiser, now in dry dock rather than floating on the river, I stood in the tiny kitchen and stared at the milky plastic as if willing the smeared mark back into existence. In the near distance came the overindulgent, powerful huff of a diesel train crossing the Ohio River. The scrape of Ford's shoes on the metallic boarding ladder was harsh, and worry pinched my brow.

The Federal Inderland Bureau had officially closed the investigation into Kisten's murder—Inderland Security hadn't even opened one—but the FIB wouldn't let me into their impound yard without an official presence. That meant intelligent, awkward Ford, since Edden thought I needed more psychiatric evaluation and I wouldn't come in anymore. Not since I fell asleep on the couch and everyone in the FIB's Cincinnati office had heard me snoring. I didn't need evaluation. What I needed was something—anything—to rebuild my memory. If it was a bloody handprint, then so be it.

"Rachel? Wait for me," the FIB's psychiatrist called, shifting my worry to annoyance. *Like I can't handle this? I'm a big girl.* Besides, there wasn't anything left to see; the FIB had cleaned everything up. Ford had obviously been out here earlier—given the ladder and the unlocked door—making sure everything was sufficiently *tidy* before our appointment.

The clatter of dress shoes on teak pushed me forward, and I untangled my arms from themselves and reached for the tiny galley table for balance as I headed to the living room. The floor was still, which felt weird. Beyond the short curtains framing the now-clean window were the dirty gray and brilliant blue tarps of boats at dry dock, the ground a good six feet below us.

"Will you hold up?" Ford asked again, the light eclipsing as he entered. "I can't help if you're a room away."

"I'm waiting," I grumbled, coming to a halt and tugging my shoulder bag up. Though he'd tried to hide it, Ford had some difficulty getting his butt up the ladder. I thought the idea of a psychiatrist afraid of heights was hilarious, until the amulet he wore around his neck turned a bright pink when I mentioned it and Ford went red with embarrassment. He was a good man with his own demons to circle. He didn't deserve my razzing.

Ford's breathing slowed in the chill silence. Wan but determined, he gripped the table, his face whiter than usual, which made his short black hair stand out and his brown eyes soulful. Listening in on my feelings was draining, and I appreciated his wading through my emotional crap to help me piece together what had happened.

I gave him a thin smile, and Ford undid the top few buttons of his coat to reveal a professional cotton shirt and the amulet he wore while working. The metallic ley line charm was a visual display of the emotions he was picking up. He felt the emotions whether he was wearing the charm or not, but those around him had at least the illusion of privacy when he took it off. Ivy, my roommate and business partner, thought it stupid to try to break witch magic with human psychology in order to recover my memory, but I was desperate. Her efforts to find out who had killed Kisten were getting nowhere.

Ford's relief at being surrounded by walls was almost palpable, and seeing him release his death grip on the table, I headed for the narrow door to the living room and the rest of the boat. The faint scent of vampire and pasta brushed against me—imagination stoked by a memory. It had been five months.

My jaw clenched, and I kept my eyes on the floor, not wanting to see the broken door frame. There were smudges of dirt on the low-mat carpet that hadn't been there before, marks left by careless people who didn't know Kisten, had never known his smile, the way he laughed, or the way his eyes crinkled up when he surprised me. Technically an Inderland death without human involvement was out of the FIB's jurisdiction, but since the I.S. didn't care that my boyfriend had been turned into a blood gift, the FIB had made an effort just for me.

Murder was never taken off the books, but the investigation had been officially shelved. This was the first chance I'd had to come out here to try to rekindle my memory. Someone had nicked the inside of my lip trying to bind me to them. Someone had murdered my boyfriend twice. Someone was going to be in a world of hurt when I found out who they were.

Stomach fluttering, I looked past Ford to the window where the bloody handprint had been, left like a signpost to mock my pain without giving any prints to follow. *Coward.*

The amulet around Ford's neck flashed to an angry black. His eyes met mine as his eyebrows rose, and I forced my emotions to slow. I couldn't remember crap. Jenks, my backup and other business partner, had dosed me into forgetting so I wouldn't go after Kisten's murderer. I couldn't blame him. The pixy was only four inches tall, and it had been his only option to keep me from killing myself on a suicide run. I was a witch with an unclaimed vampire bite, and that couldn't stand up to an undead vampire no matter how you sliced it.

"You sure you're up to this?" Ford asked, and I forced my

hand down from my upper arm. Again. It throbbed with a pain long since gone as a memory tried to surface. Fear stirred in me. The recollection of being on the other side of the door and trying to break it down was an old one. It was nearly the only memory I had of that night.

"I want to know," I said, but my voice sounded wobbly even to me. I had kicked the freaking door open. I had used my foot because my arm had hurt too much to move. I'd been crying at the time, and my hair had been in my eyes and mouth. I had kicked the door down.

A memory sifted from what I knew, and my pulse hammered as something was added, the recollection of me falling backward, hitting a wall. *My head hit a wall.* Breath held, I looked across the living room, staring at the featureless paneling. Right there. *I remember.*

Ford came unusually close. "You don't have to do it this way."

Pity was in his eyes. I didn't like it there, directed at me, and his amulet turned silver as I gathered my will and passed through the door frame. "I do," I said boldly. "Even if I don't remember anything, the FIB guys might have missed something."

The FIB was fantastic at gathering information, even better than the I.S. It had to be since the human-run institution had to rely on finding evidence, not sweeping the room for emotions or using witch charms to discover who committed the crime and why. Everyone was capable of missing something, though, and that was one of the reasons I was out here. The other was to remember. Now that I was, I was scared. *My head hit the wall . . . just over there.*

Ford came in behind me, watching as I scanned the low-ceilinged living room that stretched from one side of the boat to the other. It looked normal here, apart from the unmoving Cincy skyline visible through the narrow windows. My hand went to my middle as my stomach cramped. I had to do this, no matter what I remembered.

"I meant," Ford said as he put his hands in his pockets, "I've other ways to trigger memories."

"Meditation?" I said, embarrassed for having fallen asleep in his office. Feeling the beginnings of a stress headache, I strode past the couch where Kisten and I had eaten dinner, past the TV that got lousy reception, not that we ever really watched it, and past the wet bar. Inches from the undamaged wall, my jaw began to ache. Slowly I put a hand to the paneling where my head had hit, curling my fingers under when they started to tremble. *My head had hit the wall. Who shoved me? Kisten? His killer?* But the memory was fragmented. There was no more.

Turning away, I shoved my hand in my pocket to hide the slight shaking. My breath slipped from me in an almost-visible cloud, and I tugged my coat closer. The train was long gone. Nothing moved past the curtains but a flapping blue tarp. Instinct told me Kisten hadn't died in this room. I had to go deeper.

Ford said nothing as I walked into the dark, narrow hallway, blind until my eyes adjusted. My pulse quickened as I passed the tiny bathroom where I'd tried on the sharp caps Kisten had given me for my birthday, and I slowed, listening to my body and realizing I was rubbing my fingertips together as they silently burned.

My skin tingled, and I halted, staring at my fingers, recognizing the memory of feeling carpet under my fingers, hot from friction. I held my breath as a new thought surfaced, born from the long-gone sensation. *Terror, helplessness. I had been dragged down this hall.*

A flash of remembered panic rose, and I squelched it, forcing my breath out in a slow exhalation. The lines I'd made in the carpet had been erased by the FIB vacuuming for evidence, erased from my memory by a spell. Only my body had remembered, and now me.

Ford stood silently behind me. He knew something was trickling through my brain. Ahead was the door to the bedroom, and my fear thickened. That was where it had happened. That was where Kisten had lain, his body torn and savaged, slumped against the bed, his eyes silvered and truly dead. *What if I remember it all? Right here in front of Ford and break down?*

"Rachel."

I jumped, startled, and Ford winced. "We can do this another way," he coaxed. "The meditation didn't work, but hypnosis might. It's less stressful."

Shaking my head, I moved forward and reached for the handle of Kisten's room. My fingers were pale and cold, looking like mine but not. Hypnosis was a false calm that would put off the panic until the middle of the night when I'd be alone. "I'm fine," I said, then pushed the door open. Taking a slow breath, I went in.

The large room was cold, the wide windows that let in the light doing little to keep out the chill. Arm clutched against me, I looked to where Kisten had been propped up against the bed. *Kisten.* There was nothing. My heart ached as I missed him. Behind me, Ford started to breathe with an odd regularity, working to keep my emotions from overwhelming him.

Someone had cleaned the carpet where Kisten had died for the second and final time. Not that there had been much blood. The fingerprint powder was gone, but the only prints they had found were from me, Ivy, and Kisten—scattered like signposts. There'd been none from his murderer. Not even on Kisten's body. The I.S. had probably cleaned his corpse between when I'd left to kick some vampire ass and my bewildered return with the FIB after I'd forgotten everything.

The I.S. didn't want the murder solved, a courtesy to whoever Kisten's last blood had been given as a thank-you. Inderland tradition came before society's laws, apparently. The same people I'd actually once worked for were covering it up, and that pissed me off.

My thoughts vacillated between rage and a debilitating heartache. Ford panted, and I tried to relax, for him if nothing else. Blinking back the threatened tears, I stared at the ceiling, breathing in the cold, quiet air and counting backward from ten, running through the useless exercise Ford had given me to find a light state of meditation.

At least Kisten had been spared the sordidness of being drained for someone's pleasure. He had died twice in quick succession, both times probably trying to save me from the vampire he'd been given to. His necropsy had been no help at all. Whatever had killed him the first time had been repaired by the vampire virus before he died again. And if what I'd told Jenks before losing my memory was true, he'd died his second death by biting his attacker, mixing their undead blood to kill them both. Unfortunately, Kisten hadn't been dead for long. It might only have left his much older attacker simply wounded. I just didn't know.

I mentally reached zero, and calmer, I moved toward the dresser. There was a shirt box on it, and I almost bent double in heartache when I recognized it.

"Oh God," I whispered. My hand went out, turning to a fist before my fingers slowly uncurled and I touched it. It was the lace teddy Kisten had given me for my birthday. I'd forgotten it was here.

"I'm sorry," Ford rasped, and my gaze blurring from tears, I saw him slumped in the threshold.

My eyes squinted shut to make the tears leak out, and I held my breath. My head pounded, and I took a gasping breath only to hold it again, struggling for control. Damn it, he had loved me, and I had loved him. It wasn't fair. It wasn't right. And it was probably my fault.

A soft sound from the threshold told me Ford was struggling, and I forced myself to breathe. I had to get control of myself. I was hurting Ford. He was feeling everything I was, and I owed him a lot. Ford was the reason I hadn't been hauled in for questioning by the FIB despite my working for them occasionally. He was human, but his curse of being able to feel another's emotions was better than a polygraph or truth charm.

He knew I'd loved Kisten and was terrified of what had happened here. "You okay?" I asked when his breathing evened out.

"Fine. Yourself?" he said in a wispy voice.

"Peachy keen," I said, gripping the top of the dresser. "I'm sorry. I didn't know it was going to be this bad."

"I knew what I was in for when I agreed to bring you out here," he said, wiping a tear from his eye that I no longer would cry for myself. "I can take anything you dish out, Rachel."

I turned away, guilty. Ford stayed where he was, the distance helping him cope with the overload. He never touched anyone except by accident. It had to be a crappy way to live. But as I rocked away from the dresser, there was a soft pull as my fingertips left the underside of the dresser top. *Sticky.* Sniffing my fingertips, I found the faint bite of propellant.

Sticky web. Someone had used sticky web and smeared it off on the underside of the dresser top. Me? Kisten's murderer? Sticky web worked only on fairies and pixies. It was little more than an irritant to anyone else, like a spiderweb. Jenks had begged off coming out here on the excuse of it being too cold, which it was, but maybe he knew more than he was saying.

My heartache eased from the distraction, and kneeling, I dug in my bag for a penlight and shined it on the underside of the lip of the dresser. I'd be willing to bet no one had dusted it. Ford came close, and I snapped the light off and stood. I didn't want FIB justice. I wanted my own. Ivy and I would come out later and do our own recon. Test the ceiling for evidence of hydrocarbons, too. Shake Jenks down to find out just how long he'd been with me that night.

Ford's disapproval was almost palpable, and I knew if I looked, his amulet would be a bright red from picking up my anger. I didn't care. I was angry, and that was better than falling apart. With a new feeling of purpose, I faced the rest of the room. Ford had seen the smeared mess. The FIB would reopen the case if they found one good print—other than the one

I'd just made, that is. This might be the last time I was allowed in here.

Leaning back against the dresser, I closed my eyes and crossed my arms, trying to remember. Nothing. I needed more. "Where's the stuff?" I asked, both dreading and eager to realize what else lay hidden in my mind, ready to surface.

There was the sound of sliding plastic, and Ford reluctantly handed me a packet of evidence bags and a stack of photos. "Rachel, we should leave if there's a viable print."

"The FIB has had five months," I said, nervous as I took them. "It's my turn. And don't give me any crap about disturbing evidence. The entire department has been through here. If there's a print, it's probably one of theirs."

He sighed as I turned to the dresser and arranged the plastic bags, print side down. I took up the photos first, my gaze rising to the reflection of the room behind me.

I moved the picture of the smeared, bloody handprint on the kitchen window to the back of the stack, and tidied the pile with several businesslike taps. I got nothing from the handprint apart from the feeling that it wasn't mine or Kisten's.

The picture of Kisten was absent, thank God, and I crossed the room with a photo of a dent in the wall. Ford was silent as I touched the paneling, and I decided by the lack of phantom pain that I hadn't made it. There'd been a fight here other than mine. Over me, probably.

I slid the photo behind the stack. Under it was a close-up of a shoe imprint taken under the bank of windows. My head started to throb, and with that as a warning, I knew something was here, lurking in my thoughts. Jaw tight, I forced myself to the window, kneeling to run a hand over the smooth carpet, trying to spark a memory even as I feared it. The print was of a man's dress shoe. Not Kisten's. It was too mundane for that. Kisten had kept only the latest fashions in his closet. *Had the shoe been black or brown?* I thought, willing something to surface.

Nothing. Frustrated, I closed my eyes. In my thoughts, the

scent of vampire incense mixed with an unfamiliar aftershave. A quiver rose through me, and not caring what Ford thought, I put my face on the carpet to breathe in the smell of fibers. *Something . . . anything . . . Please. . . .*

Panic fluttered at the edge of my thoughts, and I forced myself to breathe more deeply, not caring that my butt was in the air as primitive switches in my brain fired and scents were given names. *Musky shadows that never saw the sun. The cloying scent of decayed water. Earth. Silk. Candle-scented dust.* They added up to the undead. If I'd been a vampire, I might have been able to find Kisten's killer by scent alone, but I was a witch.

Tense, I breathed again, searching my thoughts and finding nothing. Slowly the feeling of panic subsided and my headache retreated. I exhaled in relief. I'd been mistaken. There was nothing here. It was just carpet, and my mind had been inventing smells as it tried to fulfill my need for answers. "Nothing," I murmured into the carpet, inhaling deeply one last time before I sat up.

A pulse of terror washed through me as I breathed in the scent of vampire. Shocked, I awkwardly scrambled to my feet, staring down at the carpet as if having been betrayed. *Damn it.*

In a cold sweat, I turned away and tugged my coat straight. *Ivy. I'll ask her to come out and smell the carpet,* I thought, then almost laughed. Catching it back in a harsh gurgle, I pretended to cough, fingers cold as I shifted to the next photo.

Oh, even better, I thought sarcastically. Scratch marks on the paneling. My breath came fast and my gaze shot straight to the wall by the tiny closet as my fingertips started to throb. Almost panting, I stared, refusing to go look and confirm that my finger span matched the marks, afraid I might remember something even as I wanted to. I didn't recall making the marks on the wall, but it was obvious my body did.

I'd seen fear before. I'd seen fear bright and shiny when death comes at you in an instant and you can only react. I knew the nauseating mix of fear and hope when death comes slow and you frantically try to find a way to escape it. I'd grown up with old fear, the kind that stalks you from a distance, death lurking on the horizon, so inevitable and inescapable that it loses its power. But this outright panic with no visible reason was new, and I trembled as I tried to find a way to deal with it. *Maybe I can ignore it. That works for Ivy.*

Clearing my throat, I tried for an air of nonchalance as I set the remaining pictures on the dresser and spread them out, but I wasn't fooling anyone.

Smears of blood—not splattered, but smeared. Kisten's, according to the FIB guys. A picture of a split drawer that had been slid back out of sight. Another useless bloody handprint on the deck where Kisten's killer had vaulted over the side. None of them hit me like the scratches or carpet, and I struggled with wanting to know, but was afraid to remember.

Slowly my pulse eased and my shoulders lost their stiffness. I set the pictures down, bypassing the bags of dust and lint the FIB had vacuumed up, seeing my strands of red curls among the carpet fuzz and sock fluff. I watched myself in the mirror as my fingers touched the hair band in a clear evidence bag. It was one of mine, and it had held my braid together that night. A dull throb in my scalp lifted through my awareness, and Ford shifted uneasily.

Shit, the band meant something.

"Talk to me," Ford said, and I pressed my thumb into the rubber cord through the plastic, trying to keep the fear from gaining control again. Evidence pointed at me to be Kisten's killer, hence the not-quite-hidden mistrust I now felt at the FIB, but I hadn't done it. I'd been here, but I hadn't done it. At least Ford believed me. Someone had left the stinking bloody handprints.

"This is mine," I said softly so my voice wouldn't quaver. "I think . . . someone undid my hair." Feeling unreal, I turned the bag over to see that it had been found in the bedroom, and a surge of panic rose from out of nowhere. My heart hammered, but I forced my breathing to steady. Memory trickled back, pieces, and nothing of use. *Fingers in my hair. My face against a wall. Kisten's killer taking my hair out of its braid.* No wonder I hadn't let Jenks's kids touch my hair much the last five months or why I'd freaked when Marshal had tucked my hair behind my ear.

Queasy, I dropped the bag, dizzy when the edges of my sight dimmed. If I passed out, Ford would call someone, and that would be that. I wanted to know. I had to.

The last piece of evidence was damning, and turning to rest my backside against the dresser, I shook a small, unbroken blue pellet to the corner of its bag. It was filled with a now-defunct sleepy-time charm. It was the only thing in my arsenal that would drop a dead vampire.

A faint prickling of the hair on the back of my neck grew as a new thought lifted through me and a whisper of memory clenched my heart. My breath came out in a pained rush, and my head bowed. *I was crying, swearing. Pointing my splat gun, I pulled the trigger. And laughing, he caught the spell.*

"He caught it," I whispered, closing my eyes so they wouldn't fill. "I tried to shoot him, and he caught it without breaking it." My wrist pulsed in pain and another memory surfaced. *Thin fingers gripped my wrist. My hand went numb. A thump when my gun hit the floor.*

"He hurt my hand until I dropped my splat gun," I said. "I think I ran then."

Afraid, I looked at Ford, seeing his amulet purple with shock. My little red splat gun had never been missing, was never recorded as having been here. All my potions were accounted for. Someone had clearly put the gun back where it belonged. I didn't even remember making the sleepy-time charms, but this was clearly one of mine. Where the other six were was a good question.

In a surge of anger, I kicked the dresser with the ball of my foot. The shock went all the way up my leg, and the furniture thumped into the wall. It was stupid, but it felt good.

"Uh, Rachel?" Ford said, and I kicked it again, grunting.

"I'm fine!" I shouted, sniffing back the tears. "I'm freaking fine!" But my lip was throbbing where someone had bitten me; my body was trying to get my mind to remember, but I simply wouldn't let it. Had it been Kisten who had bitten me? His attacker? I hadn't been bound, thank God. Ivy said so, and she would know.

"Yeah, you look fine," Ford said dryly, and I pulled my coat closed and tugged my shoulder bag up. He was smiling at my lost temper, and it made me even madder.

"Stop laughing at me," I said, and he smiled wider, taking off his amulet and tucking it away as if we were finished. "And I'm not done with those," I added as he gathered the pictures.

"Yes, you are," he said, and I frowned at his unusual confidence. "You're angry. That's better than confused or grieving. I hate using clichés, but we can move forward now."

"Psychobabble bull," I scoffed, grabbing the evidence bags before he could take them, too, but he was right. I did feel better. I had remembered something. Maybe human science was as strong as witch magic. Maybe.

Ford took the bags from me. "Talk to me," he said, standing in front of me like a rock.

My good mood vanished, replaced by the urge to flee. Grabbing the shirt box from the dresser, I pushed past him. I had to get out. I had to put some distance between me and the scratch marks on the walls. I couldn't wear the teddy Kisten had given me, but I couldn't leave it here either. Ford could gripe all he wanted about removing evidence from the crime scene. Evidence of what? That Kisten had loved me?

"Rachel," Ford said as he followed, his steps silent on the carpet in the hall. "What do you recall? All I get is emotion. I can't go back and tell Edden you remembered nothing."

"Sure you can," I said, my pace fast and my blinders on as we crossed the living room.

"No, I can't," he said, catching up with me at the broken door frame. "I'm a lousy liar."

I shivered as I crossed the threshold, but the cold brightness of late afternoon beckoned, and I lurched for the door. "Lying is easy," I said bitterly. "Just make something up and pretend it's real. I do it all the time."

"Rachel."

Ford reached out and drew me to a surprised stop in the cockpit. He was wearing winter gloves and had only touched my coat, but it proved how upset he was. The sun glinted on his black hair and his eyes were squinting from the glare. The cold wind shifted his bangs, and I searched his expression, wanting to find a reason to tell him what I remembered, to let go of the them-versus-us attitude between human and Inderlander and just let him help me. Behind him Cincinnati spread in all her mixed-up, comfortable messiness, the roads too tight and the hills too steep, and I could sense the security that so many lives entangled together engendered.

My eyes fell to my feet and the crushed remains of a leaf the wind had dropped here. Ford's shoulders eased as he felt my resolve weaken. "I remembered bits and pieces," I said, and his feet shifted against the polished wood. "Kisten's killer took my hair out of my braid before I kicked the door off the frame. I'm the one who made the scratches by the closet, but I only remember making them, not who I was trying to . . . get away from." My hand fisted, and I shoved it in a pocket, leaving the shirt box tucked under an arm.

"The splat ball is mine. I remember shooting it," I said, throat tight as I flicked my eyes to his and saw his sympathy. "I was aiming at the other vampire, not Kisten. He has . . . big hands." A new pulse of fear zinged through me and I nearly lost it when I remembered the soft feel of thick fingers on my jawline.

"I want you to come in tomorrow," Ford said, his brow pinched in worry. "Now that you have something to work with, I think hypnosis might bring it all together."

Bring it all together? Does he have any idea what in hell he is asking? The blood drained from my face, and I pulled out of his reach. "No." If Ford put me under, I had no idea what might come out.

Fleeing, I dipped under the railing and swung my weight out and onto the ladder. Marshal waited in his big-ass SUV below, and I wanted to be in it with the heater going to try to drive away the chill Ford's words had started. I hesitated, wondering if I should drop the shirt box or keep it tucked under an arm.

"Rachel, wait."

There was the rattle of the lock being replaced, and leaving the box under my arm, I started down, watching the side of the boat as I descended. I toyed with the idea of taking the ladder away to leave him stranded, but he would probably put it in his report. Besides, he did have his cell phone.

Finally I reached the ground. Head down, I placed my boots carefully in the slush, aiming for Marshal's car, parked behind Ford's in the maze of impounded boats. Marshal had offered to bring me out after I'd complained during a hockey game that my little red car would get stuck in the ruts and ice out here, and since my car wasn't made for the snow, I'd said yes.

Guilt tugged at me for avoiding Ford's help. I wanted to find out who'd killed Kisten and tried to make me their shadow, but there were other things I wanted to keep to myself, like why I'd survived a common but lethal blood disease that was also responsible for my being able to kindle demon magic, or what my dad had done in his spare time, or why my mother had nearly gone off her rocker to keep me from knowing my birth father wasn't the man who'd raised me.

Marshal's eyes showed his concern when I got in his SUV and slammed the door. Two months ago, the man had shown up on my doorstep, back in Cincinnati after the Mackinaw Weres had burned his garage down. Fortunately he'd saved both the house and the boat that had been his livelihood—now sold to pay for getting his master's at Cincy's university. We'd met last spring when I was up north rescuing Jenks's eldest son and Nick, my old boyfriend.

Despite my better judgment, we'd been out more than a few times, realizing we had enough in common to probably make a good go of it—if it weren't for my habit of getting everyone close to me killed. Not to mention that he was coming off a psycho girlfriend and wasn't looking for anything serious. The problem was, we both liked to relax doing athletic stuff, ranging from running at the zoo to ice-skating at Fountain Square. We'd kept it friendly but platonic for two months now, shocking the hell out of my roommates. The lack of stress from not wondering will-we, won't-we was a blessing. Curbing my natural tendencies and instead keeping our relationship casual had been easy. I couldn't bear it if he got hurt. Kisten had cured me of foolish dreams. Dreams could kill people. At least, mine could. And did.

"You okay?" Marshal asked, his low voice with his up-north accent heavy with worry.

"Peachy," I muttered as I tossed the box with the teddy onto the backseat and wiped a cold finger against the underside of my eye. When I didn't say anything more, he sighed, rolling his window down to talk to Ford. The FIB officer was making his way to us. I had half a mind to accuse Ford of asking Marshal to drive me here and back, knowing I'd probably need a shoulder to cry on, and though he wasn't my boyfriend, Marshal was a hundred percent better than taking my raw turmoil back to Ivy.

Ford looked up as he angled to my door, not Marshal's, and the tall man behind the wheel silently pressed a button to roll my window down. I tried to roll it back up, but he locked the controls and I gave him a dirty look.

"Rachel," Ford said as soon as he closed the distance between us. "You won't be out of control for even an instant. That's how it works."

Damn it, he had guessed why I was afraid, and embarrassed that he was bringing this up in front of Marshal, I frowned. "We don't have to do it at my office if you're uncomfortable," he added, squinting from the bright December sun. "No one needs to know."

I didn't care if the FIB knew I was seeing their psychiatrist. Hell, if anyone needed counseling, it was me. But still . . . "I'm not crazy," I muttered as I angled the blowing vents to me and my hair flew up from under my hat.

Ford put a hand on the open window in a show of support. "You're probably the sanest person I know. You only look crazy because you've got a lot of weird stuff to deal with. If you want, while you're relaxed, I can give you a way to keep your mouth shut about anything you want under just about any circumstance. Completely confidential, between you and your subconscious." Surprised, I stared at him, and he finished, "I don't even have to know what you're keeping to yourself."

"I'm not afraid of you," I said, but my knees felt funny. *What has he figured out about me that he isn't saying?*

Shifting his feet in the slush, Ford shrugged. "Yes, you are. I think it's cute." He glanced at Marshal and smiled. "Big bad runner who can take down black witches and vampires afraid of little helpless me."

"I am not afraid of you. And you're not helpless!" I exclaimed as Marshal chuckled.

"Then you'll do it," Ford said confidently, and I made a noise of frustration.

"Yeah, whatever," I muttered, then fiddled with the vent again. I wanted to get out of here before he really figured out what was going on in my head—and then told me.

"I have to tell Edden about the sticky silk," Ford said, "but I'll wait until tomorrow."

My eyes flicked to the ladder, still propped against the boat's side. "Thanks," I said, and he nodded, responding to the heavy emotion of gratitude I knew I must be throwing off. My roommate would have time to come out with the Jr. Detective Kit she probably had stashed in her label-strewn closet and take whatever prints she wanted. Not to mention sniffing the carpet.

Ford smiled at a private thought. "Since you won't come in, how about me coming over tonight about . . . six? Somewhere after my dinner and before your lunch?"

I stared at him for his brazenness. "I'm busy. How about next month?"

He ducked his head as if embarrassed, but he was still smiling when he met my gaze. "I want to talk to you before I talk to Edden. Tomorrow. Three o'clock."

"I'm picking my brother up at the airport at three," I said quickly. "I'll be with him and my mother the rest of the day. Sorry."

"I'll see you at six," he said firmly. "By then, you'll be home trying to get away from your brother and your mom, ready for some relaxation. I can teach you a trick for that, too."

"God! I hate it when you do that!" I said, messing with my seat belt so he would take the hint and go away. I was more embarrassed than angry that he'd caught me trying to evade him. "Hey!" I leaned out the window as he turned to go. "Don't tell anyone I had my face on the floor, okay?"

From beside me, Marshal made a wondering sound, and I turned to him. "You either."

"No problem," he said, thunking the SUV into gear and moving forward a few feet. My window went up, and I loosened my scarf as the vehicle warmed. Ford slowly managed the slushy ruts back to his car, pulling his phone from his pocket as he went. Remembering my own phone, on vibrate, I dug my cell out of my bag. Scrolling through the menu to put it on ring, I wondered how I was going to tell Ivy what I remembered without both of us flaking out.

With a small noise of concern, Marshal put his SUV back into park, and my head came up. Ford was standing beside his open door with his phone stuck to his ear. A bad feeling began to trickle through me when he started back to us. It grew worse when Marshal put his window down and Ford stopped beside it. The psychiatrist's eyes carried a heavy worry.

"That was Edden," Ford said as he closed his phone and returned it to his belt case. "Glenn's been hurt."

"Glenn!" I leaned over the center console toward him, getting a good whiff of the scent of redwood coming off Marshal. The FIB detective was Edden's son and one of my favorite people. And now he was hurt. *Because of me?* "Is he okay?"

Marshal stiffened, and I leaned back. Ford was shaking his head and looking at the nearby river. "He was off duty investigating something he probably shouldn't have. They found him unconscious. I'm going to the hospital to see how much damage he's suffered to his head."

His head. Ford meant his brain. Someone had beat him up. "I'm coming, too," I said, reaching for my seat belt.

"I can drive you out," Marshal offered, but I was winding my scarf back up and grabbing my bag.

"No, but thanks, Marshal," I said, my pulse fast as I gave his shoulder a quick touch. "Ford's going out there. I'll, ah, call you later, okay?"

Marshal's brown eyes were worried, and his black hair, tight to his skull, hardly shifted as he nodded. It had been growing in for only a few months, but at least he had eyebrows now. "Okay," he echoed, not giving me any grief for ditching him. "Take care of yourself."

I exhaled, glancing once at Ford, waiting impatiently for me, then back to Marshal. "Thanks," I said softly, and gave him an impulsive kiss on the cheek. "You're a great guy."

I got out, and, pace fast, followed Ford to his car, my thoughts and stomach churning at what we might find at the hospital. Someone had hurt Glenn. Sure, he was a FIB officer and ran the risk of injury all the time, but I had a feeling this involved me. It had to. I was an albatross.

Just ask Kisten.

Two

W̶e'll take the next elevator," the tidy woman said with an overly bright smile as she pulled her confused friend back into the hall and the silver doors slid shut before Ford and me.

Wondering, I glanced at the huge lift. The thing was big enough for a gurney. Ford and I were the only two people in here. But then the woman's harsh whisper of "Black witch" came in just before the doors met, telling me all I needed to know.

"The Turn take it," I muttered, tugging my bag back up on my shoulder.

Beside me, Ford edged away, not enjoying my angry emotions as I fumed. I wasn't a black witch. Okay, so my aura was covered with demon smut. And yeah, I'd been filmed last year being dragged down the street on my ass by a demon. It probably didn't help that the entire universe knew I'd summoned one into an I.S. courtroom to testify against Piscary, Cincinnati's top vampire and my roommate's former master. But I was a white witch. *Wasn't I?*

Depressed, I stared at the dull silver panels of the hospital elevator. Ford was a dark blur beside me, his head bowed as I stewed. I wasn't a demon to be pulled back to the ever-after when the sun rose, but my children would be—thanks to the illegal genetic tinkering of the now-dead Senior Kalamack.

He had unknowingly broken the checks and balances that elves magicked into the demon's genome thousands of years ago, effectively allowing only magically stunted demon children to survive. The elves named the new species witches, telling us lies and convincing us to fight demons in their war. When we found out the truth, we abandoned the elves and demons both, migrating out of the ever-after and doing our best to forget our origins. Which we did admirably, to the point where I was the only witch to know the truth.

Ceri had filled in the gaps of Mr. Haston's sixth-grade history class, having been a demon's familiar before I rescued her. She'd read up on it between twisting curses and planning orgies.

No one knew the truth but me and my partners. And Al, the demon I had a standing teaching date with every Saturday. And Newt, the ever-after's most powerful demon. There was Al's parole officer, Dali. Mustn't forget Trent and whoever he'd told, but that was likely going to be no one, seeing that his dad's breaking of the genetic roadblock had been a stupid thing to do. No wonder they'd killed all the geneticists at the Turn. Too bad they'd missed Trent's dad.

Ford jiggled on his feet, then, looking embarrassed, he pulled a black metal flask from a coat pocket, twisted off the top, tilted his head to the ceiling, and took a swig.

Watching his Adam's apple move, I gave him a questioning look.

"It's medicinal," he said, a charming shade of red as he fumbled recapping it.

"Well, we *are* in a hospital," I said dryly, then snatched it. Ford protested as I took a sniff, then touched it to my lips. My eyes widened. "Vodka?"

Looking even more embarrassed, the slight man took it from my unresisting fingers, capped it, and tucked it away. The elevator chimed and the panels slid apart. Before us was a hallway like any other in the building, with its low-mat carpet, white walls, and banister.

My worry for Glenn came rushing back, and I lurched forward. Ford and I bumped as we got out, and I felt a wash of chagrin. I knew he didn't like to touch anyone. "Can I steady myself on your elbow?" he asked, and I glanced at the pocket he had dropped the flask into.

"Lightweight," I said, reaching out for him, careful to touch him only through his coat.

"I'm not drunk," he said sourly, linking his arm in mine in a motion that held absolutely no romance, but rather, desperation. "The emotions are sharp in here. The alcohol helps. I'm in overload, and I'd rather feel your emotions than everyone else's."

"Oh." Feeling honored, I strode forward with him and past the two orderlies pushing a hamper. My good mood soured when one of them whispered, "Should we call security?"

Ford's grip tightened when I spun to give them my opinion, and the two skittered away like I was the boogeyman. "They're just afraid," Ford said, his fingers tightening on me.

We continued down the hall, and I wondered if they could kick me out. The beginnings of a headache pulsed. "I'm a white witch, damn it," I said to no one, and the guy in a lab coat coming toward us gave us a cursory glance.

Ford was looking pale, and I tried to calm myself before they admitted him. I should step up my efforts to find a muffler for him—other than alcohol, that is.

"Thanks," he whispered as he picked up on my concern, then, voice stronger, he added, "Rachel, you summon demons. You're good at it. Get over it, then find a way to make it work for you. It's not going to go away."

I huffed, ready to tell him he had no right to sound so high and mighty, but turning a liability into an asset was exactly what he had done with his "gift." I gave his arm a squeeze, then started when I saw Ivy, my roommate, bending over the nurses' desk, not caring that a male orderly had just walked into a wall watching her. Her black jeans were low and tight, but she had the body of a model and could get away with it.

The matching cotton pullover was cut high to give a glimpse of her lower back as she craned to see what was on the computer. In deference to the cold, her long leather coat was draped over the counter. Ivy was a living vampire, and she looked it: svelte, dark, and broody. It made it hard to live with her, but I was no picnic either, and we knew each other's quirks.

"Ivy!" I called, and her head turned, her short, enviably straight hair with the gold tips swinging as she came up. "How did you find out about Glenn?"

Ford's shoulders slumped, all his tension slipping from him as he held my arm. He looked happy. But he would, seeing that he was picking up my emotions and I was happy to see Ivy. Perhaps I might invest in a little talk time about Ivy when Ford and I got together again. I could use his insight into our uneasy relationship.

I wasn't Ivy's blood shadow, but her friend. That a vampire could be friends with anyone without sharing blood was unusual, but we had an additional complication. Ivy liked both boys and girls, mixing blood and sex into one and the same. She'd been clear that she wanted me, too, in any capacity, but I was straight, apart from a confusing year of trying to separate blood lust from gender preference. That she'd bitten me more than once hadn't helped. It had seemed like a good idea at the time. The rush from a vampire bite was too close to sexual ecstasy to dismiss, and it had taken me thinking I'd been bound to Kisten's killer to wake me up. The risk of becoming a shadow was too great. I trusted Ivy. It was her blood lust I was worried about.

So we lived together in the church that was also our runner business, sleeping across the hall from each other and doing our best to not push each other's buttons. One might think Ivy would be ticked off after wasting a year chasing me, but she had a blissful happiness that vampires didn't often find. Apparently my telling her I wasn't ever going to let her sink her teeth into me again was the only way she'd believe I liked her for her and not the way she could make me feel. I just admired the hell out of anyone who could be that hard on herself and still be so incredibly strong. And I loved her. I didn't want to sleep with her, but I did love her.

Ivy came to meet us, her small lips closed and her slim boots silent on the carpet. She moved with a memorable grace, and there was a slight grimace on her usually placid face. Her features held a slight Asian cast, having an oval face, a small nose, and a heart-shaped mouth. It was seldom she smiled, afraid the emotion would break her self-control. I think that was one of the reasons we were friends—I laughed enough for both of us. That, and the fact that she thought I could find a way to save her soul when she died and became an undead. Right now, I was just looking to find the rent money. I'd get to my roommate's soul later.

"Edden called the church first," she said by way of greeting, her thin eyebrows high as she spotted Ford's arm linked in mine. "Hi, Ford."

The man reddened at the lilt she'd put in her last words, but I wouldn't let him take his arm back. I liked being needed. "He's having trouble with the background emotion," I said.

"And he'd rather be abused by yours?"

Nice. "Do you know what room Glenn is in?" I said as Ford's arm slipped away.

She nodded, her dark eyes not missing a thing. "This way. He's still not conscious." Ivy headed down the hallway with us in tow, but when we passed the desk, one of the nurses stood, determination on her no-nonsense face. "I'm sorry. No visitors except family."

A pang of fear went through me, not because I might not see Glenn, but that his condition was so serious they wouldn't let anyone in. Ivy didn't slow down, though, and neither did I.

The nurse started after us. My pulse quickened, but another waved us on, then turned to the first nurse. "It's Ivy," the second nurse said, as if that meant something.

"You mean the vampire who's—" the first nurse said, but she was pulled back to the desk before I heard the rest. I turned to Ivy, seeing that her pale complexion had shifted to pink.

"The vampire who's what?" I asked, remembering her stint here as a candy striper.

Ivy's jaw tightened. "Glenn's room is down here," she said, avoiding my question. Whatever.

An unexpected sense of panic hit me when Ivy made a sharp left into a room and vanished behind the oversize door. I stared at it, hearing the soft sounds of delicate machinery. Memories of sitting with my dad as he took his last, struggling breaths swam up, then more recent, of watching Quen fight for his life. I froze, unable to move. Behind me, Ford stumbled, as if I had slapped him.

Crap. I flushed, embarrassed that he was feeling my misery. "I'm sorry," I gushed as he stood in the hallway and held up a hand to tell me he was all right. I thanked God Ivy had already gone in and wasn't seeing what I'd done to him.

"It's okay." His eyes were weary as he came close again, hesitant until he knew I had the old pain safely tucked away. "Can I ask who?"

I swallowed hard. "My dad."

Eyes down, he guided me to the door. "You were about twelve?"

"Thirteen." And then we were inside, and I could see that it wasn't the same room at all.

Slowly my shoulders eased. My dad had died with nothing to save him. As a law enforcer, Glenn was getting the best of everything. His father was in the rocker pulled up to his bedside, ramrod straight. Glenn was being taken care of. Edden was the one in pain.

The small, stocky man tried to smile, but he couldn't do it. In the few hours since learning about his son's attack, his pale face had acquired wrinkles I'd only seen hints of before. In his grip was a winter hat, his short fingers working the rim around and around. He stood, and my heart went out to him when he exhaled, the sound carrying all his fear and worry.

Edden was the captain of the FIB's Cincinnati division, the ex-military man bringing to the office the hard, succeed-against-all-odds determination he'd gained in the service. Seeing him down to the bare bones of himself was hard. The lingering questions in the FIB as to my "convenient" amnesia concerning Kisten's death had never occurred to Edden. He trusted me, and because of that, he was one of the few humans I absolutely trusted in return. His son, unconscious on the bed, was another.

"Thank you for coming," he said automatically, his gravelly voice cracking, and I worked to keep from crying when he ran a blunt hand over his short-cropped, graying hair in a recognizable sign of stress. I came close to give him a hug, and the familiar scent of old coffee hit me.

"You know we wouldn't let you do this alone," Ivy said from her corner where she'd folded herself stiffly into a padded chair, quietly giving support the only way she could.

"How is he?" I asked as I turned to Glenn.

"They won't give me a straight answer," he said, his voice higher than usual. "He's been beaten up pretty bad. Head trauma—" His voice broke, and he went silent.

I looked at Glenn on the bed, his very dark skin standing out starkly against the sheets. There was a white bandage around his head, and they had shaved a swath of his tightly curling black hair. Bruises marked his face, and he had a split lip. A nasty swath of bruised skin ran from his shoulder to under the sheets, and his fingers resting on the blanket were swollen.

Edden sank into his chair and looked at his son's damaged hand. "They wouldn't let me in," he said softly. "They didn't believe I was his father. Bigoted bastards." Slowly his hand went out, and he cradled Glenn's hand as if it were a baby bird.

I swallowed hard at the love. Edden had adopted Glenn when he married his mother—must have been at least twenty years ago—and though they looked nothing like each other, they were exactly alike where it counted, both strong in their convictions and consistently putting their lives in danger to fight injustice. "I'm sorry," I almost croaked, feeling his pain.

In the threshold, Ford closed his eyes, clenched his jaw, and leaned against the frame.

Grabbing a chair, I dragged it across the linoleum to where I could see Edden and Glenn both. My bag went on the floor and my hand on the FIB captain's shoulder. "Who did this?"

Edden took a slow breath. In her corner, Ivy sat up. "He was working on something on his own," the man said, "after hours, in case what surfaced would be better left off the record. One of our officers died last week after a long wasting illness. He was a friend of Glenn's, and Glenn found out he'd been cheating on his wife." Edden glanced up. "Keep that to yourselves."

Ivy got to her feet, interested. "She poisoned her husband?"

The FIB captain shrugged. "That's what Glenn thought, according to his notes. He went to talk to the mistress this morning. That's where—" His voice cut off, and we patiently waited while he steadied himself. "The working theory is," he said softly, "that the husband was there and freaked out, attacked Glenn, and then they both left him for dead in their living room."

"Oh my God," I whispered, going cold.

"He was off duty," Edden continued, "so he lay there almost an hour before someone checked on him because he didn't come in to work. He's a smart kid, and one of his friends knew what he was doing and where he had gone."

My breath caught when Edden turned to me, pain etched deep in his brown eyes as he tried to find an answer. "We never would have found him otherwise. Not in time. They left him there. They could have called 911 and fled, but they left my boy to die."

The warm prick of tears hit me, and I gave the stocky, heartbroken man a sideways hug. "He's going to be okay," I whispered. "I know it." My gaze went to Ford as he came in to stand at the foot of the bed. "Right?"

Ford gripped the footboard as if struggling for balance. "Can I have a moment with Glenn alone?" he asked. "I can't work with all of you in here."

Immediately I stood. "Sure."

Ivy touched the lump that was Glenn's feet as she passed, and she was gone. Edden slowly stood, letting go of his son's hand with an obvious reticence. Leaning over Glenn, he whispered in a severe tone, "I'll be right back. Don't go anywhere, young man. You hear me?"

I drew Edden out of the room. "Come on. I'll get you some coffee. There's gotta be a machine around here somewhere."

I looked back as we left. Glenn looked like crap, but as long as his mind was undamaged, he'd be okay. Ford could tell, couldn't he?

As I escorted Edden down the hallway in Ivy's wake, I felt a moment of guilty relief. At least Glenn hadn't been hurt because of someone trying to get to me. It might sound like vanity on my part, but it had happened before. Ivy's old master vampire had raped her to get her to kill me, had given Kisten to his death for the same reason. Piscary was dead now, Kisten, too; I was alive, and I wasn't going to let others get hurt for me again.

Edden pulled out of my grip when we reached a bench across from a vending machine. Everything was done in institutional comfort: soothing shades of taupe and cushions not soft enough to encourage lingering. A wide window opened onto the snowplowed parking lot, and I sat so my feet were in the shaft of dusky sunlight coming in. There was no warmth. Edden sat beside me with his elbows on his knees, his forehead cupped in his hands. I didn't like seeing the intelligent, quick-fingered man so depressed. I didn't think he even remembered I was here.

"He's going to be okay," I said, and Edden took a deep breath.

"I know he will," he said with a forcefulness that said he wasn't sure. "Whoever did this was a professional. Glenn stumbled into something bigger than a wife cheating on her husband."

Ah hell. Maybe it is my fault. Ivy's shadow fell on us, and I looked up. Her silhouette was sharp against the bright window, and I leaned back into shadow.

"I'll find out who did this," she said, then turned to me. "We both will. And don't insult us by offering to pay for it."

My lips parted in surprise. She had tried to hide herself in shadow, but her words gave away her anger. "I thought you didn't like Glenn," I said stupidly, then went hot.

Her hand moved to her hip. "This isn't a matter of like or dislike. Someone mauled a law officer and left him for dead. The I.S. won't do anything about it, and anarchy can't be allowed a toehold." She turned and the sun came in. "I don't think a human did that to him," she said as she moved to sit across from us. "Whoever it was knew exactly how to cause an excruciating amount of pain without letting him pass out from it. I've seen it before."

I could almost hear her think, *Vampire.*

Edden's hands clenched, then he visibly forced himself to relax. "I agree."

Unable to sit still, I squirmed. "He's going to be okay," I said. Damn it, I didn't know what else to say! Ivy's entire vampiric culture was based on monsters who worked outside the law, people who treated people like boxes of chocolates. The biggest and baddest, the ones who made the rules, got away with anything.

Ivy leaned across the wide space between us. "Give me the address where he was found," she demanded. "I want to look."

Edden pressed his lips together, making his mustache bunch out. It was the first sign of him regaining himself. "Ivy, I appreciate your offer," he said, his voice firm. "But we can handle it. I have people out there right now."

Her eye twitched, and though it was hard to tell, I think her pupils were dilating in pique. "Give me the address," she repeated. "If an Inderlander did this, you're going to need Rachel and me. The I.S. won't help you."

Not to mention that the FIB will probably miss the Inderland stuff, I thought, settling myself with a soft huff more firmly in the thin padding.

Edden eyed her, clearly peeved himself. "My department is working on it. Glenn will be conscious in a few days, and then—"

His eyes closed, and he became silent. Ivy stood, agitated. Almost brutal, she said, "If you don't put the heat on whoever did this in the next few hours, they will be gone." Edden met her eyes and she added more gently, "Let us help. You're too involved. The entire FIB is. You need someone out there who can look at what happened with dispassion, not a desire for revenge."

I made a small noise and crossed my arms over my middle. Revenge was on my mind. "Come on, Edden, this is what we do for a living!" I said. "Why won't you let us help?"

A dry humor was in the short man's eyes as he looked askance at me. "It's what Ivy does for a living. You're not a detective, Rachel. You're a haul-them-in-girl, and none better. I'll let you know when we find out who it is, and if it's a witch, I'll give you a call."

That hit me with all the pleasure of a slap in the face, and my eyes narrowed. Ivy saw my irritation, and she leaned back, content to let me yell at him. But instead of standing up and telling him to get Turned—which wouldn't do anything but get us thrown out—I swallowed my pride, contenting myself with bobbing my foot in anger.

"Then give Ivy the address," I said, wanting to accidentally kick him in the shins. "She can find a fairy fart in a windstorm," I said, borrowing one of Jenks's favorite expressions. "And what if it is an Inderlander? You want to risk losing them because of your *human pride?*"

Maybe that was low, but I was tired of looking at crime scenes after the cleaning crew.

Edden looked from Ivy's mocking expectancy to my admirably contained redhead anger, then pulled out a palm-size spiral notebook. I smiled at the scratch of the pencil as he wrote something down, a pleasant slurry of contentment and anticipation filling me. We'd find whoever attacked Glenn and left him to die. And whoever it was better hope I was there with Ivy, or they'd be subjected to her own personal version of justice.

The sound of the paper tearing free was loud, and with a wry grimace, he extended the strip of white and blue to Ivy. She didn't look at it, handing it to me instead.

"Thank you," I said crisply, tucking it away.

A soft scrape of shoe on carpet brought my attention up, and I followed Ivy's gaze, over my shoulder. Ford was shuffling to us, his head bowed and my bag in his grip. I felt a moment of panic, and in response, he looked up, smiling. My eyes closed. Glenn was okay.

"Thank you, God," Edden whispered, standing up.

I had to hear it, though, and as Ford handed me my forgotten bag and took the cup of coffee Ivy gave him, I asked, "He's going to be okay?"

Ford nodded, eyeing us over the rim of the paper cup. "His mind is fine," he said, grimacing at the coffee's taste. "There's no damage. He's deep into his psyche, but as soon as his body repairs itself enough, he will regain consciousness. A day or two?"

Edden's breath shook as he exhaled, and Ford stiffened when the FIB captain shook his hand. "Thank you. Thank you, Ford. If there's anything I can do for you, let me know."

Ford smiled thinly. "I'm glad I could give you good news." Regaining his hand, he backed up a step. "Excuse me. I need to try to convince the nurses to back off on the meds. He's not in as much pain as they think, and it's slowing down his recovery."

"I'll do it." Ivy eased into motion. "I'll tell them I can smell it. They won't know the difference."

The beginnings of a smile curved my lips up as she almost sauntered down the hall, calling out to one nurse by name. Edden couldn't stop smiling, and I could see a hint of tears in his eyes as he shifted from foot to foot. "I need to make a couple of calls." He reached for his cell phone, then hesitated. "Ford, can Glenn hear me when I talk to him?"

Ford nodded, smiling tiredly. "He might not remember it, but he can."

Edden looked from me to Ford, clearly wanting to be with Glenn. "Go!" I said, giving him a happy little push. "Tell Glenn I want to talk to him when he wakes up."

His steps fast, Edden strode toward Glenn's room. I sighed, glad this story would have a happy ending. I was tired of the other kind. Ford looked pleased, and that was good, too. His life must be hell. No wonder he didn't tell anyone he could do this. They'd work him to death.

"What happened to Glenn's mom?" I asked now that we were alone.

Ford watched Edden wave to the nurses as he passed beyond the wide, smooth door and into Glenn's room. "She died fifteen years ago during a sixty-dollar stab-and-grab."

That's why he's a cop, I thought. "They've had only each other for a long time," I added, and Ford nodded, starting for the elevators. He looked whipped.

Ivy joined us after a last comment to the nurse. Falling into place on my other side, she looked across me to Ford. "What happened at the marina?" she asked as she shrugged into her long coat, and the afternoon's memories rushed back.

Her tone was slightly mocking, and I gave her a sidelong glance. I knew she was secure in her belief that her slow, steady investigations would find Kisten's killer faster than my reconstructing my memories. It was with no little pleasure that I glanced at Ford, then said to her, "Do you have time to go out tonight and smell the carpet?"

Ford chuckled, and Ivy stared, rocking to a halt at the elevators. "Excuse me?"

I punched the button for the lift. "Your nose is better than mine," I said simply.

Ivy blinked, her face blanker than usual. "You found something the FIB missed?"

I nodded as Ford pretended not to listen. "There's sticky silk stuck to the rim of the dresser's top. There might be a print, ah, other than the one I made today. And the floor under the window smells like vampire. It's not you or Kisten, so it might be his murderer."

Again, Ivy stared, looking uncomfortable. "You can tell the difference?"

The elevator doors slid open, and we all entered. "Can't you?" I said, backing up and pushing the button for the street level with a booted toe just because I could.

"I'm a vampire," she said, as if this made all the difference.

"I've lived with you for over a year," I said, wondering if I wasn't supposed to be able to tell the difference. "I know what you smell like," I muttered, embarrassed. "It's no big deal."

"Yes, it is," she whispered as the doors closed, and I hoped Ford hadn't heard.

I watched the numbers count down. "So you'll go out tonight?"

Ivy's eyes were black. "Yes."

I stifled a shiver, glad when the doors opened to show the busy lobby. "Thank you."

"My pleasure," she said, her gray-silk voice so thick with anticipation that I almost pitied the vampire who had killed Kisten.

Almost.

Three

I gripped the wheel of my car tighter in annoyance as Jenks continued to sing. Though the sun was going down and the roads had an arid frozenness, the interior of the car was hot. I had half a mind to turn off the heat. Anything to get Jenks to shut up.

"Five trolls in dra-a-a-a-ag," the four-inch man sang from my shoulder. "Four purple condoms, three French ticklers, two horny vamps, and a succubus in the snow."

"Jenks, enough!" I shouted, and from the passenger seat, Ivy snickered, idly tracing a hand on the inside of the misted window to clear a spot from which to gaze out at the evening. The street was thick with holiday lights, and it was holy and serene, in a money-oriented, middle-class sort of way. Unlike Jenks's carol. Which was thirteen-year-old humor to the max.

"'On the eighth day of Christmas, my true love gave to me—'"

I checked behind me and thunked the brakes. Ivy, with her vamp reflexes, easily caught herself, but Jenks was catapulted from my shoulder. He short-stopped himself inches from the windshield. His dragonfly-like wings were a blur of red and silver, but not a shadow of dust slipped from him, saying he'd half expected this. The smirk on his angular face was classic Jenks.

"What . . . ," he complained, hands on his hips in his best Peter Pan pose.

"Shut. Up." I rolled through the stop sign. It was icy. Safer that way. At least that was going to be my story if a zealous I.S. cop stopped me.

Jenks laughed, his high-pitched voice sounding right with the easy companionship that filled the car and the festive warmth displayed outside it. "That's the trouble with you witches. No Christmas spirit," he said, going to sit on the rearview mirror. It was his favorite spot, and I turned the heater down a smidge. He wouldn't be there if he was cold.

"Christmas is over," I muttered, squinting to see the street sign in the dusk. I was sure we were close. "I've got plenty of holiday spirit. It's just not Christian in origin. And though I'm no expert, I don't think the church would be happy with you singing about succubi."

"Maybe you're right," he said as he shifted the layers of green cloth Matalina had draped over him—her attempt at pixy winter wear. "They'd rather hear about rutting incubi."

The pixy yelped, and I jumped when he darted off the mirror, Ivy's hand just inches from smacking him. "Shut up, pixy," the soft-spoken vamp said, her gray-silk voice severe. Her working leathers made her look like a biker chick gone sophisticate, slim and sleek, and her eyes were pupil black under her Harley-logo cap. Jenks took the hint, and muttering something it was probably just as well I didn't hear, he settled on my big hoop earring to snuggle in between my neck and the soft red scarf I had worn for just this reason. I shivered when his wings brushed my neck, a whisper of chill that felt like water.

A sustained temperature below forty-five would send him into hibernation, but he could handle short, protected trips from the car to wherever. And after he'd found out about Glenn, there was no stopping him from coming out with us. If we hadn't invited him to the crime scene, I'd find his half-frozen body in my shoulder bag as a stowaway. Frankly, I think he was out here trying to get away from his brood of kids, spending the winter in my desk.

Jenks, though, was worth five FIB investigators, and that was on a bad day. Pixies excelled in sneaking around, making them experts at finding the smallest thing out of place, their curiosity keeping them interested after everyone else had come and gone. Their dust didn't leave a lasting impression, and their fingerprints were invisible unless you used a microscope, in my opinion making them excellent first-ins at a crime scene. 'Course, no one at the I.S. had cared what I thought, and it wasn't often that a pixy would work in anything other than a temporary backup position anyway. That was how I'd met Jenks, and it had been my good fortune. I would've taken him with me to the boat earlier today, but he would have had severe problems with the temperature.

Ivy sat up, inadvertently telling me we were close, and I started paying attention to house numbers. It looked like a human neighborhood, on the outskirts of Cincinnati in what was probably a lower- to lower-middle-class neighborhood. It wasn't a high-crime district, from the number of lights and the general tidiness of the homes, but it held a slightly run-down, soft comfortableness. I'd be willing to bet the area was mostly retirees or new families just starting out. It reminded me of the neighborhood I'd grown up in, and I could hardly wait until tomorrow when I'd be picking up my brother, Robbie, at the airport. He had worked through the solstice, but had somehow managed to get New Year's off.

That the lights around me now were the green and red of Christmas didn't mean it was a human neighborhood. Most vampires celebrated Christmas, and lots of humans celebrated the solstice. Ivy still had her tree up in the living room, and we exchanged presents when we felt like it, not on a specific date. Usually that was about an hour after I got back from shopping. Delayed gratification was Ivy's thing, not mine.

"That's got to be it," Ivy said softly, and Jenks shivered his wings for warmth, tickling me. Down the street on the left was a cluster of FIB cruisers, parked with their lights off and looking gray in the dim light. At the corner in a drop of light, two people stood gossiping, their dogs tugging at their leashes to go in. There weren't any news vans yet, but there would be. I could almost smell them.

Not an I.S. cruiser in sight, which was a relief since they'd probably send Denon out here. I hadn't seen the living low-blood vampire since blowing apart his cover-up of the Were murderers last summer, and I'd be willing to bet that he had suffered another demotion. "Looks like the I.S. isn't coming," I said softly, and Ivy shrugged.

"Why would they? They don't care if an FIB officer gets beat up."

I pulled to the curb and parked the car. "They might if it was an Inderlander who did it."

Jenks laughed. "Doubt it," he said, and I felt a tug on my hat as he ducked under the soft yarn for the trip inside.

Unfortunately, he was right. Whereas the I.S. policed the supernatural species, they would, and did, ignore a crime if it suited them. Hence the human-run FIB that had come into being. I had once thought that the FIB was way outclassed by the I.S., but after working with them for a year, I was impressed and shocked by the information they could dig up and put together.

It had been only forty years ago during the Turn that the combined Inderland species of vamp, witch, Were, and more had actively lent a hand to prevent humans from becoming the latest endangered species when a badly engineered, genetically altered tomato mutated and wiped out a large chunk of the human population. Though to be honest, if humans had died out, most of Inderland would suffer when vamps started preying on us instead of soft, naive, happy humans. Not to mention that Mr. Joe Vampire and Ms. Sue Were liked their high-maintenance lifestyles, impossible without the backing of a large population.

"What are you doing?" Ivy said, her hand on the door as I fumbled around under the seat.

"I've got an FIB sign in here somewhere," I muttered, fingers jerking back as they unexpectedly found something cold and squishy.

A closed-lipped smile came over Ivy. "The entire FIB knows your car."

Making a soft sound of agreement, I gave up and tugged on my gloves. Yeah, they did, seeing that they'd given it to me in payment for helping them out once, something most of them seemed to be forgetting lately. "Ready, Jenks?" I called, and got a half-heard stream of curses back. Something about my cream rinse and puking fairies.

Ivy and I got out together. The excitement of a run hit me when the doors thumped shut. Standing by my car, I pulled the sharp, dry air all the way to the bottom of my lungs. The clouds had that solid feel that they only get right before a heavy snow, and I could smell the pavement, white with salt and so dry and cold it would burn your fingers if you touched it.

Heels snapping, Ivy came around the car, and I followed her to the small house. The crunchy five inches of snow had been packed down, but a sad-looking three-foot snowman presided over a corner of the yard, his face melted and his hat covering his eyes. The curtains were open, and the yellow rectangles of light on the snow were starting to become obvious. Red and green lights from a neighbor's display made an odd counterpoint, and I could hear the conversation from the duo on the corner. Cold, I tugged my bag up higher as we walked.

More neighbors were coming out; I felt a surge of disgust when the slow-creeping lights of a van with an antenna showed under the streetlight.

Crap, they were here already? I'd wanted to talk to the neighbors before the interviewers had them thinking sensationalism instead of realism. I was sure Edden had interviewed the closest, but his people wouldn't ask the questions I wanted answers to.

"There," Ivy murmured, and I followed her gaze to the dark

shadow coming out from the garage's side door to meet us.

"Hey, hi!" I called out, pitching my voice high to give the impression we were harmless. *Yeah, right.* "Edden asked us to come out. We're from Vampiric Charms." Asked us? It was more like forced into it, but why bring *that* up.

The young FIB officer flicked on the outside lights, washing the crusty drive in an artificial glare. "Can I see some ID?" he asked, then did a double take. "Oh!" he said, tucking his clipboard back under an arm. "You're the witch and the vamp."

From my hat came a disgusted "And a really cold pixy. Can you hurry it up, Rache? I think my 'nads fell off."

I stifled a grimace, pasting on a fake smile. I'd rather be known by our company name than "the witch and the vamp," but at least Edden had told them we were coming. Maybe he wasn't going to be such a pain in the butt about us helping. I watched the officer's body language, but couldn't tell if his impatience was from the FIB's new distrust or simply the cold.

"Yes, Vampiric Charms. We're here to help with the possible Inderland connection," I said before Ivy could get all vampy. Her pulling an aura and scaring the crap out of him wouldn't help—as entertaining as it might be.

"Can we go in?" Ivy asked with a faint promise of threat, and Jenks snickered.

"Sure." The officer's head was down as he wrote something. "Put on a pair of booties, okay?"

Ivy was halfway to the door off the garage, her motions stiff at his assumption that she didn't know her way around a crime scene. I glanced back at the street, hesitating. The news crew had set up, and the huge light they had was gathering people like a bonfire. "Hey, uh, Ivy . . . ," I murmured, and she hesitated, a long, gloved hand resting on the open door.

She smiled with half her mouth. "You want to go talk to them?" I nodded, and she added, "You'll be okay, Jenks?"

"Oh crap," I swore under my breath. I'd forgotten about him.

"I'm fine!" he barked, and I felt a soft tug as he settled himself. "Nothing's going to change inside, but I want to hear what the neighbors say. Gossip, Ivy. That's where the truth is. It's all about the gossip."

I didn't know about gossip, but if he said he'd be okay, I'd rather get first impressions than stale, regurgitated comments after everyone had had a chance to think.

Ivy frowned, clearly of the opinion that crimes were solved by carefully gathered evidence, not nebulous feelings and hunches. But with a shrug, she went inside and I headed out into the night.

Pace fast, I found a spot at the back of the growing crowd, trying to stay out of the camera's line of sight. Jenks was probably hearing twice what I could, and I went on tiptoe to glimpse the man with red cheeks in the felt coat the newscaster was interviewing. I didn't think it was live, seeing that it wasn't six yet, and I eased closer, jostling for position.

"They were the nicest people," the man was saying, his eyes bright with excitement. "Nice people. I never would have expected anything like this from them. They kept to themselves and were real quiet."

My eyebrows rose, and Jenks snorted. Sounded like Inderlanders to me.

But then the kid next to me made a rude sound, and Jenks tugged my hair when the boy said snidely to his friend, "Like he knew him. The guy is a creep, and the woman is whacked."

"Got it, Jenks," I whispered so he would stop yanking on my hair. Slow and steady investigation was nice, but I wanted to find them before the sun went nova.

Smiling, I turned to find a young man in a black knit hat with the Howlers' emblem, and encouraged by the show of Inderland acceptance, I felt an unusual surge of kinship. He wasn't wearing a coat, and his hands were jammed into his jeans pockets. "Whacked?" I said, giving his friend a quick smile to include him in the conversation. "You think?"

"I know," he shot back, then fidgeted. I was guessing he was in high school, and I turned the Mrs. Robinson charm on full.

"Yeah?" I said, almost bumping into him as the crowd grew noisy when the newscaster looked for fresh meat. "Don't you love how they always say one thing in front of the camera, but at the bar, the truth comes out?"

He grinned, clearly thinking I thought he was older than he was. From under my hat came Jenks's impressed "Nice. Reel him in, Rache."

"So you know them?" I said, linking my arm in his and easing him from the news crew. I kept us close so as not to leave the highly charged atmosphere the news van was creating, angling so that if a camera should point our way, all they'd get would be my back. His friend had stayed behind, and was currently jumping to try to get in the background of the shot. He didn't have a coat either, and I thought it unfair that they were warm and I was freezing my butt off out here. Witches had a lower cold tolerance than just about everyone else, excluding pixies.

"You're not a reporter," he said, and I smiled, glad he was smarter than I'd thought.

"I'm from Vampiric Charms," I said, digging in my bag until I found a bent card and handed it to him. "I'm Rachel. Rachel Morgan."

"Righteous!" he said, his face becoming animated. "My name is Matt. I live over there. Hey, I've heard of you," he said, tapping the card against his hand. "Is that really you in that shot, being dragged down the street—"

"On my ass," I finished for him, adjusting my hat to send a whiff of cold air under it to get Jenks to stop laughing. "Yeah, that's me. But I don't really summon demons." *Much.*

"That's cool. That's cool," he said, seeming to grow three inches taller. "You're trying to find the Tilsons?"

A jolt of adrenaline made me shiver. Edden hadn't told me their names. "More than just about anything. Do you know where they went?"

He shook his head, trying to look older than he was as he gave his friend a superior look. "No, but they are weird. The entire family. I mowed their lawn this summer. The guy is a janitor at my school. He says he's allergic to grass." Matt smirked. "He's allergic to work if you ask me. But if you make him mad, stuff happens to you."

My eyes widened. "Magic?" *Were they Inderlanders, like Ivy thought?*

Matt shook his head and looked ill. "No, stuff like your dog dying. But his wife is even weirder. I don't see her much. She stays inside a lot with their kid. She talked with my mom once, and she wouldn't let my mom touch her baby."

"No kidding," I said, hoping he'd say more.

"And that baby of theirs is just as freaky as they are," he said, glancing at his friend. "Got these weird blue eyes that follow you around. She's quiet, like she's deaf or something. Her mom never puts her down. Mrs. Tilson wears the pants in the family, that's for hell sure."

"Is that so . . . ," I prompted, and Matt bobbed his head.

"Last year, someone put a firecracker in the can in the back toilet. Blew shit all over the place. Tilson was screaming about killing someone, so they sent him home. I mowed their lawn the next day. I was scared, man, but my dad made me. Tilson is nuts. He thought I knew who blew up the john and he pinned me against the fence. God, I thought I was going to die. But then *she* came out and he went all soft and stuff. He even apologized. Freakiest shit I've ever seen. She's smaller than you, and all she did was say his name and he went all meek and shit."

I blinked, my mind racing as I tried to figure it out. Mr. Tilson was a homicidal maniac with a chip on his shoulder. Mrs. Tilson was in charge. And the kid was weird. Living vampires, maybe?

"How old is the baby?" I asked, trying to keep him talking. This was pure gold.

Matt made a face. "I don't know. A year? My mom says

she's going to be a spoiled brat and Mrs. Tilson shouldn't wait five years before having another one, like she says she wants. Some kind of medical reason. She wants five or six kids, my mom says."

"Five or six?" I said, truly surprised. Maybe the Tilsons were Weres and the woman was from a highly dominant pack. But why space them out over five years? "That's a lot."

"Yeah," the kid said, scoffing. "I'm not having any kids. But if I do, I'm going to have them all right away. Get it over with. I don't want to be sixty and changing diapers."

I shrugged. There was eight years between me and Robbie, and I didn't see anything wrong with it. He'd raised me as much as my parents, and I had no complaints. But my mom was a witch, so changing diapers at sixty was about the norm. Glenn's attack was sounding more and more like an Inderland incident. "Thanks," I said, suddenly wanting to get inside. Jenks was probably freezing. "I should get in there. But thank you. You really helped."

The boy's expression became disappointed, and I smiled. "Hey, I could use someone this spring to mow my graveyard." I hesitated. "If you don't think that's too weird. My number is on the card."

He beamed, fingering it. "Yeah, that would be great," he said, then glanced at the house. "I don't think my dad will let me mow their lawn anymore."

"Call me, about April?" I said, and he nodded. "Thanks, Matt. You were a big help."

"No problem," he said, and I gave him a final smile and walked away. When I looked over my shoulder, he had his head bent to his friend's, and they were ogling my phone number. "You okay, Jenks?" I said, hoofing it away from the lights and back to the garage. Damn, wait until Ivy heard what I'd found out.

"Yeah," he said, gripping my hair harder. "But will you slow down? Unless you *want* pixy barf in your hair."

Immediately I checked my pace, tripping when I took the

curb without looking so I wouldn't have to tilt my head. Jenks swore when I stumbled, but my pulse jackhammered when my head swung up. It wasn't the almost-fall that shook me, but who was standing by my car, staring at it. Tom Bansen—it had to be—the same man who had tried to kill me by way of Al.

"Holy crap, it's Tom," I said, then shouted, "Get away from my car!" as I started to jog.

"Son of a fairy whore," Jenks swore. "What's he doing here?"

"I don't know." Caution slowed me down as I approached. "Better be quiet. If he knows you're here, all he has to do is knock my hat off and Matalina is a single parent."

Jenks became quiet. Tom continued to stand with his hands in his pockets, looking at my car as if debating something. Nervousness coated my anger as I halted a careful five feet back, puffing out white clouds in the streetlight and looking at the man like the snake he was. I'd heard he'd gotten fired from the I.S.—probably for the stupidity of being *caught* summoning demons to murder someone—but since I'd been the one Tom had been trying to off, the I.S. had done nothing more than that.

"What are you doing here?" I said, not anxious to have to defend myself, but not wanting to let him poke around in my car either.

The young man had a new hardness in his blue eyes as he stood on the shoveled sidewalk and looked speculatively at me in the lamplight. He was clearly cold in his parka and hat, the chill almost killing the redwood scent that all witches had. I'd once thought he was attractive in a tidy, almost-scholarly way—I still did, actually—but freeing Al to kill or abduct me had long since shifted the attraction to disgust.

"Trying to make a living," he answered, a tinge of red showing on his cheeks. "I've been shunned, thanks to you."

My jaw dropped and I backed up. I wasn't surprised, but I wasn't going to take the blame for it either. "I wasn't the one kidnapping girls to pay demons for black curses," I said. "Maybe you should rethink your logic, Sherlock."

He smiled in a not-nice way. Turning as if to leave, he said, "I'll be around if you want to talk." I sputtered in disbelief at the invitation and he added, "Nice car," before he walked away, hands still jammed into his big pockets.

"Hey!" I shouted, almost going after him, but the thought of his shunning and Jenks in my hat changed my mind. Rocking back on my boot heels, I exhaled loudly. *Shunned? The coven of ethical and moral standards had shunned him?* Damn! I hadn't thought they'd go that far. Sure he summoned demons, but that didn't get one shunned. It must have been kidnapping that girl for black magic. Shunning was exactly what it sounded like, and the man was in trouble. Getting the ethical and moral standards coven to reverse a decision was like surviving an I.S. death threat. He was absolutely cut off, and any witch associating with him ran the risk of being shunned in turn.

Making a living, I thought as I watched him. Tom had probably gone independent, seeing that the I.S. wouldn't touch him now, even under the table. *And looking like he was having a hard time of it,* I added as he got into a rust-cut '64 Chevy and drove away.

I headed for the Tilsons' house, jerking to a halt at a sudden thought. Fingers fumbling in my bag, I pulled out my key ring and the lethal-magic detection amulet on it. The thing had saved my life a couple of times, and Tom had a vested interest in seeing me gone.

"Rache . . . ," Jenks complained as I started to make a slow circuit around my vehicle.

"You want to be blown up smaller than fairy dust?" I muttered, and he tugged on my hair.

"Tom's a weenie," the pixy protested, but I finished my circuit, breathing easier when the amulet stayed a nice, healthy green. Tom hadn't spelled my car, but a sense of unease lingered, even as I turned to the cordoned-off house and crossed the street. And it wasn't because I might have some competition in the independent-runner arena. My car had originally belonged to an I.S. agent who died in a car bombing. Not this car, obviously, but a bomb had killed him.

Just that fast, my life can end. Tom hadn't left a charm on my car, but it wouldn't hurt to ask Edden if he'd have one of his dogs sniff around it. Boot heels clacking, I reached the door off the garage and went inside. Jenks sighed heavily, but I didn't care if I did look like a paranoid chicken when I asked Edden for a ride home.

I was done with being stupid about these kinds of things.

Four

The sudden cessation of wind as I passed into the garage was a blessed relief, and I paused, taking in the curious mix of space and clutter, the edges stacked with old boxes from grocery stores and mail-order places. Close to the steps leading inside were several large toys, bright with primary-colored plastic. The toddler sled had been used from the looks of it, but the rest was summer stuff. It had been a good Christmas, apparently.

Tracks of flattened snow showed where a big-assed truck had been on the otherwise swept cement. There wasn't room for two vehicles, and I wondered if Mr. Tilson was overcompensating for something. 'Course, maybe it was Mrs. Tilson who had the truck fetish. I sniffed deeply for the scent of Inderlander, finding only the dry smell of old concrete and dust, and I shivered.

I eyed the storage boxes, remembering what my dad had once told me when I'd tried to get out of cleaning the garage. People put things in garages that they don't want but can't get rid of. Dangerous stuff, sometimes. Too dangerous to keep inside, and too dangerous to throw out and risk someone finding. Mr. and Mrs. Tilson had a very full garage.

"Come on, Rache!" Jenks complained, tugging on my hair. "I'm cold!"

Giving the boxes a last look, I went up the cement steps.

The hum of a vacuum was a faint presence as I opened the cheerfully painted door and entered a seventies kitchen, nodding to the officer with a clipboard seated at the table. The window above the sink looked out over the front yard and the news van. A high chair done in pinks and yellows was pulled up beside the square table. A box of throw-away boot covers was on it, and I sighed, taking my gloves off and tucking them in my coat pockets.

Plush baby toys were in a large basket tucked neatly out of the way, and I could almost hear a contented, gurgling laughter. The sink held a bowl of cookie-dough-encrusted utensils. A dozen sugar cookies sat on the counter, cooling for the last eight hours. A tear-away tag was tied to the oven, the upper part signed and dated, with the time, stating that Officer Mark Butte had turned off the oven. The Tilsons had left in a hurry.

The kitchen was a curious mix of warmth and cold, the heater on to combat the in-and-out traffic, and I unzipped my coat. My first impression of the house was just as jumbled. Everything to make a home was here, but it felt . . . empty.

There was the chatter of work in the next room, and when I bent to put a blue bootie over my boot, Jenks shot out from under my hat. "Holy crap!" he swore, flitting over the entire kitchen in three seconds, giving the seated officer a coronary. "It smells like green baby paste in here. Hey, Edden!" he said louder. "Where you at?" And he darted out, his wings a gray blur.

From deeper in the house came an exclamation as Jenks probably startled another FIB officer. A set of heavy steps approached, and I straightened. I'd gotten my boots at Veronica's Crypt, and covering them in blue paper should be outlawed.

Edden's squat figure suddenly took up the archway to the rest of the house. Jenks was on his shoulder, and the FIB captain looked better now that he was doing something to help his son. He nodded to the seated officer and smiled briefly at me, but it didn't reach his eyes. He was still in his street clothes. In truth, he probably shouldn't be out here, but no one was going to tell him he couldn't oversee the investigation of his son's mauling.

"Rachel," he said in greeting, and I coyly waved a bootie-covered foot at him.

"Hi, Edden. Can I come in?" I asked, hardly sarcastic at all.

He frowned, but before he could start in on me about my lousy investigation techniques, I remembered Tom in the street. "Hey, can I ask a favor?" I said hesitantly.

"You mean more than letting you in here?" he said so dryly that I was sorely tempted to tell him about the sticky silk at Kisten's boat, which they'd missed, but I held my tongue, knowing he'd find out about it tomorrow *after* Ivy had had a chance to go out.

"I'm serious," I said as I undid my scarf. "Can someone check out my car?"

The squat man's eyebrows rose. "Having trouble with the transmission?"

I flushed, wondering if he knew I was the one who'd trashed it while learning how to drive a stick shift. "Uh, I saw Tom Bansen at my car. Maybe I'm being paranoid—"

"Bansen?" he blurted out, and Jenks nodded from his shoulder. "This is the same witch you tagged in his basement for summoning demons?"

"He was looking at my car," I said, thinking it sounded lame. "He said something about making a living, and seeing that there are lots of people who want to see me, uh, dead . . ." I let my thought trail off. I kept to myself that he'd been shunned and Jenks didn't say a word. It was a witch thing. When someone got shunned, it was an embarrassment to all of us. "I checked for lethal charms, but I wouldn't know a car bomb from an odometer cable."

The FIB captain's expression grew hard. "No problem. I'll have the dog unit come out. Actually . . ." He looked at the seated officer and smiled. "Alex, go wait by Ms. Morgan's car for the explosives team."

The man stiffened, and I winced apologetically. "Don't let anyone get within ten feet," Edden continued. "It might turn you into a toad if you touch it."

"It will not," I complained, thinking being a toad might be pleasant compared to what Tom could probably do.

Edden shook his head. "There is a news van in the street. I'm not taking any chances."

Jenks snickered, and I warmed. Chances were good nothing was wrong with my car, and I felt like a baby, but Edden's hand on my shoulder made me feel better. All the way up until he turned me back to the kitchen's door and Alex's retreating back. "Maybe Alex should take you home right now," he said, "so he can check out your church. For your own safety."

Oh for God's sake, he's trying to get rid of me. "That's why we've got a gargoyle in the eaves," I said sharply, and slipping out from under him, I resolutely paced deeper into the house. Take me home for my own safety, my ass. He was letting Ivy stay. Why couldn't I?

"Rachel," Edden protested, his compact bulk spinning to follow.

Jenks laughed, taking to the air and saying, "Give it up, FIB man. It'll take more than you to get her out. Remember what Ivy and I did to your finest last spring? Add Rachel to that, and you can say your prayers."

From behind me came Edden's dry "You think Ivy wants another stint as a candy striper?" But I was here and he was going to let me in on the evidence-gathering part of things. The FIB was confident that Mr. Tilson had attacked Glenn, seeing that it was his house, but his lawyer might try to pass it off on a burglar or something else. Not cool.

"Nice house," I said, eyes roving over the bright walls, low ceilings, and clean but worn carpet. We passed a short hallway, then stepped down into a large living room. Immediately I stopped. "Oh my God," I said, taking it in. "They have shag carpet." Green shag carpet. This might be why Mr. Tilson was nuts. It would make me nuts.

There were only a few FIB personnel still here doing their FIB thing. One of them flagged Edden over, and he left me with a stern look that said not to touch anything. The faint tickle of fingerprint dust caught in my nose. Ivy was in the corner with a tall woman who, by the twin cameras draped over her, had to be the photographer. They were both looking at her laptop and the shots she had taken earlier.

It was bright and overly warm, and Jenks left Edden to park it on top of the curtains. Warmer up there, probably. The FIB had been here most of the day before letting us in here, not wanting to chance my messing up their precious *virgin site,* but it still looked raw to me.

The green-tiled coffee table between the olive-and-orange-striped couch and the brick fireplace—painted to match the floor, incidentally— was on its side and shoved into the raised hearth. The curtains over the wide windows were open to the backyard. God help me but the curtains matched the putrid color combination. Looking at everything, I started to feel nauseous, as if the seventies had taken refuge here against extinction and were preparing to take over the world.

There was no blood except a small splatter against the couch and wall, an ugly brown against the yellowish green paint. From Glenn's broken nose, perhaps? An armchair had been shoved into an upright piano, and loose-leaf sheets of music were stacked on the bench. Leaning up against the wall by the large window overlooking the snow-covered swing set was a picture. It had fallen turned against the wall, and I wanted to see what it was in the worst way.

A Christmas tree was propped up in the corner, disheveled and clearly having fallen at some point if the dark spot on the rug where the water had drained out wasn't enough of a clue. There were a lot of decorations for one room, and they were a curious mix of style. Most were the inexpensive, mass-produced variety, but there was what was probably a two-hundred-dollar snow globe and an antique Tiffany-style mistletoe display. Weird.

Three stockings hung from the mantel, and these, too, looked expensive—too classy for most of the decorations. Only the smallest had a name. HOLLY. The baby's probably. The mantel was empty of pictures, which I thought was odd seeing as there was a new baby in the house. The top of the piano was bare as well.

Jenks had dropped down to talk with the guy at the piano. Ivy had her head next to the photographer's. Edden wasn't paying me any attention. Everyone looked busy, so I wandered to the fireplace and ran a finger over the smooth wood for evidence that the mantel had once held pictures. *No dust.*

"Hey!" the man with Edden exclaimed. "What do you think you're doing?" His face red, he glanced at Edden, clearly ticked off because he wanted to kick me out but couldn't.

Faces turned, and embarrassed, I backed up. "Sorry."

Ivy glanced up from the laptop in the sudden quiet. Both she and the photographer wore questioning expressions as they stared at me, looking like yin and yang with Ivy's short black hair and the photographer's long blond tresses. I remembered seeing the photographer at Trent's stables, taking pictures, but Ivy hadn't been there, and I wondered how she had gotten chummy enough in fifteen minutes to have their heads together discussing the niceties of angles and shadows.

Almost smiling, Edden harrumphed. Head bowed and stubby-fingered hand in the air to say he was taking care of it, he rocked into motion. Ivy gave the photographer one of our cards, then crossed the room to join me. Jenks landed on her shoulder halfway there, and I saw her lips move in a soft comment that made the pixy laugh.

By the time they all reached me, I had cocked my hip and crossed my arms over my chest. "I'm not going to touch anything else!" I exclaimed, wondering if the harsh expressions on the FIB officers' faces were for me breaking protocol or a lingering doubt about my involvement in Kisten's death. I knew Edden had done his best to squelch it, but that meant little to a lifetime of prejudice.

Rolling his eyes at Ivy, Edden took my elbow to lead me into the hallway. Ivy, too, was smiling, but as soon as the privacy of the hall took us, she became serious. "Rachel's here now, so how about showing us where Glenn was beat up?" she asked, surprising me.

"That's it," Edden said, glancing past me and into the living room. "Everything else looks untouched."

I jerked my elbow from Edden and leaned against the wall. Jenks's wings clattered as he flew to snuggle in my scarf, and Ivy shook her head. "There isn't enough emotion in the room for someone having been mauled," she said. "You say it happened this morning? No way."

Edden's face scrunched up, and I looked at Ivy. A vampire could read the pheromones left in a room, giving a qualitative, though not terribly quantitative, impression of the emotions that had been given free rein. By the way Edden looked, I guessed he knew about the ability but didn't trust it. Neither did the courts, disallowing a vampire's testimony unless they were trained, registered, and attended quarterly calibration seminars. Ivy didn't, but if she said there wasn't a sign of a struggle here, then I'd believe her over a blood-splattered wall.

"The rest of the house is undisturbed," he said, and Ivy frowned. "Do you want me to tell you what we do know while we tour the house for signs of . . . emotion?" he finished, and I smirked. Wait until they heard what I found out. But Ivy shot me a look to shut up, and my breath slipped from me. *Okay . . . I'll wait.*

"I'm listening," she said to Edden as she went down the short hall. Her stride was long and confident, and the man toting the FIB evidence vacuum pressed into the wall to let her pass. She went first into a tidy, opulent bedroom with pillows, rich drapes, rugs, and beautiful things arranged on what looked like an antique carved bedroom set. Drawers were open and the closet clearly had hangers missing. The rich femininity didn't match the rest of the house. Not at all. Well, except for the snow globe, stockings, and mistletoe display.

"The mortgage is in Mr. and Mrs. Tilson's names," Edden said, his hands in his pockets as he rocked back on his heels, clearly not interested in the incongruity of decorating styles. "They're human," he added, and I almost blurted, *No they aren't,* biting my tongue instead.

"He and his wife bought the house about a year and a half ago," Edden continued, and Jenks snorted, silent to all but me. "She's a stay-at-home mom caring for their daughter, but we've found that Holly is registered at three day cares. Mr. Tilson works as a janitor, retired from being a science teacher in Kentucky. Took early retirement, I guess, and wanted something to do and to supplement his pension."

Like clean crap from the walls of the boys' bathroom? Yeah, that sounded right.

"We have a tap on the phone and we're watching the credit cards," Edden was saying as Ivy skulked around the room. "There's no extended family that we know of yet on either side, but everyone is out for the holidays and it's taking a long time to get anything."

His words broke off suddenly, and he stared at me. "Why are you smiling?"

Immediately I forced my expression to go innocent. "No reason. What else have you got?"

"Very little." He eyed me. "We'll find them."

Ivy eased around the carved furniture like a shadow, using a pen to shift the curtains and nodding at the security-system sticker on the window. Her sleek leather made her look like a well-paid assassin against the elegant surroundings hidden inside the depths of the house. Someone had excellent tastes and I didn't think it was Mr. Tilson the janitor. Mr. Tilson the hit man, maybe.

"Here's a recent picture," Edden said, handing me a piece of paper with a copy of Tilson's school ID. Jenks startled me when he vaulted from the folds of soft yarn to hover over the nine-by-eleven paper. The face not smiling back at me was blurry, but according to the tag he was blond and blue eyed. There were some wrinkles, but not a lot, and he had a receding hairline.

"Pretty harmless looking for someone who can beat up an FIB detective," Jenks said.

"It's the quiet ones you have to watch out for," I murmured, silently asking Jenks if he was done before handing the paper back to Edden. Ivy hadn't come over to look, so she'd probably seen it already.

"We don't have anything yet on Mrs. Tilson," Edden said, starting when Ivy jerked into a fast pace and left the room. "But we're working on it."

His last words were rather distant, and I could guess why. Ivy was edging into the eerie vamp quickness she took pains to hide from me. Her unnerving speed aside, I enjoyed seeing her like this, wrapped up in thinking. Work was the only time she let herself forget the misery of her wants and needs and found a feeling of self-worth.

Edden followed me into the hallway. It wasn't hard to figure out where Ivy had gone. Jenks had already flown past the open door to the bathroom, and there was a frightened, older FIB officer leaning against a wall at the end of the hall.

"She in there?" Edden asked the man, who clearly had not been expecting an intense vampire in leather to burst in on him. Edden gave the sweating man a pat on the shoulder. "Will you find out if the fingerprints have been sent off yet?"

The officer walked away gratefully, and Edden and I entered what was clearly the baby's room.

If Ivy looked out of place in the bedroom, she looked like she was from Mars next to the crib, frilly lace curtains, and brightly colored expensive toys. The child had been lavished with attention, from the looks of it. And where Ivy stuck out, Jenks fit right in, hovering with his hands on his hips and staring in disgust at a framed shot of Tinker Bell.

"We're gathering information for a trial more than searching for a way to find them," Edden said to keep the conversation going and cover the pain in the back of his eyes. "I'm not letting a lawyer uphold the Constitution so far that we have to let them go."

I jumped when one of the toys burst into music. Jenks just about hit the ceiling in a cloud of dust, clearly the guilty party.

"You can't pack up a baby and go that fast without leaving a trail," I said, adrenaline flooding me. "I heard the woman dotes on her kid." I gazed at the mounds of toys. "All you'll have to do is post a man at the toy store. You'll have them in a week."

"I want them now," Edden said grimly. The music cut off, and seeing Jenks hovering miserably in the middle of the room, Edden added, "Don't worry, Jenks. We were done here."

Oh, sure, I get yelled at, and the pixy gets told it doesn't matter. But as Ivy poked around, I drifted to the books in the overstuffed rocking chair, smiling at a familiar title. I reached for them, not wanting to leave this spot of innocence and good taste. A feeling of melancholy had overtaken me. I knew it was from my dilemma about having kids. If it had just been my blood disease, I might have taken my chances, but I couldn't face my children being demons.

I had let the hide-and-seek book slip from my fingers when Ivy gingerly came to a halt among the stuffed animals and pastel colors, standing as if the soft domesticity might be catching. "Is this the last room?" she asked, and when Edden nodded with a tired motion, she added, "Are you sure Glenn wasn't attacked somewhere else and dropped here?"

"Pretty sure. His prints on the walk come right to the door."

Her calm face showed a glimmer of anger. "There's nothing in this room either," she said softly. "Nothing. Not even a whisper from a cranky baby."

Seeing her ready to go, I stacked the books on a small table. The thump of a small cardboard doll hitting the floor drew my attention, and I picked it up. The lavish hide-and-seek book was extravagant for a small house in a depressed neighborhood, but after seeing the bedroom, I wasn't surprised. It was obvious they spared no expense when it came to their kid. Nothing fit. Nothing made sense.

Jenks flitted to Ivy's shoulder, clearly trying to cheer her up. She was having none of it and waved him away. Edden waited for me by the door as I leafed through the book to put the doll back. But there was already a hard bump in the pocket where it belonged.

"Just a minute," I said, using two fingers to dig it out. I didn't know why, but the doll needed to go back in her bed and I was the only one who could do it. That's what the oversize print said. And I was feeling melancholy. Edden could wait.

But when my fingertips connected with the smooth bump in the pocket, I jerked my hand out, jamming my fingers into my mouth before I knew what I was doing. "Ow!" I yelped from around my fingers, then stared at the book, now fallen onto the chair.

Edden's face became wary, and Jenks flew to me. Ivy stopped dead on the threshold, staring with eyes black from the surge of adrenaline I'd given off. Embarrassed, I took my fingers out of my mouth and pointed. "Something's in there," I said, feeling quivery inside. "It moved. Something is in that book! And it's furry." *And warm, and it shocked the hell out of me.*

Ivy came back in, but it was Edden who took his pen and stuck it in the pocket. The three of us crouched over the book while Jenks stood nearby and bent to look in.

"It's a stone," he said as he straightened, looking at me quizzically. "A black stone."

"It was furry!" I backed up a step. "I felt it move!"

Edden wedged the pen in, and a black crystal came sliding out to glint dully in the electric light. "There's your mouse," he said dryly, and I felt the blood fall to my feet as I recognized it.

It was a banshee tear. It was a *freaking* banshee tear.

"That's a banshee tear," both Ivy and I said together, and Jenks gave a little yelp, taking flight to flit madly between me and Ivy until he finally landed on my shoulder.

I stepped back, wringing my hand as if I could erase having touched it. *Damn, I'd touched a banshee tear. Double damn, it was probably evidence.*

"It felt furry?" the pixy said, and I nodded, eyeing my fingers. They looked okay, but it had been a banshee tear, and it gave me the creeps.

Edden's expression of confusion slowly cleared. "I've heard of these," he said, tapping it with his pen tip. Then he straightened to his entire height and looked me directly in the eye. "This is why there's no emotion here, isn't it."

I nodded, deciding this was why it looked like a home, but didn't feel like it. The banshee tear explained everything. The love had been sucked right out. "They leave them where there's likely to be a lot of emotion," I said, wondering why Ivy had gone pale. Well, paler than usual. "Sometimes they will tip the scales and make things worse—sort of push everyone to a higher pitch. The tear soaks everything up, and then the banshee comes back to collect it." And I had touched it. *Euwie.*

"A banshee did this?" Edden said, his anger slipping through a crack in his veneer of calm. "Made that man hurt my son?"

"Probably not," I said, thinking about what Matt had told me and glancing at Ivy. "If Mrs. Tilson was cheating on her husband, that's reason enough for a banshee to leave a tear. I bet she got it in here by posing as a babysitter or something."

I looked at the tear, heavy and dark with the stored emotion of Glenn's mauling—and I shivered, remembering how warm it had felt. "The I.S. has a record on every banshee in Cincinnati," I said. "You can analyze the tear, find out who made it. The banshee might know where they went. They usually choose their victims carefully and will follow them from place to place if the pickings are good. Though they prefer to feed passively, they can suck a person dry in seconds."

"I thought that was illegal." Edden slid the crystal into an evidence bag and sealed it.

"It is." Ivy's voice was mild, but I thought she looked ill.

Jenks was picking up on her mood, too. "You okay?" he said, and she blinked her softly almond-shaped eyes once.

"No," she said, her gaze falling to the tear. "Even if Mrs. Tilson was cheating on her husband, the suspect knew exactly where to hit Glenn to hurt but not maim. The house is clean to the point of obsession, but there's too much money being spent on the little girl and the wife for him to be a wife beater. The man doesn't even have a remote for the TV, for God's sake," she said, pointing to the unseen living room, "yet they have silk sheets and a baby computer."

"You think the *woman* beat him up?" I interrupted, and Ivy frowned.

Edden, though, was interested. "If she was an Inderlander, maybe a living vampire, she could do it. She'd know how to induce pain without damage, too."

Ivy make a noise of negation. "I'd be able to smell it if a vampire had visited, much less lived here," she said, but I had my doubts. Last year, I would have said it was impossible to make a charm to cover an Inderlander's scent from another Inderlander, but my mom had spelled my dad into smelling like a witch for their entire marriage.

I stood there and tried to figure it out, both Jenks and me jumping when Edden clapped his hands once. "Out," he said suddenly, and I protested when he manhandled me into the hall. "Ivy, you and Jenks can stay, but, Rachel, I want you out."

"Wait a minute!" I complained, but he kept me moving, yelling for someone to bring the vacuum. Ivy just shrugged, giving me an apologetic smile.

"Sorry, Rachel," Edden said when we reached the activity of the living room, his brown eyes glinting with amusement. "You can poke around in the garage if you want."

"Excuse me?" I exclaimed. He knew I hated the cold. It was

an offer that really wasn't one. "How come Ivy gets to stay and help?"

"Because Ivy knows how to handle herself."

That was just rude. "You suckwad! I'm the one who found the tear!" I said as I stood in the archway to the living room and watched everyone buzz about the new development. Several heads turned, but I didn't care. I was being gotten rid of.

Edden's face darkened with emotion, but his next words were postponed when Alex, the officer he had sent to watch my car, came in, cold on his breath and snow on his boots. "Ah, they won't be able to have a dog out to look at your car for a couple of hours," he said nervously, seeing Edden's anger directed at me. "There's a big Brimstone bust out at the Hollows airport."

I jumped as, suddenly, Ivy was next to me. "What's wrong with your car?" she asked, and I let my air out in a huff.

"Tom Bansen was standing next to it," I said. "I'm being paranoid."

Ivy smiled. "Don't worry about him," she said. "You're under Rynn Cormel's protection. He wouldn't dare."

Unless the vampires want me dead, I thought, then turned back to Edden. "Edden . . . ," I complained, but the squat man put a hand on my shoulder and moved me to the kitchen.

"Alex, take Ms. Morgan home," he said. "Rachel, I'll call you if we need you. If you don't want to leave, you can wait in the kitchen, but it's going to be hours. Probably not until tomorrow. You might as well go home."

He wasn't telling *Ivy* to go home. I took a breath to whine some more, but someone had called his name, and he was gone, leaving only the faint scent of coffee.

A familiar wing clatter drew my attention to Jenks, sitting on top of a picture frame, and he dropped to me. "Sorry, Rache," he said, and I slumped back into the wall, disgusted.

"I'm staying," I said, loud enough for everyone to hear, and Alex exhaled in relief, going to stand over a heating vent. "How come Ivy gets to help?" I asked Jenks, already knowing the answer and envious of how she, a vampire who had once beaten up an entire floor of FIB guys, was fitting in better than me, a witch who had helped them bring in the city's master vampire in their own back room. It wasn't my fault Skimmer killed him.

Hell, I thought. Maybe I *should* take some classes on crime scene protocol. Anything would be better than standing on the sidelines and watching everyone else play. I was not a bench warmer. Not by a long shot.

Jenks landed on my shoulder in a show of support. I knew he wanted to help, and I appreciated his loyalty. At his movement, Edden looked up from his cell phone. "Is your finger okay?" he asked suddenly, and I glanced at it. It looked fine.

Not answering him, I pushed from the wall and stomped out. Jenks rose to follow me at head height into the empty kitchen. "Rache . . . ," he started, and I grimaced.

"Stay with Ivy if you want," I said bitterly, zipping up my coat and wrapping my scarf around my neck. I wasn't going home. Not yet. "I'll be in the garage."

His tiny features became relieved. "Thanks, Rache. I'll let you know what we find out," he said, slipping a trail of gold dust as he zipped back to the nursery.

It's so unfair, I thought as I took my blue booties off. So my protocol sucked dishwater. I was getting results faster than a houseful of FIB agents. Leaving, I slammed the screen door and stomped down the cement steps. Home. Yeah. Maybe I'd make cookies. Gingerbread men with little FIB badges. Then I'd bite their freaking heads off. But when my feet hit the cement floor, I slowed. Oh, I was still mad, but Edden had said I could look through the garage. I thought he'd offered only because he knew it was too cold, but why not?

Hands on my hips, I used a boot tip to unwedge the informal closure on the nearest box. It popped open to show a mishmash of stuff that looked like classic post-yard-sale clutter: books, knickknacks, photo albums, and several cameras. Expensive ones.

"Photo albums?" I questioned, looking at the silent walls. Who keeps their photo albums in the garage? Maybe it was temporary, for Christmas, to make room for all the baby toys.

I moved to the next box, slipping on my gloves for warmth as I opened it to find more books and clothes from the seventies—explaining their living room, perhaps. Under it was another box that contained last year's styles. I held up the first—a dress that I might find in my mother's closet—thinking that Mrs. Tilson must have been heavy once. The dress was way bigger than me, but not a maternity cut. It didn't match Matt's description. It didn't match what I'd seen in the open closet, either.

Frowning, I put the dress back, digging to the bottom to find a stack of yearbooks. "Bingo," I whispered, kneeling to feel the cold cement go right through my jeans. I didn't have to wait until Edden's office dug up a photo of them. I could see for myself.

My knees were cramping, so I pulled the kiddie sled over and sat on it, knees almost to my ears as I leafed through a yearbook with CLAIR SMITH penciled on the front flap. Clair had graduated from a high school a few hundred miles upstate, and was apparently popular if the overwhelming number of signatures meant anything. Lots of promises to write. Apparently she toured Europe before going to college.

There was another yearbook from a local college where she'd gotten her four-year journalism degree, majoring in photography, and had met Joshua, according to the hearts and flowers around his signature. My gaze slid to the box of albums. So maybe it was school stuff. It might explain the cameras, too.

She was a member of the photography club in high school, and had graduated in '82. I stared at the picture of the young woman standing on the bleachers surrounded by awkward teenagers, my finger resting on her name. Unless there was a misprint, Clair was a rather round young woman with a cheerful smile, not the slight, mild woman Matt had described. She wasn't fat, but she wasn't my size either. And if she'd graduated in '82, that would make her . . . over forty now?

I felt my face lose its expression, and I turned to look at the wall of the house as if I could pull Ivy out here with my thoughts. Over forty with one kid and wanting five more? Spacing them five years apart?

She had to be an Inderlander. Witches lived a hundred and sixty years and could have kids the entire span, apart from twenty years on either side. Maybe that was the source of strife? Mr. Tilson found out his wife was a witch? But it didn't smell like a witch lived here. Or a vampire. Or a Were.

I exhaled, setting the book aside and shuffling until I found one with JOSHUA TILSON printed on the front cover. His school had splurged for real fake-leather bindings. Nice.

Joshua had graduated from Kentucky State the same year as Clair. I thumbed through the pages, looking for him. My lips parted, and a chill tightened my muscles. Slowly I brought the page closer to my nose, wishing the light were brighter out here. Joshua didn't look anything like the photo Edden had shown me.

My eyes went to the surrounding stuff, then remembered Edden's comments about Mr. Tilson retiring. Then Matt's complaint that the same man ought to be able to mow his own lawn, the rage Mr. Tilson had fallen into, how young his family was, and how they were going to have lots more kids. Stuff in the garage they didn't want in the house but couldn't risk throwing away.

I didn't think Mr. and Mrs. Tilson were the people who lived here. They were someone else and couldn't risk being found out by calling the ambulance, so they had fled.

I shivered, the motion reaching all the way to my fingertips. "I-i-i-i-i-vy-y-y-y-y!" I shouted. "*Ivy!* Come see this!"

I listened to the silence for a moment. She wasn't coming. Annoyed, I got up, book in hand. My knees were stiff from the cold, and I almost fell, jerking myself straight when Ivy poked her head out.

"Find something?" she said, amusement in her dark eyes.

Not "Are you still here?" or "I thought you left," but "Find something?" And her amusement wasn't at my expense, but Edden's, who was now behind her.

I smiled, telling her I had indeed found something. "Glenn wasn't beaten up by Mr. Tilson," I said smugly.

"Rachel . . . ," Edden started, and I triumphantly held up the yearbook and came forward.

"Have you gotten your fingerprints back yet?" I asked.

"No. It's going to be almost a week—"

"Be sure to check them against known Inderland criminal offenders," I said, shoving the book at him, but Ivy took it. "You won't find them matching up to Mr. Tilson's record, and that's assuming he has one. I think the Tilsons are dead, and whoever is living here took their names along with their lives."

Five

"Thanks, Alex!" I shouted, waving to the FIB officer as he drove down the shadowy, snow-quiet street to leave me standing on the sidewalk outside our church. Ivy was already halfway up the walk, anxious to be on her own turf where she had her ironclad ways of coping. She'd been quiet all the way home, and I didn't think it was from us needing a ride because I was too chicken to open my car door and see if I exploded.

Alex's taillights flashed as he rolled through a stop sign at the end of the road, and I turned away. The church that Ivy, Jenks, and I lived in was lit up and serene, the colors bleeding out of the stained-glass windows and onto the untouched snow in a fabulous swirl. I studied the roofline to try to spot Bis, our resident gargoyle, but there was nothing between the white puffs of my breath. The church was pretty with its Christmas and solstice decorations of live garlands and cheerful bows, and I smiled, glad to live in such a unique place.

This last fall, Jenks had finally fixed the spotlights angling onto the steeple, and it added to the beauty. The building hadn't been used as a church for years, but it was sanctified—again. Ivy had originally chosen the church to operate our runner firm from to tick off her undead mother, and we'd never moved to more professional digs when the opportunity had arisen. I felt safe here. So did Ivy. And Jenks needed the garden out back to feed his almost four dozen kids.

"Hurry up, Rache," Jenks complained from under my hat. "I've got icicles hanging."

Smirking, I followed Ivy up the walk to the worn front steps. Jenks had been silent on the ride home, too, and I'd have almost been willing to find out what happened on the ninth day of Christmas just so I wouldn't have had to keep the conversation going with Alex all by myself. I couldn't tell if my roommates, Ivy especially, had been thinking or just mad.

Maybe she thought I'd shown her up by discovering that the Tilsons were impostors before she had. Or maybe she was upset that I wanted her to go out to Kisten's boat. She'd loved him, too. Loved him more deeply than me, and longer. I'd have thought she'd be eager for the chance to find his killer and the vampire who had tried to turn me into a blood toy.

Ivy's pace ground to a stop on the salted steps, and my head came up when a soft curse slipped from her. Halting, I sent my gaze to follow hers to our business sign, over the door. "Damn it all to the Turn and back," I whispered, seeing the spray-painted *Black Wit* and a half-scripted *c* trailing down the brass plaque to drip onto the twin oak doors.

"What is it?" Jenks shrilled, unable to see and tugging on my hair.

"Someone redecorated the sign," Ivy said blandly, but I could tell she was mad. "We need to start leaving some lights on," she muttered, yanking open the door and going inside.

"Lights?" I exclaimed. "The place is already lit up like a . . . a church!"

Ivy was inside, and I stood there with my hands on my hips, getting more and more pissed. It was an attack on me, and I felt it to my core after the hint of FIB animosity at the crime site. *Son of a bitch.*

"Bis!" I shouted as I looked up and wondered where the little guy was. "You out here?"

"Rache," Jenks said as he tugged on my hair. "I gotta check on Matalina and my kids."

"Sorry," I muttered. Pulling my coat tight about me, I passed into the church and yanked the door shut. Angry, I let the locking bar thump down, though technically we were open until midnight. There was a soft lifting of my hat, and Jenks darted off into the sanctuary. I slowly took my hat off and hung it on the hook, my mood easing at the high-pitched chorus of *hello-o-o*s from his kids. It had taken me four hours to scrape the paint from the brass the last time. Where in hell was Bis? I hoped he was okay. The "artists" had clearly been interrupted.

Maybe I should spell the sign, I thought, but I didn't think there was a charm to make metal impervious to paint. I could put a black spell on it to give whoever touched it acne, but that would be illegal. And despite what the graffiti said, I was a white witch, damn it.

The warmth of the church soaked into me as I hung my coat on a peg. Past the dark shadow of the windowless foyer was my desk, at the back of the sanctuary where the altar used to be, the oak rolltop currently covered with plants and serving as a winter home for Jenks and his family. It was safer than hibernating in the stump in the backyard, and since I didn't ever *use* my desk, it was only a matter of enduring the indignity of finding pixy girls playing in my makeup or using the hair in my brush to fashion hammocks.

Across from my desk was an informal grouping of furniture around a low coffee table. There was a TV and a stereo, but it was more of a place to interview clients than a real living room. Our undead patrons had to come around to the back and the unsanctified part of the church and our more private living room. That's where Ivy's Christmas tree was, with one present still under it. After ruining David's coat trying to tag Tom, I'd had to get him a new one. He was in the Bahamas right now, at an insurance seminar with the ladies.

One front corner of the church held Ivy's baby grand piano—out of sight from where I now stood—and across from that, a mat where I'd taken to exercising when Ivy was out. Ivy went to the gym to keep her figure. At least that's where she said she was going when she left anxious and came home rested, relaxed, and satiated. In the middle of it all was Kisten's battered pool table, rescued from the curb whereas Kisten himself hadn't been.

My mood slowly shifted from anger to melancholy as I took off my boots and left them under my coat. A passel of Jenks's kids were in the open rafters singing carols, and it was hard to stay upset with their ethereal three-part harmony mixing with the smell of brewing coffee.

Coffee, I thought as I flopped onto the couch and pointed the remote at the stereo. Crystal Method filled the air, fast and aggressive, and I tossed the remote to the table and put my feet up, out of the draft. Coffee would make everything better, but I probably had at least five minutes until it was done. After that close ride in the cop car, Ivy needed some space.

Jenks dropped down onto the elaborate centerpiece Ivy's dad had brought over one night. The thing was all glitter and gold, but Jenks went well with it, standing on the painted sticks that looped in and around. He had one of his kids with him; the little pixy boy had his wings glued shut again, tear tracks giving away his misery.

"Don't let it get to you, Rache," Jenks said as he sifted dust from himself and wedged it in the fold his son's wings made. "I'll help you clean the paint off tomorrow."

"I can do it," I muttered, not relishing the idea that whoever put it up there would probably do a drive-by to see me busting my ass on a ladder. Jenks helping me was a nice thought, but no way would it be warm enough.

"I don't get it," I complained, then did a double take at the tiny cut-out snowflakes now decorating the windows. *That's why the glue.* They were the size of my pinkie nail, and were the sweetest things I'd ever seen. "No one cares about the good stuff I do," I said as Jenks's son squirmed under his dad's attention. "So what if I had to summon a demon if it all ended well? I mean, you tell me Cincinnati isn't better without Piscary. Rynn Cormel is a way better crime boss than he was. Ivy likes him, too."

"You're right," the pixy said as he gently pulled his son's wings apart. Behind him, Rex, Jenks's cat, peeked in from the dark foyer, pulled from the belfry by the sound of her four-inch master's voice. Just last week, Jenks had installed a cat door in the belfry stairway, tired of asking one of us to open the door for his cat. The beast loved the belfry with its high windows. It made easy access for Bis, too. Not that the cat-size gargoyle came in much.

"And Trent," I said, watching Rex since Jenks was preoccupied with a flightless child. "Beloved city son and idiot billionaire goes and gets caught in the ever-after. Who has to bust her butt and make a deal with demons to get him back?"

"The one who got him there?" Jenks said, and my eyes narrowed. "Hey, kitty, kitty. How's my sweetest fluff ball?" he crooned, which I thought risky, but hey, it was his cat.

"It was Trent's idea," I said, foot bobbing. "And now it's my tail in the ever-after paying for his rescue. Do I even get one thank-you? No, I get trash painted on my front door."

"You got your life back," Jenks said, "and an end to Al trying to kill you. Got an understanding in the ever-after that any demon messing with you is messing with Al. You got Trent's silence as to what you are. He could have brought you down right there. It wouldn't be graffiti on your door but a burning stake in the front yard, with you tied to it."

I froze, shocked. *What I am?* Trent kept silent as to *what I am?* I should be *thankful* he didn't tell anyone? If he told anyone what I was, he'd have to explain how I got that way, which would put him on the stake next to me.

But Jenks was smiling at his son, oblivious. "There you go, Jerrimatt," he said fondly as he gave the youngster a boost into the air where he hung, shedding bright sparkles to pool on the table. "And if glue should somehow end up in Jack's mittens, I won't have any idea who did it."

The small pixy's wings fanned into motion and a cloud of silver dust enveloped both of them. "Thanks, Papa," Jerrimatt said, and his tear-wet eyes took on a familiar glint of deviltry.

Jenks watched his son fly away with a fond look. Rex watched, too, tail twitching. Turning back to me, Jenks saw my sour mood. *Trent kept silent as to what I am, eh?*

"I mean," the pixy backpedaled, "what Trent's dad did to you."

Mollified, I took my feet from the table and put them on the floor. "Yeah, whatever," I muttered as I rubbed my wrist and the demon mark there. I had another on the bottom of my foot, since Al hadn't traded it back for his summoning name yet, enjoying my owing him two marks. I lived with the worry that I'd be pulled into someone's demon circle some night, but no one had summoned Al and gotten me instead—yet.

The demon marks were hard to explain, and more people than I liked knew what they were. It was the victors who wrote the history books, and I wasn't winning. But at least I wasn't living in the ever-after, playing blow-up doll to a demon. No, I was just playing his student.

Leaning my head back and looking at the ceiling, I shouted, "Ivy? That coffee done?"

Rex skittered under the pool table at my voice, and at Ivy's positive call, I clicked off the music and lurched to my feet. Jenks went to help Matalina break up a fight about glitter, and I paced down the long hall that bisected the back end of the church. I passed the his-and-her bathrooms that had been converted into Ivy's opulent bathroom and my more Spartan facilities that also boasted the washer and dryer. Our separate bedrooms were next, my best guess putting them originally as clergy offices. Though the dark hallway didn't change, the feeling of the air did as I entered the unsanctified back end of the church, added on later. This was where the kitchen and private living room were, and if it had been sanctified, I would have slept here.

Put simply, I loved my kitchen. Ivy had remodeled it before

I had moved in, and it was the best room in the place. A blue-curtained window over the sink looked out on the small witch's garden. Beyond that was the graveyard. That had bothered me at first, but after mowing the site for a year, I had a fondness for the weathered stones and forgotten names.

Inside, it was all gleaming stainless steel and bright fluorescent light. There were two stoves—one gas, one electric—so I didn't have to do my spells and cook on the same surface. The counter space was expansive, and I used it all when I spelled, which was often, since the charms I used were expensive unless I made them myself. Then they were dirt cheap. Literally.

In the center was an island counter with a circle etched into the linoleum around it. I used to keep my spell books in the open rack under it until Al had burned one in a fit of pique. Now they were in the belfry. The counter made for a secure place to spell, unsanctified or not.

Up against the interior wall was a heavy antique farm table. Ivy was sitting at the back corner of it, near the archway to the hall, with her computer, printer, and stacks of carefully filed papers. When we'd moved in, I had the use of one end of it. Now I was lucky if I got a corner to eat on. So of course I'd taken over the rest of the kitchen.

Ivy looked up from her keyboard, and I dropped my bag on yesterday's unopened mail and collapsed in my chair. "You want some lunch?" I asked, seeing as it was nearing midnight.

She shrugged, eyeing the bills. "Sure."

I knew it bugged her, so I left the mail where it was under my bag, and I lurched back to my feet with tomato soup and cheese crackers in mind. If she wanted something more, she'd say so. A pang of worry went through me as I pulled a can of soup off the pantry shelves. Glenn liked tomatoes. God, I hoped he was okay. That he was unconscious had me concerned.

Ivy clicked through a couple of Web pages as I made good with the can opener. I hesitated at the sight of my copper spell pots, then reached for a more mundane saucepan. Mixing spell prep and food prep wasn't a good idea. "Research?" I asked, hearing in her silence that she was still upset about something.

"Looking up banshees," she said shortly, and I hoped she didn't know how coy she looked with the end of the pen between her teeth. Her canines were sharp, like a cat's, but she wouldn't get the extended ones until she was dead. She wouldn't get the light sensitivity or the physical need for blood to survive until then either. Ivy still had a taste for it, however, and though it made her devilishly hard to live with, she could do without.

The lid came off with a ting, and I sighed. "Ivy, I'm sorry."

Her foot moved back and forth like an angry cat's tail. "For what?" she said mildly, then stilled her foot's motion as she saw me notice it.

That my methods are getting faster results than yours, I thought, but what I said was, "For sending you out to Kisten's boat?"

I hated the question in my voice, but I didn't know what was bothering her. Ivy looked up, and I studied the rim of brown around her eyes. It was wide and full, telling me she had control of her emotions. "I can handle it," she said, and I frowned, hearing something else.

Turning my back on her, I shook the congealed soup into the pan with a dull thwap. "I don't mind going out with you." I did, but I was going to offer.

"I've got it covered," she said more forcefully.

Sighing, I searched for a wooden spoon. Ivy dealt with the uncomfortable by ignoring it, and though I wasn't averse to avoiding issues to maintain a pleasant living space, I tended to poke sticks at sleeping vampires when I thought I could get away with it.

The phone rang, and I caught Ivy's dark glare as I whipped around to answer it.

"Vampiric Charms," I said politely into the receiver. "How

can we help?" I used to answer with my name, until the first graffiti incident.

"Rachel, it's Edden," came the FIB captain's gravelly voice. "Glad you're home. Hey, we're having trouble getting the fingerprints out—"

"Re-e-e-eally?" I interrupted, making a mocking face at Ivy and turning the receiver so she could hear him with her extraordinary vamp hearing. "Imagine that."

"They keep going to the wrong office," the man continued, too intent to hear my sarcasm. "But we do know the banshee tear belongs to a Mia Harbor. The woman's been around since Cincinnati was a pig farm, and I wanted to ask you to come down tomorrow about nine and help us interview her."

I leaned against the counter with a hand to my forehead. What he wanted was for me to bring a truth amulet. Humans were adept at reading body language, but a banshee was devilishly hard to interpret. Or so I'd heard. The I.S. never sent witches after banshees.

Ivy was staring at me, brown-rimmed eyes wide. She looked surprised. No, shocked. "Nine is too early," I said, wondering what was up with her. "How about noon?"

"Noon?" he echoed. "We need to move quickly on this."

So why did you kick me out when I was making progress? "I need the morning to make up a truth charm. Those things are expensive. Unless you want a five-hundred-dollar bill for it tacked onto my consultant's fee?"

Edden was silent, but I could hear his frustration. "Noon."

"Noon," I said, feeling like I'd won some points. Actually, I had a truth amulet in my charm cupboard, two feet away, but I didn't get up until eleven most days. "As long as we're done by two. I've got to pick up my brother at the airport."

"Not a problem," he said. "I'll send a car. See you here."

"Hey, has anyone looked at my car yet?" I said, but the line had gone dead. "Tomorrow," I said with a smile, setting the phone back in its cradle. I waltzed to the fridge for the milk, then looked at Ivy when I realized she was still just sitting there. "What's the matter?"

Ivy leaned back into her chair, her expression worried. "I met Mia Harbor once. Right before I was assigned to work with you in the I.S. She's an . . . interesting lady."

"Nice lady?" I asked as I dumped in the milk. If she had been around since Cincy was a pig town, then she was probably a really *old* nice lady.

Ivy's brow was furrowed when I glanced at her, and she put her eyes on her screen. Her behavior was off. "What is it?" I asked as neutrally as I could.

The pen she was tapping stilled. "Nothing."

I made a scoffing sound. "Something's bothering you. What is it?"

"Nothing!" she said loudly and Jenks buzzed in.

Grinning, the pixy landed on the island counter between us in his best Peter Pan pose. "I think Ivy's pissed 'cause you found the banshee tear and she didn't," he said, and Ivy's pen started tapping again. It was so fast, it almost hummed.

"Nice going, Jenks," I muttered as I stirred the milk into the soup. The ticking of the burner was loud until the gas lit with a whoosh and I turned it to low. "Where's that buddy gargoyle of yours? He's supposed to keep watch at night."

"I don't know," he said, not worried at all. "But he's as hard as a rock. I wouldn't worry about him. Maybe he's visiting his folks. He does have a life, unlike some of us here."

"I think Rachel finding that tear was great," Ivy said tightly.

I glanced over my shoulder at Jenks, and at my encouragement, he went to make irritating circles around her. He could get away with a lot I couldn't, and if we didn't find out soon what was bothering her, it might be too late to head it off when we did.

"Then you're mad because you've been working on Kisten's murder for six months, and Rachel got farther in six minutes by sniffing the floor," he guessed.

Ivy leaned her chair back on two legs, balancing as she measured his flight, probably calculating where she'd have to be to catch him. "Both are valid ways of investigation," she said, her pupils widening. "And it's only been three months. I didn't look the first three."

I continued to stir the soup with a clockwise motion as Jenks rose up in a column of sparkles and darted out of the kitchen. The pixy noise in the sanctuary had reached dangerous levels, and I knew he wanted to handle it to give Matalina a break. She was doing great this winter, but we were all still worried about her. Nineteen was old for a pixy.

That Ivy hadn't done anything to find Kisten's killer for the first three months wasn't a surprise. The hurt had been that bad, and she thought she might have been the one who had done it. "I don't mind going out with you tonight," I offered again. "Ford left the ladder."

"I'm doing this myself."

I bowed my head over the soup, breathing in the acidic scent and feeling Ivy's pain now that Jenks wasn't here cluttering everything up. I'd been Kisten's girlfriend, but Ivy had loved him, too—deeper, on a gut level, with the strength of the past, not like my new love, based on the idea of a future. And here I was, making her deal with the pain. "Are you okay?" I asked softly.

"No," she said again, her voice flat.

My shoulders slumped. "I miss him, too," I whispered. I turned to see her perfect face frozen in grief. I couldn't help it, and risking a misunderstanding, I crossed the room. "It's going to be okay," I said, touching her shoulder for an instant before I withdrew and went into the pantry for the crackers.

Ivy had her head bowed when I came out, and I said nothing as I found two bowls and set them on the table with the crackers between them, shoving my bag and the mail out of the way. Uncomfortable with the silence, I hesitantly stood before her. "I'm, uh, starting to remember a little," I said, and her dark eyes flicked to mine. "I didn't want to tell you in front of Edden because Ford thinks he'll reopen the case when he finds out."

Fear flickered behind her eyes, and my breath caught. *Ivy is scared?*

"What did you remember?" she said, and my mouth went dry. Ivy was never scared. Ticked, seductive, chill, occasionally out of control, but never scared.

I shrugged, trying to look nonchalant when I pulled back, a sliver of my own fear sliding under my skin. "I know for sure it's a man. I got that today. He caught a splat ball without breaking it when I tried to shoot him. And he dragged me down the hall on my stomach after I tried to get out." I looked at my fingertips, then put a hand to my middle. Eyes on the hallway behind her, I whispered, "I tried to claw my way out through a wall."

Ivy's voice was a thin whisper. "A man. You're sure?"

She doesn't still think it was her, does she? I nodded, and her entire posture slumped.

"Ivy, I told you it wasn't you," I blurted. "God, I know what you smell like, and you weren't there! How many times do I have to say it!" I didn't care that it was really weird I knew what Ivy smelled like. Hell, we'd been living together for a year. She knew what *I* smelled like.

Ivy put her elbows on either side of her keyboard and dropped her forehead into the cradle of her fingers. "I thought it was Skimmer," she said flatly. "I thought Skimmer had done it. She still won't see me, and I thought that was why."

My lips parted as it started to make sense. No wonder Ivy hadn't been hell-bent on finding Kisten's killer. Skimmer had been both her best friend and girlfriend in high school, the two sharing their blood and bodies while Ivy was out in a private school on the West Coast. The intelligent, devious vampire had moved east to get Piscary out of prison and hopefully become a member of a foreign camarilla to be with Ivy, and the top-of-her-class lawyer would cheerfully kill Kisten or me if that's what it would take. That the petite but deadly woman had killed Piscary only added to the travesty of vampire logic. She was in jail for the crime of killing a city master—in front of witnesses—and would likely stay there until she died and became an undead herself.

"Kisten couldn't be taken down by another living vampire," I said, pitying Ivy for having lived with this alone for six freaking months.

Her deep brown eyes had lost their fear when they met mine. "He'd let Skimmer kill him if Piscary gave him to her." Ivy looked at the mirrored black square the night had turned the window into. "She hated him. She hates you—" Ivy's words caught, and she shifted her keyboard in a nervous reaction. "I'm glad it wasn't her."

The bubbling soup was threatening to run over, and I got up, giving her shoulder a squeeze of support before I went to turn it down. "It was a man," I said, blowing on the top and flicking the gas off. "It's going to be okay. We'll find him, and we can put an end to it."

My back was to her, and I froze as a faint tingle started at my neck, the scar she'd given me hidden under my curse-smoothed skin. I felt the muscles in my face grow slack, and my motion of stirring the soup slowed as the feeling deepened into a soft anticipation that struck the pit of my being and rebounded. Knowing Ivy couldn't see, I let my eyes close. I knew this feeling. Missed it, even as I struggled, against my instincts, to push it away.

In her relief that Skimmer hadn't killed Kisten, Ivy had unconsciously filled the air with pheromones to soothe and relax a potential source of blood and ecstasy. She wasn't after my blood, but she'd been uptight for the last six months, which was probably why just this hint of pheromones felt really good. I breathed them in, enjoying the rush of desire that tightened my gut and set my thoughts spinning. I wasn't going to act on it. Ivy and I had a safe, secure, platonic relationship. I wanted to keep it that way. But that wouldn't stop me from this tiny little indulgence.

Sighing, I forced myself to focus on what I was doing. I adjusted my posture and shoved the whisper of desire deep, where I could ignore it. If I didn't, Ivy would sense my willingness, and we'd be right back where we'd been six months ago, unsure, uneasy, and way too confused.

"Are you going to open your mail sometime this century?" Ivy asked, her voice distant. "You've got something from the university."

Glad for the distraction, I tapped the spoon and set it in the spoon cozy. "Really?" I said, turning to find her eyeing the half-hidden stack of mail. Wiping my fingers off on my jeans, I came closer, pulling the slim envelope with the university emblem on it out from under my bag but leaving the rest, as it so clearly bothered her. I'd registered for a couple of ley line classes right before winter break, and this was probably the confirmation. I could use ley lines, but everything I knew had been learned by the seat of my pants. I was in desperate need of some formal classes before I fried my synapses.

Ivy shifted her crossed legs and focused on her computer as I ran my finger under the seal, having to tear the envelope to actually get it open. I pulled the letter out, hesitating as my check floated to the floor. Ivy was on it in a flash, short hair swinging as she bent to pick it up.

"I've been denied entrance," I said, bewildered as I scanned the formal letter. "They say there was a problem with my check." My eyes shot to the date under the letterhead. Crap, I had missed early registration and now I'd have to tack on another fee. "Did I forget to sign it or something?"

Ivy shrugged, handing it to me. "No. I think this has more to do with the professor dying the last time you took a class."

Wincing, I jammed everything back in the envelope. Problem with my check? I had money in my account. This was crap. "She's not dead. She's in Trent's basement playing Ms. Fix-it with the elven genetic code. The woman is in heaven."

"Dead," Ivy said, smiling to show a slip of teeth.

I looked away, stifling a quiver at the sight of her fangs. "This is so unfair."

The harsh clatter of pixy wings gave us a second of warning, and I dropped the letter in disgust as Jenks buzzed in. Ivy's eyes were wide in question as she gazed at him, and turning, I was surprised to see a stream of red sparkles slipping from him. "We got trouble," he said, and I jumped, looking down when a faint bump came from under the floor.

Ivy stood and looked at the faded linoleum. "Someone's under there."

"That's what I'm telling you!" Jenks said, sounding almost snotty as he hovered between us with his hands on his hips.

There was a masculine, muffled shout and a series of thumps. "Holy crap!" I shouted, dancing backward. "That sounded like Marshal!"

Ivy was a blur headed for the back door. I jumped to follow, jerking to a halt when the rear door in the back living room thumped open unseen. Bis, who rented out the belfry, flew into the kitchen at shoulder height, his skin a stark white to match the snow and his eyes glowing like a demon's. The cat-size gargoyle beat his wings in my face, and I backed up. "Get out of my way, Bis!" I shouted, squinting at the draft and thinking about Jenks's cold sensitivity. "What the Turn is going on out there?"

There was a commotion in the living room, but Bis wouldn't get out of my way, shouting in his resonant voice about how he was sorry, and he'd clean it up. That he had followed the kids with the paint and didn't know it was a distraction. I was ready to smack him one when he landed on my shoulder.

I could barely feel his weight, but vertigo hit me and I slumped back into the counter, shocked into thoughtlessness. The sensation wasn't unexpected, but it got me every time— with Bis's touch, every single ley line in Cincinnati became clear and present in my mind. It was sensory overload, and I wavered on my feet, focus blurred. It was worse when he was excited, and I almost passed out. That Jenks's kids were darting among the hanging pots didn't help.

"Get. Off," I breathed forcefully, and looking chagrined, the gargoyle beat his wings three times and perched himself sullenly on top of the fridge. The pixy kids scattered, shrieking as if he were death itself. Bis's creased face scowled at me with teenage bad temper, and his pebbly skin shifted to match the stainless steel of the appliance. He looked like a sulky gargoyle peering over the edge like that, but that's what he was.

My head jerked up when Ivy shoved a snow-and-dirt-covered man into the kitchen. His face was hidden by a hood, and frozen chunks of dirty snow scattered across the floor, leaving streaks of mud as the kitchen's warmth thawed them. The odor of cold earth rose, and I wrinkled my nose, thinking it almost smelled like the man who had killed Kisten, but not quite.

Ivy sauntered in behind him to take a stance in the door with her arms crossed over her chest. Marshal was behind her, and he came in, sliding around Ivy with no hesitation and grinning from ear to ear, excited and bright eyed under his knit hat. His coat and knees were covered in dirt as well, but at least he hadn't rolled in it.

The unknown man in the parka lifted his head, and I almost flew at him. "Tom!" I shouted, then checked myself. It was Tom. Again. Under my house instead of looking at my car. Fear slid through me, replaced with anger. "What are you doing under my house!"

Jenks was at the ceiling yelling at his kids to get out, and when the last fled, with their wooden swords and plastic-coated straightened paper clips, Tom pulled himself upright and pushed his hood back. His lips were blue with cold, and his eyes held an irritated anger. It was then that I noticed the ley line zip-strip on his wrist, where his gloves ended. He was basically magically neutered, and my estimation of Marshal went up a notch for not only knowing what to do with an experienced ley line witch, but for having a zip-strip to begin with.

"I was coming over to drop off that box you left in my car," Marshal said, shifting to stand between Tom and me. "That's when I saw this"—he gave Tom a shove and the man caught himself against the island counter—"coming over the far wall. So I parked and watched. He gave a couple of kids a can of black spray paint and a twenty, and after Bis chased them off your front door, he snuck around back and broke the lock on your crawl space access."

Mouth open in anger, I thought about giving Tom a shove myself. "You paid someone to ruin our sign!" I shouted. "Do you know how long it took me to clean it the first time?"

Tom's lips were starting to pink up, and he pressed them together, refusing to answer. Behind him, I saw Bis sneak out of the kitchen. The small gargoyle had gone entirely white to match the ceiling, and only the rims of his ears, his long claw-like nails, and a thick stripe down his whiplike tail were still gray. He was crawling along the ceiling like a bat, wings held to make sharp angles and claws extended. It just about broke my creepy meter.

"Rachel," Marshal said gently, "he did it to get rid of Bis." Marshal took off his hat and unzipped his coat, sending a wave of redwood into the kitchen, heady from whatever magic he'd used to catch Tom. "What's important is finding out what he was doing under your church."

We all turned to look at Tom. "Good question," I said. "Got an answer, witch?"

Tom was silent, and Ivy cracked her knuckles one by one. I hadn't even known she could, but that's what she was doing, pop, pop, pop.

"Ivy," I said when it was clear he wasn't going to say anything. "Why don't you call the I.S.? They might be interested in this."

Tom snickered, his arrogance clear. "Sure, you do that," he said. "I'm sure the I.S. would love to know a shunned witch was in your kitchen. Who do you think they'll believe if I tell them I was buying charms from you?"

Oh shit. My gut twisted, and I frowned when Marshal's eyes widened at the word "shunned." Without a word, Ivy set the phone down. Her eyes a dangerous black, she eased closer. A threatening haze seemed to drift a few seconds behind her as she placed her finger under his chin and asked in a soft voice, "Is there a contract out on Rachel?"

Fear bubbled against my skull, and I caught it before it triggered something worse in Ivy. I'd lived with a death threat before, and it was hard. If not for Ivy and Jenks, I would have died.

Tom took a step back and rubbed his wrist. "She'd be dead already if there was."

Jenks bristled, his wings a sharp clatter as he came to stand on my shoulder.

"Oooooh, I'm scared," I said to hide my relief. "What are you doing here, then?"

The angry witch smiled. "To wish you a happy New Year."

My eyes narrowed, and, fist on my hip, I looked at the dirty puddles his boots were making. Gaze slowly rising, I took in his white nylon pants and his gray coat. His face was calm but the hatred was there, and when Ivy shifted her feet, he jerked, tense. "I'd start talking," she threatened. "If you're shunned, no one will care if you don't show up for church next week."

The tension started to rise, and my gaze broke from Tom when Bis flew back in.

"Tink's diaphragm!" Jenks shouted. "When did he leave? Rachel, did you even see him leave?"

"Here, Rachel," the gargoyle said as he dropped an amulet and my hand flashed out to catch it. The metallic circlet hit my palm with a cool sensation, smelling like redwood and frozen dirt. "I found it stuck to the floorboards. It was the only one."

Tom's jaw went stiff as he clenched his teeth. My anger grew as I recognized it from the days when I'd sit with my dad while he prepped his spells for a night at work. "It's a bug," I said as I handed it to Marshal to look at.

Ivy's face grew even grimmer, and spreading her feet, she

tossed her short, gold-tipped hair out of her eyes. "Why are you bugging our kitchen?"

Tom didn't say anything, but he didn't have to. I'd found him in front of the Tilsons' house. He had told me he was working. He probably thought we'd have the inside scoop on the situation, and since he didn't have access to anything magical or the Inderland database, he was going to steal what we knew and use it to jerk the tag out from under us.

"This is about the Tilsons, isn't it," I said, and I knew I was right when his eyes went to the soup, scumming over. "You want to tell me now? Save me the trouble of having Ivy beat it out of you?"

"Stay away from her," Tom said vehemently. "I've been watching that woman for five months, and *she's mine*! Got it?"

I leaned back, nodding as he confirmed my thoughts. Tom knew they weren't the Tilsons and was probably working on the murders already. He seemed to think the woman had done it. "I'm just doing my job, Tom," I said, starting to feel better. Sure he had bugged me, but my car was probably not wired to explode; dead people don't talk—usually. "Tell you what. You stay out of my way, I'll stay out of yours, and the best witch will win. Okay?"

"Sure," the man said, confidence suddenly flowing from him. "Good luck with that. You're going to come begging to talk to me before this is all over. I guarantee it."

Jenks's wings made a cool draft on my neck. "Get the cookie out of here," he said sharply, and Marshal came forward to manhandle him out. Ivy beat him to it, gripping Tom's wrist and twisting his arm into a painful angle to propel him into the hall.

"Don't forget his amulet," I called after her, and Bis darted down to take it from Marshal and fly after them. I heard a muttered comment from Ivy, and then the back door shut. Bis didn't come back. I assumed he'd gone with her.

"She can handle him okay?" Marshal asked, and I nodded, my knees suddenly shaky.

"Oh yeah. She'll be fine. It's Tom I'm worried about." My stomach hurt. Damn it, it had been ages since anyone had dared to violate the security of my home, and now that it was over, I didn't like it. Grimacing, I stirred the soup, nervous energy making me slop it over. Jenks was flitting like a mad thing, and while wiping up my spill, I muttered, "Park it, Jenks."

The kitchen grew quiet apart from the rasp of Marshal taking off his coat, but it was the gurgle of him pouring two cups of coffee that brought my attention back. I managed a thin smile when he brought me one. Jenks was on his shoulder, which was unusual, but the man had saved us a lot of trouble, and Jenks had to appreciate that since he couldn't go outside and Bis was just one gargoyle—and a young, inexperienced one at that.

"Thanks," I said, turning from the soup and taking a sip of coffee as I leaned against the counter. "For Tom as well as the coffee," I added.

Looking satisfied and smug, Marshal pulled a chair around and sat with his back to the wall and his legs in the middle of the room. "Not a problem, Rachel. I'm glad I was here."

Trailing a thin green dust, Jenks flew to land beside me, pretending to feed his brine shrimp on the sill. I knew Marshal thought my estimation of the danger I could attract was overrated, but even I'd admit that his catching a shunned ley line witch was impressive.

I breathed deep as I listened to the pixy play-by-play, filtering in from the sanctuary, of what Ivy was doing to Tom. The subtly masculine-flavored scent of redwood eased about me, a witch's characteristic smell. It was nice smelling it in my kitchen, mixing with vampire and the light garden scent I was starting to recognize as pixy. Marshal was eyeing the ceiling in an expectant way, and chuckling, I went to sit with him.

"All right," I said as I touched his hand encircling his coffee. "I admit it. You saved me. You saved me from whatever Tom had planned. You're my great big *freaking* hero, okay?"

He laughed at that, and it felt good. "You want that box from my car?" he said, starting to gather himself to stand.

I thought about what was in it, and froze. "No. Will you throw it out for me?" *I'm not throwing Kisten away,* I thought guiltily. But to keep his last gift in my bottom drawer was pathetic. "Uh, thanks again for going with me out to the boat."

Marshal shifted his chair, angling it to face me. "No problem. Is your FIB friend okay?"

I nodded, my thoughts drifting to Glenn. "Ford says he'll be awake in a few days."

Jenks had gotten himself a pixy-size mug of coffee from the still-dripping machine, and he settled between us on the box of crackers. He was unusually quiet, but he was probably keeping an ear on his kids. There was a sound of rising awe from the sanctuary when Ivy did something, and I winced.

My eyes went to the corner of the envelope, and in a sudden surge of irritation, I picked it out. "Hey, will you do something for me?" I asked as I handed it to Marshal. "I'm trying to pay for some classes, and I need to get this to the registrar's office, like yesterday."

"I thought registration ended," Jenks piped up, and Marshal's eyebrows went high as he took it.

"It did," he said, and I shrugged.

"They sent my check back," I complained. "Can you see if they will take it? Use your connections to get it in the system? I don't want to have to pay the late fee."

Nodding, he folded the envelope over and slid it into a back pocket to look at later. Brow furrowed, he leaned back in his chair, thinking. "You want some soup?" I asked, and Marshal smiled.

"No, thanks," he said, then his eyes brightened. "Hey, I've got tomorrow off. It's a teacher workday at the university, but it's not like I've got any papers to grade. You want to go do something? Blow off some steam? After I get your check in, that is? I hear they opened up a new skate park on Vine."

Whereas two months ago the offer would have tripped all

my warning flags, now my lips curled up in a smile. Marshal wasn't my boyfriend, but we did stuff together all the time. "I don't think I can," I said, annoyed that I couldn't say yes and go. "I've got this murder I'm working on . . . and my sign to clean . . ."

Jenks's wings clattered. "I said I'd help you with that, Rache," he said brightly, and I smiled and curved my hand around him.

"It's too cold, Jenks," I protested, then turned back to Marshal. "Then I've got to pick up my brother at the airport at three, talk to Ford at six, and then go back to my mom's and do the good-daughter thing by having dinner with her and Robbie. Saturday I'm in the ever-after with Al. . . ." My words trailed off. "Next week, maybe?"

Marshal nodded in understanding, and suddenly seeing a golden opportunity to avoid being badgered at my mom's, I blurted out, "Uh, unless you want to come with me to my mom's for dinner? She's making lasagna."

The man laughed. "You want me to play boyfriend so your life doesn't look pathetic, right?"

"Marshal!" I gave his shoulder a smack, but I was red-faced. God, he knew me too well.

"Well, am I right?" he needled, his eyes glinting under his hat-flattened hair.

I made a face, then said, "You going to help me here or not?"

"You bet," he said brightly. "I like your mom. Is she making pi-i-i-ie?"

He stressed the word as if it meant the world to him, and I grinned, feeling better about tomorrow already. "If she knows you're coming, she'll make two."

Marshal chuckled, and as I sipped my coffee and smiled back, content and happy, Jenks flew out of the kitchen on quiet wings, a green trail of dust spilling from him to slowly fade to nothing.

Six

The FIB's lobby was noisy and cold. Gray street slush had been tracked in, making a soggy mess of the rug and creating a slowly diminishing black path to the front desk, set back from the twin glass doors. The FIB emblem in the middle of the room was dingy from a hundred footprints. It reminded me of the emblem on the floor of the demons' law offices. A joke, Al had said, but I had my doubts. I shifted nervously in the nasty orange chairs they had out here. Saturday, and my teaching date with Algaliarept, always seemed to come up too fast. Trying to explain to Robbie and my mom why I was going to be incommunicado all day would be tricky.

I had cheerfully strode into the FIB about ten minutes before—my mood excellent since Alex had brought my car home—my snappy boots leaving prints on their emblem as I went to the front desk to announce who I was—only to be asked to take a seat, like I was some weirdo off the street. Sighing, I hunched over with my elbows on my knees and tried to find a comfortable position. I wasn't happy about being asked to wait. If Ivy had been here, they would've fallen all over themselves, but not for me—a memory-challenged witch they didn't trust anymore.

Ivy was currently out on the street trying to pick up the sixth-month-old trail of Kisten's killer. Guilt for not having done anything sooner had gotten her up long before me. Jenks had come with me today in the hopes that we'd stop at a charm shop on the way home. He wasn't interested in a charm, but the stuff that went into making them—things that a garden-loving pixy cheating hibernation can't get in December. Matalina wasn't doing well, and I knew he was upset, ready and willing to spend some of the rent money he got from Ivy and me on his wife. Sitting here in the FIB's lobby was a poor use for both our days. Not to mention that it was cold.

I straightened to swing my bag between my knees to try to burn off some irritation, and snuggled into my scarf, Jenks wiggled to life. "What's up, Rache?" he asked, landing on my hands to get me to stop swinging my bag.

"Nothing," I said shortly.

His brow rose, and he gave me a look. "Then why did your pulse quicken and your temperature rise?" He made a face. "Your perfume stinks. God, what did you do, bathe in it?"

I stared at the receptionist, avoiding Jenks's question. I couldn't tell him I was worried about his wife not making it through the winter. He buzzed his wings for my attention, and I tapped the banshee report on my knee. I had written it for Edden this morning—which only made me madder. I was here to help, and they left me waiting with distraught parents and thugs cuffed to the walls? Nice.

"Lookie here, Rache," Jenks said, not a speck of dust falling from him as he flew heavily two seats down and landed on a discarded paper. "You made some print."

"What?" Expecting the worst, I leaned over and snatched it up. Jenks laboriously flew back and settled on my hand as I held the paper up, scanning the picture. This was all I needed, but my worry eased when I found it was just a shot of the Tilsons' house with a crowd and a news van out front. The caption said YEAR-END BRIMSTONE BUST GONE WRONG, and you couldn't even tell it was me unless you knew it.

"Gonna save it for your scrapbook?" Jenks asked as I quickly read the article.

"No." I tossed the paper back where it had been, then

stretched to turn the picture side down. *Drug bust, eh? Good for them. Keep it that way.*

Hands on his hips, Jenks flew into my line of sight, but I was saved from whatever smart-ass remark he was going to gift me with when the doors cycled open and two uniformed FIB guys roughly escorted in a thin Santa. The man was shrieking about his reindeer. The cold draft hit us, and Jenks dove for my scarf.

"Tink's titties, you think you could put a little more perfume on, Rache?" he complained, and I shivered as his wings brushed my bare skin.

"It's from Ivy," I said.

"Oh."

I sighed as I settled in to wait. I'd found the new bottle of citrusy scent on the kitchen table this morning. I'd known what it meant and had immediately dabbed on a splash. Apparently, after yesterday, Ivy thought it prudent to reinstate our practice of trying to muddle the mixing of our natural scents. We hadn't had to resort to chemical warfare on her instincts for a while, but we'd been trapped in the church with the windows closed for months.

The Santa broke from the officers and bolted for the door. I jerked upright, then relaxed as the two officers fell on him. All three slid into the doors with a thump. The guy was cuffed. How far was he going to get? "Damn," I swore softly, wincing. "That's going to leave a mark."

A presence of old coffee tickled my nose, and I wasn't surprised when Edden appeared at my elbow. "The one on the bottom is Chad. He's new. I think he's trying to impress you."

My irritation at having to wait returned, and I looked up at the squat FIB captain. He was in his usual khakis and dress shirt. No tie, but his brown dress shoes were polished and he held himself with his familiar uprightness. His eyes, too, looked more determined. Tired, but the fear was gone. Glenn must be doing better.

"I'm impressed," I said, catching the drama out of the corner of my eye as Chad dragged Santa into the back. "Can't you bring the loonies in the rear door?"

Edden shrugged. "It's too icy, and we'd get sued."

From my scarf, Jenks said, "And crashing into the door like that is so-o-o-o much safer."

"Resisting arrest with lots of witnesses," he said. "I'd say that's safer." Then he tilted his head and peered at my scarf. "Hi, Jenks. I didn't see you. Kind of cold, isn't it?"

"Enough to freeze my balls together, yeah," Jenks said, peeking out at the sound of Edden's louder voice. "You got anyplace warmer? Between the cold and Rachel's perfume, I'd be more comfortable at a fairy's bris."

The short man smiled, and he extended a hand to take the banshee essay that I'd written for him in my copious spare time. "Come on back. Sorry to make you wait here. New rules."

New rules, I thought sourly as I stood. New rules or new mistrust? Old mistrust, maybe given new life. At least Chad liked me. "No problem," I said sourly, not wanting to let him know how much it bothered me. He knew it was there, I knew it was there. Why rub my nose in it? "How's Glenn doing? Has he regained consciousness yet?"

Edden had a hand on the small of my back, and where I'd usually take offense, he could get away with it. Edden was cool. "No," he said, his eyes down with a thought. "But he's doing better. More brain activity."

Once away from the cold draft, Jenks left my scarf, and I nodded, thinking I should go out and see Glenn tonight after dinner. I'd be ready for some silent company by then. Maybe tickle his feet until he woke up or peed his sheets or something. I smiled at the thought, almost missing it when Edden made an unexpected left away from the interrogation rooms.

"Aren't we going to the interrogation rooms?" I said, and Edden led me to his office.

"No. We can't find Mia Harbor."

My pace didn't slow, but me cooling my heels in the lobby

was making a lot more sense. So much for the truth amulet stuffed in my bag.

Jenks was starting to slip a thin trail of dust, telling me he was warm and in good form. "She went AWOL?" the small pixy said, flying backward to create a small commotion among the watching officers.

Edden wasn't impressed with Jenks's aerial display, and he held the door to his office open and gestured for me to enter. "Yup," he said, but he didn't follow me in. "She moved without filing her new address. We've a warrant out for her arrest, so if you want her, she's all yours, Rachel."

"A banshee?" I said, laughing. "Me? How much money you got, Edden? I don't do suicide runs."

Edden tossed my essay on his desk, hesitating as if trying to decide whether I was kidding. "You want some coffee?" he finally said. "How about you, Jenks? I think I saw a honey packet from someone's biscuits in the fridge."

"Hell yes!" he exclaimed before I could protest, and Edden nodded, leaving the door open as he went in search of it.

I gave Jenks a wry look as he buzzed over Edden's office to check out the new bowling trophy. Spinning the chair around, I plunked into it and set my bag at my feet. "I was really hoping you'd be sober for this," I said, and Jenks landed on Edden's cluttered desk with his hands on his hips.

"Why?" he said, unusually belligerent. "You don't need me if the banshee isn't here. Give me a break. Like I've been honey drunk any longer than five minutes."

I looked away in disapproval, and he buzzed a harsh flight to Edden's pencil cup to sulk. Crossing my knees, I bobbed my foot. I was waiting again, but it was warmer, quieter, and I had the promise of coffee.

Edden's office was a pleasant mix of organized clutter that I could identify with and was part of the reason I had taken to him so quickly last year. The man was ex-military, but you'd never know it by the dust and stacks of files. Still, I bet he could put his finger on anything he wanted in three seconds flat. The pictures on the walls were few, but in one of them he was shaking hands with Denon, my old boss at the I.S. It would worry me if I hadn't once heard the pleasure Edden had taken in jerking a case out from under him. The smell of old coffee seemed embedded in the gray tiles and institutional-yellow walls. A new laptop sat open on his desk instead of a monitor, and the clock that had once been behind him was now behind me. Otherwise, it was the same as the last time I had sat here, waiting for Edden to bring me coffee.

I heard Edden's footsteps before his bulky silhouette showed through the blinds between his office and the rest of the other offices, all open. The man came in with two china mugs instead of the expected foam ones. New rules again? One was clearly his by the brown-stained rim. I got the clean one with rainbows. How sweet . . .

Jenks rose up in a column of blue sparkles as Edden sat behind his desk, the pixy taking the packet almost as large as he was and retreating to a corner, out of my reach. "Thanks, Edden," he said, wrestling with the plastic to tear it open.

I leaned to shut the door with my foot, and Edden eyed me. "You have something to say in private, Rachel?" he asked, and I shook my head. Taking the packet from Jenks, I tore it open and handed it back.

"Trust me," I said, thinking that having the harried FIB officers deal with a drunk pixy was too much to ask for. My reputation was bad enough as it was.

"So," I said to draw Edden's attention from Jenks, who was humming happily and starting to list already, one wing not fanning as fast as the other. "Isn't a felony charge a little harsh for failure to register a new address?"

Edden's gaze darted from me to Jenks, and then back. "It's not for failure to register. It's because she's a suspect."

"'S good honey, Eddie," Jenks interrupted, and I set my coffee mug down loud enough to make his wings hum.

"The banshee is a suspect?" I questioned. "Why? All she did was leave a tear."

Edden leaned back in his chair and sipped his coffee. "Alex took her photo out to the neighbors to see if she had been near the scene recently. Babysitter, cosmetics lady, whatever. Every single person asked ID'd Ms. Harbor as Mrs. Tilson."

"What?" I yelped, sitting up fast.

"Holy crap," Jenks swore, almost crashing into the stack of files on Edden's desk as he took flight with his honey packet. "The banshee took a human's name? What the hell for?"

My first wash of surprise ebbed into an uneasy answer, and by looking at Edden's severe face, I knew he had the same idea. Mia had killed them and was trying to cover it up. *Good God. Tom is trying to tag a banshee? By himself? Go for it, coffin bait.* "That might explain why Tom Bansen was under our kitchen floor yesterday," I said, and Edden started.

"Under your—"

"Kitchen floor," I finished. "All dressed up like a military guy on urban-assault detail. Bis and one of my friends caught him trying to bug the church."

"Why didn't you call me?" Edden said, and I made a face while Jenks slurred something about the gargoyle.

"Because Tom's been, ah, shunned," I said, flushing. "No Inderlander will hire him, the I.S. included. He has no choice but to go independent. Bringing in a banshee will probably earn him enough money to get himself set up somewhere he can live his life out in the wilds. He warned me off the case. Now that I think about it, he told me specifically to stay away from Mia. He probably knows at least as much as we do."

"Then why bug you?" he asked, and I shrugged.

"Because if he's been shunned, he lacks the resources of both the FIB and the I.S. I guess he figured he'd listen in to what we found and act on it before we did. Tom probably knows exactly where she's gone. Maybe I should try to bug him."

Edden looked grim, rubbing his mustache, when I finally looked back. "Want a car at your house?"

Immediately I shook my head. "No, but one at my mom's might be nice."

"Within the hour," he promised, the pen almost lost in his grip as he made a note.

Jenks had started climbing Edden's desk files like a drunken mountaineer, and I blushed when I found out what happened on the tenth day of pixy Christmas. Shaking off the visual, I turned to Edden. "If Mia is Mrs. Tilson, we need to find her fast. The man with her is in danger."

Edden made an ugly sound and just about threw the pen in the cup. "I don't care."

"He's liable to wind up dead," I protested, then took a sip of my coffee now that Jenks wasn't hiding behind it. My eyes closed in bliss for a moment. I'd give the FIB one thing: They knew how to make coffee. "A banshee's live-ins never live long," I said. "And if Mia has a baby, her emotion requirements will be almost triple." I paused in my motion to take another drink. That was probably why she had to put five years between her children.

Edden's mustache was bunched up, and his expression was hard. "I'm not concerned about Mia's accomplice," he said. "He was healthy enough to beat up my son. We pulled his record this morning by way of his fingerprints. His name is Remus, and we would never have found him this fast but he's got a file thicker than my fist, starting from high school with an attempted date rape, up to about three years ago when he spent time in a psychiatric jail for an especially foul animal-cruelty charge. They let him out, and he dropped off the face of the earth. No credit card activity, no rental history, no W-2 forms. Nothing until now. So you can understand if I don't rush out and try to find him for the sake of his own health."

My stomach hurt. God, the two of them had probably killed the Tilsons together. They had killed those happy faces that were in that yearbook and taken their names, their lives, everything. Shoved what they didn't want into boxes in their garage.

Jenks dropped the empty honey packet, staggering under the desk lamp and staring up at it. Realizing that he was singing to it to get it to turn on, I flicked the switch. Jenks exploded into gold sparkles and collapsed, giggling. My expression went blank. He was stuck on the tenth day of Christmas, but finally he gave up and started singing about four purple condoms.

I looked at Edden and shrugged. "Maybe the little girl belongs to Remus," I said, and Edden jerked the topmost file out from under Jenks. The pixy rose three inches before falling down, mumbling as he pillowed his head on his folded arms and fell asleep in the artificial warmth of the light. Edden handed me the file, and I opened it. "What is this?"

He leaned back to lace his hands over his middle. "Everything we have on Mia. That baby makes her a lot easier to track. Without her, Remus wouldn't exist. We found another licensed day care that Mia frequents, making four now and at least two more informal ones."

I leafed through the small packet to read the addresses, impressed again with the FIB's investigative techniques. The day cares were mostly in Ohio, on Cincy's outskirts.

"I called them all this morning," Edden said. "Mia didn't show up anywhere yesterday, and the one she was scheduled for was concerned. Apparently she always stays to help instead of paying them for care, claiming that she wants Holly to have more socialization skills."

"No kidding?" I said, eyebrows high. I could buy that, but not if she was taking her daughter to five other day cares to do the same thing.

"No, no, no," Jenks slurred from under the glaring light. His eyes weren't open, and I was surprised he was conscious enough to listen, much less comment on the conversation. "Kid isn't socializing. The kid is sucking down emotion like . . ."

His words trailed off in confusion, and I offered, "A pixy with honey?"

Jenks cracked an eye and gave me a thumbs-up. "Yeah." His eyes closed, and he started to snore. I didn't know why, but I unwound my scarf and covered him. Embarrassment, maybe?

Edden was watching us with a questioning expression, and I lifted a shoulder and let it fall. "Mia's probably trying to spread her daughter's damage around."

Edden made a noncommittal grunt, and I continued to leaf through the information. "The neighbor kid who mowed their lawn said that Mia told his mom she wanted a lot of kids but had to space them out, five years apart," I said. "That would go along with Holly being a banshee. You can't have two kids around like that. Hell, a banshee usually has a kid once every hundred years or so, so if Mia is thinking another one in five years, she must have a really good way to keep from killing people to support her daughter's growth . . ."

My words drifted to nothing. Either that, or someone with her who knew how to abduct people in a way so that they never went reported as missing. Someone like a homicidal maniac capable of serial murders. Sort of like Remus—someone who would enjoy hunting people and bringing them back for his wife and darling baby to drain. That might be why Remus was in good enough health to beat up an FIB officer, feeding his two tigers well enough that Mia could plan on adding to her little family. This was *really* not good.

Edden was quietly waiting for me to come to just that conclusion, and I closed the file. Numb and feeling sick, I glanced at Jenks, out cold, then to Edden, silently waiting. "I'm not doing this," I said, dropping the packet on his desk. The draft shifted Jenks's hair, and the pixy grimaced in his drunken stupor. "Banshees are dangerous—apex predators. And I thought you didn't want my—excuse me—our help."

At my blatant accusation, Edden reddened. "Who is going to bring her in, then? The I.S.? I talked to them this morning. They don't care." His eyes went everywhere but to mine. "If we don't bring her in, no one will," he muttered.

And he would want justice, seeing that she had something to do with his son being in the hospital. Frowning, I slid the file back off Edden's desk and onto my lap, but I didn't open it. "Next question," I said, my tone clearly stating I wasn't taking the job—yet. "What makes you so sure the I.S. isn't covering it up?" I wasn't about to get on the I.S.'s bad side for a paycheck. I'd done that before, and was smarter now. Yeah, it had felt great showing up the I.S., but then Denon took my license and I was stuck riding the bus again.

Edden's expression went tight. "What if they are?"

My face scrunched up, and I fingered the file. Yeah, it left a bad taste in my mouth, too.

"According to the woman I talked to at the I.S.," Edden said, "there should be a trail almost eighteen months long on this woman, starting with several simultaneous deaths at the time of Holly's conception and continuing on to today. That's probably when the Tilsons were murdered. Ms. Harbor is devious, clever, and has a tremendous knowledge of the city. About the only thing going for us is that she won't leave Cincinnati. Banshees are highly territorial and dependent upon the people they've been siphoning off for generations."

I bobbed my foot and looked at the essay I had written. "Why did you ask me to write this if you already knew it?" I asked, my feelings hurt.

"I didn't know it yesterday. You were sleeping, Rachel," Edden said dryly, then hid his slight guilt behind a sip of coffee. "I talked to Audrey something or other in records this morning. She was going to make me fill out a year's worth of forms until I dropped your name." A faint smile replaced his concern, and I relaxed.

"I know her," I said. "You can trust what she said."

Edden laughed, making Jenks mumble in his sleep. "Especially after I promised you'd babysit for her." He ran a hand over his mustache to hide a smile. "She was kind of cranky. You witches aren't at your best before noon, are you?"

"No," I said, then my smile faded. Audrey had three kids last I checked. Crap. I was going to have to have Jenks help me; otherwise they'd railroad me into a closet or trick me into letting them eat candy.

"Audrey said Mia's net of people is probably so intricate that she can't risk leaving Cincy. If she does, the deaths to support the baby will be fast and easy to find, rather than the carefully chosen, hidden ones." He hesitated, and a flash of worry for his son crossed his face. "Is that true? They already killed an FIB officer. That wasting disease was probably Mia, right?"

He was too far away for me to reach out and touch his hand in support, but I wanted to. I really needed to visit Glenn and look at his aura. It wasn't as if I could help him, but I'd like to know if that's why he was still unconscious. "Edden, I'm sorry," I finally said. "Glenn will be okay, and we will find them. They won't be allowed to think they can do this with impunity."

The older man's jaw clenched, then relaxed. "I know. I just wanted to hear from you that we have a chance and that they didn't hop a plane and are in Mexico, sucking the children there dry."

From under my scarf came a high-pitched sigh, and Jenks mumbled, "On the eleventh day of Christmas, my lover gave to me . . ."

I nudged the stack of files. "Hush, Jenks," I said, then pulled my eyes to Edden, softening my gaze. "We will get them, Edden. Promise."

Jenks's mumbling grew loud, and I felt uneasy when I realized he was apologizing to Matalina. That was a hindsight better than what the drummers had been doing with the piper's pipes, but his heartfelt whining was almost worse.

"Then you'll help us?" Edden asked, rather unnecessarily, I might add.

It was a banshee, but with Ivy's help—and a lot of planning—we three could do it. "I'll look into it," I said, trying to drown out Jenks's vow that he would never touch honey again if she would get better. This was getting depressing.

Edden, too, was glancing at my scarf as he rummaged around in a top drawer. He found what he was looking for, and extended his fist, palm down. "Then you might need this," he said, and I reached for whatever it was.

The smooth feel of crystal fell into my palm, and I jerked

back. Heart pounding, I stared at the opaque drop of nothing, warming fast against my skin. I waited for my hand to cramp up or the stone to feel fuzzy or move or something, but it just sat there, looking like a cheap, foggy crystal that earth witches sell ignorant humans down at Finley Market.

"Where did you get this?" I asked, feeling squeamish even as the tear did nothing. "Is it one of Mia's?" It seemed to wiggle in my hand, and it was all I could do not to drop it, but then I'd have to tell him why, and then he might take it back. So I blinked at him, my fingers going stiff in an open cradle.

"We found a stash of them in a glass flower vase, disguised as decorative stones," Edden said. "I thought you might be able to make one into a locator amulet."

It was a great idea, and I dropped the crystal into my coat pocket, deeming I'd held the squirmy thing long enough. My held breath slipped from me, and the hesitant, almost belligerent embarrassment he was hiding gave me pause until I realized he had taken the tear from evidence.

"I'll give it a try," I said, and he grimaced, eyes lowered. I had to pick up my brother at the airport, but I might be able to squeeze in a stop at the university library as well as a charm shop for Jenks before that. A locator charm was devilishly hard. I honestly didn't know if I could pull it off. The library would be the only place I could find the recipe. Well, besides the Internet, but that was asking for trouble.

My scarf was now spouting poetry, waxing lovingly about Matalina's charms in beautifully poetic to downright lustful terms. Giving the stack of papers a push, I flicked off the light. Jenks let out a long complaint, and I stood.

"Come on, Mr. Honeypot," I said to Jenks. "We gotta go."

I flicked my scarf off him, and the pixy didn't move apart from huddling into a ball. Edden stood up, and together we eyed him. I was starting to get a bad feeling about this. Usually when Jenks got honey drunk, he was a happy drunk. This looked depressed, and I felt my face lose its expression when I realized Jenks was saying Matalina's name over and over.

"Oh crap," I whispered as he started making promises he couldn't keep, asking her to make one she couldn't. My own heart breaking, I carefully scooped him up, holding the unaware pixy in my hands, cupping him in a soothing darkness and warmth. Damn it, this wasn't fair. No wonder Jenks took the opportunity to get drunk. His wife was dying, and there was nothing he could do to stop it.

"Is he going to be all right?" Edden whispered as I stood in front of the desk, not knowing how I was going to get home with him like this. I couldn't just shove him in my bag and hope for the best.

"Yes," I said absently, deep in thought.

Edden shifted from foot to foot. "Is his wife okay?"

I brought my eyes up, unshed tears for Jenks warming them as I found a deep understanding in Edden's gaze, the understanding of a man who had lost his wife. "No," I said. "Pixies live only twenty years."

I could feel Jenks light and warm in my hands, and I wished he was bigger so I could just help him into the car, take him home, and cry with him on the couch. But all I could do was carefully slide him into the masculine glove Edden was holding out to me. The lined leather would keep him warm, whereas my scarf wouldn't.

Jenks hardly noticed the move, and I could get him to the car safely and in a dignified manner. I tried to tell Edden thanks, but the words stuck in my throat. Instead, I picked up the folder. "Thanks for the addresses," I said softly, and I turned to go. "I'll give them to Ivy. She can make sense out of rat tails in the dust."

Edden opened the door, and the noise of the open offices hit me like a slap, jerking me back to reality. I wiped my eyes and tugged my bag higher up on my shoulder. I held Edden's glove carefully. Ivy and I would map out Mia's network, starting with the day cares. Then move on to see if she worked at elderly day care centers or volunteered at the hospital. This could get really ugly.

There was a soft pull on my elbow as I rocked into motion, and I paused. Edden had his eyes on the tile, and I waited until he brought them to mine.

"Tell me when Jenks needs someone to talk to," he said, and my throat closed. Recalling what Ford had told me about Edden's wife dying in a stab-and-grab, I mustered a smile and nodded. My boots clicked fast on the tile as I made for the door, head high and eyes unseeing.

I wondered if Edden would talk to me next year when we went through the same ordeal with Jenks.

Seven

The airport was noisy, and I leaned against a support beam and tried not to fidget as I waited. Jenks and I had been here for nearly an hour, but I was glad I'd gotten here early when security stopped me at the spell-checker gate. It had either been my truth amulet or my lethal-spell detector interfering with theirs, because they were about the only invoked charms I had on me. Dumping out my bag for three uniformed stiffs to paw through was not my idea of how to meet guys. Jenks had thought it was hilarious. No one else was getting searched.

The pixy was currently down the hall at the flower cart, not a single indication that he had been honey drunk earlier. He was working a deal with the owner for some fern seed if he could entice a few people to buy roses for their departing loved ones. He had still been out cold when we passed the charm shop, and I hadn't stopped either there or the library. But if he could get the fern seed, he'd be a happy pixy.

It was cool in the drafty terminal, but vastly warmer than the blue, white, and gray world outside the huge plate-glass windows. Plows kept the runways clear, and the mounds of snow at the outskirts just begged to be played on. The people around me were a mix of hurried harassment, bored irritation, and anxious expectation. I fell into the last, and as I waited for Robbie's plane to clear checks and disembark, I felt a shiver of anticipation—though some of that might have been lingering anxiety from having been stopped at the heavy-magic detector.

Witches had always worked in aviation, both on the ground and in the air, but during the Turn they'd taken it over and hadn't given it back, changing the laws until there had to be at least one highly qualified witch on duty at each security checkpoint. Even before the Turn, witches had been using heavy-magic detectors right along with the mundane metal detectors. What had looked like a random check on a harmless-looking man or woman had often been a covert search for contraband magic. Why I'd been stopped I didn't know. Bothered, I tried to smooth out my brow and relax. Unless Robbie was in first class, it would be a while.

A cloying, too-sweet scent of cinnamon and the rich aroma of coffee gave a glimmer of contentment to the rising excitement. The conversations grew loud when the door opened and the first yawning person pushed through, intent on reaching the rent-a-car stand, his eyes glazed and his pace fast. A few feet from me was a mom with three toddlers, like stair steps, probably waiting for their dad. The eldest wiggled from his mom and ran for the huge windows, and I jumped when the mom set a circle to stop the toddler dead in his tracks.

A smile curved over my face when the little boy screamed in frustration, pounding at the faintly shimmering barrier glowing a thin blue. That had been something I'd never had to worry about when I was little. Mom sucked dishwater at making circles. I hadn't been able to walk until I was three anyway, too sick to do much more than survive before then. It was a miracle I'd made it past my second birthday—an illegal medical miracle that worried me every time I went through something like the heavy-magic detection field. There was no way to detect the tampering done to my mitochondria, but I worried anyway.

Anxious, I shifted my weight to my other foot. I was eager to see Robbie, but tonight's dinner wasn't going to be fun. At least I'd have Marshal to take some of the heat off me.

The toddler's screaming shifted from frustration to recognition, and I turned when his mother dropped her circle. She was beaming, looking absolutely beautiful despite the weariness of keeping three energetic children within society's norms. I followed the toddler with my eyes as he ran to an attractive young woman in a smart-looking suit. The woman bent to pick him up, and the five of them came together in a wash of happiness. They all began to move in a confused tangle, and after a heartfelt kiss between the two women, the one in the suit exchanged a trendy bag for a gurgling infant. It looked noisy, messy, and utterly comforting.

My smile slowly faded as they moved away, and my thoughts went to Ivy. We'd never have such a recognizable relationship, where we somehow fell into normal roles that could function within society's parameters. Not that I was looking for something so traditionally nontraditional. Ivy and I *did* have a relationship, but if we tried to make it fit her ideas or go past my limits, it would blow everything to hell.

Something older than the spoken word tickled my instinct, and I pulled my eyes from the couple's vanishing backs. My gaze landed on my brother, and I smiled. He was still in the tunnel, obvious over the shorter people ahead of him. His red hair stood out like a flag, and he had a sparse beard. Sunglasses almost made him look cool, but the freckles ruined it. Seeing his smile widen as our eyes met, I pushed from the piling and waited, anticipation tingling my toes. God, I'd missed him.

People finally moved out from between us, and I could see his narrow-shouldered frame. He had on a light jacket and was carrying a shiny leather satchel and his guitar. At the head of the tunnel he stopped and thanked a short, awkward-looking salesman-type guy who handed him a piece of luggage and vanished into the crowd, carrying it for him so he wouldn't have to check it, I suppose.

"Robbie!" I called, unable to stop myself, and his smile

grew. His long legs ate up the distance, and he was before me, dropping his things and giving me a squeeze.

"Hi, sis," he said, his hug growing fierce before he let go and stepped back. The crowd flowed around us, but no one minded. Little pockets of reunion were going on all over the terminal. "You look good," he said, tousling my hair and earning a slug on his shoulder. He caught my fist, but not until after I'd connected, and he looked at my hand, smiling at the little wooden pinkie ring. "Still not liking your freckles, eh?" he said, and I shrugged. Like I was going to tell him I didn't have freckles as the side effect of a demon curse?

Instead, I gave him another hug, noticing that we were almost the same height with me in heels and him in . . . loafers? Laughing, I looked him up and down. "You are going to freeze your butt off outside."

"Yeah, I love you, too," he said, grinning as he removed his sunglasses and tucked them away. "Cut me some slack. It was seven in the morning and seventy-two degrees when I left. I haven't had any sleep but for four hours on the plane, and I'm going to crash if I don't get some coffee in me." He leaned to pick up his guitar. "Mom still making that nasty excuse for road paste?"

Smiling as if I would never stop, I picked up the larger bag, remembering the last time I'd carried his luggage. "We'd better stop and get some now. Besides, I'm waiting for Jenks to finish up with something, and I want to talk to you about Mom."

Robbie straightened from trying to grip his satchel and guitar in the same hand, his green eyes looking worried. "Is she okay?"

I stared for a moment, then realized what my last words must have sounded like. "Mom's happier than a troll under a toll bridge. What happened out there with you, anyway? She came back tan and humming show tunes. What's up with that?"

Robbie took the bag from me, and we angled to the nearest coffee stand. "It wasn't me," he said. "It was her, ah, traveling companion."

My brow furrowed and my pulse quickened. *Takata.* I'd thought as much. She'd gone out to the West Coast to spend time with her college sweetheart, and I wasn't sure what I thought about him. I mean, I knew who he was, but I didn't *know* him.

Silently we got in line, and as I stood shoulder to shoulder with Robbie, I suddenly felt tall. Takata was birth father to both of us, a college sweetheart who gave our mom the children her human husband—and Takata's best friend, incidentally—couldn't, while Takata ran off and traded his life for fortune and fame, down to dying his hair and changing his name. I couldn't think of him as Dad. My real dad had died when I was thirteen, and nothing would change that.

But standing beside Robbie now, I snuck sidelong glances at him, seeing the older rocker in him. Hell, I could look in the mirror and see Takata in me. My feet, Robbie's hands, my nose, and both our heights. Definitely my hair. Takata's might be blond where mine was red, but it curled the same way.

Robbie turned from the overhead menu and gave me a sideways hug. "Don't be mad at him," he said, instinctively knowing where my thoughts were. He'd always been able to do that, even as kids, which had been really frustrating when I was trying to get away with something. "He's good for her," he added, shoving his luggage farther along the line. "She's moving past the guilt of Dad dying. I, uh, spent some time with them," he said, nervousness making his words soft. "He loves her. And she feels special with him."

"I'm not mad at him," I said, then smacked his shoulder just hard enough to make him notice. "I'm mad at you. Why didn't you tell me Takata was our dad?"

The businessman in front of us turned around briefly, and I made a face at him.

Robbie moved forward another foot. "Right," he murmured. "Like I'm going to call you up and tell you our mom was a groupie."

I made a scoffing noise. "That's not what happened."

He looked at me and made his eyes wide. "It makes more sense than what did happen. For Christ's sake, you would have laughed your ass off if I had told you our real dad was a rock star. Then you would have asked Mom, and then she would have . . . cried."

Cried, I thought. Nice of him to not say "go off her rocker," because that's what she would have done. It had been bad enough when the truth came out. A sigh shifted my shoulders, and I scooted forward to the counter when the guy ahead of us ordered his tall latte something or other and moved off.

"I'll have a grande latte, double espresso, Italian blend," Robbie said, his eyes on the menu. "Light on the froth, heavy on the cinnamon. Can you make that with whole milk?"

The barista nodded as he wrote on the paper cup. "This together?" he asked, looking up.

"Yeah. Um, just give me a medium-size cup of the house blend," I said, suddenly disconcerted. I couldn't be sure, but I thought that Robbie's order had sounded exactly like how Minias took his coffee.

"You want a shot of something in it?" the barista persisted, and I shook my head as I ran my card through the machine before Robbie could.

"Just black."

Robbie was struggling with his stuff, so I grabbed both cups when they came up and followed him to a table too small and sticky to encourage anything but the shortest of stays. "I *can* carry stuff now," I said as I watched him stagger under it.

He gave me a sideways smile. "Not while I'm around. Sit."

So I sat, and it felt good as he bustled about, arranging his things and asking an old couple if he could have one of their chairs. I had a moment of panic when I realized the abandoned paper on the table was folded to show that shot of the Tilsons' house. Snatching it up, I jammed it in my bag just as Robbie joined me.

Landing heavy in his chair, he took the lid off his coffee and inhaled his first deep sniff, followed by a deep draft. "That's good," he said around a sigh, and I followed suit. For a moment he was silent, and then he eyed me expectantly over his paper rim. "So, how's Mom?"

The businessman who had been ahead of us had foam on his nose as he stood and looked at the departure screens. "Fine."

Robbie silently cracked his knuckles. "Do you have anything to say to me?" he asked so smugly that I turned to look at him.

There's a cop car outside Mom's house, and you'll want to know why. I'm doing a murder investigation, and it might spill over into my home life. The university won't let me attend classes. I have a date every Saturday in the ever-after with Big Al the demon. And thanks to Trent Kalamack's dad, I'm the source of the next demon generation.

"Uh, no?" I said, and he laughed, scooting his guitar closer.

"You bailed on the I.S.," he said, green eyes showing his amusement. "I told you joining them was a bad idea, but no-o-o-o-o! My little sister has to do things her way, then work twice as hard to get out of them. I'm proud of you for realizing it was a mistake, by the way."

Oh, that. Relieved, I took the lid off my coffee and blew across the top of the rich blackness, giving him a sideways look. "Bailed" wouldn't quite be the word I would use. "Stupidly quit" might be more appropriate. Or "attempted suicide." "Thanks," I managed, though what I wanted to do was start a tirade about how it hadn't been a mistake in the first place. *See, I can learn.*

"They aren't still after you, are they?" he asked, glancing to the side and shifting uncomfortably. I shook my head, and his long face became relieved—apart from a remaining hint of caution. "Good." He took a deep breath. "Working for them was too dangerous. Anything could have happened."

And usually did, I thought as the first hot sip of coffee slipped down and I closed my eyes in bliss. "Like what I'm doing now, is that safe?" I said as my eyes opened. "Jeez, Robbie, I'm twenty-six. I can take care of myself. I'm not the puny ninety-pound nothing I was when you left." It might have been a tad harsh, but the resentment of his trying to stop me from going into the I.S. remained.

"All I meant was that the people who run it are liars and corrupt vamps," he cajoled. "It wasn't just the danger. You would never have been taken seriously there, Rachel. Witches never are. You hit that glass ceiling, and there you sit for the rest of your life."

I would have gotten mad, but looking in hindsight at the last year I spent at the I.S., I knew he was right. "Dad didn't do too bad," I said.

"He could have done a lot more."

Actually, he had done a lot more. Robbie didn't know it, but our dad had probably been a mole in the I.S., passing information and warnings to Trent's dad. *Crap,* I thought in sudden realization. *Just like Francis.* No, not like Francis. Francis had done it for money. Dad must have done it for the greater good. Which begged the question of what he'd seen in the elves to risk his life helping them stay out of extinction. It hadn't been in return for the illegal medicine to save my life. They had been friends even before I was born.

"Rachel?"

I took another sip of my coffee, scanning the busy terminal for Jenks. A sense of unease was growing in me, and I almost choked on my drink when I spotted the security guard looking at us from across the hall, just standing there, watching. *This keeps getting better and better.*

"Earth to Rachel . . . Come in, Rachel. . . ."

I gave myself a mental shake and pulled my gaze from the air cop. "Sorry. What?"

He looked me up and down. "You got quiet all of a sudden."

I forced my eyes to stay off the armed guard. Another one had joined him. "Just thinking," I hedged.

Robbie looked into his coffee. "That's a switch," he needled. But there were three rent-a-cops now. Two I could handle, but three was iffy. *Where are you, Jenks?* I wanted to get out of here, and I pretended to accidentally knock my coffee over.

"Whoops!" I exclaimed brightly, and while Robbie jumped up to avoid getting soaked, I scurried for the napkins to get a better look at the terminal police. Two Weres, I thought, and a witch. They had joined forces and were making their slow way over here. *Shit.*

"Think you can walk and drink at the same time?" I muttered to Robbie when I returned and started mopping up the mess. "We need to find Jenks and get out of here."

"The cops?" he said, and my eyes jerked to his in surprise. "You didn't have to waste good coffee like that to get me to move."

"You know?" I said, and he grimaced, his green eyes showing more than a hint of anger.

"They've been dogging me since I got to the airport," he said, his lips barely moving as he put the lid on his cup and hoisted his bag. "I was all but strip-searched at security, and I swear the air marshal was sitting beside me on the plane. What did you do, little sister?"

"Me?" I almost hissed, peeved that his first thought was that they were after me. I wasn't the one who played in Brimstone-laced dives and went on season-long tours, moving to a new city every night. No, I just stayed in little old Cincinnati, bumping into city leaders the way most people run into their neighbors at the grocery store.

"Can we just get out of here?" I said, thinking this might explain why I'd been searched on the way in.

Robbie made a noise of agreement, and as I shouldered one of his bags and picked up his instrument, he handed me his coffee and took his guitar back. "You break things," he said in explanation, and the strap slipped from my grip.

The cops swaggered behind us as we headed to the luggage claim, and it gave me the creeps. Robbie was silent until we hit one of the moving sidewalks, and in the soft hum of it, he pulled me close and whispered, "Are you sure the I.S. isn't still after you for quitting?"

"Positive," I insisted, but I was starting to wonder. I *was* working on a twin murder involving a banshee and a human. Edden said they didn't care about Mia, but what if they were covering something up? *Not again,* I thought dismally. But they would have sent Denon to threaten me by now. Maybe he'd gotten a promotion instead. The last time I'd seen the ghoul, he'd looked better.

We were nearing the end of the sidewalk, and Robbie hoisted his bag higher in such a way that he could glance at the armed men behind us. The twenty feet had become fifteen, and I was getting edgy. Jenks's distinctive wing chirp pulled my attention to a flower cart, and seeing him busy, I pointed to the baggage claim, then jerked my head behind me. He made a burst of light in acknowledgment, which delighted the woman with him, and we continued on.

"Jenks?" Robbie said softly. "That's your backup, right?"

"Yes." I frowned as I shifted Robbie's bag to a more comfortable position. "You'll like him. He's getting something for his wife. I don't know why those guys are following us."

"You're not trying to get out of dinner tonight, are you?" Robbie said loudly as we got off the walk, and I forced a laugh.

"Maybe," I said, willing to play along. "I have a few things I have to do. I've got a library book to return, and a sick friend in the hospital I want to visit tonight."

"Don't you dare," Robbie said for the benefit of security as we slowed to funnel through a small hallway by the security gates. "I need you there as a buffer in case Mom gets the photo albums out."

I smirked, knowing exactly what he meant. "Mmmm, you should have brought Cindy with you. I'm bringing someone tonight."

"Not fair," he exclaimed as we passed into the unsecured part of the airport, and I glanced behind us to see that our escort had dropped to one. *Thank God it's the witch. One witch I can handle, even without Jenks.*

"Yes fair," I said as I pointed to the hallway we had to take. "His name is Marshal, and he works at the university as a swim coach. He helped me once on a run, and he's the first guy I've ever hung with who isn't trying to get a little something, so be nice."

Robbie eyed me as we got on the escalator. "He's not . . ."

I looked over at his hesitation to see him holding the moving railing with his pinkie delicately extended, and I smiled with half my mouth. "No, he's straight. I can be with a straight guy who's single and not sleep with him. God!"

"Well, I've never seen it," Robbie said, and I shoved him, burning off a little of the adrenaline from the three security guys. "Hey!" he exclaimed good-naturedly, catching himself in time to handle the end of the escalator with no problem.

We were silent as we scanned the monitors for his flight number and carousel, then slowly joined the growing group of people angling for a good spot. *Any day, Jenks.*

"You still living in that church?"

My blood pressure spiked, and I dropped his bag with a thump. "With that vampire, yes." *How does he hit my buttons so fast?*

His gaze on the bags spilling out one by one, Robbie made a noise deep in his throat. "What does Mom think?"

"I'm sure you'll hear all about it tonight," I said, tired already. Actually, my mom was pretty cool about it. And with Marshal there, she might not bring it up at all.

"There it is," Robbie blurted out, saving me from further conversation, and then his expression became concerned. "I think it's mine," he added, and I dropped back when he wedged himself between two shorter women to lug the rolling suitcase off the belt.

The clatter of pixy wings and the soft sound of cooing people told me Jenks was around, and I wound my scarf around my neck to give him a place to warm up. The lights had been bright around the flower cart, but it was drafty here by the doors.

"Hi, Rache," Jenks said as he landed on my shoulder with the scent of cheap fertilizer.

"Get what you want?" I asked as Robbie lugged his rolling suitcase off the belt.

"No," he said, and I could hear the annoyance in his voice. "Everything had a waxy preservative on it. Why, by Tink's little red shoes, are three cops following you?"

"I have no idea." Robbie trundled his suitcase to us, his head down and looking annoyed. "Hey, Robbie, I want you to meet Jenks, my business partner," I said as my brother halted before us, disgust clear in the way he yanked the pull lever up.

"Someone broke the lock on my suitcase," he said, then forced the irritation from his face when Jenks flew down to look at it.

"Yep," the pixy said, hovering before it with his hands on his hips, then darting up, making Robbie's head snap back. "It's a pleasure to finally meet you," Jenks said.

"You're the one keeping my sister out of trouble?" Robbie said as he offered Jenks a hand to light upon, his smile honest and full. "Thanks. I owe you big."

"Naahh." Jenks's wings turned a delicate shade of red even as they hummed to life. "She's not that hard to watch. It's my kids who run me ragged."

Robbie sent his eyes to me, then back to Jenks. "You've got kids? You don't look old enough."

"Almost four dozen," he said, justifiably proud that he could keep that many children alive. "Let's get out of here before cookie-farts over there starts to have delusions of grandeur and tries to search your underwear again."

Lips parted, I glanced at the security cop standing thirty feet back—smiling at me. What in *hell* was going on? "You want to see if anything is gone?" I asked.

"No." He frowned at the busted lock. "Jenks is right. There's nothing in there but clothes and a half ream of music."

"I know," Jenks said. "I was listening to the radio chatter at the flower cart. I should have guessed it was you they were talking about, Rache."

"Did you hear why they're watching us?" I asked, heart pounding. "Is it the I.S.?"

Jenks shook his head. "They didn't say. If you go for another coffee, I can find out."

I looked at Robbie in a question, but he was shifting uneasily from foot to foot. I glanced at the security guy, now standing with his arms crossed over his chest, as if begging me to complain. "No," Robbie said as he started gathering his things. "It's not worth it. Where are you parked?"

"Idaho," I quipped, but inside I was getting upset. *Why did they search my brother's bag if I'm the one they're watching?* "So . . . tell me about Cindy," I asked as we neared the big glass doors. Jenks dove for my scarf as they slid open, and we went out into the bright but cold afternoon.

Robbie's face lost its uneasy expression, beaming as he launched into a stream of happy conversation, as I'd hoped he would. I made the right sounds at the right times, almost having to force my interest in his girlfriend as Robbie and I found our way to my car.

All the way to the lot I scanned faces, watched the horizon, checked behind me, and breathed deep for the distinctive scent of Were, vampire, or witch while trying to pretend everything was normal and keeping up my end of the conversation about new bands and what I'd been listening to. Though still uptight, I breathed easier when we got to my car and found that Denon wasn't waiting for me. It helped that my bad-mojo amulet on my key ring stayed a nice bright green.

Clearly glad to be going home, Robbie continued to chat

while we loaded his bags in the back and bundled into the front seat. I cranked the heater on full for Jenks, who immediately started cussing about perfume and left me to settle on Robbie's shoulder. I think it was more because my vastly underdressed brother had angled all the vents toward himself than my perfume. The conversation bobbled when Robbie noticed the lethal-magic detection charm hanging from my keys. He knew what it was—he'd watched our dad prep for work, too—and though his face creased in concern because his little sister had to have an amulet to warn her of car bombs, he didn't say anything.

It wasn't until we hit the expressway and started for home that I began to relax, but all the while I was checking my rearview mirror for the flashing of I.S. lights, and thinking, *Am I coming too close again to one of their cover-ups? And if I am, am I going to back off or bust it open once more?*

Eyes squinting because of the bright sun as much as my sour mood, I recalled the look of anger on Robbie's face when he saw that his stuff had been pawed through, and I decided that yup, I was going to crack it open and let the sun shine in.

Eight

The draft from the heater made my curls tickle my neck as I sat at Ivy's antique table and looked through one of my dad's old demon texts for a recipe for twisting a locator amulet. A curse, to be excruciatingly honest. Jenks was reading over my shoulder, hovering an irritating two feet up. I don't think he was pleased that even though I'd found a locator-amulet recipe in my safely mundane earth-magic books, I was still looking. Most detecting charms, be they earth or ley line magic, were sympathetic magic—using something you have to detect whatever it is you're interested in: car bombs, shoplifters, listening devices, whatever. Earth-magic *locator* charms, however, worked by finding auras over long distances. It was very sophisticated magic, and I was hoping that the demons had an easier version. Chances were good they did.

I'd escaped my mom's about an hour before, claiming I had work to do and promising that I'd be back at midnight. Robbie hadn't said anything to Mom about the airport cops, but I was still peeved his stuff had been searched. Worried, really, but I handled anger better than fear.

The sun was going down now, and a dark gloom had taken the kitchen. Past the blue curtains, the sky was a dull gray, and, wanting to get Jenks off my shoulder, I stood, open book tingling in my hand as I went to thunk on the rocker switch by the archway. Jenks's wings hummed as bright fluorescent light flickered into existence, and I shuffled to the center counter. The curse book thumped down and, still not looking up from the pages, I crossed my ankles and leaned over the book, using the end of a pencil to turn the page. I'd like to say that the book was cold from having been in the unheated belfry, but I knew better.

Jenks buzzed closer, his wings managing to sound disapproving. Rex watched from the threshold, her ears pricked and the little bell Jenks had put on her last fall gleaming. I'd try to coax her in, but I knew better. The only reason she was here was Jenks. Hovering an inch above the yellow pages, Jenks put his hands on his hips and looked at me. I couldn't help but notice that the dust he was letting slip was making the hand-penned words glow. *Interesting. . . .*

"Ra-a-a-ache," Jenks drawled in warning.

"I'm just looking," I said, waving him off before turning another page. Demon books didn't have indexes. Most didn't have titles. I was reduced to browsing. It made for slow going. Especially since I was one to linger, curious as to how bad a bad curse could be or how neutral some of them were. Some were easy to tell by just the ingredients, but others seemed to be a curse only because of the mixing of earth and ley line magic that all demon curses contained. They were black only because they threw nature's book so far out of balance. I was hoping the demon equivalent of a locator charm was one of these.

I had decided last year that I wasn't going to avoid twisting a demon curse solely on the basis of the smut. I'd been given a brain, and I was going to use it. Unfortunately, the rest of society might not agree with me. Jenks, apparently, wanted to play the part of Jiminy Cricket, and he was reading the pages as carefully as I.

"That's an excellent one," he said, sounding almost reluctant to admit it as he dusted the curse that detailed out how to twist a broomstick-size rod of redwood into flight. There was an earth charm to do the same thing, but it was twice as complicated. I'd priced it out last year, deciding the only flying this little witch was going to do would be in the seat of an airplane.

"Mmmm," I said, turning the page, "I could pay my rent for a year for just what the stick costs." The next page was a curse to turn human flesh into wood. Yuck. Jenks shivered, and I turned the page, sending his blue sparkles sifting to the floor. Like I said, some of these were really easy to tell they were black.

"Rachel . . . ," Jenks coaxed, clearly thrown.

"I'm not doing that one, so relax."

His wings buzzed fitfully, and he sank an inch in height, preventing me from easily turning the page. Exhaling, I stared at him to get him to move by my will alone. Crossing his arms over his chest, he stared right back. He wasn't going to give an inch, but when two of his kids, in front of the dark kitchen window, started arguing over a seed they'd found in a crack in the floor, the distraction lifted him up enough so that I could turn the page.

My fingertips resting on the faded yellow pages were going numb, and I curled them into a fist. But my heart started beating faster when I thought I recognized what was a locator charm under them. If I was reading it right, the demon curse used sympathetic magic, like a detection spell, not auras, like regular locator charms. Though a curse, the magic before me looked a hell of a lot easier than the aura-based one in the earth-magic book. *All the better to tempt you with, my dear.*

"Hey, look at this," I said softly as Jenks gave a warning chirp to his offspring to settle their argument. Together we read through the ingredients. "The attunement object has to be stolen?" I questioned, not liking that, so it was no surprise that I jumped when the front doorbell rang.

Hands on his hips, Jenks alternated his stern gaze between me and his two children, their faces red and wings dusting a black haze into the sink. "I'll get it," he said before I could move. "And you two better have this decided before I get back, or I'll decide it for you," he added to his kids before he darted out.

Their volume dropped, and I smiled. It was almost six, which meant human or witch. Possibly Were or a living vampire. "If it's a client, I'll see them in the sanctuary," I called after him, not wanting to have to hide my books if they should peek into my kitchen on the way to the back living room.

"Gotcha," Jenks shouted faintly. Rex had run off under him, her tail up, ears pricked, and little bell jingling. The two pixies at the window started right back up again, their hushed, high voices almost worse than their loud ones.

I gave a last look at the curse before I marked the page and closed the book. I had everything I needed, but the identifying object, in this case the crystal tear, had to be stolen. That was kind of nasty, but I wouldn't go so far as to say that made it a black curse. Earth magic had a few ingredients like that. Rue, for example, worked best when it was sown while cursing, and it didn't work in a charm unless you stole it. Which was why mine was planted by the gate for easy pilfering. Jenks stole mine for me. I didn't ask from where. The charms made from stolen rue were not considered black, so would this one be?

Standing, I crossed the room to my coat for the tear Edden had given me. He *had* stolen it from evidence. Wondering if that was enough, I pulled the tear out, shocked to see that it had lost its clarity, and had turned black. "Whoa," I whispered, and I looked up as Ford's voice became obvious in the hall. Immediately I looked at the clock. Six? Crap, I'd forgotten he was coming over today. I was in no mood for his mumbo jumbo, especially if it worked.

Ford came in with a tired smile, his dull dress shoes making wet spots as they lost the last of their snow. Rex trailed behind with feline interest, sniffing at the salt-and-water mix. A mess of Jenks's kids were with him, all talking in a swirl of silk and pixy dust. Ford's brow was creased in pain, and they were clearly sending him into overload.

"Hi, Rachel," he said, taking off his coat in such a way that it made half the pixies retreat, but they came right back. "What's this about you being followed at the airport?"

I gave Jenks a dark look, and he shrugged. Gesturing for Ford to sit, I dropped the demon book on the stack I'd brought down from the belfry and wiped my hands on my jeans. "They were just harassing me," I said, not knowing how my brother fit into it, but sure it was me they were after, not him. "Hey, what do you think about this? It was clear this morning when Edden gave it to me."

Ford sat at Ivy's spot and held out his hand, shaking his head when a trio of pixy girls asked him if they could braid his hair. I shooed them away when I came around the counter to give the tear to him, and the girls flitted to the windowsill to take sides in the seed issue.

"Tink's tampons!" Jenks yelped when he saw the tear on Ford's palm. "What did you do to it, Rache?"

"Nothing." At least it hadn't felt furry or wiggled when I touched it. Ford squinted as he held it to the artificial light. The argument at the sink was starting to spill into the rest of the room, and I gave Jenks a pointed look. The pixy, though, was with Ford, fascinated by the black swirls running through the gray crystal.

"Edden gave it to me to make a locator charm," I said. "But it didn't look like that. It must have picked up the emotions at the airport when they were following us."

Ford looked at me over the tear. "You got angry?"

"Well, a little. I was more peeved than anything else."

Jenks darted to the window as the argument reached an eyeball-hurting intensity. "Peeved, nothing. She was like a pimple on a fairy princess's ass, red and ready to pop," he said, then started speaking to his kids too fast for me to follow. Instant pixy silence ensued.

"Jeez, Jenks!" I exclaimed, warming. "I wasn't that upset."

Ford shifted the tear back and forth between his fingers. "It must have absorbed the emotions from not only you, but everyone there." He hesitated, then added, "Did the tear . . . take your emotions away?"

Seeing his hope, I shook my head. He thought it might be a way to help him muffle emotions, perhaps. "No," I said. "Sorry."

Leaning across the corner of the table, Ford handed the tear back, doing a pretty good job of hiding his disappointment. "Well," he said, settling into Ivy's chair and pulling Rex onto his lap. "I'm on the clock. Where would you be most comfortable?"

"Can't we just have coffee instead?" I suggested as I tucked the tear back in my coat pocket for lack of anywhere better. "I'm not in the mood to try to remember Kisten's killer." *Stupid cat won't let me touch her, but a perfect stranger gets head butts and kitty kisses.*

His dark eyes went to the silent coffeemaker. "Like anyone ever is?" he said softly.

"Ford . . . ," I whined, and then one of the pixy kids shrieked. Ford shuddered and turned a shade whiter. Irritated, I looked at Jenks. "Jenks, can you get your kids out of here? They're giving me a headache."

"Jumoke gets the seed," Jenks said flatly, cutting off the rising protests with a sharp wing chirp. "I said you wouldn't like it!" he exclaimed. "Get out. Jumoke, ask your mother where she hides her seeds. It will be safe there until spring."

It also would ensure that she wouldn't die without someone else knowing where she hid their valuable seed stash. Pixy life spans *sucked*.

"Thanks, Papa!" the exuberant pixy shouted, then fled, trailing the rest of them in a calliope of sound and color.

Relieved, I came around the counter to sit at my spot. Ford looked better already, and he shifted to a more comfortable position when Rex followed the pixies out. Jenks dropped down before him in his best Peter Pan pose, hands on his hips. "Sorry," he said. "They won't come back."

Ford glanced at the coffeemaker again. "One of them is still in here."

I shoved the demon texts next to the mundane university textbooks to make some space. "Cheeky bugger," I muttered, standing up to get Ford a coffee.

Jenks's brow furrowed, and he made a harsh whistle. Smirking, I waited to see who the eavesdropping pixy was, but no one showed. Maybe I could fritter all our time away, and that would be that. Talk about Jenks, maybe.

"Thanks, Rachel," Ford said with an exhale. "I could use some caffeine. It's real, yes?"

Pouring a cup, I slid it into the microwave and hit "fast cook." "Decaf is cruel and unusual punishment."

Jenks was buzzing around the kitchen like a firefly from hell, shedding sparkles to make artificial sunbeams. "I can't find anyone," he grumbled. "I must be getting old. Are you sure?"

Ford cocked his head and seemed to be listening. "Yup. It's a person."

A smile came over Jenks as the sensitive man included pixies as people. Not everyone did. "I'll go do a nose count. Be right back."

He zipped out, and I opened the nuker. Ford's cup was steaming, and leaning close as I set it by him, I whispered, "Can we go out and talk about Jenks instead of me?"

"Why?" Ford asked, as if knowing I was stalling, then took a sip. "His emotions are stable. It's yours that are jumping like bunnies in a fryer."

I frowned at the connotation, then sat in my own chair, pulling my cold coffee close. "It's Matalina," I said softly, hoping the eavesdropper couldn't hear, much less Jenks.

Ford set his mug down, but his fingers didn't leave it, seeking the warmth. "Rachel," he said even more softly, "I don't mean to sound trite, but death comes to everyone, and he will find a way to deal with it. Everyone does."

My head went back and forth, and I felt a sliver of fear.

"That's just it," I said. "He's not human, or witch, or vampire. He's a pixy. When she dies, he might go with her. Will himself to death." It was a wildly romantic notion, but I had a feeling it was standard pixy fare.

"He has too much to live for." Ford's knobby fingers tightened on the porcelain, then released. "You, the firm, his children." Then his eyes lost their focus. "Maybe you can ask one of his kids if that's common."

"I'm afraid to," I admitted.

There was the buzz of Jenks's wings darting past the arch as he went into the living room, and Ford's expression became neutral. "What's this Edden was saying about Marshal catching someone under your church?"

I rolled my eyes. "Tom Bansen, formerly of the I.S. Arcane Division, was bugging the church. Marshal was returning the box I forgot in his car and he caught him." I managed a smile despite the pang of hurt from what I'd asked Marshal to throw away. "Marshal is coming to dinner tonight with my mom and brother."

"Mmmm."

It was long and drawn out, and I brought my gaze up to see the usually stoic FIB psychologist wearing a wan smile. "What's that supposed to mean? Mmmm?" I said tartly.

Ford sipped from his mug, his dark brown eyes twinkling deviously. "You're taking someone to meet the family. It's good to see you moving forward. I'm proud of you."

I stared at him, then laughed. *He thought Marshal and I . . .* "Marshal and me?" I said with a guffaw. "No way. He's coming over as a buffer so I don't walk out of there tonight facing a blind date with my mom's paperboy." Marshal was great, yeah, but it was also nice knowing I could leave things alone if I tried.

"Right."

His voice dripped disbelief, and I set my mug down. "Marshal is not my boyfriend. We just do stuff together so no one hits on either of us. It's nice and comfortable, and I'm not going to let you turn it into anything more with your psychobabble bull."

Ford placidly arched his eyebrows at me, and I stiffened when Jenks zipped in and said, "You musta hit pretty close to the mark there, sheriff, to get her riled up like that."

"He's just a friend!" I protested.

Relenting, Ford dropped his eyes and shook his head. "That's how good relationships start, Rachel," he said fondly. "Look at you and Ivy."

I felt the muscles in my face go slack and I blinked. "Excuse me?"

"You've got a great relationship there," he said, busying himself with his coffee again. "Better than a lot of married couples I see. Sex ruins it for some people. I'm glad you're learning that you can love someone without having to prove it with sex."

"Uh, yeah," I said uneasily. "Hey, let me top your coffee off there."

I could hear him shift as I turned my back on him and went to get the carafe. And he wanted to put me under hypnosis? No freaking way. He knew too much about me already.

"Ford," Jenks said gruffly, "your spider sense is whacked. All my kids are accounted for. Maybe it's Bis." He looked at the corners. "Bis, you in here?"

I smiled as I poured half a cup into Ford's mug. "Not while the sun is up, he's not. I saw him on the front eave when I went out for the paper this afternoon."

Taking a sip of coffee, Ford smiled. "There are three emotion sets in this room other than mine. Someone's nose got counted twice. Look, it's okay," he added when Jenks started dripping green sparkles. "Forget about it."

The soft strains of ZZ Top's "Sharp Dressed Man" drifted into existence, muffled but annoying. It was Ford's phone, and I eyed him with interest, thinking it an odd sort of tune for the straitlaced guy, but then my lips parted when I realized it was coming from my bag. *My phone?* But I knew I'd had it on "vibrate." At the very least, it wouldn't be playing that song.

"Cripes, Jenks," I said, scrambling for my bag. "Will you leave my phone alone!"

"I haven't touched your phone," he said belligerently. "And don't be blaming it on my kids either. I bent their wings back last time, and they all said it wasn't them."

I frowned, wanting to believe him. Unless it was general nuisance, Jenks's kids usually didn't make the same mischief twice. Dropping my bag on my lap, I pulled out my phone, finding the call to be from an unlisted number. "Then why does it keep going off 'vibrate'? I almost died of embarrassment the night I tagged Trent." Flipping it open, I managed a courteous, "Hello?"

Jenks landed on Ford's shoulder, smiling. "It started playing 'White Wedding.' "

Ford laughed, and I pulled the phone from my ear. There was no one there. Clicking through the menu, I put it on "vibrate." "Leave it alone," I growled, and it went off again.

"Jenks!" I exclaimed, and the pixy flew up to the ceiling, grinning from ear to ear.

"It's not me!" he chimed out, but he was having too much fun for me to believe him.

It wasn't worth trying to catch him, so I dropped the phone in my bag and let it ring. Ford was very still, and a wave of apprehension swept me at the look in his eyes. Scared, almost.

"Someone else is in this room," he said softly, and Jenks's laughter cut off. I watched as Ford pulled out his amulet. It was a swirl of emotions, confusing and chaotic. No wonder he liked to work one on one. "Both of you, go back by the fridge," he said, and it was as if the warmth left my body. *Shit, what in hell is going on?*

"Go," he said, waving, and I stood up, totally creeped out. *Maybe it's a demon,* I thought. Not really here, but here on the other side of the ever-after, looking at us with his second sight. The sun wasn't down yet, but it was close.

Jenks silently landed on my shoulder, and we backed up until the amulet shifted to a frustrated black.

"And he or she is extremely frustrated," Ford said mildly. "He, I think."

I didn't believe this. How could he be so calm? "You sure it isn't a pixy?" I almost whined, and when Ford shook his head, I asked, "Is it a demon?"

Ford's amulet flashed a confused orange. "Maybe?" Ford offered, and when the amulet turned the purple of anger, he shook his head. "Not a demon. I think you have a ghost."

"What?" Jenks yelped, the burst of yellow pixy dust settling onto the floor to slowly fade. "How come we didn't know before? We've been here a year!"

"We do live next to a graveyard." I looked over my kitchen, feeling it was alien suddenly. Damn it, I should have gone with my first gut feelings when I saw the tombstones. This wasn't right, and my knees weren't feeling all that sturdy. "A ghost?" I stammered. "In my kitchen?" Then my heart did a flip-flop, and my gaze shot to my demon library, down from the belfry. "Is it my dad?" I shouted.

Ford put a hand to his head. "Back up. Back up!" he cried. "You're too close."

Heart pounding, I looked at the eight feet between us and pressed into the fridge.

"I think he meant for the ghost to back up," Jenks said dryly.

My knees started to shake. "This is freaking me out, Jenks. I don't like it."

"Yeah," Jenks said. "Like I'm all peach fuzz and nectar here?"

Ford's expression eased, and the amulet around his neck went a sorrowful brown tinged with the red of embarrassment. "He's sorry," Ford said, gaze unfocused as he concentrated. "He didn't mean to scare you." A smile came over him, unusually soft. "He likes you."

I blinked, and Jenks started to swear in one-syllable sentences in a way that only a pixy can manage. "Likes me?" I stammered, then got the willies. "Oh God," I moaned. "I've got a peeping Tom of a ghost. Who is it?"

The amulet went entirely red. Ford looked down at it as if needing confirmation. "I'd say not a peeping Tom. I'm getting that he's frustrated, benevolent, and he's starting to feel better now that you know he's here." Ford's eyes slid to my bag. "Ten to one he's the person who has been changing your ring tones."

I fumbled for a chair, yanked it to the fridge, and sat down. "But my phone has been doing this since the fall," I said, looking at Jenks for confirmation. "Months." Anger started trickling in. "He's been here all that time? Spying on me?"

Again, the amulet went an embarrassed red. "He's been trying to get your attention," Ford said gently, as if the ghost needed an advocate.

I put my elbows on my knees and dropped my head into my hands. *Swell.*

Clearly frustrated, Jenks landed on the sill beside his brine shrimp tank. "Who is it?" he demanded. "Ask him his name."

"Emotions, Jenks," Ford said. "Not words."

Taking a calming breath, I looked up. "Well, if it's not my dad . . ." I went cold. "Kisten?" I warbled, feeling my entire world take a hit. God, if it was Kisten. There was a spell to talk to the dead who were stuck in purgatory, but Kisten's soul was gone. Or was it?

Ford seemed to waver, and I held my breath. "No," he finally said, and the amulet swirled with black and purple. "I, ah, don't think he liked Kisten."

Jenks and I exhaled together, and Ford straightened in his chair. I didn't know what I was feeling. Relief? Disappointment?

"Sir," Ford said to a corner in the kitchen, and my skin crawled. "Think about your contact to this plane. Ah, that would be Rachel, probably."

Again I held my breath. Jenks was shedding gold sparkles.

Colors shifted across Ford's amulet, but I didn't know enough to interpret them when they were all mixed up like that.

"I'm feeling the excitement of a past danger shared," Ford said softly. "Of fondness, gratitude. Heavy gratitude to you." His eyes opened, and I stifled a shiver at the alien look in them. They were his, but they carried the shadow of the soul of the person he was picking up on.

"Have any of your clients died?" Ford asked. "Someone you were trying to help?"

"Brett," Jenks said.

"Peter?" I blurted out.

But the amulet went a negative gray.

"Nick," Jenks said nastily, and the color on the metal disk became a violent shade of purple.

Ford blinked, trying to divorce himself from the hate. "I'd say no," he whispered.

This was really weird. Whoever it was knew my old boy-friends. My eyes closed in a wash of guilt. I had known a lot of people who were now dead. I was a freaking albatross.

"Rachel."

It was gentle and caring, and I opened my eyes to find Ford looking at me with compassion. "You are worthy of accepting love," he said, and I flushed.

"Stop eavesdropping on me," I mumbled, and Jenks's wings hummed an agitated whisper.

"The ghost thinks so, too," Ford added.

I swallowed a lump. "Are you sure it isn't my dad?"

Ford's smile turned benevolent. "It's not your dad, but he does want to protect you. He's frustrated, watching you these past . . . months? And being unable to help."

I let out my breath in a huff. Jenks's wings hit a higher pitch, and he took to the air. Great. I really needed another white knight. Not. "Who is it?" Jenks said, almost angry. Then, in a burst of sparkles that rivaled the lights, he shouted, "Rache, where's your Ouija board?"

I stared at the wildly darting pixy, then, understanding what he wanted to do, I shuffled through Ivy's papers for the back of one she wouldn't miss. "I don't have one," I said, turning over a hand-drawn map of the conservatory and writing out the alphabet in big, bold letters. "They give me the creeps."

Feeling light-headed, I pushed the hand-drawn alphabet in front of Ford and backed up. Ford gave me a wondering look, and I said, "Run your finger under the letters. When you feel a positive emotion, that's the first letter of his name." I looked at the empty-seeming kitchen. "Okay?"

The amulet went gold in affirmation, and I sat down to hide my shaking knees. This was really, really weird.

"I'd say he's okay with that." But Ford looked uneasy for the first time. With a single finger, he began at *A*, running over them with a deliberate slowness. I watched as he paused at one, then backed up. "*P*," Ford said.

My thoughts flashed to Peter, then Piscary. One dead, the other really dead. Both impossible. But what if it was Peter? He was living as an undead, but if his soul was in purgatory, and I could get it into his body, would he be whole? Was this Ivy's answer?

I licked my lips and watched Ford reach the end of the alphabet and start over. "*I*," he said, then hesitated. "Yes, *I*."

My exhale was long. Not Peter, then. But Piscary? Ford had said the ghost was benevolent, and the vampire hadn't been. Unless it was a trick. Or Piscary had been a good man before he'd become a vampire. Did their souls renew themselves at death, not disintegrate? Revert to a state before everything went wrong?

Ford reached the end and started again. "*E*," he said, looking as if he was more relaxed. Not Piscary, then, and I felt better.

"Pie," Jenks said snidely. "Did you kill a baker we don't know about, Rachel?"

I leaned forward, breathless. "Shut up, Jenks."

Ford's finger stopped again, almost immediately. "*R*," he said, and I felt myself go cold, then hot. *No freaking way . . .*

"Oh my God!" I shouted, jumping to my feet. Jenks hit the ceiling at my outburst, and Ford covered his ears, eyes closed in pain. "I know who it is!" I exclaimed, eyes wide and my heart pounding. I could not believe it. I could not *freaking* believe it. But it had to be him!

"Rachel!" Jenks was in my face, shedding gold sparkles. "Stop! You're killing Ford! Knock it off!"

His hand to his head, Ford smiled. "It's okay," he said, grinning. "This is good stuff. From both of you."

Wonder filled me, and I shook my head as I looked around my kitchen. "Unbelievable," I whispered, then more loudly said, "Where are you? I thought you were at peace." I stopped, hands falling to my side, disappointed somehow. "Wasn't saving Sarah enough?"

Ford was leaning back in his chair, grinning as if he was witnessing a family reunion, but Jenks was pissed. "Who the hell are you talking to, Rache? Tell me or I'm going to pix you, so help me Tink."

Hand gesturing at nothing, I stood in the middle of my kitchen, still not believing it. "Pierce," I said, and Ford's amulet glowed. "It's Pierce."

Nine

The dusty box my mom had brought over last fall was pretty much empty. There was a scarily small T-shirt from Disneyland. Some bric-a-brac. My old diary, which I had started some time after my dad died and I realized pain could be remade once you gave it the permanence of words. The books that had once filled the box were now in the kitchen, but the eight-hundred-level ley line arcane textbook Robbie had given me for the winter solstice hadn't been among them. I hadn't thought it was here, but I had wanted to check before I went over to my mom's and got her stirred up by looking for it in her attic. It had to be somewhere.

But it wasn't in my closet, and sitting back on my heels, I pushed a long curl out of my eyes and exhaled, gazing at the single-paned, night-darkened stained-glass window my bedroom had. Without the book, I had no hope of re-creating the spell I'd done eight years ago to give a spirit in purgatory a temporary body. I was missing a few hard-to-find ley line tools as well. Not to mention that the charm needed a whopping big boost of communal energy.

Being at the closing of the circle at Fountain Square on the solstice would do it. I knew that from experience, but the solstice was come and gone. I was banned from the Howlers' arena, so that was out, even if they did have a game in the snow. New Year's was my next best bet. They didn't close the circle, but there would be a party, and when people started singing "Auld Lang Syne," the energy flowed. I had three days to find everything. It didn't look good.

"Well, Tink loves a duck," I said, and Jenks, resting on my dresser among my perfumes, buzzed his wings. The pixy hadn't left my side since finding out we had a ghost. I thought it was funny. Pierce had been here almost a year. Why it bothered Jenks now I had no idea.

Though our hour had come and gone, Ford was still in the kitchen, slowly talking to Pierce one letter at a time as I listened in while whipping up a batch of earth-magic locator amulets. The demon curse would have been easier, but I wasn't going to twist demon magic in front of Ford. I had a bad feeling I'd done the complex charm wrong since nothing happened when I invoked the first potion with a drop of my blood and spilled it on the amulet. Mia was probably outside the quarter-mile radius within which it worked, but I should've smelled something.

"You think the book is still at your mom's?" Jenks asked, his wings a blur though his butt was still settled on my dresser. The sound of his kids playing with Rex was loud, and I wondered how long the cat would last before she hid from them.

"I'll find out tonight," I said firmly as I refolded the box and shoved it into a pile of boots. "I must have left it at Mom's when I moved out," I said around a stretch to get the kinks out of my back. "It's probably in the attic along with the stuff to do it." *I hope.*

I stood, glancing at my alarm clock. I was meeting Marshal at his apartment in less than an hour, and from there we were driving to my mom's so it would look more like a "date." Finding an excuse to get up into the attic might be hard, but Marshal could help. I didn't want to ask my mom about the book. The first time I'd used it, I'd gotten in major trouble with the I.S.

Hands on my hips, I gazed at the unusual sight of the back of my closet. Shoes and boots were everywhere, and the thought of Newt possessing me, clearing out my closet in the search for her memory, rose up. Suddenly nervous, I shoved the box away and began carefully putting my boots back.

Jenks took to the air, his legs unfolding to reach the top of the dresser and his face tight with worry. "Why do you want to give him a body anyway? You don't even know why he's here. How come Ford hasn't asked him that? Huh? He's been spying on us."

Wondering where *that* had come from brought my head up. "Jenks, he's been dead for a hundred years. Why would Pierce be spying on us?" I huffed, nudging the last of my boots into line.

"If he's not spying on us, then why is he here?" Jenks asked, arms crossed belligerently.

Hand on my hip, I gestured in exasperation. "I don't know! Maybe because I helped him once and he thinks I can help him again. That's what we do, you know. What's with you, Jenks! You've been bitchy all night."

The pixy sighed, his wings stopping to look gossamer and silk. "I don't like it," he said. "He's been here for a year watching us. Messing with your phone."

"He's been trying to get noticed." The air pressure shifted, and Ivy's footsteps echoed in the sanctuary.

"Ivy?" Jenks said loudly, then he darted out.

Hearing Ivy's steps, I started throwing my shoes in the closet, trying to get it shut before Ivy offered to help me organize. My thoughts went back to that solstice night, trying to remember the charm. I saw Robbie pick up the rare red-and-white shallow bowl before we fled Fountain Square. But what he did with it between that and Pierce and me going to the vamp's house and saving the girl, I didn't know. The kitchen had been clean by the time I was strong enough to stand again, and I had assumed Dad's ley line stuff was back in the attic. I never did see the book again. My mom hadn't said much about me summoning a ghost out of purgatory, and it would be just like her to hide everything to keep me from doing it again.

Especially when I'd been trying to summon my dad, not a young man accused of witchcraft and buried alive in the mid-1800s.

Ivy's shadow passed my door, Jenks a small glow and a hushed voice of panic on her shoulder. "Hi, Ivy," I called as I kicked the last shoe in and forced the door shut. Then, knowing how she disliked surprises, I added, "Ford is in the kitchen."

From Ivy's room came a preoccupied "Hi, Rachel." Then a terse "Get out of my way, Jenks," followed by a soft thump. "Hey. Where's my sword?"

My eyebrows rose. Nudging my flip-flops under the bed, I went to the hall. "You left it in the belfry stairway after you oiled it the last time." I hesitated, hearing Jenks tattling on me. "Ah, what's up?"

Ivy was halfway back to the sanctuary. Her long winter coat swayed, and her boots hit the wood floor with purpose. Gold sparkles fell from Jenks as he flitted back and forth in front of her, flying backward. I hated it when he did that to me, and by her stiff arm movements, I figured Ivy did, too.

"It's a ghost, Ivy!" he shrilled. "Rachel summoned it when she was a kid, and it's back."

Leaning against the door frame with my arms crossed, I said, "I was eighteen, not a kid."

His sparkles shifted to silver. "And he likes her," he added.

Oh for God's sake, I thought, losing sight of them in the dark foyer but for Jenks's glow. "We have a randy ghost?" Ivy asked, faintly amused, and my eyes narrowed.

"This isn't funny," Jenks snapped.

"He's not randy!" I said loudly, more embarrassed by Jenks than anything else. Pierce was probably hearing every word. "He's a nice guy." But my gaze became distant as I remembered Pierce's eyes, the flinty black of them and how I'd shivered when he kissed me on my front porch, ready to go off to tag the bad vampire and thinking he could make me stay behind.

I smiled, remembering my past emotional inexperience. I'd been eighteen, and totally impressed by a charismatic witch with mischievous eyes. But it had been the turning point in my life. Together, Pierce and I had saved a little girl from a pedophile vamp—the same vampire who'd gotten him buried alive in the 1800s, which I thought beautiful justice. I'd expected the deed would have been enough to put his soul at rest, but apparently not.

That night had been the first time I'd felt alive, the adrenaline and endorphins making my body, still recovering from disease, feel . . . normal. It was then that I realized I'd risk anything to feel that way all the time—and most days, I did.

Ivy's lithe shape seemed to ghost across the dim sanctuary toward me, pixies whirling in her wake with too many questions. She had her sheathed sword in her hand, and concern hit me. "What do you need your sword for?" I asked, then froze. She'd been out to the boat. She'd found something, and was going to follow it up with cold steel before sunrise. *Crap.* "You've been to the boat."

Her perfect, oval face was placid, but the intent eagerness of her pace tightened my gut. "I've been to the boat," Ivy said. "But I don't know yet who else was out there, if that's what you're asking. Don't you have a date tonight with Marshal?"

"It's not a date," I said, ignoring Jenks hovering nearby, shedding frustrated sparkles. "He's rescuing me from my overzealous mother. How come the sword if you don't know who was at the boat?"

"The hell with the sword, Ivy," Jenks shouted, and I didn't wonder that his kids were now whispering in the sanctuary's shadowed rafters. "This is serious! It's been here for months! Changing her ring tones and scaring my cat. Spying on us!"

"Pierce is not spying on us. God, Jenks, lighten up!" I exclaimed, and Ivy came out of her room with her sword, a rag, and the cleaner she used on her steel. "I don't mind skipping dinner at my mom's. You want to take a girls' night out?" I asked, eyeing her blade.

"No, but thanks for the offer." Ivy eased the blade out an inch and the biting scent of oiled metal tickled my nose. "I got a look at the list of people who visited Piscary when he was in jail." Her smile made me stifle a shudder, and when I dropped my gaze, she added, "The sword is a conversation starter. Rynn . . ." A faint blush marred her pale complexion, and she started for the kitchen. "I'm not his scion, but he's letting me lean on him."

Lips pressed, I couldn't help but wonder what she gave him in exchange, then squelched it. Not my business. As long as Ivy was happy, I was happy.

"So did your chat with Ford bring anything to light?" Ivy asked over her shoulder, and I pushed into motion behind her, headed for the kitchen.

"Just that we've got a freaking ghost!" Jenks said loud enough to make my eyeballs hurt. Rex padded at Ivy's heels, ears pricked up and eager. "Aren't you listening? I think it's one of her old boyfriends she killed, spying on us."

"Jenks. Listen to me. Pierce is not an old boyfriend," I said, exasperated, as I followed them. "I only knew him one night. And he was dead when I found him."

Ivy chuckled. "You could fall in love in an afternoon when we worked at the I.S.," she said, then added, "But he's dead?"

"That's what I've been saying!" Jenks shouted, flitting from me to her. "Tink's little green panties! You got fairy dust in your ears?"

I entered the kitchen through a sheet of glittering sparkles. The room was a mess, and I flushed when Ivy stopped short and stared. My spelling cupboards were all open, stuff strewn across the counters, evidence of me cooking up the locator amulets. I should have just used the demon curse and been done with it, 'cause the last two hours had been a big waste of time. I hadn't even bothered invoking the last six potions, lined up at the back of the counter.

Ford looked up from the far corner where he had put himself to talk to Pierce. Beside him was the makeshift Ouija board and a pocket-size notebook with Ford's messy scrawl filling a page. Seeing us, the man brushed cookie crumbs from himself and leaned back. I wondered if I should say hi to Pierce. He was in here . . . somewhere.

"I'll tell her," Ford said softly when Rex jingled in and twined around his feet. The psychiatrist clearly wasn't talking to us, and his amulet turned a thankful blue, rich and deep.

Jenks darted about like a hummingbird on steroids. "Tell her what? What did the ghost say?" he asked, and I glared. His paranoia was getting old.

Her eyes still wide and questioning, Ivy delicately nudged a mesh sack of herbs down the counter to make room for her sword. "Doing a little cooking?" she asked mildly.

"Uh, a locator amulet to find Mia," I said, not wanting to admit that my first attempt hadn't worked. Shifting my shoulders, I started to put things away.

"If you'd let me organize your stuff, you wouldn't make such a mess," she said, and after pushing a box of candles to the back of the counter, she shifted the toaster forward. "Hi, Ford," she added, sashaying to the fridge, then coming out with the bagels. "Rachel giving you problems?"

Ford chuckled. "It wouldn't be Rachel if she wasn't."

I took in a breath to complain, catching it when Jenks unexpectedly dropped in front of me, hands on his hips. His green shirt had a tear in it, which was unusual for the usually meticulous pixy. "Tell her what you're trying to do," he demanded, putting his arms down to hide the small rip when I noticed it. "Tell her!"

Rolling my eyes, I turned to Ivy. "If I can find it, I'm going to spell Pierce a temporary body so I can talk to him."

Ivy paused with the sliced bagel in one hand, my ceremonial ley line knife in the other. The ornate handle looked odd in her fingers, and her expression was amused. "That's the ghost, right?"

A burst of light came from Jenks. "He's been spying on us!" he yelled, and I wondered why he was freaking out. Ivy and

Ford weren't. "Tink's titties! Doesn't anyone see a problem with this? He's been here a year, listening to everything! Do you have any idea the crap we've been through in the last twelve months? And you want to give this guy a voice?"

My brow furrowed as I realized Jenks had a point. Secrets. They were what kept me alive: Trent being an elf, me being a proto-demon, my arrangement with Al. Crap, Pierce probably knew Al's summoning name. Mine, too. Everything.

"Pierce wouldn't say anything," I said, but Jenks took my soft voice for insecurity, and he flew triumphantly to Ivy.

Ignoring him, Ivy shoved the bread in the toaster. "You can do that?" she said, still facing away. "Give a ghost a body . . . ?"

Her voice cut off, and she turned. The hint of hope was like thin ice, rimming her eyes, fragile. It hurt to see it there. I knew where her thoughts had gone. Kisten was dead. Seeing her hope as well, Jenks lost some of his vim.

I shook my head, and the skin around her eyes tightened almost imperceptibly. "It's a temporary spell," I said reluctantly. "It only works if a person's spirit is stuck in purgatory. And only if you have a huge amount of communal energy to work it. I'm going to have to wait until New Year's before I can even try. I'm sorry, but it can't bring Kisten back even for a night." I took a careful breath. "If Kisten were in purgatory, we'd have known it by now."

She nodded as if she didn't care, but her face was sad when she reached for a plate. "I didn't know you could talk to the dead," she said in an even voice to Ford. "Don't tell anyone, or they'll make you an Inderlander and the I.S. will put you to work."

Ford shifted uneasily on his chair, her depression probably getting to him. "I can't talk to the dead," he admitted. "But this guy?" Smiling faintly, he pointed to where Rex was now sitting in the threshold, staring at me like the creepy little cat she was. "He's unusually coherent. I've never run into a ghost who knows he or she is dead and is open to communication.

Most are stuck in a pattern of compulsive behavior, trapped in their own personal hell."

Kneeling, I stacked the still-clean copper spelling pots under the counter with my cherry red loaded splat gun nestled in the smallest. I kept it at crawling height for good reason. But when Ivy gasped, I popped back up.

"This is mine!" she exclaimed, waving the map of the conservatory I had scribbled the alphabet on. Ford was scrunched back in his chair, and her eyes were going black.

"Sorry," Ford offered, shrinking back while trying not to look as if he was.

Jenks took flight, and I brushed the salt from my knees. "I did it," I said. "I didn't know it was important. Sorry. I'll erase it."

Ivy stopped short and fumed, her short black hair with the gold tips swinging as Jenks landed protectively on Ford's shoulder. The man winced at the close contact, but he didn't move as Ivy seemed to catch herself. "Don't bother," she said stiffly, and when her bagel jumped in the toaster, she smacked the paper back down on the table in front of Ford.

Wincing, I wiped the crumbs from my ceremonial knife and slid her a table knife instead. Leave it to a vamp to slice her bagel with a ceremonial device designed for black magic. Ivy slowly lost her stiff posture as she layered a thick swath of cream cheese on the bagel. She glanced at the drawer where I had stashed my knife, and with what I thought was a huge concession on her part, she broke the silence with a terse "It's not a big deal."

Ford tucked his amulet away as if getting ready to leave. "Going out, Ivy?" he asked.

She turned with her bagel on a plate, and leaned against the far counter. "Just chatting with a few people," she said, flashing her sharp canines as she took a careful bite. "I've been out to the boat," she said around her chews. "Thanks for waiting. I appreciate that."

The man bobbed his head, and the tension in the room eased. "Find anything?"

I already knew the answer, and I dipped below the level of the counter to shove my twenty-pound bag of sea salt into a back cupboard. The deep-fat fryer went in front of it, and I shut the door with a hard thump, thinking the last couple of hours had been a real waste. I couldn't remember the last time I'd worked a charm and gotten no result. Maybe I could ask my mom. She was good at earth charms. It might be an excuse to get into the attic, too.

"An undead vampire killed Kisten," Ivy said, her gray-silk voice holding so much repressed fury it chilled me. "But we knew that already. He smells familiar," she added, and I turned with a stack of ceramic spelling spoons in hand. Her eyes were going black, but I didn't think it was from my rising pulse.

"Which is good," she said, her voice almost husky. "He's probably a Cincy vamp and still here, as Rynn Cormel suggested. I know I've smelled him before. I just can't place him. Maybe I ran into him in a blood house once. It'd be easier if the scent wasn't six months old."

That last was more than slightly accusing, and I quietly returned to putting things away. I was glad I hadn't been there to watch Ivy discover she knew the vampire who had killed Kisten. It had to be someone outside the camarilla, or she would have noticed his scent the morning we'd found Kisten.

"This wouldn't have been a problem if someone hadn't dosed me with a forget spell," I said dryly, and Jenks lit up in a burst of white.

"I said I was sorry about that!" he shouted. His kids scattered, and Ford's head jerked up. "You were going to try to stake the bastard, Rachel, and I had to stop you before you killed yourself. Ivy wasn't here, and I'm too *damned small*!"

Shocked, I reached after him as he flew out. "Jenks?" I called. "Jenks, I'm sorry. That's not the way I wanted it to sound."

Depressed, I turned to Ford and Ivy. I was acting like an insensitive jerk. No wonder Jenks was in a bad mood. Here Ivy and I were trying to find Kisten's killer, and Jenks was the one who had destroyed the easy answer. "Sorry," I said, and Ford met my guilty gaze. "That was thoughtless."

Ford pulled his legs back under him. "Don't beat yourself up. You're not the only one who makes quick decisions that come back to bite them. Jenks has a few guilt issues he needs to work out is all."

Ivy snorted as she turned her bagel to get a better grip on it. "Is that your professional opinion?"

Ford chuckled. "You're the last person to be throwing stones," he said. "Ignoring a lead for six months because you felt guilty that you weren't there to save the two people you love the most."

Surprised, I turned to Ivy. Her first startled look turned into a one-shouldered, embarrassed shrug. "Ivy," I said as I leaned against the counter, "Kisten's death is not your fault. You weren't even there."

"But if I had been, it might not have happened," she said softly.

Ford cleared his throat, looking at the archway as Jenks buzzed back in, sullen. Matalina was hovering at the lintel, her arms crossed and a severe expression on her face. Apparently the wise pixy woman was doing a bit of psychoanalyzing herself and didn't want Jenks sulking in the desk.

"Sorry, Rache," he said as he lit on my shoulder. "I shouldn't have flown out like that."

"Don't worry about it," I murmured. "I only said what I did because I was so far from putting blame on you that what I sounded like never occurred to me. You saved my life. And we'll get my memory back. You did okay. I just want to know what happened."

Ford leaned back and tucked his pencil away. "You will. It's starting to surface."

"Can we get back to the ghost?" Jenks said, his wings making my hair fly, and the wan-looking human smiled.

"He says thank you, by the way," Ford said, glancing at his notebook. "He didn't find his rest, much to his shame, but he wouldn't be allowed to walk as he is if it hadn't been for Al freeing him."

"Al!" I exclaimed, squinting to see Ford's smile through the cloud of sparkles Jenks had made, hovering in midair, in shock. Even Ivy paused, bagel halfway to her mouth. "What does Al have to do with this?" I stammered as Jenks made self-congratulatory sounds.

"I knew it!" he crowed. "I knew it all along!"

But Ford was still smiling, the faint wrinkles around his eyes making him look tired. "Nothing intentionally, I'm sure. Remember that tombstone your demon cracked?"

I shook my head, biting back my ire at his use of the term "your demon." Then I changed the motion into a nod. "The night I rescued Ceri?" I said, then blinked. "My God. Pierce is buried here? In our backyard?"

If pixies could have coronaries, Jenks was having one. Sputtering, he hovered, his face frightened and a steady stream of black sparkles puddling on the center counter to spill over and eddy about my stocking feet. "You're talking about the one with the weird-ass statue of the angel?" he managed, and Ford nodded.

No way! I thought, wondering if I had enough time to find my flashlight and go out and look at it before Marshal got here.

"The name was scratched off!" Jenks shrilled, and Rex stretched, going to twine about my feet as she tried to get closer to her tiny master.

"Take a chill pill, Jenks," I said, "before you set your dust on fire."

"You shut up!" he shouted, then flew to Ivy. "I told you! Didn't I tell you? You don't chisel off someone's name unless . . ." His eyes widened. "And he's in unsanctified ground!" he squeaked. "Rachel, he's trouble. And he's dead! Doesn't it bother you that he's dead? How come he's dead!"

Ivy's dark eyes went from me to Jenks, and then to Ford,

who was sitting back and watching it all in a rather clinical way.

"He was dead when I met him," I said dryly, "and he was nice enough then. Besides, a good slice of Cincy's population is dead."

"Yeah, but they aren't lurking in our church, spying on us!" he yelled, getting right in my face. "Why are you trying to make him real!"

I had endured just about enough. Slamming a cupboard door shut, I stepped forward to push him back. "He's been *trying* to make contact," I said, eyes narrowed and inches from him. "Making him solid is the only way I can talk to him without a frickin' Ouija board. If you have to know, he was cemented into the ground because he was accused of being a witch in the 1800s. He's probably trying to find a way to get out of purgatory and just die, so lighten up!"

Ivy cleared her throat, her bagel perched on her fingertips. "He was accused of being a witch?" she asked. "I thought you guys were really careful before the Turn."

I backed off from Jenks and took a cleansing breath. "The vamp he tagged as a blood pedophile ratted on him," I said. "Told everyone he was a witch. The ignorant SOBs cemented him into the ground alive. He's not a black witch any more than I am."

Ford's chair scraped as he rose. Grabbing his coat, he came forward as he shuffled into it. "I have to go," he said, giving my shoulder a squeeze. "I'll call you tomorrow and we can set up a time to do the hypnosis."

"Sure," I said absently, glaring at Jenks, glowing fiercely by the fridge.

"Pierce wanted me to tell you that he's been here since Al cracked his stone. It made a path a willing spirit could use, and he followed his thoughts back to you." Ford was smiling at me as if it was good news, but I couldn't smile back. Damn it, I had been in such a great mood, and now it was gone. First the thing with the failed earth charms, and now Jenks thought Pierce was a demon spy.

"This is bad, Ivy," Jenks said, lighting on her shoulder. "I don't like it."

My anger flared. I wanted him to shut up. "I don't care if you like it or not," I snapped. "Pierce is the first person I helped. The first person who needed me. And if he needs my help again, I'm going to give it." Frustrated, I threw a handful of ley line stuff in a drawer and shut it so hard Rex darted away.

Ford shifted from foot to foot. "I have to go."

No doubt, after my little show of temper. Jenks got in his way, and the man hesitated. "Ford," he said, sounding desperate. "Tell Rachel this is a bad idea. You don't bring back the dead. Not ever."

My heart seemed to clench, but Ford raised a placating hand. "I think it's a great idea. Pierce is not malevolent, and what harm can she do to him in one night?"

Jenks's wings hit an unreal pitch, and his sparkles sifted to gray. "I don't think you grasp the situation here," he said. "We don't know this guy from Tink! So Rachel feels sorry for him and brings him back for a night. He was *buried alive* in blasphemed ground. We don't know the way to bring him all the way back from the dead, but I bet a demon does. And what's to stop this guy from whispering in some demon's ear, exchanging our secrets for a new life!"

"That's enough!" I shouted. "Jenks, you need to apologize to Pierce. Right now!"

Trailing a ribbon of sparkles like a wayward sunbeam, Jenks flew to me. "I will not!" he said vehemently. "Don't do this, Rachel. You can't risk it. None of us can."

Jenks hovered before me, tense and determined. Behind him, Ivy looked at me. Suddenly, I didn't know what to say. I'd met Pierce, saved a little girl with him, but had I been looking at him through innocent, eighteen-year-old eyes, easily misled and hoodwinked?

"Jenks," Ford said, looking pained by my sudden doubt.

The small pixy darted up, his frustration obvious. "Can I talk to you in private?" he said, looking angry enough to pix the man.

Head down, Ford nodded, angling to leave the kitchen. "Let me know if you can't find the spell, Rachel, and I'll come over and you can talk to Pierce some more."

"Sure." I crossed my arms over my chest and leaned against the counter. "I'd appreciate that." My jaw was clenched, and I was getting a headache. Rex followed Jenks and Ford out, and I wondered if the cat was following them, or Pierce. The sound of Ford's feet faded, and then a soft, one-sided conversation started up from the sanctuary. Ivy could probably hear Ford clearly enough to make out the words, but I couldn't, and that's all Jenks was after.

Forcing my teeth apart, I looked at Ivy across the long length of the kitchen. She had gotten out another small plate, and as I nodded sourly, she put the other half of her dinner on it and handed it to me. I stiffly took it. "You don't think this is a bad idea, do you?" I asked, and Ivy sighed, staring at nothing.

"Is it a demon curse?" she asked. "The one to give Pierce a temporary body, I mean."

My head moved back and forth, and I took a bite of bagel. "No. It's simply hard."

Her dark eyes focused on me and she lifted a thin shoulder. "Good," she said. "I think you should do it. Jenks is a paranoid old man."

Relief brought my shoulders down and I managed a thin smile. Turning my bagel to get to the side with the most cream cheese, I took a bite, and the tart tang of cheese hit my tongue. "Pierce isn't up to anything," I said as I chewed. "I just want to help him if I can. He helped me realize what I wanted to do with my life, and I sort of owe him." I looked at her, seeing her eyes distant in thought. "You know what I mean? Owing someone for changing your life in a good way?"

Her attention flicked to me. "Uh, yeah," she said, then set her plate down to go to the fridge.

"I know I can do the spell; all I need is the recipe, the equipment, and a gathering of witches to siphon off the power." I looked at my bagel and sighed. This was going to be hard.

Ivy was silent as she poured a glass of orange juice, then said softly, "I'm sorry. This means a lot to you. Jenks is being an ass. Ignore him."

I ate another bite of my bagel and said nothing. Pierce was one of the few people who knew me before I had demon marks, or smut, or anything else. I had to help him if I could.

Ivy shifted to the sink to wash the crumbs from her plate, and knowing my agitation was hard on her instincts, I slid away a few feet. "Can't you just buy the book?" she asked, gazing at the porch light shining on the snowy garden. "If it's not demon magic, it should be out there."

My head nodded. It was nice that someone didn't think Pierce was a spy. "I'm sure it is, but level-eight-hundred Arcane ley line textbooks aren't common. They usually don't show up unless someone is teaching a class. Getting one before New Year's will be a problem. That and the crucible. If Robbie doesn't know where it is, it might take months."

The front door thumped shut, and Jenks darted in with the icy scent of a summer field on a winter night. He was in a much better frame of mind, and I couldn't help but wonder what Ford had told him.

"I'm out of here," I said, snagging my bag from the far chair before Jenks could try to start a conversation. "I probably won't be back until almost four. It's going to be bad," I said around a sigh. "Robbie has a girlfriend and my mom's nuts about her."

Ivy smiled, a closed-lipped smile. "Have fun."

I glanced at her sword on the counter, thinking I'd rather go with her and face ugly vampires than my mom and Robbie and the inevitable "when are you going to settle down" conversation. "Okay. I'm out of here." I glanced around the almost-tidy kitchen, and wondered if they would think it was weird if I said 'bye to Pierce. "You going to be okay here alone with Pierce, Jenks?" I mocked as I shoved the invoked locator amulet in my bag to ask my mom about, and Jenks flashed an annoyed red.

"Yeah, I'll be fine," he muttered. "We'll have a nice chat, Mr. Ghost and me."

"A little one-sided, isn't it?" I said, and Jenks smiled, his eagerness worrying me.

"Just the way I like it. He can't talk back to me the way my kids do."

My coat and boots were in the foyer. "Call me if you need me," I said, and Ivy gave me a wave. Jenks was already on her shoulder, and the two clearly had things to discuss. *Even more worrisome.* Giving them a last look, I headed to the front of the church, keys jingling against my lethal-magic detector.

The pixies were busy in the corner with a terrified mouse, and ignoring the drama, I wiggled my feet into my boots and tightened them up. I shrugged into my coat, and looked out from the dark room into the shadowed sanctuary, still decorated with Ivy's Christmas stuff and my solstice things. A soft, warm feeling took me, relaxing me. I wondered if I could really smell the scent of coal dust and shoe polish, or if it was just my imagination. I hesitated when the tinkling of Rex's bell joined the noise of the pixies, and I watched her sit primly in the opening to the hallway to stare at me. Maybe she was staring at Pierce?

"'Bye, Pierce," I whispered. "Don't mind Jenks. He just wants to keep me safe." And with a small smile, I pushed open the door and headed out into the cold.

Ten

The dishcloth had long since become damp, but we were almost done and it wasn't worth the effort to get a dry one. Robbie was washing, I was drying, and Marshal was putting away with the help of my mom. The truth was, she was out here supervising so Robbie and I didn't lapse into one of our infamous water fights. I smiled and handed a bowl to Marshal. The scent of roast beef and butterscotch pie was heavy in the air, a big trigger for the memories of the Sunday nights when Robbie would come over. I had been twelve and Robbie twenty. And then it had all stopped when Dad died.

Robbie saw my mood shift, and he made a fist half in the water, half out. Squeezing his hand, he made a short burst of water arc up and splash into my side of the sink.

"Knock it off," I complained, then shrieked when he squirted me again. "Mom!"

"Robbie." Mom didn't even look up from arranging the coffee tray.

"I didn't do anything," he protested, and my mom's eyes glinted when she turned.

"Then don't do anything a little faster," she complained. "Honestly, I never understood why it took you two so long to get the kitchen cleaned up. Put some hustle into it. Marshal is the only one out here working." She beamed at him, making the young man flush when Robbie muttered a good-natured "Suck-up."

Robbie and Marshal had hit it off great, the two of them spending much of the evening with talk about college sports and music. Marshal was closer to Robbie's age than mine, and it was nice seeing my brother actually approve of one of my boyfriends. Not that Marshal was a boyfriend, but watching them made me wistful, as if I was getting a glimpse of something I'd turned my back on. This was what a normal family must be like, with siblings bringing new people into the family, becoming part of something bigger . . . Belonging.

It didn't help that most of the dinner conversation had centered on Robbie and Cindy. They were obviously serious about each other, and I could just see my mother becoming happier by the moment because Robbie might start a family and find himself part of the "circle of life." I'd given up on the white picket fence after Kisten had died—finding out my kids would be demons was the nail in the coffin—but seeing Robbie getting kudos for doing something I deemed not socially responsible for me to pursue was irritating. Sibling rivalry sucked.

With Marshal here, I could at least pretend. Both Mom and Robbie were impressed that he'd just sold his own business with enough profit to put him through getting his master's without having to work at all. The swim-coach thing now was just to lower his tuition and give him a whole lot more disposable income. I'd hoped he'd heard from admissions about my declined check by now, but apparently not everyone was working over the winter break.

Giving Robbie a light smack from the back of her hand for the suck-up comment, my mother pointed out to Marshal where the glasses went, then busied herself arranging the last of the solstice cookies on a plate. The round sugar cookies were bright with solstice green and gold, and lettered with runes of good fortune. My mom put her heart into everything she did.

As soon as her back was turned, Robbie threatened to shoot

another jet of water at me. I closed my eyes and ignored him. I'd been trying to get him alone all night to ask him about that book, but between Marshal and my mother, I hadn't had the chance. I was going to have to bring in some help. Marshal wasn't devious by nature, but he wasn't slow on the uptake either.

Humming happily, my mom sashayed out with a plate of cookies. The stereo in the living room went on, and I grimaced. I had thirty seconds, tops.

"Marshal," I said, pleading with my eyes as I handed him a plate. "I've got a big favor to ask. I'll tell you all about it later, but will you keep my mom busy for about ten minutes?"

Robbie stopped what he was doing and just looked at me. "What's up, firefly?"

My mom came back in, and following the pattern we'd laid down when we were conniving kids, Robbie turned back to the sink as if I'd said nothing.

"Please . . . ," I whispered to Marshal when he came back from sliding the stack of plates away. "I've got to talk to Robbie about something."

Oblivious, my mom puttered with the coffeemaker, jostling Robbie and me aside and looking small next to us as she filled the carafe.

"Marshal," Robbie said, eyes twinkling as they met mine behind my mom's back. "You look as tired as a dead carp. Rachel and I can finish here. Why don't you go and sit in the living room and wait for coffee? Look at a few photo albums."

Immediately my mother brightened. "What a fantastic idea! Marshal, you must see the photos we took on our last summer vacation. Rachel was twelve, and just starting to have some strength," she said, taking his elbow. "And Rachel will bring the coffee out when it's done." Smiling, she turned to me. "Don't be too long, you two," she said, but the lilt in her voice gave me pause. I think she knew I was getting rid of them. My mom was nuts; she was not stupid.

I slipped my hands into the warm water and pulled out a dripping serving platter. From the front of the house came Marshal's resonant voice. It sounded good balanced against my mom's. Dinner had been pleasant, but again, almost painful listening to Robbie go on and on about Cindy, my mom joining in when they talked about her two weeks out there. I was jealous, but everyone I got attached to seemed to end up hurt, dead, or crooked. Everyone but Ivy and Jenks, and I wasn't sure about the crooked part with them.

"Well, what is it?" Robbie said, dropping the silverware so the rinse water splashed.

Quietly I ran the back of my hand across my chin. *And here I am, trying to resurrect a ghost.* Maybe I could be friends with a ghost. I wouldn't be able to kill him. "Remember that book you gave me for the winter solstice?" I asked.

"No."

My eyes came up, but he wouldn't meet them. His jaw was clenched, making his long face appear longer. "The one that I used to bring—" I started.

"No." It was forceful, and my lips parted when I realized he meant no as in "I'm not telling," not "I don't know."

"Robbie!" I exclaimed softly. "You've got it?"

My brother rubbed his eyebrows. It was one of his tells. He was either lying, or about to. "I've no clue what you're talking about," he said as he wiped off the suds he'd just put there.

"Liar," I accused, and his jaw tightened. "It's mine," I said, then softened my voice when Marshal raised his voice to cover us up. "You gave it to me. I need it. Where is it?"

"No." His gaze was intent and his voice determined as he scoured the pan the roast had been in. "It was a mistake to give it to you, and it's going to stay right where it is."

"Which is . . . ," I prompted, but he continued to scrub, his short hair moving as he did.

"You gave it to me!" I exclaimed, frustrated and hoping he wasn't going to tell me it was four time zones away.

"You have no right to try to summon Dad again." Only now

would he look at me, and his temper was showing. "Mom had a devil of a time pulling herself back together after that little stunt. Took me two weeks and almost five hundred dollars in phone bills."

"Yeah, well, I spent seven years putting her back together when you *left* after Dad died, so I think we're even."

Robbie's shoulders slumped. "That's not fair."

"Neither is leaving us for a stinking career," I said, my heart pounding. "God, no wonder she's so screwed up. You did the same thing Takata did to her. You're both exactly alike."

My brother's face became closed and he turned away. Immediately I wished I could take it back, even if it was true. "Robbie, I'm sorry," I said, and he flicked a glance at me. "I shouldn't have said that. It's just . . . I really need that book."

"It's not safe."

"I'm not eighteen anymore!" I exclaimed, dish towel on my hip.

"You sure act like it."

I dropped the dry silverware in the drawer, slammed it shut, and turned. Seeing my frustration, Robbie softened, and with his voice carrying a shared pain, he said, "Dad's at rest, Rachel. Let him go."

Peeved, I shook my head. "I'm not trying to talk to Dad. I need it to talk to Pierce."

Robbie huffed as he drained the sink and rinsed the cooking pan under tap water. "He's at rest, too. Leave the poor guy alone."

A faint excitement lifted in me at the memory of the night Pierce and I had spent in the snow of Cincinnati. It had been the first time I had really felt alive. The first time I'd ever been able to help anyone. "Pierce is not at rest. He's in my church, and has been for almost a year, changing my phone's ring tones and making Jenks's cat stare at me."

Robbie turned, shocked, and I reached to turn the water off for him. "You're kidding."

I tried not to look smug, but he was my brother, and it was

my right. "I want to help him find his rest. Where is the book?" I asked as I took the pan and shook the water from it.

He thought for a moment as he rummaged under the sink for the cleanser, dusting a little in the sink and then replacing it where it had sat for almost three decades. "The attic," he said as he started to scrub. "I've got Mom's crucible up there, too. The really expensive red-and-white one? And the bottle to hold the potion. I don't know where the watch is. Did you lose it?"

Elated, I put the roaster away half dried. "It's in my dresser," I said, trying not to sneeze at the sharp scent of cleanser as I jammed the dish towel over the rod to dry and started for the door. I was going to get everything in one go. How lucky could I get?

I was halfway to the kitchen door when Robbie caught my elbow. "I'll get it," he said, glancing past me to the unseen living room. "I don't want Mom to know what you're doing. Tell her I'm looking for my bottle-cap collection."

Snorting, I nodded. Yeah, like he'd really take his beer-bottle-cap collection on the plane with him. "Ten minutes," I said. "If you're not down here by then, I'm coming up after you."

"Fair enough." He smiled as he pulled the towel from the rack and dried his hands. "You are such a sweet sister. I truly don't know how those rumors get started."

I tried to come up with something, my mind going blank when he flicked the towel at me, scoring. "Hey!" I yelped.

"Leave your sister alone, Robbie," my mom said faintly from the living room, her voice carrying a familiar firmness, and both Robbie and I smiled. It had been too long. Smirking at his innocently wide green eyes, I grabbed the sponge and hefted it experimentally.

"Rachel!" came my mom's voice, and grinning, Robbie tossed the dish towel at me and sauntered confidently out of the kitchen. Almost immediately I heard the attic door being pulled down, and the thunk of the stairway hitting the carpet in the bedroom hallway. Confident now that I'd be going home with everything I'd need, I wiped the sink out and hung up the dish towel.

"Coffee," I whispered, sniffing at the coffeemaker and hoping she'd lightened up on the grounds in deference to having a guest.

Shoes a soft hush on linoleum, my mom came in. "What's Robbie doing in the attic?"

I pulled back from the still-dripping coffee machine. "Looking for his bottle-cap collection." Okay, so I lied to my mother. But I'd be willing to bet he'd find *something* up there to take back with him, so it wasn't a lie altogether.

She made a small sound as she pulled four white mugs from the cupboard and set them on the tray. It was the set she used for her best company, and I wondered if it meant anything. "It's nice to have you both here," she said softly, and my tension vanished. It *was* nice to have Robbie here, to pretend for a while that nothing had changed.

My mom busied herself fussing with the tray as the last of the coffee dripped into the coffeemaker, and again I noticed how young her hands were. Witches lived for almost two centuries, and we could almost pass for sisters—especially since she had stopped dressing down. "Cindy is nice," she said from out of the blue, and I started, jerked back to reality by the mention of Robbie's girlfriend. "He teases her like he teases you." She was smiling, and I went to get the cream out of the fridge. "You'd like her," she added, her eyes on the backyard, lit from the neighbor's security light. "She's working at the university while finishing up her degree."

Smart, then, I thought, not surprised. This hadn't come out in dinner conversation. I wondered why. "What is she taking?"

My mom's lips pressed together in thought. "Criminology." *Really smart. Too smart?*

"She has one year left," my mom said as she arranged a set of spoons on the napkins. "It was nice watching them together. She balances Robbie out. He's so pie in the sky, and she's so down to earth. She has a quiet beauty. Their children will be precious beyond belief."

Her smile had gone soft, and I smiled, realizing that by settling down, Robbie was setting himself up for an entirely new set of mom-wants. She might have given up on me, but now Robbie was going to take the full brunt. *Oh so sad . . .*

"Tell me," she said in a deceptively mild tone, "how are you and Marshal getting along?"

My smile faded. Okay, maybe she hadn't given up on me completely. "Fine. We're doing great," I said with a new nervousness. She'd been the one to tell me that we weren't suited for more than a rebound relationship, but after hearing at dinner how Marshal had pulled Tom out from under my kitchen, she might have readjusted her thinking.

"Robbie really likes him," she continued. "It's nice for me to know that you have someone looking after you. Able to go under your house and kill snakes for you, so to speak."

"Mom . . ." I felt trapped all of a sudden. "I can kill my own snakes. Marshal and I are friends, and that's enough. Why can't I just have a guy friend? Huh? Every time I push it, I mess it up. Besides, you told me he wasn't a long-term solution but a short-term diversion."

I was whining, and she set the sugar bowl down and turned to face me. "Sweetheart," she said, touching my jaw. "I'm not telling you to marry the man. I'm telling you to keep the lines of communication open. Make sure he knows what's going on."

My stomach, full of gravy and beef, started to churn. "Good," I said, surprised. "Because I'm not dating him, and nothing is going on. Everyone I date ends up dead or going off a bridge."

Her lips twisted into a wry expression as she took the carafe and poured the coffee into the best silver pitcher. "They do not," she chided. "I really like Marshal, and he's been good for you, but he's too . . . safe, maybe, to keep your interest, and I want to make sure he's not thinking there's more to this than there is. He's too good a person to lead on like that, and if you've given him any indication—"

"He knows we're just friends," I interrupted. God! What was it with her?

"Friends is fine," she said firmly. "And it's good to know he can come through in a pinch. This thing with the Bansen character, for example. I'll sleep better knowing you have someone to go to if I'm not around. I worry about you, sweetheart."

My jaw clenched, and I could feel my blood pressure start to rise. This was not what I wanted to talk about. "If I find any more snakes under my floorboards, I'll know who to call." Then I hesitated. *If she isn't around?*

"Uh, Mom?" I said as she fussed over the tray. "You're okay, right?"

She laughed, the sound of it pulling my shoulders down. "I'm fine!"

Not quite reassured, I set the good silver coffeepot on the tray, now knowing what it meant. She considered Marshal casual company, not a future son-in-law, and a part of me was disappointed even as I knew it was the best thing. A thump from the attic pulled my attention up. It was followed by another, and I started to fidget. I grabbed the tray as the distinctive bump of the attic door folding up into the ceiling filtered in. He was downstairs.

"I'll take it in," my mother said briskly as she plucked the tray from my hands and gave a nod to the hallway. "Poor Marshal must be bored, sitting there by himself. See if Robbie needs any help with what he pulled out of the attic. Bottle caps! I thought I threw those out!"

"Thanks, Mom." Anxious to get my hands on that book, I followed her, smiling sadly at Marshal's cheerful comment about the beautiful coffeepot as I headed in the other direction, almost running into Robbie. I gasped, and he steadied me with both hands. My eyes narrowed. *Both hands?* "Where's the book?" I whispered.

Robbie's eyes were pinched in the dim greenness of the hall, cold now from the attic. "It wasn't there."

"What?" I yelped, then lowered my voice and leaned in. "What do you mean, it wasn't there?"

"I mean, it's not where I left it. The box is gone."

Not knowing if I should believe him or not, I angled around him to look for myself. "What does the box look like?" I asked as I reached for the pull cord. Had Mom found it, or was Robbie simply telling me it was gone to keep it out of my reach?

Robbie grabbed my shoulder and turned me back. "Relax. It has to be up there," he said. "I'll check again in the morning after she goes to sleep."

My eyes narrowed, and I hesitated. From the front room came my mom's voice raised in question. "Did you find your rusty caps, Robbie? I want them out of my attic!"

Robbie's grip on my shoulders tightened, then relaxed. "Got 'em, Mom," he said. "I'll be right there. I've got something for you and Rachel."

"Presents?" My mother was suddenly in the hall, beaming as she linked her arm in mine. "You know you don't need to bring us presents. Just having you here is present enough."

Robbie grinned back, winking when I gritted my teeth. Now I'd never get up there to make sure he didn't "miss" something. Crap, he'd done this on purpose.

But my mother was happy, and I followed her back to the living room for coffee as Robbie went to rummage in his luggage. Marshal looked suitably relieved by my appearance, and I plunked myself down on the brown tapestry-covered couch, bumping into him and staying where I was, our thighs touching.

"You owe me," he whispered, his lips twisted in both fun and sly annoyance. "You owe me big."

I looked at the thick photo album of Robbie and me as kids. "Two tickets to the next wrestling event at the coliseum," I whispered back. "Front row."

"That might cover it," he said, laughing at me.

Almost humming, my mom sat and bobbed her foot until she saw me notice it and she stilled it. "I wonder what he got us?" she asked, and the last of my bad mood evaporated. I liked seeing her this way. "Oh, here he comes!" she added, eyes lighting up at the sound of Robbie's footsteps.

Robbie sat across from us and put down two envelopes, each having our names on them in a clearly feminine script. His long face was full of excitement, and he slid them to us with two fingers, one for me, one for my mom. "Cindy and I got these for you," he said as we both reached for them. "But you can't use them until June."

"June?" I mused.

"June?" my mom echoed, then let out a joyous yelp that made me jump. "You're getting married!" she shrieked, and threw herself around the coffee table. "Robbie, oh, Robbie!" she burbled, starting to cry. "Cindy is so sweet. I know you will be so happy together! I'm so excited for you both! Have you found a church yet? What are the invitations going to be like?"

I scooted away from Marshal and stared at the two plane tickets in my envelope. My eyes met Robbie's when I looked up.

"Please say you'll come," he asked me, his arms around our mother as she cried joyful tears. "It would make us both very happy."

"Look at me," my mom warbled, pulling away to wipe her face. "Son of a bitch, I'm crying."

Robbie blinked at her rough words, but I smiled. Same old Mom. "Of course I'll come," I said, standing up and moving around the table. "I wouldn't miss it for the world." Al could just suck my toes and die. So he'd have to pick me up in an unfamiliar ley line. They had ley lines in Portland, same as everywhere else.

The hug turned into a group thing, and it felt good, secure and bittersweet. The lilac and redwood scent from my mom mixed with the aroma of electric amps, but even as my thoughts rejoiced, another worry took me. Maybe I should back off from the magic completely. I mean, I'd never forgive myself if something happened to Robbie or his new bride . . . or their children.

Giving them both a last squeeze, I let go and retreated. Marshal, standing forgotten, swooped in and shook Robbie's hand, smiling as he offered his "condolences." My eyes were wet, and I smiled through the worry. "I'm really happy for you, Robbie," I said, meaning it. "When's the date?"

Robbie exhaled as he let go of Marshal's hand, becoming truly relaxed. "We haven't set it yet. It's going to be determined by the caterer, I'm afraid." He grinned, embarrassed.

My mom continued to weep happy tears, promising to help in any way she could. Robbie turned from me back to her, and I smiled awkwardly at Marshal. Nothing like your brother announcing he was getting married to make an awkward situation even better.

Someone's phone started to ring, ignored until I realized it was mine. Relishing the chance to extricate myself, I fled to the front door where I'd left my bag and searched it, thinking "Break on Through to the Other Side" must be Pierce's idea of a joke. Not bad, considering he had a hundred and fifty years of music to catch up on. "Sorry," I said when I read Edden's number. "I should take this. It's my cop friend's dad. The one in the hospital?"

My mom made flustered waving motions, and I turned my back on them for some privacy. A ping of adrenaline pulsed through me. I didn't think this was about Glenn, but I didn't want to tell them I was working on bringing in a banshee. Robbie thought I was irresponsible enough already.

My mom and Robbie's excited conversation retreated to background noise when I flipped the top open and put it to my ear. "Hi, Edden," I said in greeting, immediately recognizing that he was in the office by the faint chatter. "What's up?"

"Don't have your TV on, do you," he said, and a second flush of adrenaline built on the first.

"What is it?" I said, looking for my boots. My first thought was Glenn, but Edden sounded excited, not upset.

"Mia is at Circle Mall," he said, and my eyes darted to my bag, glad now I'd brought the charm. I didn't need it, but I'd know for sure if I'd done it right or not. "She was in the food court," Edden was saying, "her and her baby soaking up the ambient emotions. I'm guessing it wasn't enough because a fight broke out and turned into a riot. Never would have found her otherwise."

"Holy shit," I breathed, then covered my mouth. My eyes went to my mom's, and she sighed when I leaned against the wall to put on my boots. "Is Remus there?"

"Ye-e-ep," Edden said dryly. "We've got most of the by-standers out and the mall locked down. It's a mess. I'm on my way there now, and I'd like you there to help bring her in. She being an Inderlander and all. I don't have many of them on my payroll."

He didn't have *any* on his permanent payroll for legal reasons. My hands were shaking as I shrugged into my coat, but it was excitement. "I can be there in ten minutes. Five if I don't have to park my car."

"I'll tell them you're on the way," he said, and I made a noise so he wouldn't hang up.

"Wait. I'm going to be a while. I need to go back and get Jenks." If I was bringing in a banshee, I needed him. I'd like to have Ivy, too, but she was out.

"Alex is on his way to get Jenks already," Edden said, and I zipped my coat closed and dug out my keys, smacking the bad-mojo amulet with my knuckles. "I called the church first, and he wanted in on it."

"Thanks, Edden," I said, truly pleased that he was sending someone for Jenks not only because now I didn't have to, but that he'd thought of Jenks at all. "You're a peach."

"Yeah, yeah, yeah," he said, and I could hear his smile. "I bet you say that to all the captains."

"Just the ones who let me kick ass," I said, then broke the connection.

Excited, I turned to the living room. I froze, seeing Mom, Robbie, and Marshal sitting on the couch together, all staring at me. I looked at myself, already dressed for the cold, and I warmed. My keys jingled as I shifted, and I gave them a sick smile. Damn it, I was ready to walk out the door, and I had forgotten all about them. *Oh crap. We'd driven Marshal's car.*

"Uh, I have to go," I said as I put my keys away. "There's a problem at the mall. Uh, Marshal?"

Marshal stood, smiling in a rather fond way that I wasn't sure how to take. "I'll get the car warmed up while you say good-bye."

Robbie's expression was dark, like I should sit and have coffee with them instead of going to do my job, but damn it, runs happened when runs happened, and I couldn't live up to his ideas of what my life should be. "Rachel—" he started, and my mother put a hand on his knee.

"Robbie. Shut the hell up."

Marshal made a guffaw he quickly shifted into a cough, but I felt miserable. "Don't worry about it," the tall man muttered from beside me, then purposely bumped into me as he put on his shoes. "It's not a problem."

"Mom," Robbie protested.

My blood pressure spiked. Maybe we should have brought two cars, but then I'd be leaving Marshal alone here, and that wasn't any better.

Putting her hand heavily on Robbie's shoulder, my mother stood. "Marshal, I'll pack your pie up for you. It was nice to see you again. Thank you for coming over."

Marshal looked up from tying his boots and smiled. "It was a real pleasure, Mrs. Morgan. Thanks for having me. I enjoyed the pictures."

She hesitated, a hint of her worry showing, then she nodded and hustled into the kitchen.

"I'm sorry," I said to Marshal.

Marshal touched my shoulder through my coat. "It's okay. Just bring the pie out with you, okay? Your mom makes great pie."

"Okay," I whispered, and he turned and left. A brief gust of cold air blew in. It was snowing again. I still felt bad, and when I turned from shutting the door behind Marshal, I almost ran into Robbie. My head snapped up, and immediately my worry turned to anger. He was staring at me, and I stared right back, eye to eye, me in my boots and him still in socks.

"Rachel, you are such an ass sometimes. I can't believe you're walking out of here."

My eyes narrowed. "This is my job, *Bert*," I said, hitting the nickname hard. "Mom doesn't have a problem with it. You aren't around enough to have a say, so get out of my face."

He took a breath to protest, grimacing and dropping back when Mom hustled in from the kitchen, two pieces of pie on a plate covered with clear wrap. "Here you go, sweetheart," she said, elbowing Robbie out of her way to give me a hug good-bye. "Give us a call when it's over so we can sleep this morning."

Relief spilled through me that I didn't have to explain or that she wasn't trying to make me feel guilty for cutting out early. "Thanks, Mom." I breathed in her lilac scent as she gave me a quick squeeze and rocked back.

"I'm proud of you," she said as she handed me the pie. "Go kick some bad-guy ass."

I felt the prick of tears, glad she accepted that I couldn't be the daughter she wanted, and that she was proud of the daughter I was. "Thanks," I managed, clearing my throat to get the lump out of it, but it didn't work.

Giving Robbie a sharp look in turn, she said, "You two make up. Now." And with nothing more, she took the tray of coffee and returned to the kitchen.

Robbie's jaw tightened, belligerent to the end, and I forced myself to relax. I knew better than to walk out of here mad at him. It might be another seven years before I saw him again.

"Look," I said. "I'm sorry. But this is what I do. I'm not nine to five, and Mom's cool with that." He was looking at the bad-mojo amulet in my open bag, and I hid it behind my back. "You'll try to find that book, right?" I said, suddenly unsure, then I tightened my scarf.

Robbie hesitated, and then his shoulders eased. "Yeah. I will," he said around a sigh. "But I don't agree with what you're doing."

"Like you ever did," I said, finding a smile somewhere as I opened the door. "I'm happy for you and Cindy," I said. "Really. I can't wait to meet her."

At that, he finally smiled, too. "I'll give you her phone number," he said, gesturing to the night, "and you can call her. She's dying to meet you. She wants to do her thesis on you."

I jerked to a stop in the threshold and turned. "Why?" I asked suspiciously, and he lifted one shoulder and let it fall.

"Uh, I told her about your demon marks," he said. "I mean, she's a witch and all. She was going to see the smut on your aura and figure it out."

I came back inside and shut the door. "You told her what?" I said loudly, glad I had my gloves on to cover the demon mark on my wrist. I really needed to push Al into taking his name back so I could get rid of at least one of them.

"Sorry," he said smugly, not looking at all apologetic. "Maybe I shouldn't have, but I didn't want her to meet you and not have an explanation about the smut."

I waved a hand between us. "I mean, why does she want to do her thesis on me?"

Robbie blinked. "Oh! Uh, she's majoring in criminology. I told her you're a white witch with demon smut gained saving someone's life. That you can still be good and be covered in smut." He hesitated. "That's okay, isn't it?"

Giving myself a mental shake, I nodded. "Yeah. Sure."

"Here," he said, handing me the envelope with the tickets. "Don't forget these."

"Thanks." The banshee tear was a hard lump in my pocket when I shoved the tickets away. "Maybe I'll trade them in for an earlier flight."

"That'd be great! We'd love it if you came out early. Just let us know, and we'll get the guest room cleaned up." He smiled at me toothily. "You know you're welcome anytime."

I gave him a hug good-bye before I stepped away and opened the door. The night had a dry sharpness, and I looked at Marshal, waiting, as I went down the shoveled walk. The porch light flicked on, and I waved at the shadow by the window. Robbie's last words went around and around in my thoughts, and I kept repeating them, trying to figure out why they bothered me.

"The mall?" Marshal said cheerfully when I got in, probably glad that I'd pulled him out from under my mom's often one-sided conversation. I handed him the pie and he made an appreciative "Mmmm."

"Yes, the mall," I said before putting on my seat belt.

The car was warm and the windows defrosted, but cold hit me when Robbie's last words finally penetrated and I blinked fast. *I'm welcome anytime.* I knew he had meant them to be full of acceptance, but that he had felt the need to say them said much more. He was getting married. He was moving on with his life, becoming a part of it, immersing himself and finding a place on the wheel. By getting married, he was no longer just my brother, he was someone else's husband. And though we argued a lot, a bond was being broken by the simple fact that he was no longer alone. He was a part of something bigger, and by inviting me in, he had unintentionally told me I was an outsider.

"Your mom makes really good pie," Marshal said, and I smiled at him across the long seat. Mindful of the ice, he put the car in gear and slowly headed for the mall.

"Yes, she does," I said, depressed. Maybe I should look at it as if I hadn't lost a brother, but had gained a sister.

Ri-i-i-i-ight.

Eleven

I hesitated at the edge of the crowd, gaze fixed on the placid vamp being led under the yellow tape to the waiting I.S. cruisers at the curb. "I don't know," the cuffed man said, sounding bewildered. "I don't give a fuck what a Were thinks of my mom. He pissed me off."

The undead vamp's response was mostly unheard, and I watched the two meld into the lights and excitement of six I.S. cruisers, two news vans, eight FIB vehicles, and all the people who went with them. Everyone's lights were on, revolving if they could. The cold night air had the feeling of wrap-up, and I sighed. I hated being late to a riot.

I wasn't going to wait for Marshal, who was still parking his car. They wouldn't let him in. I'd be surprised if I got in without some trouble; invited or not, the FIB didn't trust me anymore. *Stupid-ass prejudice.* How many times did I have to prove myself?

Chin high and eyes scanning, I edged through the crowd to where the yellow ribbon met the wall, deciding I would just slip under the line and hope for the best. My motion to dip under the tape was halted, however, when I almost knocked heads with a familiar face doing the same thing.

"Hi, Tom," I said acerbically as I drew back. "We just keep running into each other."

The former I.S. agent dropped the tape, his shocked expression turning to frustration. He took a breath to say something, then clenched his jaw. Silent, he shoved his hands into his pockets and walked away.

Surprised, I stared after him until the snow and the crowd took him. "Huh," I muttered, then, sort of disappointed he hadn't stuck around to exchange barbs, I dipped under the yellow tape and yanked the closest door open, eager to get out of the cold. The air was still between the twin sets of doors, and I could hear voices echoing, raised in anger and frustration. A cluster of FIB uniforms gathered past the second set of doors, and I decided that was my best bet.

"Sorry, ma'am," a low voice said, and I jerked my hand from the inner door, instinct pulling me back before a thick-fingered hand could touch me.

It was a dead vampire, a fairly young one by the looks of him, set to be door guard. Heart pounding, I cocked my hip and gave him an up-and-down look. "I'm with the FIB," I said, and he laughed, the rim of his blue eyes thinning as he started to pull an aura.

"Witches don't work for the FIB," he said. "You look more like a reporter. Get behind the line, ma'am."

"I work outside the lines, and I'm not a reporter," I said, looking up at his clean-shaven face. Any other time, I would have stopped to enjoy the view, but I was in a hurry. "And knock off the aura crap," I said, ticked. "My roommate could eat you for breakfast."

The vamp's eyes went full black. The background noise of angry people abruptly vanished. The blood drained from my face, and I found my back against the outer doors. "I'd rather sip you for breakfast," the undead vampire murmured, his voice running like cool fog through my soul. A pulse from my scar sent a shock of reality through me. Damn it, I hated it when vampires didn't recognize me.

My gloved hand had covered my neck, and I forced it down and my eyes to open. "Go find a rat," I said, even as his playing on my scar felt really good. My thoughts went to Ivy, and I swallowed. This was so not what I needed.

Vamp boy blinked at my unusual resistance, and with that slight show of confusion, his hold on me broke. Damn, I had to quit teasing the dead ones.

"Hey, Farcus!" a masculine voice shouted from beyond the glass, and he turned, even as he kept me in his vision. "Leave the witch alone. That's Morgan, the FIB's whore."

Farcus, apparently, dropped back, the rim of his blue eyes growing in surprise. "You're Rachel Morgan?" he said, then started to laugh, showing his pointed canines. Somehow that irritated me more than him playing on my scar had.

I pushed forward. "And you're Farcus, rhymes with Marcus, another lame-ass vampire. Get out of my way." His laughter cut off as I bumped him, and he growled when I leaned on the door and passed into the warmth of the mall.

As far as malls go, it was nice, with the food court up front, wide aisles, and two stories to make a fun place to shop. I slowly loosened my coat and scarf as I scanned the open area. I was too late to do anything. Thick in the air was the choking scent of angry Were and the spicy tang of angry vampire, all mixing with the aroma of burgers, fries, and Asian food ruined by too much grease. Over it all was the sound of eighties pop done instrumentally. *Surreal.*

The surrounding shops on both levels had their gates down, and employees were clustered behind them, loud with gossip. The lower floor was a mess, with several tables sporting broken legs and everything shoved out of place. A red smear on the floor and pilings gave me pause until I decided the splatter pattern wasn't right for blood. It was ketchup, which might be why the humans had gathered by the ice-cream counter. Young kids wearing too much black mostly, but there were some late shoppers braving the encroaching Inderlander shopping hours, too. They looked scared, but there were no paramedics.

At the other end of the food court were the Inderlanders, and here was where the lawsuits would come from. Most had makeshift bandages pressed against their arms or legs. One was flat out on the floor. Weres and vampires. No witches, who were like humans in that they knew to get out of the way when predators fought. It was quiet over there, and most looked confused, not angry. Clearly the riot had ended as quickly as it had started. *So where's the little instigator?* I thought, not seeing anyone matching Mia's description among the walking wounded.

Stopping in the middle of the open hall, I dug the locator amulet out of my bag with a faint, foolish sense of optimism. Maybe I'd done it right and didn't know it? But as I held the smooth disk of wood in my hands, it stayed a slightly damp disk of wood. No glow, no tingle. Nothing. Either I'd flubbed the charm, or she wasn't here.

"Damn," I whispered, brow furrowed. It had been a long time since I'd misspelled a charm. Doubt in one's abilities wasn't healthy when you worked with high magic. Self-doubt led to mistakes. *Double damn.* What if I really messed up one day and blew myself to bits?

The familiar cadence of Ivy's boots pulled me around, and I shoved the amulet back in my bag. I was really glad she was here. Bringing in a banshee, even a cuffed one, was not as easy as it sounded—which was probably why the I.S. was either ignoring or covering up her activities.

"I thought you were working," I called out as she approached, and she shrugged.

"I finished early." I waited for more, disappointed when she shook her head and added, "Nothing. I didn't learn jack."

Jenks was with her, and he lit on my offered fist, looking tired and cold. "You're late," he said. "You missed all the fun."

A passing vampire with his hands cuffed snarled at us, trying to scratch at the new blisters on his neck. "Pull your damned wings off and then see if you can fly," he muttered, lunging, and making the I.S. cop with him jerk him back.

"Shove it up your ass and make a breath mint out of it!"

Jenks shouted after him, and I wondered just how much "fun" I had missed, and if it would be showing up on our doorstep in about forty-eight hours, after it posted bail.

"Making friends, I see," I said, gazing at the aftermath.

Ivy took my elbow and began leading me from the Inderlander side of things. The I.S. officers were watching me, and I felt uneasy. "What took you so long?" she asked. "Edden said he called you."

"I was at my mom's. It takes three times as long as it should to leave." I exhaled loudly, not seeing Mia anywhere. "It's over? Where's Mia? Was Remus with her?"

Jenks clattered for my attention, and he pointed to the human side of the food court. My lips parted, and I blinked. The fussing child should have clued me in even if the man standing protectively over the slight, elegant woman hadn't. *Damn, she looks midthirties, not three hundred,* I thought as I took in her slight, almost fragile-seeming frame next to the average-looking man as he held a baby bundled up in a pink snowsuit. The toddler was probably only hot, and I wondered why he just didn't take the snowsuit off her. Not a scrap of skin was showing apart from her face and her hands, gripping a sticky lollipop. Disappointment that my amulet hadn't worked filled me, then I shoved it aside.

Apart from his ever-moving eyes, Remus looked entirely unremarkable in his jeans and cloth coat. Not ugly, not attractive, maybe a little tall and bulky, but not overly so. That he could have beaten up Glenn looked doubtful, but knowing how to hurt a person and the willingness to use that knowledge, coupled with surprise, could be deadly. To be honest, he looked harmless—until I saw his eyes follow an FIB officer, hatred in the way he clenched his jaw, an almost eagerness to hurt reflected in his gaze. And then he dropped his attention and shuffled his feet, becoming a janitor standing over a woman way out of his league.

"Why are they just sitting there?" I asked, turning away before they felt my eyes on them. "Did the warrant fall through?"

Jenks slowly rose from Ivy's shoulder to see them better. "No, Edden's got it, but both of them are quiet right now, and he doesn't want to do anything until he gets more people out of here. I've been listening, and the I.S. doesn't care that Mia's killing humans."

A pang of worry made me stiff with tension. "Are they covering it up?"

"Nah. Just ignoring her. Everybody has to kill to eat, right?"

He said it with just the right amount of sarcasm, and I knew he didn't agree with their policy. Everyone had to eat, but eating people wasn't polite.

Jenks's wings fanned, to send the smell of soap to me. He was wearing his wraparound robe instead of his usual work clothes, making him look exotic, and I wondered how Bis was doing watching the church by himself. "I think she and Remus think they are going to slip out with the humans," he said as he landed on my shoulder.

Ivy laughed softly. "I call dibs on the big one."

"I don't know," I said, trying to read Mia's body language from across the large room. "They have to guess we know who they are. I mean, we've been to their house. I think they're waiting because we are."

Ivy smiled, showing a slip of teeth, potent after Farcus's play for my blood. "I still call dibs on the big one."

"Rache," Jenks said, his voice concerned. "Look at Mia's aura. Have you ever seen anything like that?"

Taking a slow breath, I willed my second sight into play. All witches could see auras. Vampires couldn't. Weres couldn't. Some humans could, gaining the ability from hybridizing with elves. Pixies saw them all the time whether they wanted to or not. If I tapped a ley line and worked at it, I could see the ever-after layered over reality. This far out from the center of Cincinnati, it would likely only be stunted trees and frozen scrub. When I'd been in my early teens, I'd spent a lot of time overlaying the ever-after on reality until a trip to the zoo cured me.

The tigers had known what I'd been doing, and they'd started for me as if they could walk through the glass to reach me.

I didn't look at auras much. It was illegal to screen employees by their auras, though I knew for a fact some food chains did. Dating services swore by them. I was of the opinion that you could tell more about people in a five-minute conversation than by looking at their auras. Most psychiatrists agreed with me, whether they were human or Inderlander.

Exhaling with a long, slow sound, I turned back to the cluster of humans. Blues, greens, and yellows predominated, with the accompanying flashes of red and black to give evidence of the human condition. There was an unusual amount of orange in a few people's outer fringes, but everyone was upset, and it didn't surprise me.

Remus's aura was a nasty, ugly red with a sheen of purple and the yellow of love at its core. It was a dangerous combination, meaning that he lived in a world that confused him and that he was moved by passion. If one believed in that kind of thing. Mia's . . .

Jenks clattered his wings, shuddering almost. Mia's was not there—sort of. I mean, it was there, but wasn't. Looking at her predominantly blue aura was like looking at the candles of a protective circle when the candles existed both here and in the ever-after. It was there, but sort of displaced sideways. And it was sucking in everyone else's aura with the faint subtlety of the incoming tide filling a tidal pool. The baby's was exactly the same.

"Look at Remus," Jenks said, shifting his wings to tickle my neck. "His aura isn't being touched at all. Even by the baby's, and he's holding her."

"That might explain why he's still alive," I said, wondering how they managed it. I'd been told that banshees didn't have any control over whose aura they sucked up along with ambient emotions, but clearly that wasn't the case.

Ivy stood beside us with her hip cocked, looking miffed that we were discussing things she couldn't see. It was with an unfamiliar enthusiasm that she straightened and smiled, saying loudly to someone behind me, "Edden. Look, she finally made it."

I dropped my second sight and turned, finding the squat, muscular man almost to us. "Hi, Edden," I said, shifting my bag up higher and unintentionally making Jenks take flight.

The captain of Cincinnati's FIB department shuffled to a stop, his khakis and starched shirt saying he was in charge as much as the badge pinned to his belt and the blue FIB hat he had dropped on his graying head. The gray seemed to be heavier now, and the few wrinkles deeper.

"Rachel," he said as he extended his hand and I shook it. "What took you so long?"

"I was at my mom's," I said, watching the cops behind him start to gossip about us, and he raised his eyebrows knowingly.

"Say no more," he said, then went silent when a Were walked past, limping and with a nasty gash on his forearm.

"You gotta keep 'em separated," Ivy murmured, then turned to us, her expression sharp. "You really think having those two in with the humans is a good idea?"

Edden put a thick hand on my shoulder and turned us away, moving slowly to the cluster of FIB officers by the kiddie rides. "I've got three plainclothes with them. We're getting people out one by one. Nice and easy."

I nodded, seeing the cops in there now. Ivy seemed less than convinced, and at her sigh he held up a hand. "We're waiting for social services to get here to take custody of the kid," he explained. "I don't want charges dropped because of a sympathy plea if it goes to trial."

His voice was grim, and I remembered that these were the people who'd put his son in the hospital.

"That's great," Ivy said, her eyes on the group, "but I don't think it can wait any longer."

Jenks spilled a yellow sifting of dust, and Edden and I turned. Remus watched from under lowered brows as two more bystanders were escorted away for "questioning." As we watched, his voice became loud, almost echoing. Holly started crying in earnest, and Mia took her, holding her close, clearly peeved.

"Edden, do something," I said, ready to go over there myself. Missing baby wagon or not, Remus had put an experienced FIB agent in the hospital. I didn't like unaware innocents surrounding him. And if I could tell who the plainclothes were, so could Remus. He was a child of the system, all grown up and made deadly. Like raising a wolf among people, society had turned something already dangerous into twice the threat.

Edden looked at the three officers in with the humans and, frowning, he bobbed his head in a meaningful way. Immediately the female cop got between Remus and the last few people. Two hefty-looking men in identical coats went for Remus, one angling to get him away from his wife and child, the other pulling his cuffs. It was way too soon, and Remus lost it.

Shouting, Remus jabbed a fist out, almost scoring on the smaller FIB agent, who stumbled back. Remus lunged after him, smacking an elbow viciously into his head, then grabbing the hand of the dazed officer and twisting it to force the man to the floor. Remus knelt on his shoulder, and at a snap of cartilage, the downed officer cried out in pain. My gut clenched. It sounded like Remus had just dislocated the man's shoulder; Jenks vaulted into motion, Ivy leapt at them, and suddenly—I was standing alone.

"Jenks, no!" I cried out, heart pounding at the thought of Remus's hand smacking into the small pixy. But he had come to a halt two feet from contact. Ivy, too, slid to a stop. The sound of fear rose from high-pitched voices, and every vampire in the place turned, their eyes black.

Remus had taken a hostage. And with one hand, he worked the gun from the downed officer's holster and stood up with it, still holding the downed officer's wrist with one foot on his shoulder. *Shit. Why had I agreed to this again?*

Mia and the baby were in the grip of the second officer, being slowly pulled back. She could kill them in an instant, but she only looked annoyed. The third officer had the humans and was hustling them out. The click of six safeties going off sounded loudly, and then Edden shouted, "Don't do it, Remus! Let him go and get your face on the floor!"

"Stay back!" Remus screamed as the remaining humans and Inderlanders dove for cover. "Let go of my wife! Let go, or so help me, I'll kill him! I broke his fucking arm, and if you don't get back, I'll shoot him!"

Ivy was between me and Remus, feet wide and hands out in a show of goodwill. Her body was tense, but she was about ten feet back—it was too far away for her to grab him easily but also far enough that she could evade all but the most accurate bullet. Jenks had vanished into the ceiling somewhere; I'd be willing to bet he could dust someone's eyes in half a second if he wanted to. Edden and the rest of the FIB officers had frozen, not wanting to trip the man into further action—but it was Mia who was the real threat. From across the court, I.S. officials were watching with concern, not wanting to have to take action. Mia sniping a human in corners and dark alleys could be overlooked to promote a greater peace. Murdering FIB officers in the mall would force them to react, and neither party was eager for a war.

Mia's lips were open and her pale eyes were narrow in anger. Holly's voice was high, complaining, and the banshee looked insulted as she jerked out of the grip of the FIB officer holding her. Upstairs, the people behind the gates pressed close, trying to see, thinking they were safe. A cool draft replaced the fleeing Inderlanders and humans.

"I said back off!" Remus shouted, glancing up at the people whispering from the second floor. "Let my wife go! You're hurting my baby! Let them both go!" Eyes wide and wild, he looked to the front of the mall. "I want a car! Get me a car!"

Edden shook his head. "Remus, we can't let you out of here.

Put the gun on the floor and lay down with your hands on your head. I promise you no one will hurt your wife or baby."

Remus looked panicked. The officer he had pinned under his knee was sweating, panting in pain, expression tight and probably kicking himself for letting Remus get his gun. The I.S. personnel inched closer. Ivy didn't move, but I saw her tense. So did Mia.

"Stop!" she shrilled, letting the toddler slip gently to the floor, where the little girl stood, gripping her mother's leg, her eyes wide, and silent at last. "Remus, stop," she said softly, her voice elegant and holding an odd accent. "This isn't going to help me. This isn't going to help Holly. Listen to me. You're going to hurt Holly if you do this. She needs a real father, Remus, not a dead memory. She needs you!"

The man brought his attention from the upper floors and focused it on his wife. Grief marked his expression. "They'll take you from me," he begged. "Mia, I can get us away. I can keep you safe."

"No." Mia started for Remus, and Ivy intercepted her, holding her in a loose but unbreakable grip, six feet back. Holly wobbled unsteadily after her, again latching on to her mother's leg for support. The I.S. personnel watched, tensing.

One hand on her daughter's blond head, Mia gave Ivy a mocking look, then focused on Remus. "Love," she said, her well-born voice full of persuasion. "It's going to be all right." She glanced at Ivy, and in a voice carrying strong conviction, she said, "Let me go. I can calm him. If you don't, he's going to kill that officer before you can move, and I will lose the only man I can love. You know what he means to me. Let me go."

Ivy's grip tightened, and Mia frowned. "I can give him peace," she insisted. "It's what I do."

"You hurt my friend," Ivy said softly, and a shiver ran through me at her anger.

"It was an accident," Mia responded coldly. "Leaving him

like that was a bad decision. We will accept our mistake and do what's necessary to make reparations. I have not lived this long by risking my life or letting my instincts rule me. I can calm him." Her voice changed, becoming softer, but her eyes were almost black with what looked like vampire hunger. "No one will get hurt," she said. "Let me go. The law can decide what is just."

Yeah, like I believe that.

Remus's breathing was harsh, and the man under him was gasping in pain, eyes trying to stay open as the agony pulled them shut. Mia hadn't said "trust me," but I'd heard it. Ivy must have, too, for she hesitated only briefly before she slowly released the banshee. My pulse hammered as the woman stood free, shaking her coat as if she were shaking off the memory of Ivy's touch.

Edden shouted, "Back off!" and I felt the tension wind tighter even as everyone retreated. A faint dusting of gold was sifting down, and Jenks dropped to my shoulder.

Mia picked up Holly, and with the toddler on her hip, she went to Remus as calmly as if they were shopping for peanut butter. "Let the officer go," she said, laying a light hand on his shoulder.

"They will separate us," he pleaded. Behind him, FIB officers were creeping closer, but Edden waved them to a stop when Mia caught sight of them. "I love you, Mia," Remus said, desperate. "I love Holly. I can't live without both of you. I can't go back to that place in my head."

Mia made a shushing noise and smiled at him. "Let the man go," she said, and I wondered if this had played out in their living room before they had fled, leaving Glenn for dead. "Once they hear what happened, we can return to the way we were."

I doubted that, but Remus shifted in uncertainty. Around me, the officers tensed.

"Let them cuff you," she whispered, the small woman on tiptoe to almost whisper the words in his ear. "I will protect you. We will not be separated. If you love me, trust me."

My eyes narrowed in suspicion. *Trust me?* Jenks's wings clattered, and I glanced at him.

"I don't li-i-i-ike this," he said in a singsong voice.

Yeah. Me either. I was a witch, damn it. Banshees were way out of my league.

Mia put a small hand against his cheek, and with Holly happily babbling between them, Remus exhaled, his shoulders slumping and his chin dropping to his chest. "I'm sorry," he said, carefully sliding the safety on the gun before tossing it to spin on the floor, away from everyone.

"Thank you, love," she said, smiling, and I wondered if the young-seeming but age-old woman was going to throw him to the mercy of the court, letting him take the blame for Glenn's injuries while she hid behind the excuse of being a bystander. She was up to something. I could feel it.

Remus let go of the man's wrist, and the FIB officer cried out in relief. Edden gestured, and the men behind Remus moved, jerking him off their fellow officer and cuffing him. From the other side of the food court, the I.S. officers buzzed, some of them swearing, most laughing. Ivy pulled herself together, trying to find her usual svelte elegance. Her eyes were black when they met mine. A pulse of fear went through me, then vanished. She looked away, and I resolved to keep my distance for a while. *I should have brought my perfume . . .*

"Be careful!" Mia demanded as the officers handled Remus roughly. A woman cop had closed in on her and Holly, and seeing it, Remus stopped, his arm muscles straining and a fearful look in his eyes.

"No," Mia demanded in a high voice before Remus could react. "Don't separate us. I can keep him calm. I never wanted to cause any trouble. We were just sitting there."

Jenks snickered from my shoulder. "Didn't want to cause trouble. Does she really think we're buying that crap?"

"Yeah, but look at him," I said, gesturing at the man. Under Ivy's watchful attention, Mia had rejoined him, and he was again docile. Meek, almost. Creepy, definitely. It was easier this way, and less embarrassing, seeing that the I.S. was watching. Not to mention the news vans out front. If it hadn't been for Ivy, this would've been a lot more difficult. As long as Mia didn't want to cause trouble, Ivy could keep her in line, and with that, Remus would do the same.

Beside me, Edden huffed in satisfaction. "Got 'em both, when they were too afraid to even try," he said to me, gesturing with his chin to the I.S. But I had my doubts that this was over. From Mia's words, I guessed she thought all we wanted was Remus. When she found out we were after her as well, things might get ugly.

"I don't like this," I murmured to Edden, thinking this was too easy, and he gave me an insulted look. Okay, so we had her walking to the door, but she was not going to meekly let us take her baby. She lived with a serial killer, for crying out loud! That she was pushing him around should be a big warning to Edden. "This isn't over," I whispered.

Edden snorted. "What do you want me to do? Cuff the baby?" he said, then shouted, "Pack it up!"

People started to move. Remus was led to the front doors, his head bowed and looking beaten with his hands cuffed before him. Ivy and Mia were six steps back, and Jenks and I fell into place after them. The baby was still on Mia's hip, and the little girl was watching me from around her mother with eyes so pale, they looked albino. Peeking from under her pink snow hat, her hair was a wispy blond that reminded me of Trent's, and it looked nothing like the jet-black severity of her mother's. Holly had her thumb in her mouth, and the child's unblinking stare was getting to me. She started to fuss when I looked away, and Mia jiggled her. Tension tightened my gut. This was too easy.

"You're losing her, pixy," Mia said, shooting a glance at us over her shoulder.

Jenks let slip a burst of green dust. "What?" he said, and I wondered at his panic.

"You've lost her already," Mia said, the banshee's voice

faint, as if she was seeing around corners to the future. "You see it in her eyes, and it's killing you slowly."

Ivy gave the woman a soft jerk to turn her back around. "Leave him alone," she said, then glanced at Jenks, her eyes crinkled up in disgust. "She's trying to feed off you," she said. "Don't listen. She's a liar."

Mia chuckled, and Jenks's wings fluttered against my neck. "I don't have to lie, and it doesn't matter if he listens to me or not. She's going to die. And you, silly vampire?" She looked askance at Ivy, and Ivy paled. "I told you that you were weak. What have you done in five years? Nothing. You think you're happy, but you're not. You could have had everything, but now she's gone, even though she's right next to you, because you were afraid. It's over. You were passive, and you lost. You may as well be what everyone wants you to be, because you aren't ever going to find the guts to be who you want."

I felt the blood leave my face. Ivy's jaw clenched, but she kept us moving forward at the same steady pace. Holly gurgled happily. Angry that Mia was hurting my friends, I snarled, "What about me, Ms. Harbor? Got anything in that bag of hate for me?"

She turned her cold blue eyes to me, and the corners of her mouth lifted. Her eyebrows arched slightly, making an expression of pure, delighted malice. Then Ivy pushed her through the double set of doors and they were gone.

It was snowing still, and I hesitated in the chill air lock. "Get in my bag, Jenks," I said, standing between the doors while FIB personnel eddied past us. The pixy seemed to be in shock, unable to move, and I reached up for him.

"I'm going!" he snarled, wings clattering as he dropped into my waiting bag and I zipped it closed. I'd put a hand heater that deer hunters use in there, and I knew he'd be all right.

My knees felt funny as I left the mall and entered the snow, and I slowed to try to see if Marshal was anywhere. No Marshal, no Tom—just faces craning to get a look at something. My breath steamed, and I was reaching for my gloves when the child-protection van pulled in under the tape the FIB had strung up.

"Mia!" Remus called out as two men tried to force him in the back of a cruiser. His voice was panicked, and I watched the banshee stiffen in Ivy's grip. Only now did she realize we were after her, too.

"Remus! Run!" she shrieked.

The baby started to cry, and Remus exploded into motion. His entire face changed. Gone was the panic, replaced by a delicious satisfaction. He moved, hooking a foot behind one of his captors and giving a yank. The man went down, slipping on the snow, and Remus went with him, slamming his fists on the man's throat. From there, he rolled to take the other man down. Just that fast, he was gone, spinning under the car and shoving through the crowd.

"Get him!" I cried, seeing him up and running awkwardly, from the cuffs.

"Run, Remus!" Mia shouted, urging him on.

Ivy shoved her at the nearest FIB officer, then leapt for the cruiser. She landed on the hood, and the car's shocks squeaked when she jumped off. I heard her booted steps in a fast cadence, then nothing.

In a belated rush, FIB officers started after them on foot or scrambled into their cars. It had been only three seconds, but Edden had lost him. The news crews were going nuts, and I looked for a place to hide. I hated news vans.

A soft thump pulled my attention from the cold parking lot. Someone gasped and pointed, and I followed a mittened finger to a blue lump on the snowy pavement.

"Edden?" I called, unheard over the noise. It was the FIB officer Ivy had shoved Mia at. The banshee was gone. Seeing several people trying to help him, I scanned the parking lot for Mia's long blue coat and a pink snowsuit. Crap on toast, I'd known this was too easy.

"Edden!" I shouted, then I saw Mia almost thirty feet away, head down and walking fast. Holy cow, how had she done that?

Adrenaline pulsed through me, and I hesitated for a split second. *It's a banshee. I shouldn't be doing this . . .* But if I didn't, who would?

"Hold on, Jenks," I said loudly, then looked for Edden's gray hair. "Edden!" I shouted again, and when he looked up, I threw my bag. "Take care of Jenks!" I exclaimed when he caught it, and then I ran after Mia. *Why am I doing this? They don't even trust me.*

"Miss, oh, miss," a news reporter said, getting in my face, and I elbowed her out of my way. Cries rose up behind me, and I couldn't help my smile.

In three seconds, I was through the ring of watchers. Darkness replaced the glare. A muffling silence pushed out the noise. Action replaced a frustrating inaction. I was moving, and I had a clear and definite goal. Mia had a good head start, and probably a car, but she also had a baby, and Holly was not happy.

Following the sound of a frustrated toddler, I ran through the parked cars, the blur of gray and falling snow quickly becoming a background nothing. The puddles of overhead light were flashes of interruption. I ran, chasing a weak prey, gaining fast.

Holly's whining grew faint when Mia's awkwardly running form vanished behind a Dumpster next to a delivery entrance. In six seconds, I was there. I skidded to a stop at the mouth of the walled parking lot, not wanting to get beaned by anything. My eyes scanned the open bay, finding Mia with her back to a padlocked door and Holly clutched to her. The small overhead light showed her proud, scared determination, and I struggled for breath. She had no way out. Ivy would catch Remus, and I would bring Mia back. It was done.

God help me if it's not that easy.

My pulse slowed, and I raised a placating hand. "Mia, think about it."

The woman clutched her daughter so tightly the baby started to cry. "You'll kill her," the banshee said, the anger a stark fury. "You can't care for her. If you take her from me, you'll kill her as surely as if you drowned her in a well like a cat."

"Holly will be fine." I took a step forward. The tall walls hiding the delivery entrances surrounded me. It seemed warmer without the wind, and the snow fell peacefully between us. "The people at social services will take good care of her. You can't raise a child on the streets. If you run, that's all that's left for you. I've seen your house, Mia, and you can't live like that. You don't want to force Holly to live like that. Give me the baby, and we'll go back. Everything will be okay. There can be a peaceful end to this."

Helpless as she looked, I couldn't bring a banshee in alone by force, but if I had her baby, she wouldn't run off again. I'd been moving forward all this time, and now only a few feet separated us.

"What do you know about peace?" Mia said bitterly, jiggling Holly in a vain attempt to get her to stop fussing. "You've never lived without running. It's all you do, run, run, run. You know you can't stop. If you do, it will kill you."

I halted, surprised. "You don't know anything about me."

Her chin lifted, and she shifted Holly so they were both facing me. Finally the little girl stopped crying, staring. "I know everything about you," she said. "I see inside you. It pours from you. You won't let yourself love anyone. Like that vamp. But unlike Ivy, who's merely afraid, you really *can't* love anyone. You're never going to have the happy ending. *Never.* No matter how you look for it, it's out of reach. Everyone you love you will eventually kill. You are alone even now, you just don't realize it."

My jaw was clenched, and my hands were fisted. "It won't work, Mia," I said, thinking she was trying to upset me to make herself stronger. "Put the baby down and your hands behind your head. I'll make sure Holly is okay." Damn it, why hadn't I brought my splat gun?

"You want my baby?" Mia mocked. "Fine. Take her."

She was holding Holly out to me, and thinking she was

starting to understand, I reached out. Holly gurgled happily. I felt the unfamiliar weight of an entirely new person fill my arms. Mia backed up a step, a harsh gleam in her eye as she glanced at the open lot behind me. A car was coming, and its lights shined into the dead end, making it bright.

"Thank you, Mia," I said, reaching to take Holly's hand before she hit my face. "I'll do what I can to keep Holly with you."

Holly's cold, sticky little fingers met mine, and my hand closed reflexively around them.

Pain came from nowhere. My heart jumped, and I gasped, unable to cry out. Fire blazed across my skin, and I found my voice.

A harsh guttural scream ripped through the icy night, and I sank to my knees. My skin was on fire, and my soul was burning. It was burning from my chest outward.

I couldn't take a new breath, it hurt that much. People were shouting, but they were too far away. My pulse was firing madly, and every beat pushed the fire through my pores. It was being stripped from me—my aura was being ripped away, and my fear was feeding it.

Holly gurgled happily, but I couldn't think to move. She was killing me. Mia was letting Holly kill me, and I couldn't stop it!

I managed a harsh gasp, and then, as suddenly as it had come, the pain vanished. I felt an icy wash of black flow through me, in time with my fading pulse. Holly cooed, and I felt her being lifted from me. Her lack of weight unbalanced me, and I slowly collapsed to the pavement. But still, the wash of black flowed through me, and it was as if I could feel the frightening nothing within me, growing larger. I couldn't stop it. Couldn't even think how.

Mia helped me down, and grateful for small favors, I stared at her exquisite boots. God, they must have cost more than my last three months of rent combined. I could feel the night air raw on my unprotected soul. And finally Holly stripped the last from me, the flood of black slowing to a trickle and stopping to leave only a fading, empty warmth.

I tried to breathe, but it wasn't enough. The snow hurt where it hit my skin, and I whimpered.

"I will *not* let them take Holly," Mia said as she stood over me. "You're *filthy* animals, and you'd kill her, even if only by accident. I worked too hard for her. She's mine."

My fingers twitched, accidentally rolling a gray pebble between my cold skin and the pavement. Mia stepped away and vanished, her footsteps fading quickly. I heard the slamming of a car door and then the car's idling away. All that was left was the falling snow, each flake making a soft tap as it landed on my eyelashes and cheeks.

I couldn't close my eyes, but it didn't seem to matter as my fingers quit moving and the heavy blackness finally smothered me.

Twelve

There was a faint scent of orange antiseptic, and the one-sided come and go of a distant, professional conversation. Closer, the sound of a TV murmured, only the low parts audible, as if through thick walls. I dozed in a pleasant muffled state, comfortable and somnolent. I'd been cold and in pain. Now I was warm and feeling pretty damn good, perfectly content to slip further into a dreamless state.

But the distinctive smell of the sheets tucked up to my chin tickled my memory, winding insidiously through my brain looking for a conscious thought. Then it found one.

"Shit!" I barked, adrenaline slamming through me. I bolted upright, eyes wide and an unreasonable fear jerking me from my drugged haze. I was in the hospital.

"Rache?"

Panicked, I turned to the sound of pixy wings, sweat beading up on me. Jenks was inches from my nose. His tiny features were pinched and afraid, scaring me. "Rache, it's okay," he said as an orange haze drifted from him to color my drawn-up knees. "You're okay. Look at me! You're okay!"

Lips parted, I focused on him and forced my breathing to slow. I was okay, and as soon as I realized that, I bobbed my head. Stringy, nasty curls shifted to block my eyes, and I pushed them back with a shaky hand. Just that effort seemed to tax me, and I let myself fall back into the slightly raised bed. "Sorry," I said softly, and he landed on my blanket-covered knee. "I thought I was in the hospital."

Jenks's expression became concerned and his wings stopped. "Ah, you are."

"No," I said as I found the controls and raised the head of the bed farther. "I mean I thought I was—" I hesitated. "Never mind," I amended, exhaling to get rid of the last of the adrenaline. I couldn't tell him I thought I was in the children's wing where I hadn't been able to cross the room to turn on the TV without going breathless. It was that memory that had shocked me awake, and I arranged the sheets to cover as much of the ugly white-and-blue-diamond gown as possible. *Jeez, Robbie visits for the first time in eight years, and I'm hospitalized?*

Jenks buzzed to the long bed table, pushed to the side. His wings stilled, and the red haze that had been hovering about one wing turned into a bit of red medical tape. I sort of remembered the ambulance. There was an IV stuck in me, and I vaguely recalled the paramedic putting it in. He had given me something, and after that, nothing. I'd had IVs before, but they usually went with an amulet if the patient was a witch. Maybe I was in worse shape than I thought.

My gaze went to the clock, right where they always put it. Noon. It didn't feel like I'd been unconscious for longer than a single night. From cold pavement to hospital. I had been there, and now I was here.

There was a stuffed giraffe on the narrow rolling table, probably from my mother. Stuffed animals were her thing. Beside it was a miniature rose sculpted of stone. From Bis, maybe? I took the stuffed animal in my hands, feeling the softness against my fingertips, in a state of melancholy. "Mia?" I asked Jenks.

The pixy's wings drooped and went a faint blue. "Gone."

I met his frown with my own. "Remus?"

"Him, too." He made the short flight to the bars on the bed, slipping slightly. "He sideswiped Ivy with a pipe; otherwise, we'd have him."

Alarmed, I stiffened, but his lack of reaction told me she was all right.

"She's madder than a jilted troll," he said with a wry expression, "but she's okay. Nothing broken. By the time she got up, he was gone. She tracked them to a busy street, and then . . . poof. Hot-wired a car and somehow slipped past the FIB roadblocks. Edden's pissed."

And baby makes three, I thought as I set the giraffe down. Crap on toast, they could be long gone. I hoped Audrey was right that banshees never left their city, or we'd never find them.

Jenks reached back to fix the red bit of tape on his wing and I flushed, remembering having thrown him at Edden. "Hey, I'm sorry about your wing," I said, and he brought his gaze to mine, his eyes green under the yellow shock of hair. "I did that, didn't I?" I added, pointing with my gaze. "I'm sorry."

"Nahhh, I'm fine," he drawled as his hand came forward. "It gave Matalina something to do besides yell at the kids. This happened in Edden's car, chasing Remus."

I wasn't sure I believed him.

"How about you?" Jenks asked, sitting cross-legged beside a mug of water bigger than his cat. "You feel okay? Your aura is . . . really thin."

I held a hand in front of my face and wished I could see my own aura. The demon mark on my wrist looked ugly, and I let my hand drop. "Holly stripped it from me," I said. "Took it along with my life's energy. That's why I passed out. I think. Has anyone looked at Glenn's aura? That's probably what happened to him, too."

Jenks nodded. "Right after you came in mumbling about your aura being gone. He's awake now. I saw him. His aura is patchy, but it will thicken. That freaky little baby can't even talk yet, and she's a born killer. She should've killed you. The doctors don't know why she didn't. They don't know why you woke up three days earlier than Glenn either. They were here staring at you and asking each other all sorts of questions, looking at your demon scars . . ." His lips pressed tight as a feeling of angst slid through me. "I don't like it, Rache."

"Me neither." Feeling violated, I tugged my blankets up a little. Had my demon marks saved me? Made my aura taste bad? I remembered a sensation of black coursing through me as Holly stripped everything, like she was sucking the last milk from a bottle, bubbles and all. I didn't like that something evil had saved me. It was bad enough that I had demon scars, but that I had to be grateful for them for saving my life was . . . perverted.

Jenks's wings hummed fitfully. Rising up, he said with forced cheerfulness, "You've got company. I can hear him in the hall."

Edden? I wondered as I was making sure I was covered when a soft knock at the cracked door turned into a soft scuffing. "Marshman!" Jenks exclaimed, a sunbeam trailing behind him when he went to the door. "How you doing? Rachel's happy to see you."

Eyebrows raised, I gave Jenks a sidelong glance. *I'm happy to see him?*

Sitting straighter, I waved sloppily at the tall man as he entered. He had his coat open, showing a flannel shirt with a wisp of curling black peeping out at the neckline. The casual lumberjack cut of the shirt hung nicely on his broad swimmer's shoulders, tucked into his jeans to show off his thin waist. There was a bouquet of flowers in each hand, and he looked awkward as he stopped before me. "Hi, Rachel," he said, smiling uncertainly, as if not sure he should be here. "Ah, you get what you needed in the mall?"

I laughed and shifted more upright. I knew how I looked in blue diamonds, and it wasn't attractive. "Thanks," I said sourly. "Sorry about that. She ran. I chased her." *Dumb.*

"And you got banshee-slapped," he said, putting the two bouquets down and sitting on the edge of the bed beside me. "Are you okay? They wouldn't let me ride with you to the hospital. You were delirious." He hesitated. "Did you really steal Mr. Ray's wishing fish?"

I blinked. "Uh, yeah, but I thought it belonged to the Howlers." My gaze dropped from his concerned brown eyes to the flowers. One was an arrangement of summer daisies, the other a carnation and mum mix. "Thank you," I said as I reached to touch them. "You didn't need to bring me flowers. They are beautiful. Did they have a 'buy one, get one free' special downstairs?"

My voice was light, and Marshal smiled. "Don't think anything because I brought you flowers. If I didn't, my mom would skin me alive. Besides, only one is from me. The daisies were sitting downstairs with your name on them, so I brought them up."

My eyes went to the florist's card, in an envelope, and I nodded. Robbie, maybe? As in "pushing up daisies"? "Thanks," I said, and he made a little jump, as if remembering something.

"I brought you this, too," he said, reaching into a coat pocket to bring out a winter-pale tomato. It was an Inderland tradition, and I couldn't help but grin. "For health," he said, then glanced at the closed door. "You're, uh, on a human floor, so watch where you put it."

The fruit was cold in my fingers, and my smile faded. *Why am I on a human floor?*

The sound of Jenks's wings rose in pitch, and he took flight. "Ah, I promised Ivy I'd tell her when you woke up," he said as he rose up. "I gotta go."

"Jenks, is she okay?" I asked, but he was gone. Rolling my eyes, I leaned to put the tomato on the table, and my knees knocked into Marshal. My eyes went to the flowers, and all my warning flags went up. He was sitting kind of close. "Um, it was awfully nice of you to come and see me," I said, nervous. "I'm not going to be here long. I was just about ready to get up and go harass the nurses."

I knew I was filling the silence with my babbling, and in a

surge of motion, I flung the covers back and pulled my knees up to get my feet past him and to the floor. I froze, looking down at those stupid pink sock slippers they give out. Damn it, I had a catheter. Even worse, just that little exertion made me dizzy.

"Easy, Rachel," Marshal said, already having stood and put his hands heavily on my shoulders. "I don't think you're ready to move yet. Your aura is really torn up."

The heady aroma of redwood cascaded over me, seeming all the more potent for the sterile smells of the hospital. "I'm fine. Marshal, I'm fine," I complained as the dizziness passed. It was almost as if I was leaving a part of myself behind when I moved, and until it caught up with me, I was naked. Exhausted, I sat with my feet dangling down and leaned my head against his chest while I tried to keep from blacking out. It felt nice when his hands rested on me. Not sexual nice—God, I was in a hospital bed with pillow hair and wearing a blue diamond pattern—it was as if I were gaining strength from his simple concern.

I settled back under his insistent, nervous hands, and he pulled the blanket up and around me. I lay there and let him do it, probably feeding his white-knight complex, but what choice did I have? If my aura was stripped, then I probably was gaining something from him. Genuine caring helped mend tears, just as the negative energy from someone who disliked me could do an equal amount of damage.

"Really," I said as he handed me the oversize mug of iced water as if it would make everything better. "I'm okay. I just need to move slower." But my hands were shaking and I was nauseous. The water seemed to help, and I took a big gulp, feeling it all the way down.

"Ivy will break my fingers if I let you hit the floor," he grumbled, taking the water back as I extended it. "Just be good for the next twenty minutes and don't get me in trouble, okay?"

I tried to smile, but I was trembling inside. Fatigue pulled at me, and memories of my early years in and out of hospitals came flooding back. "I don't even know what happened," I complained. "I mean, I remember up to blacking out, but after that? *Pfft.*"

Marshal sat on the edge of the bed again, as if I might try to get up. "No doubt. A banshee, Rachel? What were you thinking? You're lucky to be alive."

My right shoulder lifted and fell. Who else had a chance to catch her? Edden had probably checked me in. Maybe that was why I was on a human floor. I could lie in bed at home for a lot less money. David was going to be ticked when my insurance went up.

Remembering Marshal, I sighed. "Yep. A banshee. And her kid. And her homicidal husband. At the mall, no less."

He smiled, one almost of pride. "You made the news knocking over that reporter."

My eyes flicked to his and I winced. "They got it on tape?"

Leaning forward, he tucked a stray curl behind my ear, making me shiver when my thoughts went to Kisten's boat. "Knocked her right on her can," he said, oblivious. "It was good seeing you in action like that. Again."

His smile faded, and I realized this was twice now he had seen me on the news; the first time, I'd been cuffed. "Um, thanks for coming to see me," I said, sensing a growing awkwardness, as if he had stepped past our agreed-on boundaries.

Smile gone, he leaned back. He looked everywhere but at me. "Tried the pudding yet?"

"No, but I doubt it's changed since I was here last."

He chuckled, and I tried to decide if I was willing to risk taking the catheter out by myself. The one time I had, I'd hurt myself more than one would believe possible. I didn't want to stay here, and if my vitals were normal, they wouldn't keep me for simple fatigue.

The sound of Jenks returning drifted into the uncomfortable silence between Marshal and me, and we exchanged knowing smiles. Jenks was like a little kid you could hear long before you could see him. His voice was high as he talked to someone whose voice was a dull murmur, and they were moving slowly. Ivy maybe?

My pulse increased and Marshal stood when the thick oversize door creaked open. He looked nervous, and I didn't wonder why. Ivy didn't like him, and she took few pains to hide it.

"Hey!" Jenks shouted loudly as he circled the room three times. "Look who I found!"

I found myself smiling; not only was it Ivy, but Glenn, too, moving slowly and supported between Ivy and the IV stand. The black man looked awful, and it wasn't just from the hospital gown. Still, I met him grin for grin when he looked up from the floor, clearly pleased to be functioning even on this reduced level. His face was an ugly purple in places, and his hand gripping Ivy's arm was swollen, the cuts covered with stark-white bandages. "Hi, Rachel," he breathed, then focused on the tile and moving forward.

Marshal nodded his hello to Ivy, and after nudging the tomato behind the flowers before Glenn spotted it, he moved to the distant couch, built into the wall under the window, so the ailing FIB agent could have the closer chair. Oddly enough, Ivy looked like she knew what she was doing, competently shifting him around and making sure his IV didn't get tangled. She even knew to hold his gown shut while he angled to sit in the chair.

He eased into it with his arm muscles straining, and he exhaled long and loud when his weight left his feet. "Rachel," he said before he got his breath back altogether. "Ivy told me you were here, and I had to see it for myself. You look as bad as I feel, girl."

"Yeah?" I shot back. "Give me a few hours, and I'll wipe the floor with you in a game of 'round the nurses' desk.'" As far as I was concerned, he was in way worse shape than I, but he looked a whole lot better than when I'd seen him last, unconscious and surrounded by white sheets. That I couldn't stand up yet didn't mean anything. I'd be walking before sunset even if I had to crawl to do it.

Ivy came closer, and a pang of emotion went through me. The chair Glenn was now in had been pulled to the bedside when I woke up. I'd be willing to bet she'd been sitting in it all night. She looked tired, and I wondered if she had slept at all this morning. "Hi, Ivy," I said as I reached out—knowing she wouldn't. "Jenks said Remus hit you. You okay?"

Jenks clattered his wings behind the flowers, and Ivy's calm face scrunched up. "I'm fine, more mad at myself than anything." Her fingers touched mine, and I heard everything she wasn't going to say. "I'm glad you're awake," she said softly. "You had us worried."

"My pride took a hit," I said. "I'll be fine soon as I can stand." Jenks looked out around a plastic vase with a questioning expression, his hands full of pollen, and Marshal popped his knuckles. Realizing the men had become uncomfortable, I flushed. Our fingers parted.

"Marshal, you've met Glenn, haven't you?" I said suddenly. "He's the FIB's Inderland specialist. Glenn, Marshal is the swim coach at the university."

Marshal came forward. Leaning past the corner of the bed, he carefully shook Glenn's bandaged hand. "Nice to meet you," he said, and I couldn't help but notice there hadn't been a flicker of concern or reluctance in meeting an FIB officer. Not like with Nick. And I smiled.

"It's a pleasure," Glenn responded. "Have you and Rachel known each other long?"

"No," he said quickly, but I felt he deserved more than that.

"Sort of." I spoke up before Jenks, who had risen up above the flowers, could. "Marshal helped Jenks and me on that run up in Michigan. He's been in Cincinnati since Halloween, pulling snakes from under my kitchen floor and teaching me how to rock climb."

Ivy snickered at the reference to Tom, and Glenn's head

went up and down in slow consideration, his gaze becoming more accepting. I knew he believed Nick was still alive, which he was, the son of a bastard—and seeing that my ex-boyfriend and master thief had a record thicker than the phone book, I wouldn't be surprised if the FIB detective grilled Marshal later over what he knew about Nick.

Ivy made a small sound of interest when she opened the card from the second batch of flowers. I wanted to ask her about her leg, but she wasn't favoring it, and I knew she wouldn't appreciate me bringing it up in front of other people.

"Slacker," I said to Glenn, and when he gave me a tired, lopsided smile, I added, "How's your aura?"

"Thin. I don't know how it's supposed to feel, but I feel . . . weird. Three witches looked at me after you came in. Every one of them said I was lucky to be alive."

Jenks snorted. "They came in and poked Rachel, too," he said. "Left grumbling."

I exhaled slowly, bringing up my second sight without tapping a line so I didn't run the risk of seeing the ever-after. Not in a hospital six floors up. Sure enough, Glenn's aura was raggedy, leaking red around the broken edges and looking like a fluctuating aurora borealis instead of a continuous sheet. The gaps were not healthy, and until they healed, he'd be vulnerable to all sorts of metaphysical things. That I was in the same condition made my stomach turn. *And I have a date with Al in the ever-after at sunrise tomorrow.* I had to get out of it. Surely Al would give me a sick day for this. I should ask for a work excuse.

"Are you okay?" I asked Glenn, truly concerned. He looked so far out of character. The ex-military man in him peeked through when he forced himself to sit straighter, his face freshly shaved, the scent of shampoo coming faintly to me.

"I will be," he said around a heavy breath. "You went after them?"

"You know it."

"You touched the baby?" he asked, and I snorted. "Don't

touch the baby," he intoned, and the corners of my mouth lifted.

"Don't touch the baby," I echoed, realizing that that was probably what had downed him.

"It's the baby who's got the witch doctors so messed up," Glenn said, almost crossing his knees before remembering he was in a peekaboo gown. "They tell me that a banshee child has no control until she's about five. But that man was holding her when I talked to him."

Jenks's wings clattered for attention. "We saw him holding Holly, too. His aura was fine. I saw it. So did Rachel."

I nodded, not making any sense out of it. "Maybe she just wasn't hungry."

"Maybe," Glenn said, "but she drained me fast enough. You, too."

Ivy went to sit on the long bench under the window. "So what did happen in that house?" she said as she looked out, and I swear she was trying to change the subject. Her lips were parted, and her breathing was a shade too fast. Her eyes, too, held a hint of . . . guilt?

Glenn made an ugly face. "I went to talk to the suspect about the death of my friend."

Suspect, I thought, hearing the ugliness of the word. She wasn't "Ms. Harbor," or "the lady," or even "the woman," but "the suspect." Then again, Mia had probably killed his friend, put Glenn in the hospital, and allowed her daughter to almost kill me. "I'm sorry," I said, and he grimaced, not wanting the sympathy.

"Her husband didn't like some of my questions. Remus, is it?" Glenn asked, and when Ivy nodded, he continued. "Remus tried to bully me out the door. Took a swing at me, and we knocked about the house. I actually had him handcuffed, and then—"

"You touched the baby," Jenks said from somewhere in the flowers.

Glenn looked at his knees, covered with that blue diamond print. "I touched the baby."

"Don't touch the baby," I said, trying to ease the tension. No wonder Mia didn't let anyone touch Holly. Not to mention her not wanting any more kids until Holly had grown and had some control. Right now, she was like the walking plague. But Remus could hold her. What made him special?

Glenn shifted his feet in those slipper socks they give you. His were blue. "The baby put me out, not Remus," he said. "Once I fell down, I kept falling. I think he beat me slowly so they could suck it all up. If it hadn't been for the badge, I think they would have killed me and tried to hide the body." Seeing the horror in my eyes, he attempted to smile. "But you look great," he said, gesturing. "Maybe witches have thicker auras."

"Maybe," I said, unable to look at anyone. Of course I looked better. I hadn't had a psychopath maul me for the feeding pleasure of his family.

Standing awkwardly at the foot of the bed, Marshal seemed to gather himself. "Rachel, I have to go," he said, not unexpectedly. "I've got some stuff to do this afternoon, and I just stopped by to make sure you were okay." His feet shuffled, and he added, "I'll, um, see you later."

Glenn leaned back, cutting short his motion to cross his legs when he remembered the hospital gown. "Don't leave because of me," he said, his body language not matching his words. "I have to get back to my room before I'm missed. They don't like it when us rough men go past the nurses' desk and into the women's area."

Marshal shifted back and forth; then, as if making a decision, he leaned close and gave me an awkward hug. Uneasy, I returned it, hoping he wasn't trying to shift our relationship simply because I was vulnerable and he had helped me with Tom. Tom was small potatoes to what could come crashing into my kitchen. But the scent of redwood was comforting, plucking a need to go back to my roots, and I breathed it in deep.

"I'll see you later," he said earnestly. "I'm still checking into your classes, but if there's anything I can do, shopping, errands, just call me."

I smiled, touched by his concern. My mom's warning that he was a good diversion, not a good decision, echoed through me, but so did the entire comfortable evening spent with her, my brother, and Marshal. Marshal was a nice guy, and I didn't often have the chance to do stuff with nice guys. I didn't want to endanger him by close association, but what came out of my mouth was "I will. 'Bye, Marshal. Thanks for the flowers."

He nodded, waving before going with his head lowered, leaving the door open a crack.

Glenn took in Ivy and Jenks eyeing me as if in disapproval. Clearing his throat, he said, "You're taking classes? That's great. Crime scene etiquette, perhaps?"

I rubbed my eyebrow, feeling a headache coming on. "Ley lines," I said. "There was a mix-up at the registrar's office. Marshal is trying to work it out."

"That's not all he's trying to work out," Jenks muttered, and I scowled at him when he shifted to the mums. The scent of a summer meadow grew heavy, and pollen streaked his green shirt. "He's going to want to change things," the pixy said, and Glenn leaned back, mouth shut, to listen. "You being in the hospital is going to jerk him into rescue mode. Just like on that boat of his. I saw it in him right after he yanked Tom out from under our kitchen. I'm a pixy, Rachel. I may look all tough and stuff, but I got wings, and I know infatuation when I see it."

I sighed, not surprised he was warning me off Marshal. *And what do wings have to do with it?* "Well, he's not helpless," I said defensively. "Tagging a ley line witch is hard."

Jenks crossed his arms and frowned. Ivy put the giraffe down and eyed me, too.

"Yeah, yeah, yeah," I muttered, but my thoughts went zing-ing to Mia standing in the dark with her wailing child clutched to her, telling me that I'd never love anyone without killing them. "He deserves someone better than me. I know the drill."

Ivy moved uneasily, and shoving my unhappy feeling away, I turned to Glenn. The detective was very adept at reading people, and this was embarrassing. "So, how's the pudding?" I asked, reaching out and tossing the tomato to him.

Humans normally abhor tomatoes, seeing as it was a tomato that killed a good slice of their population a mere forty years ago. Glenn, however, had been shown the joys of the red fruit at fang point, and was now hooked. After his first panicked juggling to keep the tomato from hitting the ground, he cradled the fruit like a baby, in the crook of his arm.

"The pudding is nasty," he said, glad for the shift in conversation. "It's sugar free. And thank you. I don't get many of these."

"Inderland tradition," I said, wondering if I'd missed breakfast and would have to wait another six hours. I had yet to see a menu, but they'd still feed me.

Ivy sat on the foot of the bed, more comfortable now that there was one less person in here. "Flowers from Trent?" she said, her eyebrows high as she handed me the card.

Surprised, I looked at the daisies as I took it. "Ceri sent them," I said when I saw her absolutely tiny handwriting. "Trent probably doesn't even know she put his name on the card."

Jenks landed on my knee. "I bet he does," he said with a guffaw, and then we all looked up at the smart knock on the door and the woman in street clothes walking in. She had a stethoscope, and I knew she was my doctor before she opened her mouth.

She stopped short, as if surprised by the number of people, then recovered. "Ms. Morgan," she said as she came forward briskly. "I'm Dr. Mape. How are you feeling today?"

It was always the same question, and I smiled neutrally. I

could tell by the lack of a redwood smell that even the most stringent antiseptics couldn't cover that she wasn't a witch. It was unusual that they'd let a human treat a witch with human medicine, but if I'd been hit with the same thing as Glenn, I probably had his doctor. The thought seemed about right when Glenn shrank back in his chair with a guilty expression. The tomato, too, was in hiding somewhere. I didn't want to know where. I truly didn't.

"I'm feeling much better," I said blandly. "What did they use to knock me out?"

Dr. Mape pulled the blood pressure cuff off the wall, and I obediently stuck my arm out. "I don't know off the top of my head," she said in a preoccupied voice as she squished my arm with air pressure. "I can look at your chart."

I stared at the clock and tried to keep my pulse slow. "Don't bother." I knew amulets, not drugs. "Hey, can I get a work excuse?"

She didn't answer, and Glenn jumped when she ripped the cuff from me. "Mr. Glenn," she said pointedly, and I swear he held his breath. "You shouldn't be walking this far yet."

"Yes, ma'am," he said grumpily, and I hid a grin.

"Do I need to put a restriction on you?" she asked, and he shook his head.

"No, ma'am."

"Wait for me outside," the woman said severely. "I'll walk you back."

Ivy stirred from her corner. Cripes, I hadn't even seen her move there. "I'll help him to his room," she offered, and the woman's quick refusal died when she saw who it was.

"You're Ivy Tamwood?" she asked, then wrote my blood pressure on my chart. "Thank you. I'd appreciate that. His aura isn't thick enough to be mingling."

Jenks rose up from the flowers, this time covered in pollen. "Aw, we're all his friends," the pixy said, shaking in midair to create a dust cloud.

Dr. Mape started. "What are you doing out of hibernation?" she asked, shocked.

I cleared my throat dryly. "He, uh, lives in my desk," I offered, then shut my mouth when Dr. Mapes stuck a thermometer in it.

"I bet that's fun," the woman murmured as the instrument worked.

I shifted the probe to the other side of my mouth. "It's his kids who drive me nuts," I mumbled, and the thermometer beeped.

Again Dr. Mape made a note in my chart, then bent to look under the bed. "Your kidneys look fine," she said. "I'm going to leave the IV in, but I'll take the catheter out now."

Glenn stiffened. "Uh, Rachel," the man said uncomfortably. "I'll see you around, okay? Give me a day before we go racing down the halls."

Ivy got behind him, holding his gown shut as he reached for his IV and used it to haul himself up. "Jenks?" she said as they shuffled into motion. "Get your pixy ass in the hall."

He gave me a lopsided grin, then buzzed out, making circles around Ivy and Glenn. The door eased shut, and his voice faded.

I started to scrunch down to make this as easy as possible, then stopped when Dr. Mape pulled Glenn's chair back and sat, silently eyeing me. Suddenly I felt like a bug on a pin. She wasn't saying anything, and finally I offered a hesitant "You're going to take it out, right?"

The woman sighed and eased into a more comfortable position. "I wanted to talk to you, and this was the easiest way to get them to leave."

I didn't like the sound of that, and a ribbon of fear pulled through me, leaving prickles of unease. "I spent the first fifteen years of my life in hospitals, Dr. Mape," I said boldly as I sat up. "I've been told I'm going to die more often than I have pairs of boots, and I have a lot of boots. There's nothing you can say that's going to throw me." It was a lie, but it sounded good.

"You survived the Rosewood syndrome," she said, flipping back in my chart. I stiffened when she reached for my wrist, turning it over and looking at the demon mark. "Maybe that's why the banshee child didn't kill you."

Is she talking about my blood disease or my demon mark? Uneasy, I pulled my arm out of her grip. Either way, I was different, and not in a good way. "You think my aura tastes bad?"

Dr. Mape was looking at my hands, and I wanted to hide them. "I wouldn't know," she said. "From what I've been told, auras don't have a taste. I do know a banshee child will take long past when she's sated, and that's more than enough to kill a person. You and Mr. Glenn are very lucky to be alive. Ms. Harbor keeps her child well fed."

Well fed, my ass. She almost killed me.

Leaning back, Dr. Mape looked out my window and to the other wing. "She should be commended for raising a child to the age of reason, not hunted down like an animal when an accident occurs. Did you know that until a banshee reaches about the age of five, anyone who touches her aside from her mother is considered a food source? Even her own human father."

"Is that so," I said, thinking Remus had held her without a slip of his aura being taken, when everyone around was being slowly siphoned. "Forgive me if I'm not all flowers and hearts over her predicament. That woman handed Holly to me, knowing she would kill me. That *child* very nearly killed Glenn. Mia herself has killed people, they just haven't tied them to her yet. I'm all for staying alive, but I don't kill people to do it."

Dr. Mape looked at me impassively. "Of course I sympathize with you and Mr. Glenn, but in most situations, banshees take only the dregs of society. I've seen much worse human-on-human predation, and what Mia did was for her survival."

"In whose judgment?" I said snottily, then forced myself to relax. This was the woman who was going to give me my work excuse.

Again, Dr. Mape was untouched, and she leaned over to put an elbow on her knee so she could study me. "My question is why you suffered significantly less damage than Mr. Glenn. Humans and witches have the same aura strength."

"Know all about us, huh?" I said, then bit my tongue. *She's not the enemy. She's not the enemy.*

"Actually, I do. That's why I took you as a patient." She hesitated, then added, "I'm sorry, Ms. Morgan. They won't allow you on the witches' floor anymore because of your demon scars. I'm all you've got."

I stared at her. *Excuse me?* They wouldn't treat me because of my demon scars? What did my scars have to do with it? It wasn't like I was a black witch. "But you'll treat me?" I said bitterly.

"I took a vow to protect life. The same belief that causes me to look upon that banshee mother with compassion is why I agreed to treat you. I'd rather judge a person on *why* they make the choices they do rather than the cold facts of *what* they choose."

I settled back, wondering if it was wisdom or a cop-out. Dr. Mape stood, and my gaze followed her up. "I know Captain Edden from when his wife was attacked," she said. "He told me how you got your demon marks. I've seen what's left of your aura. And now I've seen your friends. Pixies don't give their loyalty lightly."

I frowned as she turned to leave. Turning back, she asked, "Why do you think you came in semiconscious and Mr. Glenn remained unconscious for three days?"

"I don't know." I really didn't think it was from the demon marks. If it had been, then black witches couldn't be harmed by banshees, and I knew that wasn't true. It had to be because I was a . . . a proto-demon, but I wasn't going to tell her that.

"Your survival of the Rosewood syndrome?" she questioned. "That's what my colleagues support."

It was too close to what I suspected, and I forced myself to look at her and shrug.

She hesitated, to be sure I wasn't going to say any more, then turned to leave.

"Hey, what about my catheter?" I shot after her, wanting some small part of myself back.

"I'll have a nurse come in," she said. "You'll be staying with us for a few days, Ms. Morgan. I hope you feel comfortable enough to talk to me soon."

My jaw dropped as she closed the door with a firm thump. So that was her game. She wouldn't release me until I satisfied her curiosity. Well, to hell with that. I had stuff to do.

The faint, familiar clatter of dragonfly wings drew my attention to the top of the tall wardrobe. "Jenks!" I said, warming. "I thought you were gone."

He flitted down, darting back and forth before landing on my knee. "I've never seen a catheter taken out," he said smugly.

"And you never will. God! Get out before the nurse gets here." But he only moved to the flowers and started to take the dead bits off.

"You're stuck here until you talk, eh?" he said. "Mind if Matalina and I borrow your jewelry box? We have got to get away from the kids for a while."

"Euwie, Jenks!" I didn't want to know. "I'm out of here as soon as I can stand up," I said as I tried to get the thought of Matalina with her feet among my earrings out of my head. "Six o'clock at the latest."

I stretched experimentally, wincing. One way or another, I was leaving. Al expected me for my lesson, and if I didn't show up in the ley line, he'd track me down. A demon in a hospital would do wonders for my reputation. 'Course that was one way to get out of here.

Jenks turned, his clever hands folding a daisy petal up to hold a handful of pollen. "Yeah? You think they're going to just let you walk out of here? Dr. Frankenstein wants you for her science experiment."

I smiled, feeling my pulse begin to quicken and anticipation warm my blood all the way to my toes. "Walk out of here is exactly what I'm going to do. I didn't spend my formative years in the hospital and learn nothing about how to sneak out."

Jenks just smiled.

Thirteen

My curls were nearly dry, and moving irritatingly slowly, I used the comb in the hospital care kit to try to smooth out the tangles. The shampoo and cream rinse had been from the kit as well, and I wasn't eager to find out how much cracking the thumb-size bottles was going to cost me. I was betting five bucks a bottle. It was worse than the amenities fridge in a five-star hotel. But asking Ivy to run home and get my stuff wasn't going to happen. The less I was carting out of here, the less likely someone would realize I was a fleeing patient.

Before the Turn, you could ask for an AMA, or Against Medical Advice discharge, and be done with it. But after the quickly spreading pandemic had ravaged the population, legislation gleefully took away a lot of patients' rights. Unless you did the paperwork ahead of time, it took forever and a day to get an AMA. If I wanted to leave, I had to sneak out. I'd likely have cops after me as the hospital tried to protect themselves from a lawsuit, but they'd go away once the AMA came in.

My shower this evening had tragically turned from the expected forty-minute indulgence in someone else's hot water into a five-minute rush; the force of the water beating into me had made me dizzy, giving me the sensation that I was washing my aura off with the soap. But I now sat reasonably comfortably on the hard couch by the night-dark window, dressed in the clothes Ivy had brought over: jeans and a black sweater she had complimented me on the first time I'd worn it.

I'd thought a hot shower would be just the thing, but the activity turned into an exercise in learning how fast I could move. Or couldn't move, rather. My aura was uncomfortably thin, and every time I shifted quickly, I seemed to lose my equilibrium. I got cold, too. Oddly so. Almost an ache. Weird, Glenn had said. That was the word for it.

Giving up, I flicked the comb into the trash and wondered if anyone had bothered to tell Pierce what had happened and that I was all right. Probably not. It was drafty by the window, and when I peeked past the curtain, the gleam of the red and white car lights against the snow made it seem all the colder.

I reached to put on my coat and found a new scrape on the right sleeve. *Crap.* Frowning, I shrugged into it, carefully levered my boots onto the couch, and sat with my arms wrapped around my knees. My smiling giraffe was sitting across from me, and memories came creeping back, memories of me sitting like this waiting for my dad to get better or die, older memories of me waiting for my mom to come pick me up and take me home. Sighing, I dropped my chin onto my knees.

My mom and Robbie had visited earlier. Mom had been shocked when I told her it was a banshee attack, and Robbie predictably went off the deep end. His exact words involved hell and an ice storm, but he'd never approved of my career choice, so what he cared didn't matter. I loved him, but he was a prick when it came to trying to make me fit into his ideas of what I should be. He'd left when I was thirteen, and I would always *be* thirteen in his mind.

At least when Marshal found out I'd be sneaking out tonight, he'd asked if he could help. After seeing him take down Tom, I was of a mind to accept his offer, but I was holding him in reserve in case I had to flee my "safe house" for a new one once the AMA police came after me.

The almost unheard squeak of the oversize door drew my attention across the dimly lit room and I lifted my head. It was

Ivy and Jenks, and I smiled and put my feet on the floor. Jenks reached me first, the slight dust from him leaving a faint trail in the dark room.

"You ready?" he said, buzzing around my damp hair before shunning my shoulder. He was wearing Matalina's latest attempt at pixy winter wear, and the poor guy had so much blue fabric wrapped around him he could hardly put his arms down.

"Just have to tie my boots," I said as I shoved the giraffe into my bag next to Bis's carved rose; I'd take it after all. "Are we set with Keasley?"

Ivy nodded as I sent my fingers among my laces. The cops would check the church. My mom's house was out, too, even if I wanted to put up with Robbie's pointed barbs, but Keasley could put us up for a few days. Ceri was spending much of her time in the Kalamack compound, and I knew he'd enjoy the company as well as the full pantry we'd leave him with.

Ivy was wearing her long leather coat over a pair of jeans and a brown sweater. I knew it was her attempt to try to blend in, but she could wear a discount special and still turn heads. She had put on some makeup, and her hair was pulled back. Apparently she was growing it out again, and the gold highlights had been colored over. Concern flickered in her dark eyes as she approached, her pupils dilated from the low light, not hunger. I'd be worried that she was vamping out from stress, but vampires treated the ill and wounded with an eerie gentleness. I think it was an instinct that evolved to help keep them from killing their chosen lovers by accident. The last place a vampire would sate themselves was a hospital.

She stood before me, evaluating my fatigue with her hand on her hip as I puffed over my boots. "Are you sure you don't want any Brimstone?" she asked, and I shook my head. Brimstone would up my metabolism, but I'd probably hurt myself when I felt better than I really was. My metabolism wasn't the problem. It was my damaged aura, and nothing could replace that but time.

"No," I emphasized when she frowned. "You didn't slip me any, did you?"

"No. God, Rachel, I do respect you."

She was glaring, so I figured she was telling me the truth. Ivy's subtle motions had a layer of hurt to them, and when Jenks clacked his wings at me I added, "Maybe later. Once I get out of here. Thanks."

That seemed to satisfy her, and I stood up, jamming my hands into my coat pockets and unexpectedly finding Robbie's plane tickets. Feeling sour after his scorn this afternoon concerning my chosen profession, I pulled the envelope out to stuff it in my bag. The banshee tear that had been in there as well came flying out, arcing through the air.

"Got it," Jenks called, then, realizing what it was, he yelped and jerked back so the tear hit the floor and skittered under the bed. "Is that the banshee tear Edden gave you?" he squeaked, unusually shaken, and I nodded. Ivy beat me to the floor, giving Jenks a dry look before she peered under the bed and retrieved it.

"It's clear again," she said, eyes wide as she rose and dropped it into my palm.

"Oh, that is just freaky." Uncomfortable, I held it in a shaft of incoming streetlight.

The small pixy hovered over my fingers, his wings a harsh blur. "That's it, Rache," he said, floating up to look me eye to eye. "The tear is why you survived, not your demon marks. The baby found the tear—"

"And took her bottle instead of me," I said, my relief absolute that it hadn't been my demon marks that had saved me. "It felt like something black was being pulled through me. I though it was the smut on my aura." Shuddering, I dropped the tear in my bag, vowing to take it out when we got home. "Maybe that's how Remus is staying alive," I muttered.

Ivy's face went almost terrifyingly blank. I looked at her in question, and feeling cold, I said, "Jenks, see if Glenn is ready."

"You got it," the oblivious pixy said, and he darted under the one-inch gap between the door and the floor.

I sank back to sit on the bed, arms crossed as I looked at Ivy, a shadow against the dark window. "You, ah, want to share something with me?" I asked.

Ivy took a slow breath. Exhaling, she sat in the corner of the long couch and looked at the ceiling, at nothing. "This is my fault," she said, her eyes black as they came back to me. "Mia going on a killing rampage to engender a child, I mean."

"You," I said. "How?"

Her hair swung forward to hide her face. "I gave her my wish. The one you gave me."

I uncrossed my arms and recrossed them the other way. "You mean from the leprechaun I let go to get out of the I.S.?" She nodded, head down, and I squinted, not understanding. "You gave your wish to a *banshee?* Why? You could have wished for anything!"

Ivy shifted her shoulders. It was a nervous reaction I didn't see often. "It was sort of a thank-you. I owed her a lot. I met Mia before I met you. My boss, Art, he was jerking me around. I was on the fast track, but he wasn't going to promote me out from under him until . . ." She hesitated, and in her silence, I heard her unsaid words. Her boss wanted a taste of her before letting her rise above him. I felt myself warm, and I was glad the room was dark.

"Office politics," Ivy said, her shoulders rounding. "I didn't want to play them. Thought I was too good to have to, and when I caught Art trying to cover up a banshee murder to help boost his bank account, I called Mia in to find out what was going on. At that point, she worked with the I.S. policing her species. Long story short, I put Art in jail to get out from under him. And I thought I had it bad in the I.S. At least I didn't have to frame my supervisor to move ahead."

"And got busted down to babysitting me," I said, embarrassed, and Ivy shook her head, leaning forward into a shaft of light. There were no tears, but she looked unhappy.

"No. I mean yes, but, Rachel, the woman told me some things about myself I was too afraid to admit. You know how banshees are. They tell you hard truths just to get you angry so they can eat your emotions, and she pissed me off by telling me I was afraid to be the person I wanted to be, someone capable of loving someone else. She shamed me into going off blood."

"God, Ivy," I said, still not believing she had given her wish to a . . . banshee! "You thought going off blood was a good thing? It nearly drove you insane."

Her eyes were black in the reduced light of midnight, and I stifled a shiver. "It wasn't the lack of blood that was driving me insane," she said. "And it *was* a good thing. The strength and confidence I gained from it was all I had to fight Piscary with. It gave me the will I use every day. Mia said—" Ivy hesitated, then softer, she said with an old anger, "Mia called me a coward, saying that *she* couldn't love anyone without killing them and that I was a whining child for having the chance to love someone but not the courage to do so. And when I met you?" Ivy shrugged. "When I realized you might love me back . . . maybe? Make my life clean somehow?" Embarrassed, she rubbed her temples. "I gave her my wish so she could have the chance to love someone, too. It's my fault she's out there killing people."

"Ivy," I said softly, frozen where I sat. "I'm sorry. I do love you."

"Stop," she said, holding out a slim hand as if to halt my words. "I know you do." She looked at me, jaw clenched and enough anger in her gaze to keep me from moving. "Piscary was right." She laughed bitterly, and I felt cold. "The bastard was right all along. But I was right, too. If Mia hadn't shamed me into it, I wouldn't have found the courage to screw Art over and let myself love you."

"Ivy." Oh God, Ivy never opened up like this voluntarily. She must have been really scared about me last night.

"You're like a master vampire, you know that?" Ivy pushed herself to the corner of the couch and stared at me, almost angry. "You scare the ever-loving crap out of me even as I want to wrap myself up in your soul and be safe. I'm sick, wanting what scares me."

"I don't want to hurt you," I offered, not knowing where this conversation was going.

"You have hurt me," she said, arms around her drawn-up knees and her chin high. "You will again. I don't care. That's the sick part. That's why I don't touch you anymore. I'm addicted to your little white lies. I want love, but I can't live with myself if I make you hurt me again. I don't want pain to feel like love. It's not supposed to."

The memory of Farcus playing on my scar lifted through me. Too close. He'd been too close. Used me like a match to light his own libido. Pain turned to pleasure—was it truly perverted if it really felt good? "I'm sorry, Ivy. I can't give any more," I whispered.

Ivy turned to the window, shifting the curtain to look outside. "I'm not asking you to, scaredy-cat," she said mildly, and I saw the signs as she closed her emotions down again. "Don't worry. I like things the way they are. I didn't tell you this to guilt you into anything; I just thought you ought to know why Mia Harbor has a husband who is immune to a banshee's attack. I gave her the wish because I owed her. She gave me the courage to fight for what I wanted. Whether I get it or not is immaterial. The only way I could thank her was to give her the chance to love. And I think she loves him. As much as a banshee can."

My hands were clenched on my arms with enough strength to cramp them, and I let go. "She loves a freaking serial killer," I said, glad the conversation had swung away from us.

Ivy smiled wanly in the streetlight. Her hand dropped from the curtain, and the shadow hid her face again. "That doesn't make it any less. Holly isn't special. Remus is. I'm sorry. I shouldn't have given it to her. I had no idea she'd use it to kill people. For all her strength, she's a monster. I owe her, but I'm still going to bring her in."

Standing, I reached out to draw her to her feet, wanting to hug her so she'd lose that awful stiffness. "Don't worry about it. You didn't know what she was going to do. No good deed and all."

"It's still my fault."

My hand touched her shoulder, and I drew back when Jenks shot under the door in a glittering of silver sparkles that left a steady stream behind as he rose up to our height. "Glenn's in the hall," he said, unusually bright-eyed in the dim room.

"Good," I said faintly, turning to get my bag. My face was warm, and I put a hand to it.

"Uh," the pixy said, hovering uncertainly in the dark. "Did I miss something?"

Ivy took my bag from me, having to jerk it free. "No," she said, then turned to me. "Stay here and I'll get you a chair."

"No you won't." She had confused me, and I didn't know how to stop her from pushing me around right now. "A chair wasn't in the plan," I added. "I can walk it."

"You're wobbling on your feet," Ivy said, and I shook my head. This was a decision I was going to stick with.

"I can't sneak out in a wheelchair," I said, eyes on the ground until I was sure it wasn't tilting. "I have to walk. Really, really slowly."

Jenks hovered before us, looking like Lawrence of Arabia with wings. "No way, Rache," he started, his eyes crinkled in worry. "You're as strong as a fairy's hard-on."

"I can make it," I breathed, hesitated, then shook my head. *Nice one, Jenks.* My head was down as I started for the door, and my thoughts were on my laundry list: Bargain with Al for the time off; reconstruct the charm to give Pierce temporary substance; remind Marshal that we weren't going to move our relationship along simply because one, I'd gotten hurt, two, he'd beaten Tom, and three, we'd had a nice dinner with my family. I also had to try making that locator charm again, not to mention, to get a lead on Kisten's killer, look through the records to track down everyone Piscary had bled or bedded during his jail time. I could do it. I could do it all. *How am I going to do this?*

Jenks was flying backward in front of me as I moved from couch, to bed, to wardrobe, gauging my aura, no doubt. It was irritating to say the least. "Tell Glenn we're on our way?" I asked, slapping at Ivy when she threatened to help me inch along.

"Already did." Jenks landed on my shoulder, puffing from the constant weight of his clothes. "You owe him big, Rachel. He was scheduled to be released tomorrow."

I clutched my bag and looked at Ivy, squashing my guilt. "Then let's go."

Ivy nodded. Touching my shoulder once, she headed out. "See you in the elevator, Rache," Jenks said, then darted out before the oversize door swung shut behind her.

Alone, I let myself lean against the wall, exhausted. I was breathing heavy and moving slow. That wasn't a problem. I could do this. I had done this lots of times, actually, with my mom when I wanted to go home and the AMA hadn't come in yet.

Sneaking out of the hospital is like riding a bike, I thought as I listened to Ivy talking to the nurse at the desk. Then I remembered that I'd never learned to ride a bike either.

"Elevator," I whispered, cementing it as my goal. I could rest there. Ride up and down until I felt like walking out. I waited by the almost-closed door, eavesdropping. It was about midnight, and since I was on a human floor, it was quiet. Perfect.

"Get a nurse!" someone shouted, and I heard a clang as something hit a wall. Jenks started shrieking, and I edged forward to peek through the crack in the door. There was a distant masculine groan, and a heavy orderly rushed past, his dreadlocks swinging.

I eased the door open with my weight, shivering when it felt like the varnished wood was stealing the heat from me right through my coat. I looked to the right, following the sound of the commotion, smiling at Glenn, on the floor at the end of the hall. Ivy was there with Jenks, two orderlies, and a nurse. The guy who delivered the food was there, too.

As I watched, Glenn groaned convincingly, cracking an eye to see me. I gave him a bunny-eared, kiss-kiss, and he flipped me off, turning his smile into a pained moan. Jenks was right; I owed him big.

Pulse racing, I hobbled to the elevator around the corner. I didn't even have to go by the nurses' desk. My pace slowly became more sure and my posture upright, while fighting the fatigue and mild sensation of walking in deep snow and trying to look as if I was sedate, not sedated.

I turned the corner, and the noise behind me grew faint. The hallway was empty, but I didn't dare use the waist-high hand-rail. Besides, the elevator was just ahead. I pushed the button, then pushed it again until the light went on.

Almost immediately the doors opened, and my heart jumped when a couple stepped out. They gave me a cursory glance, then perked up at the noise Glenn was making. Curiosity was winning when I staggered to the back of the lift and propped myself up in the corner, my bag clutched to me. The more quickly I moved, the worse I felt. Which really stunk, seeing as I was in a turtle's footrace for the door.

I took shallow breaths and stared at the couple's backs as the doors slid shut. *Jenks. Where are you? You said you'd be here.*

The pixy darted in at the last moment, nearly crashing into the back of the elevator.

"Rache!" he said in excitement, and vertigo hit me when I flung my hands over my ears.

"Not so loud!" I exclaimed, and he dropped to hover at eye level.

"Sorry," he said, looking anything but. He followed my weary gaze to the dark panel, then flew at it, hitting the button for the next level down feet first. I heard the whine of electronics click over, and we started to descend.

"Glenn is good," he said as he returned to land on my shoulder. "I don't think they'll know you're gone until they get someone to take him back to his room."

"Excellent." I closed my eyes against the vertigo. I'd been afraid the elevator might move too fast to stomach, but I couldn't take the stairs even if my aura *was* dragging behind me as we descended.

"You doin' okay?" he asked, worry thick in his tone.

"Yep," I said, propped in the corner. "It's just fatigue." I squinted to get him into focus, and then the world snapped back when the elevator dinged and the rest of my aura caught up. I took a breath, letting it slip slowly from me. "I've got things to do today, and I can't do them lazing around in a bed that moves up and down."

He laughed, and I pushed from the wall when the doors opened. If all was going well, it would be Ivy, and I didn't want her to think I was a wimp.

Ivy was standing right before the doors, and giving me a glance, she darted in and clicked the button to close the doors. "Everything okay?" she asked.

"Peachy."

Ivy exchanged a look with Jenks and hit the "lobby" button with a series of taps so rapid that they were almost indistinguishable from each other. *A little nervous, are we?*

The descent was worse this time, and I closed my eyes and leaned back in the corner as the elevator picked up speed, going almost the full height of the building.

"Rache, you all right?" Jenks asked, and I wiggled my fingers, too afraid of what might happen if I nodded. My stomach hurt.

"Too fast," I breathed, worried about the ride home. I was going to be blowing chunks if we had to drive faster than twenty miles an hour.

I started to shiver, and I clutched my bag to me, feeling every muscle I had clench when the lift lurched to a stop. The elevator dinged and the doors slid open. Relieved, I opened my eyes to find Jenks hovering at the sensor to keep the doors from shutting. The soft sounds of a nearly empty lobby filtered in, and Ivy took my arm. I would have protested, except I really needed it. Together we started out of the elevator. God, I felt a hundred and sixty years old, my heart pounding and my knees weak.

But the slow movement started to feel good, and the farther we went, the more sure I was that this was the right thing to do. I glanced around—trying not to look like I was—scopin' casual, as Jenks would say. The lobby had a few people passing through it even at midnight, and the lights shining down on the entryway illuminated the snow-covered vegetation to make it into indistinguishable blobs. It was kind of pretty with the flashing amber lights of the tow truck.

Tow truck?

"Hey! That's my car!" I exclaimed upon seeing it parked at the curb in the pickup and drop-off spot. But it wouldn't be there long from the looks of it.

At the sound of my voice, two people turned from the big plate-glass windows. They'd been watching the guy work, and my eyes narrowed when I realized it was Dr. Mape and the cop on duty. A big vamp from the I.S. Great. Just freaking great.

"Plan B, Ivy," Jenks said, then dove into the elevator.

"That's my car!" I shouted again, then gasped when Ivy spun me around and yanked me back into the elevator. My back hit the wall and I put a hand to my stomach. "Who said"—I panted through the sudden vertigo—"you could drive my car?"

The doors snicked shut and cut off the doctor's protest. I clutched at the walls when the elevator started to go up, then forced myself to let go. *Damn it, I am not going to get sick.* "Who said you could drive my car?" I said again, louder, as if I could hold off the dizziness with my voice.

Jenks's wings hummed nervously, and Ivy flushed. "What was I supposed to pick you up with? My cycle?" she muttered. "I'm in a legal spot. I had thirty minutes left."

"They're towing my car!" I shouted again, pointing, and she shrugged.

"I'll get it out of impound."

"How are we going to get home now!" I yelled, not liking the feeling of helplessness, and Ivy pulled out her cell phone from a slim case at her belt. God, the thing was the size of a credit card. "I'll call Kist—" Her voice broke, and I stared at her suddenly riven features. "I mean, Erica," she amended softly. "She'll come get us. She works near here."

Turn it to hell. Ill and heartsick, I pressed into the corner of the elevator and tried to find my equilibrium.

Jenks landed on my shoulder. "Relax, Rache," he said, his eyes darting to Ivy as she hunched in pain, her fingers tapping out a text message as fast as if she were at a conventional keyboard. "You saw the hag of a doctor. It's not Ivy's fault. They knew you were making a run for it."

Hands splayed, I propped myself against the two walls surrounding me. It felt as if we were rising through thousands of pinpricks of ice as the world hit me raw, unprotected without my full aura. It wasn't as if I was in a position to do anything. And Dr. Mape would have been a fool for not expecting this. Multiple escapes were in my record. My mom used to sneak me out all the time. "Where are we going?" I breathed, forcing myself to keep my eyes open even though they kept shifting on their own, like I had been on a merry-go-round for too long.

"The roof."

I eyed Ivy, then carefully leaned to push the button for the third floor. "There's a walkway to the children's wing on the third floor. We can go out that way," I muttered, and my eyes slid shut. Just for a moment. Ivy and Jenks's silence pulled them back open. "What?" I said. "Why should I go through the laundry chute to the basement floor when I can roll out in a wheelchair?"

Ivy shifted her feet. "You'll sit down?" she asked.

Before I fall down? Not likely. "Yes," I said, then accepted

Ivy's arm when the elevator stopped and the world magically returned to normal.

The elevator doors slid open with a ding, and Jenks flew out, darting back before we had gone three steps. "There's a chair over here," he said, and I leaned against the wall beside the fake potted plant as Ivy used one hand to keep me upright, and the other to almost throw the chair open, the locks snapping in place from the sudden shock of being jerked to a stop.

"Sit," she said, and I gratefully sat. I had to get home. Everything would be better if I could just get home.

Ivy pushed me into motion, taking advantage of the empty hall to race for the walkway. Dizziness roared from everywhere, slipping out of the corners where the walls and floor met, chasing after me as Ivy raced. "Slow down," I whispered, but I think it was my lolling head that got her to stop. Either that or Jenks screaming at her.

"What the hell are you doing!" Jenks was shouting, and I gritted my teeth, struggling to keep from throwing up.

"Getting her out of here," she snarled from somewhere far away and distant behind me.

"You can't move her that fast!" he yelled, dusting me as if he could give me a false aura. "She's not moving slowly because she's hurt, she's moving slowly to keep her aura with her. You just freaking left it back at the elevator!"

Ivy's voice was a mere whisper of "Oh my God." I felt a warm hand on me. "Rachel, I'm sorry. Are you okay?"

It was getting better surprisingly fast, and the world stopped spinning. Looking up, I squinted until she came into focus. "Yeah." I took a cautiously deep breath. "Just don't go that fast." Crap. How was I going to handle the car?

Ivy's face was scared, and I reached up to touch her hand, still on my shoulder. "I'm okay," I said, risking another deep breath. "Where are we?"

She pushed us back into motion, almost crawling. Jenks, flying a close flank, nodded. "The children's wing," she whispered.

Fourteen

Anxious, I pressed my knees together as Ivy wheeled me down the hall. We'd passed the long walkway over the service drive, and we were indeed in the children's wing. An awful feeling of dread and familiarity settled in me, and my gut clenched.

The smell was different, holding the scent of baby powder and crayons. The walls were a warmer yellow now, and the railings . . . I eyed them as we rolled past. There was a second, lower set, which just about killed me. Pictures of puppies and kittens were on the walls at seated height. And rainbows. Kids shouldn't be ill. But they were. They died here, and it wasn't fair.

I felt the prick of tears, and Jenks landed on my shoulder. "You okay?"

It isn't fair, damn it. "No," I said, forcing myself to smile so he wouldn't ask Ivy to stop. I could hear kids talking loudly with the intensity that children used when they knew they had only a short time to make their voices heard.

We were going by the playroom, the tall windows with the blinds open to show the snow, and the ceiling lights turned up to make it almost as bright as noon. It was just after midnight, and only the Inderlander kids would be up, most of them in their rooms with a parent or two, having their dinner. If they could swing it, most parents visited during meals to try to make their child's hospital room into a piece of the familiar by eating with them, and the kids—without exception—were too kind to tell them it only made home look that much farther away.

We slowly rolled by the bright room with its night-black windows. I wasn't surprised to see it empty but for the pack of kids whose parents were too far away to stop in for meals or had other responsibilities. They were an independent bunch, and they talked a lot. I smiled when they caught sight of us, but shock filled me when one of them shouted, "Ivy!"

Immediately the table in the far corner emptied out, and I sat in amazement as we were suddenly surrounded by kids in brightly colored pj's. One was enthusiastically dragging her IV stand behind her, and three had lost their hair from chemotherapy, still legal after the Turn, when more effective biomedicines were not. The oldest of the three, a skinny girl with her jaw clenched, lagged behind with a tired determination. She wore a bright red bandanna that matched her pajamas, and it gave her an endearing bad-girl look.

"Ivy, Ivy, Ivy!" a red-cheeked boy about six shouted again, shocking the hell out of me when he flung himself at Ivy's knees in an enthusiastic hug. Ivy flamed red, and Jenks laughed, spilling dust in a sheet of gold.

"Did you come to eat with us and throw peas at the parrot?" the girl with the IV asked, and I turned in my chair to see Ivy all the better.

"Pixy, pixy, pixy!" the boy on her legs shouted, and Jenks flew up out of his reach.

"Uh, I'm going to do a nurse check," he said nervously, then zipped off at ceiling height. There was a chorus of disappointment, and Ivy disentangled herself, kneeling to put us all on the same level. "No, Daryl," she said, "I'm sneaking my friend out for some ice cream, so lower your voices before they check up on you."

Immediately the shouts diminished to giggling whispers. One of the bald kids, a boy by the cowboys on his pajamas, ran to the end of the hall and peeked around the corner. He gave us a distant thumbs-up, and everyone sighed. There were only five of them, but they all apparently knew Ivy, and they clustered around us like . . . kids.

"She's a witch," the red-cheeked boy, still attached to Ivy's leg, said, pitching his tone imperialistically. His hand was on his hip, and he was clearly the floor's self-proclaimed king. "She can't be your friend. Vampires and witches don't make friends."

"She has a black aura," the girl with the IV said, backing up. Her eyes were wide, but I could tell by her plump, healthy body that she was going to survive. She was one of the kids who come in, stay, then leave, never to return. She must be special to have been accepted into what was clearly the clique of children who . . . weren't going to have an easy go of it.

"Are you a black witch?" the girl who had lagged behind asked. Her brown eyes were huge in her medicine-ravaged face. There was no fear in her, not because she was ignorant, but because she knew she was dying, and she knew I wasn't going to be the cause of her death. My heart went out to her. She was seeing around corners, but not yet ready to go. One more thing possibly to see and do.

Ivy shifted uncomfortably at her question. "Rachel is my friend," she said simply. "Would I be a friend to a black witch?"

"You might," Daryl said haughtily, and someone stepped on his foot to make him yelp. "But her aura is black!" the king protested. "And she has a demon mark. See?"

Everyone drew back with fear except the tall girl in the red pajamas. She simply stood before me and looked at my wrist, and unlike most times when someone pointed it out and I tried to hide it, I turned my hand up for all of them to see.

"I got it when a demon tried to kill me," I said, knowing most of them had to gain a lifetime of wisdom in just a few years and had no time for pretend, yet pretend was all they had. "I had to accept a very bad thing to survive."

Small heads bobbed and eyes grew wide, but the king lifted his chin and took a stance that was utterly charming—a round, chubby Jenks with his hands on his hips. "That's evil," he said, certain of his belief. "You should never do anything evil. If you do, you are evil and go to hell. My mom says so."

I felt ill when the smallest girl, with the IV, shrank back farther yet, tugging at her friend to leave with her.

"I'm sorry," Ivy whispered as she stood up and took the handles of the wheelchair. "I didn't think they would come over. They don't understand."

But the thing was, they did understand. They had the wisdom of the world in their eyes. They understood too well, and seeing their fear, I felt my heart gray.

Ivy made shooing motions with her hand, and they broke their circle. All except the skinny girl in the bright red pajamas. Seeing my misery, she reached out with her small, smooth, child hands and delicately took my wrist with her pinkie extended. Turning my hand palm up, she used a finger to slowly trace the circle and line. "Ivy's friend isn't evil for doing something to survive what hurt her," she said, her voice soft but certain. "You take poison to kill the bad cells in you, Daryl, just like me. It hurts you, makes you tired, makes you sick, but if you didn't you would die. Ivy's friend took a demon mark to save her life. It's the same thing."

Ivy's motion to push the chair stopped. The kids went silent, each thinking, assessing what they had been told with the harsh reality of what they lived with. Daryl's sure look faltered, and he pushed forward, not wanting to look like a coward, or worse, cruel. He peered over the arm of the wheelchair at my scar, then up to my face. His small round face broke into a smile of acceptance. I was one of them, and he knew it. My jaw unclenched, and I smiled back.

"I'm sorry," Daryl said, then scrambled up to sit in my lap. "You're okay."

My breath came fast, in surprise, but my hands naturally folded around him to keep him in place so he wouldn't fall.

Daryl gave a hop and settled in, snuggling his head under my chin and tracing the demon scar as if to memorize its lines. He smelled like soap, and under that, of a green meadow faraway and distant. I blinked fast to keep the tears from brimming over, and Ivy laid a hand on my shoulder.

The girl with the red pajamas smiled like Ceri, wise and fragile. "You're not bad inside," she said, petting my wrist. "Just hurt." She put her hand on Daryl's shoulder, and her gaze going distant, she murmured, "It will be okay. There's always a chance."

It was so close to what I was feeling, what I'd felt when I was growing up, that I leaned forward, and with Daryl between us, I gave her a hug. "Thank you," I whispered, my eyes closed as I held her to me. "I needed to remember that. You're very wise."

Daryl slid down and away, squirming to get out from between us, darting to stand nearby, looking uncomfortable, yet pleased to have been included.

"That's what my mom says," the girl said, her eyes wide and serious. "She says the angels want me back so I can teach them about love."

I closed my eyes, but it didn't do any good, and a hot tear slipped down. "I'm sorry," I said as I wiped it away. I'd just broken one of the secret rules. "I've been away too long."

"It's okay," she said. "You're allowed if there aren't any parents around."

My throat closed up, and I held her hand. It was all I could do. Jenks's wings clattered a warning, and all the kids sighed and drew back when he landed on my upraised hand.

"They know where you are," he said.

Ivy, almost forgotten, shifted the chair, rolling it back as she turned to look behind us. "We have to go," she said to the kids.

Instead of the expected complaints, they dutifully dropped away, all looking toward a distant clacking of heels. The king straightened and said, "You want us to slow them down?"

I looked up at Ivy, whose grin transformed her face. "If we get away, I'll tell you two stories next time," she said, and delight showed on every young face.

"Go," the girl in red pajamas said, pulling the king out of the way with the gentle hands of the mother she would never be.

"Let's save the witch princess!" the boy cried, and he ran down the hall. The others fell into place the best they could, some moving fast, others slow, the bright colors of childhood scarred with bald heads and gaits too slow for their enthusiasm.

"I'm going to cry," Jenks said, sniffing as he flew up to Ivy. "I'm going to freaking cry."

Ivy's face, as she watched them, showed a depth of emotion I'd never seen; then she turned away, divorcing herself from it. Lips tight together, she started into motion. I turned to face where we were going, and her brisk steps seemed to carry the desperation that there was nothing she could do to save them.

Jenks flew ahead to get the elevator, holding it by hovering at the sensor. Ivy wheeled me in and around. The doors shut, and the tragic wisdom of the children's wing was gone. I took a breath, and my throat tightened.

"I didn't think you would understand them," Ivy said softly. "They really like you."

"Understand them?" I said raggedly, my throat still holding that lump. "I am them." I hesitated, then asked, "You come here a lot?"

The elevator opened to show a smaller, friendlier lobby with a Christmas tree and solstice decorations, and beyond, a big black Hummer burning gas at the snowy curb. "About once a week," she said, pushing me forward.

Jenks was humming happily about a horse with no name. The lady at the desk was on the phone, eyeing us, but my worry vanished when she waved, telling whoever she was talking to that the lobby was empty. Just her and Dan.

Dan was a young man in an orderly's smock, and he opened

the door for us with a grin. "Hurry," he said as Jenks dived into my jacket and I zipped it up. "They're right behind you."

Ivy smiled. "Thanks, Dan. I'll bring you some ice cream."

Dan grinned. "You do that. I'll just tell them you hit me."

She laughed, and with that pleasant sound in my ears, we left the hospital.

It was bitterly cold, but the doors to the Hummer swung open, and two living vamps jumped out. "Uh, Ivy, that's not Erica," I said when they made a beeline for us. They were in black jeans and matching black T-shirts that all but screamed security, and I tensed.

"Erica's got people," Ivy said when Erica slid down and out from the backseat. Ivy's sister looked like a younger version of Ivy without all the emotional baggage: bright, happy, and active. Piscary had never looked her way due to Ivy intentionally distracting him, and the young living vamp was innocence where Ivy was jaded, loud where Ivy was reserved, and Ivy would do anything to keep it that way, even sacrificing herself.

"Oh my God!" the young woman squealed. "You're really breaking out of the hospital? Ivy called, and I was like, oh my God! Of course I'll pick you up. Then Rynn offered to drive, and it was a no-brainer. I mean, who wants to be picked up in their mom's station wagon?"

"Rynn Cormel is here?" I murmured, suddenly on edge, then started when the two burly living vamps in black jeans and matching T-shirts made a chair of their arms around me and I was airborne. The cold didn't seem to affect them, which seemed unfair. Old scars made an ugly mass on the neck of one man, but the other had only one, and it was relatively old.

"What happened to your mom's sedan?" I asked Ivy, and Erica fidgeted with the collar of her coat, her narrow-tipped boots marking the snow.

"A tree hit it," Erica said. "Totally totaled it. Not my fault. It was squirrel karma."

Squirrel karma?

"I'll tell you later," Ivy said as she leaned close. The intoxicating mix of vampire incense and male warmth was thick around me, and it was almost a disappointment when the two guys eased me into the back and let go. I didn't recognize them; they weren't Piscary's old crew.

"Are you okay?" I asked Erica as she slid in beside me with the scent of citrus.

"Oh, sure, but Mom almost died twice."

Ivy had gotten into the front seat, and looking remarkably relaxed, she leaned over the back. "The only person who almost died twice was you," she said to her sister, and Erica played with the thin strips of black leather dangling from her ears. She was still going Goth, complete with peekaboo lace at the neck and little tomatoes dangling among the skull and crossbones on her necklace. I wondered what she was doing with Rynn Cormel, as he was very much the sophisticate, but Ivy didn't seem worried, and Erica was as bright as ever.

There was a folded newspaper on the seat, but my sigh at the picture of the mall turned into a frown when I read, WITCH FLEES CIRCLE MALL, CAUSE OF RIOT? *Isn't that nice . . .*

"Are we all in?" came a rusty New York accent from my left, and I jumped, not having noticed Rynn Cormel in the corner. Holy crap, the attractively aged, former political leader was right next to me, and God, he smelled good. His power-colored tie was loosened and his hair was tousled, as if Erica had been in it. Smiling his world-famous, world-changing smile, which showed the barest hint of fang, he folded the newspaper and tucked it away. Shifting his eyes to the driver through the rearview mirror, he silently told her to go.

The door to my right slammed shut, and I was shoved closer to the undead vampire, making my pulse race. Ivy pushed to the middle in the front seat, and the other vamp got in beside her. With the thump of the closing door, alarm hit me. I was in a car with one dead vamp and five living ones. It was starting to smell *really* good in here. And if I liked what it smelled like, then they were liking what they were smelling, and ah . . . that would be me.

"Uh," I stammered when we crept into motion, and Rynn Cormel laughed with the practiced art of diplomacy.

"You are the last person who needs to fear anything from me, Ms. Morgan," he said, his eyes a safe brown in the street-lights. "I have other plans for you."

It might have sounded like a threat, but I knew what his plans were, and it didn't involve his teeth in my neck. Just the opposite, actually. "Yeah, but still," I protested when Erica shoved me over even more, thinking it was great fun by the amount of giggling and jumping she was doing. She was in black tights and a miniskirt, and not showing even a hint of being cold.

"Drive slowly," Ivy demanded. "She gets dizzy if you go too fast."

My focus became distant, and I suddenly realized there was only the barest hint of vertigo running through me, and we were going a lot faster than an elevator. "I'm fine," I said softly, and Ivy turned to look at me in surprise when we drove sedately under a streetlamp. I nodded, and she turned back around.

"Thanks, Ivy. Thank you, Jenks," I said as we slowed, then pulled onto the road.

"That's what we're here for," came Jenks's muffled response. "Now how about a little air?" and I unzipped my coat until he yelled that it was enough.

Remembering the kids, I leaned over to look up at the tall building behind us, knowing exactly where to look. Clustered at the wide plate-glass windows three stories up were five faces pressed against the glass. I waved, and one waved back. Happy, I settled into the seat of Rynn Cormel's car, promising myself I would come back and bring them my old tea set. Or maybe my stuffed animals. And ice cream.

"Thanks for picking us up, Mr. Cormel," I said, and the

vampire breathed deep. The almost inaudible sound seemed to dive to my middle and pluck a long-silent chord. Warmth flooded me, and I found myself gazing at nothing, completely relaxed, just existing in the hint of promise he was giving off. It wasn't anything like the lame groping of the young undead vampire at the mall, and Ivy's neck stiffened.

Rynn Cormel leaned over to touch her shoulder. "It was my pleasure," he said to me, but his fingers were on Ivy. "I was on my way to visit you, actually. I have some information."

Ivy's eyes were pupil black when she turned to see us. "You know who killed Kisten?"

I held my breath, but the man shook his head. "I know who didn't."

Fifteen

The atmosphere in the Hummer shifted dramatically after Erica was dropped off at work. Relieved, I watched the happy vampire wave good-bye, then flounce into the computer-security firm, the armed doorman holding the door for her and giving us a short nod. She acted like an airhead, she talked like an airhead, she dressed like a wealthy airhead, but there was a brain attached to the elaborate Goth costume and bright outlook. And unlike Ivy, Erica's outward demeanor wasn't a mask for a deeper depression.

"Good God," one of Cormel's security guys muttered as we started off again. "That girl doesn't shut up."

I normally would have come back with something about women having to make up for men's inabilities in that area, but he was right. If Erica was awake, she was flapping her lip.

Shoulders relaxing, I eased into the leather to enjoy the space Erica had left. It was warm, and the vampire phero-mones were building. It'd been a while since I'd been exposed to this much. My association with vamps had fallen drastically after Kisten died.

A faint alarm took root, and my eyes opened. I didn't want to get caught up with vampires again, as pleasant as that had been—as this was. It was a slow decline into passivity. It would kill me slowly or force me to react explosively. I knew it. Ivy knew it. Perhaps Kisten's death had been a blessing, as hard it had been. I couldn't say he was bad for me—he had strengthened me where I hadn't known I was weak, taught me a culture one had to learn by experience. His death broke my heart, my ignorance, and saved me from myself . . . and I didn't want it to be made meaningless by ignoring what he'd taught me.

Bittersweet memories swirled, and I sat up to put my bag firmly on my lap. Beside me, the elegant Rynn Cormel touched his mouth with the back of his hand. I think he was smiling. I warmed, guessing that he had seen me go on guard.

Rynn Cormel was not the stereotypical master vampire. He hadn't been dead long enough yet to pass the tricky forty-year barrier, and he didn't try to disguise the age at which he had died, maintaining an athletic forty-something appearance, his jet-black hair silvering slightly and his face having the first faint wrinkles that help men get higher-paying jobs and that women try to hide. He knew I had become suspicious, but he didn't pretend he hadn't noticed. He didn't make any cryptic statements that "it would do no good," making it part threat, part promise. He was just so damned . . . normal. Political.

I gave him the once-over, from his freshly arranged hair, down his black cashmere coat, to his shiny black shoes. The shoes were inappropriate for the weather, but it wasn't as if he was going to get cold. It was all for show.

Seeing my attention, Cormel smiled. The man was tall, well dressed, and had a good body. His laugh was pleasant and his manner comfortable, but he wasn't beautiful or otherwise remarkable, being too pale and wan to be attractive—until he smiled, and then he was breathtaking. His was the smile that had saved the world, literally holding it together as everything exploded and coalesced in a brand-new way after the Turn. It was the promise of gentle honesty, security, protection, freedom, and prosperity. Seeing it directed at me, I forced my eyes away and tucked a strand of hair behind my ear.

Ivy had stiffened, reading what was going on in the backseat by the signals I was unconsciously giving off. Hell, the entire car could. Her brow was pinched in concern when she turned to see us. "The hospital is going to have the cops looking for her until we can get the paperwork for an AMA," she said. "They don't want a lawsuit if she collapses."

From my coat, Jenks laughed, and I jumped, having forgotten he was there. "What are the chances that won't happen?" he quipped, then levered himself out to sit on my shoulder in the warmth of my scarf now that Erica was gone.

"We've made arrangements to stay with a friend, not too far from the church so Jenks can man the phones," Ivy said, her gaze flicking nervously from Cormel to me. There was a helpless fear there, not the raw fear Piscary had evoked in her when he'd looked at me, but the fear that Cormel might become interested in me. It wasn't jealousy—it was fear of abandonment. "If you head to the church, I can direct you when we get closer," she finished.

Jenks snickered. "How many times have you passed out this year, Rache?"

Miffed, I tried to see him, but he was too close. "You wanna pass out right now, Jenks?"

"I'd enjoy it if you would stay with me," Cormel said, his gloved hands folded quietly in his lap. "I have lots of room now that I've put the upper floors back into an apartment. There's only one bed up there, but one of you can sleep on the couch."

Couch? I thought dryly. He'd just as soon see Ivy and me sharing more than rent, but I couldn't find a hint of suggestion in his tone. Besides, I couldn't spend the night there. I had to get hold of my scrying mirror to call Al and get tomorrow off, and all before sunrise. This time of year put it at about eight, and I was starting to get anxious.

"The Chickering was delivered last week," Rynn Cormel said, shifting so his entire attention landed on me. "Have you heard Ivy play the piano, Rachel? She has such a sensitive

touch. She should have been encouraged to go professional."
Then he smiled. "Though she will have centuries to follow
that path if she ever desires."

"Yes," I said, remembering the few times I'd walked in on
Ivy lost at the keys. She quit every time; the piano left her
more open and raw than she wanted me to see her.

"Wonderful." Cormel leaned to touch the driver in direction. "Call ahead to get the heat turned up, if you would."

My eyes closed briefly at the misunderstanding and I shook
my head. "No, I mean I've heard her play, but we can't stay."

"Thank you anyway, Rynn," Ivy said softly, as if she'd been
waiting for me to say no first. "Jenks needs to get home to
mind the firm. No one will arrest a pixy, but it's likely there
will be trouble, and I don't want to be halfway across the Hollows when it hits our door."

Cormel arched his dark eyebrows, his pale complexion
making them appear stark in the dim light. "You'll have dinner with me at least? I don't have the chance since leaving office to entertain as often as I'm accustomed to. I find I miss it,
surprisingly." He smiled faintly, settling himself with the
sound of sliding cashmere. "It's impressive how many political understandings one can reach over a glass of good wine.
Tasha is out, and I don't think I can stand another evening listening to our security procedures and how to improve them."

The driver chuckled, but when I took a breath to gracefully
decline, Cormel inclined his head, stopping me. "I need a few
hours to get your AMA pushed through. You can be sleeping
in your own church this morning. Let me do this for you. I
need to speak to Ivy as well about what I learned."

Ivy's eyes flicked to mine, asking me to say yes. She obviously liked the man, and knowing how Piscary had treated
her, I found it hard to say no. Besides, I wanted to know who'd
killed Kisten, too. Thinking I was vacillating, Jenks whispered, "Why the hell not?"

Dinner was a small price to pay for my AMA and information about Kisten, and I nodded, anticipation replacing my

faint caution. Ivy smiled, and the driver made a slow U-bangy to head to the Hollows waterfront.

"Capital," Cormel said as he gave us all a closed-lipped but sincere smile. "Jeff, would you call ahead to make sure there's a bite to eat while dinner is being finished? And make sure we have two extra places, please, and something for Jenks."

The living vamp beside Ivy took out his cell phone and hit a single number. Jeff was the one with only a single visible scar, but I was willing to bet there were more hidden under his T-shirt. His low voice was pleasant and hardly audible over the blowing of the heater, turned high for Jenks or possibly me. Cormel and Ivy talked about nothing as my gut wound tighter, until Cormel cracked a window to get rid of the tension I was giving off. I thought my anticipation was from finding out what Cormel had learned about Kisten's death, but when we turned onto the waterfront, I realized where the adrenaline was really coming from.

The instant the wheels turned onto the less-used street, an old fear dripped through me, igniting memory. We were going to Piscary's.

I looked down to find that my hands were clenched, and I forced them apart as we slowed to a crawl. The place looked about the same, the two-story tavern peaceful under six inches of undisturbed snow. The lights were on upstairs, and some-one was closing the drapes. A section of the parking lot had been torn up and young trees now stood where rusty two-doors had once parked. The beginnings of a wall had been started to fence in a garden, perhaps, not done and so left until the spring and warmer temperatures. There was no boat at the quay.

"You okay, Rache?" Jenks asked, and I exhaled, forcing my hands to unclasp again.

"Yeah," I said softly. "I haven't been here since Kisten died."

"Me neither," he said, but he hadn't ever been here to begin with. Except when I was here getting into trouble, that is.

I flicked a glance at Ivy as we crept to the side entrance where trucks had once delivered produce from all over the world. She looked fine, but she'd been here often enough that the pain had dulled. Everyone was silent as we stopped before the closed door to the loading dock. A vamp got out to open it, and Jenks's wings brushed my neck as he snuggled in against the cold.

"Rachel," Cormel asked solicitously as the roll-up door noisily raised. "Would you prefer a restaurant? I hadn't considered that my home had bad memories for you. I've made changes," he coaxed. "It's not the same."

Ivy was looking at me like I was a wimp, and I glanced at his eyes, almost black in the dim light. "Just memories," I said.

"Good ones mixed with the bad, I hope?" he said as we drove into the cold, dry, and dark loading dock. I felt a faint tingle at my scar as the darkness took us. Affronted, I stared at him until the tingle vanished. Was he making a play for me? If he bound me, I'd do anything he wanted, thinking it was my idea. And when the vampire pulled the roll-up door shut to make the darkness absolute but for the headlamps, I realized how vulnerable I was. *Shit.*

"Let's get inside, and you can see what I've done with the place," Cormel said pleasantly, and as my pulse quickened, the doors to the Hummer started opening.

I slid across the long seat to the door with my bag in my hand, and as everyone milled around to make their slow way up the cement steps to the back door, I pretended to adjust my coat before I got out. This might be the last time I could have a private word with Jenks until we got home. "What's my aura look like, Jenks?" I asked, and got a pixy-size sigh in return.

"It's thin, but no holes. I think the emotion the kids stirred up in you helped boost it."

"It comes from emotion?" I murmured, deciding at the last moment to leave my bag in the Hummer as I took the hand of the vamp holding the door and made the careful slide to the cement pad.

"Where did you think it came from?" he said, laughing, from my scarf. "Fairy farts?"

I sighed, shaking my head at Ivy's inquiring look. I didn't like being out with my aura so thin, but he said it was better, and I trusted that no one was going to bite me. I was clearly ill, and that was a turnoff in the vamp world, instilling an almost overboard, lavishing sense of caring in the undead and still living alike. Maybe that was what I was seeing.

One by one, the security vamps jostled for position until they were both ahead and behind us. I obediently headed for the stairway, seeing the tires of Ivy's cycle peeking out from under a tarp. She'd parked it here for the winter after I'd nearly hit it trying to get into our carport. The snowplows had blocked me out, and I had to gun it to get through the chunky, man-made drift.

My pulse raced from the exertion, and I followed Cormel into the kitchen. At least, I was telling myself, it was from the exertion and not anticipation. I wasn't looking forward to see-ing Kisten everywhere.

The warmth of the kitchen surprised me, and I looked up from the white tiles as we entered. Most of the ovens had been taken out and a great deal of the counter space. A large, com-fortable table now took up the corner beside the stairway that led to the underground apartments. The new amber light hang-ing over it and the cotton throw rug beneath it made the spot a pleasant place to relax and eat among company, warm from the heat of the ovens and the possibility of conversation.

I breathed deep to find that it didn't smell like a restaurant anymore with its many spices and the lingering scents of unfa-miliar vampires. There was just Rynn Cormel's increasingly familiar scent and the lingering aroma of half a dozen or so living vamps, Ivy's among them.

I realized my boots were the only ones making any noise, and I nervously adjusted my collar until Jenks took to the air.

"We could eat here, but I think we will be more comfortable at the fireplace," Cormel said, watching the pixy with a polite but wary expression. "Jeff, find out why Mai hasn't started the appetizers, would you please?"

My concern eased when Ivy took off her coat, and leaving it at the table, strode directly through the old double doors. Jenks went with her and, curious, I followed. All my hesitancy vanished at the sight of the large room that had once entertained Cincy's finest partiers with gourmet pizza and mixed drinks.

The shiny bar remained, taking up one wall, the low ceiling making the dark oak look even darker. All the illuminating lights over the bar were off, and the lit fireplace pulled the eye. The little high tables had been replaced with comfortable furniture, coffee tables, and the occasional sideboard for appetizers, flower arrangements, or possible discarded wineglasses.

Cormel tossed his coat to a chair, reminding me of my dad coming home and settling in. He all but collapsed into one of the self-indulgent chairs by the fire and gestured for us to join him. His pale skin and dark, silvering hair gave him the look of a comfortable businessman home from work. *Yeah, right.*

I took off my scarf and unzipped my coat, but the winter's chill still hung in me and I kept it on. My eyes went everywhere as I followed Ivy to the hearth. To the right of the fireplace, one of the doors to what had once been a private dining room was open, and I could see a throw rug and part of a bed where a huge table once sat. One of the security vampires casually shut the door as he went by, and I guessed it was a guest room now. The floor was scratched in the old high-traffic areas and the light fixtures were still a table length apart, but it looked like a living room—a very large, low-ceilinged living room done up to look like a piece of up north with its round wooden timbers and dark paneling.

Cormel had chosen a chair, and Ivy had taken the couch before the fire. Thinking they were going to make judgments on where I sat, I carefully lowered myself onto the couch with Ivy between us, not too near her but not looking as if I was scrunched in the corner either.

The undead vampire smiled with half his mouth. Leaning forward, he rubbed his hands together and held them to the fire as if he was cold. Damn, he was good.

I felt silly in my coat, so I took it off to find it pleasantly warm. Rynn had beckoned one of his staff closer, and Ivy was giving the man my personal information so he could file for the AMA. I was just starting to get warm enough to pay attention when Jenks flew down the staircase, a content trail of gold dust spilling from him.

"You should be fine from AMA police for a while," he said as he unwound his winter wear to show the skintight black outfit he had on underneath. "He's got five vamps on security: the three who came with us plus two who were here. It wouldn't surprise me if the woman in the kitchen is security, too, by the way she's throwing the knives around."

"Thanks, Jenks," I said, knowing he was telling me this not because I was worried about the FIB or the I.S., but to tell our host we were not dumb about being here.

"Cormel has great security," he continued as more blue fabric joined the pile on the arm of the couch. "Professional. All new stuff, and don't mistake the smiles you're seeing for leniency in a stress situation."

"Gotcha," I said, then looked up when Cormel's aide nodded and left.

"I adore red tape," Cormel said, settling back with a pleased expression, "tied in a Gordian knot." I stared at him, and he added, "Any knot can be cut with a big enough sword. You'll have what you need in ten minutes."

Jenks rose an inch, then dropped when the guy with the savaged neck who had driven us here came in with an open bottle of white wine. I took my glass, vowing not to drink it, but when Cormel stood, gazing at the wine's hue, I knew he was going to make a toast.

"To immortality," he said, sounding almost forlorn. "For some, a burden; for others, a joy. Here's to long lives and long loves."

We went to drink, and Jenks muttered, "And longer lady-killers."

I choked, and Jenks rose up on a glittering column of laughter.

Ivy had heard him, and she leaned back with a sour look on her face, but Cormel had stood, and I jumped when one of his hands touched my shoulder and the other took my glass as I hacked and coughed. "Would you like a milder wine?" he said solicitously as he set it down. "Forgive me. You're still recovering. Jeff, bring out a sweeter white," he said, and I waved my protest.

"'S okay," I managed. "Went down the wrong pipe is all."

Ivy uncrossed her knees and took another sip. "Do you need to wait in the car, Jenks?"

The pixy grinned. I could see it through my watering eyes. I was probably as red as the throw pillow I wanted to smack him with. Tracking his motion to the warm mantel and out of my reach, I took another sip to clear my throat. The wine was superb, and my vow to avoid it was tempered by the knowledge that I'd probably never be able to afford a bottle like this. Ah, one glass sipped slowly wouldn't hurt. . . .

Ivy unfolded herself and went to arrange the fire, leaving me and Rynn Cormel with a wide space between us. "Are you sure you won't stay the morning?" he said across the empty couch. "I've plenty of everything but company."

"Dinner, Rynn," Ivy said. Her shape was a sharp silhouette against the fire, and when her hand came down very close to Jenks, he took to the air muttering curses. "You said you know who killed Kisten. Is he someone who will be missed?" she said.

What she was asking was if she could claim a life in return, and I stifled a shiver at the depth of her pain.

A sigh slipped from Cormel, though he didn't need to breathe but to speak. "It's not that I know who killed him, but I do know who didn't." Ivy went to protest, and the man put up a hand for her to wait. "There was no one Piscary owed a favor to," Cormel said. "He hadn't had contact with any vampire out of the city, so it was a Cincy native, and likely still here."

Seeing his fatherly concern, something in me snapped. "There's you," I said bluntly, and Ivy stiffened. "Maybe you did it."

Jenks's wings clattered a nervous warning, but the undead vampire smiled with only the barest hint of an eye twitch giving away his annoyance. "I understand you're starting to remember certain things," he said flatly, and my bravado vanished. "Do I smell familiar to you? You wouldn't forget me if I'd pinned you to the wall." His eyes tightened. "I know it."

I started to breathe again when he turned to Ivy, the shell of his humanity back in place. "You've been to the boat, Ivy," he said in a soft voice. "Was I ever there?"

Ivy was tense, but she shook her head.

I would've pointed out that he could have had someone else do it, but that wasn't how vampires worked. If Kisten had been a gift to Cormel, Cormel would have taken him without a second thought and would admit it freely. I was dining with a freaking animal, and I bowed my head with a false contriteness and muttered, "Sorry. I had to ask."

"Of course you did. No insult taken."

I felt sick. We were all pretending. Well, at least Cormel and I were. Ivy might still be living the lie. I smiled at him, and Cormel smiled back, the picture of grace and understanding as he leaned to top off my wine, and I leaned forward to accept it.

"Besides myself," he said as he retreated and Ivy relaxed, "there have been no new major political powers entering the city, and none looking for upward mobility other than what one would expect when a master vampire dies his final death. No one has more power than he or she should, which wouldn't be the case if Piscary showed favor to someone." He took a sip, considering the flavor or his next words. "Many owed Piscary, but he owed no one."

Her back to the fire, Ivy was silent. We'd learned nothing,

and I was starting to wonder if Kisten's death was another one of Ivy's *freaking life lessons*. Seeing her fidgeting in motions so subtle only Jenks or I would recognize, I hoped not. If it was, I might just dig the bastard Piscary back up and stake him again for the hell of it. Make a necklace out of his teeth and bathtub duckies out of his dried-up balls . . .

"I've met him," Ivy said, looking for a shred of hope to follow. "I just can't place him."

"Do you have a name?" Cormel asked.

I could hear faint activity in the kitchen, and Jenks flew to investigate.

"No. The scent is too old, and it's not quite the same. It's like he was alive when I knew him, and now he's dead, or maybe a large shift of status changed his diet and therefore his scent." Her head came up, showing that her eyes were red. "Maybe he tried to disguise his smell so I couldn't recognize it."

Cormel waved a hand in dismissal, his expression irate. "Then you really have nothing," he said, holding out his hand to lure her into sitting back down. "I'm sure the answer is here, but I have exhausted my leads. I'm not asking the right person. You could, though."

Ivy exhaled to try to find her composure. "And who is the right person?" she asked as she took his grip and sat.

"Skimmer," Cormel said, and my head came up sharply. "She knows all Piscary's political secrets. Lawyers . . ." The vampire sighed expressively.

"Skimmer is in jail," Jenks said as he darted back to the fire. "She won't see Ivy."

Ivy lowered her head, her brow pinched. Skimmer's refusal was tearing her up.

"She might see you if Rachel goes with you," Rynn Cormel suggested, and the hope of a possibility smoothed Ivy's expression. My mouth, though, went dry.

"You think it will make a difference?" I asked.

He shrugged as he sipped his wine. "She doesn't want Ivy to

see her in her failure. But I expect she has a few words to say to you."

Jenks's breath hissed in, but Rynn was right. Ivy's face held the hope that Skimmer would talk to her, and I set my dislike for the petite, dangerous vampire aside. For Ivy. I would talk to her for Ivy. *And to find out who killed Kisten.* "It's worth trying," I said, thinking that going in there with a thin aura wasn't the best idea in the world.

Cormel shifted his feet uneasily. It was subtle, and he probably didn't even know he had done it, but I saw it, and so did Jenks. "Good," he said, as if everything had been decided. "I do believe there is some sushi headed our way."

His words were clearly a signal, since the doors to the kitchen promptly swung open and Jeff and another vamp, in an apron, came out with trays. Jenks's wings were a shimmer of motion though he hadn't moved from the arm of the couch. "I didn't know you liked sushi," I said.

"I don't, but there's honey in one of the dipping sauces."

"Jenks," I warned as Cormel and Ivy made a spot on the coffee table before the fire.

"Wha-a-a-at," he complained, his wings slowing until I could almost see the red bit of tape. "I wasn't going to eat any. I was going to take it home for Matalina. It helps her sleep better." And seeing the flicker of concern in his eyes, I believed him.

The trays looked fabulous, and glad now I'd said yes to dinner, I took up my chopsticks, pleased I didn't have to break them apart to use them. They looked expensive. All we had at home were the ones we saved from takeout.

I watched Ivy handle her sticks with the fluency of a native language, the extensions of her fingers taking three different sashimi and several rolls with cream cheese and what looked like tuna. Remembering our first disastrous dinner as roommates, I kept my eyes down and put a few bites on my plate followed by lots of ginger. Jenks hovered over an amber sauce, and I put some on my plate, making sure he knew it was for him by pointing at him with the sticks—though how he was going to get it home was beyond me.

Cormel was still fussing with the sauces by the time Ivy and I had retreated with full plates. "I'm so pleased you stayed," he said as he moved with that eerie vampire speed and put all of three bites on his plate. "Sushi alone is not the same. You never get the variety."

Ivy was smiling, but the display of vampiric speed had me on edge. I didn't need the reminder that he was stronger than me. And he didn't need to eat. Why he was sort of bothered me.

"I love sushi," I said, not wanting him to guess he had unnerved me. "Since I was a kid."

"Really." Cormel put a bite into his mouth and chewed. "I'm surprised."

"I was eight," I said, taking a slice of ginger and enjoying the sweet zing. "I thought I was dying. Well, I was, but I didn't know I was going to get better. My brother went on this big push for me to do everything. Made it his goal one summer."

My fumbling for a roll slowed as I thought about the girl in the hospital and the look in her eyes. I should go back and tell her the chance was real. If I survived, then she had a chance. I didn't even know her name.

"You still are, you know," Cormel said, startling me.

"Dying?" I blurted, and he laughed. Ivy smiled thinly, not appreciating the joke.

"I suppose," he said, eyes on his second roll. "I'm the only one here not performing that particular trick anymore, but what I meant was, you're still pushing to try new things."

My eyes flicked to Ivy. "No, I'm not."

Ivy shifted uncomfortably between us. Determined to not back down, I took one of the more mundane crunchy pieces of fried shrimp and ate it with a great deal of noise.

Cormel smiled and set his plate aside, having eaten only one roll. "You're in a tight spot, Rachel, and I'm curious as to what your plan is for getting out."

Jenks clattered his wings in warning, and the tension went up. "I'll get the AMA whether you help me or not—" I started, and he cut me off.

"I promised you your form, and you will have it," he said, sounding insulted. "That's short-term survival, and I'm talking progress. Moving forward. Establishing yourself in a safe, long-term situation." He took his glass and sipped from it. "You have been *seen* consorting with demons. You were refused traditional treatment on the witch floors because of your demon scars. What do you think that means?"

"It means they're idiots." My chin rose, and I set the plate of sushi down. "Human medicine worked fine."

"Humans don't like demons any more than anyone else," he said. "Less. If you continue dealing with them openly, you will be silenced. Probably by witches."

I laughed at that. "Whoa, whoa, whoa," I said, waving my sticks about. "I don't know where you're getting your info, but witches don't do that to each other. They never have."

"And you know that how?" he asked. "Even so, you're acting out of character, and that will force them to do the same."

I made a scoffing sound, and returned to eating. *Why do they make these rolls so darn big? I look like a freaking squirrel.*

"Be cautious, Rachel," Cormel said, and I ignored him, continuing to try to chew a wad of rice and seaweed too big for my mouth. "Humans are vicious when cornered. That's why they survive and we don't. They came first, and they will probably persist long after we're gone. Rats, cockroaches, and humans."

Ivy rolled her eyes and ate a glob of the green stuff. Seeing her disbelief, Cormel smiled. "Ivy disagrees," he said, "but I've had to speak favorably for you more than once."

My motion to dip my last cucumber roll hesitated. "I never asked you to do that."

"It wasn't your place to give me permission," he said. "I'm not telling you this so you feel you owe me a debt, but to let you know your situation. If the witches don't react to you openly trafficking with demons, then the vampires will be pressed into it for another reason."

I set my sticks down, feeling sick. I had no choice but to traffic with demons, having bought Trent's freedom from them with a promise to be Al's student. "If you're not upset about the demons, then what's bothering you?" I asked, feeling trapped and angry.

"What you're doing to help the elves, of course."

Ivy exhaled, and I suddenly got it. "Oh." I took a steadying breath and pushed my plate away. I wasn't hungry anymore. Piscary had killed my dad and Trent's father for simply *trying* to help the elves. I had gone past trying and had actually saved them. Well, I'd gotten the sample that Trent used to do it.

"There have been three elf conceptions in the last three months," Cormel said, and my thoughts flew to Ceri. "All healthy from what I understand. Their population is going to slowly rise. The Weres, too, are poised to explode under the right circumstances. You can understand why the vampires are slightly concerned."

"David doesn't want a pack," I said, my jaw starting to clench.

Cormel crossed his knees and a grimace colored his expression. "Humans breed like flaming rabbits from hell, but we've been dealing with that for centuries. You, however, are responsible for the elves and Weres. Population wise," he amended before I could protest. "From what I understand, the elves would just as soon see you dead for some reason I haven't fathomed yet, which leaves the Weres to back you, and if they do, it will be with the power of the focus." He paused. "Which will increase their numbers," he finished.

I slumped back into the couch and sighed. *No good deed and all . . .*

Rynn Cormel mimicked my position, doing so with slow grace instead of dejected suddenness. "What can you do for us, Rachel?" he said, glancing at a very quiet Ivy. "We need something so that we may think more kindly of you."

I knew what he was asking. He wanted me to find a way for vampires to keep their souls after death, and he thought I'd do it to save Ivy. "I'm working on it," I muttered, arms crossed over my chest and staring at the fire.

"I don't see any progress."

My brow furrowed, and I gave him a look. "Ivy—"

"Ivy likes things the way they are," he interrupted, as if she wasn't sitting between us. "You need to be more aggressive."

"Hey!" I exclaimed. "That is none of your business."

Jenks took flight, hovering a careful three feet from him. "You need to keep your stick in your own flowers," he said, hands on his hips.

"Rynn," Ivy pleaded. "Please."

But the man proved who he was—what he was—when his eyes flashed black and his aura slammed into me. "Tell me you don't like this . . . ," he whispered.

I gasped, shoving away from him when his eyes touched my demon scar. I was against the back and arm of the couch, and I could go no farther. My exhalation turned into a moan as feeling shivered over my skin, delving deep where my clothes touched me. I couldn't think—there had never been anything so shockingly intimate—and my blood pounded, telling me to submit, to give in, to take what he offered and revel in it.

"Stop!" Jenks shrilled. "Stop now, or I'll jam this stick so far up your nose, you'll be able to do calculus with it!"

"Please," I panted, my knees at my chin as I nearly writhed on the couch, the leather feeling like skin against me. The sensation had come from nowhere . . . and God, it felt so good. How could I ignore this? He had flung it in my face, showing me what Ivy and I had shunned.

"Rynn, please," Ivy whispered, and the sensation cut off with the suddenness of a slap.

My gasp was harsh, and I felt the dampness of tears. I realized my face was against the couch, and I was curled up, hiding from the passion, from the ecstasy. Panting, I slowly unkinked my arms and legs. I couldn't focus well, but I found him easily enough, sitting comfortably on his chair. Jenks hovered between us with a chopstick. God, the vampire looked as unruffled as stone, and about as compassionate. He wore a superb mask, but he was an animal.

"If you touch my scar again . . . ," I threatened, but what could I do? He protected Ivy, protected me. Slowly my pulse eased, but the shaking of my legs didn't. He knew my threats were nothing, and he ignored me.

I followed his gaze to Ivy, and I felt the blood drain from my face.

"Ivy," I whispered in heartache. Her eyes were black and desperate. She was fighting every instinct she had. Her master had gone for me in front of her, then had drawn back, practically saying, "You finish." We struggled with this, and for him to callously break everything we had worked for pissed me off. "You have no right," I said, my voice shaking.

"I like you, Rachel," he said, surprising me. "I have since I first heard Ivy's impassioned description of you and then found it accurate. You're inventive, intelligent, and dangerous. I can't keep you alive if you continue to ignore the fact that your actions reach farther than next week."

"Don't do this to me and Ivy again," I seethed. "Do you hear me?"

"Why?" he said, and his confusion was too real to be faked. "I did nothing you didn't enjoy. Ivy's good for you. You're good for Ivy. I don't understand why both of you are ignoring this . . . perfect match."

I couldn't edge away from Ivy. She was balanced. Ignoring her was the only armor I could give her. "Ivy knows there can't be blood shared without dominance given. I won't, and she can't."

He seemed to think about that. "Then one of you needs to learn to bend." As if that was all there was to it. "To become second."

I thought of his scion, sent away because it was easier to do this without her here. "Neither of us will," I said. "That's why we can live together. Leave. Ivy. Alone."

A small noise came from him. "I was talking about Ivy bending, not you."

I shook my head, disgusted. "That's what I love about her," I said. "If she bends, I walk away. If I bend, she gets nothing but a shell."

His brow furrowed and the fire snapped as he thought. "Are you sure?" he asked, and I nodded, not sure if it would save or damn us. "Then maybe this won't work," he said distantly.

Jenks, silent until now, dropped the chopstick. "It will!" he protested as it clattered. "I mean, Rachel has found out so much already. She's working with a wise demon. She'll find a way for Ivy to keep her soul!"

"Jenks, don't," I said, but Cormel was thinking, even as I could see his unease that the wisdom to further his species would come from demons.

"Al might know a way for souls to be retained after death," Jenks pleaded, his angular features scrunched up in fear for me.

"Shut up!" I shouted.

Ivy was breathing easier, and I risked a look at her. Her hands were unfisted, but she was still looking at the floor and breathing shallowly.

"Ask your demon," Cormel said as Jeff cautiously came in with a fax. The man glanced at Ivy in alarm, then handed it to Cormel. Without even looking at it, the undead vampire coolly handed it past Ivy to me. "Your AMA."

I shoved it in my pocket. "Thank you."

"What good timing," Cormel said lightly, but I could see everything now. All the pretty talk and clever smiles wouldn't snare me again. "Now we can eat with relaxed stomachs."

Yeah. Right.

I turned to Ivy, and she met my eyes with a growing band of brown around her pupils, I stood. "Thank you, Rynn, but we're leaving."

Jenks dropped to the arm of the chair and hurriedly wound fabric around himself, his wings drooping and rising as he worked.

"Ivy . . . ," Rynn Cormel said, as if confused, and she backed away from him, closer to me.

"I'm happy," she said softly as she handed me my coat. "Please leave me alone."

We started for the kitchen, Jenks flying heavily behind us as a vanguard, trailing the last of his wrap along instead of sparkles. "There's more here to think about than two people's happiness," Cormel said loudly, and Ivy stopped, her hand on the swinging doors.

"Rachel won't be pushed," she said.

"Then pull her, before someone else does."

As one, we turned and left. Behind us was the sharp clatter of chopsticks and little ceramic dishes hitting the stone fireplace. The kitchen was empty, and I imagined everyone had gone somewhere else and out of Cormel's angry path. Jenks dove for my scarf as I wrapped it about my neck, and I sighed as I recalled how erotic a covered neck was to a vampire. God, I was stupid.

Ivy hesitated at the door to the loading dock. "I'll be right back," she said, a dangerous slant to her eyes.

"Are you sure?" I asked, and she strode away. Uncomfortable, I hustled into the cold garage. We weren't going to get home in the Hummer, so I got my bag out from the backseat, and with a grunt, shoved the door up, panting as the silent night met me. We'd be taking Ivy's bike, and it was going to be a very slow, very cold ride.

But I had to get home. We had to. We both needed to get back to the church and the patterns of behavior that kept us apart and together—sane. I had to call Al before the sun came up and beg for the time off. And now I had to ask him if he knew of a way to save a vampire's soul, because if I didn't, I might find myself dead.

The sound of Ivy's boots brought my attention up, and she

strode down the stairs with her arms crossed. "You okay?" I asked as I pulled the tarp from Ivy's bike, and she nodded.

From my scarf came Jenks's snotty "I'm okay, you're okay, Ivy's freaking okay. We're all okay. Can we get the hell out of here?"

Ivy stashed my bag, got on the bike, and turned to look at me, waiting.

"Are you going to pull me?" I asked, heart pounding as I stood on the hard cement with my feet going cold in my boots.

Her eyes were like liquid brown in the dim light, and I could see her misery. "No."

I had to trust her. Swinging my leg over, I got on the bike behind her and held on tight as Ivy idled the bike out of the sheltered warmth and into the cold snow of the last of the year.

Sixteen

The kitchen was warm, smelling of brown sugar, chocolate chips, and butter. I was making cookies with the excuse that they would soften Al up, but the reality was, I wanted Jenks to have the chance to get excessively warm. The ride home had been bitterly cold, and though he'd never admit it, Jenks was almost blue by the time Ivy parked her cycle in the garden shed and I hustled into the church with him. His kids had long since tired of playing in the oven's updrafts, but he was still in here, his wings slowly moving back and forth.

As expected, a stone-faced I.S. agent had been waiting for us when we cycled in, silently taking his copy of the AMA and driving off. If not for that stupid piece of paper, I'd be back in the hospital under guard, but as it was, I was pulling the last tray of cookies out and feeling better. Tired, but better. *Take that, Dr. Mape.*

It was almost four in the morning, just about the time I usually crawled into bed. Ivy was at her computer, each key getting a harder tap than the one before it as she not so patiently waited for me to call Al and ask for the night off, but talking to demons was tricky. I wanted Jenks warm and mobile before I did it. And a little comfort food never did anyone any harm.

"It's getting late," Ivy muttered, the rim of brown around her pupils narrowing as she tracked something on her monitor. "You going to do this anytime soon?"

"I've got hours," I said as I slid the last cookie onto the cooling rack. Propping the tray in the sink to sizzle, I leaned to look at the clock above me. "Relax."

"You've got four hours, sixteen minutes." Her eyes flicked to me, and she arranged her colored pens in the mug she used for a pencil cup. "I just pulled up the almanac."

Putting five cookies on a plate, I set them next to her keyboard and took the topmost for myself. "I wanted to make cookies. Everyone likes cookies," I said, and she smirked, delicately taking a cookie with her long, slim fingers.

Jenks rose up from the oven, warm at last. "Oh yeah. Cookies ought to do it." He laughed, and a slip of dust fell from him. "Al had a fit the last time you asked for a night off. He said no, too."

"That's why the cookies. Duh. I wasn't recovering from a banshee attack either. Tonight will be different." *I hope.*

Hands on his hips, Jenks got an unusually bitter look on his face as he landed by my scrying mirror on the center island counter. "Maybe you should offer him a bite out of something else? Bet he'd give you the freaking year off."

"Jenks!" Ivy snapped, and the pixy turned his back on us to look out the dark window.

"What's the matter, Jenks?" I said tightly. "You don't want me talking to the *wise demon*? Didn't I hear you tell Rynn Cormel he was a *wise demon*?" Okay, maybe that had been a little nasty, but he had been picking on me all night, and I wanted to know why.

He stayed where he was, his wings moving fitfully, and tired of it, I sat in my spot at the table and leaned toward Ivy. "What's with him?" I said, loud enough for him to hear. Ivy shrugged, and I wiped the cookie crumbs from my fingers. Rex was staring at me from the threshold, and on the off chance, I dropped my hand in invitation.

"Oh my God!" I whispered when the cat stood and, her tail crooked happily, came to me. "Look!" I said as the orange beast bumped her head under my palm as if we were great friends. Ivy leaned over to see, and feeling brave, I sent my hand under the cat's middle. Not breathing, I lifted, and without even a squirm, the cat was on my lap.

"Oh my God!" I whispered again. She was purring. The freaking feline was purring.

"It's the bloody apocalypse," Jenks muttered, and I fondled the young cat's ears. My wonder turned to contentment when Rex settled in with her paws tucked under herself. Ivy shook her head and went back to work. No way was I ruining *this* with calling Al. Al could wait. I was guessing that Pierce was in the kitchen, and he was happy.

Rex still on my lap, I ate another cookie as thoughts of Pierce sifted through me. It had been eight years, and though I'd changed—moved out, gone to school, been hired, fired, run for my life, saved a life, put my boyfriend to rest *and* learned to live again—he probably hadn't changed at all. The last time I'd seen him, he had been an attractive mix of power and helplessness, not any older than I was now.

I felt a smile grow as I recalled him busting the doors to the I.S. building with a flung spell, knocking out their security, and then sealing them inside with a ward. All with an odd awkwardness that hit my little-boy-lost button. He'd taken down an undead vampire with power he had drawn through me so subtly that I hadn't felt it, even when I'd known he was doing it.

Rex purred, and I kept my fingers moving to keep her with me. I was not stupid. I knew that Pierce, even as a ghost, had a mix of power and vulnerability that was a veritable Rachel magnet. And I wasn't so blind that I wouldn't admit I felt a twinge of attraction. But an unexpected sense of peace outweighed that. I wasn't going to run willy-nilly into a relationship, even if one was possible. Kisten had taught me the dangers of letting my heart rule me. Call it gun shy, call it growing up, but I was happy as I was. I was in no hurry. And that felt good.

Ivy looked up at me, her typing stilling as she recognized

that something had shifted in the air. Face placid, she glanced at Jenks. The pixy's wings went red in agitation, and he flew to land on the cookie plate and demand my attention. "Marshal called," he said, as if it was the most important thing in the world. "You were in the can. He says he's bringing doughnuts over tomorrow for breakfast if you get out of your thing with Big Al."

"Okay," I said as I scratched Rex's jawline, remembering that Pierce hadn't been my first kiss. He'd been my first done-right kiss, though, and I smiled.

"Trent's coming with him," Jenks said, hands on his hips, "and Jonathan."

"That's nice." I stroked Rex, then brought her to my nose so I could smell her sweet kitty fur. "Such a good kitty," I crooned. "Such a *clever* kitty to know there is a ghost in the church."

Jenks set his wings to blurring, not moving an inch. "See?" he said to Ivy, appalled. "She likes him. Rachel, he's been spying on us! Start thinking with your head, huh?"

A flicker of annoyance went through me, but it was Ivy who said, "Jenks, get off it," in an almost bored tone. "He's not spying on us."

"But she likes him!" Jenks yelped, wings so fast that the bit of red tape finally flew off.

Ivy sighed, looking up first at Jenks, then at me. "This is Rachel we're talking about," she said with a smile. "I'd give it three months, tops."

"Yeah, but she can't kill this one," Jenks grumped.

That was in extremely bad taste, but I ignored him, just delighted to have the cat finally like me. "Don't you listen to them, Rexy," I cooed, and the cat sniffed my nose. "Rachel is a smart girl. She's not going to go out with a ghost no matter how sexy he is. She knows better. Jenkskie wenskie can just get bent." I beamed at Jenks, and he made an ugly face.

"Rache, put my cat down before you mess with her kitty brain."

Smiling, I let Rex puddle out of my arms and onto the floor.

She rubbed against me, then sedately walked out. There was a cheering from the pixies up in the sanctuary, and her shadow slunk past the door to hide under the couch in the back living room.

The more agitated Jenks got, the more content I became. Smiling, I washed my hands and dropped a dozen cookies in a bag for Al, tying it with a little blue twist tie before setting them beside the scrying mirror. Seeing me getting ready, Ivy shut down her computer. "I'll get our coats," she said, and Jenks clattered his wings, angry he was going to be left behind.

"I'm doing this by myself," I said suddenly. "Thanks, though."

"Your aura is thin. Put us in a circle and do it here," Ivy said as she stood.

Putting them in a circle really didn't make them any safer. All Al had to do was shove me into it and it would fall. Same thing with standing in a circle with him. And putting Al in a circle alone wasn't going to happen—not since he'd started treating me like a person after I told him I wouldn't circle him anymore. Second-class person, but a person nevertheless.

"Why chance it?" I said, thinking of Jenks's kids. The demon might turn them into popcorn for all I knew. "You can watch from the windows." *Coat . . . in the foyer.* "It's not a big deal!" I shouted over my shoulder as I headed for the front door. My boots were there, too. It was four in the freaking morning, the coldest part of the day, and I was going to go sit in a graveyard and talk to Al. *Ah-h-h, I love my life.*

Ivy caught up with me as I shrugged into my coat. Grabbing my boots, I took a step, jerking back when I almost ran into her. "I'm coming with you," she said, eyes going dark.

I listened for Jenks's wings, and hearing nothing, I whispered, "Don't you dare make Jenks sit in here alone." She clenched her jaw, the brown rim of her eyes shrinking even more. I brushed past her and headed to the kitchen. "I'm just asking for a night off. It's not a big deal!"

"Then why don't you do it in here?" she yelled back, and I stopped at the head of the hall.

Ivy was standing by her piano. The soft glow lights on my desk made a spot of living green with pixies peeking from every nook. "Because I lost it the last time I thought you two were dead, and I'm not going to risk you if I don't have to." Ivy took a deep breath, and I turned away. "I'll be right back," I added as I paced into the kitchen.

Jenks was still atop Ivy's monitor, his wings a blur and his increased circulation making them a bright red. "Jenks, don't look at me like that," I muttered when I dropped my boots to put them on, and as my heels thumped into them, he turned his back on me. "Jenks . . . ," I pleaded, stopping when his wings buzzed. "I'll be okay," I said, and he shifted his head at the harsh sound of my zipper going up.

"This is fairy crap!" he exclaimed, rising up and spinning around. "Green fairy crap—"

"With sprinkles on top," I finished for him as I fumbled for my gloves, jammed in the pockets. "We go through this every week. Either I show up at sunrise or he comes and gets me. Hiding on hallowed ground will only tick him off and then he visits my mom. If I'm lucky, I get the night off. If I'm not, I'll send Bis back in for my things. Okay?"

Jenks hovered before me with his hands on his hips. Ignoring him, I picked up the scrying mirror and my cookies. I knew he hated being trapped by the cold, but I wasn't going to risk his family. He was so good at everything else, why this bothered him was beyond me.

"Bis will be with me," I offered, and when he crossed his arms and turned his back on me, I shouted, "I'll be freaking fine!" and stormed to the back door. *What is his problem!*

I flicked on the porch light, giving the door a tight pull to get it to latch behind me. Hesitating on the landing, I took a moment to calm myself, taking in how quiet it was out here while I put on my gloves. The moon was riding high above the horizon with an edge so sharp it looked like it could cut paper.

My breath steamed, and by the second lungful, I felt the cold all the way to my bones. Even Cincinnati, across the river and distant, seemed frozen. If death had a feeling, this was it.

Still peeved, I crunched down the salted back steps and into the garden, following the same path I'd taken out here last week. There was a good chance that Al wouldn't go for this and I'd find myself sending Bis back in for my overnight bag, giving Al a laugh and me ten additional charms to spell before sunrise tomorrow.

I looked behind me to see the kitchen window plastered with pixies, but Jenks wasn't among them. Guilt slithered out from me for having gone where he couldn't follow, but it wasn't like I was going into a dangerous situation. It was like asking your recruiter if you could skip the run today and rest up. I might get smacked for it, but I wasn't going to die.

"This is so not going to work," I muttered, then stepped over the low wall that separated the witch's garden from the grave-yard. The cold seemed to turn to knives in my chest, and I slowed before I froze my nose from breathing too fast. Fatigue was nothing new, and I had all the tricks to stave it off. I could feel the ley line shimmering in my thoughts, but I angled to Pierce's statue instead. I didn't need to be in a line to talk to Al, and the patch of unsanctified ground surrounded by God's grace would keep Al from wandering if he decided to come over.

Pierce's monolith of a kneeling, battle-weary angel was creepy, looking not quite human with its arms too long and its features starting to run from pollution and the poor grade of stone. I'd used this red-colored patch of cement to summon demons three times now, and that I was treating this as almost routine was worrisome.

"Hey, Bis?" I called, then jumped when Bis landed sud-denly on the angel's shoulder in a wash of air that smelled like rock dust.

"Holy crap!" I yelped, looking back at the church to see if anyone had noticed my surprise. "How about some warning, dude?"

"Sorry," the late-adolescent, foot-high gargoyle said, his red eyes whirling so fast in amusement that I knew he wasn't sorry at all. His pebbly skin was black to absorb what heat he could from the night, but he could change it, even when he fell into a torporlike state as the sun came up. He'd have more control over his sleep when he got older, but right now, like most teenagers, he was like a rock when the sun came up. He paid rent to Jenks by watching the grounds for the four hours around midnight when pixies traditionally slept. He'd been doing more than that since the temperatures dropped below pixy tolerance. He and Jenks got along great, seeing as Bis had been kicked off the basilica for spitting on people, and Jenks thought that was just fine.

"Why is Jenks mad at you?" he asked as he pulled his wings close, and I winced.

"Because he thinks he has to protect me, and I'm going places he can't," I said. "You can hear us from out here?"

The gargoyle shrugged and looked at the church. "Only when you yell."

Only when we yell. Brushing the snow off the base of the angel statue, I set the cookies down and brought out the mirror.

"Oh, that's ultimate!" Bis said as the wine-and-crystal-colored scrying mirror threw back the moonlight. I looked down at it, feeling the cold right through my gloves. I agreed with him, even though I thought something that called demons should be ugly. This was my second mirror, made with a stick of yew, some salt, wine, a bit of magic, and a lot of help from Ceri. The first one I'd broken over Minias's head when the demon had startled me. Ceri had helped me make that one, too. It was a contact glyph, not a summoning spell, and the double-circled pentagram with its symbols could open a path to the ever-after and any demon I wished to talk to. I didn't need to know their summoning name, just their common one. That, and the word that tapped into the demon's communal magic. Some days I really wished I didn't know the magic word.

Nervous, I hunched down to sit on the edge of the monolith, beside the cookies, and balanced the mirror on my knees. I took my right glove off and set my palm in the cave of the large pentagram. The red-tinted glass was icy cold to my naked fingers as the spelled glass transferred the cold of the night into me. Glancing up at Bis lurking above me, I said, "If Al shows up, get to hallowed ground, okay?"

The cat-size gargoyle nervously rustled his wings. "'Kay."

Satisfied, I pressed more firmly and reached to touch the nearby ley line.

Power that seemed to have picked up the chill of the night coursed in, finding a balance within me with an unusual flush of vertigo. Surprised, I leaned back until my shoulders hit the statue for balance. *What in hell?* The flow of energy was irregular, making me feel almost seasick. The odd sensation must be from my thin aura. Maybe auras functioned like filters, evening the highs and lows into a steady stream. The longer I held the line, the worse it got.

Bis dropped to stand uncertainly by my knee in concern, his clawed feet seeming to grow bigger when they hit the snow. "You okay, Ms. Morgan?" he asked, and I nodded slowly.

"Dizzy." Mirror balanced on my knees, I tucked a strand of floating hair behind my ear.

"Your aura is still thin," Bis said. "You sure you should be doing this?"

I blinked at him to get rid of the last of the vertigo. "You can see auras?" I asked, then rolled my eyes. Bis could see every ley line in Cincinnati in his mind, like I could see contrails in the daytime sky. When he touched me, I could see them, too. Of *course* he could see auras.

It was frigid out here, and since I was already connected to a line, all that was left was calling Al. Hands trembling faintly from light-headedness, I pressed my hand firmly and thought *mater tintinnabulum* to open a connection. The power of the ley line swelled in me, and my lips parted as I panted. God, this thin aura sucked—it felt like I was sick again—and I wondered how long until I was back to normal.

Shutting my eyes was worse, and I forced them open. It was as if I was in a huge space, but unlike before, when it seemed there were hundreds of whispering voices, there were only a few. *Al,* I thought again, making my goal specific, and I felt a part of me wing off in an unknown direction, a faint vibration seeming to echo through my mind.

I was contacting the demon, which was different from summoning. If I summoned Al into a circle, he'd be subject to my whims and a prisoner until the sun rose or he was able to make his escape through trickery or a lack of interaction with his summoner. He'd also be ticked, seeing as he would be taking on the payment for crossing the lines. No, I was calling him, which was cheaper, smut wise. He could ignore me, though he never refused a chance to flap his lip and show off. He could also use the connection to make the jump to our reality, which was why I was doing it out here. Us having an understanding or no, Algaliarept was a demon, and he would happily hurt Ivy or Jenks for the satisfaction of seeing me angry and impotent.

As expected, the demon picked up immediately, and the unusual vertigo from my thin aura vanished as my expanded experience narrowed to a single, tunnel-vision-like expression.

Itchy witch? his sharp thought echoed in mine. It was surprised and confused, and it was as if I could almost hear the elegant and precise British TV accent he used. I had no idea why. *It's early,* he thought, giving me the impression he was scrambling to organize his thoughts. *It is early, isn't it?* There was a hesitation, then, *It's bloody hell four in the morning! If this is about exchanging my summoning name for that old mark of Newt's, the answer is no. I like you owing me two marks, and I'm enjoying not being yanked across the lines to answer stupid questions from stupid people. You included.*

Worry that he might never make good on our agreement flitted through me, but he needed his name to make a living and would eventually want it back. He was in debt up to his eyebrows, and had the further indignity of not having a familiar to stir his spells and curses. Even better, he now lived in a dump of a two-hollow hellhole instead of the ten-room mansion deep underground that he kept bitching about. Everything but his kitchen and front room had been sold to bribe the demon muckety-mucks to let him out on parole.

Despite his numerous and loud complaints, he wasn't too unhappy, because I was the only witch alive whose kids would technically be demons . . . and I belonged to him. Sort of. I was his student, not his familiar, and he had me only one night a week. Just my luck it was Saturday. Not that I was dating or anything, but a girl liked to keep her weekends free just in case.

That I still had his summoning name meant he couldn't pursue his freelance job of luring stupid people into demon servitude and then selling them to the highest bidder. That I might get summoned out under his name didn't bother me as much as I'd thought it would. I'd scare the crap out of them so good that they wouldn't dare think to summon Al again, and they'd be safe. Soon as Al figured that out, he'd switch back. I hoped.

Curiosity got the better of him when I remained silent, and he finally added, *What do you want? I'm not letting you go early tomorrow for starting early today.*

My eyes met Bis's. The gargoyle looked concerned, shifting his clawed feet and using a wing tip to scratch the middle of his back. "Uh," I said aloud so the kid could hear at least half of the conversation. "Can I have the night off? I don't feel very well."

There was a slight background confusion in him, but Al was alone or I'd be able to pick up his thinking about whoever was with him. *You don't* feel *well?* he thought, then hesitated as I got the impression he was unhappy with the way he looked. There was a surge of minor power through his mind, followed by a flush of satisfaction, and then he added, *You want time off because you don't* feel *well? No.*

I could feel him ready to snap the connection, and I blurted, "But I made you cookies." I moaned, knowing if I played ignorant, he might give in. He knew I wasn't ignorant, but he liked it when I pretended, as if I could manipulate him. Which I could, so who was smarter after all?

The tingles of thought coming from him touched on crushed green velvet coattails and lace, and I guessed he was primping. *And what the hell do I care about that?* he thought, but there had been a flash of hidden interest, and I smiled at Bis's worried expression.

I exhaled, not caring that Al could read my relief, because he hadn't hung up on me. "Look, I was attacked by a banshee yesterday and she sucked most of my aura off. I don't feel good, and tapping a line makes me dizzy, so I don't think I can be of any use anyway."

I can think of a lot of things to do, he thought. *And none of them involve standing up.*

"Very funny. I'm serious," I said, wondering what I had interrupted. His thoughts were focused on . . . tidying up? *Good grief, is he tidying up for me?* "I would have gotten a work excuse, but I had to break out of the hospital just to get here to talk to you."

I felt a surge of annoyance, and then, quite unexpectedly, it vanished. My gaze slid to Bis. Crap, was Al coming over? "Bis, take off!" I said in alarm, then gasped as a wave of vertigo slammed into me like a cresting wave.

"Ms. Morgan!" Bis shouted.

I pushed the mirror off my lap as I struggled not to spew. Pain followed the nausea. My skin felt like it was on fire, the pulsating energy hitting me hard without my aura to even out the surges. My legs wouldn't work, and when I tried to stand, I fell over. I hit the snow-covered pavement on my side, managing to get my arms out so I didn't crack my nose open.

"Ms. Morgan?" Bis tried again, and I clenched in agony when he touched me and I felt like I was going to explode. Damn it, I'd been okay until Al tapped into me to make his crossing cheaper. The cement slab under me was hard, and my cheek burned against the snow.

I smelled burnt amber, and suddenly there was a pair of shiny, buckled shoes before my pain-clenched eyes. "Run, Bis," I panted, then sucked in air when the pain cut off with a blessed suddenness. The power of the line was gone, and it was just me lying in the snow.

"What, by my blood dame's shadow, am I doing in the snow?" came Al's refined British accent. "Morgan, get up. You look like a scullery girl down there."

"Ow," I said as his white-gloved hand grabbed my shoulder and hauled me up. I stumbled, my feet not quite finding the ground for the first second or two.

"Let go of Ms. Morgan," came a deep, gravelly voice from behind me, and still in Al's grip, I worked to look around me.

"Bis?" I stammered, and Al dropped me. Wobbling, I found my balance with a hand on Al's chest, shocked. Bis had released his body's warmth to melt a patch of snow, taking the water into him to increase his size. He was as tall as me now, a grainy black, and his wings spread to make himself look bigger. Water-filled muscles bunched and flexed, from his craggy feet to his gnarly hands. He was probably too heavy to fly, and when Al dropped back a step, the gargoyle hissed to show a long, forked tongue. Damn, there was steam coming off him.

I felt Al touch the small line running through the graveyard, and I jumped. "Al, no!" I shouted, feeling helpless as I stood between a red-eyed demon and a red-eyed, horned gargoyle, my hands outstretched to them both. *When did Bis get horns?*

"He's just a kid!" I shouted at Al. "Al, don't hurt him! *He's just a kid!*"

Al hesitated, and I flicked a look behind me at Bis, surprised by the change. Bridge trolls were able to change their size with water, too. "Bis, it's okay. He won't hurt me. Ivy wouldn't let me come out here alone if it wasn't okay. Just . . . relax."

The tension lessened as Bis stopped hissing. He slowly lost his crouch, shrinking only slightly as he closed his wings. Al's hands stopped glowing, and there was a curious sensation in me as the demon pushed a wad of force back into the line.

Al sniffed loudly, tugging his coat about him and adjusting his lace. "When did you get your gargoyle?" he said sarcastically. "You've been holding out on me, itchy witch. Bring him with you tonight, and he can have mortar cakes and tea with mine. Poor little Treble hasn't had anyone to play with in ages."

"You have a gargoyle?" I said as Bis shifted awkwardly, unused to this much mass.

"How else would I be able to tap a line so far underground?" the demon said with forced pleasantness. "And how clever of you to have one already." This last was said sourly, and I wondered what other nasty surprises he hadn't told me about.

"Bis isn't my familiar," I said, working to stay upright as my fatigue hit me anew when the adrenaline crashed. "Al, I really need the night off."

At that, the demon seemed to bring his wandering attention back from the cold night. "Stand up," he said, jerking me upright. "Get the snow off you," he added, smacking my coat to make the crusty stuff fall away. "What the devil is wrong with you, calling me out in the snow when you have that *adorable* little kitchen?"

"I don't trust you with my friends," I said. "Can we skip this week?"

His gloved hand lashed out and gripped my chin before I could think to move. I stifled a gasp, and Bis rumbled. "Your aura is nearly thin enough to tear . . . ," the demon said softly, turning my face back and forth as his goat-slitted eyes peered three inches outside my outline. "It is far too thin to work the lines, much less travel on them," he said in disgust, and dropped my chin. "No wonder you were belly down on the pavement. Hurt, huh?"

I backed up, rubbing where it felt as if I could feel him still. "So I have the night off?"

He laughed. "God's little green apples, no. I'll just pop on home and bring back a little something to make my itchy witch al-l-l-l-l better."

That didn't sound good. I had looked in my books already, finding that there was no white charm to help replace a person's aura. I didn't know any black ones either. If there were any, vampires would know about them, seeing as that's what the undead ones siphoned off their victims along with the blood.

"A curse?" I asked, backing up until I felt Bis behind me.

"It wouldn't work if it wasn't." Al eyed me over his smoked glasses and smiled to show me his blocky teeth. "I may not have much, but I do have auras, all lined up in pretty jars, like some people collect wine. I specialize in the eighteenth century. It was a good century for souls."

I stifled a shiver, telling myself it was from the cold. "I'd rather wait until mine replenishes itself, thanks."

"Like I care what you'd rather?" Turning to make his coattails furl, Al looked across the graveyard to the nearby line. "I'll be back in five minutes," he said as he started to go misty. "Soon as I remember where Ceri hid the little things. Wait for me there," he said, pointing at the nearby ley line like I was a dog. "I don't want you passing out when I come back. And have your bag with you. You're going to pay for this by starting early today. Chop-chop!"

"Al . . . ," I complained, irritated that he would try to disguise his cheapness with a supposed interest in my welfare. He didn't care if I passed out or not. But it wouldn't cost as much to cross into the ever-after if he were in a line, and though he wouldn't admit it, Al was so far up credit creek that even this minuscule difference was important.

"There," Al said, pointing at the ground. A shimmer cascaded over him, and he was gone. Only his footprints in the snow and the lingering scent of burnt amber remained.

I exhaled in annoyance and looked at the tall wall surrounding the property. It was going to be another full twenty-four hours before Ivy and I could go talk to Skimmer. Not to mention that the I.S. might find Mia during that time and get someone killed. Concerned at the sound of running water, I turned to Bis, surprised to find him spitting across the graveyard to coat individual grave markers in ice. He was getting smaller by the second, turning white as he warmed up by absorbing the warmth from the water before he let it go. Talk about weird.

"There is no way I'm taking anyone's aura," I muttered, imagining Al sitting on me and holding my nose to make me open my mouth. The truth was, I'd been over to his apartments enough times now that he probably had a strand of hair to target a spell to me. All he had to do was twist the curse and I'd be wearing someone else's aura. Nice.

Bis spit tiny little ice cubes to get his balance perfect, then flew up to land on the angel's shoulder. He looked a little ill. "You want me to come with you? To the ever-after?"

The kid looked scared to death, and my heart went out to him. "No. Absolutely not," I said firmly, looking for my discarded mirror and my forgotten bag of cookies. "Al was just jerking you around. I wouldn't take you even if you asked. It's nasty over there." His wings drooped in relief, and I added, "Look, I don't want to go into the church. It would be just like Al to show up and cause trouble. Will you tell Ivy it didn't work and bring my bag out here? It's in my closet, already packed. Oh, and make sure she calls the correctional facility to set up something for Monday."

Safety was a good reason for not going back in the church, but the truth of it was, I didn't want to have to deal with Jenks. Crap, I didn't have time to waste a day in the ever-after keeping Al at arm's length and going to parties. It seemed that's all we ever did. Al called it networking. No wonder the demon was broke.

"Sure, Ms. Morgan," the gargoyle said, his eyes downcast as

if he knew why I was sending him instead of going myself. Bis stretched his wings, going black as he drew all his warmth into his core to maintain his body heat while making the short flight to the church. His leathery wings beat once, and he was airborne, looking scary as he flew to the church.

Alone, I snatched up the scrying mirror and my bag of cookies. I wasn't looking forward to wearing someone else's aura. I'd rather just suffer the pain. Head down, I trudged through the snow, wincing when I felt the icy warmth of the line take me. Usually it was hard to feel them like this, but my aura was thin and this was my line, unused by anyone else, as it was rather small and surrounded by the dead. People were superstitious.

Finding my footprints from last week, I went a few steps beyond and set the cookies and mirror on a nearby tombstone. "Thanks, Beatrice," I whispered, reading the stone marker. Wrapping my arms around myself, I stared at the night and tried to stay warm. It was sort of like waiting at the bus stop, and I found myself falling into blank-stare mode. With a wry smile, I carefully unfocused my attention—slowly, until I knew it wouldn't hurt—to bring up my second sight, hoping to spot Al before he popped in to scare the crap out of me.

The red ribbon of power was suddenly around me, looking like an aurora borealis as it swelled and ebbed, always there, always fluctuating, running off to who knew where. Surrounding it was a broken landscape of stunted scrub and cold rock. Everything had a red sheen to it now except for the moon and the grave markers, and though the moon looked its normal silver now, when I crossed over to the ever-after, it would be an ugly shade of red. Not that we'd stay on the surface long.

I shivered, not liking it when my hair started to move in the wind from the ever-after. There was no snow, but I'd be willing to bet it was colder there. "Any time, Al," I called, then leaned against Beatrice's tombstone. He was going to make me wait. Son of a bastard.

"Ah, mistress witch," a faintly familiar voice sighed. "You're as smart as a steel trap, but I opine you won't keep body and soul together much longer. Nohow can I fix it if you maintain your course."

I spun around, going warm when I saw Al behind me, casually leaning against a tombstone with one booted foot cocked on a toe. He had made himself look like Pierce, and face hot, I gritted my teeth. But then I realized that Al didn't know about Pierce, wouldn't know to look for him in my thoughts, and wouldn't know what the man called me, or the curious accent he had—a mix of rough street talk and pre-Turn English.

Shocked, I stared at the ghost, dressed in an old-style three-piece suit and the memory of the long coat that had once belonged to my brother. He was clean shaven this time, and had a funny-looking hat on his head. Realizing I was looking at him, he jerked himself upright, his eyes wide in the moonlight. "Pierce?" I said, unsure. "Is that you?"

The small man's jaw dropped and he took his hat off as he stepped from the stone. There were no footprints behind him. "It must be the line," he whispered in wonder. "We're both in the line, and you're communing with it . . . using your second sight, aren't you?" His entire face brightened in the light from the back porch. "You don't do that very often, stand in a line."

I couldn't move, not believing it. "My dad told me not to because you never know what you'll see," I said lightly. I felt unreal, dizzy.

He shrugged, and delight filled me on a quick intake of breath. I crossed the space between us only to jerk to a stop, smile fading. It had to be a joke. It had to be one of Al's perverted jokes. "What's the word to open my dad's locket?" I asked cautiously.

Pierce leaned forward, and when his breath was cold, not warm, as Al's would be, I felt a surge of hope. "Lily white," he whispered, touching his nose, and elated, I reached out a gloved finger and jabbed his shoulder. It hit him, and he rocked back.

"Pierce!" I exclaimed, giving him a fierce hug that made

him grunt in surprise. "My God, I can touch you." Then I let him go to give his shoulder a smack. "Why didn't you do this before? Stand in a line, I mean! I'm here every week. I was going to try to stir that spell again, but now I don't have to! Damn, it's good to see you!"

The small man searched my face, grinning as the scent of coal dust, shoe polish, and redwood seeped into me. "I've been in a line when you were," he said. "I abide here most times you leave to fulfill your bargain with the demon, and I abide here when you return."

"You've been spying on me?" I asked, blushing when I remembered I'd called Pierce sexy not five minutes ago in the kitchen. Jenks's claim that he was going to sell our secrets was ridiculous, but there had been plenty going on in the church that I wouldn't want my mom to know, much less an almost stranger from the nineteenth century.

"Spying?" Pierce said, looking affronted as he put his hat back on. "No. I've been in the belfry most times. Apart from when the TV was spelled. That's a powerful fine magic there." His expression shifted to one of a satisfied appreciation as he took me in, running his eyes from my hair to my feet. "You've grown into a damned fine young woman, mistress witch."

"Well, it's good to see you, too." My eyebrows rose as I pulled my hand from his, sure now that he had been in the kitchen before I'd come out here. I went over in my mind what I'd said, deciding there'd been nothing I wouldn't want him to hear and a lot he probably ought to know—apart from me telling Jenks to get bent, perhaps. Smiling deviously, I rocked back on my heels to intentionally catch my balance a few inches back, a subtle reminder that I wasn't that eighteen-year-old-girl anymore. Trouble was, I think he was glad of it.

Sure enough, his own smile deepened as he recognized me distancing myself. Gaze intent, he inclined his head. The porch light caught his eyes, and they glinted, lingering on my face, making me wonder if I had chocolate chip cookie dough on my chin.

"Land sakes, how could you have gotten so deep so fast," he said, his brow furrowing as he shook his head in dismay and changed the subject. "Beholden to a demon? You were so innocent when I left you."

His cool fingers tucked a strand of hair behind my ear, and a shiver struck me when I took his hand out of my curls and he gripped my fingers. "Um . . . ," I murmured, then remembered what I was going to say. "I had to save Trent. I promised him I'd get him home safely. I still have my soul. Al doesn't own me."

The slamming of the back door jerked me around, but it was only Bis. His frightening, batlike silhouette lurched closer, moving heavily from the bag he was carrying. I took a breath to ask him to get Ivy, and Pierce touched my chin, turning me to him.

"Al will be back to fetch you soon," he said, his expression taking on a sudden urgency. "I beg you to be of a mind to find me when your lesson is done. I'll allow we can talk now, and that's enough. Drawing upon a coven for power to give me a body for a night isn't worth the agony until I find a way to be whole again. Just promise me you won't tell your demon about me. Don't ask for his help. I can fix this on my own hook."

Bis landed heavily atop my canvas bag, his skin black and cold and his eyes widening as he saw Pierce. *He doesn't want me to ask Al about him?* I thought. *When there might be a charm or spell that could bring him back to life?* Jenks saying he was spying for secrets rose in my mind, and my smile faded. People don't ask you to do things unless they have a reason.

Seeing me hesitate, Pierce frowned, looking between me and the startled gargoyle. "It's but a small thing, Rachel. I'm of a mind to tell you why, just not directly."

"You can be of a mind to tell me now," I said, starting to warm.

My ears popped, and I gasped as Al was suddenly behind Pierce, eyes glowing and white-gloved hand reaching out. Pierce dove for the far edge of the line, but it was too late.

"Rachel, look out!" Bis shouted, and I stumbled backward, falling over my bag, my elbow hitting the cookies. There was a whoosh of air as Bis became airborne, and I looked up at the hiss of the gargoyle, hovering between me and Al. Al's elegantly coated arm was wrapped around Pierce's neck, tightening until his feet dangled. His face went red as he struggled.

Bis landed between Al and me, his wings spread to look bigger since he was too cold to melt snow. "Al!" I shouted, moving forward until Bis hissed at me. "What are you doing?"

Al peered over his smoked glasses at us, his red, goat-slitted eyes delighted. "Getting a better apartment," he drawled, sniffing at Bis in warning.

Oh shit. "Al, you've got to stop doing this," I said, pulse hammering as I shot a glance at the church, but no one was at the windows. "Snatching people talking to me is not fair!"

Al smiled to show his thick, blocky teeth. "So?"

Pierce struggled, his hat falling from him, to vanish before it hit the snow. "Give this no mind, mistress witch," he gasped, face red and feet trying to find the ground. "This seven-by-nine demon is of no circumstance. I'll be—"

Al jerked his arm, cutting off Pierce's words, and I winced. "Busy," the demon said. "You're going to be busy." Eyes on mine, Al ran his hand suggestively under Pierce's coat, and the small man jerked.

"Hey!" I shouted, but Bis wouldn't let me get closer, pacing a line in the snow, his wings spread and placing his feet with an odd stiffness. "Let him go. This isn't fair. We need to set up some rules about you popping in and snagging people. I mean it!"

"You *mean* it?" Al laughed, shifting his grip until Pierce grunted and went still. "Looks like I don't need my name to find familiars after all," he crooned.

The thought of Pierce on the demon auction block was like ice down my back, but that Al might start popping in whenever he felt like it and snag whoever was with me was absolutely terrifying. "No way," I said, starting to get angry. "I am *not* going to be your bait. Let him go. If you want him, you catch him the old-fashioned way, but I won't be used like this. Got it, goat eyes?"

I was so pissed I could have screamed. Pierce looked pained at my words, but Al simply laughed again. "Use you as bait? Capital idea!" the demon cooed, then grimaced at Bis, still stalking back and forth between us. "The thought never occurred to me. I simply saw something I wanted and took it." His eyes narrowed. "It's what I do."

"He's worthless!" I exclaimed, almost stomping my foot and not believing him. "Pierce is a ghost. He can't tap a line. You're doing this to irritate me. Let him go!"

A slow smile grew on Al's face, and he fondled the hair about Pierce's ear, making him stiffen. "You don't know who this is, do you," Al said, sending a chill of doubt through me; he was far too satisfied. "There are curses that can cure that tiny little problem of all spirit and no body, and this piece of witchcrap . . ." Al gave Pierce a shake. "This one here? He is worth a little extra time in the kitchen. It's just a matter of finding the right curse. He's the golden boy, the one who got away, and he's going to pay my bills for the next thirty years."

I clenched my hands, cold in their gloves. *Pierce had a history with demons? Damn it!* "You know him?" I said, my words a white mist. It would explain why Pierce was so good with ley lines. But he was so nice. He was so . . . normal!

"I do not practice demonology!" Pierce exclaimed. "Let me go directly, you maggot-ridden piece of sheep liver, or you will suffer a powerful defeat. You're of no circumstance. A second-rate—"

Al flexed his arm, and Pierce choked. "I never managed to actually find this one before," Al said, regaining his usual supercilious air though Pierce dug at his fingers around his throat. "But I've heard of him, itchy witch. Everyone has heard of Gordian Nathaniel Pierce. He almost killed Newt, which is why I'm going to make enough money off him that you can keep my summoning name for the next decade. Someone will pay big for him." His voice lowered. "Even if they do nothing but poke at him."

Not a demon practitioner, but a demon killer, I thought with a weird sense of tense relief. Even Bis looked relieved. I looked at the church, but still, no movement. "Al, you can't take people talking to me," I said, and when Al laughed, I blurted, "Then *I'll* buy him!"

Bis turned to me with wide eyes, and even Pierce opened his mouth to protest, grunting when Al jerked him. "Not on your soul," the demon crooned, pulling Pierce close until the man's lips pressed together defiantly and his eyes gleamed in hate. "Well, maybe . . . ," Al mused, then shook his head. "No, not even on your soul," he affirmed. "I won't sell him to you. Despite that witch-class ceiling he has, he's more dangerous than you right now. He's at his peak. Besides, how many nasty little men do you need for your familiars?" he said lightly, looking at Bis. "He's a bad man who likes to try to kill demons."

"I'm not a demon," I said, my voice trembling, and Al's eyes narrowed.

"I am," he intoned. "Consider your night off as a thank-you for luring him to me, itchy witch. Your *lessons* are canceled until further notice. I'm going to be busy for a while."

"Al!" I shouted as they started to go misty. "Don't you walk away from me!"

Smiling at me from over his glasses, Al shook his head. "You're not in control, Rachel. I am. Of everything."

Furious, I shouted, "You're abusing your right to check on me, and you know it! Give him back and stop abducting people I'm with, or so help me I'm going to . . . to . . ."

Al hesitated, and I started to shake. "Do what?" he asked, and Pierce closed his eyes in misery. "You can't draw on a line until your aura heals, and I'm not fixing it for you." Glancing at Bis, he edged forward until the gargoyle hissed. "You're helpless, Rachel Mariana Morgan."

I dropped back, stymied. Damn it, using all three of my names was a warning, probably the only one I'd ever get. If I summoned him I might get my way, but I'd lose what little respect he'd given me and be back to being treated like a demon summoner. And I liked the respect he'd been granting me, little as it was. I enjoyed not having to fear every time the air pressure shifted. Though the parties in the ever-after were a pain in the ass, Al's kitchen was peaceful. I didn't want that to end. But his abducting of people was going to stop.

"This is not over," I vowed, trembling from frustration. "We are going to settle this, and you're going to let him go!"

"How, itchy witch?" he scoffed.

My expression twisted as I searched for an answer that wasn't there.

Seeing me without words, Al jerked Pierce up, almost off his feet. "Don't call me. I'll call you," he said, and he and Pierce vanished.

Heart pounding, I stared where he had been. "Damn it back to the Turn!" I shouted. Frustrated, I spun to the church, but there was nothing to help me there. The lights were bright, spilling out over the silent snow. Snatching up my bag and scrying mirror, I stomped to the back door, grabbing the cookies at the last moment. Al was going to be busy with Pierce for a while, but until I settled this, everyone with me was a potential target.

This was so not what I needed.

Seventeen

Ignore me, huh?" I muttered, trying for anger, not fear, as I dropped my scrying mirror and cookies on the counter, then kicked my overnight bag under the table, out of the way. The canvas sack scraped across a thin layer of salt, leaving a smear of muddy snow, and I turned to the cupboards. Salt. I didn't know how to jump a line, but I was going to use my scrying mirror to connect to Al, and I wanted to be in a circle in case he jumped to me first. Either way, we were going to get together.

From atop the fridge, Bis shifted his wings nervously. I hadn't even seen him come in with me. The sensitive kid knew I was scared, but if Al wouldn't come to me, I'd go to him. He had thrown down the gauntlet, taunting me with my inexperience, telling me I was helpless. I'd been relying on him for three months, grown complacent. I had a good idea now of how to travel the lines. I couldn't let him get away with this or he'd be walking all over me for the rest of my life. He'd crossed the line, and it was up to me to make him back up.

A whisper of presence touched my awareness, and I jerked, turning to see Ivy in the hall, hand on the archway and wonder in her eyes. "I thought you were leaving. You're still here?"

"He took Pierce," I said bitterly, and her lips parted. "Snatched him right out of the line. Damn it, I didn't know that was possible."

Her eyes flicked to the crushed cookies and back. "Pierce was in the ley line?" she asked, going to the fridge and coming out with the orange juice. "You saw him? As a ghost?"

I nodded, scanning the kitchen for my chalk. "He was solid. Al took him. I am so pissed."

The clatter of dragonfly wings grew obvious, and Jenks darted in, following three of his kids in a merry chase. He saw me, and jerked to a stop as the youngsters hid behind Bis on top of the fridge, giggling. "Rache!" he cried, clearly surprised. "What are you doing back?"

"I never left," I said sourly. "Where's my magnetic chalk?" I pulled open a drawer and shuffled around. A salt circle was out. I had melted snow all over the floor. Salt, good. Saltwater, bad. "I have to go talk to Al," I finished.

The pixy's gaze dropped to the scrying mirror. "Go? Go where?"

I slammed the drawer shut, and Bis jumped. "The everafter."

Eyes wide, Ivy turned from pouring her juice. Jenks's wings clattered, and he flew close enough to send the scent of ozone over me. "Whoa, whoa, whoa!" he exclaimed. "What, by Tink's little red shoes, are you talking about? You don't know how to jump the lines."

Peeved, I took off my coat and threw it onto my chair. "Al took Pierce. I was talking to him, and he took him. Al won't listen to me, so I'm going to go talk to him. End of story."

"End of story is right! Have you been sniffing fairy farts?" Jenks yelled as Matalina flew in, gathering the wide-eyed kids and Bis and ushering them out in a swirl of silk and leathery wings. "You're going to risk your *life* for this guy? Let him go, Rache! You can't rescue everyone! Ivy, tell her she's going to get herself killed!"

I slammed another drawer shut and pulled open the next. "I'm not doing this to rescue Pierce," I said as I shifted through my silverware and blessed candles. "I'm doing this because Al is a jerk. He used the excuse of picking me up to snatch someone. If I don't make him toe the line, then he will walk all over me. And where in hell is my *magnetic chalk*!"

Shocked, Jenks flew backward a few feet. Ivy pushed herself into motion, and, after pulling open the junk drawer, she placed a stick of magnetic chalk in my hand and retreated. Her fingers gripping her orange juice were white from pressure.

My anger abruptly fizzled as I watched her return to her corner of the kitchen. Her pace was slow and sultry, and her eyes were almost all black. I knew my being upset was hard on her instincts, and I exhaled, trying to calm myself. I wanted her here. I could talk to Al alone in the garden safely, but this had the potential to be dangerous—and I'd do it with them around.

"Why don't you just call Dali and complain?" Jenks asked.

A flash of worry flared and was gone. "I could," I said as I bent double to trace a thick layer of shiny chalk just inside the etched line on the kitchen floor. "But then I'd be whining to someone else to fix my problem. Al still wouldn't take me seriously and I'd owe Dali a favor. If I don't force Al to treat me with respect, then I'll never get it. He's been carting my ass back and forth for weeks. I can figure this out." My hands were shaking as I set the chalk on the counter beside the scrying mirror. *How am I going to do this?*

Jenks's wings blurred to nothing, but he didn't move from the counter. Worried, I leaned against the sink and took my boots off. No one said a word as I kicked one, then the other boot under the table to slide to a stop beside my packed bag. The gritty salt was obvious through my socks, and I shivered at the feel of the linoleum. If I could figure this out, I would be free. And when I showed up in Al's kitchen, he'd have to deal with me. I should be thanking him for making me do this.

If I could do this. Taking a breath, I stepped inside the circle.

Jenks rose up, red sparkles shifting from him. "Ivy, tell her this is a bad idea."

Untouched orange juice beside her, Ivy shook her head. "If

she could do this, she'd be safer. She wouldn't have to rely on us as much, Jenks. I say let her try."

The pixy made a burst of noise, and his kids, clustered at the door, vanished.

A quiver went through me, and I nervously pulled my scrying mirror close and set my hand in the cave of the pentagram. Instantly my fingers went cold, the icy chill rising from the red-tinted glass to nearly cramp them. "I can do this," I said, making myself believe. "You said the lines are displaced time. I've seen Al do it a hundred times. QED." *Think happy thoughts. Al's kitchen. The smell of ozone. The peace. Mr. Fish.*

Jenks shifted to sift a red dust onto my calling circle. If he stayed where he was, he'd be in the circle with me. "Jenks, go sit with Ivy."

He shook his head, crossing his arms over his chest. "No. Your aura isn't thick enough. You might kill yourself. Wait until your aura is better."

I blew his dust from the glass and pressed my hand more firmly to it. "I don't have the time. I have to settle this now or he will be walking all over me for the rest of my life. Get back." My knees were shaking, and I was glad the counter was between Ivy and myself.

"No. I'm not letting you do this. Ivy, tell her this is a bad idea!"

"Get out of the circle, Jenks," I said tightly. "What if Al decides he wants a pixy, huh? Or someone he knows develops a taste for vampires? What's to stop him from popping over during dinner and just taking you or one of your kids! I thought he had some scruples about this, but I was wrong. And by God I'm going to make him treat me with some respect. The only reason Al hasn't done this before is because he hasn't seen anyone with me worth his while. But now he's broke! He's going to start snatching. Get out of my circle!"

Jenks made a noise of frustration, and in a burst of dust that lit up the kitchen, he left. From the sanctuary came a brief uproar of pixy shouting, then nothing.

My blood pressure dropped, and Ivy opened her eyes as I looked at her. They were black with fear. "How long do you want me to wait before I have Keasley summon you back?"

I looked at the window, then the clock. "Right before sunrise." My head hurt, and I forced my jaw to unclench. This was going to be the most difficult thing I'd ever done. And I didn't even know if I could do it. I looked at the clock above the sink, and with a slow exhale of breath, I tapped the line out back.

I shuddered as it spilled into me with that new, raw coldness of jagged metal scraping back and forth along my nerves. The sensation seemed worse than before, the nauseating irregularity making me sick.

Jenks's wings hummed as he came back in, hovering beside Ivy with black sparkles drifting from him. My circle wasn't set yet, but he stayed with Ivy. I blinked and shuddered, waiting for my equilibrium to return. "Dizzy," I said, remembering the sensation. "But I'm okay." *I can do this. How hard can it be? Tom can do it.*

"It's your thin aura," the pixy said. "Rache. Please."

Jaw clenched and vertigo rising, I shook my head, becoming even dizzier. I made myself stand straighter, and when Ivy nodded at me, I awkwardly pulled the sock off my right foot and put my big toe on the smooth tang of the magnetic chalk.

Rhombus, I thought firmly. The trigger word would spell the circle in an eyeblink.

Pain sliced through me. I jerked my hand from the mirror, doubling over as the energy from the line roared in, unfiltered and without the cushion of my aura. "Oh God . . . ," I moaned, then fell to the cold linoleum when a new wave hit me. It hurt. Holding the circle hurt, and hurt bad, the entire, dizzying, sharp pulses smacking into me with the force of a Mack truck. You could survive being hit by a Mack truck. In fact, I had. But not without the cushion of an air bag and an inertia charm. My aura had been that cushion. Now it was so thin as to be useless.

"Ivy!" Jenks was shouting as my cheek ground into the salt-gritty linoleum when another spasm hit me. "Do something! I can't get to her!"

I didn't let go of the line—I shoved it out of me. A silent wave of force exploded from my chi, and I gasped in relief as the pain vanished. The electricity went out, and an unexpected snap of power echoed through the church.

"Down!" Jenks shouted, and a sharp pop hurt my ears.

"Shit," Ivy hissed, and my cheek scraped the salty floor when I blearily looked up at her quick steps into the pantry behind me. My attention, though, never left the fridge. It was on fire, the ghastly gold-and-black glow of my magic lighting the powerless kitchen as the door swung open, hanging from one bolt. *I broke our fridge!*

"Jenks?" I whispered, remembering the force of the line I'd shoved out of me. *I think I just blew every fuse in the church.*

I heard the hum of pixy wings over me as Ivy put the magically induced fire out with the fire extinguisher. Behind me, I could hear the pixies, but I closed my eyes, content to lie on the floor in a fetal position as the lights flickered back on. The choking hiss of the extinguisher ceased, and all that was left was my ragged breathing. No one moved.

"Damn it, Ivy, do something," Jenks said, the draft from his wings hurting my skin. "Pick her up. I can't help her. I'm too damned small."

At the edge of my awareness, Ivy's boots ground the salt in agitation. "I can't," she whispered. "Look at me, Jenks. I can't touch her."

I took another breath, grateful the pain was gone. Sitting up, I wrapped my arms around my shins and dropped my head to my knees, shaking from the lingering memory of the pain and shock. *Damn it, I broke our fridge.*

No wonder Al had been so confident. He had said I was helpless, and he was right. And as I sat there, beaten, I felt the first tear of frustration trickle down my face. If I couldn't get Al to treat me with more respect, I *would* be alone. I couldn't have a deeper relationship with Marshal because I'd make him a target. Pierce wasn't even alive, and he was now going to live out eternity in the ever-after, plucked from my backyard. Eventually Al would turn to Ivy and Jenks. Unless I forced him to conform to common decency, everyone around me was living on a demon's whim.

I couldn't seem to catch a break.

Depressed, I sat on my kitchen floor and tried to keep from shaking. I needed someone to hold me, someone who would wrap me up in a blanket and take care of me while I figured it all out. And having no one, I held myself, holding my breath so another tear wouldn't leak out. I was hurt and in pain, both in my body and heart. I could cry if I wanted to, damn it.

"Ivy," Jenks said, panic in his small voice. "Pick her up. I'm too small. I can't help her. She needs to be touched or she's going to think she's alone."

I am alone.

"I can't!" Ivy shouted, making me jump. "Look at me! If I touch her . . ."

Eyes wet, I looked up. A shiver ran through me as I saw her before the broken fridge, spent CO_2 dripping from the shelves. Her eyes were full, vampire black. Her hands were clenched with repressed need. Instinct triggered by Rynn Cormel earlier tonight warred with her desire to comfort me. The instincts were winning. If she made one move to help me, she'd end up at my throat.

"I can't touch you," she said, tears slipping from her, making her look beautiful. "I'm so sorry, Rachel. I can't . . ."

Jenks darted to the ceiling when she shifted into motion. She was fleeing, and in an eyeblink, the kitchen was empty. Wobbling, I got to my feet. She had fled, but I knew she wasn't leaving the church. She just needed the time and space to find herself again.

"It's okay," I whispered, not looking at Jenks as I lurched to my feet. "It's not her fault. Jenks, I'm going to take a shower. I'll be better after a hot shower. Don't let your kids near me until the sun comes up, okay? I couldn't live with myself if Al snatched them."

Jenks hovered where he was as I used the counter and then the wall for balance to stagger to the bathroom, my head down and my eyes unseeing. Behind me, I left the wreckage of the kitchen. A shower wouldn't help, but I had to get out of the room.

I needed someone to hold me and tell me it was going to be okay. But I was alone. Jenks couldn't help me. Ivy couldn't touch me. Hell, even Bis couldn't touch me. Everyone else I had come close to was dead or not strong enough to survive the crap my life dished out.

I was alone, just like Mia had said, and I always would be.

Eighteen

It had been hard staying asleep with Ivy's crashing around this morning, coming in about ten, showering, by the sound of it, and leaving an hour later. Jenks's kids hadn't helped either, flying up and down the hall playing tag with Rex. Nevertheless, I buried my head in my pillow and stayed in bed as seven pounds of kitty fur slammed into walls and knocked over an end table. I was tired, aura sick, and depressed—and I was going to sleep in.

So several hours later, when Jenks locked Rex in my room to get his kids to shut up for their noon nap, I barely heard the front door open and the soft steps pass my door. *Ivy,* I assumed, and I sighed, snuggling deeper under my coverlet, glad that she'd found a shred of kindness and was going to let me sleep. But no. I was never that lucky.

"Rachel?" came a high-pitched whisper, and the sound of dragonfly wings susurrated into my dream of amber-tinted fields of grain. Pierce was stretched out in them, a stalk of wheat between his teeth, gazing up at red clouds. "You can't kill me, mistress witch," he said, smiling before he vanished with my conscious thought and I fully awoke.

"Go away, Jenks," I mumbled and pulled the blanket over my head.

"Rache, wake up." There was the scrape of my drapes being

opened and the harsh clatter of Jenks's wings. "Marshal is here."

"Why?" Lifting my head, I squinted through my hair at the sudden light.

The memory of steps in the hall resurfaced, and I rolled to see my clock. Ten after one. *Not much of a sleep-in.* The sun was bright through my stained-glass window, and it was cold. Rex was a warm puddle at my feet, and as I watched, she stretched, ending it with an inquiring trill to Jenks, now standing beside the stuffed giraffe on my dresser.

"Marshal is here," he repeated, his angular face looking concerned. "He brought breakfast. You know, doughnuts?"

I propped myself up on an elbow and tried to figure out what was going on. "Oh yeah. Where's Ivy?"

"Out pricing new refrigerators." His wings blurred into motion, and he rose, his reflection in the mirror making twice the glow. "She spent the morning at Cormel's, but she came back to shower before she went out. She told me to tell you that since you're not in the ever-after today, she got an appointment to see Skimmer at six."

Six? After sunset. Nice. I had wanted to have lunch with my mom and Robbie today, but I could postpone it a little. "I heard her come in." I sat up and blearily looked at the clock again. I didn't like that Ivy had been with Rynn Cormel, the pretty monster, but what could I say? *And why does my mouth taste like apples?* Leaning over, I pulled Rex across the mounds of covers to me for a cuddle hello. I liked her a lot more now that she would let me touch her.

"Are you going to get up?" Jenks added, his wings hitting a pitch akin to nails on a chalkboard. "Marshal is in the kitchen."

Doughnuts. I could smell coffee, too. "I'm not even dressed," I complained as I let go of Rex and swung my feet to the cold floor. "I'm a mess." *Thank God it's daylight, or Al might come over and decide to take him, too.*

The pixy crossed his arms over his chest, giving me a superior look as he stood beside my giraffe. "He's seen you look worse. Like the time you rolled your snowmobile into those fir trees. Or when he took you ice fishing and you got minnow guts in your hair?"

"Shut up!" I exclaimed as I stood. Rex jumped to the floor and went to stand under the doorknob, waiting. "And stop trying to fix me up with him," I said, fully awake and irritated. "I know you asked him to come over."

He shrugged with one shoulder, looking embarrassed. "I want you to be happy. You aren't. You and Marshal have a good time when you do stuff together, and Pierce is dangerous."

"I'm not interested in Pierce," I said, glaring at Jenks as I shoved my arms into the sleeves of my blue terry-cloth robe and tied it closed.

"Then why are you hell-bent for pixy dust on trying to rescue him?" he asked, but the severe attitude he was trying for was ruined by the smiling stuffed animal beside him. "If it wasn't for him, you wouldn't have hurt yourself last night."

"Last night was me trying to keep Al from abusing his right to check on me to abduct other people," I said in a huff. "That it might get Pierce back is no small thing, but do you really think I'm only going to rescue people I want to jump in the sack with? Not that I'm looking to jump in the sack with Pierce," I amended as Jenks raised a pointed finger. "I rescued Trent, didn't I?"

"Yeah, you did." Jenks dropped his hand. "I never understood that either."

Rex stretched on her hind feet to pat the doorknob, and I went to my dresser for a set of undies. "Hold on, Rex," I crooned. I knew how she felt. I had to go, too.

"Rache, even if you do help him, I don't trust the guy. I mean, he's a ghost!"

My eyebrows rose. *This is why he's suddenly gung ho on Marshal,* I thought. Jenks thought he was the safer of the two. Irritated, I slammed the drawer shut, and he rose up in a burst of light. "Will you get off it!" I exclaimed. "I am not attracted to Pierce." *At least, not enough to do anything about it.* "If I don't make Al treat me with respect, everyone around me is in jeopardy. Okay? That's why I'm doing this, not because I need a date."

Jenks's wings hummed. "I know you," he said in a hard voice. "You can't get to a happy ending from here. You're self-sabotaging by chasing something you can't have."

Self-sabotaging? Is he not even listening to me? Black socks in hand, I looked up at him, finding we were eye to eye. "You watch too many daytime talk shows," I said, then shut the drawer. Hard.

Jenks said nothing, but his words kept pricking me as I yanked a pair of jeans off a hanger. Mia had said I was running, afraid to believe someone could survive being with me, that I'd be alone out of fear. She said that even though I lived with Ivy and Jenks, I was still alone. Upset, I looked at my sweaters, stacked up in the organizer Ivy had gotten me, not really seeing them. "I don't want to be alone," I breathed, and Jenks was suddenly at my shoulder.

"You aren't," he said, his voice heavy with concern. "But you need someone besides me and Ivy. Give Marshal a chance."

"This isn't between Marshal and Pierce," I said as I pulled out a black sweater. But my thoughts kept returning to Jenks yelling at Ivy to pick me up because he was too small to do it. Ivy couldn't touch me or show me she loved me without that damned blood lust kicking in. I had good friends who would risk their lives for me, but I was still alone. I'd been alone since Kisten died, even when Marshal and I did stuff together. Always alone, always separate. I was tired of it. I liked being with someone, the closeness two people could share, and I shouldn't feel I was weak for wanting it. I wouldn't let what Mia said become the truth.

Tucking my clothes under my arm, I smiled thinly at Jenks. "I hear what you're saying."

Jenks rose up and followed me. "So you'll give Marshal a chance?"

I knew his being too small to help me had torn him up. "Jenks," I said, and his wings went still. "I appreciate what you're trying to do, but I'm okay. I've been picking myself up off the floor for twenty-six years. I'm good at it. If Marshal and I were to change things, I'd want it to be for a real reason, not because we were both lonely."

Jenks's wings drooped. "I just want you to be happy, Rache."

I glanced at Rex, twining about herself under the knob. "I am," I said, then added, "Your cat needs to go out."

"I'll get her," he muttered, and when I opened the door, both he and the cat darted out.

"Marshal?" I peeked around the door frame to find that Jenks and Rex had already reached the back living room and that the hall was empty. "I'll be right there."

From the kitchen came the sound of a sliding chair, followed by Marshal's familiar, resonant voice saying, "Take your time, Rachel. I've got coffee, so I'm happy." There was a hesitation, and as I waited to see if he was going to look into the hall, he added in a preoccupied voice, "What's in the potions? It smells like carbonic wax."

"Uh," I stammered, not wanting to tell him they didn't work. "Locator charms for the FIB. I have to invoke them and put them in disks," I added so he'd leave them alone.

"Cool," he said softly. The squeak of Jenks opening the pixy/kitty door was obvious, and confident that Marshal wasn't going to peek into the hall, I made the dash to my bathroom, easing the door closed when I heard Jenks and Marshal start to talk.

"Oh, that's nice," I whispered when I saw my reflection. Black rings made an obvious showing under my eyes, and I was as pale as Jenks's ass. I'd showered before bed to try and warm up, and sleeping with damp hair had left it looking like snakes had been in it. Thank God Marshal hadn't come out of the kitchen. My complexion amulet would take care of the circles, and I got the water going and slowly undressed while I waited for it to warm.

Carefully, until I knew how dizzy it would make me, I sent my awareness to my ley line out back. Vertigo eased in, and I let go of the line immediately. I wasn't going to be setting a circle any time today, but it was better than last night, and I hoped I wasn't putting myself in danger by walking around not able to set one.

"Nothing different from the first twenty-six years of your life," I whispered, but then again, I hadn't had vampires, demons, and freaked-out elves gunning for me then either.

Because I was mindful of Marshal waiting, my usual twenty-minute indulgence became a hasty five-minute splash-and-dash. My thoughts kept cycling between Marshal in my kitchen and Pierce in the ever-after. Complaining to Dali wasn't a good option. Neither was trying to jump the lines until I could hold one without pain. Al wasn't playing fair, and it was up to me to make him. There had to be a way to get him to respect me other than resorting to Dali.

But my mind stayed blissfully empty all the way through the shampoo, rinse, and repeat.

It was finally the low rumble of Marshal's voice as I was toweling my hair that reminded me I had a more immediate problem sitting in my kitchen drinking coffee. I swung my hair around and wiped the mirror clear, wondering what I was going to do about this. Jenks had probably filled his head with nonsense. I couldn't be Marshal's girlfriend. He was too good a guy, and though he was able to react in a crisis, Marshal probably never had people trying to kill him.

I dressed quickly, then yanked a brush through my damp hair and left it to dry. Jenks's voice was clear as I opened the door and padded stocking-footed to the kitchen. I entered the sun-drenched kitchen to see that the fridge was duct-taped shut, but otherwise normal looking. Jenks was at the table with Marshal, and the tall man looked like he belonged, sitting with the pixy and one of Jenks's kids fighting his noon nap.

Marshal met my eyes, and my smile faded. "Hi, Marshal," I said, remembering how he had helped Jenks and me in Mackinaw when we really needed it. I'd always be grateful for that.

"Morning, Rachel," the witch said as he stood. "New diet plan?"

I followed his eyes to the fridge, reluctant to tell him I'd blown it up. "Yup." I hesitated, then, recalling him visiting me in the hospital, I gave him a quick hug, hardly touching him. Jenks rose with his kid and moved to the sink and the slice of sun. "Any news on my classes?"

Marshal's broad shoulders lifted and fell. "I haven't checked my e-mail today, but I'm going in later. I'm sure it's just a glitch."

I hoped he was right. I'd never heard of a university refusing money. "Thanks for breakfast," I said as I looked at the open box of doughnuts on the counter. "That's really nice."

Marshal ran a hand over his short black hair. "Just checking on you. I've never known anyone to sneak out of the hospital before. Jenks said you had a run-in with Al last night?"

"You made coffee?" I said, not wanting to talk about Al. "Thanks. Smells good." I headed for the carafe beside the sink.

Marshal clasped his hands in front of himself and then let go, as if realizing how vulnerable it made him look. "Ivy made the coffee."

"Before she left," Jenks offered, sitting on the spigot with a kid sleeping on his lap.

I leaned against the sink and sipped my coffee, eyeing the two men at opposite ends of the kitchen. I didn't like my mom playing matchmaker. I liked it even less when Jenks tried it.

Marshal sat back down. He looked uncomfortable. "So, your aura looks better."

A sigh slipped from me, and I relented. It had been nice of him to visit me in the hospital. "It's getting there," I said sourly. "That's why I was asking Al for today off, actually.

Apparently my aura is too thin to travel the lines safely. I can't even make a circle. Dizzy." *And it puts me in so much pain I can't breathe, but why bring* that *up?*

"I'm sorry." Marshal took a doughnut and held the box out to me. "It will be okay."

"So they tell me." Coming forward, I leaned over the center counter to take a glazed. "I'm thinking next week it will be back to normal."

Marshal glanced at Jenks before he said softly, "I meant about Pierce. Jenks told me you saw him in the line, and then Al took him. God, Rachel. I'm sorry. You must be really upset."

I felt the blood drain from my head. Jenks had the decency to look discomfited, and I set the doughnut on a napkin. "That's an understatement. I didn't know I had that particular hole to plug. Just one more thing for Ms. Rachel to fix." *Along with finding Kisten's murderer. I am a freaking albatross.*

The witch rubbed a hand over his short hair, only two months long. "I understand. When someone you care about is in danger, you'll move the world for them."

My blood pressure spiked, and frowning at Jenks, I put a hand on my hip. "Jenks, your cat is at the door."

The pixy opened his mouth, looked at my grimace, then took the hint. He exchanged some male look with Marshal that I couldn't interpret, and with the sleeping child on his hip, he flew out. He looked kinda nice with a sleeping child, and I wondered how Matalina was doing. Jenks had been very closed-lipped about her lately.

I waited until even the humming of his wings was gone, then sat across from Marshal. "I only knew Pierce one day," I said, feeling like I owed him an explanation. "I was eighteen. Jenks thinks I'm looking for men I can't have a real relationship with so I don't have to feel guilty about not having one in my life, but really, there's nothing between Pierce and me. He's just a nice guy who needs some help." *Because he has the misfortune to know me.*

"I'm not trying to be your boyfriend," Marshal said to the floor. "I'm just trying to be your friend."

That hit every single guilt button I had, and I closed my eyes to try to figure out what I could say to that. Marshal as a friend? Nice thought, but I'd never managed to have a male friend I didn't end up in the sack with. Hell, I'd had thoughts about Ivy, for that matter. Marshal was the longest I'd ever seriously known a guy without letting it spill into the physical. But we weren't really dating. *Were we?*

Confused, I exhaled slowly. Wondering how I was going to handle this, I looked at his hand. It was a nice hand, strong and tanned. "Marshal," I started.

The phone rang in the living room, and the extension in the kitchen blinked, on mute from last night. Jenks shouted he'd get it, and I dropped back in my chair.

"Marshal," I repeated when Rex padded in since her master wasn't eavesdropping on us in the hall anymore. "I love what you're trying to do, and it's not that I don't find you attractive," I said, flushing and starting to babble. "But I study with demons, I've got their smut all over me, and my aura is so thin I can't tap a line and do anything! You deserve better than my crap. You really do. I'm not worth it. Nothing is."

My gaze jerked up when Marshal leaned over and took my hand.

"I never said you weren't hard to be with," he said softly, his brown eyes gazing earnestly at me. "I knew that the moment you walked into my shop with a six-foot pixy and bought a dive with a Vampiric Charms credit card. But you're worth it. You're a good person. And I like you. I want to help you when I can, and I'm getting better at staying out of the way and not feeling guilty when I can't."

His hand on mine was warm, and I gazed at it. "I needed to hear that," I whispered so my voice wouldn't break. "Thank you. But I'm not worth dying for, and it's a distinct probability."

The clatter of pixy wings intruded, and when Jenks flew in,

Marshal drew back. Warming, I hid my hands under the table.

"Ah, Rache," Jenks said, glancing between us. "It's Edden."

I hesitated, my first impulse to have him call me back. Maybe he had something on Mia.

"It's about a banshee," Jenks continued. "He says if you don't pick up the phone, he's going to send a car."

I stood, and Marshal smiled and took a doughnut. "Is it about Mia?" I asked as I reached for the extension. My eyes flicked to the useless locator potions lined up on the counter, and I blinked. They were gone.

"Where's my—" I started, and Marshal waved a hand for my attention.

"Hanging in your cupboard. I invoked them for you." His eyes widened at my suddenly worried expression. "Sorry. I should've asked, but you said they were done. I thought I could help, you know . . ."

"No, it's okay," I said, distantly hearing Edden on the line talking to me. "Um, thanks," I said, flushing. Great, now he knew I had messed up on them. He made his own charms and would know by the lack of redwood scent that they were duds.

Embarrassed, I turned to the phone. "Edden?" I said, mortified. "Did you find her?"

"No, but I want your help this afternoon with one of these banshee women," Edden said without preamble, his gravelly voice a mix of preoccupied gratefulness, sounding odd with the original line still open in the living room. "This one's name is Ms. Walker. She's the iciest woman I've talked to since my mother-in-law, and that was just from our phone conversation."

I glanced at Marshal, then turned my back on him. Jenks was sitting on his shoulder, his kid probably in the desk where he belonged.

"She called the department this morning," Edden was saying, drawing my attention back. "And she's flying in this afternoon from San Diego to help me find Ms. Harbor. Can you be here when I talk to her? Banshees police themselves, same as vampires, and she wants to help—seeing as the I.S. won't do anything."

The last was said rather sourly, and I nodded though he couldn't see it. This was making sense, but I wasn't sure I wanted to meet this woman if a freaking *baby* of her species had almost killed me. "Uh," I hedged, uneasy, "I'd really like to help and all, but my aura is still thin. I don't think talking to another banshee is a good idea." *Besides, I've got to come up with a way to make Al behave today.*

Jenks buzzed his wings in approval, but Edden wasn't happy.

"She wants to meet you," he said. "Asked for you. Rachel, she made you being there a stipulation for talking to me. I need you."

I sighed, wondering if Edden was above stretching the truth to reach an ending he wanted. Putting a hand to my head, I thought for a moment. "Jenks?" I asked, not sure about this, "can you tell if she starts sucking on me?"

The pixy's wings brightened. "You bet, Rache," he said, clearly glad he could help.

I bit my bottom lip and listened to the echo of the open line as I weighed the risks. I'd like to see Mia get her own for letting her kid try to kill me, and Ms. Walker could help. "Okay," I said slowly, and Edden made a pleased rumble. "Where and when?"

"Her plane comes in at three, but she's on West Coast time, so how about a late lunch," Edden said confidently. "On the FIB."

"You mean my lunch, or your lunch?" I asked, rolling my eyes.

"Uh, say four at Carew Tower?"

Carew Tower? This has to be some woman.

"I'll send someone to pick you up," Edden was saying. "Oh, and good job on the AMA. How did you get one so fast?"

I glanced at Jenks, sitting on Marshal's shoulder. "Rynn Cormel," I said, hoping Marshal was starting to understand how risky it was to be around me.

"Damn!" Edden exclaimed. "You do have pull. See you this afternoon."

"Hey, how's Glenn?" I asked, but the phone had clicked off. *Four at Carew Tower,* I thought, mentally going through my closet for something to wear as I hung up the phone. *I can do that. How am I going to do that?* I was exhausted, and I'd just gotten up.

My gaze darted to the island counter where I'd once kept my spell books. Ivy had moved them all back into the belfry when I'd been in the hospital, and the thought of bringing them all down again made me sigh. Al had said there wasn't a spell to supplement a person's aura, but maybe there was something to protect a person from a banshee.

I stood to go check, and from the living room came the beeping of the open line. Jenks buzzed out to take care of it, and I froze, remembering I had company. "Uh, I'm sorry," I said, staring at Marshal's amused expression as he sat comfortably in his chair and ate a doughnut. "I have to go up to the attic and get some books. To look for a, uh, spell."

"Want some help bringing them down?" he asked, already stretching into a stand.

"It's just a couple of books," I hedged, thinking about the demon texts in with the others.

"Not a problem." He headed to the sanctuary, pace casual and confident, and I scrambled to follow. *Crap, how am I going to explain why I have demon texts?*

The sanctuary was silent, warm from the space heater cranked up for the pixies. Jenks had hung up the phone, and he was sitting with his two eldest kids in the rafters on sentry duty. "I can do this by myself," I said when I caught up with Marshal, and he gave me a sideways look.

"It's just a couple of books," he said, then took a bite of the doughnut he had brought with him. "I'll bring them down, and then if you want me to leave, I will," he added around his full mouth. "I know you've got work to do. I just wanted to check on you was all."

His tone had held a measure of hurt in it, and I felt bad as I followed him through the cold foyer and into the unheated circular stairway that led into the belfry. I had spelled up there once before, when I'd been hiding from demons last Halloween. Marshal had just come into town and was looking for an apartment. Cripes, had it been two months that we'd been doing stuff? It seemed longer.

"Marshal," I said as we found the top and I clenched my arms around me in the chill of the unheated belfry. Dang, it was cold up here, and my breath steamed. I searched the open rafters above the huge bell that made a false roof over the space, but Bis was elsewhere. He'd probably put himself on the eaves last night, where the sun would hit him all day. The adolescent gargoyle didn't come in apart from inclement weather, and when he got older, he probably wouldn't come in even then.

"Hey, this is nice!" Marshal said, and I dropped back, pleased as he looked the hexagonal room over. The rough floor was the color of dust, and the walls had never been finished, still showing the two-by-fours and the back of the siding. It was the same temperature as the outside, about fifty something, refreshing after the steamy warmth downstairs.

The slatted windows let in slices of light and sound, making it a nice hidey-hole where one could sit and watch the day happen. I wasn't surprised when Marshal bent one of the slats to look out. Next to him was the folding chair I'd left up here for when I had to get away. The middle of the ten-by-ten space held an antique dresser with a green marble top and an age-spotted mirror. My library was on the mahogany shelf propped up in one of the spaces between the windows. Beside it, next to the door, was a faded fainting couch. Other than that, the space was empty of everything except the almost subliminal hum of the bell resonating faintly.

Tired, I sat on the couch and pulled one of the books onto my lap, content to sit while Marshal satisfied his curiosity. My thoughts sifted back downstairs to the useless charms in my cupboard. "Um, Marshal, about those locator charms," I said softly.

Marshal turned, smiling. "My lips are sealed," he said, crossing the room. "I know the stuff you do for the FIB is confidential. Don't worry about it."

Okay, that's weird, I thought when Marshal sat beside me, taking the book out of my hand and opening it. How could he not know the charms were bad?

"What are we looking for?" he asked cheerfully, then looked at his hand when it probably started to tingle. Demon books were like that.

"A spell to protect my aura," I offered. "Um, that's a demon text you've got there."

Marshal blinked, stiffening as he realized what he'd opened. "That's why you keep them up here," he said, looking at it, and I nodded.

Much to my surprise, he didn't give the book back, but turned the page, curiosity getting the better of him. "You don't need a charm to help your aura," he said. "What you need to do is get a massage."

My shoulders eased, and glad he wasn't running screaming into the afternoon, I murmured, "A massage?"

"Full body, head to toe," he said, starting when he turned the page and found a curse to destroy an army with a single note of music. "You really think this works?"

"If you do it right, sure." Reaching, I picked up a university textbook and turned to the index. My fingers were cold, and I blew on them. "A massage will make it all better, huh?"

Marshal chuckled and turned a yellowed page. "If you do it right, sure," he said, mimicking me, and I looked up to find him smiling. "Scout's honor. Massage triggers the digestive and sleep rhythms. That's when your aura replenishes itself. You get a massage, and your aura will be better."

I eyed him, trying to figure out if he was joking or not. "Really?"

"Yup." His confident assurance faltered when he saw the next curse to blow up a wind strong enough to topple buildings. He looked at me, then the curse. "Uh, Rachel?" he stammered.

"What?" I said as my warning flags started going up. I wasn't a black witch, damn it.

"This is some creepy-ass shit," he said, brow furrowed, and I laughed, sliding the demon book back onto my lap and the university text onto the floor.

"That's why I don't do it," I said, grateful that he didn't think I was bad just because I had a book that told me how to twist a curse to cause the black plague.

He made a small sound and scooted down to read over my shoulder. "So, running the risk of opening a wound, what did Robbie think about you being in the hospital?"

I turned a page and blanched. HOW TO CREATE WOLF PREGNANCY IN HUMANS. *Damn, I didn't know I had that one in my library.* "Uh," I stammered, quickly turning the page. "Robbie said it was par for the course and told me to stop doing dangerous things because it might upset Mom. He's the one upset, though. Not her."

"That's about what I thought he'd say." Marshal leaned into my space and turned the page for me. I breathed deep, enjoying both the extra body heat in the cold belfry and the rich scent of redwood. He'd been spelling recently, and I wondered if he had a modified warmth amulet keeping him from shivering.

"I like your brother," he said, unaware that I was breathing him in. "It irks me, though, seeing him treat you like you're the same kid you were when he left. My older brother does that to me. Makes me want to pound him."

"Mmmm." I let the weight of our bodies slide us together a little bit more, thinking it suspicious that he was saying all the right things. "Robbie moved out when I was thirteen. He hasn't had the chance to see me as a grown-up." Our arms touched as I turned the page, but he didn't seem to notice. "And then I go and put myself in the hospital the week he comes for a visit. Really good, huh?"

Marshal laughed, then peered more closely at the text describing how to make bubbles last till sunrise, and I felt better as he saw that not all curses were bad. I suppose you could make them appear in someone's lungs and suffocate them, but you could also entertain children.

"Thanks for coming with me to my mom's," I said softly, watching him, not the curses he was flipping through. "I don't think I could have taken sitting there all night and listening to Cindy this, Cindy that, followed by the inevitable, 'And when are you going to get a steady boyfriend, Rachel?'"

"Moms are like that," he said in a preoccupied tone. "She just wants you to be happy."

"I am happy," I said sourly, and Marshal chuckled, probably trying to memorize the curse to turn water into wine. Good for parties, but he wouldn't be able to invoke it, lacking the right enzymes in his blood. I could, though.

Sighing, I pushed the book entirely onto his lap and dragged a new one onto mine. It was cold up here, but I didn't want to go downstairs and risk waking up four dozen pixies. *Am I jealous that Robbie seems to have everything? Has it so easy?*

"You know," Marshal said, not looking up from the book he was searching for me, "we don't have to keep things the way they are . . . with us, I mean."

I stiffened. Marshal must have felt it, seeing as our shoulders were touching. I didn't say anything, and emboldened by my lack of a negative response, he added, "I mean, last October, I wasn't ready for anyone new in my life, but now—"

My breath caught, and Marshal cut his thought short. "Okay," he said, sliding to put space between us. "Sorry. Forget I said anything. I'm lousy at body language. My bad."

My bad? When did anyone ever say my bad anymore? But

letting this go without saying anything was easier said than done, especially when I'd been thinking the same thing off and on in stupid-Rachel moments for weeks. So licking my lips, I said carefully to the book on my lap, "I've had fun with you, these last couple of months."

"It's okay, Rachel," he interrupted, edging farther down the long fainting couch. "Forget I said anything. Hey, I'll just go, okay?"

My pulse quickened. "I'm not asking you to leave. I'm saying I've had fun with you. I was hurting then. I still am, but I've laughed a lot, and I like you." He looked up, slightly red-faced and with his brown eyes holding a new vulnerability. My mind went back to me sitting on the kitchen floor with no one to pick me up. I took a deep breath, scared. "I've been thinking, too."

Marshal exhaled, as if a knot had untwisted in him. "When you were in the hospital," he said quickly, "God help me, but I suddenly saw what we'd been doing the last couple of months, and something hurt me."

"It didn't feel that good to be there," I quipped.

"And then Jenks told me you collapsed in your kitchen," he added with a worried sincerity. "I know you can take care of yourself and that you've got Ivy and Jenks—"

"The line ripped through my aura," I explained. "It hurt." My mind jerked back to my jealousy when I sat all night beside Marshal and listened to Robbie go on about Cindy, almost glowing. Why couldn't I have some stability like that?

Marshal shifted to take my hand, the space between us looking larger for it. "I like you, Rachel. I mean, I really like you," he said, almost scaring me. "Not because you've got sexy legs and know how to laugh, or because you get excited in chase scenes, and take the time to help get a puppy out of a tree."

"That was really weird, wasn't it?"

His fingers tightened on mine, drawing my gaze down.

"Jenks said you thought you were alone and you might do something stupid trying to rescue that ghost."

At that, I gave up on all pretense of levity. "I'm not alone." Maybe Mia was right, but I didn't want her to be. Even if I was, I could still stand alone. I'd done it all my life and I could do it well. But I didn't want to. I shivered, from the cold or the conversation, and Marshal frowned.

"I don't want to ruin what we have," Marshal said, his voice soft in the absolute stillness of a winter's afternoon. He slowly slid closer, and I set the book on my lap on the floor to lean up against his side, testing the feeling though I was stiff and uncertain, trying it on. It felt like it fit, which worried me. "Maybe friends is enough," he added, as if really considering it. "I've never had as good a relationship with a woman as I've got with you, and I'm just smart enough, and old enough, and tired enough to let it ride as it is."

"Me, too," I said, almost disappointed. I shouldn't be resting against him, leading him on. I was a danger to everyone I liked, but the Weres had backed off, and the vamps. I'd get Al to see reason. I didn't want Jenks to be right about me chasing the unattainable as an excuse to be alone. I had a great relationship with Marshal right now. Just because it wasn't physical didn't make it any less real. *Or did it?* I wanted to care about someone. I wanted to love someone, and I didn't want to be afraid to. I didn't want to let Mia win.

"Marshal, I still don't know if I'm ready for a boyfriend." Reaching out, I touched the short hair behind his ear, heart pounding. I'd spent so much effort trying to convince myself that he was off limits, that just that small motion seemed erotic. He didn't move, and my hand drifted down until my fingers brushed his collar, a whisper from touching his skin. A small spot of feeling grew, and I drew my gaze back to his. "But I'd like to see if I am. If you do . . ."

His hand came up to pin mine against his shoulder, not binding but promising more. His free hand dropped lower, suggestively crossing the invisible boundary of my defenses and retreating to give me his answer. That we'd spent the last two months keeping our distance made that simple move surprisingly intense.

Marshal reached to tilt my head up to his, and I let my head move easily in his grip, turning to face him. His fingers were warm on my jawline as he searched my gaze, weighing my words against his own worries. I shivered in the chill. "You sure?" he said. "I mean, we can't go back."

He had already seen the crap of my life, and he hadn't left. Did it matter if this didn't last forever if it gave me peace right now? "No, I'm not sure," I whispered, "but if we wait until we are, neither of us will find anyone."

That seemed to give him a measure of assurance, and I closed my eyes as he gently turned my face to his and tentatively kissed me, tasting of sugar and doughnuts. Feeling raced through me, heat from wanting something I said I never would pursue. His hand pulled me closer, and the slip of a tongue sent a dart of desire to my middle. Oh God, it felt good, and my mind raced as fast as my heart.

I didn't want this to be a mistake. I'd been with him for two months and proved neither of us was here for the physical stuff. So why not see if it worked?

Tension plinked through me, sharpening my thoughts and arraying an almost-forgotten possibility before me. Despite— or maybe because of—our platonic relationship, I wasn't ready to sleep with him. That would be just too weird, and Jenks would tell me I was overcompensating for something. But he was a ley line witch—I wasn't a slouch either—and though the age-old technique of drawing energy from one witch to another probably had its origins in our ancestral past to assure that strong witches procreated with strong witches to promote species strength, nowadays all that remained was insanely good foreplay. There was only one problem.

"Wait," I said, breathless as our kiss broke and reason filtered back into me.

Marshal's fingers slowed and dropped. "You're right. I should go. Dumb idea. I'll, uh, call you if you want. In about a year, maybe."

He sounded embarrassed, and I put a hand on his arm. "Marshal." Looking up, I shifted closer until our thighs touched. "Don't go." I swallowed hard. "I, uh, I haven't been with a witch in ages," I said in a small voice, unable to look up. "One who could pull on a line, I mean. I'd kind of like to . . . you know. But I don't know if I remember how."

His eyes widened as he understood, and his chagrin at my supposed rebuff was pushed out by something deeper, older: the question our DNA had written that begged to be answered. Who was the more proficient witch, and how much fun could we have finding that out?

"Rachel!" he said, his soft laugh turning me warm. "You don't forget stuff like that."

My mortification grew, but his gaze was one of understanding, and it gave me strength. "I didn't practice ley lines much then. Now . . ." I shrugged, embarrassed. "I don't know my limits. And with my aura being damaged . . ." I let my words trail off to nothing.

Marshal put his forehead against mine, his hands on my shoulders. "I'll be careful," he whispered. "Would you rather pull than push?" he said softly, hesitantly.

I flushed hot, but I nodded, still not looking at him. Pulling was more intimate, more soul stealing, more tender, more dangerous in terms of confusing it with love, but it was safer when the two people didn't know each other's ley line limits.

He leaned in slowly for an inquisitive kiss. My eyes closed as his lips met mine, and I exhaled into it, my grip on his shoulders tightening. I shifted to face him. Marshal responded, his hand going to the back of my head, possessive yet hesitant. His redwood scent sparked in me a rise of emotion, pure and untainted by the fear that had always lurked with Kisten. The kiss lacked the adrenaline push of fear, but it struck just as deep, hitting emotion born in our beginnings. There was danger in this not-so-innocent kiss. There was the potential for ecstasy or an equal amount of pain, and the dance would be very careful, as trust was only a promise between us.

My pulse leapt at the chance to see this through. A power pull didn't have to include sex, but it was probably the reason female witches always came back after playing with invariably more well-endowed human males. Even if humans could work the lines, they couldn't do a power pull. My only worry besides embarrassment was my compromised aura . . . It might hurt instead. It was basically the same thing Al used for punishment, forcing a line into me to cause pain, but it was like comparing a loving kiss to rape.

A trill of anticipation lit through me and was gone. *Oh God. I hope I remember how to do this, 'cause I really want to.*

I drew him to me even as I broke our kiss. My breath came fast, and eyes still shut, I leaned my head against his shoulder, lips open as I breathed in his scent. One of his hands held my waist, the other was lost in my hair. I tensed at the feel of his fingers. He knew I wasn't going to hit him with a blast of ley line force to repel him and his advances, but several millennia of instinct were hard to best with only a lifetime of experience, and we'd go slow.

I shifted, straddling his legs, pinning him to the back of the couch. A spike of anticipation dove deep. It was followed by worry. What if I couldn't loosen up enough to do this? My breath was fast, and with my hands laced behind his head, I opened my eyes to find his. Their deep brown was heady with a desire to match my own. I shifted, feeling him under me. "You ever done this with a friend before?" I asked.

"Nope, but there's a first time for everything," he said, and I could hear the smile in his voice as well as see it. "You need to be quiet."

"I . . . ," I managed to get out before his hands edged under my shirt and he kissed me again. My pulse hammered, and as the rough-smoothness of his hands explored my midriff and rose higher, his mouth on mine grew intense. I met his aggression with my own, sending my hands to his waist, dipping a finger beneath his jeans to prove I might do more someday.

I pressed into his warmth, deciding not to think anymore, but just to be. My chi was utterly empty, so with the soft hesitancy of a virginal kiss, I reached out my awareness and found the simmering energy his chi held. Marshal felt it. His hands on me tightened and relaxed, telling me to draw it from him, to set his entire body alight with the rush of adrenaline and the ecstasy of endorphins when I forcibly took it.

I exhaled, willing it to come.

The warmth of his hands on me flashed into tingles. In a sudden rush that shocked us, the balances equalized. Adrenaline spiked out of control. Marshal groaned, and, frightened, I tightened my awareness. Barriers clamped down, and I warmed in embarrassment. But the energy had come in smooth and pure, lacking the sickening nausea that a ley line left me in. Coming from a person, it had lost its jagged edges.

"Marshal," I gushed, totally miserable. "I'm sorry. I'm not good at this."

Marshal shuddered, opening one eye to focus on me. He had gone utterly pliant under me, frighteningly so. "Who says?" he whispered, sitting up to pull me farther onto his lap.

I was ready to throw myself out the window. I could feel the energy from him in my chi, scintillating and tasting of masculinity in my thoughts. It wanted to go back to him, but I was afraid. I'd closed myself to him, and it was going to be harder, now.

"Rachel," Marshal soothed, his hand running up and down my arm. "Relax. You've been carrying around chunks of everafter with the intent of hurting people if they attack you, and because of that, you've built one hell of a wall."

"Yeah, but—"

"Just shut up," he said, giving me little kisses that distracted and sent tingles of desire building in me. "It's okay."

"Marshal—" *This is so weird, kissing him,* and I walled the thought off.

"Use your lips for something other than talking, will you? If it doesn't work, it doesn't work. No big deal."

"Mmmmph," I mumbled, surprised when he wrapped his arms around me and hiked me farther onto him, silencing my protests with his mouth. Giving up, I kissed him, feeling myself relax and tense up all at the same time.

My breath came faster as Marshal's hands started exploring, running across my jeans to drag me up where I could feel him pressing into me. I took his mouth with my own, finding a kiss, slowly tasting him as his redwood scènt filled me. His tongue slipped into my mouth, and I pushed back. It was my undoing.

I gasped, hands flying to his shoulders to shove away when he pulled on my chi. With an exquisite ping of adrenaline, I fought him, even as he gripped me harder, forcing me to stay. The shock was heady, and with a sound of desperation, I broke our kiss. Panting, I stared at him, breathless in the chill winter afternoon. *Damn, that had felt good.*

"Sorry, sorry," I panted, sexual excitement pounding in me.

"For what?" Marshal asked, heat in his gaze.

"I pulled away," I said, and he smiled.

"Take it back," he whispered, teasing me. His fingers touched everything, running smoothly over me to make me shiver in the dusky light coming through the slats. Here, there, never long anywhere, to drive me almost mad. *Oh God, I'll make him beg for it.*

Shivering from anticipation and desire, I leaned in. Marshal's scent was everywhere. I breathed him in, shutting off my thoughts. His hands were on my waist, and as I grew comfortable with our new closeness, I exhaled in a soft sound of pleasure as he found my breasts, nuzzling one of them through my shirt, then the other, bringing me stiff with anticipation until I couldn't take it anymore. I wanted to wait, to make him ask for it with his body if not his words, but instead I exhaled, pulling from him every last erg of power in his chi.

Marshal groaned as the exquisite fulfillment of it rolled into me, mixed with the wicked feeling of domination and possession. He opened his eyes; the hot need showing in them set my heart pounding. I had taken from him, and now he was going to take from me.

He didn't wait. One hand behind my neck, he drew me down to kiss him. I knew it was coming, but I couldn't help my whispered cry as he touched my chi with his awareness and pulled everything from me, running it through my body and into his to leave glittering trails of loss and heat to spiral through me like smoke from an extinguished candle.

I didn't fight him. I was able to share this, and with our kiss holding, I steadied myself to wrestle it back. My knees pressed into his thighs, demanding it, taking it, making it mine.

Power pulled fast through him with the crack of a whip, and he gasped, his arms jumping up to imprison me. I breathed him in, feeling him inside me everywhere. I could taste him in my mind, in my soul. It was glorious. I could hardly stand it.

"Take it," I whispered, wanting to feel him do the same, but he grunted no. My moan turned into a pant of want, and spurred on, he gripped me more intensely until he touched my chi again, taking all of it in a wash of scintillation to leave only a trail of sparkles in my mind and an aching emptiness.

It was my turn to steal it back, but he took control of everything. In a mind-numbing pulse of force, he pushed the energy into me. I sucked in my air in shocked surprise, clutching him. "Oh God, don't stop," I gasped. It was as if I could feel him inside me, outside me, all around me. And then he drew it back again, leaving me almost weeping for it. "Marshal," I panted. "Marshal, please."

"Not yet," he groaned.

I gripped his shoulders, wanting everything. Wanting it all. Wanting it now.

"Now," I demanded, out of my mind with the self-enforced deprivation. He had my line energy, he had my fulfillment. His mouth found mine, and I begged. Not with my words, but with my body. I writhed for it, I pressed into him for it, I did everything but take it, finding the exquisite ache of unfulfilled need chiming through me, driving me to a fevered pitch.

And then he groaned, unable to deny it anymore. I moaned in release as the energy from his chi filled mine as we both climaxed. A rush of endorphins cascaded through us, bringing me to a back-arched, gasping halt. Marshal's grip on me shook, and I trembled as wave after wave smothered me, pulling me into a hyperalert state where nothing was real.

I heard a panting moan, then realized, embarrassed, that it was me. Slumping into him, I felt my senses return. Marshal was breathing hard, his chest rising and falling under me as his hand lay on my back, still at last. I exhaled, feeling the flow of energy between us sift back and forth without hindrance, leaving little tingles that faded to nothing as the forces balanced perfectly.

I lay against him with my head on his shoulder, listening to his heartbeat and deciding there were probably not too many more enjoyable ways to mess up your life than this. And fully clothed, too. Feeling the icy cold of the afternoon against me, I stirred. "You okay?" I asked, smiling as I felt him nod.

"How about you?" he asked, his voice more of a rumble than a real sound.

I listened for a moment, hearing nothing. No pixy wings, no roommate stomping around downstairs. "Never better," I said, feeling more at peace than I had in a long time. Marshal's chest began to bounce, and I pushed myself up when I realized he was laughing. "What?" I said, feeling like I was the butt of the joke.

"Marshal, I don't know if I remember how," he said in a falsetto. "It's been so long."

Relieved, I sat up and mock-punched his shoulder. "Shut up," I said, not minding that he was laughing at me. "I didn't."

Marshal eased me off his lap, and I snuggled up to him,

both of us slouched with our heads on the back of the couch and our feet intertwined on the floor.

"You sure your aura is okay?" Marshal asked, almost too soft to hear. He turned to look in my eyes, and I smiled.

"Yeah. That was . . . Yeah." Marshal's arms wrapped around me as I made a move to get up, and giggling, I fell back into him.

"Good," he whispered in my ear, holding me all the closer.

I wasn't going to worry about what happened next. It truly wasn't worth it.

Nineteen

The sun was arching toward the horizon, painting the buildings at Cincinnati's waterfront in red and gold as I headed for Carew Tower for a quick bite and that interview with Edden. If it had been a normal Sunday, I'd be just about ready to head home from the ever-after and Al's and my weekly push-and-shove contest, and though I was glad to have gotten out of it, I was worried about Pierce. Pierce, Al, Ivy, Skimmer, Kisten's killer, and Mia. They all swirled in the back of my head, problems demanding to be solved. Most days, the overload would have had me tense and snappish, but right now? Smiling, I gazed at the sun reflecting on the buildings and fiddled with the radio as I followed the guy ahead of me over the bridge. *All in due course,* I thought, wondering if my calm was from Marshal, or Marshal's massage therapist.

Edden's meeting was in about half an hour, then the I.S. lockup was at six, followed by an early dinner with Robbie and my mom at ten—I'd heard Robbie complaining in the background when I'd called to say I'd have to miss lunch, and he could just suck dishwater. Eventually Mia would surface, and then I'd nail her ass, but until then, I could enjoy a snack at Carew Tower. The massage I'd indulged in earlier had been fantastic, and I felt twinges of guilt all afternoon that I'd been enjoying myself under the excuse that it might help my aura. The feeling of relaxation was still with me, making it easy to tell Marshal that he'd been right, yada, yada, yada . . . He was going to call later. It felt good, and I wasn't going to think any more about it than that.

I was feeling dressy in the silk-lined pants and shiny top I had put on for Ms. Walker. I hadn't gotten a chance before to wear the long felt coat my mom had given me last winter, and I felt elegant, driving over the bridge into Cincinnati, aiming for Carew Tower and a business meeting at the top of the city. Jenks, too, had dressed up, wearing a black top and pants that flowed, hiding the insulating layers of fabric under it. Matalina was improving at making winter wear he could fly in, and the pixy was perched comfortably on the rearview mirror, fussing with the black fisherman cap she'd concocted out of a scrap of felt from the inside lining of my coat. His blond hair was peeking out rather charmingly, and I wondered why he didn't wear a hat all the time.

"Rache," he said, looking suddenly nervous.

"What?" I fiddled again with the radio as we came off the bridge, cutting in front of a semi to get onto the exit ramp at a fast forty-five miles an hour. There was a guy on my tail in a black Firebird, and he followed, riding my bumper. *Really safe in the snow, bud-dy.*

"Rache," he repeated, wings fanning.

"I see him." We were both headed for the exit ramp, and giving me the one-fingered salute, the guy accelerated, trying to get ahead of me before the lane disappeared.

"Rachel, just let him in."

But he ticked me off, so I maintained my speed. The semi behind us blew his horn as the off-ramp approached. The guy wasn't going to make it, and the weenie shoved me into the curb.

Gravel and rock salt hit the undercarriage of my car. The wall slid close, and I caught my breath, hands clenching as the lane narrowed to one. I thunked the brakes, jerking the wheel at the last moment to slip in behind him. The guy roared ahead and ran the yellow light at the end of the exit ramp. Face flaming, I waved to the irate semi driver behind me who had seen the whole thing from a sort-of-safe distance. Jenks was shedding a sickly yellow dust as he stood on the rearview mirror and held the stem as if it were his life. I slowed to a halt at the red light and glared at the Firebird, a block ahead of me, stopped at the next light. *Ass.*

"You okay, Rache?" Jenks asked, and I turned down the heater.

"Fine. Why?"

"'Cause you don't usually career into other cars unless you're going more than sixty," he said, dropping to land on my arm and walk up it to sniff me. "You on some human medicine? Did that massage therapist slip you an aspirin or something?"

Not as upset as I thought I'd be, I glanced at him and then back to the street. "No." Marshal was right. I should get a massage more often. It was really relaxing.

Jenks made a face and sat down in the crook of my elbow, wings fanning to keep his balance. The massage had been wonderful, and I hadn't realized how tense I'd been until the stress was gone. God, I felt good.

"Green light, Rache."

I pushed the accelerator, noticing that the Firebird was still at the red light. A smile curved over my face. I checked my speed, the sign, and the street. I was legal.

"It's red," Jenks said as I barreled down the street to the next light.

"I see it." Glancing behind me, I shifted lanes so Mr. Ass was parked in the lane next to me. No one was in front of me, and I maintained my speed.

"It's red!" Jenks exclaimed as I didn't slow down.

My fingers gripped the wheel casually, and I watched the crossing light start to blink. "It'll be green when I get there."

"Rachel!" Jenks shouted, and as smooth as white icing, I blew past Mr. Firebird two seconds after the light changed, going a nice forty miles per hour. I made the next light while he raced his engine and tried to catch up. Making a sedate left on an early yellow, I turned to go downtown. Mr. Firebird had to stop, and I couldn't help my feeling of satisfaction. *Dumb ass.*

"Holy crap, Rachel," Jenks muttered. "What's gotten into you?"

"Nothing," I said as I turned up the radio. I felt really good. Everything was A-OK.

"Maybe Ivy could pick us up at the restaurant," Jenks muttered, and I took my eyes from the road, mystified.

"Why?"

Jenks looked at me like I was crazy. "Never mind."

I zipped around a bus, changing lanes halfway down the block. "Hey, how does my aura look?" I asked, slowing as I tapped the nearby university line. It flowed in with an uncomfortable pinch, but at least I wasn't dizzy from the ebb and flow of energy. There was a car ahead of me, and I checked both ways before I shifted lanes and took a yellow light. Plenty of time.

"Stop playing with the line and drive!" Jenks exclaimed. "Your aura's a lot more even than before, and thicker, but only because it's been compacted down to a bare inch off your skin."

"Huh. It's good, though?"

He nodded, his tiny features looking irate. "Good enough if no one takes any more. You just missed the turn for the parking garage."

"Did I?" I mused, seeing a black Firebird roaring up a block behind me. "Look, there's a space right out front," I said, eyeing an open spot on the other side of the street.

"Yeah, but by the time you circle around, it will be gone."

I looked behind me, then smiled. "If I circle around," I said, then cut a sharp U-bangy. The road was slick, and the car spun just as I thought it would, turning to face the opposite direction as it drifted into the spot with a soft jiggle when the wheels met the curb. *Perfect.*

"Good God, Rachel!" Jenks shouted. "What the hell is wrong with you? I can't believe you did that! Who do you think you are? Lucas Black?"

Grabbing my bag, I turned off the engine and adjusted my scarf. I didn't know where the confidence for that had come from, but it had felt damn good. "Coming?" I said sweetly.

He stared at me, then pried his fingers off the rearview mirror. "Sure."

Jenks's wings were cold as he snuggled in between my neck and scarf, and after a last look, I got out. Chill air smelling of wet pavement and exhaust hit the bottom of my lungs as I took a deep breath, scenting the coming night and calling it good. It was freezing out here, and feeling confident in my best coat and boots, I waved at Mr. Firebird before I headed for Carew Tower.

My boots squishing in the melting slush, I squinted at the light as I adjusted my sunglasses. The bright storefront of an independent charm shop caught my eye, and I wondered how early we were. "Jenks?" I questioned as my steps slowed. "What time is it?"

"Three thirty," he said, muffled from the yarn he was hiding in. "You're early."

Jenks was better than a watch, and my thoughts shifted to the coming meeting with the banshee. Marshal and I hadn't found anything in my books to supplement my aura after we got ourselves together and actually looked at them. But maybe the owner of a spell shop had something to increase "digestive and sleep rhythms." There was that failed locator amulet I wanted to check on, too. Maybe I'd just used the wrong kind of carbonic wax.

"You want to stop at a spell shop?" I asked Jenks. "See if they have any fern seed?"

"Oh, hell yes!" Jenks said so enthusiastically that I felt a twinge of guilt. He was so damned independent that it probably never occurred to him to ask us to take him shopping. "If they don't have fern seed, I'll get some tansy," he added as his wings brushed my neck. "Matalina likes tansy tea. It keeps her wings moving well."

I angled to the small front door, the memory of his ailing wife rising in me. The man was hurting, and there was nothing I could do about it. Not even hold his hand. Taking him to a charm shop was the best I could do? It wasn't enough. Not by a long shot. "Almost there," I said, and when he swore at me for my concern, I pulled open the single glass door and entered.

Immediately I relaxed at the tinkling of the bell and the scent of cinnamon coffee. The soft buzz of the charm-detection spell was a mild alarm reacting to my bad-mojo amulet. I took my hat off, and Jenks flew from my scarf to land on a nearby rack and stretch his wings.

"It's nice in here," he said, and I smiled as he ruined his tough-guy image by standing on top of dried rose petals and using the word "nice."

I undid my scarf and took off my shades, scanning the shelves. I liked earth-charm shops, and this was one of the better ones, right downtown, in the middle of Cincy. I'd been here a few times and had found the clerk to be helpful and the selection more than adequate, with a few surprises and the odd pricey item I didn't have in my garden. I'd rather buy local than use mail order. If I was lucky, they might have that red-and-white stone crucible. Worry pinched my brow at the thought of Pierce with Al, but it wasn't as if I could do the spell if he was trapped in the ever-after.

Or could I? I thought suddenly, my fingers, running over a stand of planting seeds, going still. I'd be willing to bet Al hadn't given Pierce a body yet, in effect preventing him from tapping a line and becoming more dangerous than he already was. If he was still a ghost, maybe the charm could pull him back from the ever-after the same way it did from the hereafter. Ever-after, hereafter. What's the difference? And if I did that—Al would come to me.

A smile overcame me, and excitement zinged down to my

toes. *That* was how I was going to get Al to grant me some respect. If I snatched Pierce from him, Al would come to me. I'd be in a position of power, whether real or pretend. New Year's Eve was tomorrow night. All I needed was the recipe to make sure I did it right! I didn't even need to tap a freaking line!

Excited, I turned to the door. I needed that book. *Robbie.* Suddenly wanting to be somewhere else, I jiggled on my feet, settling back into an anxious bother. I'd see Robbie tonight, and I wouldn't leave until I had that book and everything that went with it.

Jenks zipped around a display, almost running into me. He was spilling a bright copper glow and I figured he had found something. Behind him, the woman next to the register looked up from her newspaper, tucking her straight purple-dyed hair back behind an ear as she eyed Jenks's sparkles. "Let me know if you need any help," she said, and I wondered if her hair was really that enviably straight or if it was a charm.

"Thanks, I will," I said, then held out my hand for Jenks to land on. He was darting back and forth like an excited kid. He must have found something he thought would help Matalina.

"Over here," he said, zipping off the way he had come.

Smiling at the woman behind the counter, I followed Jenks's trail of slowly sifting gold sparkles. My boots clunked on the dark hardwood as I passed the racks of herbs to find him at a nasty-looking weed hanging in the corner beside the gnarly lengths of witch hazel.

"This one," he said, hovering over the sparsely leafed, mangy-looking sprig of gray.

I eyed him, then the tansy. Right next to it was a much nicer sheaf. "Why don't you want this one?" I asked, touching it.

Jenks buzzed harshly. "It's hothouse grown. The wild one is more potent."

"Gotcha." Being careful not to break anything off, I set it gently into one of the woven baskets stacked at an end cap. Satisfied, Jenks finally parked on my shoulder. I slowly headed to the front, lingering over a pouch of dandelion seed and smiling. We had a little time yet. I should ask her about the carbonic wax.

The hushed sound of the clerk on the phone drew my attention. She was arguing with someone, and Jenks buzzed his wings nervously.

"What's going on?" I asked softly as I pretended to look at a display of rare-earth muds. Holy crap, they were expensive, but they were certified and everything.

"I'm not sure," he said. "Something doesn't feel right all of a sudden."

Much as I hated to admit it, I agreed. But the question of what I'd done wrong with the locator amulet still remained, and I headed to the register.

"Hi," I said brightly. "I've been having some trouble getting a locator potion to work. Do you know how fresh the carbonic wax has to be? I've got some, but it's like three years old. You don't think a salt dip would ruin it, do you?" She stared at me, like a deer caught in the headlights, and I added, "I'm working a run. Do you need to see my runner's license?"

"You're Rachel Morgan, aren't you," she said. "No one else has a pixy with them."

A faint feeling of apprehension slid under my skin at how she'd said it, but I smiled. "Yup. This is Jenks." Jenks buzzed a wary greeting, and she said nothing. Uncomfortable, I added, "You really have a great store."

I set the tansy on the counter, and she backed away, looking almost embarrassed. "I-I'm sorry," she stammered. "Will you please leave?"

My eyebrows rose, and I went hot. "Excuse me?"

"What the hell?" Jenks whispered.

The young woman, eighteen at the most, fumbled for the phone, holding it like a threat. "I'm asking you to leave," she said, voice firm. "I'm calling the I.S. if you don't."

Sparkles dripping, Jenks got between us. "What for? We didn't do nothing!"

"Look," I said, not wanting an incident, "can we pay for this first?" I nudged the basket, and she took it. My blood pressure eased. It lasted all of three seconds—until she set the basket out of my reach, behind her.

"I'm not selling you anything," she said, eyes darting to tell me she was uncomfortable. "I have the right to refuse anyone service, and you need to leave."

I stared at her, not understanding. Jenks was at a loss. But then my eyes fell on the newspaper with yesterday's story of the riot at the mall. There was a new headline. BLACK MAGIC AT CIRCLE MALL—THREE IN HOSPITAL. And suddenly I got it.

I reeled, putting a hand to the counter for balance. The university returning my check. The hospital refusing to treat me on the witch floor. Cormel telling me he had to speak on my behalf. Tom saying he'd be around if I wanted to talk. They were blaming me for the riot. They were publicly blaming me, and calling it black magic!

"You're shunning me?" I exclaimed, and the woman went red. My eyes flicked to the paper, then back to her. "Who? Why?" But the why was kind of obvious.

Her chin lifted, the embarrassment gone now that I'd figured it out. "Everyone."

"Everyone?" I yelped.

"Everyone," she echoed. "You can't buy anything here. You might as well leave."

I retreated from the counter, my arms slack at my side. *I've been shunned?* Someone must have seen me with Al in the garden, seen him abduct Pierce. Had it been Tom? The freaking bastard! Had he gotten me shunned so he'd have a better shot at Mia?

"Rache," Jenks said, close to my ear but sounding faraway and distant. "What does she mean? Leave? Why do we have to leave?"

Shocked, I licked my lips and tried to figure it out. "I've been shunned," I said, then looked at the tansy. It might as well have been on the moon. I wasn't going to get it, or anything else in the store. Or the next. Or the next. I felt sick.

I shook my head in disbelief. "This isn't right," I said to the clerk. "I've never hurt anyone. I've only helped people. The only one who gets hurt is me." *Oh my God, what am I going to tell Marshal? If he talks to me again, he might be shunned, too. Lose his job.*

My demon mark seemed heavy on my foot and wrist, and I tugged my sleeves down. Red-faced, the clerk dropped the tansy in the trash because I'd touched it. "Get out," she said.

I couldn't seem to find enough air. Jenks wasn't much better, but he at least found his voice. "Look, you lunker," he said, pointing at her and dripping red sparkles that puddled on the counter. "Rachel isn't a black witch. The paper is printing trash. It was the banshee that started the riot, and Rachel needs this stuff to help the FIB catch her!"

The woman said nothing. I put a hand to my stomach. Oh God. I didn't want to spew in here. I'd been shunned. It wasn't a death sentence, like it had been two hundred years ago, but it was a statement that what I was doing was not approved of. That no one would help me if I needed it. That I was a bad person.

Numb, my grip tightened on the counter. "Let's go," I whispered, turning to the door.

Jenks's wings were a harsh clatter. "You need this stuff, Rache!"

I shook my head. "She won't let us buy it." I swallowed. "No one will."

"What about Matalina?" he said, panic icing his voice.

My air slipped from me, and I turned back to the counter. "Please," I said, Jenks's wings making my hair tickle my neck. "His wife is ill. The tansy will help. Just let us buy this one thing, and I'll never come back. It's not for me."

Her head shook no. All her fear was gone, washed away by the confidence she found when she realized I wasn't going to give her trouble. "There are places for witches like you," she said tartly. "I suggest you find them."

She meant the black market. It wasn't to be trusted, and I wouldn't seek it out. Damn it, I had been shunned! No witch would sell to me. No witch would trade with me. I was alone. Absolutely alone. Shunning was a tradition that stretched back before the days of the pilgrims, and it was 100 percent effective; one witch couldn't grow, find, or make everything. And once shunned, it was seldom revoked.

Her chin lifted. "Get out or I'll call the I.S., for harassment."

I stared at her, believing she'd do it. Denon would love that. Slowly I pulled my hand off the counter.

"Come on, Rachel," Jenks said. "I probably have some tansy under the snow somewhere. If you don't mind getting it for me."

"It's wet," I said, bewildered. "It might be moldy."

"It will be better than the crap they sell here," he shot back, flipping the woman off as he flew backward to the door.

Feeling unreal, I followed him. I wouldn't be able to check anything out of the library either. This was so not fair!

I didn't feel Jenks snuggle in between my scarf and my neck. I didn't remember opening the door or the cheerful tingling of the bells. I didn't remember walking to my car. I didn't remember waiting for traffic before I edged into the street. Suddenly, though, I was standing at the door to my car with my keys in my hand, the bright sun gleaming on the red paint, making me squint.

I blinked, going still. My motions slow and deliberate, I stuck the key in the lock and opened it. I stood there a moment with my arm on the fabric roof, trying to figure it out. The sun was just as bright, the wind just as crisp, but everything was different. Inside, something was broken. Trust in my fellow witches, maybe? The belief that I was a good person, even if there was black on my soul?

I had an appointment in twenty minutes, but I had to sit for a while, and I didn't know if the coffee shop on the tower's first floor would serve me. Word of a shunning traveled fast. Slowly I got in and shut the door. Outside, a truck rumbled past where I'd been moments before.

I was shunned. I wasn't a black witch, but I might as well have been.

Twenty

I t was with a new feeling of vulnerability that I stood before the double glass doors of the Carew Tower and adjusted my hat in the murky reflection, and I jumped when the doorman leaned forward and opened it for me. A warm gust of air blew my hair back, and he smiled, tipping his hat in salute when I came in with small steps and whispered, "Thank you."

He answered me cheerfully, and I forced myself to straighten up. So I had been shunned. Edden wouldn't know. Neither would Ms. Walker unless I told her. If I walked up there looking like prey, she would chew me up and spit me out.

My jaw clenched. "Stupid department of moral and ethical standards has their head up their ass," I muttered, determined to fight this all the way to the Supreme Court—but the reality was, no one would care.

The restaurant at the top of the tower had its own dedicated elevator, and I could feel the doorman's eyes on me as I clicked and clacked my way to it, forcing myself to find a confident posture. The elevator, too, had a doorman of sorts, and I told him who I was and gave Edden's name as he checked his computer for reservations.

I hiked my bag up higher on my shoulder and read the restaurant's events sign as I waited. Apparently someone had reserved the entire restaurant for a party tomorrow.

My flagging confidence took another hit as I remembered

Pierce. I was shunned, my ex-boyfriend's killer was roaming free, I was doubting my ability to stir something as complex as a locator amulet, Al was abusing our relationship . . . I had to start fixing things.

Jenks moved, startling me as he wiggled out and sat on my shoulder. "Your pulse just dropped," he said warily. "Is your blood sugar low?"

I shook my head, smiling thinly at the doorman when he got off the phone and pushed the button to open the elevator. "I've got a lot to do today," I said as I got in the small, opulent lift.

"And we're late," Jenks grumbled as he took off his cap and tried to arrange his hair in the reflection of the shiny walls. He had flitted to the wide banister circling the inside of the elevator, and twin pixies made an impressive display of winged physique.

I forced myself to straighten as I checked that my complexion charm was in place. *Shun me, would you?* "It's called arriving fashionably late, Jenks," I murmured as I took my own hat off and tucked a curl behind an ear.

"I hate being late," he complained, making faces to pop his ears as the pressure shifted.

"It's a five-star restaurant," I came back with. "They won't have a problem waiting."

The lift chimed and the doors slid open. Jenks moved to my shoulder with a huff, and together we looked out onto the revolving restaurant.

My posture relaxed in pleasure, and I stepped out, smiling, as my worries seemed to pale. Below me the river wound a slush gray ribbon through the white hills of Cincinnati. The Hollows lay beyond, peaceful in the coming dusk. The sun was nearing the horizon, painting everything with a red-and-gold sheen, and clouds reflected it all. Beautiful.

"Ma'am?" a masculine voice prompted, and I brought my gaze inside. He looked like the twin of the guy downstairs, right down to the black suit and blue eyes. "If you'll follow me?"

I'd been up here only once before, with Kisten for breakfast, and I silently walked behind the host, taking in again the rich fabrics; the Tiffany lights; and the mahogany, pre-Turn tables with carved feet. Rosemary and pink rosebuds were on every table. The sight of the booth where Kisten and I had shared morning conversation over French toast made a surprisingly soft ache in me, more fond remembrance than hurt, and I found I could smile, glad that I could think of him without heartache.

The place was empty but for the staff setting up for tonight, and after passing a small stage and dance floor, I spotted Edden at a window table with an attractive older woman. She was Ceri's size, dark where the elf was light, with very thick black hair, falling straight on her back. Her nose was small, and she had thick lips and luscious eyelashes. It wasn't a young face, but her few wrinkles made her look wise and venerable. Graceful, aged hands moved when she talked, and she wore no rings. She sat across from Edden, slim and upright in her stark white, full-length dress, not resting against the back of her chair. Ms. Walker had the view—as well as the poised presence that said she was in charge.

Jenks's wings brushed my neck, and he said, "She looks like Piscary."

"You think she's Egyptian?" I whispered, confused.

Jenks snorted. "How the Turn should I know? I meant she is in control. Look at her."

I nodded, disliking the banshee already. Edden hadn't noticed us, fixated on what she was saying. He looked good in his suit, having worked hard to keep his shape through the late-thirties meltdown and into his midfifties. Actually . . . he seemed captivated by the woman, and a warning flag went up. Anyone as self-possessed and beautiful as she was was dangerous.

As if hearing my unspoken thoughts, the woman turned. Her heavy lips closed and she stared. *Evaluating me, are you?* I thought, sending my eyebrows high in challenge.

Edden followed her gaze, and his demeanor brightened. Getting to his feet, I heard him say, "Here she is," and he came to greet me.

"Sorry I'm late," I said as he took my elbow to hustle me to the table. "Marshal made me get a massage to help with my aura." *Yes. Blame it on Marshal, not me needing to recoup after finding out I'm shunned.*

"Really?" the squat man said. "Does it help? How do you feel?"

I knew he was thinking about his son, and I set my hand atop his. "Wonderful. Jenks said my aura looks tons better, and I feel great. Don't let me leave without giving you the woman's phone number. She makes hospital calls. I asked. No extra charge for the FIB."

Jenks made a scoffing sound. "She says she feels great?" he said. "More like stinking drunk. The damned woman nearly smashed her car drifting it into a parking spot."

"How's Glenn?" I asked, ignoring Jenks as Edden helped me out of my coat.

"Ready to go home." Edden gave me a look up and down. "You look good, Rachel. I never would have guessed that you had to get an AMA."

I beamed as Jenks rolled his eyes. "Thanks."

The waiter holding out his hand for my coat was eyeing Jenks. Edden saw his gaze and moved his chin to make his mustache bunch up. "Can we get a honey pot?" he asked, trying to put Jenks at ease.

"I appreciate the offer, Edden," Jenks said. "But I'm working. Peanut butter would be good, though." His gaze went to the table in its white-and-gold perfection, and his expression became panicked, as if he'd asked for grits and pig's feet instead of the source high in protein he needed because of the cold.

The waiter, of course, picked right up on his unease. "Pe-e-e-ea-nut butter-r-r-r?" he said in a patronizing tone, and Jenks let a wisp of red dust slip.

My eyes narrowed as the man implied with those two words that Jenks was a bumpkin, or worse, not even a person. "You *ha-a-ave* peanut butter, don't you?" I drawled in my best Al impression. "Freshly ground, absolutely nothing out of a jar will *do*! Low salt. I'll have a raspberry water." I had sampled Kisten's raspberry water after finding my French toast not to my taste. It had some fancy glaze on it. Okay, maybe *I was* a bumpkin, but making Jenks feel like one was rude.

The man's face went blank. "Yes, ma'am." Gesturing for a second waiter to get my water and Jenks's peanut butter, he helped me with my chair, and then a menu—which I ignored since he'd given it to me. I had a view, too. Jenks hovered by my place setting as if reluctant to set down on something so fine. His flowing black outfit looked great among the china and crystal, and after I turned an empty water glass over for him, he gratefully sat on the elevated foot. Edden was to my right, the banshee to my left, and my back was presently to the door. But that would change as the hour advanced and the restaurant turned.

"Ms. Walker, this is Rachel Morgan," Edden said as he settled back in his chair. "Rachel, Ms. Walker has been adamant about meeting you. She's the administrative coordinator of banshee internal affairs west of the Mississippi."

Edden seemed unusually flustered, and another flag went up. Jenks, too, didn't seem to like that the usually levelheaded man looked almost twitterpated. But she was a banshee, beautiful and alluring in her sophistication and exotic beauty.

Shoving my increasing dislike away, I extended my hand across the corner of the table. "It's a pleasure, Ms. Walker. I'm sure you know we can use all the help we can get. Mia Harbor turning rogue has us in a tight spot." Jenks smirked, and I flushed. I was trying to be nice. So sue me. I hadn't said anything that wasn't true. It was obvious I couldn't bring Mia in if she resisted.

The older woman took my hand, and I tensed, searching for any sensation of her siphoning off my aura or emotions. Her eyes were a rich brown, and with the bone structure of a super-model and her wrinkled but clear complexion, she was classi-cally alluring.

"You can call me Cleo," she said, and I drew my hand away before I shuddered. Her voice was as exotic as the rest of her, a low slurry of warmth insinuating a promise of naughty but nice. God, the woman was like a vampire. Maybe that was what was putting me on edge.

That I had pulled away was not missed by Edden or Ms. Walker, and a faint, knowing smile curved the edges of her mouth up. "It's good to meet you," she said, shifting to lean forward. "I'll help find little Mia, but I'm here for you. Your reputation is worth investigating."

My fake smile faded, and Edden, hunched over and guilty, started to play with his drinking glass. Slowly I turned to him, calming my anger before the banshee noticed it. But she did anyway.

The cool woman put her elbows charmingly on the table and eyed him almost coyly. "You lied to get her here?"

Edden glanced at me, then back down to the river. "Not at all," he grumped, his neck going red. "I stressed certain things is all."

Stressed certain things, my ass. But I smiled at the woman, keeping my hands below the table, as if she'd soiled them with her touch. "Is this because I survived Holly's attack?" I asked.

"In large part, yes," she said, lacing her fingers together and propping her chin on them. "Would you mind if I felt your aura?"

I stiffened. "No. I mean yes, I would mind," I amended. "I don't trust you."

Edden winced, but Ms. Walker laughed. The comfortable sound of it made the waiters just out of earshot look up, and my stomach clenched. She was too perfect, too assured. And her eyes were dilating like a vampire's.

"Is that why you brought your pixy?" she said, the first hint of distaste wrinkling her nose as she grimaced at Jenks. "I won't be sampling your aura, Ms. Morgan. I simply want to run my fingers through it. Find out why you survived an attack from a child banshee. Most don't."

"Most don't have a black banshee tear in their pocket," I said stiffly, and the woman made a small sound of interest.

"That's why . . . ," she said, and it was as if an until-now hidden tension slipped out of her. "The emotion went sour as she killed you, and finding a sweet source, one familiar—"

"Holly took that instead," I finished for her. Jenks's heels were tapping out a distress signal, and I twitched my fingers to acknowledge it. He had seen the woman lose her tension, too. She'd been afraid of me, and now she wasn't. Good. It would make taking her down easier if it came to that. *Stop it, Rachel. You can't tag a banshee.*

The woman sat upright in her chair and sipped her tea with a thousand years of grace. She and Ceri would get along famously. "Even so, your aura is extremely tight," she said as she set it down. "If I hadn't known you were recovering from an attack, I'd say you were insane."

That was just rude, and when Jenks shifted uncomfortably, Ms. Walker's eyes went from him to me, squinting softly in the bright light. "Your pixy didn't tell you a tight aura is a sign of instability?"

Knowing she was goading me, I let my anger dissipate before I smiled back. "He's my business partner, not my pixy," I said, and Edden miserably shrank into his chair while we had our polite, sophisticated catfight.

Jenks, though, couldn't help himself, and he rose with his hands on his hips. "Why should I tell Rachel what a tight aura means? She's not insane. She had a massage today and it condensed it down. Lighten up—you *hag* of a washerwoman."

"Jenks!" I exclaimed, but Ms. Walker took it in stride. *What is up with him?*

Ignoring Jenks but for a warning twitch of her fingers, she focused on me, her brown eyes going black. I clamped down on my sudden fear. This woman could probably kill me as we sat, and she would get away with it though Edden sat two feet away. "I don't care what they say you are," she said, her low voice entirely devoid of anything but scorn. "We are more powerful than you. That you survived was a fluke."

She stood amid Edden's protests, but I sat, frozen in fear. *Who I am?* She knew. She knew I was a proto-demon.

Standing above me, Ms. Walker closed her eyes and breathed deep, sucking in my fear like a drug. Jenks rose up in a clattering of wings.

"Stop," he intoned as he hovered between us, and the woman's eyes flashed open. "Leave Rachel's aura alone or I will kill you."

Ms. Walker's eyes went even blacker, and my fear slid deeper and twisted. She had Ivy's eyes, full of an unsated hunger. She was a predator chained by her own will, and she didn't mind letting herself off the leash once in a while. But not me. She wouldn't have me. I wasn't prey. I was a hunter.

While Edden winced, the woman gathered up her small handbag. Today's paper was folded up next to it, and my gut clenched. *Great, she knew I'd been shunned, too.* As she looked at Jenks, her disgust poured forth. "Bug," she said simply, hiding her eyes behind a pair of dark glasses. "Shouldn't you be sleeping in a hole in the ground?"

"Shouldn't you be extinct, like the rest of the dinosaurs?" he snarled back. "Want some help getting there?" he added, and I cleared my throat even as I bristled at her racial slur.

"Ms. Walker," Edden was saying, having stood up and moved to her side of the table. "Please. The FIB could really use your help, and we would be most grateful. Ms. Morgan and her associate's opinions aside, one of your own is accused of murder."

The elegant woman stopped two steps from the edge of the revolving ring, her eyes hidden. "I've seen what I've come to see, but I'll look for little Mia tonight. It's unlikely she's left her city, and I'll inform you when I've dealt with her."

Dealt with her? I didn't like the sound of that. By his expression neither did Jenks.

"In return, any assistance you can give me in streamlining the adoption process will be appreciated," she finished, turning away and accepting the hand of a nearby waiter to make the step to the unmoving core of the building.

Adoption? Alarmed, I stood up. "Whoa, wait up," I said caustically, and the woman turned back with cheeks flushed in anger. "Adoption? You mean Holly? Holly has a mother."

Edden's hands went loose at his sides, his posture becoming threatening without his making one overt move. "Ms. Walker, we never discussed you taking the child."

The woman sighed before she stepped back down to our level, moving with crisp, precise motions. "The child can't be held by anyone other than another banshee until she gains control," she said with a wave of her hand, as if we were simpletons. "Almost five years. What are you going to do, put her in a bubble?"

"You are underestimating the child's control," Edden said. "Her father holds her."

Interest arched her eyebrows, and she took her sunglasses off. "Does he really?"

Great. Now she really wanted Holly. It was almost impossible to engender a child under the laws of humanity, and now Ms. Walker thought Holly was special. Mia wasn't going to live out the week, and Remus would probably die defending them if we didn't find them first.

"It's not Holly," I said quickly. "It's her dad. There's a wish involved."

Edden turned to me with accusation in his expression, and I shrugged. "I found out yesterday. I was going to tell you."

Ms. Walker's eyes squinted in the glare, making wrinkles at the corners, and Jenks smiled wickedly as a flash of worry crossed the banshee's face before she hid it away. "Your own son hospitalized, Captain Edden," she said, as if it might make us want to give the child to her. "You yourself, Ms. Morgan, attacked and nearly killed. How many lives will you sacrifice before you accept it? I can control her. You can't. In return, I will give the child a home."

"Temporarily," I said, and Ms. Walker's smile twitched.

"If Mia is cooperative."

Like I believe that would happen?

"Ms. Walker," Edden said, his earlier fluster washed away, leaving his usual hard-assed self. "We all want what's best for Holly, but neither Mia nor Remus has had due process yet."

The woman made a huff, clearly thinking that due process wasn't going to enter into it if she found Mia alone. "Of course," she said, her voice and posture regaining their earlier grace and self-assurance. "Good afternoon, Ms. Morgan, Captain Edden. I'll send word when I have Mia contained." Giving us an icy smile, she turned and walked sedately to the elevator, two waiters trailing behind her.

Jenks's wings clattered as he exhaled and flew back to the table. Red sparkles sifted from him as he stomped from where he'd landed to a small dish of peanut butter that had magically appeared while we argued. Sitting cross-legged on the rim of the plate, he reached over and helped himself with the pair of pixy-size chopsticks he had somewhere on his person. "Damned banshees," he muttered. "Worse than fairies in your outhouse."

Edden put a hand to the small of my back and directed me back to my chair. "Why do I have the feeling we need to find Mia before Ms. Walker does?" he said worriedly.

Someone had set a glass of rose-tinted water by my plate, and I sat down. Slouching, I took a sip, almost getting a lap of water when the ice shifted. "Because banshee babies are rare and precious," I said, then wondered if they'd laugh at me if I asked for a straw. "Giving Holly to that woman would be a mistake, banshee or not. I don't trust her."

Edden snorted. "I think the feeling was mutual."

"Yeah, but according to her, I don't matter." Maybe it was better to not matter to a banshee. "We have to find Mia before that woman does. She's going to kill her to get Holly."

Edden looked at me sharply. "That's a strong accusation."

I reached for the bread basket, hoping we still got to eat even if our Most Important Guest had left. "You can wait until Mia is dead, or you can believe me now. But ask yourself who you'd rather have Holly grow up with." I pointed at him with my pinkie, and he frowned.

"You think so?

Tearing a bit of bread from the loaf, I ate it, thinking it was too dry. "I know so."

Edden's eyes shifted to the elevator, then back to me. "It would be easier if we had a locator amulet. Any progress on them?"

I nearly choked, and as I scrambled for words, Jenks chimed up with a cheerful "Yeah—"

My knee smacked the underside of the table, and his wings burst into motion. "I just have to finish them up," I said. Edden looked from my hot cheeks to the pixy, now silently staring at me. Grunting, the man pushed away from the table, his thick fingers looking out of place on the white linen.

"I'll send a car to pick them up as soon as you have them done," he said as he stood. "I know you don't have the license to sell them, but let me know how much it cost you, and I'll add it to your check. We're having a devil of a time finding her. They keep slipping past us." He rocked back, looking at the elevator again. "I'll be right back."

"Okay," I said, helping the dry bread down with a sip of raspberry water, but my thoughts were elsewhere as the squat man tried to catch up with Ms. Walker.

Jenks snickered, settling in and looking more relaxed. "Want me to tell you what he says to her?" he asked, and I shook my head. "Then you want to tell me why you don't want him to find Mia?" he added.

I brought my gaze back from the elevator. "Excuse me?"

"The amulets?" Jenks licked his fingers free of the peanut butter. "Duh? Marshal invoked them."

Grimacing, I started brushing the crumbs I had made into a pile. "They're duds. I screwed up. They don't work."

Jenks's eyes went wide, and his heels swung back and forth. "Uh, yes, they do."

I didn't look up from brushing the crumbs off in my napkin. "Uh, no, they don't," I mimicked him. "I tried one at the mall, and it was just a hunk of wood."

But Jenks was shaking his head, dipping for another clump of peanut butter with his chopsticks. "I was there when Marshal invoked them. They smelled okay to me."

Exhaling, I leaned back in my chair and shook my napkin out under the table. Either the tear Edden had given me was from another banshee, or the amulet I put the potion into was bad. "It smelled like redwood?"

"Absolutely. The amulets even turned green for a second."

The elevator dinged, and I pulled myself closer to the table. "Maybe the one I invoked was a bad amulet," I said softly as Edden said good-bye to Ms. Walker, and Jenks nodded, satisfied.

But a faint sense of unease wouldn't let go as we waited for Edden to rejoin us. There was a third possibility I didn't even want to think about. My blood wasn't *entirely* witch blood, but proto-demon. It was possible that there were some earth charms I couldn't invoke. And if that was true, then that was one more mark that said I wasn't a witch, but a demon.

Better and better.

Twenty-one

I pulled my car into one of the open, back spots at the correctional facility, right under a light, and making a best guess as to where the lines were since they hadn't plowed the last few inches of snow. The heater was going full blast since Ivy had the window cracked for air, and turning it and the car lights off, I killed the engine and dropped the keys into my bag. Ready to face Skimmer, I sighed, hands in my lap and not moving as I looked at the low building before us.

Ivy sat rigidly still, staring at nothing. "Thank you for doing this," she said, her eyes black in the dim light.

I shrugged and opened my car door. "I want to know who killed Kisten, too," I said, not wanting to talk about it. "I haven't been much help, but I can do this."

She got out as I did, and the thump of our doors was muffled by the mounds of snow that turned the world black and white under the puddles of security lights in the thickly populated lot—employees, probably, though I supposed they could be visitors; it was a low-security facility. Sure, Skimmer had killed someone, but it had been a crime of passion. That, and being a lawyer, had gotten her here instead of the high-security prison outside Cincinnati.

About a quarter mile back, the hospital was hazy with dusk and falling snow. Seeing the peaceful buildings, I had the sudden idea to take my old stuffed animals to the kids. They'd know how precious they were and would take good care of them. I could pick the toys up tonight when I was looking for that spell book. It would be a good excuse for me to get up there, too.

Ivy was still standing beside her closed door, gazing at the building as if it held her salvation or her damnation. She looked sleek and lanky in her working leathers, all in black, with a biker cap to add some spice. Feeling my questioning gaze on her, she pushed into motion, and we met at the front of my convertible. Together we angled through the parked cars toward the shoveled sidewalk. "I'm sorry to make you do this," she said, hunched from more than the cold. "Skimmer . . . she's going to be ugly."

I choked back my laughter. Ugly? She was going to be positively poisonous. "You want to talk to her," I said stiffly, shoving my fear down where I hoped it wouldn't show.

I had way too much to do tonight to be visiting Skimmer, if not for the information we might get from her, but at least I wouldn't have to restir the locator charms. The relief that the problem was likely with my blood—not my skills—was starting to outweigh the worry of *why* the problem was with my blood. Jenks was the only one who knew that the charm I invoked had failed, and he thought it was a bum amulet. By now, the locator charms Marshal had invoked were in the hands of six FIB guys cruising the city. I doubted they'd come within the needed hundred feet to engage the amulet, but it had improved my standing with them immeasurably.

Dinner with my mom and Robbie later tonight would hopefully give me the book and equipment and I could move forward on stamping out *that* fire. I'd been concerned that Al might show up and snag whoever was with me now that it was again dark, but he hadn't done so before finding Pierce, and it was unlikely he would now.

I *so* wanted to be at my mom's looking for that book, not here talking to an angry vampire, but I resolutely walked beside Ivy to the low-security Inderland correctional facility. All the safeguards must be on the inside, because the outside looked like a research building, its stucco walls and accent lights shining on low, snow-covered evergreens. It probably made for better neighbor relations, but not being able to see the fences gave me the creeps.

We walked in silence but for our boots on the crushed ice and salt. The pavement gave way to gray sidewalk, and then the glass double doors with visiting hours and rules about what could be brought into the building. My lethal-amulet detector was going to be a problem.

The woman behind the desk looked up from her phone conversation as we entered. Mild alarms were already going off, reacting to my amulets, and I smiled to try to defuse the situation. Redwood, and a faint smell of unhappy vampire, drifted to me. Ivy grimaced, and I swung my bag around to drop it on the desk while we signed in. There was a TV on in the corner, set to the weather map and talking to itself. More snow tonight.

"Rachel Morgan and Ivy Tamwood to visit Dorothy Claymor," I said, handing her my ID as I noticed the sign asking for it behind her. No wonder the blond vampire wanted everyone to call her Skimmer. "We have an appointment."

Ivy handed me the pen, and I signed in under her. My thoughts went back to the last time I'd put my name in a register book, and I added a solid period after my signature to symbolically end any psychic connection it might have to me. Crossing it off would be better, but I wouldn't be able to get away with that here.

"Right through there," the woman said as she ran our IDs through a scanner and handed them back. "Keep your ID out," she added, gesturing to a pair of thick plastic doors, clearly anxious to get back to her phone conversation.

I'd rather have gone to the right, where the floor was covered in carpet and there were fake potted plants, but Ivy, who clearly knew the drill, was already headed for the sterile, ugly hallway to the left with its white tile and milky-plastic doors.

They were magnetically sealed, and when I caught up to Ivy, the woman buzzed us through.

My jaw clenched when the doors opened and the scent of unhappy vampire and angry Were worsened. I shuddered as I passed the threshold and the prison's safeguards started to take hold. The magnetic door snicked shut behind us, and the air pressure shifted. We were probably in prison air now. Swell. There could be anything in it up to and including airborne potions.

At the end of the room was another set of those doors and a guy behind a desk. The old woman with him started our way, clearly in charge of the standard-looking spell checker before us—which was probably anything but standard. I couldn't help but notice that the woman really stank of redwood, and that, if the gun on her hip wasn't enough, would keep me minding my p's and q's. She might look like an old woman, but I bet she could give Al a run for his money.

"Anything to declare?" the woman asked as she looked over our IDs then gave them back.

"No." Ivy's mood was tight as she handed her coat and purse to her, ignoring the little claim check and walking unhesitatingly through the spell checker and to the desk at the end of the room. *More paperwork,* I thought as I saw her take a clipboard and start filling in a form.

"Anything to declare?" the guard asked me, and I brought my attention back. God, the woman looked a hundred and sixty, with nasty black hair that matched the color of her too-tight uniform. Her complexion was a pasty white, and I would've wondered why she didn't invest in a cheap complexion spell except I didn't think they allowed them anything while on the job.

"Just a lethal-amulet detector," I said, handing her my bag and taking the little slip of paper and jamming it in a jeans pocket.

"I'll bet," she said under her breath, and I hesitated, eyeing her. I didn't like my stuff in her care. She'd probably go through it as soon as I was out of sight. I sighed, trying not to get upset. If this was the crap you had to go through to see a low-security inmate, I didn't want to know what was needed to see someone in the high-security prison.

Smiling, making herself look almost ugly, she nodded to the spell checker, and I reluctantly approached it. I couldn't see the cameras, but I knew they were here—and I didn't like the casual carelessness she used to bag my stuff up and drop it in a bin.

The wave of synthetic aura cascading over me from the spell checker gave me a start, and I jumped. Maybe it was because I didn't have much of an aura right now, but I hadn't been able to stifle my shudder, and the guy at the desk smirked.

Ivy was waiting impatiently, and I took the form the guy shoved across the desk at me. "And who are we visiting today?" he snarkily asked me as he handed Ivy her visitor's pass.

My attention jerked up from the release form. I was not the one in jail here. Then I saw where he was looking and went cold. My visible scars were less than a year old, clear enough, and I stiffened when I decided he thought I was a vampire junkie on my way to get a fix. "Dorothy Claymor, same as her," I said as if he didn't know, signing the paper with stiff fingers.

The young man's smirk grew nasty. "Not at the same time you aren't."

Ivy took a stance, and I set the clipboard down with a tap. Peeved, I looked at him. *Why is this becoming so difficult?* "Look," I said, using one finger to slide the form back to him. "I'm just trying to help a friend, and this is the only way Dorothy will see her, okay?"

"She likes threesomes, eh?" the guy said, and seeing me drumming my fingers on my crossed arm, he added in a more businesslike voice, "We can't let two people visit an inmate at once. Accidents happen."

Much to my surprise, it was the woman who came to my rescue, clearing her throat like she was trying to get a cat out of it. "They can go in, Miltast."

Officer Miltast, apparently, turned. "I'm not losing my job over her."

The woman grinned and tapped her paperwork. "We got a call. *She* can go in."

What in hell is going on? Concern wound tighter in my gut when the man looked from me to my scrawl and back again. Face scrunching up, he turned to Ivy, then handed me the visitor's badge the tabletop machine spit out.

"I'll escort you to the visiting rooms," he said as he rose and patted his shirt front for his key card. "You got this okay?" he asked the woman, and she laughed.

"Thank you," I muttered as I peeled the backing off my badge and stuck it to my upper shoulder. Maybe me being an independent runner just got me in, but I doubted it. My man Miltast opened the door, and hoisting his belt up, waited for us to pass through. God, he was only thirty-something, but he was swaggering around like he was fifty, with a gut.

Again the vampire incense hit me, with a hint of unhappy Were and decayed redwood. It was not a good mix. There was anger, and desperation, and hunger. Everyone was under mental stress so thick I could almost taste it. Ivy and I going in together suddenly didn't seem like a good idea. The vamp pheromones were probably hitting her hard.

The door shut behind me, and I stifled a shudder. Ivy was silent and stoic as we paced down the corridor, jittery under her facade of confidence. Her black jeans looked out of place in the white corridor, and her dark hair caught the light, looking almost silver. I wondered what she was hearing that I wasn't.

We passed through another Plexiglas door and the corridor got twice as wide. Blue lines blocked the floor into sections, and I realized that the clear doors we were passing led to cells. I couldn't see anyone, but it all looked clean and sterile, like a hospital. And somewhere down here was Skimmer.

"The solid doors cut down on the pheromones," Ivy said, noticing me eyeing them.

"Oh." I missed Jenks, and I wished he was here watching my back. There were cameras in the corners, and I bet they weren't fake. "So how come they've got witches working as guards?" I said, realizing that the only vamp I'd seen outside a cell so far had been Ivy.

"A vampire might be tempted to do something stupid for blood," Ivy said, her gaze distant and not paying me much attention. "A Were can be overpowered."

"So can a witch," I said, watching our escort take an interest in our conversation.

Ivy looked sideways at me. "Not if they tap a line."

"Yeah," I protested, not liking that I couldn't right now, "but even the I.S. doesn't send a witch after an undead. There's no way I could even come near besting Piscary."

The man walking behind us made a small noise. "This is an aboveground, low-security facility. We don't house dead vampires here. Just witches, Weres, and living vampires."

"And the guards are more experienced than you, Rachel," Ivy said, her gaze lighting on the cell numbers, counting them down probably. "Officer Milktoast here probably has clearance to use charms that aren't street legal." She smiled at him, chilling me. "Isn't that right?"

"It's Miltast," he said sharply. "And if you ever get bitten," he added, looking at my neck, "you lose your job."

I wanted to jerk my scarf up, but knew that to a hungry vampire, dead or alive, that was like wearing a negligee. "That is so unfair," I said. "I get labeled a black witch for getting a smutty aura saving people's lives, but you can use a black charm with impunity?"

At that, Miltast smiled. "Yep. And I get paid for it."

I didn't like what he was saying, but at least he was talking to me. Maybe he had a smutty aura, too, and my own greasy coating didn't scare him. That he was even talking to me was odd. He had to know I was shunned. That's probably why they'd let me in with Ivy. They simply didn't care what happened to me. *God help me. What am I going to tell my mom?*

We passed through another set of doors, and my claustrophobic feeling doubled. Ivy, too, was starting to show the strain and was beginning to sweat. "You okay?" I asked, thinking she smelled great. Evolution. You've gotta love it.

"Fine," she said, but her nervous smile said different. "Thank you for doing this."

"Wait to thank me until we both get back in the car in one piece, okay?"

Our escort slowed to check the numbers painted on the outside of the doors, and leaning to the side, he used a two-way radio to check something. Satisfied, he looked through the glass, pointed his finger at someone in warning, then ran his card to open the door.

There was a soft hiss of equalizing pressure, and Ivy immediately went in. I moved to follow Ivy, and Miltast stopped me. "Excuse me?" I said snottily, letting him grip my arm like that because he was the only one armed with magic.

"I'm watching you," he threatened, and I started. Me? He was watching me? Why?

"Good," I said, confirming that he knew I'd been shunned. Maybe they let us in together hoping we would all kill each other. "Tell them that I'm a white witch and to get off my case."

Miltast didn't seem to know what to say, and with a final squeeze of pressure, he let me go in. Knees shaking, I passed over the threshold. The door hissed shut, and I swear I heard it seal with a vacuum. The better to contain the pheromones, I guess.

The white chamber was a mix of interviewing room and conjugal-visit trailer. Not that I knew what the latter looked like, but I could guess. There was a second, solid door in the back with a peephole. A white couch took up one side wall, two chairs and a table between them filled the opposite. Lots of room to touch. Lots of room for mistakes to be made. I especially didn't like the transparent door we had come through or the camera on the ceiling. It smelled like burnt paper, and I wondered if it was to help mask the pheromones.

Skimmer sat coyly in a corner white chair. Her white jumpsuit looked good on her, making her seem both small and devilish. Standing in the middle of the room, Ivy was her polar opposite. Skimmer was confident where Ivy was unsure. The blond vamp was coy where Ivy was pleading for understanding. Skimmer wanted to rip my face off, and Ivy wanted to save it.

No one said anything, and I realized I could hear the circulation fans. Skimmer stayed silent, knowing from her courtroom past that he who spoke first was probably the neediest.

"Thank you for seeing me," Ivy said, and I sighed. *Here we go.*

Skimmer shifted to cross her legs the other way. Her blond hair hung about her face, and her complexion was blotchy. They didn't allow them much in here. "I didn't want to see you," she said. Smiling wickedly, she stood to show she'd lost some weight. Never heavy, the woman was now skinny. "I wanted to see *her,*" she finished.

I licked my lips and edged away from the closed door. "Hi, Skimmer." My pulse was quickening, and I forced my breathing to slow, knowing tension was a trigger.

"Hi, Rachel," the smaller vampire mocked as she sashayed closer.

Ivy jerked her arm up, and I fell back in shock when she blocked Skimmer's blurring arm, lashing out at me. Thin fingers with long nails swung inches from where my face had been, and I pressed against the wall. Crap, I didn't want to walk out of here with a scratch or a bite. I was having dinner with my mom and Robbie, and he'd never let me live it down.

"Don't," Ivy said, and I forced myself from the wall. This was going to be bad. Skimmer's eyes had flashed black, and a thread of warning drifted through me, tightening my muscles when I realized Ivy's eyes had dilated to match hers. *Damn.*

Ivy let go of Skimmer's arm, and the white-clad vampire backed up, smelling Ivy's scent on her wrist and smiling. *Double damn.*

"So, Ivy," Skimmer said, shifting her body in its tight jumpsuit to look sultry. "She's still stringing you along like a pull toy, baby?"

Ivy jerked when I moved a step closer. "Can you be decent for once?" my roommate said. "Who visited Piscary but wasn't on the official list? He got blood from someone."

"Other than you?" Skimmer mocked, and my pulse jerked again. "Hurts, doesn't it?" she said as she settled herself in her chair, making it a throne of power. "Seeing what you want and knowing they don't care a shit about you."

I took a deep breath, unable to let that stand. "I care."

"Don't argue with her," Ivy said. "It's what she wants."

Skimmer smiled to show her fangs, and that, combined with her dark eyes, caused a shiver to slide through me. She wasn't dead yet, so she couldn't pull a full vampiric aura, but it was close.

"But here you are," the small woman almost purred, "asking what I know. How bad do you want it, Ivy girl?"

"Don't call me that." Ivy had gone pale. That was Piscary's pet name for her, and she hated it. My scar started to tingle, and I clenched my jaw, refusing to let the tendrils of feeling slip any deeper in me. Skimmer must have noticed my panicked expression.

"Feels good, doesn't it?" she said coquettishly. "Like a lover's long-absent touch. If you knew how it was hitting Ivy in this little tiny locked room, you'd be scared shitless."

In a surge of pique, the vampire rose. I took an involuntary step back before I could stop myself. This was so not good. I think they'd bent the rules and let me in here hoping I'd get killed, thus ending the problem of what to do with Rachel Morgan.

Ivy's stance stiffened. "You said you'd tell me who visited Piscary."

"But I didn't promise . . ."

Ivy's face became closed. "Let's go," she said, her tone crisp as she spun to the door.

"Wait," Skimmer said petulantly, and Ivy halted. There'd been panic in Skimmer's voice, but instead of making me feel better, my tension ratcheted higher. This was so not safe.

Skimmer came forward, to take the middle of the room, and Ivy stood almost in front of me with her hands on her hips. "I can't give you anything, Skimmer," my roommate said. "You killed Piscary. That was a mistake."

"He treated you like shit!" Skimmer exclaimed.

Ivy was calm and sedate. "He was still important to me. I loved him."

"You hated him!"

"I loved him, too." Ivy shook her head, making the tips of her hair shift. "If you're not going to tell me who visited him off the lists, then we're done."

Again Ivy turned her back on Skimmer. She took my arm and started me to the door. *We're leaving?*

"Ivy likes her new toy," Skimmer said bitterly. "She doesn't want to play with her old dolls anymore."

I didn't think we were going to get anything out of Skimmer, but Ivy stopped. Her head was down as she gathered her thoughts, and slowly she spun around to the angry, frustrated vampire. "You were never a toy," she whispered, pleading for understanding.

"No, but you were." Skimmer's confidence flowed back, and she stood before us tall and proud. "Once. When we first met. I turned you back into a person."

Her eyes were black again, and my scars, both visible and hidden beneath my perfect skin, were tingling. Backing up, I found the wall. I felt safer, a false security.

Skimmer moved forward as I moved back, and the woman stopped right before Ivy. "I want you to hurt, Ivy," she breathed. "I want restitution for what you did to me."

"I didn't do anything to you."

"That's the point, love," Skimmer said, hitting Kisten's accent perfectly.

Ivy took a breath and held it, frozen as Skimmer started circling her. "You aren't going to have one good thing in your life," the smaller vampire said, and I knew she was talking about me. "Not one. And I'm going to take her from you. Know how?"

"If you touch her," Ivy threatened, and Skimmer laughed.

"No, silly Ivy girl. I'm better than that. You're going to do it for me."

I didn't get it. Skimmer had already tried to warn me off Ivy, and it hadn't worked. There wasn't anything she could do, but as the slinky woman wound herself more tightly around Ivy, I wondered what the intelligent vamp was thinking.

The satisfied noise coming from deep within her set my scars warming in memory. Her motions sultry and slow, Skimmer stopped, facing me, with Ivy between us, draping her arms around Ivy's neck. Ivy didn't move, frozen, and my gut tightened. "You want to know who visited Piscary?" Skimmer asked, her eyes flicking over Ivy's shoulder to me. "Bite me."

My face went cold. I didn't think she meant it in the negative sense.

"Right now," the small woman said, "in front of your new girlfriend. Show her the blood, the savagery, the monster you really are."

I took a breath and held it. I knew how ugly Ivy could be. I didn't want to see it again.

"I told you," Ivy whispered. "I'm not practicing anymore."

A surge of panic rose through me, and I jerked from the wall. "Since when?" I exclaimed, pretty much ignored. "I want you to practice. God, Ivy, it's who you are."

Skimmer just smiled, showing a slip of fang. "But it's not who she wants to be." Watching me, she played with the hair behind Ivy's ears until my blood pounded in anger. She was toying with Ivy, and I could do nothing. Ivy couldn't move, couldn't bring herself to pull away. Skimmer was in complete control.

"I want you to bite me," Skimmer said, "or you get—nothing."

Ivy's hands, fisted at her sides, trembled. "Why are you doing this to me?"

Her eyes fixing on me, Skimmer wound even more tightly against Ivy, kissing her neck. "Please?" she whispered, soft and petulant. "It's been ages, Ivy. And you're the best. I'd kill for you."

I pressed into the wall, wanting to escape. Skimmer put her mouth on an old scar under Ivy's ear, and a rush of remembered ecstasy rose through me at Ivy's tormented intake of breath.

"Don't do this," Ivy whispered, her hands rising to take Skimmer's elbows, but she couldn't push her away. It was too much. I knew it felt too good, and I leaned against the wall, unable to look away as the pheromones lit through my own scars and dove to my groin.

"I'm not *making* you do anything," Skimmer said. "You *want* to do this. How bad do you want to know who killed that bastard Kisten? How much did you love him? Was it real? Or was he just another one of your toys?"

I clenched my jaw harder. My neck was flaming, sending tendrils of promised ecstasy down my long muscles, making them tremble. "That's not fair," I managed. "Stop it."

Skimmer moved to Ivy's earlobe. "Life seldom is," she said, and I watched, fixated, as she bit down gently on Ivy's lobe, her white teeth on Ivy's skin. "Push me away," Skimmer whispered into her ear. "You can't do it. You're a monster, my sweet, and only I will love you. Little Bo Peep will lose her sheep if the sheep can see inside her. You'll be all alone, Ivy. And I'm the only one who loves you."

I exhaled, but the vampire scent I pulled in after it only made things worse. My eyes closed and I held myself, almost rocking with the pain of not wanting to be here. Too late I saw Skimmer's plan. She was going to drive Ivy into biting her, thinking if I saw Ivy rip open Skimmer's throat in a release of blood lust that I'd abandon her. Or if it turned into sex, the same result. This was ugly. It wasn't love, it was manipulation, using Ivy's instincts against her will. And Ivy couldn't stop it.

The soft sounds of Skimmer coaxing Ivy made my stomach clench as private moments from their past were laid out before me. My focus went blurry as I tried to divorce myself from it, but the combination of my fear and the vampire pheromones ripped through the barriers my mind had made, and with the suddenness of a slap, a memory of Kisten surfaced.

I gasped, holding my breath as I felt my face go blank. Slowly I slid down the wall until I found a corner. It was a memory not of Kisten, but of his killer, one so close to what Skimmer was doing to Ivy that it had triggered a memory of my own struggle.

Oh God, I thought as I clenched my eyes, trying to keep the memory from growing on itself, but I couldn't . . . stop it, and as I sat, my knees to my chin, I remembered.

Kisten's killer tried to blood-rape me, exactly like Skimmer is trying to do to Ivy. Breath held, I put a hand to my neck as the memory of him playing on my scar slithered into my conscious mind. I remembered him holding me against the wall, bespelling me. I remembered the waves of passion he sent through me with only the lightest of touches, passion mixed with loathing, disgust, and desire. His fingers had been rough and aggressive, and I had been confused. The sound of Ivy's ragged panting as she struggled to say no ignited a memory of me doing the same. They were so familiar, so god-awful familiar.

"No," Ivy whispered, and I felt my own lips form the word. I had said no, too, and then I had begged him to bite me, hating myself as I writhed for it. I could almost feel the boat rocking as I recalled standing with my back to the wall, my hands clenched upon him, as they were clenched about my knees right now. Tears started. I had begged for it, just as Ivy was about to.

And Kisten, I remembered, *hadn't let me.* In my thoughts, I had a vision of Kisten, confused and not himself, knocking us apart so I could regain my will. He had done it knowing the other vampire would end his life a second time, but he had loved me so deeply that just the shadow memory of it had broken past his first death and he had made the sacrifice.

Anger burned through my misery, driving the Skimmer-and-Ivy-induced, pulse-pounding ecstasy deep, where I could see beyond it. Head up, I wiped the tears away, wishing I could do the same for my fragmented memory, but it was there now, and I'd never forget. I focused on Skimmer and Ivy, heart breaking at what Ivy had to suffer simply because of who she was, her vulnerabilities tied closely to her strengths. Kisten had saved me. I could do no less for Ivy.

Ivy was trembling, her lips parted and her eyes closed as she forgot how to say no, tasting the sweetness she couldn't refuse. Victory was in Skimmer's face as she nuzzled Ivy's neck, and her eyes were black with the power she had over Ivy, taking herself higher by dragging Ivy down to her swill.

My teeth clenched, and the remembered scent of damp cement spilled through my memory. I staggered to my feet, and it was as if I could taste cold, dry iron on my tongue. I strode forward, making my hands into fists as the memory of running my hands through Kisten's killer's short black hair filled me.

Skimmer gasped and arched into Ivy, encouraging her, blind to me coming at her.

It was almost too late. Ivy's fangs were wet, glistening, and a flash of remembered heat sparked through me at the memory of them sliding cleanly into me, mixing pleasure and pain in an unreal surge of adrenaline and endorphins. Shaking, I took a breath.

"I'm sorry, Ivy," I whispered, then punched her in the gut.

Ivy's breath whooshed out. Hands on her middle, she stumbled, struggling to breathe.

"You bitch!" Skimmer screamed, too shocked to move as

the expected rush of a bite had been ripped from her. If I had hit her, she would have instinctively reacted and I'd probably be dead. Even dying, Kisten had taught me one more lesson. He had gone after his murderer, and it had cost him his undead existence. He had died for me. *He had died for me.*

Ivy took in an ugly gasp of breath. I spared her a glance, then fell into a defensive stance between them. "Leave Ivy alone."

Skimmer screamed in frustration, her eyes black and her hands cramped into claws, but I had knocked her on her butt once before, and she knew I could take her.

"Ivy?" I called, risking a glance back to see that she was still lost in the throes of blood lust even as she struggled for air. Crap on toast. I hadn't expected to have to handle both of them at once. "Ivy!" I shouted, angling to get her out from behind me yet keeping an eye on Skimmer, too. "Look at me. Look at me! Who do you want to be tomorrow?"

Her hands still on her middle, Ivy peered at me from around the curtain of her hair. She got one clean breath, then another. To my right, Skimmer started shaking in frustration. Ivy looked at her, her face horrified.

"Who do you want to be tomorrow?" I asked again, seeing her awareness return. "You haven't lost anything, Ivy. It's okay. You didn't lose. You're still the same."

She blinked, and a rim of brown showed about her pupils. "Oh my God," Ivy whispered, then straightened. "You sorry little . . . vampire!" she shouted. "How could you do that to me!"

Ivy took three steps, and I got between them. Behind me, Skimmer was pressed into a corner in fear. "Ivy, don't!" I demanded.

Her eyes were still black, the fear heavy that she'd almost lost herself, to be ruled by her instincts, and a shiver lifted through me. "Let it go," I said, and her jaw unclenched. My breath slipped from me in relief, and I inhaled. She smelled delicious when she was pissed.

Skimmer saw Ivy regain her will, and knowing that I'd given it to her, something in her broke. "She's mine!" the vampire shouted, and she leapt, fangs bared and snarling.

I ducked, and I heard a soft "Ooff." Skimmer fell to the floor beside me in a crumpled heap. I looked up at Ivy from my crouch. Pain and betrayal had replaced her hunger, and deeper than that, gratitude.

"You can't have her!" Skimmer was crying, pushing into a folded ball of misery. "She's mine. She's mine! I'll kill you. I'll kill you just like I killed Piscary!"

Ivy extended a shaking hand to help me rise. "Are you okay?"

I looked up at her, standing between me and a jealous death. Her eyes were mostly brown, the pain at what was happening mirrored in her gaze, familiar. I turned to Skimmer, sobbing and scared. Taking a shallow breath, I put my hand into Ivy's and let her help me up. "Yes," I whispered as I stumbled until I found my balance. I didn't feel so good.

Ivy wouldn't look at Skimmer. "I think we should go."

She moved to the door, and I glanced at Skimmer. "We didn't get what we came for."

"I don't care."

Ivy tapped on the door, and when that brought Miltast, though the screams hadn't, Skimmer rallied. "Bitch!" she shouted, lunging at me again. Ivy was ready, and Skimmer ran right into Ivy's stiff-armed palm. My pulse hammered at how fast it had been.

Gasping, Skimmer fell back. Her hands covered her face, but blood leaked from her nose. Crying now in earnest, the small vampire collapsed onto the couch. Her back was to us, and as I almost ran through the open door, Ivy hesitated. I watched from the hall as she put a loving hand on Skimmer's shoulder.

"I'm sorry," I heard her whisper. "I loved you, but I can't do this anymore."

Skimmer hunched deeper. "I'll kill her," she sobbed. "If you stay with her, I'll kill her."

A chill ran through me. Not at her words, but at the love in Ivy's arms as she curved them around Skimmer. "No, you won't. Rachel isn't the one who showed me I deserved to be loved. You did. Tell me who came to visit Piscary."

"Get out," Skimmer sobbed, pushing weakly at Ivy. Blood stained her white jumpsuit, and Miltast stiffened upon seeing it.

"Who visited Piscary off the lists?" Ivy insisted.

Skimmer's shaking stopped as she gave up. "No one but Kisten came," she said, her high voice bland. "Once a week, three days after you. No one else."

I exhaled, and a sorry-assed depression took hold. Nothing. We had gotten nothing.

"I loved you, Ivy," Skimmer whispered in a dead voice. "Get out. Don't come back."

Ivy stood, her head bowed. Steadying herself, she turned and strode to the door, passing me in a wash of sour, unhappy-vampire incense. Boots clacking on the hard floor, she continued down the hallway alone.

I jumped to follow. I heard Miltast lock the door and then his booted steps. I caught up to Ivy at the locked door where we waited for Miltast. "Are you all right?" I questioned, not knowing what she was feeling.

"She'll be okay," Ivy said, jaw tight and not looking at me.

Miltast fumbled for the door lock, swiping his card and falling back when Ivy pushed through it ahead of him. "I can't believe you didn't get bitten," he said in apparent awe.

My eyes narrowed and I decided that they'd let me in there expecting me to come out hurt or dead. He was a white witch who had the government's blessing to do black magic. And if I made one wrong move, he'd react. Disgusted, I turned on my heel and followed Ivy.

I could hear his steps slow behind me, and my skin prickled. I finally caught up with her at the first door. The old woman at the spell checker, standing up and getting the checkout forms ready, seemed surprised to see us.

"Ivy," I said as we waited for Miltast to catch up, her head down and silent. "I'm sorry."

Finally her stoic expression cracked and she looked at me, unshed tears glinting. "I didn't know she was going to do that," she said. "Thank you for hitting me. I . . . couldn't say no. Damn it, I couldn't. I thought—"

She cut her thought short when Miltast slid the glass door aside. The air wasn't much fresher, but I pulled it in deep as I crossed into the middle ground, trying to rid myself of the accumulated vampire pheromones. Sighing, I put a hand to my neck and let it drop. "You're not serious about going on a blood fast," I asked as I handed Miltast my badge.

Ivy's fingers shook as she peeled off her name tag and handed it to the officer. "I was thinking about it," she said evenly.

Even Miltast knew it was a bad idea, and he eyed me as we signed our forms again and headed to the final door. If she was on a blood fast, living with her was going to be a lot harder.

"What a waste of time," Ivy said softly as we passed back through the spell checker and the woman gave us our stuff; but it hadn't been, and my pulse quickened. I remembered. I had remembered a lot. Ignoring my shaky knees, I wound my scarf around my neck, and with my bag under my arm, I headed for the double glass doors and the brutal but honest chill of the night. Milktoast and his friend had been privy to too much of our drama already.

"Actually," I said as I wrangled my gloves on while Ivy held the door open for me, "it wasn't a waste. Seeing you and Skimmer . . . I remembered something."

Ivy stopped dead in her tracks, pulling me to a halt in a puddle of light just outside. It seemed to have gotten colder in the hour we'd been inside, and the night air cut into my lungs like a knife, making my thoughts crystal clear after the heated confusion behind the glass walls. I pulled the dry air, smelling of snow and exhaust, in deep, relishing it and seeing the past moments with a clearer eye.

"Kisten—" I said, warming, then flushed. God, this was hard, and I closed my eyes to keep them from filling. Maybe I could say it if I couldn't see her. "Kisten's killer had dry hands," I said. "Rough. He smelled like damp cement, and his fingertips tasted of cold iron." I knew this because I'd had them in my mouth. *God help me, I had begged him to bite me.*

My jaw clenched, and I forced it to relax as I opened my eyes. "Kisten was dead," I said as the snow started to show on Ivy's black-clad shoulder. "I think it was an accident. His killer hadn't touched his blood yet, and he was really mad about that. . . . So he was going to make me his shadow instead. He . . . he was making me beg for it." I took a shaky breath. If I didn't tell her now, I might not ever. "He was playing on my scar to make me beg him to bite me. Kisten stopped him. He knew it might end with him dead twice, but he did it anyway."

Ivy's head dropped, and she rubbed her forehead.

"I'm sorry," I said, not knowing why. "He let himself be killed again because he loved me."

The light glistened on Ivy's tear-wet eyes when she looked up. "But he couldn't remember why he loved you, could he?"

I shook my head when a remembered feeling of mental pain drifted up. "No, he couldn't."

Ivy silently took that in. Deep in her shadowed eyes I could see her wish that I might find a way to save her from that fate. "I don't want to live not remembering why I love," she finally said, her face pallid as she looked ahead to her own soul death.

"I'm sorry, Ivy," I whispered as I fell into step beside her while we headed for my vehicle.

"It's what we are," she said stoically.

But it wasn't who she wanted to be.

Twenty-two

Ivy's head was down as we walked into the parking lot, aiming for my red convertible under a distant security light. Snow had covered all but the warm cars, and the world was white and black. "I'm sorry," she said, not looking at me. "I could have gotten you killed in there."

I breathed in another lungful of cold air to try to clear my head. "I'm fine. You didn't."

"I could have." She slowed to let me go first between two cars, looking at me with her face deceptively placid. "Your aura was compromised and you can't make a circle. I'm sorry. Asking you to do that when you're not well was a mistake. They were expecting you to die in there, or worse."

Linking my arm in hers, I pulled her after me, angling for the shortest path to my car. I could see it, its bright red paint looking gray in the streetlight and the snow sticking only to the cooler roof. "I guess we fooled them, huh?"

Ivy stiffened, but I wouldn't let her pull out of my grip in the narrow passage. If I didn't touch her, she wouldn't believe that she was worth the emotional baggage she brought to both our lives. "I'm fine," I said, becoming serious. "I wanted to know who killed Kisten, too. Now we know more." *Not exactly how I would have chosen it, but okay.* "Don't worry about it."

Ivy predictably pulled out of my grip the moment we came out from between the two cars, glancing over her shoulder through the snow to the quiet building. "I'm not going to be that person anymore," she said, and my eyes widened when she wiped her eyes with the back of a gloved hand to show a glint of moisture in the security light. "I can't do this," she whispered, clearly shaken to her core. "Rachel, I'm sorry. I understand that I can't bite you again. I'm sorry I ever tried. You're better than that, and I'm bringing you down."

"You are the strongest person I know!" I protested, but she shook her head, wiping her eyes again. She was down to the bare bones of herself. Skimmer had shaken her to her core.

"Anyone I once called a friend wouldn't have been able to do what you did in there," she said, chin trembling. "Or if they did break us apart, it would have been to take Skimmer's place. I don't want to be that person, and I won't be. I'm off blood. Completely."

My eyes widened, and I felt a slip of fear. Sensing it, Ivy's jaw clenched and she strode away. "Wait, Ivy. That's not necessarily a good idea," I called after her.

"Piscary is dead, I can be who I want," she said over her shoulder.

"But you're a vampire," I protested as I followed, worried. "It's what you are!"

She stopped, turning to stare at me, and I came to a halt, a car between us.

"Look, I'm not saying I want you to bite me," I said, gesturing. "But I've lived with you while you're on a blood fast, and the more you try to be what you aren't, the more confused you get and the harder it is to live with you."

Ivy's mouth opened. Betrayal shone in her eyes. "Abstinence is all I've got, Rachel." Turning, she paced to the car, a shadow of black among the gray and white of falling snow.

"Nice one, Rache," I muttered, thinking there had to be a better way to have said that. Hands jammed into my pockets, I slowly pushed myself into motion. The ride home ought to be swell. There was only so much a little green cardboard tree could do. Ivy on a blood fast was not fun, but she was right to be pissed at me. How could I not support her desire to be who she wanted to be? I did support her, but going on a blood fast wasn't the answer. She needed to break the cycle. She had to end the addiction completely. There had to be something in Al's books for this. *Or maybe Trent . . .*

My bag smacked the taillight of the car I was passing, and I followed Ivy's footprints into the frozen slush of the aisle. The sliding sound of a van's door opening brought my head up. Ten feet from my car, a man lurched out of a white minivan beside Ivy. She wasn't paying attention, her head down and looking vulnerable. *Shit.*

"Ivy!" I exclaimed, terrified by the glint of a pistol in his hand, but it was too late. The man shoved her, and she was pushed into the side of a nearby SUV parked half a car away. "Hey!" I shouted, but then I spun at the soft sound of snow compacting beside me. My instinctive crouch put me eye to eye with Mia.

"Witch," she said, lips blue with cold, and then she reached out.

Adrenaline pounded, and I flung myself backward, my right foot slipping out from under me when I hit the bumper of the car I'd just passed. I went down, arms flailing and purse falling from me. The banshee grabbed my wrist, where my glove and coat parted, and I froze, kneeling before her. Her baby had almost killed me. *Shit, shit, shit!*

Mia's hood had fallen back, and her eyes were wisps of blue under the spotlights. Cold fingers encircling my wrist, she leaned closer. "Who did you talk to today?" she asked, her voice precise and angry.

Heart pounding, I looked past her. Ivy had her face against the window of the SUV, her arm twisted and a gun to her head. There was a baby car seat in the open van, and the happy babble of a baby drifted out. *Why in* hell *hadn't I brought my splat gun?* "You're wanted for questioning," I said, thinking one swift kick and she'd be off me. "If you come in, it will look good."

The words sounded stupid the moment they left my mouth, and Mia squinted, making the skin around her eyes tighten. "You think I care?" she said imperially. "Who did you talk to?"

I tensed to smack her, and Mia's eyes, almost white in the dim light, dilated to pupil black. My breath hissed in, and I almost collapsed. A scintillating flood tingled through me, rising up my arm. Cold followed close behind it, and the feeling of being pulled inside out turned my stomach. Like a puppet with cut strings, I sagged, my arm stretched out with my wrist in Mia's grip.

"S-stop," I stammered, head bowed as I struggled to just breathe. Damn it, what was I doing? I never should have taken this case. She was a freaking predator. A top-of-the-line, ancient predator, like an alligator. As I knelt there, going cold and thick, I could feel myself dying in stages, watching, and unable to stop it.

I gasped as the pulling sensation quit. Warmth eased back, but it was less, settling like a sloshing tub over my soul. Haggard, I brought my head up to find Mia's blue eyes waiting. They were cold and uncaring. Reptile eyes. Behind her, Ivy watched. Her cheek was against the tall vehicle, and her jaw was clenched, making her look helpless, frustrated, and really mad. We were in front of a freaking jail—the woman had enough guts to rule the world. Maybe she thought she already did.

"Someone is following me," Mia asked coldly. "Who did you talk to?"

My knee had gone wet, and my arm hurt. An ache was spreading from it to my back. Mia withdrew a step, drawing me into the slush-rutted aisle, and I rose to my feet like a pull toy. Her other hand went around my throat, her wedding band catching the light. "Wait," I blurted in panic when the first threat of my aura leaving lifted through me again.

Seeing my understanding, Mia smiled. She was beautiful in the falling snow, smaller than me, but cold—so cold and uncaring. "That's *me* taking your life, witch," she said, snow melting on her upturned face. "The more you struggle, the stronger I am. Who did you talk to? Someone is following me. Tell me or you die right here."

A cold sweat broke out on me. The woman was like a slip-knot. I was a rabbit in a raptor's talons.

"Rachel, just tell her!" Ivy shouted, then grunted when Remus encouraged her to keep her mouth shut.

"Don't hurt her!" I called out, eyes fixed on Ivy, helpless against the SUV. My fear grew worse when I remembered what Remus had done to Glenn. *Son of a bitch. Why shouldn't I tell Mia?* I licked my lips, and Mia tightened her grip. A soft ache pulled through me, and I said, "A banshee named Ms. Walker. It was another banshee, from the west."

Mia's eyes widened, and her grip almost fell away. "In my city? That . . . *thing* is in my city?" she said, her high voice carrying a shocking amount of hatred. Her eyes had gone vampire black—clear in the lights from the parking lot—and I wondered if the two species were related.

"I think she's going to kill you for Holly," I said, wondering if a quick palm thrust to her chin while she was distracted might break me free, but I was too scared to try. She didn't have to touch me to take my aura. "You and Remus both. Your only chance to keep her is to come in now. The FIB will take her temporarily, but you'll get her back. Let me go." *Please, let me go.*

Her focus returned to me, hatred making her look like a wronged queen. "You brought The Walker here," the slight woman accused, and I felt myself go weak, sparkles showing at the edges of my sight. "You're working with her!"

"I didn't bring her here!" I cried, and I heard Ivy grunt in pain. "You did," I panted. *Damn it, how do I get into these situations? And don't they monitor their parking lot?* "She heard I survived a banshee attack and thought it was because Holly had gained control. I told Ms. Walker it wasn't Holly but the dark banshee tear in my pocket, but she still wants Holly.

Mia, I can help you if you let me go." *Though only God knows why I'm doing this. Survival?*

Mia's breath steamed as she gauged my words. In a quick burst of motion, she let go of my throat and took two steps away. I gasped and fell back against the trunk. Weight supported on an elbow, I held a hand to my throat and looked at the small woman, trying to decide how much aura I had left. It didn't feel like a lot, but I was able to stand up and move without becoming dizzy. She didn't need to touch me to kill me, but at least I had some room now.

Behind her, Remus took the gun from Ivy's head and backed up out of her reach. His weapon was still pointed at her, though. I watched Ivy visually measure the distance between them, and knowing the gun would beat her, she fell into a tense pose. Behind Remus, Holly gurgled, excited by the emotions reaching her.

Mia stood in the falling snow, disgust clear in her expression. "I would have stayed to make sure you were dead if I'd known The Walker would find out about Holly."

"We all make mistakes," I said, knees weak. "You mean Ms. Walker?"

"The Walker," she corrected me. I could almost hear the capital letters, and Mia's disgust grew. "She's an assassin who kills with the grace of a falling log. If she's east of the Mississippi, in *my* city, your assessment that she wants Holly is correct." Her delicate jaw clenched. "She won't have her. Holly is special. She's going to give us back our power, and I'm not going to let that bitch take the credit."

The whining complaint of a tired Chevy trying to start in the snow broke the stillness. At the far end of the lot, a pair of headlights lit up and a big engine roared to life. Suddenly nervous, Remus called out, "Mia?"

I shook my head, trembling. The cold was eddying about my feet, telling me Mia was still sucking in my aura, but at least she wasn't actively taking it. "I'm sorry, Mia," I whispered as Holly started fussing in the open van. "We know it's

Remus who's special, not Holly. We know it's a wish that lets him hold her. Ms. Walker doesn't care. She wants your daughter, and she's going to kill you to get her."

Ivy shifted from foot to foot, probably blaming herself. No one moved as the car drove past, two aisles over, headed for the exit. An idle thought drifted through me. Why hadn't I seen anyone come out of the building? Remus, too, wasn't liking it. "Mia . . . ," he prompted, the security light showing his worried features.

Mia watched the car's taillights as they hesitated at the street, then slowly drove away. The banshee brought her attention back to me, her expression shifting to show an inner excitement. "Holly *is* special," she insisted. "And you're going to make sure I keep my daughter, Rachel Morgan."

"Why would I help you?" I said dryly. "You're a freaking parasite."

"Predator, not parasite, and you need me," she said, reaching out.

"No!" I cried out, backpedaling until I found the car behind me again. Panic grew at the soft pop of a gun, muffled in the snow. "Ivy!" I shouted, then jerked when Mia found my throat again. "What have you done?" I whispered, seeing her inches away.

"Don't move," she demanded, eyes wild. "Or Remus will kill her."

She's alive? I squirmed, and my energy left me. I didn't care. "Ivy," I panted. "I can't see her. Let me see her, you cold bitch!"

Mia's face grew ugly, but from behind her I heard Ivy say, "I'm okay!" followed by a soft "Ow," and then an aggressive "Hurt her, and you'll find yourself worse than dead, human!"

Mia's cold fingers never leaving my throat, she sent her gaze to the van, where Holly was now crying. My heart pounded when her attention returned to me. Hand still around my neck, she reached out, her palm coming for my forehead. "Don't," I pleaded, thinking she was going to kill me. "Please, don't!"

Smiling wickedly, Mia put her cold hand to my cheek in an almost loving gesture. "This is why you're going to help me, witch. This is what I can give you."

Tiny pinpricks exploded in my cheek, and I gasped, stiffening, as I reached for the car behind me. Warmth was spilling into me, familiar and soothing. It was my aura returning, filling the cracks and making me whole. It spilled in with the pain of a healing scab, and my eyes flashed wide as I looked into Mia's clear blue ones. I exhaled, thinking it sounded like a sob, and I held my next breath so I could taste the incoming energy better. She was giving it back. The energy wasn't coming from a ley line—it was coming right from her soul. She was giving me back my life's energy. *Why?*

The tingles quit with a surprising suddenness, and I realized that I was pressed up against a car in a cold parking lot, a small woman holding me hostage with the power of my soul.

Mia made a fist of her hand and backed up, hunched over and looking tired. "That's what Holly taught me," she said proudly. "Because her father cannot be harmed by a banshee, Holly was born knowing how to push energy into a person, not just take it. I learned by example."

"So?" I said, still not understanding. God, it felt good, and I suddenly realized I could tap a line. Relief spilled into me as I did, taking in a huge amount of ley line force, spindling it in my head. At the end of the lot, a car pulled in, its lights dim in the falling snow. Moving slowly, it crept down the aisles, looking for a space.

"Mia?" Remus called, clearly nervous.

"Be still," the woman said. "I'm impressing upon the witch the reason she's going to convince the FIB to back off." She wore a smile when she turned back to me, but it was the smile of someone who thinks they control you, and my mood hardened. "I've fed extremely well these last few months," Mia said with an unremorseful satisfaction. "Humans are stupid, trusting animals, and if you give a little, they think you love them, and then it's a simple matter of taking what they give you. Natural causes," she said coyly, "heart attack, brain aneurysm, simple fatigue. We have fasted for forty years since the Turn, but Holly will give us back our strength, the cunning to take what we want with impunity instead of this thin tracing the law allows us. Those who protest will be silenced. The I.S. knows it. I'm charging you to impress upon the FIB the error of their thinking."

Behind her, Ivy shook with anger, Remus's hold tight on her. "You monster," she seethed. "You're making them think you love them, then killing them? That's not why I gave you the wish!"

"Shut up," Remus said, and Ivy grunted in pain. My face paled and the cold night seemed darker. That's how she had been feeding herself and her child. Damn it, how were we supposed to tell the banshee-induced deaths from the natural ones? "You think I'm going to help you?" I said, appalled. "Are you nuts?"

The car drove slowly past, following the path of the one that had just left, tracks upon tracks, and my skin started to tingle. It was going too slowly. And it looked, no, *sounded* familiar. Early model, dripping rust. It turned at the end of the lot, and the lights shown on Ivy and Remus. In the van, Holly cried, her hands reaching up for someone.

"Mia!" Remus shouted. "We have to go!"

"Help me is exactly what you're going to do," Mia said, and a second wave of warmth filled me as she moved closer. "Tell the FIB I'm gone. Tell them aliens came down and abducted me. I don't care, but if they don't leave me alone, I'll kill you, right here if need be, then start on that man's son, and move on from there."

"Touch Glenn, and you'll find yourself dead!" Ivy snarled, and Mia eyed her in disgust.

"Don't presume to threaten me," she said condescendingly. "I watched your Piscary set foot in my city, and I watched him buried in it. Keep that in mind."

I shook my head. "I won't help you, Mia. If you don't come

in, you and your daughter will be forever living outside society and on the run."

Mia's pale eyebrows rose. "Witch, I made this society. If they touch me, I won't live outside it. I'll bring it down."

I felt the strength of the line in me, and it made me bold. "Then you can go to hell."

A sigh lifted through Mia. She turned to Remus, who was fidgeting, wanting to leave. "You can lead a pig to water," she said, then turned back to me. "I'll ask the vampire to pass on my words, then."

My breath caught as I realized she was going to kill me. "Wait!"

Panicked, I scrambled back among the cars, but she followed. Still not touching me, she reached out a hand, and eyes glistening in rapture, she ripped my aura away. Everything she had given me, she took back.

Mouth open, I fell to my knees as the ley line in me became a ribbon of fire, and screaming, I shoved it at her, unable to hold it anymore. Mia swore delicately, and I had a moment of respite, but then cold avalanched in behind it, and my arms and legs went numb. The force of the line hadn't slowed her at all. She was taking my aura slowly, painstakingly, making me suffer so there would be more to feast on.

Ivy was shouting, a savage sound against Holly's piercing cries. Behind it was the roar of a car. I couldn't think, kneeling on the snow as Mia stripped me bare. I looked up as a brilliant white light grew. *I'm dying,* I thought, and the light shifted and the car that was making it smashed into the front corner of the van.

Metal groaned and plastic shattered. Mia's attention was diverted, and the pain of my aura being ripped from me vanished. I looked up, on my hands and knees, sucking in air as if it might coat my soul. "Look out!" I called in warning as the van slid on the ice, toward Ivy. Crap, it was going to pin her between it and the SUV.

Ivy jumped straight up, landing on the hood of the SUV.

Remus dropped to roll under it. Holly howled as the van jolted to a halt. In the aisle, an ugly green, rusty Chevy steamed. Radiator fluid poured out, but the engine still ran. The thing probably weighed more than the van and the SUV put together and would take an atomic bomb to kill.

"Holly!" Mia screamed, running to her daughter.

Pulling myself up to lean against the car, I stared as Tom emerged from the Chevy. *Son of a bitch!* It hadn't been Ms. Walker Mia had felt following her, it had been Tom.

With an ugly snarl, Ivy launched herself from the top of the SUV, landing on Mia.

"God, no," I whispered. I was shaky, hardly able to walk, and I staggered forward. Mia had a grip on Ivy's throat, her face savage as she started to kill her. The light from one head-lamp threw everything into a stark light. Ivy was fighting back, teeth shining as she struggled.

The harsh sound of Holly screaming continued, and my eyes jerked to Remus and Tom. The ley line witch's fist was smothered in a purple haze, but the incensed man had grabbed it and squeezed until Tom screamed in pain. Giving him a solid kick in parting, Remus left Tom kneeling over his broken hand. I moved, and Remus's head swung up to me. Black eyes fixed me where I was, warning me to not move. They were the eyes of a wolf, and I froze. He turned away. From the jail, a loud claxon started hooting, and the lot was suddenly bathed in a harsh glow of blue krypton bulbs. *Where in hell have they been?*

Calm and soothing, the mass murderer coolly got his screaming child from the ruined van. Singing a lullaby, he looked to his wife.

"Ivy," I breathed, seeing her down and unmoving. Mia was kneeling beside her with her back to me, her blue coat spread, looking like the wings of a bird covering her prey. Staggering, I started for them, yelling, "Get away from her!"

Remus got there first, and with one hand, he yanked Mia up.

"Let me go!" the woman yelled, fighting him, but he dragged her to Tom's running car, opening the passenger-side door and nearly throwing her in. Holly's crying competed with the jail's alarm system, but her cries became faint when Remus handed her to Mia and slammed the door. Giving me a sour look, he paced to the other side and got in. The engine roared. Tom rolled out of the way as Remus gunned it, headed for the road. Frozen slush pelted us, and they were gone.

Feeling as if my heart was going to explode, I got to Ivy, and fell to kneel in the pressed snow. "Oh my God, Ivy. Ivy!" I exclaimed, turning her over and pulling her upright, against me. Her head lolled, and her eyes were shut. Her skin was pale, and her hair was in her face. "Don't you leave me, Ivy! I can't live with you being dead!" I shouted. "Ivy, you hear me?"

Oh God. Please no. Why do I have to live like this?

Tears were falling from me, and I choked back a sob when her eyes opened. They were brown, and I rejoiced. She wasn't dead, or undead, or whatever. White and pale, she looked up at me, eyes glassy and not seeing. In her grip was a faded purple ribbon with a coin laced on it. Her fingers gripped it as if it was life itself, holding on with a white-knuckled strength. "I got it back," she rasped, victory in her vacant gaze. "She doesn't deserve love."

The building behind us was still making that awful noise, and I could hear men coming this way. Ivy took a breath, then another. "I need . . . Rachel?" she whispered, and then her focus on me cleared. "Shit," she breathed, and I held her closer, rocking her and knowing she was still alive. She hadn't died, and I wasn't holding an undead.

"You're going to be all right," I said, not knowing if it was the truth. She looked so pale.

"I'm not. I have to have it," Ivy said, and I looked at her, seeing the tears making tracks down her face and her fangs wet with saliva. It was obvious what she was talking about. Blood. She needed blood. Vampires were the banshee's closest relative, and they had a way to replenish auras. They took them in when they fed. Ivy needed blood.

Unafraid, I pulled her farther up off the pavement, and she started to cry in earnest, knowing she couldn't be the person she wanted and mourning the loss of a dream. "I wanted to be clean, but I can't," she said as I rocked her. "Every time I try to be someone else, I fail. I need it," she said, eyes glowing black. "But not you. Not you," she begged even as her eyes started to dilate and her hunger took hold. "I'd rather die than have you give me your blood. I love you, Rachel. Don't give me your blood. Promise me—you won't give me your blood."

"You're going to be all right," I said, frantic. I could smell antifreeze from the busted Chevy, and the faint smell of hot engine was fading.

"Promise me," she said, trying to touch my face. "I don't want you to give me your blood. Promise me, damn it!"

Shit. I looked up, only now seeing the flashlights and the men behind them. My bag with my keys was across the aisle. "I promise."

There was a crunching of boots on ice, and from behind me came an authoritative "Ma'am, get away from the woman. Lie down and put your face on the pavement! Keep your fingers spread and where I can see them!"

Face wet with tears, I looked up and behind me into the bright security lights, seeing a big shadow behind it. "Go ahead and shoot me!" I screamed. "I'm not letting go of her!"

"Ma'am," the voice said, and the light dropped to Ivy, then back to me.

"She's been hurt!" I exclaimed. "I was just in your offices, you idiots. Check your security tapes. You know who I am. You watched the entire thing. You think I ran that jack-shit car into myself!"

"Ma'am—" he tried again.

I started to get up, dragging Ivy with me. "If you call me that one more time," I huffed, straining until I got her upright, leaning against the SUV.

"Down! Get down!" someone shouted.

A boom shifted the air, and I jerked Ivy closer, managing to keep both of us on our feet. The man with the light turned it toward the sound of the explosion. Men and women were shouting, and the guy with the light looked ticked off that he wasn't involved. A purplish green haze of Tom's aura covered a nearby decorated tree, and my stomach turned as the tree started to steam and dissolve. The holiday lights flickered and went out. *Holy crap! What had Al taught him?*

My keys were in my bag, three cars away. "Stay here," I told Ivy, and after seeing her leaning upright, under her own power, I started for my keys. "That's Tom Bansen," I said as I walked between the man and the sight of the melting tree. "He did this. You want answers, go talk to him. I'm in a city parking lot. You have no jurisdiction, and I'm leaving." I scooped up my bag and got out my keys. The lethal-amulet detector was a bright, shiny red. *No kidding.* "You want my ID?" I said as I headed back to Ivy. "It's in your file. Have a freaking nice day and a happy New Year!"

Shifting my shoulder under Ivy's arm, we started for my car. Her feet dragged through the puddle of antifreeze, and she was starting to pant. Leaving her leaning against the hood of my car, I opened it. She mumbled for her purse, and after helping her inside, I went back for it. I looked up at the click of a safety going off, but they couldn't shoot me if I was just walking away.

"Ma'am!" the man tried again, and my blood pressure spiked. But a second voice intruded.

"Let her go. She's been shunned."

A bitter sensation filled me, but no one stopped me. "Hold on, Ivy," I whispered as I got in my car and reached across to shut her door. "The hospital is right next door."

"Rynn Cormel," she said, eyes closed as tears coursed down her face. "Take me to Rynn. I don't care about him. He's just a vampire."

Just a vampire? I hesitated, then fumbled with the key

twice before I got it in the ignition and the car came to life. Around us, the security people were having fits. Apparently Tom had gotten away, and they didn't have the authority to detain me.

"Rynn," Ivy said, staring at me, her head propped up against the door. Her eyes were glassy, and hunger sent a shiver through me. It was starting to take hold. If not for her weakened state, she'd be having a much harder time.

"Okay," I said, sniffing back my tears. I knew how she felt. She didn't want to be this person, but to survive, she had to be. "I won't let him hurt you."

"Please hurry," she said, shutting her eyes as they turned a full, hungry, vampire black. Her long pianist's hand clenched on the door handle, and she pressed herself as far away from me as she could.

Lights on, I pulled out and headed for the exit. The speedometer crept upward, and I waited for a dizzy feeling, but it never came. Apparently Mia hadn't taken enough from me to affect my balance, but a quick tap on a ley line told me I was still compromised and I dropped it before I threw up from the pain.

"Call him." Ivy's voice sent a chill through me. It was low and sultry, in wide contrast to her weakened state. "Use my phone."

I was starting to see some traffic, and at a red light, I pulled her purse to me, finding her slim phone and opening it up. Five bars. *How come my phone never has five bars?* Eyeing the bright screen and the traffic light both, I scrolled through the numbers, then hit "RC."

My heart pounded, and as the phone rang, the light changed and I pulled out into a snow-rimmed street. I didn't get more than fifteen feet before the line clicked open and a cultured, interested voice said, "Yes, Ivy?"

Shit. I jiggled the phone closer, gunning the engine to make the next yellow light. "Ivy's been hurt," I said tersely. "She needs blood."

Rynn Cormel made an odd sound. "Then give it to her, Rachel."

Son of a bastard. "She doesn't want my blood!" I said, looking at her and seeing her in pain. "She wants you. I'm bringing her to you, but I don't know if she can make it." I wiped my eyes when the streetlights went blurry. "That damn banshee got her. You're going to keep her alive, or so help me, I'm going to kill you, Rynn Mathew Cormel. Don't mess with me on this. I mean it! I can't save her soul yet. I need more time."

I didn't care if I sounded like a demon, using all three of his names like that. Managing the icy roads, I heard the undead vampire take a slow breath he didn't need. "Take the I-75 bridge. We'll find you."

The phone clicked off, and I tossed it in the direction of Ivy's purse. Blinking furiously, I clamped my hands on the wheel and pushed down on the accelerator. Horns blew as I tore through town, but the FIB guys wouldn't stop me and the I.S. didn't care anymore.

"Hold on," I said through gritted teeth as I took a turn too fast, having to push on her shoulder to keep her from falling into me.

Ivy's eyes opened as my hand touched her, and fear plinked through me. "Hurry," she panted. "Rachel, I'd rather die than bite you now. Please hurry. I don't know how long I can stop myself. It hurts. Oh God . . . She took everything."

"It's going to be okay," I said as I saw a sign for bridge traffic. "He's coming. We're almost there."

She was silent, and then a ragged "Are you okay?" came out of her.

Astonished, I looked across the car. She was worried about me? "I'm fine," I said, beeping my horn to keep some guy from pulling out in front of me. He rocked to a halt, and after I swerved around him, I looked at her, brow furrowed. "Ivy, why did you do it? You should have let her go. She's a freaking banshee!"

"This was my fault," she panted, her eyes dropping to the coin, still clenched in her fist. "Mia, Remus, everything. It was my fault that Mia learned how to kill people with impunity. And she hurt you. I'll take care of this. You can't risk yourself anymore."

"You're going to take care of her alone?" I said, feeling distant and unreal inside. "This is as much my fault as yours. I gave you the wish in the first place. We're going to get her, Ivy, but not apart. We have to do it together." *Who am I kidding? It would take a demon to take down a banshee. But then again . . .*

She didn't say anything, but her expression behind the hunger was determined. I flicked the heater on, and a blast of warm air billowed out. In the distance, I saw the lights of an oncoming car flashing. Relief so strong it hurt washed through me. I could tell it was a Hummer by the spacing of the lights. It was them. It had to be. "I see them!" I exclaimed, and Ivy tried to smile. Her teeth were clenched and her eyes were wild, and it twisted my heart to see her red-rimmed, pain-filled eyes as she struggled.

Fumbling, I put on my own flashers and pulled into a fast-food place. Two cars pulled in behind me, black in the streetlight. I came to a halt, not slamming on the brakes, but close. Before I could put the car in park, two men were at Ivy's door. There was a crack of breaking metal, and the door swung open, the lock broken.

Vampire incense rolled into the car, and with a savage sound, Ivy lunged for the man stooping to pick her up. I turned away, tears falling. I heard a groan, and when I looked back, the second man with them was supporting the first as he carried Ivy back to the black Hummer. She was on his neck, blood slipping past her lips. The second man opened the door for them, and Ivy and the man she was clutching to her vanished inside. He turned to look at me, his expression unreadable, before he followed them in and closed the door.

The snow fell between us, and I sat there, my passenger-side door open, staring out my front window, hands on the wheel and crying. Ivy had to be all right. She had to be. *This is so messed up.*

A soft tap on my window jerked my attention away and I looked to see Rynn Cormel standing outside my closed door. His cashmere coat had the collar turned up against the snow and the hat on his head was just showing the first few flakes. He looked good standing there, but the memory of his callous treatment of me—me and Ivy, actually—was too new for me to be taken in. He was an animal, and now I understood what Ivy had meant when she'd said, "He's just a vampire."

Though wealthy, powerful, and attractive, he was nothing, not worth anyone's love or affection. I wouldn't allow Ivy to become like that.

Wiping my nose, I rolled down my window. I was numb inside.

Rynn Cormel bent over so our faces were closer. Seeing me in a state, he pulled a handkerchief from an inside pocket and handed it to me. "Why didn't you let her bite you instead of all this drama?" he said, his gaze flicking to the unmoving Hummer. "All she needs is blood."

Animal or no, I still needed to treat him with respect. "She doesn't want that," I said as I used his hanky and shoved it away. He might get it back after I washed it. Maybe. "She doesn't want to lose her soul, and biting me brings her closer to that."

He frowned and stood, dropping back a few steps so he could see me. "It's what she is."

"I know." I took my hands from the wheel, placing them quietly in my lap. "She knows it, too."

Eyebrows high, Rynn Cormel made a soft sound. Rocking on his feet, he made motions to leave. "Rynn," I said, and he stopped. "She accepts what she is, and by God, I'm going to find a way to help her be who she wants to be."

My heart was pounding, but his worried expression melted into one of his famous smiles, and I wondered if I had just saved my own life with my promise to find a way for her to keep her soul. If he thought I meant to find a way to keep it after she died, then that was his prerogative. I was thinking something a little more immediate. Something we could both benefit from.

"Good," he said, hands in his pockets, looking harmless. "Enjoy your evening with your family, Rachel. Ivy will be fine."

I sat straighter, hope making my eyes wide. "Are you sure?"

His gaze never moved from the Hummer. "Her aura will be replaced as she satiates herself, and her strength will return in time. It's my people with her I'm worried about."

I couldn't help my smile at that, but it faded fast. She was out of control in that car, and she was going to hate herself when she came home. What she was pinning her sanity on now was that she hadn't allowed her hunger to rule her and satisfy it by savaging me. Her vow to abstain from blood had lasted thirty seconds.

"Rynn, don't push her," I said. "Please? Just make her better and send her back to me. I'll find a way for her to die with her soul. If it's possible, I'll find a way. I promise." *Damn it, I'm going to have to talk to Trent.* He had a way to make the vampire virus dormant, but from there, he might find a way to remove it. I wasn't sure if Ivy would agree to becoming human to lose her blood lust, but after tonight . . . she might.

The tall man inclined his head to acknowledge my words. Smiling, he jauntily returned to his second car. The driver emerged to open his door for him, and in a moment, both vehicles were gone.

I glanced at the clock, then noticed that Ivy's purse was still with me. I picked it up off the floor and put it on the seat where she'd been, then reached across and closed my broken door. Ivy's scent lingered, and I breathed it in, wondering how she was. My hands started to shake with the remaining adrenaline. I was late for my already postponed lunch. Robbie was going to have a field day.

Clearly I wasn't ready to risk the road yet. I was deathly worried about Ivy, but that was probably fair play. Ivy had been worried about me when I was in the hospital. Rynn Cormel said she was going to be all right, and I had to believe it. A vampire was a banshee's closest rival in terms of strength, having a fast way to rebound after an attack—blood to renew her aura, and Brimstone to revitalize her strength.

I slowly thunked the car into gear and crept up to the exit, turning my blinker on and sitting there, waiting for a break in traffic. As I sat there, it hit me that this was probably the turning point in our relationship. Ivy was a vampire who wanted to be more. Or maybe less. But she could never be who she wanted unless I could find a way to get the virus out of her. By magic or medicine, I was going to have to do that. I might not be able to be the person I wanted to be, but if I had to be a demon, I was, by God, going to make sure Ivy could be who she wanted to be.

Having to deal with stuff like this was just crappy.

Twenty-three

The scent of beef stew was heavy in my mom's kitchen, but even that, combined with the homemade biscuits Mom had pulled out of the oven when I walked in the door, hadn't blunted my worry for Ivy. Dinner might have been pleasant; I didn't remember. I'd been there for over an hour, and still no one had called about Ivy. Just how long did it take to replenish an aura?

Adding to my state was the fact that somewhere in this house was an eight-hundred-level arcane textbook that my brother was hiding from me. My life was falling apart, and I wasn't leaving without it. I should just tell my mom and have her make Robbie give it to me, but the last time I'd used it, I'd gotten into a lot of trouble. I didn't need any more trouble tonight. I'd maxed out on it. I was wound so tight a hangnail might have sent me over the edge.

I handed Robbie the last of the glasses and fumbled in the dishwater for the bowls. The shifting-eyed witch above the sink ticked, and from the back of the house, I heard my mom thumping around, trying to find something. It was odd standing here, like I had while I was growing up. I washed; Robbie dried. 'Course, I didn't need to stand on a footstool anymore, and Robbie wasn't wearing grunge. Some changes were good.

Heels clicking on the tile, my mom came in looking happy and satisfied. I couldn't help but wonder what she was up to—

she looked far too pleased with herself—though just having me and Robbie here at the sink like old times might account for it.

"Thanks for lunch, Mom," I said as I slipped a plate into the rinse water before Robbie could take it. "I'm sorry for dragging it out this late. I really thought I'd get over here sooner."

Robbie made a rude noise, but my mom beamed as she sat with her cold cup of coffee. "I know how busy you are," she said. "I just threw everything into the slow cooker, figuring we could eat whenever you got here."

I glanced at the ancient brown pot plugged into the wall, trying to remember the last time I had seen it, and if it had held food or a spell. God, I hoped it was food. "Stuff kept getting in the way. Trust me, I really wanted to be here earlier." Boy, did I want to be here earlier. I hadn't told them why I was late. Not with Robbie looking for a reason to needle me about my job. His mood tonight was bordering on smug, worrying me even more.

Robbie shut the door to the cupboard too hard. "Stuff always seems to happen to you, little sister. You need to make some changes in your life."

Excuse me? My eyes narrowed. "Like what?"

"It wasn't a problem, Robbie," my mom interrupted. "I knew she was probably going to be late. That's why I made what I did."

Robbie made that noise again, and I felt my blood pressure rise.

My mom got up and gave me a sideways squeeze. "If I knew you weren't trying to do ten things before the Turn, I'd be miffed. Want some coffee?"

"Yes. Thanks." My mom was pretty cool. It wasn't often that she took sides between Robbie and me, but he'd been on my case all night.

I handed him a plate, not letting go until he looked at me and I gave him a glare to get him to shut up. I really thought he'd been lying when he told me the book wasn't where he'd left it, trying to make me do things his way by force instead of persuasion—because persuasion wasn't going to work. I had to get up in that attic without my mom knowing. I didn't want to worry her. Snatching a ghost to get a demon to talk to you didn't sound safe even to me.

So when I handed the last dish to my brother, I used my perfect excuse, smiling as the sink drained. "Mom," I said as I dried my hands, "are my stuffed animals still in the attic? I have someone I want to give them to."

Robbie jerked, and my mom beamed. "I expect so," she said. "Who? Ceri's little girl?"

I allowed myself one superior look at Robbie, then went to sit across from my mom. We'd known Ceri was having a girl since last week, and my mom was as delighted as if it were one of her own. "No," I said as I fiddled with my mug. "I want to give them to some of the kids in the children's wing of the hospital. I met the brat pack yesterday. The ones who spend more time there than at home? It just seems right. You don't think Dad would mind, do you?"

My mother's smile turned beautiful. "I think he'd say that was the right thing to do."

I stood, restless and invigorated. Finally I was doing something. "Mind if I get them now?"

"Go right ahead. And if you find anything else up there you want, bring it on down."

Bingo! With her carte blanche to rummage, I was in the hall before she could call after me, "I'm putting the house on the market, and a clean attic sells better than a full one."

Huh?

The string to pull down the attic stairs slipped through my fist, and the ceiling door slammed shut. Not believing I'd heard her right, I went back to the kitchen. Robbie was smirking, his ankles crossed as he leaned against the sink with a cup of coffee. Suddenly I saw my mom's stilted conversation tonight in an entirely new way. I wasn't the only one hiding bad news. *Shit.*

"You're selling the house?" I stammered, seeing the truth in her downcast gaze. "Why?"

Taking a resolute breath, she looked up. "I'm moving out to the West Coast for a while. It's not a big deal," she said as I started to protest. "It's time for a change, is all."

Eyes squinting, I turned to Robbie. God! He looked too satisfied to live, leaning against the counter like that. "You . . . selfish brat," I said, furious. He'd been trying to get her to move out there for years, and now he'd finally gotten his way.

My mom shifted uncomfortably, and I reined in my anger, shoving it down to bring out when he and I were alone. This was where we'd grown up. This was where my memories with Dad were, the tree I had planted with his ashes. And now a stranger was going to have it? "Excuse me," I said stiffly. "I'll get my things out of the attic."

Ticked, I strode into the hall. "I'll talk to her," I heard Robbie say, and I made a sarcastic puff. *I* was going to do the talking, and *he* was going to listen.

This time I jerked the stairs all the way down and flipped on the light. A memory of Pierce came from out of nowhere. He had opened the attic for me when I'd been looking for my dad's ley line stuff to help him save a girl and his soul both. At least he had saved the girl.

Cold spilled down, and as Robbie came into the hallway, I stomped up the ladder and out of his reach. Chill silence enveloped me, doing nothing to cool my temper. The space was lit by a single bulb, making shadows on the stacked boxes and dark corners with angled support beams. My brow furrowed as I decided someone had been up here recently. There were fewer boxes than I remembered. Dad's stuff was missing, and I wondered if Robbie had thrown it all away in his efforts to keep me from using it.

"Selfish brat," I muttered, then reached for the topmost box of my stuffed animals. I'd gathered the toys one by one during my stints in the hospital or home sick in bed. Many bore the names and pretend personalities of my friends who hadn't made it out one last time to feel the wind push on their face. I hadn't taken them when I'd moved out, which was just as well. They wouldn't have survived the great salt dip of '06.

My pulse was fast as I took the box to the hole in the floor. "Catch," I said, dropping it when Robbie looked up.

He fumbled it, and the box smacked noisily into the wall. I didn't wait to see him glare up at me. Spinning away, I went for the next one. Robbie had gained the attic by the time I turned back around. "Get out of my way," I said, frowning at his tall height, hunched in the low ceiling.

"Rachel."

He wasn't moving, and unless I wanted to take the direct route to the hallway by way of crashing through the ceiling, I was stuck here. "I always knew you were a prick," I said, drawing on years of frustration. "But this is pathetic. You come back here and get her all stirred up and convince her to move out there with you and your new wife. *I'm* the one who held her together when Dad died, not you. You ran off and left me to cope with her. I was thirteen, Robbie!" I hissed, trying to keep my voice down but failing. "How *dare* you come out here and take her from me now, just when she's gotten herself together."

Robbie's face was red, and he shifted his thin shoulders. "Shut up."

"No, you shut up," I snapped. "She's happy here. She's got her friends, and this is where all her memories are. Can't you just leave us alone? Like you used to?"

Robbie took the box from me and set it beside him. "I said shut up. She needs to get out of here for every reason you just mentioned. And don't you be so selfish, keeping her here when she finally finds the courage to do it. Do you like seeing her like that?" he said, pointing to the unseen kitchen. "Dressing like an old lady? Talking like her life is over? That's not who she is. I remember her before Dad died, and that old lady isn't her. She's ready to let Dad go. Let her."

Arms crossed over my chest, I exhaled.

"I'm not taking her from you," he said, softer now. "You

held her together when Dad died. I was a coward. I was stupid. But if you don't let her go now, then you're the coward."

I didn't like what I was hearing, but figuring he was right, I looked up at him. My face was twisted and ugly, but that's how I felt.

"She wants to be closer to Takata," he said, and I puffed in disgust. Sure, bring him into it. "She wants to be closer to Takata, and Takata can't live in Cincinnati," he said persuasively. "She doesn't have any friends here. Not really. And thanks to you, she can't sell her charms—now that you've been shunned."

Shock washed cold through me, and my expression blanked. "Y-you know about that?"

His eyes dropped from mine, then returned. "I was with her when we found out. They won't sell to her anymore, won't buy. She may as well be shunned herself."

"That's not fair." My stomach was hurting, and I held it.

Turning sideways, Robbie put one hand on his hip, the other on his forehead. "For Christ's sake, Rachel. You've been shunned?"

Embarrassed, I dropped back. "I-I didn't know they would . . . ," I stammered, then realizing he had turned the tables on me, I lifted my chin. "Yes. Because I talk to demons."

Robbie sucked his teeth and looked at my demon-scarred wrist.

"Okay," I admitted. "And maybe make deals with them when I'm forced into it. And I've spent some time in the everafter. More than most."

"Uh-huh."

"And a demon prison," I added, feeling a twinge of guilt. "But it was a run for Trent Kalamack. He was there, too. No one got mad at him."

"Anything else?" he mocked.

Wincing, I said, "You saw the news, huh?" The agony of my defeat, or in my case, being dragged down the street on my ass by a demon, had been worked into their opening credits.

Robbie's anger vanished in an amused snort. "That must have hurt."

I smiled, but it faded fast. "Not as bad as what you're doing to me does."

He sighed and nudged the box closer to the hole in the floor. "There isn't anything here for her, Rachel."

My pique came back. "There's me."

"Yeah, but thanks to your mess-ups, she can't make a living anymore."

"Damn it, Robbie," I swore. "I didn't want this to happen! If she leaves, I don't have anyone."

He edged to the stairway. "You've got your friends," he said, head down and shoving the box with his foot across the plywood floor to the door.

"Friends you've made abundantly clear you don't approve of."

"So make new ones."

So make new ones, I mocked in my thoughts. Bothered, I went to get the last box of stuffed animals I'd named after dead or dying friends. There were so many of them. My thoughts went to Marshal, then Pierce. How was I going to tell Marshal I'd been shunned? So much for *that* friendship. I never should have done a power pull with him.

Robbie lifted the second box. "You need to change something."

The scent of dust was thick as I took a breath to protest. "Like what? I try. I try damn hard, but there isn't anyone decent who can survive the crap my life can turn into."

Again Robbie's long face went hard, and he started down the stairs. "That is an excuse. You've been shunned, and you're hurting Mom. This goes deeper than who your friends are. On second thought, maybe that's all there is to it."

"You leave Ivy and Jenks out of this," I snapped, my worry for Ivy coming out as a hot anger. "They have more courage in one day then you will have in your entire life!"

Robbie's attention came up, and he scowled at me, his head

just above the floor. "Grow up," he said. "Burn your demon books and get a real job. If you don't start thinking inside the box, you're going to end up in one."

Angry, I shifted the toys to my hip. "You are a piece of work. You know that? You don't know anything. You have no idea what I've done or what I'm capable of. And that comes at a cost. Nothing is free. I'll tell you what. You just take Mom and fly on back to your safe girlfriend, in your safe house, in your safe *trendy* neighborhood, and live your safe, predictable life and have safe, predictable kids, and die a safe, worthless death after doing absolutely nothing with your safe life. I'm going to stay here and do some good, because that's what people do when they are alive and not just going through the motions. I am *not* going to find myself on my deathbed, wondering what would have happened if I hadn't played it *safe!*"

My brother's face darkened. He took a breath to say something, then changed his mind. Sliding the waiting box into his arms, he descended the stairway.

"Thanks a hell of a lot, Robbie," I muttered. "Look at me. I'm shaking. I come over here for lunch, and now I'm shaking."

I headed for the stairway with my last box of dead friends. I could hear Robbie and my mother talking, but not their words. Halfway down the ladder, I stopped. My head even with the floor, I took one last look. The book I wanted wasn't up here. Robbie had it, and damn it, he wasn't going to give it to me. Maybe I could find something online. It wasn't the safest thing to do, but seeing it might trigger my memory enough that I could reconstruct it.

Knees watery, I descended into the green hallway backward off the ladder, almost backing up into my mom.

"Oh crap!" I stammered, knowing by her miserable expression she had heard everything. "I'm sorry, Mom. Don't listen to me. I'm just mad at him. I didn't mean it. You should go to Portland. Be with Takata, ah, Donald."

My mom's misery shifted to teary-eyed surprise at the pop star's real name. "He told you his name?"

I smiled back, though I was really upset. "Yeah. After I punched him."

The thump of the back door closing made me jump. It was Robbie going out to cool off. Whatever. "I'm sorry," I muttered as I edged by her and headed for the kitchen. "I'll apologize. It's no wonder he lives on the other side of the continent."

My mom closed the attic door with a bang. "We need to talk, Rachel," she said over her shoulder as she went in the opposite direction, to my old room.

Sighing, I came to a halt on the green carpet, depressed as she disappeared into my room. My head was starting to hurt, but I shifted the box on my hip and resolutely followed her, ready for the coming lecture. I hadn't meant to get into a fight with Robbie. But he'd ticked me off, and things needed to be said. Things like "Where in hell is my book?"

But when I entered my old room to find my dad's stuff piled up on my bed, I froze.

"This is for you," she said, gesturing to the dusty boxes. "If you want it. Robbie—" She took a slow breath and put a hand to her forehead briefly. "Robbie thinks I should throw it away, but I can't. There's too much of your dad in them."

I set the box of stuffed animals down, feeling guilty. "Thank you. Yes, I'd like it." I swallowed hard, and seeing her distress, I blurted, "Mom, I'm sorry I was shunned. It's not fair! They're being stupid, but maybe I should just drop it all and walk away."

She sat on the bed, not looking at me. "No. You shouldn't. But you do need to find a way to get your shunning removed. For all your rebel tendencies, you're not cut out for living outside society. You like people too much. I heard what you told Robbie. He's scared that he's a coward when he sees you live by your own convictions, so he yells at you to be safer."

I came close and shoved a box over so I could sit beside her. "I shouldn't have said that," I admitted. "And I really think you should go out to . . . Portland." My mouth felt nasty saying it, and I got depressed. "Maybe . . ." I swallowed a lump in my throat. "Maybe I should just scrap the whole thing. They might take the shunning off if I walked away from everything."

But I'd have to leave Ivy and Jenks, and I can't do that.

My mom's eyes were bright when she took my hand. "I'm going. And you're staying. But I'm not leaving you here alone."

I stifled a wince as I thought of her matchmaking attempts, and as I took a breath to protest, she handed me a smooth, shiny textbook. "Is this the one you're looking for?" she said softly.

My mouth dropped open, and I stared. *Arcane Divination and Cross-Tangential Science,* volume nine. That was it! This was the one I needed!

"That's the book Robbie gave you on the solstice when you were eighteen, right?" she was saying. "I made Robbie give it to me, but I didn't know if it was the right one. I think you'll need this, too."

Eyes wide, I took the red-and-white rock with the small dip in it with shaking hands. She wanted me to rescue Pierce? "Why?" I managed, and my mom patted my knee.

"Pierce was good for you," she said instead of explaining. "I watched you find more strength and personal resolve in that one night together than the entire eighteen years before. Or maybe it was always there, and he simply brought it out. I'm proud of you, sweetheart. I want you to do wonderful things. But unless you have someone to share them with, they don't mean a dog's ass. Trust me on this."

I couldn't say anything, and I just stared at the book and the crucible. *She thinks Pierce would make a good boyfriend?* "Mom, I only want this to prove to Al that he can't just jerk people into the ever-after," I said, and she smiled.

"That's a good start," she said as she stood up, drawing me to a stand in her wake. "Save him, and if it works, then it does. If it doesn't, then no harm done. The important thing is that you try." My mom leaned forward and gave me a hug, smothering me in a heady redwood scent.

I was pretty sure she was talking about trying Pierce on as a boyfriend, not trying to summon him out, and I absently hugged her back.

"You need someone a little dirty, honey, with a heart of gold," she whispered in my ear as she patted my back. "I don't think you're going to find it in this century. We don't make honest men who are that strong in their convictions anymore. Society seems to just . . . twist them bad."

She let go and stepped back. "Mom," I managed, but she waved me off.

"Go. Go on. You still have the watch, don't you?"

I nodded, not surprised she knew it was part of the spell. It was my dad's watch, but it had been Pierce's before that.

"Do it exactly like before. Exactly. If you added something by accident, do it again. If you stirred it with your finger, do it again. If you got your hair into it, add a strand. It has to be exact."

Again I nodded. There were tears in both our eyes, and she walked me to the hall with her arm over my shoulders. "Don't worry about the rest of this. I'll bring everything over tomorrow in the Buick. Your little car would need three trips."

Blinking, I smiled at my mom and pulled the book and stone tight to me. "Thanks, Mom," I whispered. And with the knowledge that my mom believed in me even if the rest of the world didn't, I headed for the door.

Twenty-four

I winced at the clatter of the three black potion storage bottles in the sink. Looking up at the night-darkened window, I listened for the whine of adolescent pixy wings. It was just after midnight; Jenks's kids were asleep, and I wanted to keep it that way. Hearing nothing, I shoved my sleeves up higher and dipped my hands into the warm suds. I wouldn't be able to invoke Pierce's charm until tomorrow night, but I had to do something to distract myself from my worry over Ivy, and prepping the charms would help. I still hadn't heard from Cormel, and if no one called me soon, I was calling them.

A box of cold pizza with one piece gone lay open atop Ivy's papers, and a two-liter bottle of pop sat, barely touched. The fridge was gone, leaving an empty space; our food was outside on the picnic table. Behind me on the center counter were the partially prepared bits and pieces of my spell, making a wide semicircle around the open university textbook. There was enough stuff to make three substance charms, and I was going to use it all.

New Year's Eve was my best chance to find enough ambient energy to work the spell, and I wasn't going to bet everything on one go. Not after the locator charms had failed to work. Yes, it had probably been my blood that had been the problem, seeing that Marshal's worked and mine hadn't, but the mere thought that I might do a spell wrong was enough for me to spend the time to stir a little insurance.

Oh God, Marshal, I thought, almost dropping the slippery storage bottle as I remembered my shunning. What was I going to tell him? Or better yet, *how* was I going to tell him? *Hey, hi, I know we just had sex with our clothes on, but guess what I found out!* Shunning was contagious. I didn't want him to lose his job because of me. Actually, I didn't want him to lose his job *again* because of me. I was the freaking black plague.

Mentally tired, I rinsed the bottles in salt water and reached for the dishcloth. And things had been going so well, too—apart from my latest mess, that is. I'd finally gotten the Weres off my case by returning the focus to them. Thanks to my saving Trent, the elves weren't bothering me despite my potential demon, ah, liabilities. The vampires were edgy, but I think I had just taken care of that. Ivy was going to be okay, and our relationship was going to get a lot less chaotic. Just when everything was under control and I might be able to have something normal with a normal guy doing normal things, my own people had come down on me.

"Must have been Tom," I muttered, shoving my sleeves back up and pulling out the drain plug.

Young, attractive guys who have a good job and don't mind a girl who spends a night in the ever-after once a week were hard to find. It wasn't as if Marshal and I had been planning a life together, but damn it, there'd been the chance that it might have gone that way. Eventually. Not anymore. What was wrong with me?

Standing at the black window, I closed my eyes and sighed. That power pull had been fantastic, though. *What am I going to tell him?*

Grimacing, I turned back to the center counter and the spells waiting to be put together, bottled, and stoppered for tomorrow. I'd take them out to Fountain Square, find an alley, and when the crowd started singing "Auld Lang Syne," I'd invoke them all if I had to. And then Al and I would talk. Get a few things settled.

But even as I was looking forward to it, the thought of arguing with Al in the snow with a naked ghost and a square full of witnesses made me cringe. Maybe I could rent a van and do it in the parking garage. It wasn't as if Al was giving me any choice. I'd tried to call him earlier, but all I'd gotten for my trouble was a lingering headache and a "go away" message. Fine. We could do it the hard way. I had agreed not to summon him, but he hadn't said anything about stealing his latest chunk of meat out from under him.

The soft hum of pixy wings got my attention, and I gave Jenks a closed-lipped smile as he flew in. "Hi, Jenks," I said as I shook the black bottle to get the water out and dried the exterior, impatient to get to the fun stuff on my counter. "I didn't wake up your kids, did I?"

Jenks glanced over my spelling supplies, and a slip of silver dust sifted from him as he hovered over the table. "No. Have you heard from Cormel yet?"

"No." The word was flat, carrying all my worry. "But she'll be fine." *And if she isn't, I'm taking up the new profession of master-vampire killer.*

He landed on the open pizza box, making a face at the unused garlic dipping sauce. "Fine. Yeah. Going after a banshee is fine. You're both lucky to be alive."

I set the bottle upside down in the cold oven and turned it on low, letting the door shut with a hard thump. There was a clatter as the bottle fell over. "Don't you think we know that?" I said, irritated. "Mia came after us, we did not go after her. What would you like us to have done? Roll over and play dead?"

"Ivy might be okay if you had," he muttered, just within my hearing, and I shook the last drops of water out of the next bottle before giving it a cursory swipe with the towel. It went in beside the first, this time propped up against the wall, and I reached for the last black bottle.

"Ivy thinks it's her fault that Mia learned how to kill without a trace," I said. "She tried to bring her in. She tried, failed, and learned from it. Next time, we'll do it together." I looked at his drooping wings, and added, "All of us. It's going to take all of us. That's one wicked bitch."

His wings blurred into nothing, and feeling better, I set the last bottle in the oven with the others and carefully shut the door. They'd be dry by the time I was ready for them.

Whether from the pixies being asleep, or Ivy being gone—or maybe because Pierce was in the ever-after—the church felt empty. Turning to the center counter, I wiped my hands on my jeans and looked at the clock. Spelling on the back side of the night wasn't the best of times, but it would be okay. "Wine," I said as I reached for the cheap bottle and unscrewed the top. Not one of the finest wines to have graced our kitchen, but it was local, the grapes grown in the soil where Pierce had lived and died.

Squinting, I crouched to put my eyes level with the graduated cylinder and filled it until the meniscus settled right where it should, and as Jenks watched, I dribbled in a little extra.

"You overfilled it," he said dryly, wings clattering as he looked from it to the recipe.

"I know." Not bothering to explain, I picked up the cylinder and made the big no-no of putting it to my lips and doing my impression of "The Drunken Chef." The hint of warmth slipped down my throat as I sipped the level back to where it should be. My mom had said to do the spell exactly the same, and being stupid at eighteen, that's how I had leveled it. Who knew? It might be why it had worked. Arcane earth spells were notoriously difficult to reproduce. It might be something that nebulous that had made it possible the first time.

Three separate batches of the yew and lemon mix were already waiting, and leaving them where they sat, I dumped the wine into the mortar already holding the snipped bits of holly leaf I'd taken from Ivy's Christmas centerpiece earlier. "Don't get your dust in that," I said, waving Jenks off from the top of the open bottle, and the pixy shifted to alight on the overhead rack of spelling utensils instead. Ivy had replaced the tacked-together rack with a solid redwood mesh, and my spelling supplies were again where they should be instead of shoved in cupboards.

"So-o-o-orry," he muttered, and I nodded, more concerned with the spell than his pique.

"Ivy roots," I murmured, reaching for the little measuring cup full of the tiny little rhizomes from one of Jenks's plants in the sanctuary. It had to be airborne roots, not underground, and Jenks's kids had been delighted to harvest them for me. The knobby roots went in, and with a few twists, the scent of chlorophyll mixed with the cheap wine.

It was a lot easier to crush everything this time, not being sick now like I'd been at eighteen. My thoughts went back to Pierce as the soft sounds of rock against rock filled the kitchen, and a whisper of worry lifted through me that tomorrow might be too late. I didn't think Al would give Pierce a body until he had a buyer, enabling him to work the cost of the expensive curse into the deal. Not to mention that Pierce couldn't tap a line given the state he was in. Why would Al make him stronger if he didn't have to? I knew Al wouldn't sell to the first buyer, wanting to up the going price as far as he could. It would take a few days at least.

A curl drifted between me and the mix, and remembering something, I carefully drew a single hair into the mortar and gave the pestle two twists, grinding it before I pulled the hair out. My hair had been to my waist the first time I had done this charm, and it had gotten caught. It might be important. I was betting it was. With this and my spit, I might be investing part of myself in the spell. It was going to be hard enough getting this to work.

I straightened to crack my back. "Holy dust," I murmured, looking for it among the clutter. Jenks's wings hummed and he dropped to hover over the envelope that I'd gathered from the slats under my bed, the only place the pixies didn't clean. It was on sanctified ground, so I figured it was holy enough. And God knew my bed hadn't seen any action lately.

"Thanks," I said absently as I pulled the flap to open it. I wiped the pans of my scales with a tissue, then frowned. A thin smear of lotion showed in the bright overhead lights. Not only would it add aloe, but the dust would stick to it and I wouldn't get enough in the mix.

Sighing, I took the pans to the sink to give them a quick wash. Jenks moved back to the overhead rack, and in the black mirror the window had become, I could see a sifting of dust falling from him. He was worried.

"Ivy is going to be fine," I said over the chatter of running water. "I'll call before I go to bed, to find out how she is, okay?"

"I'm not worried about Ivy, I'm worried about you."

Metal pans swathed in a dish towel, I turned. "Me? Why?" He made an exasperated gesture that encompassed my spelling, and I huffed. "You want Al popping over anytime with the excuse of checking on me and then snagging whoever he wants? Can you imagine the trouble I'd be in if Al showed up and took, say, Trent, when I'm telling the little shoemaker to get lost?"

Jenks's small angular features pulled into a tight grimace. "Al is going to be more pissed than a fairy who finds acorns in his spider sack."

That was a new one, and I frowned as I replaced the pans and weighed out the dust, carefully tapping the envelope until the delicate balance started to shift. "He left a loophole, and I'm going to use it," I said as the instrument leveled. "Al's not taking my calls, and this is the only way I can think of to get his attention. Not to mention, this will save Pierce, too. Two birds with one stone. He'll probably treat me to dinner for outsmarting him." *After he smacks me around.* I looked up, seeing an unsure look on his tiny features. "What's the worst he's going to do to me? Ground me? Cancel our weekly sessions?" A private smile curved across my face and I tapped the dust from the pan into the wine medium. "Bully for him."

"Rachel, he's a demon. He might just pull you into the ever-after and not let you back."

The fear in Jenks's voice broke through my nonchalance, and I turned to him. "Which is why I told you and Ivy my summoning name," I said, surprised that this was bothering him so much. "He can't hold me even with charmed silver, and he knows it. Jenks, what's the matter? You're acting like there is more to this than there is."

"Nothing."

But he was lying, and I knew it.

The dust turned black when it hit the wine and sank. Jenks flew to the sill and looked out into the snowy garden, only a small patch lit by the back-porch light. All that was left besides invoking the charm was adding the identifying agent—in this case, metal shavings from the back of my dad's watch.

I drew the old pocket watch from my back jeans pocket, hefting the weight and feeling the warmth of my body in the metal. It had belonged to my dad, but it had been Pierce's before that, hence his being pulled from purgatory the night I had tried to make contact with my dad. I turned the watch over to find that the scratches I'd made eight years ago were now tarnished. I tried to remember what I had used to scrape the tiny bits into the spell pot the last time, guessing it had been my mom's scissors.

"It's the thought that counts," I said as I reached for Ivy's pair, jammed into her pencil cup, and scraped a new three marks into the old silver. The almost-unseen shavings made dimples on the wine half of the brew, and I stirred it until they settled. Almost done, and I pulled a warm, and now dry, bottle from the oven and dumped in both the lemon-yew mix and the wine, dust, roots, and holly.

Jenks hovered over it, his expression blank. "It didn't work," he said, and I waved him off before his dust could get in it.

"It's not done yet. I have to add my blood to invoke it, and I can't do that until tomorrow night," I said as I wedged a glass stopper into it and set it aside. Fortunately it was an earth charm and I could do it without tapping a line. He was frowning, and tired of his mood, I asked, "What's your problem, Jenks?"

His face tightened, and he flew to land on the book. Standing sideways to me, he crossed his arms and fumed, wings drooping. Silently I waited. "This isn't going to work," Jenks finally said.

My breath slipped from me, and I turned away, brow furrowed. "Gee, thanks, Jenks."

"I meant with Pierce."

Understanding him now, I straightened after carefully pouring a second portion of wine into the graduated cylinder. "You think I'm cooking up a boyfriend in my kitchen? Grow up."

"You grow up!" Jenks said. "Let's just say he's a nice ghost who needs a little help and is not spying on us for some demon. I know you, Rache. He is a ghost. You're a witch. He needs help, and I'd be willing to bet the first time you met him, he did something strong and powerful. And now he needs help, which turns him into freaking Rachel candy."

I couldn't help a flush from creeping up my face. Okay, maybe once, but I was smarter now. But seeing it, Jenks rose an inch.

"He's Rachel candy. And I don't want to see you hurt when you realize you can't have him."

"You think I'm doing this because I like him?" I said, mentally backpedaling. "It's not always about sex!"

"Then it's a good thing you didn't sleep with Marshal, isn't it."

Silently I reddened, eyes fixed on the wine level. *Damn it!*

"Tink's titties, Rache!" he exclaimed. "You slept with the guy? When?"

"I didn't sleep with him," I protested, but I couldn't look at him as I sipped the wine to the right amount. "It was just a really involved kiss." *In a broad sort of way.* Crap, Ford had said Pierce spent a lot of time in the belfry. I sure hoped he hadn't been up there when Marshal and I had— No, Al had abducted him before that.

Jenks landed on the bottle I'd just capped, and with his hands on his hips, he stared disapprovingly at me. "I thought you were going to leave it at friends," he said, then he slumped. "Crap, Rache, can't you just have a guy friend?"

"I did have a guy friend," I snapped, my hair swinging as I dropped the ivy roots and a holly leaf into the mortar and started grinding. "I spent two months doing friend stuff because I thought my life was too dangerous, and I found out that yeah, I can keep it friendly, but I also found out he was a really nice person. Maybe someone I might want to spend my life with. Maybe not. *I* didn't know I was going to get shunned. Excuse me if I thought I might finally have my *freaking* life together enough that I could share it with someone other than just you and Ivy!"

Jenks's wings buzzed, then went guiltily silent. Feeling bad for yelling at him, I set the pestle down and crouched to put us on the same level. "I thought I had my life together," I whispered. "I really liked him, Jenks."

"Me, too." In a soft hum, he landed by my hand. "Don't put him in the past tense."

My focus sharpened on him and I stood. "He is," I whispered. "Ever since I became shunned." Depressed, I straightened and looked to the holy dust. Ashes and dust. It sort of fit.

Jenks watched as I shook the envelope over the weighing pan, then rose up on a column of amber-tinted sparkles. "The phone is going to ring. You want to get it before it wakes up my kids?"

I looked up, not sure I believed him. The trill of the phone broke the silence, and I reached for the receiver, adrenaline jumping through me. *Cormel?* "God, I hate it when you do that," I said, as I hit the button to open the line.

"Hello, yes?" I blurted as Jenks darted from the kitchen to check on his kids. Then remembering we were a business, I cleared my throat. "Vampiric Charms," I said politely. "This is Rachel. We can help, dead or alive."

"Alive would be better," came Edden's voice, and disappointment that it wasn't Cormel slumped my shoulders. Tucking the phone between my shoulder and my ear, I went back to my set of scales.

"Hi, Edden. How is Glenn doing?" I asked, trying not to breathe on the scales as I tapped a little more dust out.

"Great. They released him this afternoon. The massage worked, though it raised a few eyebrows. It's going into the SOP for aura trauma."

"That's fantastic!" I said as I stood and dumped the dust in with the wine mix. Wine to give life, dust to give substance, ivy to bind, and holly to be sure nothing bad came in on the souls of the dead. "Thanks for calling me." I looked at the clock, wanting to keep the line open, but clearly Edden didn't get the hint.

"It was only right, seeing as you helped get him out." He hesitated, and when I didn't say anything, he added, "I'm sorry about Ivy. Is she okay?"

My motions to scrape the metal shavings into the mix were harsher than I had intended, and I warmed, gaze flicking to Jenks as he flew in. *Oh yeah. He would have heard about that.* "Ah, she's okay." I winced, adjusting the phone and remembering to grind a strand of my hair in with everything. "Um, how much trouble am I in over that?"

He laughed. "Just come in tomorrow and fill out a statement. I told them you were working for me, and they cut you a lot of slack."

I sighed in relief. "Thanks, Edden. I owe you."

"Yeah, you do . . . ," he said, and my tension ratcheted up again at his sly tone.

"What," I said flatly. My eyes flicked to Jenks, listening to the entire conversation from across the room, and the pixy shrugged.

"I'd like your help on the next step in bringing Mia in," he said. "We can go over it tomorrow. See you at my office at eight."

"Whoa, whoa, whoa, Edden," I said, holding the phone tight to my ear. "There is no *next step*. Until my entire team is functioning, none of us is going after her."

"Our three best profilers say Ms. Harbor will be at a party tomorrow," Edden said as if not having heard me. "I want you there."

Jiggling the phone, I pulled a bottle from the oven and turned it off. Jenks's wings had hit a high pitch, and I tried to tell him with my eyes that this was not going to happen. "On New Year's Eve?" I quipped. "How much are you paying these guys? Half of Cincinnati is going to be at a party."

"I want you to come with me to one in particular," he continued, his voice tired.

"Golly, Edden. I don't date people I work with."

I could hear him puff his breath out in annoyance. "Morgan, stop messing with me. There's an eighty-three percent chance Mia will show up at this one."

The bottle was warm in my hands as I filled it, and I gave the mix a good shake before setting it beside the first with a sharp tap. "I've got spelling to do tomorrow. Personal spelling."

"I'll give you time and a half," he coaxed.

I crossed one arm over my middle. He wasn't getting it. "That woman's *baby* almost killed me," I said, trying the direct approach. "She tried to finish the job last night in front of a freaking jail, damaging my new aura and pretty much stripping Ivy's down to nothing. Do you know how hard it would be to live with Ivy if she were dead? I'm not going to risk us on some lame attempt to tag her and her psychotic boyfriend. Did you know I can't tap a line without convulsing if I don't have a good aura? I'm helpless, Edden. Not going to happen."

"Make some charms. I'll double your rate," he said, and I heard a burst of muffled noise when someone came into his office.

Make some charms. Stupid human. "No," I said, eyeing my potions. "Maybe when it gets warmer and all three of us can work."

"Rachel . . . People are dying. Don't you want to get even with this piece of work for what she did to your roommate?"

I got mad at that. "Don't you guilt me, Edden," I said, hearing Jenks's wings clatter. "There's a reason the I.S. is ignoring her. She's a freaking apex predator, and we are zebras at the watering hole to her. Trying to goad me into it by waving the flag of revenge is low. You can just take your guilt and your manipulation and shove it!"

Jenks looked pained, and I lowered my voice so I wouldn't wake up his kids. From the phone came Edden's cajoling voice saying, "Okay, okay, that was unfair. I'm sorry. Can I come over and talk to you about it? Bring you flowers? Candy? Does bribery work with you?"

"No. And you can't come over. I'm in my pajamas," I lied. God, I couldn't believe he had tried to use revenge to get me to do what he wanted. Thing was, last year, it might have worked.

"You are not. It's only midnight."

I leaned to look at the clock. *By golly, he's right.* "I took a bath," I lied again. Tired, I turned to look at my reflection in the black window. "Remus is a psychotic murderer, but Mia is a power-hungry psychotic murderer who is also an Inderlander. She thinks she owns this city, built it, even, and she's been alive longer than most undead vampires. Edden, she said if you don't back off, she's going to start picking targets according to her political agenda instead of thinning the herd. You need to slow down and think. I know people are dying, but bringing her in is going to take a lot of finesse and luck, and I'm fresh out of both."

Apart from a slow breath, there was silence on the other end. "Her threatening the FIB doesn't surprise me. It goes along with the profilers' report."

I rolled my eyes. *Damned profilers' report.* Upset, I put my back to the window and leaned against the sink. *I am not going to do this. It is too risky.* "Mia is not your average psychotic killer. She doesn't need to go to a party," I said, tired. "If she goes out at all, it will be to a private party where she already knows the victim, and the poor guy will probably die of a heart attack or choke on an olive."

He said nothing, and I blurted, "Look, I agree, we have to get her, but staking out parties isn't going to do it! You can't catch her! The I.S. can't catch her. She keeps slipping your lines because she knows the city better than you, and she's like a poisonous snake you can't get within ten feet of. You've got to get her to come in voluntarily." Frustrated, I looked at my demon books beside Ivy's maps and charts. "I've done the research, and there's nothing I can do to protect your auras from her, so short of gunning her down, you don't have a chance."

"Then we'll dart the bitch with an animal sedative," he said grimly. "Don't you guys do that with Weres?"

"No. We don't," I said tightly, thinking it was barbaric to even suggest it. "Listen to me. You cannot risk alienating this woman. Even if I do hit her with a sleepy-time potion and down her for you, in about eighteen years, you're going to have another one of these women on the street, and you won't be able to distinguish her kills from natural causes. You saw Remus. He's alive because of some stupid wish, and from watching Holly interact with him, Mia learned how to push energy into people, not just take it."

"So," the FIB officer prompted. "That sounds good to me."

"So like every good thing we can think up to make our lives better, it can be turned into a weapon. Mia goes in, makes some poor sap think she's in love with him, and because she's feeding him emotion, he believes it. His guard goes down, and he dies without a whimper or an emotional stain. Of natural causes."

"Like Glenn's friend," he said, and I picked up the bottle of wine, looking at it. *No, Rachel. You'll have a migraine in the morning.*

"Exactly," I said, filling the graduated cylinder right to the top. Not looking at Jenks, I drank half of it, then topped it off to get to the right mark. Who would have thought that so much trouble could come from one lousy wish? No wonder Ivy felt responsible.

Edden was silent, and I let him stew while I dropped another leaf of holly and some ivy roots into the mortar and started working them over. "I have to get this woman," he finally said. "Will you just come with me to the party?"

Frustrated, I shifted the phone to the other ear. He wasn't getting it. "Mia is not afraid of you," I said. "The only thing you have to bargain with is Holly, and that's pretty thin. The woman doesn't want The Walker to have her. If you can promise me that there will be no wards of the court, no temporary custody, and that you can keep Holly with Mia all the time, she might come in just so she can impress you with how low and scummy you are."

"I will not promise that woman *anything*," Edden said, his anger so deep that Jenks clattered his wings in concern. "She left my son to die. Her child is social service's problem, not mine."

Angry, I huffed, "That's right. You'll be retired by the time Holly is out on her own." *Me, I'll probably be just coming into my own—if I am still alive.* "Come on," I coaxed when he was silent. "Look at the bigger picture. You tell me Mia's daughter can stay with her, and maybe I can get Mia to come in as a gesture of goodwill. Everyone wins, and you look like a benevolent human being allowing a helpless woman in jail to keep her baby. She'll do her time for beating up Glenn, and then peacefully reenter society, promising to be good. You'll have a handle on her, and better yet, one on Holly."

"What about the Tilsons?" he asked, and I made a face he couldn't see. *Oh yeah. I forgot about them.*

I continued to grind away, shoulder starting to hurt. "She'll probably blame it on Remus, and God knows he deserves whatever comes to him. Once you have her behind bars, you have control. One step at a time."

Again there was a long silence. "I'll see what I can do."

It had been a sour-sounding admission, and the circuit clicked closed. "Edden!" I exclaimed, but it was too late. I couldn't go to Mia with "I'll see what I can do," and upset, I set the phone in its cradle and made a frustrated noise at the ceiling. "CYA bull crap," I muttered.

Jenks flew to the island counter, stilling his wings when I finished weighing out the last bit of dust. "Why are you helping her, Rachel?"

Eyes on the scale, I blew some of the dust off, then held my breath until it gave me a reading. "I'm not." I said, satisfied with the amount. "I'm trying to not get blamed for the resurgence of a deadly Inderlander species. If we can keep her in jail long enough, Remus will be dead when she gets out, and she can't easily have another child."

I dumped the dust into the wine mix, watching it turn black and the clumps settle to the bottom. Jenks rose high again, bringing me a strand of my hair. I carefully put it in the mix and gave a couple of twists with the pestle.

The shavings from the watch were next, and finished, I opened the oven for the last bottle. Jenks came close to ride the updraft from the heat, and as I dumped everything into it and stoppered it up, I felt a twinge on my awareness. It wasn't someone tapping my ley line out back, but rather a sensation that I could sense it almost without trying. My eyes went to the ceiling, and I wasn't surprised to see Bis crawling in, his usually dark skin a pale white to match the color of what he was clinging too. My welcoming smile faded when his red eyes met mine and I noticed that his huge, white-tufted ears were at a worried slant, almost parallel to his head.

Seeing me notice him, the young gargoyle dropped to the counter.

"Holy sweet mother of Tink!" Jenks yelped, shooting halfway across the kitchen and leaving a spot of dust like an octo-pus inking. "Bis! What the hell is wrong with you?"

I set the bottle beside the first two, lined up beside my dis-solution vat, and wiped my hands on my jeans. "Hi, Bis," I said. "Come in to get warmed up?"

Bis shook his wings straight and wound his lionlike tail around a back haunch, as if nervous. "There's two cars out front. I think it's Rynn Cormel."

My breath hissed in and a spike of adrenaline jumped, mak-ing my head hurt. "Is Ivy with them?" I asked, already mov-ing.

"I don't know."

Jenks was way ahead of me, and I almost jogged to the front of the church, hitting lights as I went. The gong of the farm bell we used as a doorbell clinked once, not very loud, and I brushed bits of the spell off my shirt.

Though the sanctuary was blazing with light, the foyer was dark. Relief that Bis had gotten the graffiti off the sign flitted through me. It was followed by the thought that I really needed to invest in a peephole. Or some lighting. Pulse racing, I reached for the handle, ducking when Bis landed beside the door to cling to the wall like a huge bat. His ears were pinned to his head, and he shifted upward to hang at head height. Jenks was at my shoulder, and hoping the pixies stayed asleep, I opened the door.

Rynn Cormel was on my front porch, standing somewhat sideways in the yellowish light shining on the sign above the door. He looked about the same as he had a few hours ago: long coat, round hat, snow dusting his shiny shoes, hands in his pockets. Behind him were two long cars in the dark street. Not limos, but close.

Giving us a welcoming smile, he inclined his head at Jenks and me, his eyes flicking briefly to where Bis was lurking in-side, almost as if he could see through the paint and shingles.

"Is she okay?" I said breathlessly.

"More than," he said in his rough voice, his New York accent obvious. "She's a masterpiece." Bringing a gloved hand from a pocket, he gestured to the second car.

Jenks's wings clattered as he dropped beside my neck to find some warmth, and my eyes narrowed. People were getting out of the second car, but there was no sign of Ivy, and I hadn't appreciated his comment.

Rynn Cormel smiled at my obvious anger, ticking me off all the more. "I did not take advantage of her, Rachel," he said dryly. "Piscary is an artist, and I can appreciate a work of art without having to get my fingers on it, spoiling it."

"She is a person," I snapped, arms crossed over me against the cold, and not going out on the stoop.

"And a magnificent one at that. You have a discerning eye."

God! This was just sick. Jenks's wings moved against me, and I looked past Rynn to the street, seeing in the dim light Ivy slumped in a husky guy's arms. He was in a black T-shirt, arms bulging while he carried Ivy as if she were nothing. Behind him was a second man with her boots and coat.

"You said she was okay!" I accused, realizing she was unconscious.

The master vampire moved aside as they mounted the steps, and I got out of their way as they walked in, nice as you please, the heavy scent of vampire trailing behind them. "She is," he said as they passed me. "She's asleep. She will likely stay that way until well after sunrise. Her last words made it quite clear that she wanted to come home." He smiled, ducking his head to look perfectly normal, perfectly alive. Perfectly deadly. "She used words that left no doubt. I didn't see the harm in it."

I could imagine. "Her room is on the left," I called after them, not wanting to follow and leave a past U.S. president standing on my porch. Jenks took off from my shoulder, and dusting heavily from indecision, he finally took off after them.

"I'll show you," he said. "This way."

I turned back to Cormel, arms still over my chest. I didn't care if I looked defensive. "Thank you," I said stiffly, thinking

I'd give him something more sincere once I found out how messed up she was.

Again the tall man inclined his head. "Thank you."

He said nothing else, and the silence became uncomfortable. Bis twitched his ear, and Cormel's eyes shifted. There was a soft thump from inside the church, then nothing.

"I am going to try to find a way for her to keep her soul after death," I said.

"I know you are." He smiled the smile that saved the world, but I saw beyond it to the monster underneath. I had to keep Ivy from becoming this. It was foul.

I didn't look away from Cormel as the sound of footsteps and pixy wings grew behind me. Standing in the middle of my threshold with my feet spread and my arms crossed, I refused to move as the men brushed past me and went down the cement steps and into the dark. With a last inclination of his head, Rynn Cormel slowly spun on a heel and followed, getting in the first car when one of his men opened the door. Two more doors thumped shut, and they slowly accelerated down the street.

Jenks landed on my shoulder as I exhaled long and loud. "In or out, Bis?" I asked, and the gargoyle launched himself deeper into the church. There was a delighted laugh from the open support beams, and I shut the door, sealing out the night. Jenks's wings were cold, and I decided I'd bake cookies or something to warm up the church.

Feet slow, I went into the sanctuary. Bis was on one of the support beams, three of Jenks's older kids with him. His ears were flat as he tried to decide what to make of them, and it looked sweet as he tried to appear harmless, shifting to a bright white and holding his wings close. Bis didn't come in often, but the entire church had the feeling of closing in, circling the wounded, bracing for a fight.

"Is she okay?" I asked Jenks as I tiptoed into the hall.

"She stinks like vampire" was his opinion. "But her aura looks really thick."

Really thick. Thicker than usual? I mused, not knowing if that was good or bad, sighing as I touched Ivy's closed door in passing. I was glad to have her home. The church felt . . . almost right.

Just a few more days, I thought as I reached the kitchen and turned the oven on to preheat. Just a few more days, and everything will be back to normal.

But as I looked at the stoppered bottles all lined up and ready to go, I wondered.

Twenty-five

"Oh God. I think I'm going to be sick," I whispered, head bowed over my lap, making my hair drape onto the scrying mirror. The morning chill made me feel ill as it mixed with my nausea, and my hand shook as I pressed it into the cave of the pentagram engraved on the scrying mirror. The ley line spilling into me was still ragged lurches and jumps. Obviously my aura wasn't yet back to normal.

Rachel calling Al, come in, Al, I thought sarcastically, in a last-ditch effort to reach the demon, but as before, he refused to answer, leaving me in this dizzy, uncomfortable morass of existence. I hunched, as it felt like the world suddenly dropped out from under me. My stomach gave a heave, and I broke the connection before I vomited on the kitchen floor.

"Damn it all to the Turn and back!" I exclaimed, barely above a whisper. Shaking, I curbed my desire to fling the mirror across the kitchen, and instead leaned to shove it roughly away on the open shelves under the island counter. Slumping back in my chair, I stared at the silent room. It was about three in the afternoon. Ivy wasn't up yet, but the pixies were at it, trying to be quiet so as not to wake her. I eyed the open box of cold pizza from last night, and feeling my nausea leave as fast as it had come, I yanked a piece and ate the point. "Crap, this is awful," I muttered, tossing it back in the box. I was too old for this.

It was really quiet. And cold. 'Course, being in my robe didn't help. Rex appeared in the doorway, sitting on the threshold and curling her tail around her feet. Pulling a pepperoni off my abandoned slice, I offered it to her, and the cat padded in, taking it with a finicky precision. "Good kitty," I whispered, giving her ears a little rub after she ate the morsel.

I had way too much to do today to be sitting around in my robe feeding the cat cold pizza, and taking my cup, I refilled it, standing at the sink to look out at the glittering snow. Our perishables, stacked on the picnic table, looked funny, and I sighed.

Tonight was New Year's, and I was shunned. What a nice way to start the year. No wonder, really, if I was considering doing a spell to force a demon to come to me—in a public place. Maybe I should break into a vacant office that overlooked the square. *Maybe I am a black witch.*

Mood souring, I took a sip of coffee, eyes closing as it slipped down and eased the last of my nausea. Turning, I started, almost spilling my coffee when I found Ivy standing in the doorway in her black silk robe, her arms crossed, watching me.

"Holy crap!" I exclaimed, flustered. "How long have you been there?"

Ivy smiled with her lips closed, her eyes dilating slightly at the pulse of adrenaline I'd probably given off. "Not long," she said, picking up Rex and giving her a cuddle.

"You freaking scared the crap out of me," I complained. *And why were you just standing there, watching me?*

"Sorry." Dropping Rex, she eased into the kitchen, going to the sink and warming up her coffee mug in a steady stream of hot tap water.

I casually moved back to my chair and sat, trying not to look like I was avoiding her. She didn't look sorry. She looked . . . gorgeous, her alabaster white skin having a hint of rose. Casual in her black robe, her motions had an unusual edginess to them. Sharp. Obviously her night at Cormel's had done more than save her life.

"How are you feeling?" I asked hesitantly, eyeing the pizza and deciding I couldn't stomach it. "Cormel brought you home about midnight. You, ah, look great."

The gurgle of the coffee as it filled her cup was loud, and she said without turning, "I'm feeling really, really good. Every last itch scratched, every last bubble burst." Her voice was tight and depressed, and she carefully replaced the carafe. "I hate myself. But tomorrow will be better. I took blood from someone to keep from dying. My only consolation was that it wasn't you." Now she turned, and holding her cup high in salute, she added, "Small victories."

I didn't know what to do, seeing her standing at the sink with the island counter between us. "I'm sorry," I said softly. "I don't care what you did. I'm just glad you're okay." But I couldn't bring myself to cross the room and give her a hug. Not yet.

Her eyes dropped to the mug in her hand. "Thank you. We both know the monster is there. No need to have to look at it, right?"

She sounded resigned, and I protested, "Ivy, you're not a monster."

Her gaze flicked to mine, and she looked away. "Then why do I feel so damn good right now? After what I did last night?"

I didn't know the answer. My thoughts went to the brat pack, comparing black magic to chemo treatments. "All I know is that it saved your life, and I'm glad you're okay."

She took her coffee to her computer. Lips pressed in a tight line, she moved two books off her chair and sat before a blank screen. More needed to be said, but I didn't know how to bring it up. I listened for the sound of wings, but Jenks was either in the sanctuary with his kids or being especially quiet in his eavesdropping. "Um, Ivy, I have something to ask you."

Tossing the hair from her eyes, she shook the mouse and woke up her computer. "Yes?"

Yes? It sounded innocent enough, but my pulse was racing, and I knew she knew it and was feigning disinterest. Hands around my warm mug, I took a slow breath. "If you could, would you leave everything to become human?"

Mouse unmoving, she stared at me with empty eyes. "I don't know."

A dry clattering of pixy wings interrupted and Jenks darted in, spilling silver sparkles. "What!" he exclaimed, hovering in midair between us in his Peter Pan pose. "Rachel says she can take away the blood lust, and you say you don't know? What's wrong with you!"

"Jenks!" I exclaimed, not surprised he'd been listening. "I didn't say I could make her human. I asked if she could, would she do it. And quit eavesdropping on us, okay?"

Ivy shook her head. "So I'm human, and the blood lust is gone. What does that leave me with? It's not the blood lust that warped me, it was Piscary. I'd still be mixing savagery with feelings of love. Only now, if I hurt someone in passion, it would hurt. At least the way things are, it would feel good."

Jenks's wings dropped in pitch, and a slip of dust turned green for a moment. "Oh."

"Not to mention I'd be frail and lower on the food chain," she added, a soft blush coloring her skin, attention going to the screen, avoiding us. "Anyone could take advantage of me and probably would, seeing as I've got a past. The way things are now, no one dares."

Cold, I tugged my robe closed. "You can feel strong without the vampire virus."

"Yeah, right," she said, and my expression froze at her flash of anger. "I like being a vampire. It's losing my soul that scares me. If I knew I wouldn't lose it when I die, I might try harder to . . . conform." Her eyes met mine, my magic books stacked between us, all brought down this morning from the belfry. "You really think you can make me human?"

Jenks's kids came rushing in with a burst of noise and silk, and I shrugged as he corralled them, pushing them out ahead of him as he went to see what had them in a tizzy. "I don't know," I said in the abruptly quiet kitchen. "Trent has a treatment. It only has an eleven percent success rate, and it only makes the virus and neurotoxins dormant. If you survived taking it, you'd still become an undead and lose your soul when you died. Rynn Cormel would say it was a failure." I smiled thinly, thinking it sucked to be a vampire, even one as respected as Ivy. "It might make your life easier. Or it might kill you." I wasn't going to risk an 11 percent chance of success. Not with Ivy.

"Actually," I said, hesitant to bring it up, "I was thinking along the lines of a curse that can turn you human."

"Or witch?" Ivy said, surprising me. There was a soft vulnerability in her and I blinked.

"You don't want to be a witch," I said quickly.

"Why not? You are."

Jenks came back in with one of his kids, her wings tangled up in what was probably spiderweb. "I think you should be a pixy," he said, fingers sifting dust as they gently ran over Jrixibell's wing to clean it. "You'd look so cute with your little wings and your sword. I'd let you fight in my garden anytime."

A smile quirked her lips, then died. "A witch can't be turned," she said shortly.

"Neither can a Were," said Jenks, smiling as he boosted his child into the air and the little girl zipped out, hurting my ears with her shout to wait for her.

Ivy was lost in thought, and I couldn't help my smile as I thought of David. I think she was, too, when she turned to her computer, blushing. Cormel would freaking kill me if I turned Ivy into anything other than a vampire with an eternal soul. But seeing as I couldn't be what I wanted, why not use my liability to give Ivy the chance to be what she wanted?

Feeling like something had been settled even though it

hadn't, I pushed myself up and went to the pantry. Everything that had been in our fridge was outside. "You want pancakes? I feel like cooking."

"Sure." Her fingers were clicking on the keys, but her eyes were on the three bottles of potion against the wall by the disillusion pot of salt water. "You got the book?" she asked.

I came out of the pantry with the box of mix. "Last night. I'm going out to try it tonight at Fountain Square. You want to come?"

"Will there be news vans and screaming?"

"Probably," I said sourly.

"Count me in," she said, and Jenks snorted from the sill where he was feeding his sea monkeys. The tiny tank of brine had taken the place of honor at the window ever since I'd moved Mr. Fish to the ever-after as my canary, to know if the ever-after was poisoning me.

Leaning against the counter, I read the back of the box. If we had eggs, they were frozen. "Actually, I'm going to rent a van and park it in the garage. Could you help keep people away?"

"If the van's a rockin', don't come a knockin'!" Jenks said, gyrating beside me.

"God, Jenks," I said. "We do have kids in the church."

"How do you think they got here, baby?" he said, laughing.

I set the box down hard, and the mix puffed up into him. "Hey!" he shouted, dusting heavily as he shivered his wings and the mix made a cloud.

Ivy was smiling with closed lips. This was nice. We'd come a long way in a year—all of us. "After you whip that demon's ass, I'll take you and Pierce out for pizza," she offered.

"Deal." Bending, I got the frying pan out from under the counter and put it on the stove. My thoughts went to what spells I could make today to help ensure that Al wouldn't get so pissed he took his mistake out on me. They'd be earth charms, so I wouldn't have to tap a line, but that was where I excelled. Sleepy-time charms for sure.

Ivy stood in a fast motion, and Jenks and I jumped. Either she wasn't hiding her vampire speed, or she was having trouble controlling it. Seeing Jenks's and my alarm, her face scrunched in amusement. "Glenn's car is at the end of the street," she said, and Jenks rose higher, his expression one of disbelief. "I'm getting dressed." Coffee in hand, she walked out.

"Tink's little red thong," Jenks blurted, following her. "You can hear that from here?"

"Today I can," she said, her words fading as she went into her room.

I tightened the tie on my robe. Would I give up being that special in order to love someone, or would I just find someone new to love?

The creaking of the front door and the ensuing pixy uproar told me Jenks had let the FIB detective in, and I was smiling when the tall man entered, a paper grocery bag in his grip. Pixies wreathed him, noisy as they darted in and out of the bag while he set it on the counter. His eyes went to the empty space where the fridge had been, a question in his expression. "Where's your fridge?"

"I blew it up," I said, taking in his fading bruises and bare scalp, newly shaved to even out the mess the hospital had left. I didn't think I'd ever seen him in jeans before, and a dark sweater showed from underneath a leather coat. "You look better," I said as he eyed my robe.

"Uh, it's three in the afternoon," he said, suddenly unsure.

"It sure is." I gave him a hug, truly glad to see him. "How are those locator amulets I gave your dad working? You want some coffee? Pancakes? I owe you for helping me get out of the hospital. Thanks for that." I couldn't stop smiling. I'd thought he was going to die or be hospitalized for months, and now he was standing in my kitchen with a bag of groceries and only the faintest hint of stress showing in his face.

Glenn's gaze slid to the coffeepot, then back to the empty spot. "Uh, amulets are working, I guess, you're welcome for the help breaking out, and no thanks on the coffee. I can't stay. The department heard what happened last night with you and Ivy, and the guys wanted me to bring you both something. You're not invincible, you know. There's no big *S* on your chest." He hesitated, brow furrowing as he leaned close enough that I could smell his aftershave. "How's Ivy? I heard she was hit hard."

"She bounced right back," I said dryly, peeking into the bag with the pixies to find . . . Tomatoes? *He bought tomatoes with the FIB's gift fund?* "Ah, she's getting dressed," I added, surprised. *Where did Glenn get tomatoes?*

"Damn, vampires heal fast," he said, his dark eyes interested as he leaned to see into the bag while I poked around. "It took me five days. No wonder Denon wants to be one."

"Yeah, well, we all make mistakes." Three of Jenks's kids rose up with a cherry tomato, arguing over who got the seeds. "Glenn, did you get all this by yourself?"

He grinned, rubbing a hand behind his neck. "Yeah. Too much?"

"Not if you're going to have a family reunion," I said, smiling so he'd know I was messing with him. "Damn, Mr. Man! I'm proud of you! You actually went in a store and everything?"

He came close to the bag, leaning to look in, his eagerness charming on a big black man. "You should have seen the looks I got," he said as he reached in and the bag crackled. "Did you know there is more than one kind of tomato? This one is a beefsteak." A huge tomato the size of my two fists hit the counter. "It's good for slicing up on sandwiches. And the lady at the store said you can quarter them and grill them."

"No kidding," I said, hiding a grin as his dark fingers pulled out a bag of plum tomatoes.

"These long ones are Romas," he said as he set them down. "You cut these up and put them in salads, on pizza, and in sauces. And the little ones here are cherry tomatoes. You can put them in salads or eat them like candy."

I had never eaten a tomato "like candy," but I ate one now, the acidic fruit not mixing at all well with the coffee. "Mmmm, good," I said, and Jenks laughed, hovering at the lintel with the tomato his kids had swiped. Behind him, one of his daughters waited, wringing her hands.

"I've got three that were vine ripened," Glenn said, showing me the top of his bruised and cut head as he looked for them. "Those babies were expensive, but they're really red."

"Don't you want some of these for yourself?" I asked, and he looked up, grinning. The smile went all the way to his eyes, and it felt good to see it on him.

"I've got another bag in the car. You're going to have to find someone else to blackmail into giving you law enforcement tools."

"So you don't mind if I tell your dad, then?" I teased, and his smile vanished.

Jenks came in, easily handling the weight of the cherry tomato. "Here, Glenn. My kids are sorry. They won't do it again."

I caught the fruit as he dropped it. "They can keep it," I said, and five pixy bucks and Jenks's daughter swooped in, arguing in high-pitched voices as they snatched it from my palm.

"Hey!" Jenks shouted, following them out.

"Are you sure you don't want some coffee?" I said as I heard Ivy's door creak open. "I think the rani of recycling has a foam cup around here. You can take it with you."

Glenn took his fingers out of the bag of tomatoes, his hands going behind him in sort of a parade rest, his back to the door. "No, I have to go. But I want your opinion on last night."

He was starting to look like a cop. Frowning, I thought about Ivy and my frantic drive to the bridge. "It sucked. Why?"

"Not your personal night," Glenn said dryly. "Don't you ever look at a paper?"

Interested, I pushed off from the counter and found this

morning's paper still in its little plastic bag on the table. Under it was the picture of Jenks and me standing before the Mackinaw Bridge, rescued from yesterday's burning fridge. Carefully moving the photo, I opened up the paper. "Where am I looking?" I asked, standing hunched over it.

"The front page," he said wryly.

Oh goodie. Wincing, I read, THREE IN HOSPITAL. EARLY MORNING BLACK MAGIC TO BLAME. There was a picture of ambulances in the dark, the scene lit by a car on fire. People were milling around in front of a business. From my shoulder, Jenks whistled, back from his kids.

"Uh, I was home all night," I said, thinking I was going to get blamed for this somehow. Whatever it was. "I talked to your dad about midnight. He can vouch for me." I leaned forward, recognizing the roof's outline. *Aston's roller rink?* "You're not working this, are you?" I asked, worried now. "Glenn, you might feel better, but your aura is still thin."

"I appreciate your concern," he said, his attention moving from the paper to the open box of cold pizza. "Hey, uh, can I have a slice of that? I'm starving."

"Sure." I squinted at the black-and-white shot as Glenn crossed the kitchen and wrangled a slice from the pizza. "Jenks, did you know about this?"

Jenks shook his head and landed on the paper, hands on his hips and his attention directed downward as he read.

"From what we've gotten from the I.S.," Glenn said around a bite of pizza, "it seems Ms. Walker ran into Ms. Harbor. Three people in intensive care with damaged auras."

"That's terrible," I said, glad I wasn't being blamed for it. "Do you need me to come down and look at the crime scene?" I asked, brightening. "It's Aston's roller rink, isn't it?"

Glenn laughed, turning it into a choke, and I kept my eyes on him—not on Ivy, suddenly standing in the doorway. She was dressed in jeans and a black sweater, looking nice, her hair brushed and wearing a little bit of makeup. "No, but thanks," he said, oblivious to Ivy.

Affronted, I sat in my chair and said, "You didn't have to laugh."

Jenks was in the air with the paper, struggling to turn it over and get to the rest of the article. "Yes, he did. You need to take a class on crime scene etiquette, Rache."

Ivy ghosted up behind Glenn as he started to take another bite, her feet soundless. "Thanks for the tomatoes, Glenn," she whispered in his ear, and the man jumped.

"Sweet mother of Jesus!" he exclaimed, spinning, his hand smacking his hip where his pistol would have been. The slice of pizza went airborne, and he scrambled to catch it. "Damn, woman," he complained as it hit the floor. "Where did you come from?"

Ivy smiled with her lips closed, but I was laughing. "My mother always said I came from heaven," she said, then delicately stepped over the pizza to reach the coffeemaker. Motions sultry, she refilled her cup and turned, standing in front of the cupboard door to the trash.

Glenn was holding the slice of pizza cradled in his big hand like it was a favorite pet—dead but still beloved. Ivy slid sideways and opened the cupboard door, and the man sighed as he threw it away. Amused, I extended the pizza box, and he brightened, taking another slice.

"So what's up?" Ivy asked as she sipped her coffee, eyeing him over the rim as if she wanted to eat him up like pie.

"Yeah, why are you here, Glenn, if you don't want me to check out that crime scene?" I asked, putting my feet up on the adjacent chair and adjusting my robe to cover my legs.

"Can't a guy bring over a get-well tomato without getting the third degree?" he said with a false innocence.

"Six freaking pounds of get-well tomatoes," Jenks muttered, and Ivy set her cup down, turning to the sink to fill a small pan to wash the red fruit. She wanted to stay and needed something to do.

"It better not be about working tonight," I said, looking

askance at the paper. "I already told your dad I was not working his lame-ass party."

"No way!" Jenks darted from the paper to hover an inch before Glenn's nose. "There is no way I'm letting Rachel work with her aura that crappy. You want her facedown again? She may look all tough and shit, but her aura peels off like a banana skin."

I hadn't known that, and I wondered if it was a species thing or just me.

"Which is exactly why I'm not doing what my dad sent me to do, asking you to work that party," Glenn said as he stood unperturbed in our kitchen and mowed down his pizza crust. Wings clattering, Jenks backed down, and Glenn glanced at me. "If he calls, swear a lot and tell him I gave you a hard time, will you? He has no idea what it's like to have a compromised aura. I'm glad you're both staying in tonight."

I didn't shift my eyes from him, but it was hard not to look at Ivy, who had turned with that beefsteak swathed in a towel, a smile quirking her lips. "Yeah, a nice and quiet night," I said, hoping he didn't see my spell books. Fingers slow, I folded the paper up and set it deliberately on top of them.

Ivy turned her back on us, but I think she was still smiling as she continued washing the tomatoes, setting them to dry one by one.

"Well, I gotta go," Glenn said, dusting his hands and looking at the leftover pizza. "Thanks, ladies. Don't let my dad get to you. He really wants to nail this woman and doesn't realize what he's asking of you."

"No problem." Now I felt guilty, and I stood up, handing him the pizza box. His eyes lit up as he took it, but I wished he'd get out of here. I had to prep for tonight. Sure, I had agreed not to circle Al, but there were other ways to catch a demon, and I wondered if turning him into a mouse would work. I knew I could do that one. "Have a great New Year's, Glenn."

The FIB detective smiled. "You, too." He picked up one of the clean tomatoes and tucked it in his pocket. Winking, he said, "Don't tell my dad about the tomatoes, okay?"

"I'll take it to my grave." *Which might be as soon as to-night . . .*

Ivy turned from folding up the grocery bag and sliding it under the sink. "Glenn, are you headed in to work?" she asked, and he hesitated.

"Ye-e-es," he hedged. "You want a ride?"

"I have a few words of wisdom for Edden about that little bitch of a banshee," she said, grimacing, then added, looking at me, "Unless you need me to stick around?"

Jenks's wings clattered in agitation, and mystified, I glanced at my spell books. "I'm just going to play with my junior cook books," I said, and then worried that guilt might make her try to face Mia alone, I added, "You'll be back before the ball drops, right?"

The rim of brown around her eyes shrank slightly. "You know it. I'll get my coat," she said, and turning, she strode out of the kitchen, moving with that eerie grace.

From the paper, Jenks muttered, "Need her to stick around? Who does she think she is?"

"I heard that!" Ivy shouted from the sanctuary, and there was a squeal of pixies.

Glenn was moving to the door. "Take care of yourself, Rachel," he said, and I angled for a hug, my bad mood squeezed out by the big man who now smelled like pizza.

"You, too," I said, my smile fading as I became serious and rocked back. "Glenn, I want to get this woman, but it needs some solid planning."

"You don't need to tell me twice."

He turned to follow Ivy, and I touched his sleeve, stopping him. "Hey, if you see Ford today, will you tell him I'm ready to make an appointment?"

A smile holding what looked like pride came over him. "I will. Good for you, Rachel."

"Glenn?" came from the sanctuary, and he rolled his eyes.

"Coming, Mother," he called, and headed out, pizza box in hand. I heard his feet in the hall, a chorus of tiny good-byes, and the door closing. Content, I slid the pancake mix away.

Jenks sat on the rim of the coffeemaker, his wings fanning in the rising warmth. "You might want to get dressed if you're going to fight demons today," he said, and I looked at him from around my sleep-stringy hair.

"Will you watch the door while I shower?" I asked, and he buzzed his wings.

"Duh."

The pixies were loud, playing with the cherry tomatoes as I shuffled into my bathroom to get the water going. I was looking forward to a long soak, and I blissfully lost myself in lather, rinse, and repeat. Eyes closed, I stood under the hot water and breathed in the steam, reluctant to get out and get back to my life. I'd spent four years using a crappy, low-volume shower thanks to Mrs. Talbu, and the high-output, energy-inefficient head that Ivy had installed even before I'd moved in was better than therapy. Not that I needed therapy. Na-a-a-ah. Not me.

The spray suddenly went cold, and gasping, I pushed from the wall, making my back smack the one behind me. "Jenks!" I shouted in a burst of adrenaline. "Knock it off!"

The water hitting my feet grew warm, but my mood had soured and I got out and reached for my towel. My motions were rough as I dried my hair and worked my way down. Apparently Jenks thought I was clean enough. Wrapped in a towel, I swiped at the mirror to take stock. Not too bad, I decided, apart from lingering circles under my eyes. Not too bad at all for having been bitch-slapped by a banshee twice in as many days.

From outside the door came the clatter of pixy wings and a hesitant "Rachel?"

My towel slipped as I rummaged for a complexion spell. "Very funny, Jenks. I could have slipped and cracked my head open." The humming of wings grew louder, and I snatched my towel higher. "Jenks!" I exclaimed as he darted under the door. "I didn't say to come in!"

His wings a bright red, Jenks turned his back on me. "Sorry. Uh, I thought you ought to know Marshal is here," he said apologetically.

Panic iced through me, and I tightened my grip on my towel. "Get him out of here, Jenks!" I just about hissed. "I've been shunned!"

The pixy glanced over his shoulder, then revolved in the air to face me. "I think he knows already. He wants to talk to you. Rache, I'm sorry. He looks mad."

Shit, I'd been shunned. Marshal hadn't come over to hold my hand and tell me he could make it all better. I'd told him I was a white witch, and I was, but now . . ."

"Tell him to go away," I said, chickening out. "Tell him to leave before someone knows he's here and they shun him, too." But the pixy only shook his head.

"No. He has a right to tell you to your face."

I took a breath. My head started to hurt. *This is going to be way fun.* Turning to the mirror, I started brushing my hair. Arms crossed, Jenks waited for the right answer. The brush got tangled in my hair, and frustrated, I smacked it on the tiny counter. "I'll be out in three minutes," I said to get him to leave.

Nodding, he dropped to the floor. A faint glimmer of light, and he was gone.

I had underwear in the dryer and a camisole hanging over the industrial-size tub. My bathroom was really a glorified laundry room, but it was easier than sharing the more traditional bathroom across the hall with Ivy. Besides, I had jeans fresh from the dryer most days. *No socks, though,* I thought as I gave my hair a last brush and let it hang damp.

Worried, I quietly opened the door and looked hesitantly down the hall. It was cool out here compared to the moist warmth of the bathroom, and I could smell fresh coffee. Padding down the hall on silent bare feet, I peeked into the kitchen to find Marshal sitting with his back to me. I was out of his peripheral eyesight, and I hesitated.

He looked empty, or maybe just deep in thought as he stared at the grimy floor where the fridge had been, probably wondering what happened. His long legs were bent comfortably under the table, and the reflected sun glinted on his short curly hair. This was going to be hard. I didn't blame him for being mad at me. I'd told him I was a white witch and he had trusted me. Society said different.

Resolute, I pushed myself off the archway and into the kitchen. "Hi."

Marshal pulled his feet under him and spun. "Hey, you gave me a start," he said, his eyes wide and color flashing into his face. "I didn't expect you out for another ten minutes."

Giving him a tiny smile, I looked for something to hide behind, but all that was between us was space. Lots of new space. "You want some coffee?"

The cups scraped as I got two new ones out, and he said nothing as I filled them. He remained silent as I slid one in front of him. "I'm sorry," I said as I retreated, putting the island counter between us. Scared, almost, I took a sip. Hot bitterness slipped down. Gathering my courage, I set the mug by the sink. "Marshal—"

His eyes met mine, cutting me off. They weren't angry, they weren't sad, they were . . . empty. "Let me say something, and then I'll go," he said. "I think I'm allowed that much."

Depressed, I crossed my arms over my middle. My stomach hurt. "I'll get the shunning removed," I said. "You know this is a mistake. I'm not a black witch."

"When I went to the registrar's office about your classes this morning, my supervisor came in. He told me not to see you anymore," he said abruptly. "I think that's funny."

Funny. That's what he'd said, but his face was grim. "Marshal . . ."

"I don't like people telling me what I can't do," he added, sounding angry this time.

"Marshal, please."

His broad chest expanded and contracted, and he looked past me, toward the snowy garden. "Don't worry about it." Bringing his focus back into the kitchen, he shifted forward to reach into a back pocket of his jeans. "Here's your check. It will be a rainy day in the ever-after before they will cash it."

Swallowing, I stared at the envelope, feeling unreal as I took it. It was heavier than it should be, and I looked inside. My eyes widened. "Two tickets to the party at the top of the Carew Tower?" I said, shocked he even had them, much less was giving them to me. "Why?"

Marshal grimaced, eyes on the floor. "I was going to ask you if you wanted to come with me to a New Year's Eve party tonight," he said, "but why don't you just take both tickets. You're going to need a lot of ambient energy to make that charm work. The top of the tower ought to be close enough."

My lips parted, and I stared at the formal invitations in my hand. I didn't know what was going on anymore. Jenks had said he was mad. Why was he helping me? "I can't take these."

He cracked his neck and backed up a step. "Sure you can. Put them in your pocket and say thank you. My supervisor is going to be there." Marshal sniffed. "You should meet him."

An uncertain smile came over my face. He wanted me to meet his supervisor? Maybe get a picture of us together? "And I thought I was wicked," I said, eyes warming. *Damn it, he's leaving me. Well, what did I expect?*

Marshal didn't smile back. "He's got red hair. Can't miss him." Gaze distant, he took up his coffee. "It's a fund-raiser for the university. Kalamack will be there. He's a major bene-factor, so he's always invited. He's not a witch, so he probably won't care if you're shunned. You'll have someone to talk to until someone tells him."

My face lost expression at the utter blankness he had given the word "shunned," like it meant nothing. "Thank you," I said meekly. "Marshal, I'm sorry," I said as he reached for his coat, on the back of his chair, and I just about died when he put up a hand to stop me before I could get close. I froze where I was, feeling the hurt.

"It was fun," Marshal said, eyes down. "But then you got shunned, and, Rachel . . ." His gaze rose to mine, anger in it. "I like you. I like your family. I have fun when we get together, but what *pisses* me off is that I let myself start to think about spending my life with you, and then you go do something so stupid that it gets you shunned. I don't even want to know what it was."

"Marshal." I never had a choice. I never had a *damned choice!*

"I don't want to do this," he said, not letting me interrupt. "And trust me," he said, gesturing, "I thought hard about it, really weighed what I wanted and what I was willing to give for a possible life with you. I came over here ready to curse the world, to try to find out who did this to you and find a way to get the shunning rescinded, but then . . ." Marshal gritted his teeth, making his jaw muscles bunch. "I'm only going to get myself shunned. I can't live outside society. You're a fun, beautiful, fabulous woman," he said, as if trying to convince himself. "Even if you do get the shunning rescinded, what are you going to do next? I like my life." He looked at me, and I blinked fast. "Now I'm just angry that you can't be a part of it," he finished.

I couldn't seem to breathe, and I held the edge of the center counter to hide my vertigo.

"No hard feelings, okay?" he said as he turned.

I nodded. "No hard feelings," I breathed. Marshal wasn't a bad man for wanting out. He wanted to be part of something, and I clearly wasn't able to put *my* needs aside and put *ours* first. Maybe if my life wasn't so crappy, it wouldn't show as much and we could have tried, but not now. It wasn't his fault. I'd screwed up, and asking him to pay the price with me wasn't fair.

"Thanks, Marshal," I whispered. "For everything. And if

you ever need help from the dark side . . ." I gestured help-lessly as my throat closed. "Call me."

A faint smile turned the edges of his mouth up. "No one else."

And then he was gone, his steps fading as he walked away from me. I heard a soft murmur as he said good-bye to the pix-ies, and then the closing of a door.

Numb, I sank into my chair at the table. Eyes unseeing, I pulled my spell book closer, covering up the letter from the university. Wiping my eyes, I opened it and started searching.

Twenty-six

The wind funneling between the tall buildings down by the river picked up tiny bits of ice and grit, and they hit my legs like pinpricks. I hated nylons. Even black ones with glitter. Hunching into my dressy long felt coat, I hustled after Ivy, head down and pace fast. Trying to do this charm in the parking garage would have been miserable, and I was glad for the invitations if only for that, but now that we'd be inside, Jenks could come. He was currently in my bag sitting on one of those hand warmers hunters use. With him at my back and Ivy guarding the ladies' bathroom door, this would be a snap. That is, if we got up there in time. If we didn't hurry, we'd be in the elevator at midnight.

A gust of wind brought me the scent of fried vendor food, and I squinted ahead to one of Carew Tower's street entrances. Carew Tower was right over Fountain Square, and people were everywhere, milling through the closed-off streets as both FIB and I.S. cruisers blocked the way. It wasn't as bad as the solstice, when they closed the circle by lottery, but the uproar at midnight ought to be a big enough collective emotion to do the spell. Actually, it was a lot like the night I had first summoned Pierce, trying to bring my dad back for some parental advice, weather and all.

Reminded, I held my bulging bag tighter, trying not to squish Jenks. I had everything in it I'd need to do the charm, including a set of clothes for Pierce, and my splat gun. Beside me, Ivy's steps were short and fast because of her heels.

"Sure are a lot of witches," she said as we made our way across the street.

"Any excuse to party, right?" I said, then took a longer look. She was pale in her long coat with her hair whipping in the wind. And worried. "We make you nervous, don't we?"

She met my eyes as we stepped up onto the curb. "You don't."

I smiled. "Thanks." I understood. Most vampires made me nervous, especially when they gathered.

The doorman opened the glass doors for us so we didn't have to use the revolving entryway, and we entered together. The cessation of the wind was a blessed relief, and I immediately opened my bag. "You okay, Jenks?" I said, peering down to find him sitting awkwardly beside the warmer.

"Freaking fantabulous," he muttered. "Tink's tampons, I think my wing snapped off. What are you doing out there? Jumping jacks?"

"Stay put until we get up there," I said so he wouldn't come out to prove that the echoing entryway wasn't too cold—which it was. "I only have two invitations."

"Like they could stop me?" he said, and I smiled at Ivy's snicker.

I left the bag unzipped as Ivy and I clacked our feminine way to the restaurant's elevator, where the man in the white uniform checked our invitations and then our coats. The night air from the revolving door was cold on my bare shoulders, and I let my coat go with regret. The doors to the elevator had been polished to a shine, and I resisted the urge to adjust my nylons as I shifted to get a better appreciation of the work I had done to look like this.

My heels, nylons, and a long black dress with no shoulders and a choker neckline looked good. I'd picked it out last week, almost able to feel Kisten in my thoughts as I shut out the clerk's enthusiastic recommendations for something with more flash. I'd nearly gotten the little dress that showed off my butt, but I'd listened to Kisten's memory instead. I looked great with my hair up off my neck in a complicated braid that had taken five of Jenks's kids to do. It had even held up in the wind.

Ivy was dressed just as dramatically, having pulled a bright red dress out of her closet, and going from workout tights to glamorous sophisticate in ten minutes. Her neckline was cut low, and the slit in the dress went to midthigh. A lace shawl graced her shoulders. I knew the shawl was for a vampire's benefit, more enticing around her neck than bare skin. Apart we looked good. Together we looked fantastic, with her Asian heritage standing as a beautiful contrast to my pale, dead-fish complexion.

An older couple smelling of too much perfume and after-shave stood ahead of us as the silver doors opened and we all got in. A spike of adrenaline went through me, and I shifted my lumpy bag to my front. This had to work. I'd prepped Pierce's substance spells in exactly the same way, and I had my splat gun loaded with sleepy-time charms. Ivy would man the bathroom door, Jenks would help me with Al. Nothing would get past them. And when it was over, we could party the new year in together, ghost, vamp, witch, and pixy.

There was another doorman inside the elevator in case we didn't know how to push a button, and as I nervously stood in the dead center of the small lift, the hairs on the back of my neck pricked. I slowly turned to see the couple who had gotten in with us, the woman's lips pressed tight and the man staring straight ahead with a strained look on his face. I turned back around, and Ivy snickered.

"You're a fun date," she whispered as she leaned sideways. "People look at you."

Whatever. Embarrassed, I stared at the elevator man while he hid a grin. Finally the doors opened. The older woman, who looked good in her own right, gave her husband a smack on the shoulder with her beaded handbag as they got out. He took it like a man, but I noticed he was already ogling the serving ladies in their modestly short skirts.

The murmur of conversations and the scent of high-calorie appetizers hit me first, and my shoulders eased in the warmth. Hidden around the curve of the restaurant, a live band played slow jazz. The tables were gone but for a ring around the windows. Elegantly dressed people mingled, holding little plates of food or champagne flutes, the occasional feminine laugh mixing with the clinking of expensive china to invoke a feeling of high class. Servers moved sedately or darted about, depending on what they were doing. And behind it all as a backdrop was Cincinnati herself.

Forgetting myself, I stood for a moment and took in the view. It had been pretty during the day, but now, with the black of the sky and the lights . . . it was riveting. The Hollows was glittering, showing the contours of the land as it rose up and away. A ribbon of illumination on the expressway ran as an informal border. The river was a black shadow, and I could see where it had cut into the hills over the millennium.

A woman's laugh and the flash of Jenks darting from my bag drew my eyes away. Immediately the conversation seemed to grow loud. Jenks flew two circles around me to stretch his wings, then landed on Ivy's shoulder. She was staring at the city, mesmerized. "It looks peaceful from up here," she said when her line of sight was broken by a member of the waitstaff.

Jenks snorted. "It looks peaceful when you get up real close, too," he said, and I thought of my garden. "It's only the middle ground that's ugly."

A woman with a tray was slowly passing, and I met her eyes. She smiled at Jenks and handed me a little plate. "We've got twenty minutes," I said, nervous, as I put a few bites of food on it. "Jenks, you want to scope out the bathrooms?"

"You got it, Rache," he said, and he was gone.

By the looks Ivy and I were getting, it was growing obvious that this was almost an office party. Everyone seemed to know everyone else, and they were all dressed alike, too. Elegant, but a little out of date—classy geek, maybe? No wonder Ivy and I were getting eyed.

Slowly we made our way onto the revolving floor. Balloons were netted to the ceiling for midnight, and the lights were low to keep the view fabulous. I didn't see anyone I recognized, but it had been a long time since I'd been in school, and I'd taken only one class at the university. I'd flunked it, but that was because the teacher had faked her own death before finals.

Ivy snagged two light amber glasses as we moved. She handed one to me without looking, and as soon as we found the band, I stopped beside a potted plant at the window. There was a small dance floor, and I turned when the woman started singing "What's New?" Crap, it was the same band that had been playing at Trent's wedding-rehearsal dinner—minus most of the players. There were only five this time. But it was her. The woman's voice bobbled as she caught sight of me, and I looked away. Being recognized shouldn't cause fear.

"Nice music," Ivy said, seeing my flush. Taking a deep breath she added, "Edden's here."

My back to the band, I stared at her. "Edden? You can smell him?"

She smiled. "He's standing behind you."

Startled, I spun, almost spilling my drink. "Edden!" I cried as I set my glass down and took in his tux. There was a thickening at his chest that told me he was wearing a sidearm in a holster, but he looked great with his hair slicked back and his almost squat figure standing shoulder to shoulder with mine. "What are you doing here?" I asked.

"Working," he said, clearly glad to see me. "I see Glenn got through to you. Thanks for coming in. You look nice." Attention going to Ivy, he added, "Both of you."

Ivy smiled, but I was flustered. "That's not why I'm here," I said. "I told Glenn no. I'm here doing some personal spelling. I didn't know this was the party you were talking about, and even if I did, I wouldn't be working it. Mia isn't going to show. Ivy, tell him Mia won't be here."

Ivy adjusted her little clutch purse, hanging on a thin strap. "She won't be here."

Oh yeah. That was a big help.

Captain Edden rocked back in his dress shoes to look mildly irritated. He had a plate with a stuffed puff on it, and showing a thinning spot in his short hair, he took a bite. "Personal spelling. What is that? Witch speak for washing your hair?"

"I *am* spelling," I said. "Jenks is here somewhere, Ivy's chaperoning, I guess, and my date will be along about midnight. I've got his clothes in my bag."

Edden's gaze dropped to my oversize shoulder bag that didn't match my shoes, my dress, or my hair. "I bet you do," he said dryly, clearly still upset I'd turned him down, then showed up at the same party he wanted me to come to with him. "Well," he said as he wiped his fingers on his napkin and set his plate aside, "if you aren't here for Mia, then I'm going to guess your *personal spelling* involves Trent." I shook my head, and he sighed. "Rachel, don't make me arrest you tonight."

"Trent has nothing to do with this," I said as I watched Ivy mentally map out the floor, "and Mia isn't going to be here. Your profilers are way off. She's not worried about you bringing her in. She's fighting her own personal war with Ms. Walker, and, Edden, you need to back off and let things cool down. You hire me for my opinion, well, there it is. Don't you have one of those amulets I gave you? It's blank, isn't it?"

Edden frowned, telling me it was. His eyes scanned everywhere with the skill and patience of the military officer he'd once been. "After the incident at Aston's, three independent profilers put Mia here or at another highly visible party," he said, as if not having heard me. "We'll catch her, with or without your help. Enjoy your evening, Ms. Morgan. Jenks. Ivy."

His last words, though dry, held a hint of anxiety, and my instincts kicked in. "How's Glenn?" I asked, and Edden's jaw clenched. Ivy saw it, too, and when Jenks flew up, we all faced him square on, not letting him leave. "My God. You didn't put Glenn back on duty, did you?" I looked over the edge of the windows to the party below and the FIB cruisers. "Is he down there? At Fountain Square? With his compromised aura? Edden, are you crazy? I told you I'm not ready to face a banshee, and Glenn sure as hell isn't."

Ivy set her plate down, and Edden's squat form shifted uncomfortably. "He's fine. He's got one of those amulets and he knows what she looks like. The minute she shows, he calls. Lower your voice."

My pulse quickened, and I put my face right by Edden's. "He is not fine," I almost hissed. "And I'm not so sure those amulets are all working."

Feeling the tension rise, Ivy gave us a professional smile. "Rachel, it's getting stuffy in here," she said pleasantly. "I'm going to go downstairs and get some air. Jenks, you got this okay?"

"Tink's panties, yes," he said as he landed on my shoulder protectively.

My breath slipped out in relief. She'd watch him. Good. I didn't think Mia would show, but she sure as hell wouldn't be up here. Jenks and I could handle Al. Pierce, if he wasn't hurt, could help, too.

"My son is fine," Edden said, his brow furrowed and his posture hunched.

"I like watching *fine* men," Ivy said, and checking that her phone was on, she slid it away in her clutch purse and started for the elevator. "You're the one who wanted us to work the party. I'll be downstairs. Call me if you need me."

Edden took that with a bad grace, muttering, "You do the same. I have a warrant for both of them now."

She nodded, and sashayed off. Not three steps away, and two guys approached her. *Don't do it,* I mentally warned them, but she laughed like the happy woman she'd never be, and the two men thought they had it made. They were going to be made all right. Made into happy little burgers if they weren't careful.

"I want to talk to Ivy before she goes," Jenks said, spilling heavy dust as he hovered beside me. "Be nice to Trent, okay? You're going to need his help someday."

"Trent?" I asked, stiffening at the faint scent of wine and cinnamon. Jenks inclined his head to someone behind me before darting off to join Ivy in the elevator, and Edden and I turned. My jaw clenched, and I forced my teeth apart. It was Trent, and oh my God, he looked good.

"Hi, Trent," I said wryly as I tried not to show my appreciation, as hard as that was, seeing him in a slim tux that showed off his height and frame. The fabric looked silky and free moving, making me want to run my hand down his shoulder just to feel it. A sharp, professional-looking tie with a pattern that said he wasn't uptight gave the impression of a clever, witty man, but it was his bearing that made it all work. He had a nearly full wineglass in hand, and he was clearly comfortably in control with no doubts about who he was and what he wanted—and how to get it.

Feeling his eyes on me, I stood a little straighter and remembered how good we had looked together the night Kisten had blown up the casino boat we'd been on. Kisten hadn't known we were on it, but thanks to Ivy's warning, Trent and I had survived. We'd been the only two to do so. My brow furrowed as I considered that. We had gotten out of the ever-after together, as well. We were survivors.

Trent saw my frown, and the cocky boyish front that he used to beguile grew stilted. He touched his baby-fine hair to make sure it was lying flat, and I knew he was nervous. "Ms. Morgan," he said, saluting me with his glass so I wouldn't shake his hand.

That just ticked me off. And I wasn't happy he'd been keeping Ceri away from me like I was the plague. Even if I was.

"We've shared a cell in the ever-after," I said. "I think we ought to be on a first-name basis, don't you?"

A single pale eyebrow rose. "They're dressing the help nicely this year," he said, and Edden disguised a laugh as a cough. It was all I could do to not give the FIB captain a backhanded swat.

The distinctive click and whine of a shutter snapping pulled my head around and I froze. It was the *Cincinnati Enquirer*, the photographer looking odd dressed in a full-length sequined gown with two cameras draped over her. "Councilman Kalamack," she said enthusiastically. "Can I get a picture of you, the lady, and Captain Edden together?"

Edden shifted closer, hiding a smile as he muttered for me alone, "She ain't no lady. She's my witch."

"Stop that," I whispered. Then I stiffened as Trent sidled closer, slipping his hand about my waist so that his fingers would show for the camera. It was possessive, and I didn't like it.

"Smile, Ms. Morgan," the woman said brightly. "You might make the front page!"

Swell. Trent's touch was light compared to Edden's heavy pressure on my shoulder. I sucked in my gut and turned a little sideways to put my back to Trent to balance out his hand on my waist. He smelled like the outdoors. The shutter clicked several times, and I stiffened when I spotted Quen, Trent's bodyguard, watching. Jenks zipped over us to talk to Quen, and the woman snapped another picture when his dust glittered upon us. My tension eased; Jenks was back.

"Wonderful," the photographer said as she looked at the back of the camera. "Thank you. Enjoy the party."

"Always a pleasure to talk to the press," Trent said as he started drifting away.

The woman looked up. "Captain Edden, if I could get a picture of you and the dean of the university? I promise I'll leave you alone after that."

Edden gave me a severe look that told me to behave myself, then smiled benevolently as he talked to the woman about the FIB's annual fund-raiser while she led him away.

Trent was gazing at nothing in the hope that either I would go away or someone would come rescue him, but the photographer had given everyone the idea that we were here together and they were leaving us alone. I wanted to talk to him about a Pandora charm to possibly return my memory, but I couldn't come right out and ask. Cocking my hip, I tapped my heel once, then turned to him.

"How is Ceri?"

He hesitated, and still not looking at me, he said, "Fine."

His voice was beautiful, and I nodded as if waiting for more. When he remained silent, I added, "My calls are being stopped at the switchboard."

He didn't even twitch. "I'll look into it." His eyes were mocking when they met mine, and then he started to walk away.

"Trent," I said as I jumped to keep up with him.

"Don't touch me, Morgan," he said without moving his lips, waving pleasantly at someone across the room.

Jenks made a noise of affronted surprise, and angry, I got in front of Trent. The man rocked to a halt, clearly bothered. "Trent," I said as my heart pounded. "This is stupid."

Again his eyebrows rose high. "You are a demon. If I could, I'd have you jailed on that alone. Shunning is hardly justice."

My expression became stiff, but I wasn't surprised he knew I'd been shunned. "Take me down and you go with me, eh?" I said as Jenks landed on my shoulder in support.

Trent smiled mirthlessly. "That's about it."

"I'm not a demon," I protested softly, aware of the people around us.

The man sniffed, as if smelling something rank. "You're close enough for me."

He started to push by me again, and I muttered, "It was your dad's fault."

At that, he jerked to a stop. "Ooooh," Jenks mocked, sparkles sifting down my front as his wings made a draft, "don't you talk about my daddy!"

"He saved your life," Trent said, clearly affronted. "It was a mistake that cost him his own. My father didn't make you. You were born what you are, and if you need any more proof, just look at who you settled into an apprenticeship with."

I felt that keenly, but I swallowed my anger. I'd been trying to talk to him for months to clear the air, but he wouldn't take my calls, wouldn't let me talk to Ceri. This might be my last chance to explain myself.

"You just don't get it, do you?" I said, leaning close since my words were barely above a whisper, and Jenks took off. "I did what I did to save your life. Laying claim to you was the only way to get you out of there, and to do that, I had to agree to a very tight tie to Al."

"Tight tie?" he mocked under his breath. "You're his student."

"I did it to save your *damned freaking life!*" My knees were shaking, and I locked them. "I don't expect any thanks from you, as you're so irritatingly unable to thank anyone when they do something you're afraid to do, but stop taking your guilt or shame out on me."

I was done, and kissing good-bye my chance at getting a Pandora's charm or him to understand, I turned my back on him and stomped to the window. The restaurant had shifted, and I was looking right down at the square. Damn it, why wouldn't he at least listen?

The familiar wing hum of Jenks brought my head up, and I wiped an eye an instant before he landed on my shoulder again. "You have a way with him, don't you," the pixy said.

I sniffed, wiping my eyes. "Look at that," I muttered. "The bastard made me cry."

Jenks's wings made a cool spot on my neck. "Want me to pixy him?"

"No. But now I don't have the chance of a ghost's fart in a

windstorm to get that Pandora charm." That's not really what was bothering me, though. It was Trent. Why did I even *care* what he thought?

The soft scuff of a shoe on flat carpet and Jenks's soft oath brought me around, shocked to see Trent. He had a glass in his hand, and he extended it. "Here's your water," he said loudly, his jaw clenched.

I looked him up and down, wondering what the devil was going on. Behind him, Quen was doing his security thing, arms crossed and expression severe. It was obvious that Quen had made him come over. Sighing, I took the glass, turning to look out the window in the attempt to divorce myself from everything. I needed to find a quiet place, out of the way. "Jenks, could you see if the bathroom is clear?"

The pixy's wings buzzed a warning, but he lifted from my shoulder. "Sure, Rache."

In an instant he was gone, leaving in his path delighted coos of sound from some of the older ladies. "I don't have anything to say to you right now," I said softly to Trent.

Trent shifted to stand shoulder to shoulder with me. Together we looked over the edge to the mass of people down below. I should have just taken my chances in the parking garage as I had originally planned. This was starting to have all the signs of one of my famous backfires.

"I don't have anything to say to you either," Trent said, but tension was showing. I could play this game. I'd already lost, so it didn't matter.

"You need a Pandora charm?" the man said casually, and I jerked. *Cripes, he heard me?*

Pretending indifference, I breathed on the glass to fog it up. "Yes."

Trent put a shoulder against the glass and faced me. "That's a rare branch of magic."

Why does he have to be so insufferably smug? "I know. Elven, my mother says."

He was silent while the band took a break. "Tell me what you need to remember, and maybe I'll look into it."

I'd been down this path with him before and had gotten burned every time. I didn't want to owe him anything, but what harm would it do if he knew? Sighing, I faced him, thinking that leaning against the window like that looked really dangerous. "I'm trying to remember who killed Kisten Felps."

Trent's jaw unclenched. It was a small move, but I caught it. "I thought you'd want to remember something from the make-a-wish camp, or your father," he said.

I looked out the window again. They had a band down there. Ivy was probably having a lot more fun than me. "What if it was?" I whispered.

"I might have said yes."

Behind us, the party continued, excitement growing as the serving people started distributing champagne for the upcoming toasts. My eyes searched the ceiling for Jenks. I had to move. No one would be in the ladies' restroom when the clock ticked over.

Nervous, I tightened my grip on my bag. "What do you want, Trent?" I asked, trying to hurry this up. "You wouldn't offer if you didn't want something. Other than me dead, that is."

He smiled with half his mouth, then became serious. "How do you figure I want something? I'm just curious as to what makes you tick."

My head tilted, and for the first time all night, I felt in control. "You've approached me twice. You've touched your hair three times. You had a drink in your hand when we had our picture taken. That will be a first if it goes to press. You're nervous and upset, not thinking clearly."

Trent's face lost all expression. He dropped his head as if in irritation, and when he pulled it back up, there was a new tightness to his eyes. He glanced at Quen, and the older man shrugged.

"Is it Ceri?" I asked. Mocked almost.

His brow furrowed, and he looked out the window.

"You want to know what she really thinks of you." Still he said nothing, and I felt a sloppy smile come over me. Hiding it, I took a sip of water and set it on the tiny railing. Slowly it started to move away as the restaurant turned. "You won't like what I say."

"I don't like a lot of things."

I sighed. I couldn't do this to him. I really couldn't. Much as I would like to see Trent hurt, betraying Ceri's trust was not going to happen. I didn't think he had a Pandora charm anyway. "Ask Ceri. She'll tell you a pretty story that will save your pride."

Okay, so I wasn't above a little dig.

"Rachel."

He was reaching out, and I pulled back a step. "Don't touch me," I said coldly.

Jenks flew up, the glow of his dust reflected in the black glass. He hovered uncertainly, and he tapped his wrist like he'd seen Ivy do when we were running late. He had his sword bared, and though it looked like a shiny olive pick, it could be deadly. My pulse jumped. It was almost time.

"If you will excuse me," I said tightly. "I have to use the little girls' room. Happy New Year, Trent."

Without a backward glance, I walked away, my head high and my bag in my grip. Jenks landed on my shoulder almost immediately.

"Get on the elevator," he said, and curiosity filled me. People were getting out of my way with whispers and stares, but I didn't care.

"Elevator?" I echoed. "Why? What's wrong?"

He took off, flying backward so I could see him grin. "Nothing. There's a maintenance floor where they store the tables. I wouldn't have been able to find it if they hadn't left the key wedged atop the frame holding the inspection notice." He grinned. "I sat on it when I took Ivy downstairs."

Arms swinging, I smiled at the elevator man as I entered the lift, and with no regret, shoved him out with a well-planted foot. The poor guy hit the carpet face-first, his loud complaint cutting off as the doors shut. Excited, I held my hand out, and the key dropped into it.

"Thanks, Jenks," I said as I keyed the panel and hit the button he indicated. "I don't know what I would do without you."

"Probably die," he said, grinning.

Maybe I could pull this off yet.

Twenty-seven

The elevator hardly moved, dropping a floor before the silver doors slid apart to show a dark, low-ceilinged entryway. "Jenks," I said as I edged to the opening lit by the elevator itself. "Are you sure about this?"

The hum of his wings rose over the faint sound of machinery as he lifted off from my shoulder. "I'll get the lights. Hit the button for the lobby before you come out so it looks like you left, okay?"

I did what he said, and his faint glow darted out and was lost. There was undoubtedly a camera in the elevator, but Jenks would've taken care of it. I followed the pixy's sifting dust, holding my bag more tightly to me. It was cooler down here. Not like outside, but worrisome.

"Jenks?" I called, hearing my voice come back from hard walls and surfaces. "You okay with this temp?" There were chairs stacked up everywhere, with a wide path leading out. Low carpet. I didn't think the floor was moving, but if it was like upstairs, there would be only a ring of mobile floor, moving with the steady pace of an hour hand.

Jenks's faint voice came back, "Tink's panties. You're worse than my mother, Rache."

"I'm just saying it's cold." The chairs gave way to tables stacked surface to surface. I moved to an open spot before the bare, black windows. It had the same view as the restaurant above, and I could see Fountain Square if I pressed my head to the glass. We weren't moving, but the grinding of machinery was loud. Maybe it was too noisy to use this level.

"Found the lights!" Jenks shouted, and with that as warning, bright light flashed into existence from the recessed fixtures overhead.

I jerked, shrinking down below the level of the windows. "Uh, is there a dimmer? All of Cincinnati can see me!"

Immediately the lights went out, and before I could stand, Jenks's wings were humming by my ear. "No. Sorry. You want me to keep looking?"

Squinting to see with my light-blinded vision, I fumbled for a chair stacked on an upside-down table. "No, there's enough ambient light." I said. "I'll just do this by the window."

He shook himself to light a small circle, and I set the chair in it, dropping my bag on top. A second chair went beside it, and a third about five feet to the side. "What's our time look like?" I asked, tension knotting my stomach as I dug in my bag. Finally my eyes readjusted.

Jenks landed on the back of the chair. I recognized the pattern of brocade from having sat on it only yesterday. "Less than two minutes."

"Why do I always cut these things so darn close?" I said, dropping a pair of jeans on the chair beside me. The eight-year-old memory of Pierce naked in the snow rose up in my thoughts, and I forced it away, setting the rest of his clothes there as well. The shoes had come from Ivy, and they smelled like vampire. I hadn't asked, I'd just said thank you. My splat gun topped the pile, and Mom's red-and-white crucible/stone went on the chair across from me. Pulse quickening, I set the three bottles on the window ledge. *Almost ready.*

I ran my hands down my dress to dry my palms. Despite it being chilly, I was starting to sweat, and in this dress, it was going to show. "Okay. I can't make a protective circle, so you're going to have to keep yourself intact," I told Jenks.

The pixy's wings blurred into invisibility. "Give me a freaking break."

A sigh slipped from me. "When Al shows, get yourself out of sight until he agrees to leave people with me alone. Got it?"

Jenks looked at me. "Sure, whatever."

Like I believed that. "Time?" I asked.

"Half a minute."

The bottles clinked as I chose one, and Jenks flew to the window, looking down at Fountain Square as I twisted the ground-glass stopper out and poured the liquid into the crucible. The tinkling of the potion drew Jenks back, and hovering so that the draft from his wings shifted the surface, he said, "It doesn't smell like it worked."

He looked worried, and I remembered the failed locator charms. "I have to invoke it when they all start singing."

"Gotcha." Reassured, he lit on the back of the chair. "And he's going to be naked."

"Yup." I rolled the finger stick between my thumb and forefinger, waiting. Man, I hoped I did this right. If I could get Al to agree to this, it would be the first time I'd gotten anything from him without leaving a bit of my soul behind.

From above, I could hear the faint whisper of a countdown, the concrete and machinery between us making the enthusiastic shouting hardly audible. *Ten seconds.* I snapped the top to the finger stick and pricked my finger. The sharp jab was a jolt, and I massaged the tip.

"Wait for it," Jenks admonished. "Wa-a-a-ait for it . . . Now!"

Heart pounding, I let one, two, and then three drops of blood into the crucible. "Think happy thoughts," I whispered as Jenks flew to me, and we both waited for the redwood scent that would tell me if I had done the spell right. Like a wave, the warm scent rolled out.

"There it is!" Jenks said brightly, then his expression, lit by his own dust, faded. I backed up from the chair. Okay, I'd done it. Now we'd see if I was as smart as we all hoped I was.

"Holy crap!" the pixy said as the liquid started to spontaneously steam. My pulse quickened, and I picked up my splat gun. Al was going to be pissed. If this didn't get his attention, nothing would.

"Let me know when you smell burnt amber, okay?" I muttered, but Jenks was fascinated, hovering between me and the rising mist, unseen but for the faint dust slipping from him.

"Here he comes!" the pixy said excitedly, and I got behind one of the chairs. Somewhere in the spell, the dust was being used to give Pierce material to form his temporary body around. The mist started to take on a more human silhouette in the faint ambient light. Every second he looked more there. I didn't know what kind of shape he was going to be in. Al could've beaten him badly by now. I was going to have my hands full with Al and wouldn't be able to help Pierce.

"Jenks, get back," I demanded, and the pixy zipped to me and away again. The mist was thickening, and Jenks swore as the misty shape seemed to shrink an inch all around—and suddenly, Pierce was there, his bare feet standing on the brocade fabric with his head near the ceiling facing away from me. Naked as a jaybird.

The man spun, holding on to the back of the chair as he turned. His eyes lit on me, and he let go of the chair, wobbling as he covered himself. "Holy manure," he said, tossing his head to get the black tangle of hair out of his eyes, his face creased in what looked like anger. "I'd be of a mind to know, what the devil are you doing, mistress witch?"

Jenks rose up, his sword bared. "You scrawny ungrateful piece of crap!"

"Jenks!" I shouted, breathing deep for any sign of Al as I leaned over the chair and tossed Pierce the clothes. He caught them with one hand, and in a smooth motion, he jumped to the floor, putting his back to me as he fumbled to put the pants on.

I was scanning the dark, cluttered floor for demon-sign, but Jenks was more interested in Pierce, shocking the man as he flew to face him, shedding bright sparkles. "We're saving your ass, that's what we're doing," he said. "And the correct vernacular is holy shit."

Adrenaline spiked when I caught a whiff of burnt amber, but it was coming from Pierce.

The solid ghost was shoving his legs into the pants, not bothering with the underwear. I couldn't help but notice—even in the dark—that they were nice legs. Strongly muscled. Used to work.

As if feeling my eyes on him, he turned, trying to get the zipper up. "What are you doing?" he said, clearly aghast. "I opine that it's not your responsibility to save me. I can take care of myself."

Still no Al. "Good," I said, anxious, "because in about three seconds, Al is going to show up, and you need to take care of your own ass. I'm going to be busy. Get behind me and stay out of the way, okay?"

Pierce gave up on the zipper and snatched a white, collared shirt up from the floor. "You rescued me without a plan?" he said, his old-world accent making him sound exotic as he shoved his arms into the sleeves and started buttoning it up. "This is a powerful fix. Nohow around it."

"Of course I have a plan, but rescuing you wasn't the point," I said, affronted. "It's the catalyst. Get behind me!"

Pierce grabbed the shoes and half-hopped beside me as he put one on. His shirt was untucked to hide his open zipper. The socks, too, he had ignored. "You didn't rescue me, then?"

"Not really."

"Do tell," he said, sounding almost unhappy. His angular, thin face was wearing disappointment as he got his last shoe on and looked up. In the dim light, I could see his dark hair was mussed, and his narrow chin smooth. Though his blue eyes looked innocent, I knew behind them was a devious mind, clever and wicked. And he was looking at me. *Damn it to the Turn and back. Stop it, Rachel.*

"Pierce. I'm sorry. Can we talk about this after I take care of Al?"

He stood, matching my height. "After?" he questioned.

I looked over the dark storage room, gripping my gun tighter as I started to sweat. "Al wouldn't talk to me, and pulling you out from under him was the only way I could think of to force the issue. Will you get behind me? I can't tap a line or set a circle. My aura is too thin."

"You're taking on a demon with a thin aura? I can't commune with the ever-after either! Are you plum mad?"

From above us, Jenks muttered, "I ask myself that at least three times a week."

His expression going empty, Pierce looked up at Jenks, unknown thoughts sifting behind his blue eyes, looking black in the dim light from the windows.

"I'm not taking him on," I said as I scanned for signs of Al. "I'm talking to him."

Thick eyebrows furrowing, Pierce took a breath to say something. My eyes narrowed, but he stopped, holding his breath, as if listening to something I couldn't hear. Jenks's wings hit a higher pitch, and the skin on the back of my neck crawled.

"Rache?" Jenks had his sword out as he revolved in midair. "He's coming . . ."

"Make yourself scarce, Jenks. I mean it."

With a boom of sound, the air pressure shifted. My instinctive hunch straightened, my eyes going first to the quivering windows, and then the new shadow standing before us in the open space. In one quick lurch, Pierce was beside me. Al was here. *About freaking time.*

"Student!" Al shouted, his red goat-slitted eyes glowing as he looked over his smoked glasses. He was poised in anger, his velvet coat and lace looking ominous against the black windows. Seeing Pierce, his jaw clenched. "There you are, you little runt. We had an agreement!"

"It wasn't me!" Pierce shouted indignantly. "She did it!" he added, pointing as he took three steps away.

Agreement? I thought as Jenks started swearing. *She did it?* "Al, I can explain," I said even as I leveled my gun at him. I wanted to talk to him, but I wasn't going to be stupid about it.

"You slimy little slug!" Jenks was saying, hovering over us to light the scene.

Al's growl of annoyance was loud, and his white-gloved hands clenched. "I am going to pulp one or both of you," he said in a low voice.

Pride that I had snatched Pierce mixed with a healthy dose of fear. Adrenaline was running, and I felt alive. I thought I'd kicked this particular high, but apparently not. Al made a grab for Pierce, and I jerked him back. Jenks darted up, and the shadows grew darker.

"You're mine, little runt," Al intoned. "The longer it takes, the longer you're going to suffer."

"Mistress witch summoned me," he said defiantly. "I have until sunrise before I am obliged to return."

I had a bad feeling about this. It sounded as if Pierce had already made a deal with Al, and worse, that he was comfortable with it. *Damn it, I did it again.*

"I told you, Rache!" Jenks said as I shoved Pierce behind me and the pixy dropped down. "I'm sorry, but I told you!"

"I don't have time for this," Al growled. He gestured, and Pierce seized, falling to the flat carpet in convulsions at my heels.

"Hey!" I shouted, shifting to stand so Al couldn't just scoop him up. "Do you not see this gun I've got? Knock it off, Al. I'm trying to talk to you."

Al wasn't listening, a black haze pulsing as he clenched his white-gloved hands together, and Pierce groaned, tightening into a ball. This was so not working. "Al, if you don't knock it off and pay attention to me, I'm going to plug you!" I threatened.

His red eyes flicked to mine. "You wouldn't dare."

I squeezed the trigger. Al dove for the side, falling into a roll and landing on his feet, facing me. Behind me, Pierce gasped. "I missed on purpose!" I shouted. "Stop tormenting Pierce and talk to me."

"Rachel, Rachel, Rachel," Al said from the dark, his low voice making me shudder. "That was a mistake, my itchy witch."

Never taking my eyes off the incensed demon, I fumbled for Pierce, helping him up. "You okay?"

"As a summer day in the meadow," he breathed heavily, wiping his face.

Jenks hovered between Al and me, his face ugly. "Let Al have him, Rache. He's slug slime. You heard him. He's already got a deal going."

Like I don't? "This isn't about Pierce," I said tightly. "It's about Al snagging people." I turned to the demon. "And you're going to listen to me!"

"You should listen to the pixy," Al said, pulling the lace from his sleeves before making a backward kick to send six tables sliding into the distant wall like dominoes. "If you were wise, you'd throw that pile of refuse to me and beg for leniency. He's going to kill you."

The shakes were starting, and I pushed Pierce farther behind me. Soon as Al got him, they would be gone. And I wanted to talk to Al. "Pierce isn't going to hurt me," I quavered, and Al smiled, his blocky teeth catching a glint of ambient light.

"Tell him what you are, itchy witch."

Doubt filled me. Seeing it, Al reclined against a table. Slowly I lowered my gun. "I just want to talk to you. Why are you making this so dramatic?"

"He's going to betray you," Al prophesied, taking a step closer, and my gun came up again.

"Why should he be any different from any other man?" I said.

Jenks made a tiny huff, and hearing it, Pierce turned, his

expression sour. "If you would give me a hooter of a moment, I could explain."

"Yeah, I'll bet," I said, then, more charitable, I added, "Later, okay? I want to talk to Al." I focused on the demon. "That's the only reason I snatched him. The *only* reason," I affirmed when Jenks buzzed his disagreement. Seeing Al listening, I eased my posture. "Al, you can't snatch people when you're checking up on me. It's not fair."

"Wahh, wahh, wahh," he mocked. Snapping his fingers in an unusual showmanship, he vanished.

Jenks's wings clattered a warning. "Ah, Rache, he's not gone."

"Really? You think?" I whispered, then spun when Pierce made a choking sound.

"Damn it, Al!" I shouted, falling back in frustration upon seeing that the demon had Pierce by the neck, his feet dangling three inches above the floor.

"This one is already mine," he snarled, bringing Pierce close to his face. "Let me jump you to a line, worm. A year in my oubliette will teach you not to stray."

"It wasn't me," he gasped, his face going purple in the dim light. "She spelled me here. That's how we met," Pierce forced out. "When . . . she . . . was . . . eight . . . teen."

His last words warbled as he shook, and I was seriously wondering how much damage even a solid ghost could take. "Al! Stop it!" I said, putting my gun down and tugging on Al's velveteen-hidden arm. "I wouldn't have even taken him if you hadn't ignored me and picked up your damned line. I just want to talk to you. Will you listen to me!"

"This is for your own good," the demon said, eyeing me from over his glasses, Pierce still hanging in his grip. "He'll kill you, Rachel."

"I don't freaking care! Knock it off and pay attention to me!"

Pierce gurgled, and Al's focus became distant. Nervous, I let go of his arm and backed up into Jenks's dust. "You didn't rescue him to be your boyfriend?" Al asked, shifting his blood-smeared, white-gloved fingers around Pierce's throat.

"No!" I exclaimed, glancing at Jenks. "Why does everyone think he's my boyfriend?"

Pierce collapsed as Al dropped him. The demon stepped elegantly over the crumpled man, and I backed to the window as elegant swearwords in an old-world accent spilled out from the downed witch. Jenks's eyes widened, the pixy clearly impressed.

Al was looking at me in disbelief. "Not your lover?"

"No."

"But he is Rachel candy," Al said, his confusion too honest to be faked.

Behind him, on his hands and knees, Pierce pulled his head up. His blue eyes were vivid, and his hair was mussed. "Go to hell. You can't kill me until I'm alive."

"Looks like I can make you hurt, though," Al said, and Pierce clenched into a ball.

My neck started to sweat. Okay. Al was here, he was listening. "Al," I said loudly, trying to get the demon's attention back on me as he leaned over Pierce and poked him. "We need to talk about you snagging people. You need to stop it. Not only is it going to get me worse than shunned, but do you really want to be known as the demon who snatches instead of the demon who cleverly outwits stupid humans and Inderlanders? Come on. This is your reputation we're talking about."

On the floor, Pierce took a heaving breath of air and relaxed as Al quit whatever he was doing to him and straightened. "You can't have this one here," he said.

"Neither can you. Let him go."

Pierce's eyes met mine. "Mistress witch . . . There are things you don't understand. If you could only allow it in yourself to let me explain."

Al put a foot on his neck, and Pierce choked. Jenks flew down from the unseen rafters, his dust lighting the small space. "It doesn't make a difference," I said, my thoughts going to Nick and his belief that you can outsmart demons and wondering how he was doing. "We all do what we have to in order to survive. It's up to me to become involved or not, and I'm not."

"I'm sorry, Rache," Jenks whispered.

A thick smirk was on Al's lips. "Dali wouldn't help you, eh?"

"I didn't ask him."

"No?" Al questioned, and he pulled his foot from Pierce's neck.

I shrugged, though it was hard to see in the dark. "Why bother him when I can talk to you, demon to student." Cocking my hip, I made sure he could see my silhouette before the lighter darkness of the window. "The only student. In five thousand years. Yours. Not Dali's."

Worried, Jenks began dusting even more heavily, lighting a small space. Al made a small noise in thought. "You wouldn't," he said confidently, but there was doubt.

My heart pounded, and I gave him a mocking look. I doubt he could see it, but my posture was clear enough. Behind Al, Pierce opened one eye, finding mine immediately. There was defiance in him yet, helpless as he was. Strong beyond belief, but needing my help. Damn it, he was classic Rachel bait. "I only snatched him to get your attention," I said. "Now that I've got it, this is what I want."

"Damn my dame!" Al shouted, hands raised to the ceiling. "I knew it! Not another list!"

Jenks had let a burst of light go in his surprise, and in the new glow, I held up a finger. "Number one," I said. "Don't you *ever* not pick up when I'm trying to get in touch with you. I don't call unless it's important, so answer your line, okay?"

Al brought his attention back down from the ceiling. "You really don't want to have sex with him? Why? What's wrong with him?"

I flushed and held up a second finger. "Two, I want a little respect. Stop hurting people with me. And no more snatching."

"Respect," Al huffed. "Too bad. So sad. Respect needs to be earned, and you haven't given me anything to buy it from me."

Behind him, Pierce edged away, but before he could gain his feet, Al jabbed his foot backward, and the witch went sprawling.

"Respect?" I echoed. "You think I still need to earn your respect? How about me not summoning you even when I wanted to talk to you? How about me knowing all your friends' names and not summoning them? How about me not working with them so they can get their own bloody familiars? I could walk away from you and go to any of them. At any time. Done."

Leaving him was an empty threat, but because I had snatched Pierce from him, with no ley line magic and limited resources, he was listening. I didn't want another teacher. Maybe I should tell him that.

The light from Jenks's last dusting had faded, and I couldn't see Al's face. He wasn't moving, though. "Three," I said softly, "I want to stay your student. You probably want to keep it that way, too, huh? Don't push me on this, Al. I'll leave, and I don't want to."

Pierce looked riven, and Al's expression became unreadable.

Taking a breath, I focused on Al—who had been listening intently. "So what's it going to be? Are you going to be nice, or naughty?"

In a smooth motion, Al swooped toward Pierce, grabbing him by the shirtfront and hoisting him up. "Sorry about that, little runt," he said, zipping up his pants and arranging his collar in motions so fast that it left Pierce shocked, and scrambling. "Terrible misunderstanding."

He gave Pierce a smack on the back, to send him stumbling. Face red, Pierce caught his balance and pushed Al's hands off him. Stiff with pride, he turned his back on us as he tugged his clothes back where they should be, ran a hand over his hair, and then turned around. I wouldn't look at him.

Jenks had moved closer to me in the fast exchange, and he hovered suspiciously. I wasn't satisfied, though, and I stayed where I was, my back to the window. "So you agree, no snatching, smacking, killing, or scaring people with me. I want to hear it."

"This one doesn't count," Al said. "It's not retroactive."

"Good God! This is an addition!" I exclaimed, but seeing I'd pushed him far enough—and that he and Pierce already seemed to have an agreement—I nodded. "Say it," I insisted.

Pierce was edging away from Al. The motion wasn't lost on the demon, and he jerked him back. "I won't snatch, harm, or scare to death people with you or use checking up on you as an excuse to cause trouble. You're worse than my mother, Rachel."

"Mine, too," Jenks muttered.

"Thank you," I said formally. I was shaking inside. I'd done it. I'd freaking done it. And it hadn't cost me my soul, or a mark, or anything. *Hallelujah, she can be taught!*

Al gave Pierce a shove away and strolled closer to me. I tensed, then relaxed, putting my gun away. I could smell the burnt amber flowing from him, and Jenks hovered backward, sword hefted as if ready to throw it. I didn't move, numb as Al sidled up alongside me and together we eyed Pierce, nervous under our combined scrutiny. "If you give him a body," he said lightly, "I will kill him."

I looked at Al. His eyes didn't look strange anymore, and it scared me. "I don't know that curse," I said blandly.

Al's jaw clenched and released. "He will eventually try to kill you, Rachel. Let me save you the trouble of killing him in turn."

Tired, I started tucking things away. The empty bottle, the crucible, the used finger stick. My hands were shaking, and I made a fist. "Pierce isn't going to kill me."

"You got that right," Al and Jenks said simultaneously.

"Tell him what you are, itchy witch," Al added after a wary look at the pixy. "See what happens."

Pierce had been in my church for almost a year. I doubted very much he didn't know what I was. It was only just after midnight, but I was ready to go home. "Why don't you leave before someone recognizes you," I said as Jenks landed on my shoulder. My adrenaline was gone, and I was cold in my little black dress. I looked around, but apart from the two bottles of potion still on the sill, there was nothing of mine except Pierce standing stoically by the window, trying not to look naive as he gazed down at the streets of Cincinnati full of people partying. "I'm already shunned, thanks to you," I finished.

A beautiful smile came over the demon, and looking at me from over his smoked glasses, he said, "Leave? But it is such a spectacular night!" That smile still on his face, he strode to the window and picked up my potion bottles. I held out my hand for them as he lifted them to the faint light and squinted.

"You made more than one potion to give him substance?" Al asked, and when I said nothing, he cracked one of the seals and breathed. "Nice presentation," he murmured, then slid them into a jacket pocket.

"Hey! Those are mine!" I protested, jolted out of my complacency. Jenks launched himself off my shoulder, but Pierce gave me what was almost a nasty look, as if I should have known better and was being stupid.

Al didn't even bother to acknowledge me as I stood with my arms crossed over my middle and sulked in a drop-dead gorgeous dress underneath Cincinnati's premier restaurant. "These are mine," he finally said. "You're my student, and I can claim anything you make."

I jumped when I suddenly became aware that Pierce was behind me. He gave me a heartfelt look, trying to take my hands as he said, "Rachel, might I have a word with you? My heart is breaking to explain."

"I'll bet," I said sourly, pulling my hands away. "Why don't you vamoose so Al will go with you and leave me the hell alone?"

"I'll allow that this looks powerful suspicious," he admitted. "And anyone would be in a fine pucker, but you yourself have a mind to deal with the devil spawn upon occasion. I have until sunrise to convince you that I'm honorable." He looked at Al. "You agreed to no snatching. I have until sunrise."

Al gestured grandly. "If you must. But I'm not leaving you alone with her."

My eyebrows rose, and even Jenks made a tiny squeak of a sound. "Whoa, boys. I have plans tonight, and they don't include a demon and a ghost."

"Yeah!" Jenks launched himself from my shoulder and hovered to brighten the area. "We got reservations at the Warehouse." He flitted to the window and looked down, staying in flight and dusting heavily.

"Sounds like fun," Al said, rubbing his white-gloved hands together. "Pierce, get the lift."

"No way!" I shouted. "Pierce, will you just go? I can talk to you next week."

The man's jaw was set as he ducked out from under Al's attempt to shove him to the elevator, and he straightened, saying, "I'll not be moseyin' until I have a chance to settle this. And that is all I'm saying about it."

I sighed, leaning back against the cold window with my butt on that narrow sill. The last thing I needed was to put this circus on rails. "Fine," I said sourly, crossing my ankles. "I'm listening."

Al started pouting, unable to leave and cause mischief lest Pierce "kill me," I suppose. More likely it was to keep the witch from telling me something that Al didn't want me to know.

Seeing me listening, Pierce took a breath he really didn't need. His arms fell to his sides as he exhaled, and his expressive face softened into one of persuasion.

"Uh, guys?" Jenks said, hovering at the window. "Fountain Square is on fire."

"What?" I jumped to my feet and turned in one motion. Al rushed to the window, and we pressed our foreheads to the glass, looking down, Jenks between us. From overheard, the groaning of machinery became loud and obvious. Faint calls were sifting down through the concrete or perhaps vibrating through the glass. I could imagine that the entire party upstairs was now leaning against the glass as we were.

It was hard to see, but Jenks was right. The stage was on fire. People were gathering in the street. From beside me, Pierce said, "I thought that was what it was supposed to look like."

Shit. Ivy was down there. And Glenn.

"I gotta go," I said, turning to the elevator. My phone rang, and I jerked to a stop. It wouldn't work in the elevator. The little screen lit up, and Al peered over my shoulder. "It's Ivy," I said, my relief obvious. "Ivy?" I called as I flipped the phone open, and the sound of screams and sirens filtered out.

"I need you," she said loudly, over the chaos. "Your locator amulets just lit up. Mia is here."

I stood at the window and looked down. "Jenks says there's a fire," I said.

She hesitated, and then calmly said, "Oh. Yes. The stage is burning. Rachel, I'm watching Glenn, but if he gets too close to a banshee . . ."

Crap. "Got it." I started walking to the elevator, Jenks hovering close so he could hear both ends of the conversation.

"I think The Walker is calling Mia out," Ivy added, and I punched the button for the lift.

"I'm on my way." Breathless and fidgety, I closed the phone and jammed it in my bag. *Where's the stupid elevator? I'm not going to run down thirty flights of stairs.*

Al cleared his throat, and I spun around, just now remembering them.

"Oh, uh, Pierce," I said, feeling myself warm. "I'm sorry. I have to go."

Al jiggled the man's elbow, beaming from ear to ear. "This

is going to be entertaining. I've never watched Rachel work. Apart from when she was working on me, of course."

"Entertaining?" Pierce slid away from him. "You have an almighty odd vision of entertainment, demon."

"I told you to call me Al," he said, looking at his blurry reflection and adjusting his lace.

Jenks's features scrunched up in annoyance, and I rubbed my forehead. I could not take the two of them down into Fountain Square. Pierce didn't have a coat, and Al . . . Thanks to a couple of news shots, the entirety of Cincinnati knew his face. "Pierce, can't we do this another time?" I asked, distracted. *Where is the damn elevator!* I thought, hitting the call button again, my elbow smacking into it with undue force.

But Pierce inclined his head, dropping back to give me a half bow, his eyes never leaving mine as he almost smiled. His look reminded me of the night we had met, racing off to save a young girl from a vampire. He had liked my "fiery spirit," and clearly things hadn't changed. I had, though.

"You summoned me, mistress witch, whether by intent or secondary purpose. I'm not leaving until I have a chance to explain."

Swell.

Al straightened as the elevator dinged behind me. "I'm staying with him," he affirmed.

Peachy keen.

The elevator doors opened, and Jenks whistled, long and slow. "Tink's contractual hell," he whispered, and I turned to see who Al was making bunny-eared kiss-kiss gestures to.

Unbelieving, I started shaking my head. "Trent. This isn't what it looks like."

The young man had pressed himself to the back of the elevator, his terror showing for an instant before he pulled himself together and decided that if he was going to die, he might as well do it looking good.

"This just keeps getting better and better," Jenks said, and I pushed the call button again.

"We'll take the next one," I said, smiling.

"Plenty of room!" the demon exclaimed, and my heels clattered on the steel frame of the door when Al shoved me. Trent fended me off, pressing into a corner as Pierce and Al followed me in. Jenks rose up high to sit on the top of the controls, his feet tapping the screen that showed what floor we were on.

"I do not believe this," Trent said, his unbreakable composure shattered. "Rachel, you are unbelievable!"

"Believe it, you little cookie maker," Jenks chimed out, and then to Pierce, "Hit the 'close' button, will you, Pierce? We don't have all day."

Pierce didn't have a clue, and Jenks flew down and hit the button feet first. The doors slid shut, and we started to drop. "Holy shit!" Pierce exclaimed, pressing into the opposite corner and clutching the rail. "We're falling!"

I slid away from his suddenly green face, bumping Trent. The elevator wasn't that big, and everyone was giving Al lots of room as he hummed the theme song to . . . *Dr. Zhivago*?

"Summoning your demon at the top of Carew Tower?" Trent hissed in my ear.

Peeved, I shifted a little more to stand between him and Al. "I'm trying to make the world a little safer," I muttered, then beamed as Al looked at us, my smile fading the instant the demon looked away. "He's not abducting you, is he? Turning you into a toad?" My voice was getting louder. "I've got this *under control!*" I smacked the "lobby" button, praying we didn't stop anywhere between here and there. There was no way this elevator could go fast enough.

"You will be jailed for this," Trent was saying, still having kittens in the corner.

"Nonsense." Al polished his glasses with another bit of red cloth. "I'm here to party on this side of the lines, eat a little something, but mostly"—he looked at me and put his glasses back on—"I'm here to keep our itchy witch from killing herself with an ash-to-flesh spell."

Jenks's wings buzzed in the sudden silence, and I turned to Trent. The man was pale, and his hair was in disarray, but he was staring at Al and me. His eyes flicked to Pierce, white-faced in the corner, and he said, "You can bring the dead to life? That's black magic."

"Not at all," Al protested grandly. "Where do you think our itchy witch found this tricky little runt of a bastard?" He gave Pierce a shove, and the witch gagged. "He's a ghost." The demon sniffed. "Can't you smell the little worms on him?"

My head thumped into the wall. This was so not going well.

"You're a ghost?" Trent said, and Pierce shakily extended his hand from his corner.

"Gordian Pierce. Coven of moral and ethical standards. You are, sir?"

"You're what?" I exclaimed, my face warming.

Al started laughing, and Jenks dropped down to my shoulder.

Jenks tickled my ear, almost getting smacked. "Rache!" he hissed. "Isn't that the coven that got you shunned?" I nodded, and he added, "Maybe he can get your shunning rescinded."

I thought about that. Having been buried in blasphemed ground and dealing with demons didn't stand well in his favor, but he had worked for the coven of moral and ethical standards. They were kind of like the I.S. Once a member, always a member. You couldn't retire. But you could die.

Trent shook his hand, looking positively stunned. "Ah, I'm Trent Kalamack. CEO of—"

Pierce jerked his hand from Trent and pushed himself straight. "Kalamack Industries," he said, expression twisted as he wiped his hand on his pants. "I knew your father."

"I do not freaking believe this," I said, shifting to stand where I could see both of them.

Al beamed. "Amazing who you can meet in an elevator," he said, and Trent eyed me.

"You have a charm to bring the dead to life. And it's white," the elf stated.

I took a breath to answer, and Al interrupted smoothly. "And it's for sale, at apprentice rates. No guarantees. I have two right here," he said, patting his coat pocket. "It's temporary. The curse to give them a lasting body is a far sight trickier. Someone has to die, you see. I'd imagine that would make them black, but you don't seem to worry about killing people for your own ends, do you, Trenton Aloysius Kalamack?" he said with a simper. "Funny how you call my witch black, when you kill for profit, and she kills . . ." He hesitated in mock thought. "Why, she hasn't killed anyone who didn't ask her to! Imagine that."

Color spotted Trent's cheeks. "I don't kill for profit."

From the corner, Pierce muttered, "You kill for progress, if you're anything like your father."

As one, we all looked at Pierce. The elevator dinged, and our attention was diverted as the doors opened. "Splendid! A fire!" Al cried cheerfully, striding out into the noisy crowd that had filled the downstairs lobby. The smell of smoke hit me, and I lurched to follow, not wanting Al to get out of my sight. It was crowded as people in evening gowns and suits talked loudly, mixing with people in jeans and heavy coats coming in to get warm but not ready to leave. Or perhaps they couldn't with the streets blocked off.

Trying to watch Al and Pierce both, I shuffled over to the coat clerk. Pierce's hand landed on my arm as I extended my ticket, and I spun, almost smacking him. "Best stay away from that one, mistress witch. His father was a devil on earth," the dead witch said, his eyes going to Trent.

"No kidding." *Who should I believe, a ghost, or my dad?* My dad was a good man, wasn't he? He wouldn't work for the devil on earth. *Would he?*

Confused, I took my coat and scanned the crowd for Al's velveteen one. Seeing Quen, I gave Trent's security a little shrug to try to tell him everything was okay and to keep him from going into battle mode when he saw Al. The demon had once mauled Trent.

Trent was making his way to Quen, his pace slow for being recognized and delayed. I pointed him out to Quen, and the security officer jumped into motion, his employer's coat over his arm.

I finally spotted Al by the doors, chatting up a pair of twins wearing baby bonnets for the year's end, and I unzipped my bag. "Inside, Jenks," I offered as I went to rescue the twins, and the pixy dropped down, cold and probably ready for that hand warmer. I knew it killed him being shoved in a bag like this, but he had no choice. And as I zipped it up, I vowed to be very careful with him tonight.

I shuffled into my coat as we went, jerking from Pierce's reach when he tried to help me. "I've got this okay," I said, then winced when Al grabbed my shoulder, pinching me into submission as he helped me into my coat. "Let go," I demanded, but my options were limited by the crowd. My last arm went sliding into the cold sleeve, and Al leaned in, reaching over my shoulders to fasten my top button.

"I admire the way you are breaking Trent," Al whispered from behind me, his white-gloved fingers moving to my chin to force my gaze to Trent and Quen. "So slow, like melting ice. And with his own pride. Masterful. I didn't know you had it in you, Rachel. Pain gets old after a time, but it's faster, and profit is the name of the game unless you're making art."

"I'm not breaking him," I said softly as Al backed up and I shifted my shoulders to get my coat to hang right. Trent and Quen were leaving, and the security officer looked back once before they vanished, his expression blank. I breathed easier when they were gone. At least I wouldn't be responsible for Trent's death. Not tonight, anyway.

The wail of sirens grew louder, and I turned to a second door. Pierce jumped ahead of us to open it, and I did a double take. "Where did you get a coat?"

Pierce's face reddened, but it was Al who leaned forward, saying, "He stole it, of course. The man has many talents. Why do you think I'm so interested in him? Or you, my itchy witch?"

Mood sour, I headed out into the cold, ducking down into my scarf and wishing I was anywhere other than here. If Ivy and Glenn weren't okay, I was going to freaking kill someone.

Twenty-eight

This is not going to go well, I thought, glancing ruefully at Al beside me as we strode down the closed-off street toward Fountain Square. I was cold, and I hunched into my coat and squinted through the flashing lights for Ivy. Pierce trailed behind us, trying not to look like a goober, but he was wide-eyed and clearly from out of town, if not from out of this century.

The square was organized chaos, with what looked like five I.S. vehicles just arriving, the original two FIB and I.S. cruisers stationed at the event, the expected news vans and ambulance. Topping it off, we now had fire trucks, and the spray from the hoses was turning into little pinpricks of ice on my face. It was the cold that made it miserable, the wind going right through my coat and to my core. Even in my bag, Jenks was going to have a hard go of it.

There were fewer people than one might have expected, Inderlanders being good at disappearing and naturally avoiding anything that breathed of scandal. A handful of onlookers vied for the news crews' attention. Avoiding eye contact, I quickened my pace to get behind the yellow tape where they could only shout questions I could pretend not to hear.

There was a cluster of people at the dry fountain being treated for burns and what looked like smoke inhalation. The fire was out, but the firemen were still hosing down the stage, performing, I think, for the news crews. I spotted Edden's squat form at the edge of the cordoned-off area, and he turned when I shouted. Looking cold but sharp in his tux, he held the yellow tape up for me, and we slipped under. Immediately I felt protected, and when my guard went down, I shivered violently from the cold.

"Glad you could join us," he said, eyeing the two men behind me. "Where did you find the twins?"

Twins? I thought, breath catching as I spun around to see a sullen Pierce in jeans standing next to a laughing one with dark sunglasses and a brilliant red tie. *Holy cow,* I thought, feeling a sliver of worry slip through me. Al put a finger to his lips, and I whipped back around to Edden, willing to play the game since it would keep me out of trouble for a few minutes longer.

"Oh, you know us witches," I said, not knowing why but only that I had to say something. "Hey, is that Tom?" I said as I spotted what I thought was a familiar face among the wounded.

"Where?" Edden looked where I pointed. The man in the black trench coat was getting his hand bandaged, but when he saw us notice him, he quickly strode away, the person attending him shouting for him to come back.

"Well, I'll be damned," Edden cursed, whistling and pointing to get someone to go after him, but it was too late.

"That was Tom. Tom Bansen," I said in affront, glaring at Al when he chuckled. The man had once summoned and released Al to kill me. "That's the third time he's beat me to a crime scene this week," I mused uneasily.

"He must have better intel," Al said, giving Pierce a shove to stay behind him.

"Are you giving Tom information?" I asked Al as Edden snagged a passing officer and started shooting off questions.

A mock-hurt expression came in his eyes as Al peered at me from over his glasses. "Everything I do, I do for you, love."

I wasn't sure if that was an answer or not, and I slowly let out my breath, flicking a glance at Pierce, now gazing up at the Carew Tower restaurant. There were three I.S. agents headed our way, and I had a moment of worry about Al until Edden flashed his badge and the men turned away.

The officer with him jogged away, and Edden put his hands on his hips to assess the situation. Standing there he looked like a squat Jenks without the wings. With a stiff mustache. And a round face. And a tux too cold for the weather. Okay, so he didn't look anything like Jenks, but the same protector-of-the-world attitude was there.

Seeing Glenn's tall form with a bunch of FIB personnel, I tapped Edden's arm and we headed that way. The poor guy looked colder than I was with his knit hat pulled low and his eyes pinched. People were listening to him, though, and he looked like he was in charge.

Ivy was next to him, her vampire need to protect the weak just about flaming from her, and making me smile. Her red dress flashed from under her coat as the wind whipped it. She didn't look cold at all. As if noticing my gaze on her, her eyes rose to mine, then shifted to Al. Pierce was lagging behind, eyes on the fountain. Her words never stopped as she talked to the surrounding FIB agents.

"The I.S. is lying," she said firmly as the wind brought her voice to us when we got close enough. "No evidence of a banshee being involved is an outright lie. There should be tons of emotion here, and there isn't. Barely enough to cover a fender bender. It's as if it's a Tuesday night, not New Year's Eve after the ball has dropped and there's been a fire. Emotion should be echoing between the buildings, and it isn't. There's nothing here. Someone sucked it up."

The circle of FIB officers shifted to let us in, and we rocked to a stop with Al uncomfortably close behind me and Pierce still at the fountain. The missing emotion was exactly the force I'd used to catalyze Pierce's spell, but unlike a banshee, I hadn't used it up, simply borrowed it to push the spell into working. I wondered if that made witches and banshees some-how related.

I could see the shift of attention to Edden as he approached, and Glenn stifled a sigh. "Glenn, where are we?" the FIB captain asked to shift it back, and his son's mood eased.

Ivy frowned and crossed her arms over her middle. "Someone sucked the emotion out of here, and it wasn't Rachel," she said. "Her magic doesn't work like that."

Not exactly, anyway.

Glenn wiped a mittened hand under his nose, absolutely miserable with the cold. "I know it was a banshee," he admitted. "I'm not arguing with you, Tamwood. But you aren't licensed to give court evidence, and I'm stuck using what the I.S. is telling me. All we have right now is conflicting testimony from multiple witnesses. We know Mia was here."

"My amulet lit up," an FIB officer said, his words echoed by another as the man brought out the spell and showed it to everyone. It was black now, but it was gratifying to know for sure that I'd done the spell right. *Yet my blood wasn't able to invoke it.*

Ivy huffed. "Okay, she was here. But that doesn't mean she started the fire."

Arguments erupted, and Ivy took the opportunity to step out of the circle and come around to where we stood. Nodding to Al, she gave me a distracted smile. "It worked," she said. "Good. I'm glad for you, Rachel. Pierce, welcome to the chaos of Rachel's life. The next few hours ought to be fun."

I shook my head, but before I could explain, Al took her hand and kissed the top of her black glove. "Your welcome means more to me, Ivy Alisha Tamwood, than a thousand souls. Watching Rachel work is a wonder of one catastrophe after another."

That was kind of insulting. "This isn't Pierce," I said softly. "It's Al. Pierce is at the fountain."

Ivy jerked her hand from him. Glenn heard, as did most of

the FIB agents, but only Glenn knew what Al was. His instruction cut off in midphrase, and I shrugged to tell him that gathering FIB souls wasn't on the demon's agenda today. Edden's expression became questioning. Glenn thought for a moment before remembering what he was saying, then continued, shifting to keep Al in his sights. Al huffed when the cautious man undid the snap to his holster. It didn't go unnoticed by the surrounding FIB officers either. Ivy flicked her attention between the demon and Pierce, now gaping at the fire trucks.

This was so not right, and I glanced around the square not wanting to believe that Mia had been here. That she'd kill a man to feed her daughter, I might understand, but up to now, she'd always been focused on the individual, not the collective. Even if I wanted to believe she was responsible for this, logic said it wasn't her.

Edden broke away from the FIB group as his son's voice took on the sound of instruction. His gaze tight on Al, he approached. "Rachel, I'm sorry," he said as he brought his gaze back to me. "I am going to do what's best for the sake of the child, within the limits of the law, but I'm not putting my neck out for Mia. Not after this."

I was too cold to protest, shivering. Glenn was giving out a final instruction, and the men looked grim. "Look for anyone with a baby, probably a woman, but it could be a man, or a man and a woman together," he was saying. "There shouldn't be too many infants out here."

Ivy had her hip cocked. "Mia did not set the fire," she said bluntly.

"More vampire vibes?" Edden mocked, and Al grinned.

"There is more than one banshee in this city," Ivy continued. "I saw her. Tall, scary woman with long hair. Dressed like she should be surrounded by security. Not Asian. More Mayan than anything else. She'd look Hispanic to most people."

Mayan? I mused, my thoughts immediately going to the top of Carew Tower and the lunch I'd had with Edden yesterday. "That's Ms. Walker," I said, feeling my pulse quicken. "Edden, Mia might have been here, but so was Ms. Walker. Which makes perfect sense! Walker doesn't have her usual haunts, so she's feeding where she can, stirring up trouble to make herself stronger."

Edden's face was thoughtful, but he waved to Glenn to get the men moving. With a chorus of agreement, they dispersed. It suddenly felt a whole lot colder.

"Of course Ms. Walker would be here," Edden said gruffly, but I could hear a note of doubt in it. "She's tracking Mia. I'd be surprised if she wasn't here."

Ivy sighed and shifted her weight, but I was a lot more direct. "Damn it, Edden!" I shouted. "Why are you being so bullheaded about this? Are you so smitten with that woman that you can't look at things logically?"

The few FIB personnel within earshot turned, and Glenn's eyes went wide. I suddenly felt nervous as the stocky man forced his clenched jaw to loosen. "Are you so bleeding-heart stupid that you can't do the same?" he barked back.

I suddenly realized that Al was quietly arranging the snowflakes on his sleeve, turning them into blue butterflies. The doomed insects flew from him only to die a few feet away, their wings fluttering briefly before being covered by snow.

"Mia hurt me, too," I said to Edden, nervous that someone might see Al's show of demon skill. "Whether you like it or not, Holly is going to grow up to be one hell of a predator. You can either make her a friend, or a foe. Think about it."

Edden shook his head, zipping up his coat and walking away. "With friends like her, we don't need foes."

That was one of the lamest things I'd ever heard him say, and I took several mincing steps to keep up with him. "Stop thinking like a human," I said roughly. "It's not a human world anymore. We don't have any proof it was Mia, but you're ready to put her in jail for it. Banshees are territorial, and I think Walker set the stage on fire to get a quick fix and call Mia out."

Edden stopped. Not looking at me, his eyes tracked the ambulance people, packing up. Behind him, Al was strolling forward, and Pierce was hotfooting it to us as well. "Don't you love how Rachel sides with the underdog?" the demon said, then brushed the garden of tiny blue butterflies from his sleeve. They fluttered to the ground, dead before they touched the snow-caked cobbles. "It's going to kill her someday," he said lightly, bending to pick one up. "But not tonight," he added as he pulled my hand from my coat pocket to put a chrysalis into it, curving my cold fingers protectively around it.

I glanced at the blue chrysalis, then shoved it into my coat pocket to deal with later. "Edden . . . ," I pleaded.

Wincing, he sighed. Five steps away, someone waited for him with a clipboard. "I can't promise Mia anything. Especially now. Rachel, go home."

I licked my lips and the wind made them into ice. "You can't prove she did this."

"I can't prove Ms. Walker did either. Go home." I hesitated, and he exclaimed, "Rachel, go home!"

"Bad dog," Al whispered, mocking me, and my face flamed. Pierce slid up beside us, and I gritted my teeth, not liking the ghost seeing me being treated like this.

"Fine," I said bitterly. "Do what you want." *This is a crappy New Year's.* "Ivy, I'm going home. Are you staying?"

Ivy looked from Pierce to the beaming demon. "Ah, you don't mind if I hang here for a while, do you? Glenn wants my opinion on something."

Crime scene slut, I thought bitterly, more than a little jealous that they would let her stay but wanted me to leave. I didn't want to be alone in a car with Al and Pierce, but I gave her a wave good-bye and turned. Edden had already walked away in a huff, and Glenn was waiting uncomfortably for Ivy.

Ticked, I turned my back on all of them and started walking.

Twenty-nine

This was the second time I had suffered a demon in the back of my car, and I didn't like it any better than the first. Al was more obnoxious than Minias had been, leaning forward between Pierce and me to point out red lights and shortcuts through human and Inderland slums that only an idiot would take this time of night—though with a demon along, it might be safe. The smell of burnt amber slowly grew in my small car despite whatever charm he was using, but I didn't dare crack a window to let in the freezing night. Though the heater was cranked, Jenks was still cold. He really shouldn't have been out of my bag, much less sitting on the rearview mirror.

"You could have made that light if you had gunned it," Al said.

No one was behind me, and I let the car coast forward a foot to the red light before I jammed on the brakes. Al's nose smacked into the headrest, and Pierce's arm, already extended to brace himself against the dash, stiffened. "I'm driving," I muttered with an apologetic glance at Jenks. *My toes are freezing in these stupid heels. What was I thinking?*

"Yes, but you're not doing it *properly*," the demon protested, in a better humor than I liked. He hadn't given me any trouble about getting in the backseat, but maybe he could keep a better eye on Pierce that way. Honestly, the man was not going to hurt me. Even now, when I glanced at him, his frustrated expression shifted to one of anxious hope.

"Mistress witch," he said as our eyes met, and my phone vibrated, almost unheard.

"Do you know how to get that?" I asked him, giving Al's hand a tart smack when he reached for it in my bag. The demon had gone back to looking like himself, and my fingers were soundless as they hit his white-gloved, thick hand.

The light changed, and I eased forward, driving carefully as it was icy near the bridge.

"I'll help him," Jenks said, dropping down into my bag. "You've seen Rachel use it, right?" he said sarcastically. "You've been spying on us for a year."

Pierce frowned as he pulled the slim pink phone from my bag. "It's not a powerful trick," he said indignantly. "And I've not been spying. Rachel, if I could explain."

"Just open the top, okay?" Jenks said, and I frowned at him to be a little nicer.

The scent of burnt amber grew when Al put the flat of his arms on the two seats to make a bridge for his head to rest on. "May I use your phone when he's done?" he asked sweetly.

I debated what might happen if I slammed the brakes on again. "No. Sit the way you're supposed to, or we're going to get pulled over for a Breathalyzer."

"No fun," he simpered, slumping back.

I breathed easier, wishing Pierce would simply leave so I could go home and forget this day had ever happened. What a waste.

From the backseat came Al, humming the tune to *Jeopardy!* until Pierce found the seam and wrangled the top open. Motions hesitant, he went to put it to his ear, stopping when Jenks hovered before the phone, hands on his hips as he barked, "This is Rachel's secretary. The lazy-ass witch is currently busy. Can I take a message?"

"Jenks!" I complained as Al snickered and Pierce looked

appalled, but Jenks—the only one who could really hear whoever it was—had become serious.

"Where?" he asked, and a bad feeling trickled through me, chilling me though the heater was cranked and sending my hair to tickle my face. From the back came an unearthly, satisfied chuckle. All I could see in the rearview mirror was a dark shadow with red goat-slitted eyes. Fear slithered through me. *Shit, I have a demon in my backseat. What in hell am I playing with?*

"Good witch," Al said, his voice coming from nothing, and I stifled a shudder. "You're starting to understand."

"I'll tell her," Jenks said, then stomped on the "end" button. I jumped when Pierce snapped the phone closed, then jerked the car back into the proper lane when a horn blew.

Jenks rose up, looking eerily dark in the chill car with no dust slipping from him. "That was Ford," he said, surprising me; I had thought Edden, or maybe Glenn. "He's at a coffee shop downtown with Mia. She wants to talk to you. I think Ms. Walker gave her a good scare."

Oh God. It's starting. "Where?" I said, tension knotting my gut. Ivy. I had to call Ivy.

Jenks laughed, filling the car with the sound of bitter wind chimes. "You're not going to believe me," he said.

I checked behind me, then in front. "Junior's place, right?" I said dryly, then did a U-bangy. Pierce reached for the dash, his long face going white, but Al didn't shift an inch, ramrod straight, dead center, in my tiny backseat. The car swung wildly, finding its new direction as another horn blew. "That's past Edden's blockade, isn't it?" I asked. "How does she do that! The woman must have a way with the force." *I'm not the banshee you seek. I may pass.*

Jenks walked Pierce through calling Ivy to tell the FIB as I made my way back over the bridge into Cincy and down to the shopping district. I doubted very much that Mia was giving up. More likely, she was sacrificing Remus to buy her way out of trouble, and my tension ratcheted up as we pulled into Junior's place.

It was packed, but Al did something involving Latin and what looked like the same gesture I occasionally used on people who cut me off in traffic on Vine, and the Buick ready to pull into the last parking spot changed its mind. My pulse quickened when I spotted Ford's gray car three vehicles down. *Ivy.* We should wait for Ivy and the FIB, but that might be too late.

"Both of you stay in the car," I said as Jenks dove for my bag and I zipped it up. I didn't even see the demon get out. One moment, I was snatching up my bag and slamming my door shut, and when I turned, he was there—standing way too close. The security lights shone on his hair, carefully styled and ridged, his jaw tight and his demon eyes almost glowing in the dim light. He didn't say a word. Waiting. On the other side of the car, Pierce got out and gave me a worried look.

"I'll get you a coffee," I said as I pushed around Al. "Then stay out of my way." I didn't hear Al following when Pierce took my elbow as I slipped in my heels, but he was there.

The door jingled a welcome, and the four of us entered, me in my Carew Tower restaurant finery, Al in his usual velveteen and lace, Pierce in jeans and a stolen coat, and Jenks in my bag. We didn't get as many looks as one might think. It was New Year's, and there was a wide span of dress. Junior's wasn't far from Fountain Square, and the place was busy, voices fast-paced and excited because of the fire downtown and the blockades. If Mia was here, I was sure she was soaking up the excitement.

"Rachel, if I could have but a moment."

"Not now, Pierce," I said as I let Jenks out. The pixy rose, not a speck of dust coming from him as he flew heavily to the nearest light fixture and parked himself beside the hot bulb. He gave me a thumbs-up, but it was obvious he was suffering as he put his elbows on his knees and hunched over. I was on my own till the FIB got here. Worse, I was babysitting Al.

I shoved my gloves in my pockets and scanned the floor

while standing in line. A spike of adrenaline shot through me when I found Mia smack in the middle of the place, Remus on one side of her, Ford on the other. Holly was on her lap, the infant resting, her eyes closed and at peace with the world. I met Ford's eyes, and he nodded before getting up and trying to find a chair for me. That table looked too small to talk to two serial murderers.

Pierce brushed my arm, and I jerked. "Mistress witch?"

"Don't call me that," I muttered, conscious of the people around us. There were too many people in here. Someone was going to get hurt.

"Rachel, I'll allow that my situation looks dire, but I'm of a mind to help you."

My attention swung back to him, remembering the night we'd met. He was basically a runner—member of the coven of moral and ethical standards aside. Even if he couldn't tap a line, he could help. I didn't think Mia had arranged for this meeting to kill me, so it was likely Remus was going to be the biggest threat. Him I could handle, and I'd put my best undies online if Mia wasn't about to sacrifice him to remain out of jail and off the grid.

"Think you can do what I say?" I asked, and he grinned, tossing his hair from his eyes in a way that wasn't like Kisten's at all, but reminded me of him all the same.

"You're not alone," he said, eyes darting to Ford's table. "I'll help you settle your hash, and then we might talk."

His hand reached for mine, and Al shoved between us. "Two grande lattes, double espresso, Italian blend," he said to the clerk. "Light on the froth, extra cinnamon. Use whole milk. Not two percent or half-and-half. Put a shot of raspberry in one for my itchy witch here."

And put it in porcelain, I thought, wondering if this was the only way demons liked their coffee. Minias had ordered something similar, minus the raspberry.

"The runt will have a juice box." He turned to Pierce. "It will make you big and strong, won't it, little fella."

Pierce's jaw clenched and his blue eyes narrowed, but he swallowed the insult.

"Anything else?" the clerk asked, and I looked to find that it was Junior himself.

"Espresso," I said, remembering Jenks. Swinging my bag around, I dug out my wallet. The light caught the glitter on my dress, and I thought how stupid it all seemed. At least my toes had thawed.

"Hey," Junior said suddenly, backing up a step when he saw the gun in my bag. "I heard about you. You're shunned. Get out of my shop."

Shocked, I looked up, blinking. *Could he have said it any louder, maybe?* But my mood quickly turned to anger. "Look, Junior," I said bitterly, my bile finding an easy outlet. "I'd really like to. Going home and taking a bubble bath sounds really great right now." I leaned in close so only he, Pierce, Al, and probably Jenks could hear me. "But two of those *good* people sitting in the middle of your *freaking* shop are wanted for the assault of an FIB officer, a double murder, causing a riot at the mall, and are the number one suspects in that fire at Fountain Square tonight. Why don't you get everyone else out of here so I can take care of it?"

His eyes were wide, and he stared at me. "Do me a favor and forget that I've been shunned," I said, shaking inside. "Think for yourself and do something for the greater good? Huh? Can you do that?"

Our coffee was up, and after I dropped a twenty on the counter, I handed Pierce his juice box and Al one of the paper cups. There were three people behind the counter, and they were looking at us like we were . . . demons. "Thanks," I said, shaking as I picked up my drink with the big *R* for raspberry on it and Jenks's espresso. I hated it when my temper got loose like that. Al seemed to think it was funny.

The smell of coffee seemed to pull Jenks from the light fixture, and he dropped heavily onto my shoulder, catching his balance with a sudden tugging on my hair. "You okay?" I breathed, and he shivered his wings.

"Just cold," he said, and I nodded, agreeing. My coat wasn't doing much to cut the chill either. There was too much in-and-out traffic for my comfort, mostly in.

Halfway to the table, I realized there was no way we'd all fit, and in all truthfulness, I didn't want Pierce or Al near Mia or Remus. "Jenks, can you and Pierce get people out of here?" I asked, trying to get rid of two birds with one stone.

"I'm not babysitting ghost boy!" Jenks exclaimed from my shoulder.

Pierce added a quick "I suspect you think me less than likely, mistress witch."

Both of them were frowning when I stopped dead still in the store and turned, coat bumping my calves. Al was smiling. "Jenks, you're so cold you're not dusting," I said, trying not to sound worried. "I need to get people out of here quietly, and you can do that. By the time I need you, you'll be warm." *I hope.* "Until then, let me know if Mia touches my aura."

I handed Pierce Jenks's coffee and added, "I'm giving you my phone. Ivy will probably call when the FIB is here. Let me know, and tell them not to barge in here, okay?"

"Jenks can do that," he said grudgingly.

I put a hand to my forehead, feeling a headache coming on. "If I'm right, ugly guy over there is going to have a hissy long before the FIB gets here. I'm going to need your help, and at that point, you can let your testosterone rip. Meantime, Jenks can brief you on what Remus has occupied his last twenty years with so you don't get smeared. 'Kay?"

I handed Pierce my phone, and when he looked at me wryly, Jenks's wings clattered to life. "Okay," the pixy conceded, laboriously making the flight to the wary man, eyeing him before landing on his shoulder and telling him to start at the front.

Two down. I turned to Al and the demon beamed. "Al, why

don't you be a good boy and take the seat of the first people Pierce gets out of here."

"I *want* to be *closer,*" he said, then looked over his glasses at the couple the next table over. Their chairs scraped as they beat a hasty path to the exit, and Al sat, taking meticulous care in arranging his coat.

Okay. Time to earn your rent, I thought as I exhaled heavily. I took a moment to loosen another button on my coat and feel for the comforting weight of my splat gun in my bag as I approached Ford, Mia, and Remus. Ivy would probably tell Edden to be circumspect, but it wouldn't surprise me that if in their zeal, six FIB cars pulled up with lights on and sirens going.

If Mia didn't behave herself, this was going to be over really quickly. She had tried to kill me twice, and I knew I should've been concerned when I said hi to Ford and sat down in the chair he had pulled up for me, but the only thing I was feeling was tired. That Edden had a warrant and I could shoot them now was a comfort. Eyes were heavy on me as I took the lid off my drink and sipped it. My shoulders relaxed as the hot, rich coffee slipped down. With a little effort, I could see the door and counter both.

Either Mia was going to sacrifice Remus and promise to be good, or this was a plot to see me dead, but I didn't think Ford would read the situation wrong. The door jingled when a couple left with frightened backward glances, and Jenks gave me a distant thumbs-up. Damn, this was good stuff, and I made a mental note of what it was in case I survived. *Raspberry Italian latte?*

My eyes rose over the rim of the paper cup. Remus's expression was both angry and frightened—a bad combination as his attention flicked from me to Al and back. Mia had an unsettling confidence about her as she held the sleeping Holly in her little pink snowsuit. One would never guess they were wanted for assault and possible murder. She was going to bail on him. I knew it. What did she know of love?

"Mia," I said, seeing that no one else was talking. "Did you set the fire?"

"No." Her voice was soft to keep Holly from waking, and the toddler's hands moved in her sleep. Mia's eyes were fixed on mine, trying to impress me with what I already believed was the truth. "The Walker did. She's trying to pit my own city against me. I told you she had the skill of a falling log." Her high voice held a shocking amount of hatred. "She wants Holly."

Mia held her daughter closer, and the child shifted into a more comfortable position, lips pouting in her sleep. Remus's hands clenched, and when he saw me notice their white-knuckled strength, he moved them out of my sight.

I put my hands under the table, keeping my elbows still while I pulled my splat gun out and set it atop my knees. "I didn't think it was you," I said to try to get them to relax. "I'm trying to stop Ms. Walker, Mia, but you were seen at the fire. The FIB isn't going out of their way to help anymore. You need to come in. Someone's going to get hurt." *Like me.*

Remus stood, and my heart jumped. "We need to go, Mia. People are leaving."

A faint, musty scent drifted from the angry man at his movement, tickling my memory. Fear pinged through me, and I froze. It smelled like cement. Cold and rough. Mia felt my fear, the woman going almost slack as my emotions puddled out from me. Ford did too, but his expression was of confusion, not satisfaction. He knew my fear didn't stem from Mia, but something else, and I shoved the emotion away. *Kisten. It's from Kisten. I don't have time for this.*

Mia moved Holly to a more comfortable position, ignoring Remus. The baby's eyes opened. Silently, she stared, and as I watched, Holly's pale blue eyes became the pupil black of hunger. "Did you tell the FIB to drop their investigation?" Mia asked me.

I jerked my attention from Holly, surprised. "Ah, yes, but someone needs to go to jail for the Tilsons. You were living in their house. You beat up an FIB officer." *Tried to kill me twice. Jeez, what am I doing here?*

Beside me, Ford swallowed hard, feeling everyone's emotions and having a hard time separating himself. He was better than a truth amulet, but something was shifting, and I gripped my gun, setting my free hand casually around my cup. "Mia, let me tell them you are ready to cooperate," I tried again. I didn't want to shoot her unless I had to. "The captain of the FIB knows you're sorry." *Liar, liar.* "He knows the lengths to which Ms. Walker will go to gain custody of Holly." *Pants on fire.* "He's angry about what happened to his son, but if you come in, as a sign of trust, he will look past it. We can keep you and Holly together."

Remus bent over his wife, hissing in her ear, "They lie to get what they want, then tell you you're a liar when you ask for it. I won't have my daughter pushed from foster home to foster home, sleeping on stained mattresses and beat up for not having a real mom or dad."

I doubted that would happen with Holly, and Mia reached up and touched his hand. "Remus, love," she said, eyes on mine. "I'm not turning us in. I'm finding out if the FIB is taking me seriously. She warned them, and if they come, I'll know their answer."

Oh. Shit. Heart pounding, I dropped my hand below the top of the table and gripped my gun with both hands. *Show of lethal force or not, if you twitch, I'll down you both.* "Think about it, Mia . . . You broke the law. You either live by society's punishments or live outside it in the abandoned stretches, off scraps. You said you made this city. You're really going to leave it? Killing me won't help you. It will tick them off."

Ford stood, and Remus tensed, held in check by Mia's hand on his, atop her shoulder. "You told me you weren't going to hurt anyone," the psychiatrist said. "I believed you."

Mia jiggled Holly as she fussed. "At the time, I thought the FIB was smarter than that. Clearly the FIB won't listen until scores of them are dead. But they will listen. The witch is shunned, dross I can kill with impunity."

She's nuts! She is freaking insane! Behind me, I felt Pierce turn. It was the eeriest thing I'd ever felt, but I swear, I felt him turn. In an instant, Jenks was before me, shedding hot sparkles. "I wouldn't say impunity," the pixy said, blade pointing at her.

"I'm of a mind to agree with the pixy," Pierce said from behind me.

I watched Remus assess them, but it was Mia who said, "What the devil are you? You don't even have an aura!"

"So I've been told, and if you're powerful smart, you'll pull foot and not look back."

Holly started to whimper, and Mia jiggled her, gaze rising up to Remus. Behind me, I heard the clatter of boots and the jingle of the door as someone left. They were going voluntarily now, and the place was almost empty. I turned to the counter. Junior was there, staring, frightened. "Call the I.S.," I mouthed. This was too much for the FIB. No way.

Remus saw, and in a bellow of rage, he ran at Junior.

I bolted upright, gun tracking Remus, but I didn't have a clear shot. Ford dropped, staying out of the way. A woman gasped and ducked under her table.

Junior's eyes widened at Remus. Shouting a word of Latin, made strong in his fear, he set a circle. Remus ran right into it as he tried to jump over the counter. Blood spurted from his nose as he fell back, bellowing as he hit the floor. Pierce grabbed his arm, and Remus smacked him with an unfocused blow that sent him reeling. Catching his balance, the small man licked his thumb and fell into a boxer's stance. He was going to get himself killed. Again.

"Git the blood out of your eyes and stand so I can row you up salt river," Pierce said, then made a face at me to get on with it. Jenks, too, was shrilling at me to shoot him. But it was too late. I couldn't hit one without hitting the other.

"Don't kill him, Remus," Mia was saying calmly. "I think I know the little man."

"Back up, Rache!" Jenks exclaimed, darting from one end of the shop to the other. "Before she starts sucking on you!"

And Al was laughing, almost choking on his grande latte as he clapped.

A chair scraped as Mia stood. The scent of cold cement and mold flowed from her and Holly. I backed up. My hand had crept up to my throat, as if I could feel cold fingers there. "Killing me isn't going to stop the FIB, Mia," I said, thinking this was a great time to be having a flashback to Kisten's killer.

Mia stood, the table between us, Holly holding tight to her as the baby howled. Behind me, Pierce grunted as he took a blow, and something crashed. "You're mistaken," she said, eyes on me, not the fight behind me. "Killing you will stop everything. Remus, quit playing with that dead man and hold the witch down. Holly is hungry."

Oh my God. That's why she hadn't touched me yet.

There was a thump and Pierce groaned again. I turned to see Pierce slumped against the wall among the remnants of a table. Grinning, Remus came at me with grasping hands. I shoved a chair aside for some room and kicked off my heels. Pissed, I swung the barrel up, and at the bottom of an exhale, I pulled the trigger.

"No!" Mia shouted, but the little blue plastic ball hit him square in the chest. Potion soaked his shirt and splashed up to his neck—and the man dropped. I danced back as he fell into the table, and from there to the floor. Coffee went everywhere. *Thank you, God.* Now for Mrs. Bitch.

The door jingled, and I turned. "Damn it!" I shouted as Mia's silhouette raced past the window. Ford was tight behind her. What in hell was he doing? "Pierce? Jenks?"

Pierce was getting up, shaking his head from Remus's blow. Jenks hovered over him, dusting heavily to stop the cut on his head.

"Jenks, stay put. Tell them to bring some salt water. I'm downing her."

"Rache! Wait!"

He couldn't come with me. My arm hit the door, and it crashed open. I raced after them in my feet, bare but for nylons, and my splat gun in my grip. To the left, a fast patter of heels drew my attention. I took a deep breath and ran through the snowy parking lot. In an instant, I'd passed the cars and was on the sidewalk.

The cold cement numbed my feet, and I ran faster. My breath puffed out, and my body fell into a rhythm I could keep up for an hour. My slit dress hiked up as I ran, and I was glad my stupidity in choosing fashion over functionality had stopped at my shoes. Ahead, the smallest movement in the light a block up told me where they'd gone. God, how had she gotten ahead so fast?

A toddler wailed, the odd cadence telling me she was being held in the arms of someone running. I couldn't help but gain on them. Ford's silhouette was clear in the light for an instant. Then they were past the light, and they were gone.

I gripped my splat gun as I followed, slowing so I didn't run into them. Coming to a stop under the light, I listened. It was dark in all directions. New Year's celebrations were going on all over the city, but here, on the outskirts of an old industrial park, it was dark.

A baby cried, and I heard the crack of cold metal.

Heart pounding, I spun. "Ford?" I called. He didn't answer, and I jogged to the end of the street. A small cement hut surrounded by a chain-link fence was the only logical option. Though the chain-link door was shut, I could see in the snow the track it had made when it opened. Footprints marked the otherwise-pristine snow.

Slower yet, I approached, my feet hurting from the cold. "Ford?" I whispered, then edged into the tiny fenced yard. It was no bigger than a dog run, and I guessed this was a switching house for the city's electric or phone lines.

But the small room was empty when I stood on tiptoe and looked in the high window, my fingertips numb from the cold. Two sets of prints had tracked in the snow. I licked my lips. Going in alone was really stupid. I looked back toward the coffeehouse. No FIB. No I.S.

I couldn't wait. "Dumb," I said as I started to remove my coat, then, shivering, hiked up my dress and stripped off my nylons instead, hanging them over the tall fence for them to find and know where I'd gone. "Dumb. You are a dumb witch," I muttered, and, shivering, I pushed the heavy metal door open and went in.

Thirty

The smell of damp stone hit me, and I recognized the scent that had been coming off Mia and Remus tonight. They'd been here before, and I moved quickly to the conventional steel door at the back of the empty room. The doorjamb had been broken from the inside, and feeling this was really wrong, I pulled it open to see a staircase going down.

"Down," I muttered as I hiked my dress up. "Why is it always down?" Gun in hand, I felt the rough cement walls as I descended. There was a bare bulb glowing, showing that the way was straight and even. Wires ran along the sloping ceiling, as if put in after the building was constructed. My steps were silent because I was barefoot, and my feet were numb on the old but unworn cement. It stank like mold and dust.

People were talking, their voices unclear but echoing. I heard a small, feminine gasp, and then Ford shouted, "Mia! It's just me. It's okay. I'm trying to help you. You have to come in, but I promise I won't let them take Holly from you."

"I don't need your help," Mia said tightly. "I never should have wished for love. How do you live like this? He's dead. That witch killed Remus!"

"He's not dead, Mia," Ford said. "It was a sleeping charm."

"Not dead?" Mia said.

It was a pain-filled whisper, and thinking Mia was ready to break, I ghosted down the rest of the stairs. The light from the bulb in the stairway was overpowered by the shifting beam of a high-powered flashlight. Slowing, I crept to the end of the stairway, and with my hands on my splat gun, I peeked around the archway.

The echoing room was huge, stretching fifteen feet high at least, with beautiful vaulted ceilings. Mia was standing in the middle with a lanternlike flashlight in her grip—Ford was before her with his back to me. I think he sensed my emotions, but he didn't turn.

Behind Mia was a sunken tunnel stretching in two directions. It looked like a subway tube, but there were no rails or tracks. There was no electricity, no benches, no graffiti. There was nothing but empty walls and forgotten bits of trash smelling of dust.

Mia's face was proud and determined in the light reflecting off the walls as she tried to soothe the toddler, to no avail since she was upset herself. She hadn't had the lantern in the coffee shop. It must have been in the little room upstairs. And it suddenly hit me that this was how Mia and Remus had been getting around, moving under the city to evade the FIB and the I.S. I hadn't even known the tunnels existed, but Mia had probably witnessed their construction.

Mia's eyes flicked to mine, and discovered by my emotions, I stepped out. "Remus is fine, Mia. You have to turn yourself in."

"No I don't," she said, the defiant pride in her voice telling me she wasn't giving up. Ever. "This is my city."

I shook my head. "Things are different." I slowly moved forward. It was frigid down here, and I shivered, edging closer yet. Almost close enough to make the splat ball gun a sure thing. "If you don't come in, the FIB will bring everything against you. I know they look stupid, but they aren't. Without a show of goodwill, Ms. Walker will leave with Holly." I stopped when Mia's chin lifted. "Mia, I swear I will do everything I can to keep Walker from taking her, but you have to help me."

Mia shook her head and backed up. The light in her hand swung wildly over the cold walls, and Holly started to cry. "Remus is right. I'm going back to the old ways. They've kept me alive for hundreds of years. Give me Remus, and leave me and my child alone, or there will be more deaths. You've been warned."

Turning her back on us, Mia headed for the black arch of the tunnel.

My gun swung up, and Ford got in my way. "Mia!" he exclaimed as I tried to edge around him for a clear shot. "Think about your future."

"My *future*?" The words were a cold, imperialistic bark, and she stopped at the edge of the three-foot drop. "You are children! You are *all* children! I saw the birth of this city, when she was a wallowing hole that pigs ran through heedlessly. I helped her grow by removing the people who would keep her ignorant and small. This is *my* city. I built her. How dare you think to put your laws and rules on me and lecture me about the future! I'm not running away. Tell Captain Edden that if the FIB follows me, his son will be in a casket, not a hospital bed. You," she said, child on one hip and light in her hand, "are nothing. Animals to be culled and sucked dry. I am still living among pigs."

I had my gun aimed at her, but I'd have to hit her face for it to do any good with her wearing that heavy winter coat.

"Mia," Ford said in his best psychologist voice, "I'm not as old as you are, but I've lived more heartache and joy than you can comprehend. Don't do this. Love is worth the trial. It's what defines us. Nothing can stain your love for Holly. And you do love her. It is as clear as your voice. Isn't that purity worth some pain? Don't risk losing that from pride!"

From behind me in the stairway came the soft scuffing of shoes. Adrenaline surged, but I couldn't take my eyes from Mia. I'd give anything for Edden or Glenn right about now. Mia's eyes tracked behind me, and her face grew even more determined as I heard the presence of only one person, not the ten I wanted.

"The Turn take it, Morgan, you are worse than my mother," a masculine voice mocked. "Always showing up at the wrong place at the wrong time to mess up my day."

I spun around. I couldn't help it. "Tom!" I exclaimed, backing up and not knowing who to point my gun at anymore. "Get out of here. Mia is my tag!"

Mia's brow furrowed. Dropping my nylons, Tom came even with Ford, his bandaged hand out in warning to me and pointing his wand at the banshee, looking like a bad actor in a fantasy flick. His expression was far too condescending for him to get out of this alive. "You can have her," he said. "All I want is the baby."

Mia's face went white, and my jaw dropped as it all came together. He wasn't trying to bring in Mia. He was working for The Walker. He was a freaking baby snatcher. He hadn't been spying on me when I kept finding him at crime scenes; I'd been messing up his takes.

My face burned, and I shifted the aim of my weapon to him. *Slime. And how is the FIB going to find me now?* "What do you think you are doing?" I said, but it was obvious. "You can't touch Holly, and Mia sure as hell isn't going to help you."

"Unlike you, Morgan, I don't mind a little smut on my soul," he said grimly, his brow furrowing to tell me that whatever was in his wand wasn't legal—not to mention nasty enough that it bothered him. "Ms. Harbor is going to walk up those stairs and hand that kid to whoever I say." He smiled an ugly smile at the angry woman, standing with her heel at the edge of the drop-off.

"And you walk away with a pocketful of change, huh?" I said, backing up to better get him in my sights. "Subjection spells are nasty, Tom. Did you take the tongue out of the goat yourself, or did you pay someone to do it?"

Tom's jaw clenched, but he didn't move. "What's it going to

be, Mia?" he said. "Either walk up those stairs on your own, or you do it charmed."

"Bloody hell witch," she cursed, her head lowered to eye him from under her hair. It was the look of a predator, her eyes black and her muscles tense. Mia let Holly slide from her, and I retreated—getting out of the way; Ford was doing the same. "You won't have her," Mia said, setting her lantern down as well. Hands free, she stepped forward. "I earned this child with blood and death."

Oh, this isn't looking good . . . Oblivious, Holly patted the floor where the light fell, fascinated with the shadow her chubby hand made and trying to catch it. Getting to her knees, she started crawling, chasing the echoes. I eyed the drop-off. It was far too close for my comfort. "Mia . . . ," I warned, but she wasn't listening.

Mia's eyes had narrowed and her stance shifted. Pulling herself up tall, she became a wronged goddess, her face beautiful and calm, savage and without pity. She was a queen, a giver of life and death, and her eyes shone like black coals. Oh, she was pissed.

"Tom, look out!" I shouted as Mia leapt at him, her hands bent like ugly claws.

Tom panicked, and Mia easily knocked the wand from him. It skittered to the base of the stairs. "You will all die to feed my child," she said, looking small as she stood in front of him. "And I will weep tears to suck your life for all of eternity."

"Mia! Stop!" I shouted, my gun pointed at her. "I won't let you kill him. I'm not going to let him take your baby either. Just stop. Back off and we can find a way. I promise!"

Mia hesitated, either considering it or trying to think of a way to kill us all at once.

"I mean it, Mia," I intoned, and her grip on Tom trembled. A bead of sweat rolled down his face. He understood how close he was to death, not knowing if I'd really bother to save his sorry ass or not. I honestly didn't know why I cared.

Holly squealed in delight, and my eyes darted to her. Fear

pulsed through me, and I almost jerked into a run. Oblivious to the anger of the adults, immune to it because of her history, the child was contentedly playing in the shifting light, wobbling on her feet and entranced as she reached for the shadows we were making on the curved wall of the tunnel. She was at the edge of the drop-off. Teetering, she cooed, and Mia's face was riven with indecision. If she moved, Tom would run for his wand. If she didn't, her baby would fall.

"Ford! No!" I shouted as he lunged for the little girl in her pink snowsuit.

"Got you," he exhaled as she tipped into a fall and he pulled her back at the last instant. The two of them landed against the cold floor with a puff of Ford's breath. Holly thumped into his chest, safe. But Ford was holding her.

"Oh God . . . Ford," I breathed as the little girl peered up at him and smiled that same smile she had given me—right before she pulled my aura away and ate my soul. I couldn't move. If I did, Mia would kill us all.

Holly's chubby hand reached up and patted Ford's face. Ford gasped in pain. Mia's eyes narrowed in satisfaction. My anger burned, and I tightened my grip on my gun. Damn it, I didn't know who to shoot. *Maybe the girl,* and throat tight, I swung my gun to her.

"No," Ford breathed, and my finger, tightening on the trigger, jerked loose. *He's okay?*

We all stared as Ford hunched around Holly, shaking in a spasm before he took a deep breath. "It's gone," he moaned, the words almost a sob. Oblivious to us, the tears ran down his tired, lined face. "Not that one, Holly," he whispered, sounding exhausted. "That's mine. Take the rest. You're an angel. You're a beautiful, innocent angel."

My pulse hammered. Mia stared at Ford in stark, shocked wonder. The little girl was patting his face, feeling the beginnings of his six o'clock shadow and babbling. She wasn't killing him. She was . . . I didn't know what she was doing, but Ford's tears were in relief, not pain.

"What the hell is going on?" Tom said, and I felt him tap a line.

Damn it, I couldn't tap a line. I was playing patty-cake with a black arts witch, and all I had was a sleepy-time charm?

"I don't know." I shifted my attention to Mia. "Maybe she's gotten control of herself."

Mia's lips parted. Clearly the woman was stunned to see another man holding her child. "It's too soon," she breathed. Her feet scuffed as she turned to them. "Holly?"

Holly babbled in Ford's arms, the purity of the sound echoing against the curved, cold ceilings far overhead.

"Then I guess I don't need you anymore, do I?" Tom said suddenly.

I felt a drop in the ley line. Instinct kicked in. I swung my gun around and pulled the trigger. A little blue ball hit Tom squarely in the chest, but it was too late. A nasty green ball of something was already in the air.

"Down!" I shouted, then dropped to the hard cement as an explosion of green sparkles pushed my hair back. My ears hurt, and I looked to see Mia picking herself up off the floor. Ford was out cold, a shimmering green haze marking his aura. Tom's spell apparently. Tom wasn't moving either. *Tag, you're it.*

Pushing myself up, I went for Mia, landing a side kick squarely in her gut. I fell from the impact, and the woman was shoved into the wall. Her head hit the cement, and she collapsed. *Whoops. My bad.* But damn, that had felt good.

I turned to Ford to see that the green shimmer was gone and that Holly was crying beside him, in the curve of his body. Ford shifted his face off the cement and relief spilled into me. He was alive. *Thank you, God.* I got to my feet and tugged my coat straight, rubbing my sore hand where a new scrape and probably another bruise would run come morning. But it was done. All that was left was the mopping up.

He was going to snatch her baby? I thought, shivering as I turned Mia over with a foot. Glancing at the gun in my hand, I debated hitting her with one of my few remaining sleepy-time potions since I couldn't make a circle to contain her. But if I'd given her a concussion, the charm might send her into a coma. I'd just have to watch her like the predator she was until the FIB caught up with me. And Mia *was* a predator. A freaking tiger. A crocodile shedding crocodile tears.

"Stay there, sweetheart," I whispered to Holly when she crawled to pat at her mother's face and cry baby tears. I couldn't help her. God help me, why did I feel like such a bad guy?

The soft scrape of wood on cement whispered, and I spun, gun pointed. Not only was Tom awake, but he was moving, and I gaped at him as he scooped his wand up from the floor with his bandaged hand and looked at me from under his raggedy bangs, hatred in his every motion. I'd hit him. I knew I'd hit him! This wasn't fair!

"Anticharm gear," he explained, rubbing his nose and wiping away the blood. "You think I'd come against you without something to defuse your infamous little blue sleepy-time charms? You need to diversify, Rachel."

My eyes narrowed, and my grip shifted. "It will probably hurt if I hit you in the eye," I threatened.

"Don't. Move," he said, and I froze. That wand was a lot more dangerous. Seeing Holly unattended, his eyes took on a satisfied glint.

"Tom," I said, shaking my head in warning. "Don't be stupid. You give Holly to Walker, and Mia will freaking kill you."

"I think she'll be more angry at you than me," he said, twirling the wand dexterously. "Or at least she will be when I get done with her. Back up. Get away from the kid."

I had nothing. Well, I could talk him to death, maybe. "This is a bad idea," I said as I edged away while he moved closer, pushing me from Holly with his presence. "Think about this. You're not going to walk away from it, and if you do, you won't be alive for long."

"Like you know a bad idea from a good one," he said, motioning with his wand for me to keep moving back. "If a human can touch the kid, then I can, too," he added as he scooped her up.

"Tom, don't!" I exclaimed, and Holly keened, an eerie coo of pleasure and delight that chilled me to my core. The man stiffened. His eyes bulged, and his mouth opened in a silent scream. He fell to his knees, and I tensed to knock the child from him, only to fall back and cower as a wave of bright force burst from him. I couldn't see it—my eyes were blind to it—but it was there. I could feel it, and my skin tingled, as if a thousand summers were pressing on me in the smothering dark of the sunken room.

Tom's cry of pain echoed against the curved ceiling and came again a thousand times. Back arched, he hung poised as Holly pressed her hand to his cheek, rapture infusing her.

"Holly, no!" Remembering my gun, I aimed at Holly and pulled the trigger. The ball went wild when someone hit my arm.

Shocked, I dropped back when I saw Al. Pierce was behind him, looking afraid, and that chilled me to my core. "What are you doing?" I asked, shocked.

But the demon, in his green velvet and with his reddish complexion, only smiled. *"Celero inanio,"* he whispered, and I yelped, dropping my suddenly hot gun.

"Damn it, Al," I said, frustrated as I shook my hand. "What are you doing?"

"Keeping you alive, itchy witch." He held a warning hand out behind him at Pierce, and the man rocked back. "Stay put, or the deal is off and you're really dead."

Deal?

Tom moaned in pain. I didn't care if he was a black witch. No one should die like that. Giving up on any help from Al or Pierce, I ran to help him, only to fall when Al tripped me. Gasping, pain whitened the world as my cheek scraped the cement when I didn't turn my head fast enough. I looked up, shocked into stillness.

It's Tom's life, I thought in despair as I shook the hair from my eyes. Holly was taking him, like she had tried to take me. The room pulsed with the force of Tom's soul, a hidden heartbeat of intent that measured his life. I could feel it as his aura was sucked away and nothing was left to hold his soul to his will. And it was fading.

A soft scuff behind me was my only warning, and I yelped again when Al roughly pulled me up. He grinned, his flat blocky teeth glinting in the light from Mia's lantern. "Too late," he said, smiling as he watched in macabre rapture, almost salivating at the death of the black witch and making me wonder if Al was here to collect on a debt. "Too late and perfect timing."

Ford was out cold, the emotions of the room having brought him to his knees. The air pounded with white-light thoughts, a lifetime of whispered conversations at the edge of my awareness. But they were fading. Holly made a delighted squeal of surprise when Tom completely collapsed. The black pulse echoing in my head was sucked into oblivion, and I staggered, unwittingly pushing back into Al. The small child awkwardly got to her feet and wobbled to her kneeling mother, now smiling and holding out her arms to her. God help us. Tom was dead. Mia was awake. And Holly was walking.

"Let me go, Al. I have to . . . get her," I finished lamely. But with what? The heat had probably popped the sleepy-time charms in my gun.

The demon's grip on my arm tightened when I tried to pull away. "Not yet," he said, and pain shot up my arm as I twisted in his grip. "I need something."

I stared at him, my heart pounding. "Need what?"

"This."

He unexpectedly swung at me, and my head rocked back. My ears rang, and I staggered. Pierce protested, but it was the smooth, clean touch of velvet against my neck that caught and cradled me as I fell. "So sorry, itchy witch," Al said as he gently eased me to the floor. The scent of burnt amber and mold made me ill, and I tried to focus. Dizzy, I was dizzy.

The cold seeped up through my back, my coat doing little to keep me warm. I felt a moment of panic when I saw the shiny gold knife in Al's hand as he knelt by me, but I was helpless. Al gave me a little pat on the cheek that stung, and I pushed ineffectively at him.

"You are a font of opportunity," he said, in a wonderful mood as he caught my wrist. "Never would I have been able to plan this, itchy witch, but good things just seem to follow you like a puppy."

Good? I wondered. Was he crazy? "What are you doing . . . ," I panted, trying to pull my arm from his grip.

Temporarily putting the knife between his teeth, Al pulled from his coat pocket the black potion bottle he'd taken from me. "I need a wee bit of your blood, love," he said when he took the knife from his mouth. "Something to invoke the excellent charm you cooked up for me."

Pierce's charm? Panic slid through me when he set the potion aside and took the knife. Behind him, Pierce stood with his hands fisted, clearly upset but not going to do a thing. "S-stop," I said, then jerked at the icy pain of the blade. "Al, stop!" I cried, trying to pull my wrist from him.

Al stood. I tried to follow, but he put a booted foot across my throat, and my upward surge ended in a gurgle and a thrashing of legs.

"Master's prerogative," he said as he swirled the potion with the three drops of blood in it. "I can claim any spell you make. We've been over this before." Tilting his head, he looked at me from over his smoked glasses. As if in a toast, he held up the potion. "Mine."

His foot lifted, and I gasped, putting a hand to my throat and sitting up. My finger throbbed, and I looked, seeing that he had cut right across the closed loop of my fingerprint. He wasn't doing the charm right. It should be spilled into a hollowed-out stone and allowed to disperse. He was using my potion, but for what?

"What are you doing?" I said, truly horrified when he

yanked Tom's body up and dumped the potion into the corpse's mouth. Was he trying to resurrect him?

Al dropped the body and turned in a jaunty motion. "I can't have a corpse for a familiar. How gauche would that be? People would talk. And with you idling your time away, I need a real familiar. Thanks, love. This will do fine. Enjoy the rest of your night. This one is mine. Preexisting agreement, you see. It's not a snatch, itchy witch." And he laughed.

I scrambled upright with a hand to my stomach. Al was using my potion, but for what?

"Ta, love," he said, and with a wicked smile, he yanked Tom to him and vanished.

He took Tom. Holy crap, he took Tom! And I think he used my potion to keep him from dying. "Al!" I cried, panicked that it had been my charm to do it. This was not my fault! You play with black magic, you pay the cost.

The light shifted, and I turned to find that I was alone down here with an unconscious FIB agent and one extremely pissed banshee. Pierce was gone. A pile of clothes and the stolen coat marked where he had been, and I cursed Al, thinking he had snagged both witches and left, Tom, apparently, being more important than keeping his word.

Mia had Holly on her hip, and the child watched me with eyes as black as her mother's, as innocent and unforgiving as death itself. Backing up, I looked at my now-useless splat gun. I couldn't make a circle, and running after a banshee without backup—or better yet, angry—was going to bite me on the ass. But I'd gone out tonight intent on talking Al into agreeing to stop snatching people, not to rescue the world from a banshee having a bad day.

"You will die for your part in this," the woman snarled.

"I tried to help," I said, grabbing the back of Ford's shirt and dragging him out of her reach. He was conscious, but not going to be of any help, unable to sit under his own power yet.

"You are alone," the woman said, letting Holly slip from her.

"So?" I said stupidly, then gasped and backpedaled when the woman lunged forward, hands grasping.

"Rachel!" Ford called with a slurred shout, and I stumbled, tripping over his legs.

I went down, Mia on top of me.

We hit the floor. My breath whooshed out, and I tapped a line, frantic. Pain hit me as the heat of the ley line suddenly burned across my unprotected neurons and synapses, and when her hands touched my face, I screamed as my aura pulled through my soul. "You think you can kill me!" I screamed defiantly. "Go ahead," I panted. "Make my freaking . . . day."

Her teeth bared, inches from me. Her breath came in a pant, her gaze wild, fevered with savage instinct. But I had fought off Ivy, and this didn't scare me. The line was humming through me, and I let her have it. I let her have it all.

Mia screamed. Her fingernails dug into my jaw, her agony reverberating through me like her voice echoing against the curved ceilings of stone over us. She screamed again, and I clenched my teeth, refusing to let go of the line even as it burned me. Power flowed into her, burning her mind and body, but she wouldn't let go. The scent of cold dust and forgotten air filled me, and then her eyes opened against the torment.

Blacker than the sin of betrayal, she fixed her gaze on mine, panting from the agony. "If it was that easy," she said, clearly hurting, "I would have died before my twenties."

I had a second of doubt, and feeling it, she attacked.

It was as if the world flipped over. With a curious twist of vertigo, she ripped my thin aura from me. Pain lit through me as the ley line I was pulling on hit me, completely raw and unfiltered. I jerked, instinct shoving her away, but she had me and pinned me to the floor. The line still flowed, but I wouldn't let go as it was clearly hurting her, too. Pain was etched on her forehead and sweat beaded up. Her breath came in a pant, and she held it. Behind her pain, I could see my soul slipping into her, my strength going with it. If I couldn't stop her from taking my soul, she would freaking kill me, line or no.

"Rachel . . . ," I heard from behind the roaring in my ears, and then someone knocked us apart. Mia's grip tore away as she fell back. The cool air of the tunnel hit me, and I groaned as the strength of the line boomeranged back into me. Unable to breathe, I curled into myself and rolled to my stomach, clenching in hurt. My face rubbed into the dusty cement, and I sucked in the air as if it would help me find my soul. I still had it. I still had some of my aura, or I'd be dead. I didn't think I was dead. I hurt too much.

Only now did I let go of the line. A pained sob escaped me as the incoming force ceased and I pushed enough out of me so I could think, but even so, it hurt. Power leaked from my muscles, cramping them when I tried to move. In the distance, I could hear Holly crying. Or maybe it was me.

"I'm sorry, Mia," Ford was saying faintly as I tried to breathe without taking in the dust. "You've had all the chances I can give a person. Holly will be fine. She's—"

"Give her to me!" Mia screamed, her raw voice scraping my awareness. I turned my head and cracked my eyes. It hurt. God, it hurt to do even that little bit, but I found them. Ford was holding Holly, the young girl blinking at her raging mother but not upset. Ford had my splat gun and was holding Mia off. The charms must not have popped, or he would have knocked himself out picking up the gun. How he could hold the baby and Tom couldn't was beyond me.

"Holly, take him!" the banshee shouted, and Ford shifted her higher on his hip.

"She is," the man said, his face screwing up with emotion, and then he forced his expression to calm. "She's taking everything from me but what is mine. There are no thoughts in me but my own. And, Mia, you are a criminal. You helped make our society, and you will live by our rules."

"No!" she howled, then lunged. The flash of the lantern was red against my eyes as it fell over. My sight went gray as the pain in my head almost made me black out. It was either that or the light was busted. Groaning, I didn't see but heard the puff of my splat-ball gun and the thump of someone hitting the floor.

"It's okay," I heard Ford whisper, his voice pitched high to tell me he was talking to Holly. "Your mommy is okay. She's going to sleep for a while. And you'll see her every day, Holly. I promise. Stay with her. I'll be right back."

I couldn't breathe. My chest hurt so bad.

"Rachel. Are you okay?" Ford said, his voice heavy with heartache, and I felt him turn me over, lifting my head from the cold cement. Masculine fingers traced my face, but I couldn't tell if my eyes were open or not. I was so cold, and I shivered violently, making the pain worse.

The dust on his hands turned to damp grit as he wiped my tears away, and the scent of wet cement rose higher. It trickled through my thoughts, mixing with my pain in a slurry of confusion. I breathed, not knowing if I was in my past or my present. I was going unconscious. I could feel everything shutting down. The light was gone, and I couldn't see. But someone held me, and he smelled like cold cement.

"Kisten?" I forced my lungs to work. Someone in Kisten's boat had smelled like this. Like old, abandoned cement. I struggled and he pulled me closer, holding my wrists when I tried to fight him. "We have to go!" I sobbed, but he only pressed me into his chest as he cried with me, telling me to remember, that he had me, and that he wouldn't let me remember alone. That he would bring me back.

The stink of cement filled me, pulling a memory into existence. It trickled painfully through me, drawn by the scent of wet stone and dust. And I panicked.

We had to get away! The vampire was coming, and we had to go now. I struggled to break from Kisten but he held me close, his voice mixing with my frustration as he wiped my tears. I jerked when a memory surfaced. *Kisten had wiped my tears away. He wouldn't leave with me, and then it was too late.*

I couldn't think, that dammed dust caking my thoughts,

mixing my past and now. I couldn't . . . think. Was I here or on Kisten's boat? I'd been crying. I had tried to save him, and he had loved me. But it hadn't made a difference. He had still died. And I was alone.

Not alone, echoed in my mind. *Go. I'll bring you back.*

Tears leaked out even as I fought oblivion, and my mind rebelled, dropping me into a memory lost for an instant in time, triggered by the scent of dust, the sensation of pain, and the feeling of love turned into the pain of sacrifice.

My heart beat, and I closed my eyes, falling.

Thirty-one

You son of a bastard!" I exclaimed in frustrated anger, wiping the helpless tears away and shaking from adrenaline as I faced Kisten, his blue eyes pinched in distress because I'd found him in this tiny backwater of the Ohio River. "I don't care what vampire law says, you're not a box of candy. I've got everything we need. My car is in the lot. Just put on the disguise charm and we'll get the hell out of here!"

But Kisten smiled at me with his bright blue eyes and ran a shaking hand under my eye to leave the cool breath of drying skin. "No, love," he said, voice utterly devoid of his fake accent. "I can't live outside my society's rules. I don't want to. I'd rather die among them. I'm sorry you think I'm a fool."

"You're being stupid!" I yelled, stomping my foot. God, if I was stronger, I'd knock him out and drag him away. "There's no reason for it!"

Kisten stiffened, and when his eyes went over my shoulder, I remembered the boat's oh-so-subtle shift of motion and the sound of water lapping. The smell of vampire rose thick, and I turned, pressing my back into Kisten's chest. My chin trembled, and I clenched my jaw.

Kisten's killer wasn't a big man. Kisten could probably take him in a fair fight. I knew there would be no such thing. His eyes were black from blood lust, and there was a faint trembling in his hands, as if he was holding himself back, relishing the last drawings out. Faint wrinkles marked the corners of his eyes. His suit looked like it was from the eighties, and his tie was wide, stuffed into his shirt. For an undead, he looked sloppy and out of date. But he was hungry. Blood lust apparently never went out of style.

"Piscary said I might get a taste of witch," he said, and I swallowed at the angry bitterness just beneath his softly aggressive voice. He might look the fool, but he was a predator, and as he moved slowly into Kisten's low-ceilinged bedroom at the back of his cruiser, I realized how deep in the crapper I'd fallen. Eyes unmoving, I felt in my bag for my splat gun. It would down him as fast as anyone else, but only if he didn't see it coming. Undead vampires were fast, and I was sure he'd been dead long enough to pass the tricky forty-year ceiling that killed most of the undead. Which meant he was smart, too. Oh God. Why hadn't I just left when Kisten told me to? But I knew that answer, and I fumbled for Kisten's hand.

"Rachel, leave. He has no claim on you," Kisten said as if he was still in control, and the vampire facing us smiled at his innocence. His fangs were a stark white, gleaming in the low-voltage lights, wet with saliva. And my neck . . . Oh God. It was starting to tingle.

My hand pressed to my old scar and I retreated, my only thought to put enough distance between us so I could get out my splat gun. The vampire lunged.

Gasping, I flung myself to the side. My arm burned as I found the carpet, facedown. A terrifying sound filled the boat, and whipping my hair from my eyes, I watched them grapple. I couldn't breathe, and still on the floor, I sat up and fumbled in my bag. But my fingers wouldn't work, and it took an agonizingly long time to find my gun. I cried out in relief, shoved my bag aside, and pointed the muzzle at him. I'd shoot them both if I had to.

"Not like this," the older vampire said with a snarl.

"You got that right, coffin breath," I said, and I pulled the trigger.

His face an ugly mask of anger, the vampire shoved Kisten. He flew backward across the room, and his head made a loud thump as it hit the boat's metal wall, behind the paneling. "Kisten!" I shouted as his eyes rolled back and he slumped to the floor, out cold.

Shaking, I got to my feet. "You son of a bitch," I said, hardly able to point the gun.

"You have no idea," the vampire said, then showed me the splat ball, safely in his hand, unbroken and worthless. He set it gently on the dresser, and it rolled, falling behind it. Eyes slitted, he breathed deeply of the fear I was filling the room with.

Tears of frustration started leaking out. I had to let him get closer or he'd just catch the next ball, but too close, and he'd have me. Kisten wasn't moving, and I backed up. "Kisten," I said, nudging him. "Kisten, please wake up. I can't keep both of us alive. I need your help."

The smell of blood drew my eyes down, and I felt my face go pale. Kisten wasn't breathing.

"Kisten?" I whispered, shock filling my entire world. "Kisten?"

My eyes warmed, and hot tears slipped down as I realized he was dead. The vampire had killed him. The son of a bitch had killed Kisten.

"Bastard!" I shouted, in agonized pain and anger. "You son-of-a-bitch bastard. You killed him!"

The vampire stopped short and stared at Kisten. His black eyes widened as he realized he had, and his mouth twisted into a grimace. An ugly rumble of anger, almost a growl, lifted through the air. "You puking little witch," he snarled. "He was mine to kill, and you made me do it before I had even tasted him!"

I couldn't stop shaking, and as I stood with my feet spread wide before Kisten, I aimed my gun at him. "I'm going to—"

"Kill me?" he taunted, his expression so full of hate it was frightening. "Right."

He moved. My back hit the same wood that had crushed Kisten's brain against his skull, killing him instantly. The air left my lungs. The flat of the vampire's arm was at my throat, pinning me there. My eyes bulged, and I struggled to breathe. His weight let up, and I got a gasp of air in as the world spun and suddenly he had my front against the wall.

Pain exploded in my wrist, and my hand opened. I heard the dull thump of my gun hitting the carpet, and the pressure vanished.

"You ruined my entire evening," the vampire said, leaning against me so I could see the thin rim of brown around his eyes. "I was promised someone's last blood, and Kisten's is gone. Guess what that means?"

He was feeding off my fear, bringing himself to a higher pitch. I struggled, and he pressed his entire body length against mine. I couldn't move, and my fear edged into panic. My fingers dug at the paneling, and my tears slipped down.

"It means," he said, sending the scent of damp cement over me, "I'll drain you instead." I jerked as he pulled the last of my braid apart and ran his dust-scented fingers through my hair. "I'd rather have played with Kisten," he said as he breathed deeply of my curls. "Piscary has been at him a good long time, and the boy has so much saliva in him that I could probably cut out his heart and he would writhe for more."

"Bastard," I said to the wall, terrified.

He sucked in air as he ran the flat of his nose along my neck to breathe in my scent. I shuddered as his pheromones dove deep and brought the scar to life. Tension shifted to adrenaline, and I stifled a moan of what might have been ecstasy. But there could be no ecstasy here. This was evil. I was not turned on. I was scared shitless. "Leave me alone," I said, but it was a powerless demand, and he knew it.

"Mmmm," he said as he turned me around and I could see the lust reflected in his eyes. "I've a better idea. I'm going to keep you alive as my shadow. Take my revenge on sweet Ivy slowly. Piscary's little bitch needs to be taught her place."

He knows Ivy? Terror gave me strength, and I fought him. He let me go. He had to have. I couldn't have gotten away otherwise. *He's playing with me,* I thought as I ran for the door. I was on the water. I couldn't tap a line unless I could get off the boat. *I am so lost.*

Stars exploded, and I stumbled, falling on the bed. He had hit me. I hadn't even seen him move, but the freaking bastard had hit me, and I felt my face grow hot as I tried to figure out where the floor and walls were.

The bed dipped as he landed on it, and I rolled, finding myself farther from the door. I was going the wrong way. I had to get our positions reversed. I had to make a run for it.

His eyes glinted as he reached out, and with a soft exhalation, he said, "Ivy's bitten you, hasn't she? Maybe we can have some fun after all."

My face lost its expression, and I forced my hand from creeping up to hide my neck.

"Got a taste for vampires?" he mocked, and I made the mistake of taking a deep breath. Vampire incense tinged with the scent of cement filled me, lighting a path from my neck to my groin.

"Oh shit," I moaned, and my back hit the wall. Kisten lay dead at my feet, and I had a sexual high running through me, twisting, perverting my fear into pleasure. No wonder Ivy was screwed up. "Get the hell away from me," I panted.

The vampire had followed me, and he touched my shoulder, making my knees almost give way. "Soon you'll be begging me to sleep with you," he promised in a soft whisper.

Tears filled my eyes, and he kissed them away, his fingers smelling of damp cement as my tears moistened the dust from his fingers. I brought my hand up to claw at his eyes, and I gasped when he crushed them. "Stop," I said, begging him. "Please stop."

His wide hand splayed across my face, he forced my jaw open. One finger rubbing my neck, he slipped a dust-tasting finger in my mouth, feeling inside me.

"Don't," I panted, even as I writhed in his grip, and he forced his mouth to mine now that he knew I wasn't going to bite off his tongue. His rough hand pressed fully into my neck, and he gave a hard rub. Ecstasy surged. It wasn't him. It was like hitting a reflex, and I hated myself for the lust that hit me even as I struggled to get away, struggled to take a breath that wasn't full of him. *To just get away!*

I was crying, and he pulled away with my lip between his teeth. The sharp spike of pain through my lip was like an electric shock. He probably expected me to swoon at his feet, but it had the opposite effect.

Fear overrode the breath-stealing surge, and I lashed out. My nails raked his eyes. He swore and stumbled back. He had bitten me. God, he had bitten me!

Hand over my mouth, I ran for the door.

"I'm not done yet!" the vampire bellowed, and I lunged down the narrow hall. Falling into the living room, I ran for the door to the galley and my freedom. I tried to turn the handle, but my wrist wouldn't work, still numb from where he had forced my gun from me. The fingers on my other hand were purple and unresponsive.

Sobbing, I kicked at the door. Pain stabbed through my ankle, but I aimed again with a sidekick. I screamed as it hit, and this time the doorjamb splintered.

My numb fingers scrabbled for the door, and I shrieked when a heavy hand jerked me from the broken wood. I struggled for consciousness as my head hit the far wall, and I fell.

"I said, I'm not done yet," the vampire said as he dragged me back to the bedroom by my hair. Fighting like a mad thing, I tried to grab the door to the bathroom as we passed, but he gave a yank and my fingers scraped the carpet until they burned. He didn't let go of my hair until he jerked me up by the arm and threw me on the bed. I bounced off before I could find my balance, and I hit the floor on the far side, between the bed and the wall. My eyes went to Kisten, and my panic paused. He was gone. The floor was empty.

Shaking, I peered over the bed to find my love standing calmly at the window, staring at the night. "It's beautiful," he said softly, and my heart broke to hear his familiar voice coming from the mouth of a stranger. He was dead. Kisten was an undead. "I can see everything, hear everything. Even the mosquitoes over the water," he added in wonder, and he turned.

My chest clenched at the familiar smile, but the eyes behind it had lost something. If he could hear mosquitoes, then he had heard me scream and had done nothing. His blue eyes were without recognition, a confused, beautiful angel. He didn't know me.

And my tears wouldn't stop.

The vampire who had killed him had an irate expression, almost bothered. "You need to leave," he said brusquely. "You're worthless now. Used up. Get out."

One by one the tears fell, and I stood, not expecting any help from Kisten.

"I know you," Kisten said suddenly, and his eyes lit with remembrance. My bruised hands clasped at my chest, and I closed my eyes, weeping. They flashed open when his soft touch on my chin came too soon for him to have crossed the room, but there he was, his head cocked as he puzzled it through.

"I loved you," he said, with the wonder of the sun's first rising, and I caught back a sob.

"I love you, too," I whispered, dying inside. Ivy was right. This was hell.

"Piscary," Kisten said, confused. "He told me to kill you, but I didn't." He smiled, and my soul was crushed to nothing by the familiar twinkle. "In hindsight, that might have been a stupid thing to do, but it felt right at the time." He took my other hand and frowned at my swollen fingers. "I don't want you to hurt, but I don't remember why."

It took me three times before I could make the words come out. "You're dead," I said softly. "That's why you don't remember."

Kisten frowned, confused. "It makes a difference?"

My head hurt. It was a nightmare. A freaking nightmare. "It shouldn't," I whispered.

"I don't remember dying," he said, then let me go and turned to the vampire who had killed him. "Do I know you?" he asked, and the vampire smiled.

"No. You need to leave. She's mine, and I'm not sharing. Your blood needs are not my problem. Go take a long walk in a short shadow."

Again Kisten frowned, puzzling it through. "No," he finally said. "I love her, even if I don't remember why. I won't let you touch her. She doesn't like you."

I held my breath as I realized what was going to happen. Shit. I was going to be bound either to Kisten or to his killer. My fear coloring the air, I started backing up.

"She'll adore me in a few moments," the vampire said with a low growl. He dropped his head to eye Kisten from under his brows, and his hair swung forward. Kisten hunched, mimicking him, turning into an animal on two legs. The beauty and allure were gone. It was pure savagery, and I was the prize.

The vampire silently jumped at Kisten, shifting at the last moment to lunge over his head. He was headed right for me. Eyes wide, I ducked, swearing when his fist smacked my shoulder and sent me spinning into the wall. My head hit, and I struggled to focus.

I started to slide down the wall, but propped my feet against the carpet and locked my knees. I wouldn't go down. If I did, I might never get up. I watched, riveted, as the two fought. Kisten was not as fast, but he was ferocious. Barroom brawls had given him dirty fighting techniques that kept him moving and upright as the attacking vampire struck hard enough to break bones. Each block and punch did damage that the vampire virus mended.

"Get out, Rachel," Kisten said calmly when he finally got the vampire pinned in a corner.

Crying, I went for my bag instead. I had charms in there.

My numb hand fumbled for something to save Kisten, to save myself. Seeing what I was doing, the attacking vampire took a hit and lunged at me. Terrified, I dropped the bag. I had the bottle of sticky silk in my hand from when I had pasted Jenks to my bathroom mirror so he wouldn't follow me.

I dodged out of the way and sprayed the vampire. The man screamed in shock as it hit him squarely in the eyes, but he was between me and the door again. I tried to edge by, and his arm flashed out, flinging me into the dresser. My gut landed squarely on the edge, and my momentum flung my head into the mirror. Pulse hammering, I spun, going stock-still when I saw Kisten in the other vampire's grip, his arm around Kisten's throat in what could easily become a neck-snapping grip. Fear took me again.

"Come here or he dies again," the vampire said to me, and I obediently took a step forward. Kisten had only one life left.

Kisten's eyes were wide. "You love me," he said, and I nodded, wiping the tears from my eyes so I could see.

The vampire smiled, long and toothy, as he held Kisten close, like a lover. "It would have been so distracting to take your last blood," he said into Kisten's ear, lips brushing the hair that I had once run my fingers through. "The only thing I'd have enjoyed more would be to take Ivy's, that bitch, but I can't have her," he snarled, jerking Kisten so his feet were on tiptoe for an instant. "She's Piscary's fucking queen. But this will hurt. I owe her some pain for the years I spent in prison, living off scraps and discarded shadows who bleed for anyone. Killing you is a good start. Making a puppet out of her roommate is better, and when she's a whining bitch with dead eyes and no soul, I'll move on to Ivy's sister, and then every last person she ever loved."

Kisten became frightened, the emotion crossing death, where love couldn't. "Leave Ivy alone," he demanded.

Kisten's killer's lips brushed his hair. "You're so young. I remember loving someone. But they died, and now all I have is the purity of nothing. My God, you're still warm."

Kisten looked at me, and from somewhere, more tears welled forth. We were all so very lost. It shouldn't end like this.

"So take my blood instead of hers," Kisten said, and the other vampire laughed.

"Right," he said sarcastically, and shoved Kisten away like the poison his blood now was to him.

Kisten gathered himself. "No," he said softly, in a voice I had heard only once before, on a cold snowy night when he'd fought off six black witches. "I insist."

He jumped at the vampire. The man stumbled, arms raised and almost helpless from the shock of the attack. Kisten's fangs flashed, still short for an undead, but they were enough.

"No!" the vampire screamed, and Kisten's teeth sank into his neck. I stared, pressed into the wide windows as Kisten's killer jammed a palm into Kisten's chin. I heard a sickening snap, and Kisten fell.

He hit the floor, convulsing before he even found the carpet. The other vampire clutched his neck and stomach as he staggered to the door. I heard him stumble down the hall, fleeing as he fell into dry heaves. The boat rocked, and I heard a splash.

"Kisten!" I dropped down beside him, dragging his head up into my lap. The convulsions slowed, and I wiped his face with my hands. His mouth was red with blood, but it wasn't his, it was his killer's, and now they both would die. Nothing could save him. The undead couldn't feed upon each other. The virus attacked itself, and both would die.

"Kisten, no," I sobbed. "Don't do this to me! Kisten, you sweet idiot, look at me!"

His eyes opened, and I stared, breathless, into their precious blue depths. The haze of death quavered, and cleared. My chest clenched as I saw a moment of lucidity return to him, as he teetered on his final, true death.

"Don't cry," he said, his hand touching my cheek as he looked up, and it was Kisten. He was himself, and he remembered why he loved. "I'm sorry. I'm going to die, and so will that fucking bastard if I got enough of my saliva into him. He won't be able to harm you or Ivy."

Ivy. This was going to destroy her. "Kisten, please don't leave me," I said, my tears spotting his face. His hand fell from my cheek, and I grabbed it, holding it to me.

"I'm glad you're here," he said, his eyes closing as he took a breath. "I didn't mean to make you cry."

"You should have left with me, you dummy," I sobbed. His skin was hot to the touch, and he convulsed once and took a rasping breath. I couldn't stop it. He was dying in my arms, and I couldn't stop it.

"Yeah," he whispered, his finger twitching against my jaw where I held it. "Sorry."

"Kisten, please don't leave me," I begged, and his eyes opened.

"I'm cold," he said, fear rising in his blue eyes.

I held him tighter. "I'm holding you. It's going to be okay."

"Tell Ivy," he said with a gasp, clenching in on himself. "Tell Ivy that it wasn't her fault. And tell her that at the end . . . you remember love. I don't think . . . we lose our souls . . . at all. I think God keeps them for us until we . . . come home. I love you, Rachel."

"I love you, too, Kisten," I sobbed, and as I watched, his eyes, memorizing my face, silvered, and he died.

Thirty-two

Somewhere I could hear Mia and Holly, each screaming different lyrics to the same song of frustrated anger and loss, the smooth rhythm of the FIB's Miranda serving as a background chorus. My eyes opened, and it took me a moment to focus on the moving patterns of light playing over the ugly cement walls and ceilings. The tight chatter of two-ways was loud, and the room was echoing, Mia's tirade and Holly's unhappy complaints being the least of the noise.

I bolted upright, going dizzy when I clutched the blue FIB blanket draped over me. People were everywhere, ignoring me, flashing their lights up and down the tunnel, pointing their weapons at Mia as they read her her rights. She was being led away by I.S. agents, and Ford was standing across the room with Holly. The little girl wasn't happy, but Ford was holding her with impunity. His expression was pained for his part in separating mother and child, but with him able to touch Holly, The Walker wouldn't have her.

Beside me on the cold cement floor, like an offering, was my splat gun. My eyes widened as I saw it, and a second wave of vertigo took me as I remembered. *Oh God. Kisten's dead.*

Bile rose, and I fell into dry heaves. I tried to rise but never made it up, too dizzy to get off my hands and knees when I rolled over to try to stand. No one noticed me, fascinated by Mia's threats and struggles as she was pulled up the stairway like a wet wildcat, four undead vampires holding her leash, two before, two behind, so she couldn't touch anyone. Their policy of ignoring her had shifted, forced by the FIB to take action.

Staring past my stringy hair at the filthy floor, I struggled to breathe, to work the memory of Kisten's death into my existence, but it hurt like a broken knife across my soul. *Ah, crap. I'm crying now.* I looked at my hand, half expecting to see it pulped and bruised, but only Al's cut was there.

"Holly!" Mia wailed as if giving my grief voice, and I looked past my lank hair at her, shocked by the fear coming from the woman. We were all having a fabulous New Year.

Ford's words rose above Holly's soft crying, stilling the woman's struggles. "Your daughter is beautiful, Ms. Harbor," he said, easily containing the little girl's struggles, and the vampires pulling at her paused. "I will protect her with my life."

"She's mine!" Mia cried out, distress turning her from a power-crazed banshee to a mother watching her child being taken from her, and the tears pricked again, for Holly this time.

"She's your child," Ford said calmly. "I'm holding her in trust, and I *will not* turn her against you. She's . . . my sanity, Mia. She quiets the emotions that hurt me. She will never want for emotion around me, and I will not twist her against you as The Walker would have."

Mia's face was stark with fear, but under it was hope. "She won't have my daughter?"

Ford shifted Holly to a more comfortable position. "Never. The paperwork is being pushed through. Unless Walker can prove that she's related to Holly, she doesn't have a chance, banshee or not. I will have custody of Holly until you're able to become her mother again, and I'll bring her to see you whenever you ask. And Remus, if they will let me. As long as I am alive, that woman will not have her."

"Holly?" Mia said tremulously, her voice holding only love,

and the little girl turned, her pale skin red from tears. Ford moved close, and mother and child touched one last time. Tears leaked from Mia, and she brushed them away, shocked to find them wet. "My daughter," she whispered, then pulled her hand back when the two vampires in the lead gave a tug.

Ford backed behind the security of the armed FIB officers. "It's not forever," he said. "You killed people to make your life easier, making your task of finding enough emotion to raise your child simple rather than the chore it rightfully should be. If you live in society, you have to live by its rules. Those same rules will let you go if you're willing to abide by them. Right now, Holly is safe. You won't get her away from me without killing me or those who watch you. Kill me, and The Walker will have Holly when they catch you again—and we will catch you. There are too many of us, and we know what to look for now."

Mia nodded. She looked back only once as she headed up the stairs, the two I.S. agents before and behind her. Her eyes were black with tears that turned silver as she wept for herself.

The tension in the room dropped. I moved to sit against the wall. In an angry motion, I pulled my knees to my chin, and, not caring what anyone thought, I put my head down and cried, the wool of my coat rough against my scraped cheek. *Kisten.* He had died to save my life. He killed himself to keep me alive.

"Rachel."

There was the rasp of dress shoes. Head down and hair covering my vision, I shoved whoever it was away, but they came right back. Thin, masculine fingers landed on my shoulder, gripping briefly, then falling away. Someone smelling of cookies and aftershave eased himself down to sit beside me with his back to the wall. I could hear Holly's soft fussing, and I figured it was Ford. Wiping my nose on the corner of the blue blanket, I snuck a look. Ford said nothing, gazing over the FIB people as they packed up and started moving out. The show was over, apparently. I'd woken in time for the last act.

Ford sighed when he noticed me looking at him, and making sure Holly couldn't touch me, he reached into a coat pocket and pulled out a package of Handi Wipes. I sniffed loudly as he worked one free and handed it to me. Taking it, I held my breath and leaned my head back against the wall as I washed the dust and tears from my face, the soap stinging against my scraped face and cut finger. I took a breath, and the clean smell went right to my core, pulling some of the pain away. Either that, or just walling it off. The tight band around my chest seemed to ease and I could breathe again.

"You okay?" Ford asked, and I shrugged, feeling as miserable as Holly looked. *I'm alive,* I thought as I clenched the wipe into a tiny ball.

"I'm okay." I sighed, exhaling as if it were my last breath, but I took another, then another. The thought of Ford's presence with mine as I remembered surfaced, and his promise that I wouldn't have to live through it alone. "Is Ivy here?" I breathed. I had to tell her. I'd tell Edden, too, but not until Ivy and I had a chance to deal with this first.

"Upstairs, talking to the I.S."

My wandering gaze landed on an FIB agent tagging and bagging Pierce's clothes and my nylons. They could have them for all I cared. And Tom's abduction wasn't my fault. "How did they find me?" I asked, tired.

Ford smiled, and Holly leaned against him in exhaustion, quiet at last. "Your locator amulets and footprints in the snow, apparently. Your feet must be freezing."

I nodded, glad I had the blanket to rest them on. My gaze rose from the lumps my feet made to find his eyes, remembering him taking Holly for the first time, tears flowing in relief as she devoured every last emotion he had but his own. "You can hold her," I said, my heart aching that something good might come from this. "Holly, I mean. Even when she's upset."

Walker wasn't going to get Holly after all, and wouldn't she be pleased about that?

Ford's gaze was beautiful when he looked at the sleeping little girl. "She absorbs everything before it gets to me," he said, his voice carrying awe. "I don't really need to hold her, just be close. But I'm not going to put her on the floor."

I smiled and tugged the blanket up higher around my shoulders. It was freezing down here. I was glad for Ford, but I was cold, bitterly disillusioned, and aching from a memory I'd thought I wouldn't have to deal with. The last of the FIB guys was leaving, and I gathered myself. "Hey, you probably have a diaper to change, huh?" I said as I got to my feet. Dizzy, I put a hand to the wall to find my balance. My stomach clenched, and I sat back down fast. Mia had stripped my aura again, damn it.

"You want a stretcher?" Ford asked, and after I reluctantly nodded, he went to talk to one of the departing FIB officers. I couldn't make it up the stairs like this, pride be damned.

Slowly the dizziness abated, and I concentrated on breathing as I looked over the room. I wasn't sure how I was going to explain Pierce's clothes. Tom's abduction was going to be even harder. It wasn't like I could pretend he hadn't been here. Both Ford and Mia had seen him. That Al had taken both of them was not going to look good for me at all. *Damn it, I am so not going to take the blame for this.*

Ford came back as the last FIB agent headed upstairs. Setting Mia's lantern by me, he sank back down with Holly to wait. "This is unbelievable," he said. "I don't know for sure what you're feeling. I can see it in your face, but not feeling it? That's freaky." He dropped his eyes as I noticed they were filling with emotion. "He's not dead anymore, you know."

The shadows shifted as I banked the lantern to focus the light ahead and toward the stairs. "Tom?" I said, glad he couldn't feel my emotions while he was holding Holly. It had to be Tom he was talking about. Kisten was gone, gone, gone, and I'd just relived his death. "I know. Al took him." A pang of fear hit me, fear that if the I.S. knew, they would use it against me.

"Not Tom," Ford said, and my head jerked up. "Tom is dead. I felt him die. I'm talking about Pierce."

Startled, I turned to him. "Al snagged him," I said. "Broke the charm and took him. His clothes were right over there."

Ford's smile widened and he shifted the sleeping child higher. "That wasn't Tom the demon pulled into the ever-after, it was Pierce."

This wasn't making sense, and I just stared at him, hunched in the blue FIB blanket.

"Your potion was targeted to Pierce," Ford explained. "Tom died and Al used your summoning charm to force Pierce into his body. I felt Tom's emotions die. Pierce's emotions took their place, coming from Tom's body. I'd know his thought signature anywhere. He's a unique individual."

I looked to where Pierce's clothes had been, a chill rippling through me as I shivered. "That's black magic," I whispered, hearing it echo in the tunnels behind me, like sin itself. "It was my spell! I didn't know it was black. It was in a university textbook!"

Ford leaned back against the wall, clearly not bothered. "It was your spell, and it was white, but the demon perverted it. He loves you, you know."

"Al?" I yelped, and Ford laughed. Holly smiled in her sleep, and the man's face calmed.

"No, Pierce."

I was dizzy from my outburst, and I looked at the stairway, wishing they would hurry. Kisten had loved me. Pierce was a teen crush. "Pierce doesn't even know me," I said softly, heart aching. "Except for that one night. God, I was eighteen."

Ford shrugged. "It would explain your troubled history with men. You saw what you wanted at eighteen, and no one now is measuring up."

I sighed. I was sitting on my butt on the cold, dusty concrete, waiting for a stretcher, and he was analyzing me. "Ford,

I don't love Pierce. It was teenage infatuation. Attraction to a charismatic power. I loved . . . Kisten."

"I know." His hand touched my shoulder, shocking me. "I'm sorry."

I turned away, forcing my thoughts from Kisten lest I start to cry again. "Pierce had a deal going with Al. Probably about getting a body in return for service." I felt my face scrunch in hopelessness. "And I helped. How nice is that? I don't even know why he did it. He was better off as a ghost." I looked to the stairway. There was the distinct possibility they might forget we were down here.

"I told you why," Ford said, grimacing as he shifted Holly's weight. "He loves you. I guess he figured being a familiar to your demon and having a body was better than being a ghost without one in your graveyard. Give the man a break, Rachel. He's been hanging around your church for almost a year."

A smile threatened, then disappeared. I was cold, dizzy, and numb from thoughts of Kisten. It stank down here, like cold dust. Like Kisten's killer. All I wanted was to go home and take a bath.

"I think they forgot us," I said. "Help me up?"

Ford grunted, getting to his feet. Holly cooed in her sleep as he extended his free hand and I slowly found my balance, leaning against the wall until I was sure I wouldn't fall over. The cement was cold on my feet, and I shifted to stand on a corner of the blanket.

"We'll take it slow," he said, clearly unused to Holly's unfamiliar weight.

"Yeah," I whispered, my thoughts turning to him and the relief Holly was giving him. It was beautiful, and I wondered if Ford was truly a human, or a very rare type of Inderlander who hadn't been discovered yet. One who balanced out a banshee. Vampires balanced Weres. Pixies balanced fairies. Witches . . . okay, maybe there wasn't anything to balance banshees either. Unless witches balanced out demons?

"Ford," I said as we started for the stairs, Mia's light bobbing. "I'm happy for you."

He smiled that blissful smile again when he glanced over his shoulder. "Me, too. She's a gift, and I'll have to give her back someday. But even this little bit is heaven. I'll try to repay Mia by teaching Holly what love is. I can show her that, though I believe Mia and Remus were already doing that admirably. In their own way."

My pace bobbled when Ivy's and Edden's voices filtered down the stairs. Kisten had died to save us both, to keep some lame-ass vampire from screwing our lives up any more than they already were. And he had loved us enough to give his life in exchange for ours. How could I tell Ivy?

My strength pooled out of me, and blinking fast, I stopped, slumping against a pillar. Ford looked uneasy. "Rachel, you're a good person," he said from out of the blue, surprising me. "Remember that. Just . . . don't worry about the next few hours."

I stared at him, becoming frightened. What did he know that I didn't?

"Call me tomorrow if you need to talk," he said before I could ask. "There's nothing that will ever make me think you're not a good person. That's what's important, Rachel. Who we love and what we do for them."

A last smile, and he started up the stairs with Holly. I heard him speak to Ivy and Edden on the stairs, and then Ivy's familiar steps continued down. She rounded the bottom of the steps, and I smiled thinly when her pace quickened. "Are you okay?"

Kisten, I thought, and my eyes teared. "Yeah," I said softly, and she stood there, looking helpless. Throat thick, I gave her a hug.

And this time, Ivy returned it, her grip almost pressing the air from me.

My first startled reaction shifted to heartache, and I hugged her back, my eyes closed and my heart clenched all the harder.

Her vampire incense lifted through me, soothing and exciting at the same time. "You scared me," she said when she let go and backed up a step. Edden was now behind her, playing his flashlight over the ceiling. "I don't like it when you tag someone without backup. Jenks said you tore out of there like a bat out of hell."

"Is he okay?" I asked, and she let go, head bobbing as she wiped her eyes. My own tears threatened as I tried to find the words to tell her I remembered Kisten's death. Thoughts of him were ringing from one ear to the other, making me dizzy.

Knowing something was wrong, Ivy took my arm and didn't let go. "Where's Pierce?" she asked as her eyes lingered on the scrape on my cheek.

My thoughts went to Tom, hanging in the demon's grip, and I hesitated. Had it really been Pierce? Either way, Tom was gone and Mia had seen the entire thing. Misreading my sudden worry, Ivy said, "Al took him, didn't he."

I shook my head. "Yes. No. It wasn't my fault," I said, and Edden squinted at me.

"Rachel . . . ," the FIB officer warned as he took the lantern and gestured to the stairs. "Tell me now, or I'll make you fill out paperwork."

I swallowed hard and shifted my feet because of the cold. The stairs were only thirty steps away—it looked like a mile. My finger throbbed where Al had cut it, and I curled my hands into fists. "Tom Bansen was down here. He was working a deal with Walker to get Holly. He saw Ford touch Holly, so he thought she was safe. Holly killed him."

Edden grunted. "Where is he? Corpses just don't get up and walk away."

"Yes they do," Ivy said, and I leaned heavily on her arm as I looked up the long stairway.

Forcing my breath to stay even, I decided a little lie wouldn't hurt anyone. No one needed to know I'd made the spell that put Pierce inside the shunned witch. "Al got him breathing again and dragged him off," I said softly.

Edden's mouth dropped open, but Ivy snorted. "It's not my fault," I protested.

Crap, I was tired, and as Edden winced, I started for the stairs, muttering, "I'm going home." I wanted to move fast, but it was barely a crawl as Ivy and I shuffled along.

The light swung in Edden's grip as he waited for us to actually reach the stairs. "I want a statement before you leave," he said, and I made a noise of disgust.

Hours. I'd be here for freaking hours if I had to give a statement. Beside and a little behind us, Edden played his light over the tunnel. "So this is how Remus and Mia did it," he said, gazing back at the vaulted ceilings, going shadowy behind us.

I hoped there'd be someone upstairs in a hospital coat. If I moaned enough, they'd cart me out of here and I could slip away, statement or not. "How they did what?" I asked, wincing when my foot found a chunk of concrete.

Edden took my other arm and gestured to the tunnel stretching into the black. "How they kept slipping through our lines," he explained.

I nodded, head down as I walked between them. "What are these, anyway? A vamp underground? I never knew this was down here."

"It's an old mass-transit plan started in the 1920s," he said, sounding like an instructor as the walls of the stairway closed in around us. "Too little money, too much political infighting. Unexpected structural damage when they drained the canal. A war and a depression. It never got finished. Some of the tunnels are filled in, but stretches of it still exist here and there. It's cheaper to inspect them once a year than destroy them. Some carry water pipes now."

"And Mia would know because she was here when it was built," I said sourly.

Edden chuckled. "I'd be willing to bet she was on the committee to beautify it or something." Making a little grunt of remembrance, he thumbed the two-way on his belt and said loudly, "Hey, someone call utilities and tell them we need a new lock out here!" and then to me, "Rachel, I'm not one to say I told you so—"

A flash of anger lit through me. "Then I'll say it for you," I snapped as my foot almost slipped off the stair. "I told you so. She is a bad seed. A spoiled brat with a goddess complex. She wants to live above the law, and I should have treated her like an animal and gunned her down on sight!" Heart pounding, I shut my mouth and concentrated on the next step.

"And yet you stopped her with just your earth magic," Edden said, completely unruffled as he took my other arm. "You're becoming a superhero, witch."

I winced as I remembered Holly's plaintive cries for her mama when they'd hauled Mia upstairs, roped like a tiger. "That's funny," I said sourly. "I so totally feel like crap."

No one said anything. Another step behind me, I took a breath and let it out. We were almost to the top, and all I wanted was to go home. "Edden, can I give my statement later?"

Eye to eye with me, he nodded. "Go home. I'll send someone tomorrow."

"After noon, right?" I reminded him, wobbling when the stairway opened up and the tight confines of the small room took us. The cold was worse up here, and I clenched my coat closer. I'd never be warm again.

"You okay, Rachel?" Ivy asked.

I exhaled heavily, thinking of Jenks and missing his support. Making a face, I leaned harder on Ivy's arm and started to shake. I was cold. My feet were numb and would probably have cuts when they thawed out. And Kisten's death, once safely removed from my mind, had reached out and bitch-slapped me with all its broken promises and shattered beauty.

"No," I said, wondering if I'd have to walk all the way back to the coffee shop in my bare feet. Edden followed my gaze to my bruised, white toes, and after murmuring something about socks, he set the lantern down and left me with Ivy. Alone at last, I caught Ivy's eyes. She saw my fear, and they dilated. "While I was unconscious, I remembered the night on Kisten's boat," I whispered. "All of it."

Ivy's breath caught. Outside I could hear Edden on his radio yelling for a car to come the hell back and pick us up.

I swallowed hard, barely able to force the words out. "Kisten's murderer had been in the tunnels before he came to take Kisten's last blood," I said, my soul as cold as the snow drifting in. "That's what I've been smelling," I added as I dismally brushed at the filth on me. "It's this damned dust. He'd been in it, and it was all over him."

Ivy didn't move. "Tell me," she demanded, her eyes black and her long hands clenched.

I gave her an evaluating look, wondering if this might be better at home with some wine, or even in a car with some privacy, but if she was going to vamp out, I'd rather have a few dozen FIB agents with guns around. Voice low, I said, "The vampire had come for Kisten, and I was in the way. Kisten died from a blow to the head before the vamp could do more than sniff his blood. He was really mad," I said, my voice going high so I wouldn't start crying again as I remembered his grip on me and my helpless rage, "but then he decided to make me his shadow to hurt you. Kisten woke up . . ."

Blinking fast, I wiped the sting of tears from my scraped cheek as I remembered his confused eyes and his angelic grace. "He was beautiful, Ivy," I said, crying. "He was innocent and savage. He remembered he loved me, and on that alone he tried to save me, save us, the only way he could. Remember, Jenks said I told him Kisten bit his attacker? He did it to save us, Ivy. He died in my arms as his attacker ran away."

My voice broke and I went silent. I couldn't tell her the rest. Not here. Not now.

Ivy blinked fast. It almost looked like panic in her slowly widening pupils. "He killed himself to save you?" she asked. "Because he loved you?"

I clenched my jaw. "Not me. *Us.* He chose to sacrifice the rest of his existence to save *both* of us. That vampire hates you, Ivy. He was going on and on about how you were Piscary's queen and he couldn't touch you, but killing Kisten wasn't enough, and how he was going to make you pay for his going to jail and living off discarded shadows for five years."

Ivy backed up. Frightened, she put a hand to her throat. "It wasn't someone who went to visit Piscary. It was someone who was in jail at the same time," she whispered.

Her eyes went utterly black in the dim shadows of the lantern-lit room, and I stifled a shiver. "The psycho was going to kill everyone you had ever loved, including your sister, just to hurt you. After Kisten bit him, he ran away. He fell off the boat. Kisten didn't know if he got enough saliva in him to start a rejection of the virus. He might still be alive. I don't know." Drained, my voice trailed off at the end.

For a moment, Ivy said nothing. Then she turned to the door, yanking it open with enough force to send it crashing into the wall.

"Edden!" she shouted into the snowy darkness. "I know who killed Kisten. He's down here. Bring me another flashlight."

Thirty-three

I t's Art. It's got to be Art," Ivy said as she paced beside me in the empty tunnel, fretting at my slow pace. We'd make faster time if she carried me, but that wasn't going to happen.

"Why are we just now hearing about him?" Edden asked, and I blanched as she turned her anger-black eyes to him.

"Because I'm a stupid ass," she said caustically. "Any more questions?"

"I don't understand why you didn't recognize his scent," I said to distract her, but having her glaring at me wasn't a vast improvement.

Ivy took a slow breath. The shadows of Mia's lantern moved with us, making it seem as if we weren't moving at all. Edden had his own flashlight, and I was shaking too much to hold one. The FIB captain had predictably wanted us to wait for a car, but Ivy was predictably so sure she knew where he was that she headed down before they could get back here. So of course we predictably went with her. At least I had Edden's socks on now, something I hadn't predicted but greatly appreciated.

Slowly Ivy eased her tension, and once calm, she answered, "It was five years ago, and smells change, especially when you go from living in a nice house in the city to a dank hole in the ground. He was my I.S. supervisor." Ivy clenched her jaw, seeing not the darkness ahead of us but her past, fidgeting so subtly that only Jenks or I would notice. "I told you, remember? I put him in jail for one of Piscary's accidental deaths so I wouldn't have to sleep with him to move up in the I.S. hierarchy."

My eyes narrowed, and Edden took an aggressive stance. "Y-you . . . ," he stammered. "That's not legal," he added.

Ivy was nonplussed. Unvoiced thoughts flitting behind her eyes, she glanced at me and said, "Vampires have a different outlook on legal."

It was making a lot of ugly sense, and a slow burn of anger took root as I hiked my coat closer and put one cold foot before the other. The deeper we went, the thicker the dust and dirt were. "So you put him in jail for Piscary's crimes, and then got demoted to me, huh."

Ivy jerked. Mouth open in embarrassment, she said, "It wasn't like that."

"Yes it was," I said, hearing the bitterness as my words echoed back. "I was your punishment. No one puts a witch working with a vampire. I wasn't blind those first few weeks until you . . . lightened up." I was shivering violently, but I wasn't going to go back and wait in a car.

Shadows on her face, Ivy looked at me. "I could have gone to the Arcane. I chose to be a runner. That I was assigned to you is one of the best things in my life."

Edden cleared his throat uncomfortably, and my face warmed. What could I say to that? "Sorry," I muttered, and she looked ahead.

"Ivy?" Edden's voice was tired. We'd been walking for a good five minutes. His radio wasn't working, and I knew he wasn't happy. "No one is down here. I understand your desire to search, but they inspect the tunnels every year. If there was a vampire here, living or dead, they would have found evidence of it by now."

Ivy glared at him as if he might turn around and walk off. "Who inspects the tunnels?" she said, determination etched on her tight brow. "The FIB? Humans? Inderlanders made these tunnels as much as humans did. There will be oubliettes for destitute vampires. A place to hide before hope is abandoned to the sun. Art is down here. I've been searching the city for three months. I wasn't looking for him, but if he was around, someone would have seen him." Her face went frighteningly still. "It's the only place left."

Edden stopped, placing his feet wide, tucking his flashlight under his arm, and becoming immovable. He took a breath, and suddenly Ivy was right in front of him. Surprised, he let his breath out and backed up a step.

"Don't think you're big enough to get me to go upstairs so you can come down here and find him yourself," she said softly. "You won't find the safe hole without me. If you ask the I.S. for help, they will walk right on by and come back without you later."

She was right, and I shifted to stand on my other foot as Edden thought about it. Clearly bothered, he exhaled long and slow. "Okay. Five more minutes."

We started off again, Ivy bolting ahead before she remembered me and slowed down. I ought to be in Carew Tower partying the new year in, but no, here I was, slogging under the city looking for a dead vampire. Anger was what was keeping me moving now. Ford had said I was a good person. It was what I wanted to be. I wasn't so sure anymore that he was right.

With no warning, Ivy's head came up and she stopped, breathing deeply. The lantern in her grip swung to make fast shadows, and the whisper of our feet echoed eerily as Edden and I stopped. Adrenaline jabbed me. My roommate smelled the air, backtracking a few steps with her hand running at shoulder height along the uniform wall.

Her eyes were black in the gloom, and I picked up the lantern when she set it down to run both hands against the stone.

"Close," she whispered, and I stifled a shudder when she moved to the other side of the tunnel's wall with that vampire speed. "Here." My heart pounded at the raw hatred in her voice. Edden and I came nearer, lights held high. My shadow stretched behind me, and I shivered again.

The wall looked utterly unmarked, apart from a small indentation where someone had chipped a hunk of stone away, but if it was a vampire oubliette, it wouldn't have a neon arrow pointing to it. It was going to be a secret door, and it was likely locked.

Ivy put her fingers in the indentation and pulled. Nothing happened. Her head came up and she tossed the hair from her cold, dark eyes. Damn, she was ready to vamp out. "Please get this door open for me, Rachel," she whispered.

Okay. If it was a door she couldn't open, it was going to be witch magic, which meant I was going to have to cut my finger or tap a line. My thumb felt the rough edges of the cut on my finger as I thought. Drawing blood while she was like this was not a good idea, but tapping a line was going to hurt.

I looked at the door and placed a hand on it. *Speak, friend, and enter,* ran through my mind, and I choked back a bark of laughter. "Nice," I said when a quiver in my middle brought forth a twin pull from the magic stored in the door. The wall had been built with a ley line charm in it. Buried in the concrete was one hell of a charmed circle of iron. I'd have to tap a line.

My hand dropped, and I got a sick feeling. Whatever was behind the door was going to be nasty. "It's a charmed door," I said, glancing from Ivy to Edden, and the squat man frowned.

"What's that?" he asked, looking defensive.

I shifted uneasily. "Just what it sounds like. Remember when I told you that all Inderland magic runs on witch magic?" I thought of the elves, and added, "Mostly, anyway. Vampires love witch magic. They use it to look young after they die, to call demons to beat up helpless witches, and when they want to hide themselves, they use it to lock themselves in." I was going to have to tap a freaking ley line, but a little pain would be a small payment for finding Kisten's killer.

Edden tucked his flashlight under his arm and angled it to

the line between the wall and the floor. There was a shifting of dust to show where the door had been opened once, how long ago was up for debate, invisible unless you were looking. Hand shaking, I put my palm against the smooth rock. The FIB captain's bulk shifted to take an aggressive stance by the door.

"Edden," I complained, "if there is an undead vampire in there, he will kill you before the door even finishes opening." *Ugly, but true.* "Back up."

The FIB captain frowned. "Just open the door, Morgan."

"Your funeral," I muttered, then took a deep breath. This was going to hurt. My fingers were numb from the cold, and they cramped as I pressed them deeper into the stone. Taking a breath and gritting my teeth against the coming pain, I locked my knees and tapped a line.

I gasped, jerking straight as the line hit me. I tried not to, but I did.

"Rachel?" Ivy said, close and concerned.

My stomach was rolling, and I panted to keep from vomiting. The undulating surges of power from the nearby line were making me seasick, and every nerve felt the power grating across it. "Fine," I gasped, unable to even think of the right words. There were three charms that were generally used, and my dad had taught me them all, plus one that wasn't used except for the most dire situations. Oh God, this was awful.

I took a heaving breath and held it, fighting to think past the pain and dizziness. Ivy's cool hand touched my shoulder, and my breath exploded out as I felt her aura slip to cover me, soothing.

"I'm sorry!" Ivy shouted, her hand leaving me, and I almost fell when the pain returned.

"No," I said as I reached to grasp her hand and the pain again vanished. "You're helping," I said, watching her fear that she'd hurt me replaced with wonder. "It doesn't hurt when I'm touching you. Don't let go. Please."

There in the lamp-lit dark, she swallowed hard and her fingers in mine became firmer. It wasn't perfect. I could still feel the waves of ley line coming at me, but at least it wasn't so raw and the agony across my nerves was muted. My thoughts returned to last Halloween, when she had bitten me that last time. Our auras had become one before she lost it. Was I seeing a lingering effect of that? Were Ivy's and my auras the same? Able to protect each other when one was compromised? Was it love?

Edden stood beside us, not sure of anything, and taking a steadying breath, I put my free hand more firmly on the door.

"Quod est ante pedes nemo spectat," I whispered, and nothing happened.

I shifted my feet. *"Quis custodiet ipsos custodes?"* I tried again, and still nothing.

Edden scuffed his feet. "Rachel, it's okay."

My hand quivered. *"Nil tam difficile est quin quaerendo investigari possit."* That one did it, and I pulled my hand back when I felt a quiver of response rise up from the charm buried in the cement and ping through my soul. *Nothing is so hard that it can't be found by searching.* It figured that it would be that one.

I stepped back and dropped the line, and Ivy searched my face before she let go of my hand and I fisted it. Edden put his fingers into the curve of the handle and pulled. The door cracked, and Ivy flung herself back with her hand over her face.

"Holy crap!" I exclaimed, gagging and falling back as well. I almost tripped Edden as he reared back at the stench. The light from the lantern showed Edden's expression, twisted in distaste. Whatever was in there was long dead, and anger started trickling in. Kisten had succeeded in killing our attacker. Now who would I yell at?

"Hold this," the FIB captain said as he shoved the flashlight at me. I set my lantern down and took it. Edden pulled the door farther open to show a black archway and little else. The stench rolled out, old and putrid. It wasn't the smell of decay, which would have been muted from the cold and perhaps sheer time, but the stink of vampire death that lingered until the sun or wind had a chance to disperse it. It was incense gone bad. Decaying flowers. Spoiled musk and dead sea salt. We couldn't go in, it was that bad. It was as if all the oxygen had been replaced with thick, poisonous, decaying oil.

Edden took his flashlight back. Holding a hand across his nose, he played the light over the floor to find the edges of the room. I stayed where I was, but Ivy came forward to stand at the threshold. Her face was damp from tears, and her expression was blank. Edden moved to get his shoulder in front of hers, but it was the smell that was keeping her out, not his presence.

The floor was the same dust-colored stone, and the walls were cement. A black scum stained the floor, crinkled and cracked, the color of old blood. Edden followed it to the wall to find scratches gouged in the concrete.

"Neither of you go in there," Edden said, then gagged from the deep breath he had taken to say the words. I nodded, and he quickly played the light over the rest of the room. It was a nasty hole of a place with a made-up cot and a cardboard box table. On the bare floor beside another smaller puddle of dried blood was the body of a big black man, faceup and spread-eagled. He had on a lightweight shirt, open to show that his throat had been completely torn out. His lower body cavity had been opened as well, almost as if an animal had been at him, though I expected the small mounds of something piled beside him were probably his insides.

I couldn't tell if he had been attacked while not wearing any pants or if his attacker had eaten through them. Vampires didn't do this. At least not that I'd heard. And this wasn't the man who I'd remembered at Kisten's boat.

Edden's light shook as I held it on the body. Damn it, it had all been for nothing.

"Is that Art?" Edden asked, and I shook my head.

"It's Denon," Ivy said, and my gaze jerked from the corpse to her and back again.

"Denon?" I gasped, feeling my gore rise.

Edden's light dropped away. "God help him. I think it is."

I leaned against the wall as my knees went wobbly. That's why I hadn't seen him lately. If Denon had been Art's scion, assigning Ivy to his stable of runners would make it really easy to watch her. And insulting to assign her to me.

"The cot," Ivy said, her hand over her face. "Bring your light to the cot. I think it's a body on there. I'm not . . . sure."

I came close and carefully angled the lantern's light to the cot, but my hand was shaking and it wasn't clear. Edden had known Denon. Had a friendly rivalry with him. Finding him torn apart was hard. I heard him take a shallow breath, and his light found the bed as well.

I squinted, trying to figure out what I was seeing. What had first looked like a bundle of forgotten clothes and straps . . . "Shit," I whispered as my mind shifted and it made sense. It was a gray, grotesquely twisted body, the bones warped into unnatural curves as the two viruses had fought for control, each trying to make the vampire into its version of perfection. Pale white parchment skin had flaked off in sheets, drifting slightly in the draft that opening the door had created. The black hair was puddled around the skull, and there were no eyes in the sockets gazing at the ceiling. Canines twice as long as a normal vampire's spouted from the jaw. The mouth had been ripped wide and the jaw was hanging at a broken angle. A hand with several fingers missing hung from the corner of it. God, had he done it to himself?

Ivy jerked, and I swung the light wildly as she tried to go in. Edden grunted, grabbing her arm and using her momentum to fling her to the opposite wall of the tunnel. She hit with a thump, her eyes wide and angry, but he had his arm under her chin and wasn't letting up.

"Stay out of that room!" he shouted, pinning her to the wall, his voice echoing in what sounded like pity. "You are not going in there, Ivy! I don't care if you kill me. You are not going in that . . . filthy"—he took a gasping breath, trying to find words—"cesspit of a hole." He finished, tears shining in his eyes. "You're better than that," he finished. "You have nothing to do with that perversion. *It's not you.*"

Ivy wasn't trying to move. If she'd wanted to, she could have broken his arm without a thought. Tears shimmered in the light as I angled the flashlight down. "Kisten died because of something I did," she said, anger shifting to pain. "And now I can't do anything to make the hurt go away. He's dead! Art even took that from me!"

"What are you going to do!" Edden shouted at her, his voice echoing. "The vampire is dead! You can't get revenge from a dead body. You want to tear him apart and throw chunks of him at the wall? He's dead! Let it go or it will ruin your life, and then he wins again."

Ivy was crying silently. Edden was right, but I didn't know how to convince her of it.

Edden snatched the lantern from me and turned. "Look at that, Ivy!" he said, shining it directly on the corpse. "Look at that and tell me that is a victory."

She tensed as if to scream, but then the tears flowed and she gave up. Arms wrapped around herself, she whispered, "The son of a bitch. The fucking son of a bitch. Both of them."

The deep chill took the core of my being as I stared at the twisted pieces of what remained. The dusty scent of Art's fingers on me was heavy in my memory as I looked at his broken hand and the flesh pulled tight to the bone. I could feel his touch on my throat, my wrist. It had been a hard death, leaving him mummified, a gross caricature of twisted limbs and contorted bones as the two strains of vampire virus fought for control, breaking him until he couldn't survive even as an undead.

It was easy to imagine what had happened. Dying from the undead blood Kisten had given him, Art called his scion. Denon died by accident or design as Art tried to gain enough strength to fight off Kisten's undead blood. No wonder Ivy wanted a way out. This was ugly.

Edden let the light fall from the cot. His eyes were tired as he flicked it off and only Mia's lantern lit the tunnel. He looked at Ivy's raw misery, then hiked his belt up to try to find a semblance of his usual demeanor. "We'll let the room air out, then get a shoe for a print match. We're done here."

Ivy was against the wall, staring at the black doorway. "He never would have touched Kisten if it hadn't been for me."

"No," I said firmly. "Kisten said it wasn't your fault. He said it, Ivy. Told me to tell you." Setting the lantern down, I crossed the tunnel, my shadow blanketing her. "He said so," I repeated as I touched her shoulder, finding her ice cold. Her eyes were black, but they weren't looking at me, they were focused on the dark hole across from us. "Ivy, if you take this on your conscience, it will be one of the dumbest things I've ever seen you do."

That got through to her, and her gaze flicked to me.

"He didn't blame you," I said as I gave her bicep a squeeze. "If he did, he wouldn't have sacrificed his life to kill the bastard for you and me both. He loved me, Ivy, but it was thinking of you that made his decision. He did it because he *loved you*."

Ivy's expression cracked, and her face twisted in pain. "I loved him!" she shouted, voice echoing. "I loved him, and there's nothing I can do to prove it! Art is dead!" she said, gesturing. "Piscary is dead! I can't do anything to prove I loved Kisten. This isn't fair, Rachel! I want to hurt someone, and no one is left!"

Edden shifted uneasily. My throat was tight. I wanted to hug her and tell her that it was going to be okay, but it wasn't. There was no one to take revenge on, no one to point to and say, I know what you did and you are shit for it. That Piscary was dead and Art was a twisted corpse didn't come close to being enough.

"Ladies . . . ," Edden prompted, gesturing down the tunnel with his light. "I'll get a forensics team down here tonight.

Once we are sure of the identities, I'll let you know." He took a step to leave, hesitating to make sure we would follow.

Clearly exhausted, Ivy pushed herself from the wall. "Piscary gave Kisten to Art as compensation for me putting him in jail. It was political. God, I hate my life."

I stared at the black hole in the wall, tension rising in me. She was right. Kisten had died in a political power play. His bright soul just starting to learn its own strength had been snuffed out to soothe an ego and bring Ivy to her knees. Revenge I might have understood, but this . . .

Whispering good-bye to Kisten, Ivy dropped her head and passed me. I didn't move, staring at the black hole. Edden's hand fell on my shoulder. "You need to get warmed up."

I jerked out from under him. Warmed up. Good idea. I wasn't ready to walk away. Kisten's soul was at rest because he had fought back and won. But what about those of us who were left behind? What about Ivy and me? Didn't we have the right to satisfaction, too?

My heart pounded, and I clenched my jaw. "I am not going to live with this pain."

Ivy's boots scuffed to a stop, and Edden squinted suspiciously at me.

Shaking, I pointed at the dark hole. "I'm not going to let the I.S. cover this up, put them in the ground with pretty headstones and dignified names and dates and say that Kisten was murdered to further someone's political agenda."

Ivy shook her head. "It makes no difference."

It made a difference to me. The room was cloaked in black, hiding the depravity of what happened when a lifetime was spent afraid of death, when one's entire existence was bent to the selfish desires of the self, when the soul was exchanged for the mindless drive to survive. Real lives were ruined in the wake of these ugly caricatures of power. Kisten's soul lost just as he found the strength in himself, Ivy winding the noose tighter in her attempts to find peace. Darkness wouldn't cover this up. I wanted the room bright. Bright with a savage truth so that it would never be consigned to the shelter of the earth.

"Rachel?" Ivy asked, and shaking, I tapped a line. It touched me, tearing my thin aura like a flame. I went down on a knee, but gritting my teeth, I stood, letting the pain flow through me, accepting it.

"Celero inanio," I shouted, giving the force an outlet of a black charm gesture. I'd seen Al do it. How hard could it be?

The line roared into me, pulled by the charm. Agony flamed, and I convulsed, refusing to let go of the line as the spell worked. "Rachel!" Ivy shouted, and I fell back at the white-light explosion in the middle of the room. My hair blew back, then shifted forward as the air in the room burnt itself out and new air rushed in to replace it. Like heaven itself, the glory of fire burned white, a tiny spot of black at the center of my rage.

I fell to my knees, eyes fixed on the doorway and the hard stone going unnoticed as my knees bruised. And then Ivy had me. Her arms cushioned me, and I gasped, not at their icy softness, but at the sudden cessation of pain from the line. She had me again, and her aura protected me, filtering the worst of it.

"You stupid witch," she said bitterly as she held me. "What the hell are you doing?"

I stared up at her, the line cool and clean in me. "Are you sure you can't feel anything?" I questioned, not believing her aura was protecting me from this.

"Just my heart breaking. Let it go, Rachel."

"Not yet," I said, and with her arms around me, I pointed at the hellhole. *"Celero inanio!"* I said again.

"Stop!" Ivy shouted, and I screamed as her hands left me and the pain bent me double. I gasped, feeling my lungs burn. But I couldn't let it go. It wasn't done yet.

The cot burst into flame, a glowing haze of orange hovering over it, looking like a body contorting in torment. The blood on the floor was a puff of black that whirled up as more air was sucked in to replace that which was burnt. Ivy's hands found me from behind, and I took a clean breath as the pain was muted and I could bear it again.

"Please don't let go," I said, tears of pain and heartache trickling down, and I felt her nod.

"Celero inanio!" I cried again, my tears evaporating as they fell to make glittering sparkles of salt, and still the rage burned in me, pulsing in time with my heart. The ley line streamed in like vengeance, burning, trying to take me with it like a mindless flood. I could smell my hair starting to burn. The scrape on my cheek felt like fire.

"Rachel, stop!" Ivy screamed, but I could see the sparkle of Kisten's eyes in the flames, smiling at me—and I couldn't.

A shadow darted between me and the roaring inferno. The heat beat at me as it blinked past. I could hear Edden swearing, and then the stone door shifting. A sliver of cool shade touched my knee, crept up my leg, and kissed the edge of my cheek. I leaned into it as the band of white vengeance narrowed. My balance left me and I collapsed. But I held on to the line. It was the only clean thing I had.

Ivy gave me a little shake to bring my attention to her. Her eyes were black with fear, and I loved her. "Let go of the line," she pleaded, her tears burning as they hit me. "Rachel, let go of the line! Please!"

I blinked. *Let go of the line?*

The tunnel was plunged into darkness as Edden finally got the door shut. A wave of cold air burned my skin. My eyes slowly recognized the outline of her face as she held me. Edden's silhouette grew more defined as a red glow became brighter, showing where the wall was thinnest, at the door. My fire still raged behind it, and the glow of the heat lit the tunnel with a soft haze.

Edden's shape stared at the door, his hands on his hips. "Sweet mother of Jesus," he breathed, then drew his hand back when he went to touch the lines the spell had etched in the door. I could see the bright ring of the charmed circle of iron embedded in the door. Radiating out from it were black threads making a spiral pentagram with arcane symbols. In the middle was my handprint, and it was molding to the spell, making it wholly mine. No one would open the door again.

"He's gone! Let it go!" Ivy shouted, and this time, I did.

I gasped as the power shut off, jerking as the cold swarmed in to replace the heat. I clenched in on myself, whispering, "I take it. I take it. I take it," before the imbalance could strike me. Tears leaked out through my clenched eyes as I felt the ugly black slither over me like a cool silk sheet. It had been a black curse, but I had used it without thought. Even so, the tears weren't for me: they were for Kisten.

Silence apart from my rasping breaths. My chest hurt. It felt like it was burning. Nothing flowed in me. I was a burnt-out shell. Everything was silent, as if the sounds themselves had been turned to ash.

"Can you stand?"

It was Ivy, and I blinked at her, unable to answer. Edden leaned over us, and I cried out in pain when his arms slipped between Ivy and me, raising me up as if I were a child.

"Oh shit, Rachel," he said when I fought back a wave of nausea. "You look like you've got a bad sunburn."

"It was worth it," I whispered. My lips were cracked, and my eyebrows felt singed when I touched them. The wall was still glowing as Edden shifted into motion. A spiderweb of black was etching through the door, turning the rock silver as it cooled. It was the curse that I had spoken, slowly lightening like stretch marks as the stone cooled. The door was fused shut, and my mark would warn anyone away from tampering with it. Not that I thought there was anything behind the door now.

I caught my breath in pain when Edden almost tripped and my tender skin was rubbed. Ivy touched my arm as if needing to reassure herself that I was okay. "Was that a ley line?" she asked hesitantly. "You did that with power right off a line, right?"

My chest hurt, and I hoped I hadn't damaged my lungs. "Yeah," I said softly. "Thank you for cushioning it."

"You have that kind of power all the time?" she said, almost a whisper.

I went to nod, then thought better of it when my skin pulled. "Yes." The memory of the black magic symbol etched on the door rose through my thoughts. So it was a black charm. So what? I might be a black witch, but at least I was an honest one.

Edden slowly carried me back to the surface, silent but for his breathing. Everyone who knew Kisten had been murdered to satisfy a political agenda was either dead or in this hallway. My love would be remembered for dying to save Ivy's and my life. That was why he had died, not because of someone's whim. That was who Kisten was. Had been.

And no one would ever say different.

Thirty-four

Though my mom was hundreds of miles away by now, my room still smelled like her light lavender perfume, wafting up from the dusty boxes stacked where Robbie had left them beside my bed. It had been nice of him to bring them all in while Mom showed me the brochure of the apartment she had waiting for her in Portland.

Kneeling beside my bed, I pulled the top box to me, reading my adolescent scrawl before I shoved the box aside to take to the brat pack at the hospital later. The moving van had shown up at my mom's house yesterday, and I was tired of packing peanuts and bubble wrap, depressed by all the good-byes. Mom and Robbie had brought the last of my things over early this afternoon, waking me up and taking me out for a bon voyage breakfast at an old-lady eatery, since by Robbie's guess her kitchen was already in Kansas. I think we got bad service because of my shunning, but it was hard to tell unless your waitress wrote BLACK WITCH on the back of your napkin. It didn't matter. We weren't in any hurry. The coffee sucked dishwater, though.

Robbie had been in a good mood because he'd paid for the moving van. Mom had been in a good mood because she had some excitement in her life. I was in a bad mood because she wouldn't have had to do this if I hadn't gotten shunned. It didn't matter that my mother had been apartment hunting since getting back from visiting Takata. She was moving because of me. Robbie and my mom had probably landed by now, and all that remained of them in Cincinnati were six boxes, her new fridge in my kitchen, and her old Buick out front.

Melancholy, I pulled new tape off an old box, peeking inside to find my dad's old ley line stuff. Making a pleased sound, I stood and hoisted the box onto a hip to take it to the kitchen.

The pixies were noisy up front in the sanctuary as I made my way to the back of the church, and I didn't even bother to turn on the lights as I shoved the box on the center counter. In the corner, the little blue lights on my mom's fridge glowed. It had a through-the-door ice dispenser, and Ivy and I had been thrilled when she gave it to us. The pixies had taken all of six seconds to discover that if three of them hit the ice dispenser together, they'd get a cube, which they then used like a surfboard to skate around the kitchen floor. Smiling at the memory, I left the box and went back to my room. I'd unpack it later.

The entire back part of the church had a chill air about it that couldn't all be blamed on the late hour. Ivy being out might account for some of it, but most was because we had inherited my mom's space heater along with half her attic. The electric heater was going full tilt up front, and the pixies were enjoying a hot summer evening in January, but since the thermostat for the entire church was in the sanctuary, the heat hadn't clicked on in hours. It was cool away from the reach of the space heater, making me shiver in my still-tender skin. Coffee would be nice, but since having that grande latte . . . raspberry . . . thing, nothing seemed to taste good anymore.

Thoughts of cinnamon and raspberry dogged me back to my room, and I pulled the tape from the next box to find music I'd forgotten I ever had. Pleased, I shoved the box into the hall to go through with Ivy later.

Ivy was doing well, having borrowed my mom's Buick after

sundown to go talk to Rynn Cormel. I didn't expect her back until after sunrise. She had told him about the oubliette last week, how Denon had been Art's ghoul set to watch her until she quit the I.S., and how Art had died. I hoped she'd kept quiet about how her aura had protected me when I pulled on a line so hard that it melted stone, but I bet she'd told Rynn Cormel that, too. Not that I was embarrassed or anything, but why advertise to the city's master vampire that you can do that sort of thing?

Had it surprised me that her aura could shield my soul? I'd never heard of such a thing before, and a search on the Internet and in my books yielded nothing, but since our auras had blended the last time she had bitten me . . . I wasn't surprised— I was scared. There was the potential here to find a way to reunite her mind, body, and soul after her first death. I just didn't see how yet. Kisten had his soul when he died that second time. I knew it. What I didn't know was if it was me and our love for each other, or if it had been because he had died twice in quick succession, or if it had been something completely different. It wasn't worth risking Ivy's soul to find out. Just the thought of her dead terrified me.

A third unmarked box turned out to be more stuffed animals, and I sat back on my heels as my fingers went to pick one up. My smile became sad, and I brushed the unicorn's mane. This one was special. It had graced my dresser for most of my high school years. "Maybe I'll keep you, Jasmine," I whispered, then I straightened at a zing of adrenaline.

Jasmine. That was her name! I thought, elated. That was the name of the black-haired girl I'd hung around with at Trent's dad's make-a-wish camp. "Jasmine!" I whispered, excited as I held the stuffed animal close and smiled with a bitter happiness. The toy made a small spot of warmth against me. I remembered it covering a much larger area when I was younger. Happy, I stretched to set it next to the giraffe on my dresser. I'd never forget again.

"Welcome home, Jasmine," I whispered. Trent had wanted

to know Jasmine's name as much as I had, having had a crush on her and nothing to remember her by. Maybe if I told him her name, he might tell me if she'd survived—once he looked her up in his dad's records.

I ought to try to mend that fence, I thought, rummaging to find a toy that didn't have a name or face associated with it that I could take to Ford and Holly. I knew *he'd* appreciate something to distract and help socialize the young banshee. The two of them were doing great the last time I'd called, though Edden wasn't happy about Ford taking sick days or setting up a nursery in the corner of his office. Not to mention the potty chair in the men's room.

I grinned. Edden had ranted for an entire fifteen minutes about that.

Pulling out the elephant named Raymond and the blue bear named Gummie that had nothing but happy memories associated with them, I set them aside, folding the box closed and setting it atop the other box to take to the hospital. My aura was just about back to normal, and I really wanted to see the kids. The girl in the red pajamas, especially. I needed to talk to her. Tell her the chance was real. If her parents would let me, that is.

I held my breath against the dust as I hoisted the two light boxes, nudging my door open with a foot and taking them to the foyer. The pixies chorused a cheerful hello as I entered the sanctuary, and Rex darted through the cat door to the belfry stairway, spooked when I dropped the boxes on top of the one already there. Her head poked back through the door, and I crouched and extended my hand.

"What's up, Rex?" I crooned, and she came out, tail high as she sedately made her way to me for a little scritch under her chin. She'd been in the foyer when I brought the first box in, too.

The hum of pixy wings pulled our attention up. "Toys for the kids?" Jenks said, his wings a bright red from sitting under the full-spectrum light I had put in my desk lamp.

"Yup, you want to come with me and Ivy when we take them?"

"Sure," he drawled. "I might raid the witch's floor for some fern seed, though."

I harrumphed as I stood. "Be my guest." It was harder to get stuff now that I was shunned, and Jenks was already planning out a third more garden space to compensate for it. There was the black market, but I wasn't going there. If I did, then I'd be saying I agreed with what they'd labeled me as, and I didn't.

Rex went to stand under my coat, and I hesitated when she stood on her hind legs to pat the pocket. My eyebrows rose, and I looked at Jenks. I'd chased her out of the foyer twice now.

"Is one of your kids in there?" I asked Jenks, then jumped for the cat when her nails hooked the felt and started to pull. Her claw disengaged when I scooped her up, but I had to drop her when her back claw dug into my arm. Tail bristled, she ran for the back of the church. There was a brief shout from Jenks's kids, and then disappointment. Having the sanctuary warmer than the rest of the church was better than putting them in a bubble.

Jenks was laughing, but when I pushed my sleeve up, I found a long scratch. "Jenks," I complained. "Your cat needs her nails trimmed. I said I'd do it."

"Rache, look at this."

I tugged my sleeve down, head coming up to find Jenks hovering before me with a blue something in his hands. If I hadn't known better, I would have said it was a little bambino, wrapped up in a blue blanket by the way Jenks was carrying it. "What is it?" I asked, and he dropped it into my waiting hand.

"It was in your pocket," he said, landing on my palm, and we looked at it together in the light coming from the sanctuary. "It's a chrysalis, but I don't know what species," he added, nudging it with his booted toe.

My confusion cleared, and I took a breath, remembered Al

curling my fingers around it on New Year's Eve. "Can you tell if it's alive?" I asked.

Hands on his hips, he nodded. "Yup. Where did you get it?"

Jenks flew up as my fingers closed over it and I started for the kitchen to wash my scratch. "Uh, Al gave it to me," I said as we passed through the sanctuary and into the cooler hall. "He was making little blue butterflies out of snow, and this was the only thing that survived."

"Tink's a Disney whore, that is the creepiest thing I've seen since Bis got stuck in the downspout," he said softly, his wings a soft hum in the dark.

I thunked the lights on in the kitchen with my elbow, and not knowing what to do with it, I set it on the windowsill. "Didn't see Ivy's last date, huh?" I asked as I turned on the taps and grabbed the soap. The window was black, throwing back a skewed vision of myself and Jenks.

Rex jumped up onto the counter, and I splashed her when she reached for the chrysalis.

"No! Bad kitty!" Jenks shouted to make the cat leap for the floor, and arm dripping, I set one of Mr. Fish's oversize brandy snifters upside down over it. Mr. Fish was still in the ever-after, and if he was dead when I got back there, I was going to be pissed. It had been a week now because of my thin aura. At least that's what Al was saying. Personally, I think he was breaking in Pierce and didn't want me around, mucking things up.

"Jenks, she's just being a cat," I said as the pixy scolded the orange ball of unrepentant fur. She stared lovingly up at her pixy master, licking her chops and twitching the tip of her tail.

"I don't want her to eat it!" he said, rising to be even with me. "She might turn into a frog or something. Tink's knickers, it's probably full of black magic."

"It's just a butterfly," I said, drying my arm and pulling the sleeve back down.

"Yeah, with fangs and a thirst for blood, for all you know," he muttered.

I scooped up the cat and fondled her ears, wanting to be sure that we were still friends. Rex hadn't been watching me from doorways all week, and I kind of missed it. The more I thought about it, the more I believed I had played right into Al's plans. Pierce would want a body, and Al could give it to him. I could easily imagine that the two had come to an agreement, body for servitude. Win-win all the way around. Al got a useful familiar, Pierce got a body and a chance to see me once a week. And knowing Pierce, he thought he'd find a way to slip Al's leash eventually, leaving me in the middle to suffer the fallout. I'd be willing to bet most of Al's bluster and anger at me for snatching Pierce had been an act. I had freaking made the charm that he corrupted to make the curse work.

That Pierce was now in Tom Bansen's body was just squeamy. Even worse, he'd done it to himself. No wonder his plight wasn't hitting any of my rescue impulses. *Stupid man.* I'd find out what happened come Saturday and my stint with Al.

The faint tingling of Rex's bell caught my interest, and I looked at the pretty thing before letting her slip to the floor. My eyes widened at the pattern of loops and swirls that made up its shape. It looked exactly like the bell Trent had found in the ever-after. I'd never noticed before. "Ah, Jenks?" I questioned, not believing it. "Where did you get this bell?"

He was on top of my dad's box of stuff, trying to wedge it open. "Ceri gave it to me," he said, puffing. "Why?"

I took a breath to tell him where it had come from, then changed my mind. "No reason," I said, letting Rex slip from me. "It's really unique, is all."

"So, what's in the box?" he asked, giving up and putting his hands on his hips.

I smiled and crossed the kitchen. "My dad's charms. You should see some of this stuff."

As Jenks and I talked, I brought out wrapped gadgets and

utensils, laying them down for him to unwrap. Jenks buzzed around in the cupboards to find nooks and crannies, his wings slowly losing their red tint to become their normal grayish hue. He was better than a flashlight for seeing what was at the back of a cupboard.

"Hey, Jenks," I said as I set a box of uncharmed ley line amulets and pins at the back of my silverware drawer. "I'm, uh, really sorry about pasting you against my bathroom mirror with sticky silk."

The pixy flashed red, the dust slipping from him mirroring his embarrassed color. "You remember that, huh?" he said. "It sure made the decision easy to down you with that forget charm." He hesitated, then added softly, "Sorry about that. I was only trying to help."

The box was empty, and not seeing Ivy's scissors, I ran my ceremonial knife along the tape lines to collapse the box so the rani of recycling wouldn't yell at me. "It's okay," I said as I wrestled the thing flat. "I've forgotten about it already. See?" I quipped.

Tired, I tucked the box in the pantry and began sorting the remaining charms. Jenks landed beside me, watching. The sound of his kids was nice. "I'm sorry about Kisten," Jenks said, surprising me. "I don't think I said that yet."

"Thanks," I said, grabbing a handful of spent charms. "I still miss him." But the pain was gone, burned to ash under the city, and I could move on.

The old spells went into my dissolution vat of salt water, making a soft splash. I missed Marshal, too. I understood why he'd left. He hadn't been my boyfriend, but something more— my friend, one I'd really messed up with. Doing a power pull with him made the entire situation look worse than it really was.

I held nothing against him for leaving. He hadn't betrayed me by walking away, and he wasn't a coward for not sticking around. I'd made a very large mistake by getting shunned, and it wasn't his responsibility to fix it. I didn't expect him to wait for me until I did. He hadn't said he would. He was rightfully ticked at me for screwing up. If anything, I'd betrayed him, breaking his trust when I told him I could keep everything under control.

"Rache, what does this one do?" Jenks said as he messed around with the last charm I'd left on the counter.

Finding my keys in my bag, I came closer. "That one detects strong magic," I said, pointing out the rune scratched on it.

"I thought that's what that one does," he said as I wedged it on my key ring beside my original bad-mojo, or rather, lethal-amulet, detector.

"This one detects lethal magic," I explained, flipping the original earth-magic amulet and letting it drop. "The one from my dad detects strong magic, and since all lethal magic is strong, it will do the same thing. I'm hoping it won't set off the security systems at the mall, like the lethal amulet does, since they're both ley line based. I'm going to take them shopping and see which works best."

"Gotcha," he said, nodding.

"My dad made it," I said, feeling closer to him as I dropped my keys back in my bag. The charm was over twelve years old, but because it had never been used, it was still good. Better than batteries. "You want some coffee?" I asked.

Jenks nodded, and a chorus of pixy shouts pulled him into the air. I wasn't surprised when the front bell rang. The pixies were better than a security system.

"I'll get it," Jenks said, darting away, but before I could do more than get the coffee grounds out, he was back. "It's a delivery service," he said, slipping a thin trace of silver pixy dust as he came back in. "You need to sign for something. I can't do it. It's for you."

A pang of fear slipped into me, and vanished. I'd been shunned. It could be anything.

"Don't be a baby," Jenks said, instinctively knowing my warning flags had been tripped. "Do you have any idea of the penalty for sending a bad charm through the mail? Besides, it's from Trent."

"Really?" Interested now, I flicked on the coffeemaker and followed him out. A bewildered human was standing on my doorstep in the light from the sign overhead. The door, gaping open, was letting out the heat, and pixies were darting in and out on dares.

"Stop it! Enough!" I called, waving them back inside. "What's wrong with you?" I said loudly as I took the pen and signed for a thickly padded envelope. "You all act like you were born in a stump."

"It was a flower box, Ms. Morgan," one of Jenks's kids said merrily, perched on my shoulder, out of the cold night and nestled in my hair.

"Whatever," I muttered, smiling at the confused man and taking the package. "Everyone inside?" I asked, and when I got off a round of counting up to fifty-something, I shut the door.

A good dozen of Jenks's kids braved the chill of the kitchen, curiosity winning out over comfort, and they all wove in and out before me in a nightmare of silk and high-pitched voices that scraped along the inside of my eyelids. It wasn't until Jenks made that awful screech with his wings that they quit. Nervousness hit me as I tossed the manila-wrapped package on my spot at the table to deal with later. I'd wait until Ivy got home so she could pick me up off the floor when the joke charm Trent had sent me exploded in my face.

Arm around my middle, I got my Vampiric Charms mug out of the cupboard. I hadn't had a good cup of coffee in a week. Not since the last one at Junior's. I wanted another one, but was afraid to go back. Not that I remembered what it was, anyway. Cinnamon something.

Jenks buzzed close, then away. "You going to open it?" he prompted as he hovered over the table. "It's got bumps inside."

I licked my lips and looked askance at him. "You open it."

"And get blasted by whatever nasty elf charm he put in there?" he said. "No way!"

"Elf charm?" I turned around, curious. Crossing the kitchen, I dug my keys out of my bag, watching the heavy-magic amulet glow a faint red. The lethal one was quiet, though. Interested, I waved the pixies off it. It wasn't lethal . . . but still.

"Open it, Rache! Tink's tampons!"

The coffeemaker finished with a hissing gurgle, and enduring the complaints of twenty-some pixies, I smiled and poured myself a cup. I took a careful sip as I brought it to the table, frowning. Maybe I could get some raspberry syrup to put in it the next time I was at the store.

Pixies clustered on my shoulders, shoving each other as I used my ceremonial knife, still out on the counter, to cut the brown envelope open. Not looking inside, I angled the envelope and cautiously shook whatever it was out and away from me.

"It's a rope!" Jenks exclaimed, hovering over it, and I peeked inside the envelope to make sure there wasn't a note. "Trent sent you a rope? Is that a joke?" he said, looking so angry that his kids started to back off, whispering. "To hang yourself with, maybe? Or is it an elven version of getting a horse head in your bed? It's made out of horsehair."

I cautiously picked up the short length of rough rope, feeling the knotted bumps. "It's probably made from his familiar," I said, remembering Trent once telling me that his familiar was a horse. "Jenks," I said, heart beating fast. "I think it's a Pandora charm."

Immediately Jenks lost his anger. From behind us, I heard a rumble and chunk of an ice cube dropping onto the floor, and his kids swarmed it. Rex appeared at the doorway and hunched down, watching Jenks's kids push and shove to be the first five on the long cube of ice. Wings going in tandem, they shot across the floor, under the table, and around the island. Pixy squeals rose high, and they all flew off an instant before the cube hit the wall, out of control.

"He just gave it to you?" Jenks said as he landed beside me, kicking it. "Are you sure that's what it is?"

"I think so," I said, not sure what to make of it. "You undo the knots, and a memory returns." I picked it up, looking at the gray strand knotted with complex figures that reminded me of the sea. I'd be willing to bet Trent had made it himself. I could feel the rising tension of wild magic, making a quiver in me as it tickled my compromised aura. Or maybe elf magic always felt that way.

Jenks looked from the black-and-silver strand of knotted rope to me. "You gonna do it?"

I shrugged. "I don't know what memory it's for."

"Kisten's murder," he said confidently, but I shook my head.

"Maybe." I ran the string through my fingers, feeling the bumps like notes of music. "It might be something about my dad, or his dad, or the make-a-wish camp."

Carefully, I set it down. I didn't want to know what memory was there. Not yet. I'd had enough of memories. I wanted to live for a while without them, dealing with the present without the hurt of the past.

My phone rang from my bag, and I eyed Jenks when ZZ Top's "Sharp Dressed Man" jingled out. The pixy gave me an innocent stare, but when Rex perked up, sitting to stare at the corner of the room with a familiar intensity, my expression left me, and I drew back from answering my phone. "Pierce?" I whispered.

The air pressure shifted, and with a soft pop, a misty shape in the corner grew, solidified, and turned into Pierce. Rex stood with a little kitty trill, and I jumped to my feet, shocked. It had to be Pierce. Unless it was Al disguised as him.

"Pierce?" I asked again, and he turned to me, his eyes twinkling, and dressed to the nines in mid-nineteen-hundreds high fashion. He looked like himself. I mean, he didn't look like Tom, and I wondered what in hell was going on.

"Mistress witch," he said, darting across the kitchen to take my hands. "I can't stay," he said breathlessly, eyes glinting. "Al will be of a mind to track me down faster than a dog trees a coon on a moonlit night, but I had to visit you first. To explain."

"You took Tom's body," I said, pulling away. "Pierce, I'm glad to see you, but—"

He nodded, his hair sliding into his eyes until he tossed it back roguishly. "It's black magic, yes, and I'm not proud of it, but it wasn't me who killed the black witch. He killed himself."

"But you look—"

"Like myself, yes," he finished, drawing me into almost a dance, he was so happy. "That was part of the deal. Rachel . . ." His expression suddenly became concerned. "You've been burned," he said, every last other thought clearly out of his head. His hand went out, and I stopped it before it touched my face.

My pulse was hammering, and I was hot. "Kisten's pyre," I said, flustered.

Pierce gave me a firm look. "It is ended, then."

I nodded. "Please don't tell me you sold your soul for this. . . ." I looked him up and down, and he dropped my hands and stepped back.

"That is a matter of some debate. You must be able to hold what you claim, and though I entered into an agreement, he can't hold me. None of them can hold me."

His smile was way too smug, and I felt a quiver in myself. "You escaped!"

"Once I had obtained a body and could commune with a line, it was only a matter of time. Nothing can hold me forever. Except perhaps you."

Beaming, he pulled me close, and knowing he was going to kiss me, I blurted, "Jenks is here."

Immediately his hands flashed from me. Blue eyes wide in charming shock, he dropped back a step. "Jenks!" he said, flushing. "My apologies."

I followed the sound of an angry humming to see Jenks hovering over the middle counter, staring at us with his hands on his hips and a grimace on his face. "Get out," he said flatly. "I just got her normal again. Get out before you turn her into a sniveling, twitterpated . . . twit!"

"Jenks!" I exclaimed, and Pierce put a calming hand on me.

"That is my intent, Jenks," he said gallantly, and I wondered if Pierce meant his intent was to leave or to turn me into a twitterpated twit.

Pierce bent to Rex, who was twining about his ankles. "I have to go," he said as he rose with her in his arms. "I was of a mind to explain before Al fills your head with his view of what happened this past week. I will see you as soon as I can. Al is a devilishly fine demon. More fun than a nest of bunnies to outwit."

He's playing with Al? "Pierce . . . ," I said, almost laughing. I was so confused. He had escaped him? He had used Al to gain a body, and then escaped him?

Pierce brought his gaze back to me. "I must pull foot, but until I find myself in a better situation, I will think of you every evening between candle lighting and dawn."

"Wait a minute, Pierce. I'm not—"

But he had swooped forward, and as Jenks angrily dusted silver sparkles on us, he kissed me soundly. He stole it. That was the only way I could describe it. He stole a kiss, wrapping his arms about me and holding me tight as he took a kiss from me and left me breathless.

"Hey!" I exclaimed, not shoving him away but pulling back. Letting go, he inclined his head . . . and vanished with the soft scent of coal dust and shoe polish.

I stared at where he had been. From behind me, a forgotten cube of ice slipped down and hit the floor. "Uh, Jenks?" I warbled. He had come. He had befuddled me. He had escaped Al on his own and come to crow to me about it. Oh-h-h-h-h crap. I was in trouble.

"No!" Jenks shouted. "Damn it to the Turn and back!" he shrilled, throwing a hot-sparkled tantrum two feet above the counter. "I'll not have you falling for him, Rachel. No!"

But as I ran my fingers over my lips, remembering his there, I thought it might be too late. He was just so . . . Rachel-ly. Hitting a spot in me that hadn't been alive since I was eighteen. And with that thought, my face went blank. Damn it, Ford had been right. This was why I hadn't had any luck with guys. I had been measuring them against Pierce all this time, and they had all come up lacking. I was in big trouble. Big. Maybe as an eighteen-year-old I thought it was romantic to be involved with a smart, intelligent, devil-may-care, handsome witch who could take on demons, vamps, and the I.S., but I was smarter now, right? Right?!

The air pressure shifted with a bang. I cowered below the level of the counter, and Jenks shot up to the ceiling.

"Witch!" Al bellowed, and I peeked over the counter. His eyes met mine, and he yelled, "Where is my familiar?"

I stood, a smile quirking the corners of my lips. "Uh, he was here," I said. "I didn't summon him, he just kind of showed up." My focus sharpened on Al, and he narrowed his eyes, trying to gauge the truthfulness of my words. "Kind of like how you just did," I added. "He popped in, and then he left."

"Where did he go!" he bellowed, gloved hands clenching. "I had him in a snare that would take Alexander the Great a lifetime to untwist, and he did it in a week!" Al took a step, pinwheeling as his booted heel found an ice cube.

"I don't know," I said, then shouted, "I don't know!" when Al growled at me. "I think he went that way." I pointed off in a vague direction.

Making an mmmm of discontent, Al tugged his frock coat. "I'll see you Saturday, Rachel," he said roughly. "And bring a silver-core rope to tie Gordian Nathaniel Pierce down with. If I ever find him, I'm going to sell him to Newt. I swear, if I didn't need him, I'd kill him myself!"

With a foul-smelling gust of air, Al vanished.

I stared at the spot, blinking.

"Sweet mother of Tink," Jenks whispered from the ladle. "What just happened?"

Leaning against the counter, I shook my head. From the front of the church came the sound of the door opening. "Rachel?" Ivy's voice filtered in. "I'm home. Why did Pierce pop into the car and tell me to pick up a grande latte, double espresso, Italian blend, light on the froth, heavy on the cinnamon, with a shot of raspberry?"

My lips curved up in a smile.

I loved my life.

Don't miss the continuing
Hollows adventures of Rachel Morgan with
BLACK MAGIC SANCTION
Kim Harrison
Available now
wherever books are sold

One

Tucking my hair back, I squinted at the parchment, trying to form the strange angular letters as smoothly as I could. The ink glistened wetly, but it wasn't red ink, it was blood— my blood—which might account for the slight tremble in my hand as I copied the awkward-looking name scripted in characters that weren't English. Beside me was a pile of rejects. If I didn't get it perfect this time, I'd be bleeding yet again. God help me. I was doing a black curse. In a demon's kitchen. On the weekend. How in hell had I gotten here?

Algaliarept stood poised between the slate table and the smaller hearth, his white-gloved hands behind his back. He looked like a stuffy Brit in a murder mystery, and when he shifted impatiently, my tension spiked. "That isn't helping," I said dryly, and his red, goat-slitted eyes widened in a mocking surprise, peering at me over his smoked spectacles. He didn't need them to read with. From his crushed green velvet frock, to his lace cuffs and proper English accent, the demon was all about show.

"It has to be exact, Rachel, or it won't capture the aura," he said, his attention sliding to the small green bottle on the table. "Trust me, you don't want that floating around unbound."

I sat up to feel my back crack. Touching the quill tip to my throbbing finger, my unease grew. I was a white witch, damn it, not black. But I wasn't going to write off demon magic just because of a label. I'd read the recipe; I'd interpreted the invocation. Nothing died to provide the ingredients, and the only person who'd suffer would be me. I'd come away from this with a new layer of demon smut on my soul, but I'd also have protection against banshees. After one had nearly killed me last New Years, I'd willingly entertain a little smut to be safe. Besides, this might lead to a way to save Ivy's soul when she died her first death. For that, I'd risk a lot.

Something felt wrong though. Al's squint at the aura bottle was worrisome, and his accent was too precise tonight. He was concerned and trying to hide it. It couldn't be the curse. It was just manipulating an aura—captured energy from a soul. At least . . . that's what he said.

Frowning, I glanced at Al's cramped handwritten instructions. I wanted to go over them again, but his peeved expression and his soft mmmm of a growl to get on with it convinced me it could wait until the scripting was done. My "ink" was running thin, and I dabbed more blood from my finger to finish some poor slob's name, someone who trusted a demon . . . someone like me. *Not that I really trust Al*, I thought, glancing at the instructions once more.

Al's spelling kitchen was right out of a fantasy flick, one of four rooms he had retained after selling everything else to keep his demon-ass out of demon-ass jail. The gray stone walls made a large circular space, most of which were covered in identical tall wooden cabinets with glass doors. Behind the rippled glass Al kept his books and ley line equipment. The biological ingredients were in a cellar accessed through a rough hole in the floor. Smoky support beams came to a point over a central fire pit, a good forty feet up. The pit itself was a round, raised affair, with vent holes to draw the cold floor air in by way of simple convection. When it got going, it made a comfortable spot to read at, and when fatigue brought me down, Al let me nap on the benches bracketing it. Mr. Fish, my beta, swam in his little bowl on the mantel of the smaller fire. I don't know why I'd brought him from home. It had been Ivy's idea, and when an anxious vampire tells you to take your fish, you take your fish.

Al cleared his throat, and I jumped, fortunately having pulled my quill from the parchment an instant before. Done, thank God. "Good?" I asked, holding it up for inspection, and his white-gloved, thick fingered hand pinched it at the edge where it wouldn't smear.

He eyed it, my tension easing when he handed it back. "Passable. Now the bowl."

Passable. That was usually as good as it got, and I set the painstakingly scribed bit of paper beside the unlit candle and green bottle of aura, taking up Al's favorite scribing knife and the palm-sized, earthen bowl. The knife was ugly, the writhing woman on the handle looking like demon porn. Al knew I hated it, which was why he insisted I use it.

The gray bowl was rough in my hand, the inside cluttered with scratched off words of power. Only the newly scribed name I was etching would react. The theory was to burn the paper and take in the man's name by way of air, then drink water from the bowl, taking in his name by water. This would hit all four elements, earth and water with the bowl, air and fire with the burning parchment. Heaven and earth, with me in the middle. Yippy skippy.

The foreign-looking characters were easier after having practiced with the parchment, and I had it scratched on a tiny open space before Al could sigh more than twice. He'd taken up the bottle of aura, frowning as he gazed into the swirling green.

"What?" I offered, trying to keep the annoyance from my voice. I was his student, sure, but he would still try to backhand me if I got uppity.

Al's brow furrowed, worrying me even more. "I don't like this aura's resonance," he said softly, red eyes probing the glass perched in his white-clad fingers.

I shifted my weight on my padded chair, trying to stretch my legs. "And?"

Al's focus shifted over his glasses to me. "It's one of Newt's."

"Newt? Since when do you need to get an aura from Newt?" I asked. No one liked the insane demon, but she was the reigning queen of the lost boys, so to speak, and knew everything—when she could remember it.

"Not your concern," he said, and I winced, embarrassed. Al had lost almost everything in his effort to snag me as a familiar, ending up with something vastly more precious but broke just the same. I was a witch, but a common, usually lethal, genetic fault had left me able to kindle their magic. Al's status was assured as long as I was his student, but his living was bleak.

"I'll just pop over and find out who it is before we finish this up," he said with a forced lightness, setting the bottle down with a sharp tap.

I looked at the assembled pieces. "Now? Why didn't you ask her before?"

"It didn't seem important at the time," he said, looking mildly discomforted. "Pierce!" he shouted, the call for his familiar lost in the high ceilings coated in shadows and dust. Mood sour, he turned to me. "Don't touch *anything* while I'm gone."

"Sure," I said distantly, eyeing the green swirling bottle. He had to borrow an aura from Newt? Jeez, maybe things were worse off than I'd thought.

"The crazy bitch has a reason for everything, though she might not remember it," Al said as he tugged his sleeves over his lace cuffs. Glancing at the arranged spelling supplies, he hesitated. "Go ahead and fill the bowl. Make sure the water covers the name." He looked at the image of an angry, screaming face scribed into his black marble floor. It was his version of a door in the door-less room. "Gordian Nathanial Pierce!"

I pushed back from the table as the witch popped into the kitchen atop the grotesque face, a dishtowel over his shoulder and his sleeves rolled up. "I'd be of a mind to know what the almighty hurry is," the man from the early 1800s said as he tossed his hair from his eyes and unrolled his sleeves. "I swan, the moment I start something, you get in a pucker over nothing."

"Shut up, runt," Al muttered, knowing to backhand him would start a contest that would end with Pierce unconscious and a big mess to clean up. It was easier to ignore him. Al had snared the clever witch within the hour of his first escape, the demon taking great pains to keep us apart during my weekly lessons until Al realized I was ticked with Pierce for having willingly gone into partnership with Al. Partnership? Hell, call it what it was. Slavery.

Oh, I was still impressed with Pierce's magic that far outstripped mine. His quick one-liners in his odd accent aimed at Al when the demon wasn't listening still made me smirk. And I wasn't looking at his long wavy hair, or his lanky build, much less his tight ass. Damn it. But somewhere shortly after seeing him naked under Carew Tower's restaurant, I'd lost the teenage crush I'd had on him. It might have been his insufferable confidence, or that he wouldn't admit how deep in the crapper he was, or that he was just a little too good at demon magic, but for whatever reason, that devilish smile that had once sparked through me now fell flat.

"I'm stepping out for a tick," Al said as he buttoned his coat. "Merely checking something. A tidy curse is a well-twisted one! Pierce, make yourself useful and help her with her Latin while I'm gone. Her syntax sucks."

"Gee, thanks." The modern phrases sounded odd with Al's accent.

"And don't let her do anything stupid," he added as he adjusted his glasses.

"Hey!" I exclaimed, but my eyes darted to the creepy tapestry whose figures seemed to move when I wasn't looking. There were things in Al's kitchen that it was best not to be alone with, and I appreciated the company. Even if it was Pierce.

"As the almighty Al wishes," Pierce said dryly, earning a raised eyebrow from Al before he vanished from where he stood, using a ley line to traverse the ever-after to Newt's rooms.

In an instant, the lights went out, but before I could move, they flashed back to life, markedly brighter as Pierce took over the light charm. *Alone. How . . . nice.* I watched him meticulously drape his damp dishtowel to dry on the top of the cushioned bench that circled the central fire pit, and then, jaw clenched, I looked away. Standing, I moved to keep the slate table between us as Pierce crossed the room with the grace of another time.

"What is the invocation today?" he asked, and I pointed to it on the table, wanting to look at it again myself but willing to wait. His hair fell over his eyes as he studied it.

"Sunt qui discessum animi a corpore putent esse mortem. Sunt erras," he said softly, his blue eyes shocking against his dark hair as he looked up. "You're working with souls?"

"Auras," I corrected him, but his expression was doubtful. *There are people who believe that the departure of the soul from the body is death. They are wrong,* I silently translated, then took it from him to set it with the bottle of aura, bowl, and the name scribed with my blood. "Hey, if you can't trust your demon, who can you trust," I said sarcastically, gathering up the pile of discarded signature attempts and moving them out of the way to the mantle. But I didn't trust Al, and I itched to look at the curse again. Not with Pierce, though. He'd want to help me with my Latin.

The tension rose at my continued silence, and Pierce half-sat on the slate table, one long leg draped down. He was watching me, making me nervous as I filled the inscribed bowl from a pitcher. It was just plain water, but it smelled faintly of burnt amber. *No wonder I go home with headaches,* I thought, grimacing as I overfilled the bowl and water dribbled out.

"I'll get that," Pierce said, jumping from the table and reaching for his dishtowel.

"Thanks, I'm good," I snapped, snatching the cloth from him and doing it myself.

He drew back, looking hurt as he stood before the fire pit. "I'll allow I've gotten myself in a powerful fix, Rachel, but what have I done to turn you so cold?"

My motion to clean the slate slowed, and I turned with a sigh. The truth of it was, I wasn't sure. I only knew that the things that had attracted me once now looked childish and inane. He'd been a ghost, more or less, and had agreed to be Al's familiar if the demon could give him a body. Al had shoved his soul into a dead witch before the body even had the chance to skip a heartbeat. It didn't help that I'd known the guy Al had put his soul into. I didn't think I could take another person's body to save myself. But then, I'd never been dead before.

I looked at Pierce now, seeing the same reckless determination, the same disregard for the future that had gotten me rightfully shunned, and all I knew was I didn't want anything to do with it. I took a breath and let it out, not knowing where to start. But a shiver lifted through me at the memory of his touch, ages ago but still fresh in my mind. Al was right. I was an idiot.

"It's not going to work, Pierce," I said flatly, and I turned away.

My tone had been harsh, and Pierce's voice lost its sparkle. "Rachel. Truly. What's wrong? I took this job to be closer to you."

"That's just it!" I exclaimed, and he blinked, bewildered. "This is *not* a job!" I said, waving the cloth. "It's slavery. You belong to him, body and soul. And you did it intentionally! We could have found another way to give you a body. Your own, maybe! But no. You just jumped right into a demon pact instead of asking for help!"

He came around the table, close but not quite touching me. "I swane, a demon curse is the only way to become living again," he said, touching his chest. "I know what I'm doing.

This isn't forever. When I can, I'll kill the demon spawn, and then I'll be free."

"Kill Al?" I breathed, not believing he still thought he could.

"I'll be free of him and have a body both." He took my hands, and I realized how cold I was. "Trust me, Rachel. I know what I'm doing."

Oh my God. He is as bad as I am. Was. "You're crazy!" I exclaimed, pulling out of his grip. "You think you're more powerful than you are, with black magic and whatever! Al is a *demon*, and I don't think you grasp what he can do. He's *playing* with you!"

Pierce leaned against the table, arms crossed and the light catching the colorful pattern of his vest. "Do tell? You opine I don't know what I'm doing?"

"I opine you don't!" I mocked, using his own words. His attitude was infuriating, and I looked at the bowl behind him— the remnant of others who had thought they were smarter than a demon, now just names on a bowl, bottles on a shelf.

"Fair enough." Pierce scratched his chin and stood. "I expect a body needs proof."

I stiffened. Shit. Proof? "Hey, wait a minute," I said, dropping the rag to the table. "What are you doing? Al brought you back, but he can take you out again, too."

Pierce impishly put a finger to his nose. "Mayhap. But he has to catch me, first."

My eyes darted to the band of charmed silver around his wrist. Pierce could jump ley lines where I couldn't, but charmed silver cut off his access to them. He couldn't leave.

"What, this?" he said confidently, and my lips parted when he ran his finger around the inside of the silver band, and the metal seemed to stretch, allowing him to slip it off.

"H-How," I stammered as he twirled it. Crap on toast. I'd be blamed for this. I knew it!

"It's been tampered with so I can move from room to room here. I tampered with it a little more is all," Pierce said, sticking the band of silver in his pack pocket, his eyes gleaming. "I've not had a bite of food free of burnt amber in a coon's age. I'll fetch you something to warm your cold heart."

I stepped forward, panicking. "Put that back on! If Al knows you can escape, he'll—"

"Kill me. Yeah, yeah, yeah," he said, hitting the modern phrase perfectly. His hand dipped into another pocket, and he studied a handful of coins. "Al will tarry with Newt for at least fifteen minutes. I'll be right back."

His accent was thinning. Clearly he could turn it off and on at will—which worried me even more. What else was he hiding? "You're going to get me in trouble!" I said, but with a sly grin, he vanished. The lights he had been minding went out, and the ring of charmed silver he had stuck in his pocket made a ting as it hit the floor. My heart thumped in the sudden darkness lit only by the hearth fire and the dull glow of the banked fire pit. He was gone, and we were both going to be in deep shit if Al found out.

Heart pounding, I watched the creepy tapestry across the room. My mouth was dry, and the shadows shifted as the figures on it seemed to move in the firelight. *Son of a bitch!* I thought as I went to pick up the ring of charmed silver and tuck the incriminating thing in a pocket. Al was going to blame me. He'd think I took the charmed silver off him.

Edging back to the small hearth fire, I fumbled for the candle on the mantel, pinching the wick and tapping a ley line to work the charm. *"Consimilis calefacio,"* I said, voice quavering as a tiny slip of ley-line energy flowed through me, exciting the molecules until the wick burst into flame, but just as I did, the ley-line powered lights flashed high, and I jumped, knocking the lit candle off the sconce.

"I can explain!" I exclaimed as I fumbled for the candle now rolling down the mantel and into Mr. Fish. But it was Pierce, tossing his hair from his eyes and two tall lattes in his hands. "You idiot!" I hissed as the candle hit the scraps of paper, and in a flash, they went up.

"Across lots like lightning, mistress witch," Pierce said, laughing as he extended a coffee.

God, I wish he'd speak normal English. Frantic, I brushed the bits of paper off the mantel, stepping on them once they hit the black marble floor. The stink of burning plastic joined the mess, and I grabbed the bowl of water, dumping it. Black smoke wisped up, stinging my eyes. It helped mask the reek of burning shoe, so maybe it wasn't all bad.

"You ass!" I shouted. "Do you realize what would happen if Al came back and found you gone? Are you that inconsiderate, or just that stupid! Put this back on!"

Angry, I threw the ring of charmed metal at him. His hands were full, and he sidestepped it. With a thunk, it hit the tapestry, and then the floor. Pierce's hand extending the coffee drooped, his enthusiasm fading. "I'd do naught to hurt you, mistress witch."

"I am *not* your mistress witch!" Ignoring the coffee, I looked at the bits of burned paper in a soggy mess on the floor. Kneeling, I snatched the rag from the table to sop it up. I could smell raspberry flavored Italian blend, and my stomach growled.

"Rachel," Pierce coaxed.

Pissed, I wouldn't look up at him as I wiped the floor. Standing, I tossed the rag to the table in disgust, then froze. The aura bottle wasn't green anymore.

"Rachel?"

It was questioning this time, and I held up a hand, tasting the air as my eyes stung. Shit, I'd burned the name and gotten the charged water all over me. "I think I'm in trouble," I whispered, then jerked, feeling as if my skin was on fire. Yelping, I slapped at my clothes. Panic rose as an alien aura slipped through mine, soaking in to find my soul—and squeezing.

Oh shit. Oh shit. Oh shit. I'd invoked the curse. I was in so-o-o-o much trouble. But this didn't feel right; the curse burned! Demons were wimps. They always made their magic painless unless you did it wrong. Oh God. I'd done it wrong!

"Rachel?" Pierce touched my shoulder. I met his eyes, and then I doubled over, gasping.

"Rachel!" he cried, but I was trying to breathe. It was the dead person, the one whose name I'd scribed in my own blood. It hadn't been his aura in the bottle, but his soul. And now his soul wanted a new body. Mine. Son of a bitch, Al had *lied* to me. I knew I should have trusted my gut and questioned him. He said it was an aura, but it was a soul, and the soul in the bottle was pissed!

Mine, echoed in our joined thoughts. Gritting my teeth, I bent double and tapped a ley line. Newt had once tried to possess me, and I burnt her out with a rush of energy. I gasped when a scintillating stream of it poured in with the taste of burning tinfoil, but the presence in me chortled, welcoming the flood. *Mine!* the soul insisted in delight, and I felt my link to the line sever. I stumbled, falling to kneel on the cold marble. It had taken control, cutting me out!

No! I thought, scrambling for the line in my mind only to find nothing to grasp. My chest hurt when my heart started to beat to a new, faster rhythm. What in hell was this thing! What sort of mind could make a soul this determined? I couldn't . . . stop it!

"Rachel!"

Eyes tearing, I blinked at Pierce, struggling to focus. "Get. It. Out of me!"

He spun, motions fast as he found the unburnt signature still on the table. There was a swallow of water left in the bowl. It had to be enough.

I am Rachel Morgan, I thought, teeth gritted as the soul rifled through my memories like some people shake old books for money. *I live in a church with a vampire and a family of pixies. I fight the bad guys. And I will not let you have my body!*

You can't stop me.

The thought was oily—hysteria set to discordant music. It hadn't been my thought, and I panicked. It was right, though. I was powerless to stop it, and as soon as it looked at everything and claimed what it wanted, I was going to be discarded.

"Get out!" I screamed, but its fingers reached into my heart and brain for more, and I groaned, feeling control over my body start to slip away. "Pierce, get it out of me!" I begged, clenched on the cold black floor, the silver etchings decorating it like threads under my cheek. Everything I didn't concentrate on was gone. The moment I lapsed, I would be too.

I smelled the scent of burnt paper, and the soft murmur of Latin. *"Sunt qui discessum animi a corpore putent esse mortem,"* Pierce said, his hand shaking as he brushed the hair from my face. Beside him was the empty bowl. *"Sunt Erras."*

"This is mine!" I cried gleefully, but it wasn't me, screaming. It was the soul, who had found, and held aloft like a jewel, the knowledge that my blood could invoke demon magic. I got in one clean gasp of air as it was distracted, and I opened my eyes. "Pierce . . . ." I whispered desperately for his attention, then choked when the soul realized I still had some control.

"Mine!" the soul snarled with my lips, and I backhanded Pierce across the cheek.

Oh, God, I'd lost, and I felt myself pull my legs under me to crouch before the fire like an animal. I'd lost my body to a thousand year old soul! My lips curled back, and I grinned at Pierce's horror, even as I tried to claw my way back into control. But even my connection to the ley line belonged to it.

"Get away from her!" I heard Al exclaim, and with the sound of smacking flesh, Pierce slid backward against the tapestry. *Al.*

Hissing, I spun to him, crouched and hands turned to claws. *It is a demon*, echoed in my thoughts, and hatred bubbled up, a thousand years of hatred demanding revenge.

P9-DNO-631

In a Land of Honor, War and Heroism, One Powerful Samurai Would Master the Way of the Sword . . .

Sasaki Kojirō: The deadly samurai knew no shame or pity. He had come to Edo to make his fame and fortune—and he would kill anyone who stepped in his way . . .

Akemi: In Edo's red-light district she had known the touch of countless men. But no man could frighten her as Kojirō did—and no man could quench the flame in her heart for Musashi . . .

Zushino Kōsuke: Musashi came to him to have his sword sharpened and polished. But the old man refused, telling him, "I only polish souls . . ."

Yagyū Sekishūsai: He was the founder of the most powerful school of swordsmanship in Japan. But now he was dying, and a nation was crying out for a new master . . .

Iori: Mystical, rustic, full of the arrogance of youth, he and Musashi were bound by the earth they tilled together—and by the way that lay ahead . . .

MUSASHI

BOOK IV:
—THE—
BUSHIDO
CODE

EIJI YOSHIKAWA

Translated from the Japanese by Charles S. Terry
Foreword by Edwin O. Reischauer

POCKET BOOKS

New York   London   Toronto   Sydney   Tokyo

Map design by Ray Lundgren Graphics, Ltd.
Map research by Jim Moser

POCKET BOOKS, a division of Simon & Schuster Inc.
1230 Avenue of the Americas, New York, NY 10020

Published by arrangement with Kodansha International
Library of Congress Catalog Card Number: 80-8791

ISBN: 0-671-67722-5

First Pocket Books printing July 1989

10 9 8 7 6 5 4 3 2 1

POCKET and colophon are trademarks of
Simon & Schuster Inc.

Printed in the U.S.A.

CONTENTS

Contents

PLOT SUMMARY
Book I: *The Way of the Samurai*

Wounded in the great battle of Sekigahara, Takezō (later Musashi) and Matahachi were taken in by a beautiful girl, Akemi, and her lascivious mother, Okō. After a violent confrontation with local bandits, in which he slew the leader, Takezō left his friend with the two women and traveled back to his home province of Mimasaka. There, he was accused of having murdered Matahachi. A wild and undisciplined youth, Takezō was hunted by his own townspeople, and reacted with bitter rage—until the Buddhist town monk, Takuan Sōhō, was able to capture him without a single blow. Takuan tied Takezō up in the branches of a tall tree, but Matahachi's beloved, Otsū, took pity on him and freed him. Begging him to run away with her, she forsook Matahachi forever, but the eccentric Takuan had an even greater power over Takezō—and led him to Himeji Castle. There, by the light of a single lamp in a windowless room, Takezō began to study Suntzu's *The Art of War*, the Books of Zen, and the history of Japan. Weeks stretched into months, and gradually Takezō was transformed. When the day came for him to leave, he took the name Miyamoto Musashi and set off for Kyoto—and his first tests as a man of the sword . . .

PLOT SUMMARY
Book II: *The Art of War*

Musashi, Otsū and Takuan are in the beautiful Yagyū
Valley, unaware of one another's presence, drawn by the
master swordsman Sekishūsai. But a violent fight with
the lords of Yagyū forces Musashi to flee—and leave Otsū
behind. Outside Kyoto, Matahachi is working as a day
laborer when he witnesses the brutal killing of a samurai
by a crowd of workers. The dying samurai gives Matahachi a letter and a sack of gold, sending the half-starved
man on a journey to Osaka, where his money is stolen
from him. More destitute than ever, Matahachi learns
that his former friend Takezō is traveling nearby under
the name Musashi. Meanwhile, Osugi and Uncle Gon
have come to Osaka, too, determined to bring back
Matahachi and kill Musashi. Near the ridge of Mount
Suzuka, Musashi is confronted by the brother of a man
he killed years before. In Kyoto his friends, admirers and
enemies are waiting for him, and so are the swordsmen
of the House of Yoshioka—whom Musashi has challenged to a duel to the death . . .

PLOT SUMMARY
Book III: *The Way of the Sword*

The most powerful swordsman of the House of Yoshioka, Denshichirō, is searching for Musashi, while Musashi has fallen in with Kyoto's rich artistic crowd. Osugi and Matahachi are reunited and meet Otsū by the edge of a steep ravine. Osugi urges her son to kill the woman who betrayed him, but when he strikes out he spills the blood of the wrong person. In the company of a strange and brilliant artisan, Hon'ami Kōetsu, Musashi visits a house of pleasure, where he meets the most beautiful courtesan in Japan. But Musashi must leave her side to face Denshichirō, whom he kills in a duel. Now the Yoshiokas' very existence is threatened, and they set an extraordinary trap for Musashi. On a hill outside Kyoto he defeats their entire force, but in the process is forced to slay a young boy who is the symbolic head of the Yoshiokas. Stunned and confused, Musashi sets off for Edo. On the way he is challenged to a duel by a crude farmer and nearly loses his life. Suddenly Musashi knows his own utter fallibility—and that he has yet to learn the true essence of the samurai spirit.

CHARACTERS AND LOCALES

AKEMI, the daughter of Okō
DIAZŌ, a robber
EDO, the Shōgun's capital city
ISHIMODA GEKI, a retainer of Date Masamune
YAGYŪ HYŌGO, grandson of Yagyū Sekishūsai
TOKUGAWA IEYASU, the Shōgun, ruler of Japan
SANNOSUKE IORI, a peasant boy
JŌTARŌ, a young follower of Musashi
JŪRŌ, one of Hangawara Yajibei's thugs
OBATA KAGENORI, military instructor for the Shōgun
IWAMA KAKUBEI, a vassal of the House of Hosokawa
HON'AMI KŌETSU, an artisan
SASAKI KOJIRŌ, a young samurai
ZUSHINO KŌSUKE, a sword craftsman
KOROKU, one of Hangawara Yajibei's thugs
DATE MASAMUNE, a wealthy lord
HON'IDEN MATAHACHI, childhood friend of Musashi
YAGYŪ MUNENORI, son of Yagyū Sekishūsai and
    samurai of the Shōgun
MIYAMOTO MUSASHI, a swordsman of growing fame
HON'AMI MYŌSHŪ, the mother of Hon'ami Kōetsu
OKŌ, a lascivious woman
HON'IDEN OSUGI, the mother of Matahachi and bitter
    enemy of Musashi
OTSŪ, a young woman in love with Musashi
NAGAOKA SADO, aide to Hosokawa Tadatoshi

Characters and Locales

SEKIGAHARA, battle in which Ieyasu defeated the combined armies of the western daimyō for control of Japan

YAGYŪ SEKISHŪSAI, aging master of the Yagyū style of swordsmanship

HŌJŌ SHINZŌ, student of Obata Kagenori and son of Lord Hōjō Ujikatsu

TAKUAN SŌHŌ, an eccentric monk

KIMURA SUKEKURŌ, a swordsman of the House of Yagyū

HOSOKAWA TADATOSHI, eldest son of Lord Hosokawa Tadaoki

LORD HOSOKAWA TADAOKI, a powerful daimyō, or regional ruler

SHIMMEN TAKEZŌ, former name of Musashi

GION TŌJI, samurai of the Yoshioka school and suitor of Okō

HŌJŌ UJIKATSU, Lord of Awa and a renowned military strategist

HANGAWARA YAJIBEI, a powerful boss in Edo

OBATA YOGORŌ, son of Obata Kagenori

FOREWORD[1]
by Edwin O. Reischauer[2]

Musashi might well be called the *Gone with the Wind* of
Japan. Written by Eiji Yoshikawa (1892–1962), one of
Japan's most prolific and best-loved popular writers, it is
a long historical novel, which first appeared in serialized
form between 1935 and 1939 in the *Asahi Shimbun*,
Japan's largest and most prestigious newspaper. It has
been published in book form no less than fourteen times,
most recently in four volumes of the 53-volume complete
works of Yoshikawa issued by Kodansha. It has been
produced as a film some seven times, has been repeatedly
presented on the stage, and has often been made into
television mini-series on at least three nationwide net-
works.

Miyamoto Musashi was an actual historical person,
but through Yoshikawa's novel he and the other main
characters of the book have become part of Japan's living
folklore. They are so familiar to the public that people
will frequently be compared to them as personalities

---

[1]This foreword has been taken in its entirety from the original single-
volume American hardcover edition of *Musashi: An Epic Novel of
the Samurai Era.*

[2]Edwin O. Reischauer was born in Japan in 1910. He has been a
professor at Harvard University since 1946, and is now Professor
Emeritus. He left the university temporarily to be the United States
Ambassador to Japan from 1961 to 1966, and is one of the best-
known authorities on the country. Among his numerous works are
Japan: The Story of a Nation and *The Japanese.*

everyone knows. This gives the novel an added interest
to the foreign reader. It not only provides a romanticized
slice of Japanese history, but gives a view of how the
Japanese see their past and themselves. But basically the
novel will be enjoyed as a dashing tale of swashbuckling
adventure and a subdued story of love, Japanese style.

Comparisons with James Clavell's *Shōgun* seem inevitable, because for most Americans today *Shōgun*, as
a book and a television mini-series, vies with samurai
movies as their chief source of knowledge about Japan's
past. The two novels concern the same period of history.
Shōgun, which takes place in the year 1600, ends with
Lord Toranaga, who is the historical Tokugawa Ieyasu,
soon to be the Shōgun, or military dictator of Japan,
setting off for the fateful battle of Sekigahara. Yoshikawa's story begins with the youthful Takezō, later to be
renamed Miyamoto Musashi, lying wounded among the
corpses of the defeated army on that battlefield.

With the exception of Blackthorne, the historical
Will Adams, *Shōgun* deals largely with the great lords
and ladies of Japan, who appear in thin disguise under
names Clavell has devised for them. *Musashi*, while
mentioning many great historical figures under their true
names, tells about a broader range of Japanese and particularly about the rather extensive group who lived on
the ill-defined borderline between the hereditary military
aristocracy and the commoners—the peasants, tradesmen and artisans. Clavell freely distorts historical fact to
fit his tale and inserts a Western-type love story that not
only flagrantly flouts history but is quite unimaginable in
the Japan of that time. Yoshikawa remains true to history
or at least to historical tradition, and his love story, which
runs as a background theme in minor scale throughout
the book, is very authentically Japanese.

Yoshikawa, of course, has enriched his account with
much imaginative detail. There are enough strange coin-
cidences and deeds of derring-do to delight the heart of
any lover of adventure stories. But he sticks faithfully to

such facts of history as are known. Not only Musashi himself but many of the other people who figure prominently in the story are real historical individuals. For example, Takuan, who serves as a guiding light and mentor to the youthful Musashi, was a famous Zen monk, calligrapher, painter, poet and tea-master of the time, who became the youngest abbot of the Daitokuji in Kyoto in 1609 and later founded a major monastery in Edo, but is best remembered today for having left his name to a popular Japanese pickle.

The historical Miyamoto Musashi, who may have been born in 1584 and died in 1645, was like his father a master swordsman and became known for his use of two swords. He was an ardent cultivator of self-discipline as the key to martial skills and the author of a famous work on swordsmanship, the *Gorin no sho*. He probably took part as a youth in the battle of Sekigahara, and his clashes with the Yoshioka school of swordsmanship in Kyoto, the warrior monks of the Hōzōin in Nara and the famed swordsman Sasaki Kojirō, all of which figure prominently in this book, actually did take place. Yoshikawa's account of him ends in 1612, when he was still a young man of about 28, but subsequently he may have fought on the losing side at the siege of Osaka castle in 1614 and participated in 1637–38 in the annihilation of the Christian peasantry of Shimabara in the western island of Kyushu, an event which marked the extirpation of that religion from Japan for the next two centuries and helped seal Japan off from the rest of the world.

Ironically, Musashi in 1640 became a retainer of the Hosokawa lords of Kumamoto, who, when they had been the lords of Kumamoto, had been the patrons of his chief rival, Sasaki Kojirō. The Hosokawas bring us back to *Shōgun*, because it was the older Hosokawa, Tadaoki, who figures quite unjustifiably as one of the main villains of that novel, and it was Tadaoki's exemplary Christian wife, Gracia, who is pictured without a shred of plausibility as Blackthorne's great love, Mariko.

Foreword

The time of Musashi's life was a period of great transition in Japan. After a century of incessant warfare among petty daimyō, or feudal lords, three successive leaders had finally reunified the country through conquest. Oda Nobunaga had started the process but, before completing it, had been killed by a treacherous vassal in 1582. His ablest general, Hideyoshi, risen from the rank of common foot soldier, completed the unification of the nation but died in 1598 before he could consolidate control in behalf of his infant heir. Hideyoshi's strongest vassal, Tokugawa Ieyasu, a great daimyō who ruled much of eastern Japan from his castle at Edo, the modern Tokyo, then won supremacy by defeating a coalition of western daimyō at Sekigahara in 1600. Three years later he took the traditional title of Shōgun, signifying his military dictatorship over the whole land, theoretically in behalf of the ancient but impotent imperial line in Kyoto. Ieyasu in 1605 transferred the position of Shōgun to his son, Hidetada, but remained in actual control himself until he had destroyed the supporters of Hideyoshi's heir in sieges of Osaka castle in 1614 and 1615.

The first three Tokugawa rulers established such firm control over Japan that their rule was to last more than two and a half centuries, until it finally collapsed in 1868 in the tumultuous aftermath of the reopening of Japan to contact with the West a decade and a half earlier. The Tokugawa ruled through semi-autonomous hereditary daimyō, who numbered around 265 at the end of the period, and the daimyō in turn controlled their fiefs through their hereditary samurai retainers. The transition from constant warfare to a closely regulated peace brought the drawing of sharp class lines between the samurai, who had the privilege of wearing two swords and bearing family names, and the commoners, who though including well-to-do merchants and land owners, were in theory denied all arms and the honor of using family names.

During the years of which Yoshikawa writes, however, these class divisions were not yet sharply defined. All localities had their residue of peasant fighting men, and the country was overrun by rōnin, or masterless samurai, who were largely the remnants of the armies of the daimyō who had lost their domains as the result of the battle of Sekigahara or in earlier wars. It took a generation or two before society was fully sorted out into the strict class divisions of the Tokugawa system, and in the meantime there was considerable social ferment and mobility.

Another great transition in early seventeenth century Japan was in the nature of leadership. With peace restored and major warfare at an end, the dominant warrior class found that military prowess was less essential to successful rule than administrative talents. The samurai class started a slow transformation from being warriors of the gun and sword to being bureaucrats of the writing brush and paper. Disciplined self-control and education in a society at peace was becoming more important than skill in warfare. The Western reader may be surprised to see how widespread literacy already was at the beginning of the seventeenth century and at the constant references the Japanese made to Chinese history and literature, much as Northern Europeans of the same time continually referred to the traditions of ancient Greece and Rome.

A third major transition in the Japan of Musashi's time was in weaponry. In the second half of the sixteenth century matchlock muskets, recently introduced by the Portuguese, had become the decisive weapons of the battlefield, but in a land at peace the samurai could turn their backs on distasteful firearms and resume their traditional love affair with the sword. Schools of swordsmanship flourished. However, as the chance to use swords in actual combat diminished, martial skills were gradually becoming martial arts, and these increasingly came to emphasize the importance of inner self-control and the character-building qualities of swordsmanship rather than its untested military efficacy. A whole mystique of the sword grew up, which was more akin to philosophy than to warfare.

Yoshikawa's account of Musashi's early life illustrates all these changes going on in Japan. He was himself a typical rōnin from a mountain village and became a settled samurai retainer only late in life. He was the founder of a school of swordsmanship. Most important, he gradually transformed himself from an instinctive fighter into a man who fanatically pursued the goals of Zen-like self-discipline, complete inner mastery over oneself, and a sense of oneness with surrounding nature. Although in his early years lethal contests, reminiscent of the tournaments of medieval Europe, were still possible, Yoshikawa portrays Musashi as consciously turning his martial skills from service in warfare to a means of character building for a time of peace. Martial skills, spiritual self-discipline and aesthetic sensitivity became merged into a single indistinguishable whole. This picture of Musashi may not be far from the historical truth. Musashi is known to have been a skilled painter and an accomplished sculptor as well as a swordsman.

The Japan of the early seventeenth century which Musashi typified has lived on strongly in the Japanese consciousness. The long and relatively static rule of the Tokugawa preserved much of its forms and spirit, though in somewhat ossified form, until the middle of the nineteenth century, not much more than a century ago. Yoshikawa himself was a son of a former samurai who failed like most members of his class to make a successful economic transition to the new age. Though the samurai themselves largely sank into obscurity in the new Japan, most of the new leaders were drawn from this feudal class, and its ethos was popularized through the new compulsory educational system to become the spiritual background and ethics of the whole Japanese nation. Novels like *Musashi* and the films and plays derived from them aided in the process.

Foreword

The time of Musashi is as close and real to the modern Japanese as is the Civil War to Americans. Thus the comparison to *Gone with the Wind* is by no means far-fetched. The age of the samurai is still very much alive in Japanese minds. Contrary to the picture of the modern Japanese as merely group oriented "economic animals," many Japanese prefer to see themselves as fiercely individualistic, high-principled, self-disciplined and aesthetically sensitive modern-day Musashis. Both pictures have some validity, illustrating the complexity of the Japanese soul behind the seemingly bland and uniform exterior.

Musashi is very different from the highly psychological and often neurotic novels that have been the mainstay of translations of modern Japanese literature into English. But it is nevertheless fully in the mainstream of traditional Japanese fiction and popular Japanese thought. Its episodic presentation is not merely the result of its original appearance as a newspaper serial but is a favorite technique dating back to the beginnings of Japanese storytelling. Its romanticized view of the noble swordsman is a stereotype of the feudal past enshrined in hundreds of other stories and samurai movies. Its emphasis on the cultivation of self-control and inner personal strength through austere Zen-like self-discipline is a major feature of Japanese personality today. So also is the pervading love of nature and sense of closeness to it. *Musashi* is not just a great adventure story. Beyond that, it gives both a glimpse into Japanese history and a view into the idealized self-image of the contemporary Japanese.

January 1981

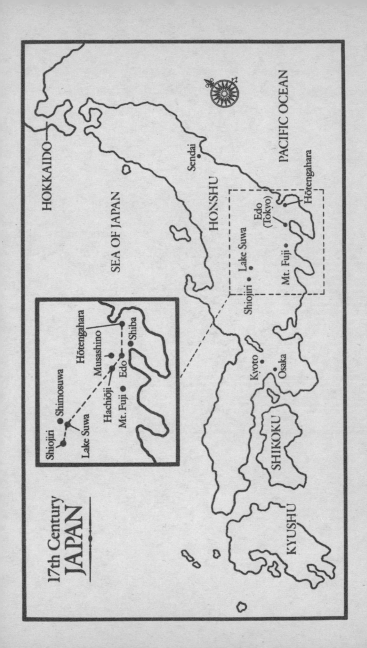

17th Century JAPAN

HOKKAIDO

SEA OF JAPAN

HONSHU

Sendai

PACIFIC OCEAN

Edo (Tokyo)

Hōtengahara

Lake Suwa

Shiojiri

Mt. Fuji

Kyoto

Osaka

SHIKOKU

KYUSHU

Shiojiri

Shimosuwa

Lake Suwa

Hōtengahara

Musashino

Shiba

Hachiōji

Mt. Fuji

Edo

1

A One-Night Love Affair

Musashi's injury was painful, so instead of spending time in Kamisuwa to make inquiries about Otsū and Jōtarō, he went on to the hot springs at Shimosuwa. This town, on the banks of Lake Suwa, was quite a large one, with the houses of ordinary townsmen alone numbering over a thousand.

At the inn designated for use by daimyō, the bath was covered by a roof, but otherwise the pools situated along the roadside were open to the sky and available to anyone who wanted to use them.

Musashi hung his clothes and swords on a tree and eased himself into the steaming water. As he massaged the swelling on the right side of his abdomen, he rested his head against a rock on the edge of the pool, closed his eyes and savored a groggy, pleasurable sense of well-being. The sun was beginning to set, and a reddish mist rose from the surface of the lake, which he could see between the fishermen's houses along the shore.

A couple of small vegetable plots lay between the pool and the road, where people and horses were coming and going with the usual noise and bustle. At a shop selling lamp oil and sundries, a samurai was purchasing straw sandals. Having selected a suitable pair, he sat

1

down on a stool, took off his old ones and tied the new ones on.

"You must have heard about it," he said to the shopkeeper. "It happened under the great spreading pine at Ichijōji near Kyoto. This rōnin took on the entire House of Yoshioka all by himself and fought with a spirit you rarely hear about anymore. I'm sure he passed this way. Are you certain you didn't see him?"

For all his eagerness, the samurai seemed to know little about the man he was looking for, neither his age nor how he might be dressed. Disappointed when he received a negative reply, he repeated, "I must find him somehow," two or three times while he finished tying his sandals.

The samurai, a man of about forty, was well dressed and sunburned from traveling. The hair at his temples stood out around the cords of his basket hat, and the toughness in his facial expression matched his manly build. Musashi suspected his body bore the marks and calluses that come from wearing armor. "I don't remember ever seeing him before," he thought. "But if he's going around talking about the Yoshioka School, maybe he's one of their students. The school's had so many students, a few must have some backbone. They may be hatching another plot for revenge."

When the man had completed his business and left, Musashi dried himself and put on his clothes, thinking the coast was clear. But when he walked out onto the highroad, he almost bumped into him.

The samurai bowed and, looking intently into his face, said, "Aren't you Miyamoto Musashi?"

Musashi nodded, and the samurai, ignoring the suspicion written on his face, said, "I knew it." After a short paean to his own perspicacity, he continued familiarly, "You can't know how happy I am to meet you at last. I've had the feeling I'd run into you somewhere along the way." Without pausing to give Musashi a chance to speak, he urged him to spend the night at the same inn with him. "Let me assure you," he added, "you don't have to worry about me. My status, if you'll forgive me for saying so, is such that I usually travel with a dozen attendants and a change of horses. I'm a retainer of Date Masamune, the lord of Aoba Castle in Mutsu. My name is Ishimoda Geki."

When Musashi passively accepted the invitation, Geki decided they would stay at the inn for daimyō and led him into the place.

"How about a bath?" he asked. "But of course, you've just had one. Well, make yourself comfortable while I take one. I'll be back shortly." He took off his traveling clothes, picked up a towel and left the room.

Though the man had a winning way about him, Musashi's head was full of questions. Why would this well-placed warrior be looking for him? Why was he being so friendly?

"Wouldn't you like to change into something more comfortable?" asked the maid, proffering one of the cotton-stuffed kimonos furnished to guests.

"No, thank you. I'm not sure I'll be staying."

Musashi stepped out onto the veranda. Behind him he heard the maid quietly setting the dinner trays. As he watched the ripples on the lake change from deep indigo to black, the image of Otsū's sad eyes formed in his mind. "I suppose I'm not looking in the right place," he thought. "Anyone evil enough to kidnap a woman certainly has the instinct to avoid towns." He seemed to hear Otsū calling for help. Was it really all right to take the philosophic view that all things happen as a result of heaven's will? Standing there doing nothing, he felt guilty.

Coming back from his bath, Ishimoda Geki apologized for having left him alone and sat down before his dinner tray. Noticing that Musashi still wore his own kimono, he asked, "Why don't you change?"

"I'm comfortable in what I have on. I wear this all

3

the time—on the road, inside the house, when I sleep on the ground under the trees.''

Geki was favorably impressed. "I might have known," he said. "You want to be ready for action at any time, no matter where you are. Lord Date would admire that." He stared with unconcealed fascination at Musashi's face, which was lit from the side by the lamp. Remembering himself after a moment, he said, "Come. Sit down and have some sake." He rinsed off a cup in a bowl of water and offered it to Musashi.

Musashi seated himself and bowed. Resting his hands on his knees, he asked, "Could you tell me, sir, why you're treating me in such a friendly manner? And if you don't mind, why you were inquiring about me out on the highroad.''

"I suppose it's only natural for you to wonder, but there's really very little to explain. Perhaps the simplest way to put it is that I have a sort of crush on you." He paused for a moment, laughed and went on. "Yes, it's a matter of infatuation, a case of one man being attracted to another.''

Geki seemed to feel this was sufficient explanation, but Musashi was more mystified than ever. While it did not seem impossible for one man to be enamored of another, he himself had never experienced such an attachment. Takuan was too severe to inspire strong affection. Kōetsu lived in an entirely different world. Sekishūsai occupied a plane so far above Musashi's that either liking or disliking was inconceivable. Though it could be Geki's way of flattering him, a man who made such statements opened himself to the charge of insincerity. Still, Musashi doubted that this samurai was a sycophant; he was too solid, too manly in appearance, for that.

"Precisely what do you mean," Musashi asked with a sober air, "when you say you are attracted to me?"

"Perhaps I'm being presumptuous, but ever since I heard of your feat at Ichijōji, I've been convinced that you're a man I would like, and like very much.''

"Were you in Kyoto then?"

"Yes, I arrived during the first month of the year and was staying at Lord Date's residence on Sanjō Avenue. When I happened to drop in on Lord Karasumaru Mitsuhiro the day after the fight, I heard quite a bit about you. He said he'd met you and remarked on your youth and what you'd been doing in the past. Feeling this strong attraction, I resolved that I must make an effort to meet you. On my way from Kyoto, I saw the sign you put up at Shiojiri Pass."

"Oh, you saw that?" Ironic, thought Musashi, that instead of bringing him Jōtarō, the sign had brought him someone of whose existence he had never dreamed.

But the more he considered the matter, the less he felt he deserved the esteem in which Geki seemed to hold him. Painfully conscious of his own mistakes and failures, he found Geki's adulation embarrassing.

With perfect honesty, he said, "I think you're rating me too highly."

"There are a number of outstanding samurai serving under Lord Date—his fief has an income of five million bushels, you know—and in time I've met many a skilled swordsman. But from what I've heard, it would seem that few can be compared with you. What's more, you're still very young. You have your whole future before you. And that, I suppose, is why you appeal to me. Anyway, now that I've found you, let's be friends. Have a drink, and talk about anything that interests you."

Musashi accepted the sake cup in good humor and began matching his host drink for drink. Before long, his face was bright red.

Geki, still going strong, said, "We samurai from the north can drink a lot. We do it to stay warm. Lord Date can outdrink any of us. With a strong general in the lead, it wouldn't do for the troops to fall behind."

The maid kept bringing more sake. Even after she'd trimmed the lamp wick several times, Geki showed no inclination to stop. "Let's drink all night," he suggested. "That way, we can talk all night."

"Fine," agreed Musashi. Then, with a smile: "You said you'd talked to Lord Karasumaru. Do you know him well?"

"You couldn't say we're close friends, but over the years I've been to his house any number of times on errands. He's very friendly, you know."

"Yes, I met him on the introduction of Hon'ami Kōetsu. For a nobleman, he seemed remarkably full of life."

Looking somewhat dissatisfied, Geki asked, "Is that your own impression? If you'd talked with him at any length, I'd think you'd have been struck by his intelligence and sincerity."

"Well, we were in the licensed quarter at the time."

"In that case, I suppose he refrained from revealing his true self."

"What's he really like?"

Geki settled himself in more formal fashion and in a rather grave tone said, "He's a troubled man. A man of sorrows, if you will. The shogunate's dictatorial ways disturb him greatly."

For a moment, Musashi was conscious of a lilting sound coming from the lake and the shadows cast by the white light of the lamp.

Abruptly Geki asked, "Musashi, my friend, for whose sake are you trying to perfect your swordsmanship?"

Never having considered the question, Musashi replied with guileless candor, "For my own."

"That's all right as far as it goes, but for whose sake are you trying to improve yourself? Surely your aim is not merely personal honor and glory. That's hardly sufficient for a man of your stature." By accident or design, Geki had come around to the subject he really wanted to talk about. "Now that the whole country's under Ieyasu's control," he declared, "we have a semblance of

6

peace and prosperity. But is it real? Can the people actually live happily under the present system?

"Over the centuries, we've had the Hōjōs, the Ashikagas, Oda Nobunaga, Hideyoshi—a long string of military rulers consistently oppressing not only the people but the Emperor and the court as well. The imperial government has been taken advantage of, and the people mercilessly exploited. All the benefits have gone to the military class. This has been going on since Minamoto no Yoritomo, hasn't it? And the situation today is unchanged.

"Nobunaga seems to have had some idea of the injustice involved; at least he built a new palace for the Emperor. Hideyoshi not only honored the Emperor Go-Yōzei by requiring all the daimyō to pay obeisance to him, but even tried to provide a measure of welfare and happiness for the common people. But what of Ieyasu? To all intents and purposes, he has no interest beyond the fortunes of his own clan. So again, the happiness of the people and the well-being of the imperial family are being sacrificed to create wealth and power for a military dictatorship. We seem to be at the threshold of another age of tyranny. No one worries about this state of affairs more than Lord Date Masamune or, among the nobility, Lord Karasumaru."

Geki paused, waiting for a response, but none was forthcoming except for a barely articulate, "I see."

Like anyone else, Musashi was aware of the drastic political changes that had occurred since the Battle of Sekigahara. Yet he had never paid any attention to activities of the daimyō in the Osaka faction, or the ulterior motives of the Tokugawas, or the stands taken by powerful outside lords like Date and Shimazu. All he knew about Date was that his fief officially had an income of three million bushels per year but in fact probably yielded five million, as Geki had mentioned.

"Twice every year," Geki went on, "Lord Date sends produce from our fief to Lord Konoe in Kyoto for presentation to the Emperor. He's never failed to do this, even in times of war. That's why I was in Kyoto.

"Aoba Castle is the only one in the country to have a special room reserved for the Emperor. It's unlikely, of course, that it'll ever be used, but Lord Date set it aside for him anyway, built it out of wood taken from the old Imperial Palace when that was rebuilt. He had the wood brought from Kyoto to Sendai by boat.

"And let me tell you about the war in Korea. During the campaigns there, Katō, Konishi and other generals were competing for personal fame and triumph. Not Lord Date. Instead of his own family crest, he wore the crest of the rising sun and told everyone he'd never have led his men to Korea for the glory of his own clan or for that of Hideyoshi. He went out of love for Japan itself."

While Musashi listened attentively, Geki became absorbed in his monologue, describing his master in glowing terms and assuring Musashi that he was unexcelled in his single-minded devotion to the nation and the Emperor.

For a time he forgot about drinking but then suddenly looked down and said, "The sake's cold." Clapping his hands for the maid, he was about to order more.

Musashi hurriedly interrupted. "I've had more than enough. If you don't mind, I'd rather have some rice and tea now."

"Already?" mumbled Geki. He was obviously disappointed but, out of deference to his guest, told the girl to bring the rice.

Geki continued to talk as they ate. The impression Musashi formed of the spirit that seemed to prevail among the samurai of Lord Date's fief was that, as individuals and as a group, they were vitally concerned with the Way of the Samurai and with the problem of disciplining themselves in accordance with the Way.

This Way had existed since ancient times, when the warrior class had come into being, but its moral values and obligations were now little more than a vague memory. During the chaotic domestic strife of the fifteenth and sixteenth centuries, the ethics of the military man had been distorted, if not totally ignored, and now almost anyone who could wield a sword or shoot an arrow from a bow was regarded as a samurai, regardless of the attention—or lack of it—given to the deeper meaning of the Way.

The self-styled samurai of the day were often men of lower character and baser instincts than common peasants or townsmen. Having nothing but brawn and technique to command the respect of those beneath them, they were in the long run doomed to destruction. There were few daimyō capable of seeing this, and only a handful of the higher vassals of the Tokugawas and the Toyotomis gave any thought to establishing a new Way of the Samurai, which could become the foundation of the nation's strength and prosperity.

Musashi's thoughts returned to the years when he had been confined in Himeji Castle. Takuan, remembering that Lord Ikeda had in his library a handwritten copy of *Nichiyō Shūshin-kan* by Fushikian, had taken it out for Musashi to study. Fushikian was the literary name of the celebrated general Uesugi Kenshin; in his book, he recorded points of daily ethical training for the guidance of his chief vassals. From this, Musashi had not only learned about Kenshin's personal activities but also gained an understanding of why Kenshin's fief in Echigo had come to be known throughout the country for its wealth and military prowess.

Swayed by Geki's enthusiastic descriptions, he began to feel that Lord Date, besides equaling Kenshin in integrity, had created in his domain an atmosphere in which samurai were encouraged to develop a new Way, one that would enable them to resist even the shogunate, should that become necessary.

"You must forgive me for going on and on about matters of personal interest," said Geki. "What do you think, Musashi? Wouldn't you like to come to Sendai, see for yourself? His lordship is honest and straightforward. If you're striving to find the Way, your present status doesn't matter to him. You can talk with him as you would with any other man.

"There's a great need for samurai who will devote their lives to their country. I'll be more than happy to recommend you. If it's all right with you, we can go to Sendai together."

By this time the dinner trays had been removed, but Geki's ardor was in no way diminished. Impressed, but still cautious, Musashi replied, "I'll have to give it some thought before I can reply."

After they had said good night, Musashi went to his room, where he lay awake in the dark, his eyes glistening.

The Way of the Samurai. He concentrated on this concept as it applied to himself and to his sword.

Suddenly he saw the truth: the techniques of a swordsman were not his goal; he sought an all-embracing Way of the Sword. The sword was to be far more than a simple weapon; it had to be an answer to life's questions. The Way of Uesugi Kenshin and Date Masamune was too narrowly military, too hidebound. It would be up to him to add to its human aspect, to give it greater profundity, greater loftiness.

For the first time, he asked whether it was possible for an insignificant human being to become one with the universe.

2

A Gift of Money

Musashi's first waking thought was of Otsū and Jōtarō, and though he and Geki carried on a convivial conversation over breakfast, the problem of how to find them was very much on his mind. After emerging from the inn, he unconsciously scrutinized every face he encountered on the highroad. Once or twice he thought he saw Otsū ahead, only to find he was mistaken.

"You seem to be looking for someone," said Geki.

"I am. My companions and I got separated along the way, and I'm worried about them. I think I'd better give up the idea of going to Edo with you and search some of the other roads."

Disappointed, Geki said, "That's too bad. I was looking forward to traveling with you. I hope the fact that I talked too much last night won't change your mind about visiting Sendai."

Geki's manner, straightforward and masculine, appealed to Musashi. "That's very kind of you," he said. "I hope I have the chance someday."

"I want you to see for yourself how our samurai conduct themselves. And if you're not interested in that, then just regard it as a sightseeing trip. You can listen to the local songs and visit Matsushima. It's famous for its scenery, you know.'' Geki took his leave and headed briskly for Wada Pass.

Musashi turned around and went back to where the Kōshū highroad branched off from the Nakasendō. As he stood there mapping out his strategy, a group of day laborers from Suwa come up to him. Their dress suggested they were porters or grooms or bearers of the primitive palanquins used in these parts. They approached slowly, arms folded, looking like an army of crabs.

As their eyes rudely sized him up, one of them said, ''Sir, you seem to be looking for someone. A beautiful lady, is it, or only a servant?''

Musashi shook his head, waved them off with a slightly disdainful gesture and turned away. He did not know whether to go east or west, but finally made up his mind to spend the day seeing what he could find out in the neighborhood. If his inquiries led nowhere, he could then proceed to the shōgun's capital with a clear conscience.

One of the laborers broke in upon his thoughts. ''If you're looking for somebody, we could help you,'' he said. ''It's better than standing around under the hot sun. What does your friend look like?''

Another added, ''We won't even set a rate for our services. We'll leave it up to you.''

Musashi relented to the extent of describing Otsū and Jōtarō in detail.

After consulting with his fellows, the first man said, ''We haven't seen them, but if we split up we're sure to find them. The kidnappers must've taken one of the three roads between Suwa and Shiojiri. You don't know this area, but we do.''

None too optimistic about his chances of success in such difficult terrain, Musashi said, ''All right, go look for them.''

''Done,'' shouted the men.

Again they huddled, ostensibly deciding who was to

go where. Then the ringleader came forward, rubbing his hands together deferentially. "There's just one little thing, sir. You see . . . I don't like to mention it, but we're just penniless laborers. Why, not one of us has had anything to eat yet today. Wonder if you couldn't advance us half a day's pay and, say, a little something extra. I guarantee we'll find your companions before sundown."

"Of course. I was planning to give you something."

The man named a figure, which Musashi found, after counting his money, was more than he had. He was not unmindful of the value of money, but being alone, with no one to support, his attitude was on the whole indifferent. Friends and admirers sometimes donated travel funds, and there were temples where he could often obtain free lodging. At other times, he slept in the open or went without ordinary food. One way or another, he had always managed to get by.

On this trip, he had left the finances to Otsū, who had received a sizable gift of travel money from Lord Karasumaru. She had been paying the bills and giving him a certain amount of spending money each morning, as any ordinary housewife might do.

Keeping only a little for himself, he distributed the rest of his money among the men, and though they'd expected more, they agreed to undertake the search as a "special favor."

"Wait for us by the two-story gate of the Suwa Myōjin Shrine," the spokesman advised. "By evening we'll be back with some news." They made off in several directions.

Rather than waste the day doing nothing, Musashi went to see Takashima Castle and the town of Shimosuwa, stopping here and there to note features of the local topography, which might come in handy at some future date, and to observe the methods of irrigation. He asked several times whether there were any outstanding military experts in the area, but heard nothing of interest.

As sundown drew near, he went to the shrine and sat down, tired and dispirited, on the stone stairway leading up to the two-story gate. No one showed up, so he took a turn around the spacious shrine grounds. But when he returned to the gate, there was still no one there.

Though not loud, the sound of horses stamping the ground began to get on his nerves. Descending the steps, he came upon a shed, obscured by the trees, where an ancient horsekeeper was feeding the shrine's sacred white horse.

He glanced at Musashi accusingly. "Can I help you?" he asked brusquely. "Do you have some business with the shrine?"

Upon hearing why Musashi was there, he broke out in uncontrollable laughter. Musashi, seeing nothing at all funny about his predicament, made no attempt to conceal a scowl. Before he spoke, however, the old man said, "You've no business being on the road by yourself. You're too innocent. Did you really believe roadside vermin would spend the whole day looking for your friends? If you paid them in advance, you'll never see them again."

"You mean you think they were just putting on an act when they divided up and left?"

The horsekeeper's expression changed to one of sympathy. "You've been robbed!" he said. "I heard there were about ten vagrants drinking and gambling in the grove on the other side of the mountain all day today. They're most likely the ones. These things happen all the time." He went on to tell some stories of travelers being cheated out of their money by unscrupulous laborers, but concluded mildly, "That's the way the world is. You'd better be more careful from now on."

With this sage advice, he picked up his empty pail and departed, leaving Musashi feeling foolish. "It's too late to do anything now," he sighed. "I pride myself on my ability not to give my opponent any opening, and then get taken in by a gang of illiterate workmen!" This evidence of his gullibility came like a slap in the face. Such lapses could easily muddy his practice of the Art of War. How could a man so easily deceived by his inferiors effectively command an army? As he climbed slowly toward the gate, he resolved to henceforth pay more attention to the ways of the world about him.

One of the laborers was peering around in the dark, and as soon as he caught sight of Musashi, he called to him and ran partway down the steps.

"Glad I found you, sir," he said. "I've got news about one of the people you're looking for."

"Oh?" Musashi, having just reprimanded himself for his naiveté, was astonished but gratified to know that not everyone in the world was a swindler. "By one of them, do you mean the boy or the woman?"

"The boy. He's with Daizō of Narai, and I've found out where Daizō is, or at least where he's headed."

"Where might that be?"

"I didn't think that bunch I was with this morning would do what they promised. They took the day off to gamble, but I felt sorry for you. I went from Shiojiri to Seba, asking everybody I ran into. Nobody knew anything about the girl, but I heard from the maid at the inn where I ate that Daizō passed through Suwa about noon today on his way to Wada Pass. She said he had a young boy with him."

Embarrassed, Musashi said rather formally, "It was good of you to let me know." He took out his money pouch, knowing it contained only enough for his own meal. He hesitated a moment, but reflecting that honesty should not go unrewarded, gave the laborer his last bit of cash.

Pleased with the tip, the man raised the money to his forehead in a gesture of thanks and went happily on his way.

Watching his money go down the road, Musashi felt he had used it for a purpose worthier than that of filling his stomach. Perhaps the laborer, having learned that right conduct can be profitable, would go out on the road the next day and help another traveler.

It was already dark, but he decided that instead of sleeping under the eves of some peasant's house, he would cross Wada Pass. By traveling all night, he should be able to catch up with Daizō. He started off, savoring once again the satisfaction of being on a deserted road at night. Something about it appealed to his nature. Counting his footsteps, listening to the silent voice of the heavens above, he could forget everything and rejoice in his own being. When he was surrounded by crowds of busy people, his spirit often seemed sad and isolated, but now he felt alive and buoyant. He could think about life coolly and objectively, even appraise himself as he might appraise a total stranger.

A little after midnight, his musings were distracted by a light in the distance. He had been climbing steadily since crossing the bridge over the Ochiai River. One pass was behind him; the next one, at Wada, loomed up in the starry sky ahead, and beyond that the even higher crossing at Daimon. The light was in a hollow that ran parallel to the two ridges.

"It looks like a bonfire," he thought, feeling pangs of hunger for the first time in hours. "Maybe they'll let me dry off my sleeves, give me a bit of gruel or something."

As he drew near, he saw that it wasn't an outdoor fire but the light from a small roadside teahouse. There were four or five stakes for tying horses, but no horses. It seemed incredible that there would be anyone in such a place at this hour, yet he could hear the sound of raucous voices mingling with the crackling of the fire. He stood hesitantly under the eaves for a few minutes. If it had been a farmer's or a woodcutter's hut, he would have had no qualms about asking for shelter and some leftovers, but this was a place of business.

The smell of food made him hungrier than ever. The warm smoke enveloped him; he could not tear himself away. "Well, if I explain my situation to them, maybe they'll accept the statue as payment." The "statue" was the small image of Kannon he had carved from the wood of an ancient plum tree.

When he barged into the shop, the startled customers stopped talking. The interior was simple, a dirt floor with a hearth and fire hood in the middle, around which huddled three men on stools. Stewing in a pot was a mixture of boar's meat and giant radish. A jar of sake was warming in the ashes. Standing with his back to them, slicing pickles and chatting good-naturedly, was the proprietor.

"What do you want?" asked one of the customers, a keen-eyed man with long sideburns.

Too hungry to hear, Musashi passed by the men and, seating himself on the edge of a stool, said to the proprietor, "Give me something to eat, quick. Rice and pickles'll do. Anything."

The man poured some of the stew over a bowl of cold rice and set it before him. "Are you planning to cross the pass tonight?" he asked.

"Um," mumbled Musashi, who had already seized some chopsticks and was attacking the food with gusto. After his second mouthful, he asked, "Do you know if a man named Daizō—he comes from Narai—passed here this afternoon, going toward the pass? He has a young boy with him."

"I'm afraid I can't help you." Then, to the other men, "Tōji, did you or your friends see an older man traveling with a boy?"

After a bit of whispering, the three replied in the negative, shaking their heads in unison.

Musashi, filled and warmed by the hot food, began to worry about the bill. He'd hesitated discussing it with the proprietor first, due to the presence of the other men, but he didn't for a moment feel he was begging. It had simply seemed more important to tend to his stomach's

THE BUSHIDO CODE

needs first. He made up his mind that if the shopkeeper would not accept the statue, he'd offer him his dagger.

"I'm sorry to have to tell you this," he began, "but I don't have any cash at all. I'm not asking for a free meal, mind you. I have something here to offer in payment, if you'll take it."

With unexpected amiability, the proprietor replied, "I'm sure that'll be all right. What is it?"

"A statue of Kannon."

"A real statue?"

"Oh, it's not the work of a famous sculptor—just something I carved myself. It may not be worth even the price of a bowl of rice, but take a look at it anyway."

As he began untying the cords of his bag, the one he had carried for years, the three men left off drinking and focused their attention on his hands. Besides the statue, the bag contained a single change of underwear and a writing set. When he emptied out the contents, something fell with a clunk to the ground. The others gasped, for the object that lay at Musashi's feet was a money pouch, from which several gold and silver coins had spilled out. Musashi himself stared in speechless amazement.

"Where did that come from?" he wondered.

The other men craned their necks to gape at the treasure.

Feeling something else in the bag, Musashi pulled out a letter. It consisted of a single line, saying, "This should take care of your travel expenses for the time being," and was signed "Geki."

Musashi had a pretty clear idea of what it meant: it was Geki's way of trying to buy his services for Lord Date Masamune of Sendai and Aoba Castle. The increasing probability of a final clash between the Tokugawas and the Toyotomis made it imperative for the great daimyō to maintain sizable numbers of able fighters. A favorite method used in the cutthroat competition for the few really outstanding samurai was to attempt to get such

18

men in debt, even for a small sum, and then forge a tacit agreement for future cooperation.

It was common knowledge that Toyotomi Hideyori was providing large sums of money to Gotō Matabei and Sanada Yukimura. Though Yukimura was ostensibly in retirement on Mount Kudo, so much gold and silver was being sent to him from Osaka Castle that Ieyasu had undertaken a full-scale investigation. Since the personal requirements of a retired general living in a hermitage were fairly modest, it was all but certain that the money was being passed on to several thousand indigent rōnin, who were idling away their time in nearby towns and cities waiting for the outbreak of hostilities.

Finding an able warrior, as Geki believed he had, and somehow enticing him into his lord's service was one of the most valuable services a retainer could perform. And it was for just this reason that Musashi had no interest in Geki's money: using it would incur an unwanted obligation. In a matter of seconds, he decided to ignore the gift, to pretend it did not exist.

Without a word he reached down, picked up the pouch and restored it to his bag. Addressing the proprietor as though nothing had happened, he said, "All right then, I'll leave the statue here in payment."

But the man balked. "I can't accept that now, sir!"

"Is there something wrong with it? I don't claim to be a sculptor, but—"

"Oh, it's not bad, and I would have taken it if you didn't have any money, like you said, but you've got plenty. Why do you throw your cash around for people to see if you want them to think you're broke?"

The other customers, sobered and thrilled by the sight of the gold, vigorously nodded their agreement. Musashi, recognizing the futility of arguing that the money was not his, took out a piece of silver and handed it to the man.

"This is far too much, sir," complained the proprietor. "Don't you have anything smaller?"

A cursory examination revealed some variation in the worth of the pieces, but nothing less valuable. "Don't worry about the change," Musashi said. "You can keep it."

No longer able to maintain the fiction that the money didn't exist, Musashi tucked the pouch into his stomach wrapper for safekeeping.

Then, despite urgings to linger awhile, he shouldered his pack and went out into the night. Having eaten and restored his strength, he calculated that he could make it to Daimon Pass by sunrise. By day, he would have seen around him an abundance of highland flowers—rhododendrons, gentians, wild chrysanthemums—but at night there in the immense sea of darkness he could see only a cottonlike mist clinging to the earth.

He was about two miles from the teahouse when one of the men he'd seen there hailed him, saying, "Wait! You forgot something." Catching up with Musashi, the man puffed, "My, you walk fast! After you left, I found this money, so I brought it to you. It must be yours."

He held out a piece of silver, which Musashi refused, saying it certainly wasn't his. The man insisted that it was. "It must have rolled into the corner when you dropped your money pouch."

Not having counted the money, Musashi was in no position to prove the man wrong. With a word of thanks, he took the silver and put it in his kimono sleeve. Yet for some reason he found himself unmoved by this display of honesty.

Though the man's errand had been completed, he fell in alongside Musashi and began making small talk.

"Perhaps I shouldn't ask, but are you studying swordsmanship under a well-known teacher?"

"No. I use my own style."

The perfunctory answer failed to discourage the man, who declared that he had been a samurai himself, adding, "But for the time being I'm reduced to living here in the mountains."

"Is that so?"

"Um. Those two back there too. We were all samurai. Now we make our living cutting trees and gathering herbs. We're like the proverbial dragon biding its time in a pond. I can't pretend to be Sano Genzaemon, but when the time comes, I'll grab my old sword and put on my threadbare armor and go fight for some famous daimyō. I'm just waiting for that day to come!"

"Are you for Osaka or Edo?"

"Doesn't matter. The main thing is to be on somebody's side, or else I'll waste my life hanging around here."

Musashi laughed politely. "Thanks for bringing the money."

Then, in an effort to lose the man, he started taking long, rapid strides. The man stayed right beside him, step for step. He also kept pressing in on Musashi's left side, an encroachment that any experienced swordsman would regard as suspicious. Rather than reveal his wariness, however, Musashi did nothing to protect his left side, leaving it wide open.

The man became increasingly friendly. "May I make a suggestion? If you'd like, why don't you come spend the night at our place? After Wada Pass, you've still got Daimon ahead of you. You might make it by morning, but it's very steep—a difficult road for a man not familiar with these parts."

"Thanks. I think I'll take you up on that."

"You should, you should. Only thing is, we don't have anything to offer in the way of food or entertainment."

"I'd be happy to have a place to lie down. Where is your house?"

"About a half mile off to the left and a little higher up."

"You really are deep in the mountains, aren't you?"

"As I said, until the proper time comes, we're lying

21

low, gathering herbs, hunting, doing things like that. I share a house with the other two men.''

"Now that you mention it, what became of them?''

"They're probably still drinking. Every time we go there, they get drunk, and I wind up lugging them home. Tonight I decided to just leave them. . . . Watch out! There's a sharp drop there—stream down below. It's dangerous.''

"Do we cross the stream?''

"Yes. It's narrow here, and there's a log across it just below us. After we cross, we turn right and climb up along the riverbank.''

Musashi sensed that the man had stopped walking, but he did not look back. He found the log and started across. A moment later, the man leaped forward and lifted the end of the log in an attempt to throw Musashi into the stream.

"What are you up to?''

The shout came from below, but the man jerked his head upward in astonishment. Musashi, having anticipated his treacherous move, had already jumped from the log and lit as lightly as a wagtail on a large rock. His startled attacker dropped the log into the stream. Before the curtain of flying water had fallen back to earth, Musashi had jumped back onto the bank, sword unsheathed, and cut his assailant down. It all happened so quickly that the man did not even see Musashi draw.

The corpse wriggled for a moment or two before subsiding into stillness. Musashi did not deign to give it a glance. He had already taken a new stance in preparation for the next attack, for he was sure there would be one. As he steeled himself for it, his hair stood up like an eagle's crown feathers.

A short silence ensued, followed by a boom loud enough to split the gorge asunder. The gunshot seemed to have come from somewhere on the other side. Musashi dodged, and the well-aimed slug hissed through the space he had been occupying, burying itself in the embankment behind him. Falling as though wounded, Musashi looked across to the opposite side, where he saw red sparks flying through the air like so many fireflies. He could just make out two figures creeping cautiously forward.

3

A Cleansing Fire

Clenching his teeth tightly on the sputtering fuse, the man made ready to fire his musket again. His confederate crouched down, and squinting into the distance, whispered, "Do you think it's safe?"

"I'm sure I got him with the first shot," came the confident reply.

The two crept cautiously forward, but no sooner had they reached the edge of the bank than Musashi jumped up. The musketeer gasped and fired but lost his balance, sending the bullet uselessly skyward. As the echo reverberated through the ravine, both men, the other two from the teahouse, fled up the path.

Suddenly one of them stopped in his tracks and roared, "Wait! What are we running for? There's two of us and only one of him. I'll take him on and you can back me up."

"I'm with you!" shouted the musketeer, letting go of the fuse and aiming the butt of his weapon at Musashi.

They were definitely a cut above ordinary hoodlums. The man Musashi took to be the leader wielded his sword with genuine finesse; nonetheless, he was a poor match for Musashi, who sent them both flying through the air with a single sword stroke. The musketeer, sliced from shoulder to waist, fell dead to the ground, his upper torso hanging over the bank as if by a thread. The other man sped up the slope, clutching a wounded forearm, with Musashi in hot pursuit. Showers of dirt and gravel rose and fell in his wake.

The ravine, Buna Valley, lay midway between Wada and Daimon passes and took its name from the beech trees that seemed to fill it. On its highest point stood an exceptionally large mountaineer's cabin surrounded by trees and itself crudely fashioned of beech logs.

Scrambling rapidly toward the tiny flame of a torch, the bandit shouted, "Douse the lights!"

Protecting the flame with an outstretched sleeve, a woman exclaimed, "Why, you— Oh! You're covered with blood!"

"Sh-shut up, you fool! Put out the lights—the ones inside too." He could hardly get the words out from panting, and with a last look behind him, he hurtled past her. The woman blew out the torch and rushed after him.

By the time Musashi arrived at the cabin, not a trace of light was visible anywhere.

"Open up!" he bellowed. He was indignant, not for being taken to be a fool, nor because of the cowardly attack, but because men like these daily inflicted great harm on innocent travelers.

He might have broken open the wooden rain shutters, but rather than make a frontal attack, which would have left his back dangerously exposed, he cautiously kept at a distance of four or five feet.

"Open up!"

Getting no answer, he picked up the largest rock he could handle and hurled it at the shutters. It struck the crack between the two panels, sending both the man and the woman reeling into the house. A sword flew out from beneath them and was followed by the man crawling on his knees. He quickly regained his feet and retreated into the house. Musashi bounded forward and seized him by the back of his kimono.

"Don't kill me! I'm sorry!" pleaded Gion Tōji, his whining tone exactly that of a petty crook.

He was soon back on his feet again, trying to find Musashi's weak point. Musashi parried each of his moves, but when he pressed forward to hem in his opponent, Tōji, mustering all his strength, pulled his short sword and made a powerful thrust. Dodging adroitly, Musashi swept him up in his arms and with a cry of contempt sent him crashing into the next room. Either an arm or a leg struck the pot hanger, for the bamboo pole from which it hung broke with a loud crack. White ashes billowed up from the hearth like a volcanic cloud.

A barrage of missiles coming through the smoke and ashes kept Musashi at bay. As the ashes settled, he saw that his adversary was no longer the bandits' chief, who was flat on his back near the wall. The woman, between curses, was throwing everything she could lay her hands on—pot lids, kindling, metal chopsticks, tea bowls.

Musashi leapt forward and quickly pinned her to the floor, but she managed to pull a bodkin from her hair and take a stab at him. When he brought his foot down on her wrist, she gnashed her teeth, then cried out in anger and disgust at the unconscious Tōji, "Haven't you any pride? How can you lose to a nobody like this?"

Hearing the voice, Musashi abruptly drew in his breath and let her go. She jumped to her feet, grabbed up the short sword and lunged at him.

"Stop it, ma'am," said Musashi.

Startled by the oddly courteous tone, she paused and gaped at him. "Why, it's . . . it's Takezō!"

His hunch was right. Apart from Osugi, the only woman who would still call him by his childhood name was Okō.

"It *is* Takezō," she exclaimed, her voice growing syrupy. "Your name's Musashi now, isn't it? You've become quite a swordsman, haven't you?"

"What are you doing in a place like this?"

"I'm ashamed to say."

"Is that man lying over there your husband?"

"You must know him. He's what's left of Gion Tōji."

"That's Tōji?" murmured Musashi. He had heard in Kyoto what a reprobate Tōji was, and how he had pocketed the money collected to enlarge the school and absconded with Okō. Still, as he looked at the human wreck by the wall, he couldn't help feeling sorry for him. "You'd better tend to him," he said. "If I'd known he was your husband, I wouldn't have been so rough with him."

"Oh, I want to crawl in a hole and hide," simpered Okō.

She went to Tōji's side, gave him some water, bound his wounds, and when he had begun to come around, told him who Musashi was.

"What?" he croaked. "Miyamoto Musashi? The one who . . . Oh, this is awful!" Placing his hands over his face, he doubled up abjectly.

Forgetting his anger, Musashi allowed himself to be treated as an honored guest. Okō swept the floor, tidied up the hearth, put on new kindling and heated some sake.

Handing him a cup, she said, in accordance with the accepted rules of etiquette, "We haven't a thing to offer, but . . ."

"I had quite enough at the teahouse," Musashi replied politely. "Please don't go to any trouble."

"Oh, I hope you can eat the food I've prepared. It's been such a long time." Having hung a pot of stew on the pot hanger, she sat down beside him and poured his sake.

"It reminds me of old times at Mount Ibuki," said Musashi amiably.

A strong wind had come up, and though the shutters were again securely in place, it came in through various cracks and teased the smoke from the hearth as it rose to the ceiling.

"Please don't remind me of that," said Okō. "But

tell me, have you heard anything of Akemi? Do you have any idea where she is?"

"I heard she spent several days at the inn on Mount Hiei. She and Matahachi were planning to go to Edo. Seems she ran away with all his money."

"Oh?" said Okō disappointedly. "Her too." She gazed at the floor, sadly comparing her daughter's life with her own.

When Tōji had recovered sufficiently, he joined them and begged Musashi's forgiveness. He had, he avowed, acted on a sudden impulse, which he now deplored. There would come a day, he assured his guest, when he would reenter society as the Gion Tōji the world had known before.

Musashi kept quiet, but he would have liked to say that there didn't seem to be much to choose from between Tōji the samurai and Tōji the bandit, but if he did return to the life of a warrior, the roads would be that much safer for travelers.

Somewhat mellowed by the sake, he said to Okō, "I think you'd be wise to give up this dangerous way of life."

"You're quite right, but of course, it's not as though I'm living this way out of choice. When we left Kyoto, we were going to try our luck in Edo. But in Suwa, Tōji got to gambling and lost everything we had—travel money, everything. I thought of the moxa business, so we started gathering herbs and selling them in the town. Oh, I've had enough of his get-rich-quick schemes to last a lifetime. After tonight, I'm through." As always, a few drinks had introduced a coquettish note into her speech. She was beginning to turn on the charm.

Okō was one of those women of indeterminate age, and she was still dangerous. A house cat will romp coyly on its master's knees so long as it is well fed and cared for, but turn it loose in the mountains, and in no time it will be prowling the night with flaming eyes, ready to feast off a corpse or tear the living flesh off travelers who have fallen sick by the wayside. Okō was very much like that.

"Tōji," she said lovingly, "according to Takezō, Akemi was headed for Edo. Couldn't we go there too and live more like human beings again? If we found Akemi, I'm sure we'd think of some profitable business to go into."

"Well, maybe," was the unenthusiastic reply. His arms were wrapped pensively around his knees; perhaps the implied idea—peddling Akemi's body—was a little raw even for him. Tōji, after living with this predatory woman, was beginning to have the same regrets as Matahachi.

To Musashi, the expression on Tōji's face seemed pathetic. It reminded him of Matahachi. With a shudder, he recalled how he himself had once been enticed by her charms.

"Okō," said Tōji, lifting his head. "It won't be long till daylight. Musashi's probably tired. Why don't you fix a place for him in the back room, so he can get some rest?"

"Yes, of course." With a tipsy sidelong glance at Musashi, she said, "You'll have to be careful, Takezō. It's dark back there."

"Thanks. I could use some sleep."

He followed her down a dark corridor to the back of the house. The room seemed to be an addition to the cabin. It was supported by logs and projected out over the valley, with a drop of about seventy feet from the outer wall to the river. The air was damp from the mist and the spray blowing in from a waterfall. Each time the groaning of the wind rose a trifle, the little room rocked like a boat.

Okō's white feet retreated across the slatted floor of the outdoor hallway to the hearth room.

"Has he gone to sleep?" asked Tōji.

"I think so," she replied, kneeling by his side. She whispered in his ear, "What are you going to do?"

"Go call the others."

"You're going through with it?"

"Absolutely! It's not just a matter of money. If I kill the bastard, I'll have taken revenge for the House of Yoshioka."

Tucking up the skirt of her kimono, she went outside. Under the starless sky, deep in the mountains, she sped through the black wind like a feline demon, her long hair streaming out behind.

The nooks and crevices on the mountainside were not inhabited solely by birds and beasts. As Okō raced along, she made contact with more than twenty men, all members of Tōji's band. Trained for night forays, they moved more quietly than floating leaves to a spot just in front of the cabin.

"Only one man?"

"A samurai?"

"Does he have money?"

The whispered exchanges were accompanied by explanatory gestures and eye movements. Carrying muskets and daggers and the type of lances used by boar hunters, a few of them surrounded the back room. About half went down into the valley, while a couple stopped halfway down, directly below the room.

The floor of the room was covered with reed mats. Along one wall were neat little piles of dried herbs and a collection of mortars and other tools used to make medicine. Musashi found the pleasant aroma of the herbs soothing; it seemed to beckon him to close his eyes and sleep. His body felt dull and swollen to the tips of his extremities. But he knew better than to give in to the sweet temptation.

He was aware there was something afoot. The herb gatherers of Mimasaka never had storage sheds like this; theirs were never located where dampness accumulated and were always at some distance from dense foliage. By the dim light of a small lamp resting on a mortar stand beside his pillow, he could see something else that disturbed him. The metal brackets holding the room together at the corners were surrounded by numerous nail holes. He could also discern fresh wooden surfaces that must previously have been covered by joinery. The implication was unmistakable: the room had been rebuilt, probably a number of times.

A tiny smile came to his lips, but he did not stir.

"Takezō," Okō called softly. "Are you asleep?" Gently sliding the shoji aside, she tiptoed to his pallet and placed a tray near his head. "I'll put some water here for you," she said. He gave no sign of being awake.

When she was back in the cabin itself, Tōji whispered, "Is everything all right?"

Closing her eyes for emphasis, she replied, "He's sound asleep."

With a satisfied look, Tōji hurried outside, went to the back of the cabin and waved a lighted musket fuse, whereupon the men below pulled the supports out from under the room, sending it crashing down into the valley—walls, frame, ridgepole and all.

With a triumphant roar, the others sprang from their hiding places, like hunters from behind portable blinds, and rushed down to the riverbank. The next step was to extricate the corpse and the victim's belongings from the debris. After that, it would be a simple matter to gather up the pieces and rebuild the room.

The bandits jumped into the pile of planks and posts like dogs falling on bones.

Arriving from above, others asked, "Have you found the body?"

"No, not yet."

"It's got to be here somewhere."

Tōji shouted raucously, "Maybe he struck a rock or something on the way down and bounced off to the side. Look all around."

Rocks, water, the trees and plants of the valley, were taking on a bright reddish cast. With startled exclamations, Tōji and his henchmen looked toward the sky.

Seventy feet above, bright flames spouted from the doors, windows, walls and roof of the cabin. It had turned into a huge ball of fire.

"Quick! Hur-r-ry! Get back up here!" The piercing summons came from Okō, and sounded like the howl of a woman gone mad.

By the time the men had made their way up the cliff, the flames were dancing wildly in the wind. Unprotected from the shower of sparks and embers, Okō stood tied securely to a tree trunk.

To a man, they were dumbfounded. Musashi gone? How? How could he conceivably have outwitted them all?

Tōji lost heart; he did not even send his men in pursuit. He had heard enough about Musashi to know they'd never catch him. On their own, however, the bandits quickly organized search parties and flew off in all directions.

They found no trace of Musashi.

4

Playing with Fire

Unlike the other principal routes, there were no trees lining the Kōshū highroad, which joined Shiojiri and Edo by way of Kai Province. Used for military transport during the sixteenth century, it lacked the Nakasendō's network of back roads and had only recently been upgraded to the status of a main artery.

For travelers coming from Kyoto or Osaka, its least agreeable feature was a dearth of good inns and eating places. A request for a box lunch was likely to bring forth nothing more appetizing than flat rice cakes wrapped in bamboo leaves or, even less appealing, balls of plain rice done up in dried oak leaves. Despite the primitive fare—probably not much different from that of the Fujiwara period, hundreds of years earlier—the rustic hostelries swarmed with guests, most of them bound for Edo.

A group of travelers was taking a rest above Kobotoke Pass. One of them exclaimed, "Look, there's another batch," referring to a sight he and his companions had been enjoying almost daily—a group of prostitutes on their way from Kyoto to Edo.

The girls numbered about thirty, some old, some in their twenties or early thirties, at least five in their middle teens. Together with about ten men who managed or served them, they resembled a large patriarchal family.

There were in addition several packhorses loaded down with everything from small wicker baskets to man-sized wooden chests.

The head of the "family," a man of about forty, was addressing his girls. "If your straw sandals are giving you blisters, change into zōri, but tie them tight so they don't slip around. And stop complaining that you can't walk any farther. Just look at the children on the road, the children!" It was clear from his acid tone that he was having a hard time forcing his usually sedentary charges to keep moving.

The man, whose name was Shōji Jinnai, was a native of Fushimi, a samurai by birth, who had for reasons of his own abandoned the military life to become a brothel keeper. Being both quick-witted and resourceful, he had succeeded in gaining the support of Tokugawa Ieyasu, who often took up residence at Fushimi Castle, and had not only obtained permission to move his own business to Edo but had also persuaded many of his colleagues in the trade to do likewise.

Near the crest of Kobotoke, Jinnai brought his procession to a halt, saying, "It's still a little early, but we can have our lunch now." Turning to Onao, an old woman who functioned as a sort of mother hen, he ordered her to pass out the food.

The basket containing the box lunches was duly unloaded from one of the horses and a leaf-wrapped ball of rice dealt out to each of the women, who scattered themselves about and relaxed. The dust that had yellowed their skin had also turned their black hair nearly white, though they wore broad-brimmed traveling hats or had tied hand towels around their heads. There being no tea, eating entailed a good deal of lip smacking and tooth sucking. There was no suggestion of sexual wiles or amorous thrills. "Whose arms will embrace this red, red blossom tonight?" seemed utterly beside the point.

"Oh, this is delicious!" cried one of Jinnai's younger

charges ecstatically. Her tone of voice would have brought tears to her mother's eyes.

The attention of two or three others wandered from their lunch to focus on a young samurai passing by.

"Isn't he handsome?" whispered one.

"Umm, not bad," replied another, of more worldly outlook.

A third volunteered, "Oh, I know him. He used to come to our place with men from the Yoshioka School."

"Which one are you talking about?" asked one lustful-eyed creature.

"The young one, strutting along there with the long sword on his back."

Unaware of the admiration, Sasaki Kojirō was pushing his way through a throng of porters and packhorses.

A high, flirtatious voice called, "Mr. Sasaki! Over here, Mr. Sasaki!"

Since there were lots of people named Sasaki, he didn't even turn.

"You with the forelock!"

Kojirō's eyebrows shot up, and he spun around.

"Watch your tongues!" Jinnai shouted angrily. "You're being rude." Then, glancing up from his lunch, he recognized Kojirō.

"Well, well," he said, rising quickly. "If it isn't our friend Sasaki! Where are you headed, if I may ask?"

"Why, hello. You're the master of the Sumiya, aren't you? I'm going to Edo. And what about you? You seem to be engaged in a full-scale move."

"That we are. We're moving to the new capital."

"Really? Do you think you can make a go of it there?"

"Nothing grows in stagnant waters."

"The way Edo's growing, I imagine there's plenty of work for construction workers and gunsmiths. But elegant entertainment? It seems doubtful there's much demand for it yet."

"You're wrong, though. Women made a city out of

Osaka before Hideyoshi got around to taking any notice of it."

"Maybe, but in a place as new as Edo, you probably won't even be able to find a suitable house."

"Wrong again. The government's set aside some marshland in a place called Yoshiwara for people in my business. My associates have already started filling it in, putting in streets and building houses. From all reports, I should be able to find a good street-front location fairly easily."

"You mean the Tokugawas are giving the land away? For free?"

"Of course. Who'd pay for marshland? The government's even providing some of the construction materials."

"I see. No wonder you're all abandoning the Kyoto area."

"And what about you? Or do you have some prospect of a position with a daimyō?"

"Oh, no; nothing like that. I wouldn't take one if it was offered. I just thought I'd see what's going on up there, since it's the shōgun's residence and the place where orders are going to come from in the future. Of course, if I were asked to be one of the shōgun's instructors, I might accept."

Though no judge of swordsmanship, Jinnai had a good eye for people. Thinking it just as well not to comment on Kojirō's unbridled egotism, he averted his eyes and began prodding his troop into movement. "Everybody up now! It's time we were going."

Onao, who had been counting heads, said, "We seem to be missing one girl. Which one is it, now? Kichō? Or maybe Sumizome? No; they're both over there. This is strange. Who could it be?"

Kojirō, disinclined to have a party of prostitutes for traveling companions, went on his way.

A couple of the girls who had gone back down the road to search returned to where Onao was.

Jinnai joined them. "Here, here, Onao, which one is it?"

"Ah, I know now. It was that girl named Akemi," she replied contritely, as if the fault were hers. "The one you picked up on the road in Kiso."

"She must be around here somewhere."

"We've looked everywhere. I think she must have run away."

"Well, I didn't have a written commitment from her, and I didn't lend her any 'body money.' She said she was willing, and since she was good-looking enough to be marketable, I took her on. I suppose she's cost me a bit in traveling expenses, but not enough to worry about. Never mind her. Let's get moving."

He began hustling his group along. Even if it meant traveling after sundown, he wanted to reach Hachiōji within the day. If they could get that far before stopping, they could be in Edo the next day.

A short way down the road, Akemi reappeared and fell in with them.

"Where have you been?" Onao demanded angrily. "You can't just wander off without telling anyone where you're going. Unless, of course, you're planning to leave us." The old woman went on to explain self-righteously how they had all been so worried about her.

"You don't understand," said Akemi, from whom the scolding brought nothing but giggles. "There was a man I know on the road, and I didn't want him to see me. I ran into a clump of bamboo, not knowing there was a sudden drop-off there. I slid all the way down to the bottom." She corroborated this by holding up her torn kimono and a skinned elbow. But all the time she was begging forgiveness, her face showed not the slightest sign of contrition.

From his position near the front, Jinnai caught wind of what had happened and summoned her. Sternly he said, "Your name's Akemi, isn't it? Akemi—that's hard to remember. If you're really going to succeed in this business, you'll have to find a better name. Tell me, have you really resolved to go through with this?''

"Does it require resolution to become a whore?''

"It's not something you can take up for a month or so and then quit. And if you become one of my girls, you'll have to give the customers what they ask for, like it or not. Don't make any mistake about that.''

"What difference does it make now? Men have already made a mess of my life.''

"That's not the right attitude at all. Now, you give this some careful thought. If you change your mind before we reach Edo, that's all right. I won't ask you to pay me back for your food and lodging.''

That same day, at the Yakuōin in Takao, an older man, apparently free of the pressures of business, was about to resume his leisurely journey. He, his servant and a boy of about fifteen had arrived the previous evening and requested overnight accommodations. He and the boy had been touring the temple grounds since early morning. It was now about noon.

"Use this for roof repairs, or whatever is necessary,'' he said, offering one of the priests three large gold coins.

The head priest, immediately apprised of the gift, was so overwhelmed by the donor's generosity that he personally hastened out to exchange greetings. "Perhaps you would like to leave your name,'' he said.

Another priest, saying this had already been done, showed him the entry in the temple registry, which read: "Daizō of Narai, dealer in herbs, resident at the foot of Mount Ontake in Kiso.''

The head priest apologized profusely for the poor quality of the fare served by the temple, for Daizō of Narai was known throughout the country as a lavish contributor to shrines and temples. His gifts always took the form of gold coins—in some cases, it was said, as many as several dozen. Only he himself knew whether he did this for amusement, to acquire a reputation, or out of piety.

The priest, eager to have him stay longer, begged him to inspect the temple's treasures, a privilege accorded to few.

"I'll be in Edo awhile," said Daizō. "I'll come see them another time."

"By all means, but at least let me accompany you to the outer gate," insisted the priest. "Are you planning to stop in Fuchū tonight?"

"No; Hachiōji."

"In that case, it'll be an easy trip."

"Tell me, who's the lord of Hachiōji now?"

"It's recently been put under the administration of Ōkubo Nagayasu."

"He was magistrate of Nara, wasn't he?"

"Yes, that's the man. The gold mines on Sado Island are also under his control. He's very rich."

"A very able man, it would appear."

It was still daylight when they came to the foot of the mountains and stood on the busy main street of Hachiōji, where reportedly there were no fewer than twenty-five inns.

"Well, Jōtarō, where shall we stay?"

Jōtarō, who had stuck to Daizō's side like a shadow, let it be known in no uncertain terms that he preferred "anywhere—as long as it's not a temple."

Choosing the largest and most imposing inn, Daizō entered and requested a room. His distinguished appearance, together with the elegant lacquered traveling case his servant carried on his back, made a dazzling impression on the head clerk, who said fawningly, "You're stopping quite early, aren't you?" Inns along the highroads were accustomed to having hordes of travelers tumble in at dinnertime or even later.

Daizō was shown to a large room on the first floor, but shortly after sundown, both the innkeeper and the head clerk came to Daizō's room.

"I'm sure it's a great inconvenience," the innkeeper began abjectly, "but a large party of guests has come in very suddenly. I'm afraid it'll be terribly noisy here. If you wouldn't mind moving to a room on the second floor . . ."

"Oh, that's perfectly all right," replied Daizō good-naturedly. "Glad to see your business is thriving."

Signaling Sukeichi, his servant, to take care of the luggage, Daizō proceeded upstairs. He had no sooner left the room than it was overrun by women from the Sumiya.

The inn wasn't just busy; it was frenetic. What with the hubbub downstairs, the servants did not come when called. Dinner was late, and when they had eaten, no one came to clear away the dishes. On top of that, there was the constant tramping of feet on both floors. Only Daizō's sympathy for the hired help kept him from losing his temper. Ignoring the litter in the room, he stretched out to take a nap, using his arm for a pillow. After only a few minutes, a sudden thought came to him, and he called Sukeichi.

When Sukeichi failed to materialize, Daizō opened his eyes, sat up and shouted, "Jōtarō, come here!"

But he, too, had disappeared.

Daizō got up and went to the veranda, which he saw was lined with guests, excitedly gaping with delight at the prostitutes on the first floor.

Spying Jōtarō among the spectators, Daizō swiftly yanked him back into the room. With a forbidding eye, he demanded, "What were you staring at?"

The boy's long wooden sword, which he did not take off even indoors, scraped the tatami as he sat down. "Well," he said, "everyone else is looking."

"And just what are they looking at?"

"Oh, there're a lot of women in the back room downstairs."

"Is that all?"

"Yes."

"What's so entertaining about that?" The presence

40

of the whores didn't bother Daizō, but for some reason he found the intense interest of the men gawking at them annoying.

"I don't know," replied Jōtarō honestly.

"I'm going for a walk around town," Daizō said. "You stay here while I'm gone."

"Can't I go with you?"

"Not at night."

"Why not?"

"As I told you before, when I go for a walk, it's not simply to amuse myself."

"Well, what's the idea, then?"

"It has to do with my religion."

"Don't you get enough of shrines and temples during the daytime? Even priests have to sleep at night."

"Religion has to do with more than shrines and temples, young man. Now go find Sukeichi for me. He has the key to my traveling case."

"He went downstairs a few minutes ago. I saw him peeking into the room where the women are."

"Him too?" exclaimed Daizō with a click of his tongue. "Go get him, and be quick about it." After Jōtarō had left, Daizō began retying his obi.

Having heard the women were Kyoto prostitutes, famous for their beauty and savoir faire, the male guests were unable to leave off feasting their eyes. Sukeichi was so absorbed with the sight that his mouth was still hanging open when Jōtarō located him.

"Come on, you've seen enough," snapped the boy, giving the servant's ear a tug.

"Ouch!" squealed Sukeichi.

"Your master's calling you."

"That's not true."

"It is too. He said he was going for a walk. He's always taking walks, isn't he?"

"Eh? Oh, all right," said Sukeichi, tearing his eyes away reluctantly.

The boy had turned to follow him when a voice called, "Jōtarō? You're Jōtarō, aren't you?"

The voice was that of a young woman. He looked around searchingly. The hope that he would find his lost teacher and Otsū never left him. Could it be? He peered tensely through the branches of a large evergreen shrub.

"Who is it?"

"Me."

The face that emerged from the foliage was familiar.

"Oh, it's only you."

Akemi slapped him roughly on the back. "You little monster! And it's been such a long time since I saw you. What are you doing here?"

"I could ask you the same question."

"Well, I . . . Oh, it wouldn't mean anything to you anyway."

"Are you traveling with those women?"

"I am, but I haven't made up my mind yet."

"Made up your mind about what?"

"Whether to become one of them or not," she replied with a sigh. After a long pause, she asked, "What's Musashi doing these days?"

This, Jōtarō perceived, was what she really wanted to know. He only wished he could answer the question.

"Otsū and Musashi and I . . . we got separated on the highroad."

"Otsū? Who's she?" She had hardly spoken before she remembered. "Oh, never mind; I know. Is she *still* chasing after Musashi?" Akemi was in the habit of thinking of Musashi as a dashing *shugyōsha*, wandering about as the mood suited him, living in the forest, sleeping on bare rocks. Even if she succeeded in catching him, he'd see right away how dissolute her life had become and shun her. She had long since resigned herself to the idea that her love would go unrequited.

But the mention of another woman awoke feelings of jealousy and rekindled the dying embers of her amorous instinct.

"Jōtarō," she said, "there're too many curious eyes around here. Let's go out somewhere."

They left via the garden gate. Out in the street, their eyes were regaled by the lights of Hachiōji and its twenty-five hostelries. It was the liveliest town either had seen since leaving Kyoto. To the northwest rose the dark, silent forms of the Chichibu Range and the mountains marking the boundary of Kai Province, but here the atmosphere was replete with the aroma of sake, noisy with the clicking of weavers' reeds, the shouts of market officials, the excited voices of gamblers and the dispirited whining songs of local street singers.

"I often heard Matahachi mention Otsū," Akemi lied. "What kind of person is she?"

"She's a very good person," Jōtarō said soberly. "Sweet and gentle and considerate and pretty. I really like her."

The threat Akemi felt hanging over her grew heavier, but she cloaked her feelings with a benign smile. "Is she really so wonderful?"

"Oh, yes. And she can do anything. She sings, she writes well. And she's good at playing the flute."

Now visibly ruffled, Akemi said, "I don't see what good it does a woman to be able to play the flute."

"If you don't, you don't, but everybody, even Lord Yagyū Sekishūsai, speaks highly of Otsū. There's only one little thing I don't like about her."

"All women have their faults. It's just a question of whether they honestly admit to them, the way I do, or try to hide them behind a ladylike pose."

"Otsū's not like that. It's just this one weakness of hers."

"What's that?"

"She's always breaking into tears. She's a regular crybaby."

"Oh? Why is that?"

"She cries whenever she thinks of Musashi. That makes being around her pretty gloomy, and I don't like it." Jōtarō expressed himself with youthful abandon, heedless of the effect this might have.

Akemi's heart, her whole body, was afire with raging jealousy. It showed in the depths of her eyes, even in the color of her skin. But she continued her interrogation. "Tell me, how old is she?"

"About the same."

"You mean the same age as me?"

"Um. But she looks younger and prettier."

Akemi plunged on, hoping to turn Jōtarō against Otsū. "Musashi's more masculine than most men. He must hate having to watch a woman carry on all the time. Otsū probably thinks tears will win a man's sympathy. She's like the girls working for the Sumiya."

Jōtarō, very much irked, retorted, "That's not true at all. In the first place, Musashi likes Otsū. He never shows his feelings, but he's in love with her."

Akemi's flushed face grew bright crimson. She longed to throw herself into a river to quench the flames that were consuming her.

"Jōtarō, let's go this way." She pulled him toward a red light in a side street.

"That's a drinking place."

"Well, what of it?"

"Women have no business in a place like that. You can't go in there."

"All of a sudden I have the urge to drink, and I can't go in alone. I'd be embarrassed."

"*You'd* be embarrassed. What about me?"

"They'll have things to eat. You can have anything you want."

At first glance, the shop seemed empty. Akemi walked right in, then, facing the wall rather than the counter, said, "Bring me some sake!"

One cup after another went down as fast as was humanly possible. Jōtarō, frightened by the quantity, tried to slow her down, but she elbowed him out of the way.

"Quiet!" she yelped. "What a nuisance you are! Bring some more sake! Sake!"

Jōtarō, insinuating himself between her and the sake jar, pleaded, "You've got to stop. You can't go on drinking here like this."

"Don't worry about me," she slurred. "You're a friend of Otsū's, aren't you? I can't stand women who try to win a man with tears!"

"Well, I dislike women who get drunk."

"I'm so sorry, but how could a runt like you understand why I drink?"

"Come on, just pay the bill."

"You think I've got money?"

"Don't you?"

"No. Maybe he can collect from the Sumiya. I've already sold myself to the master anyway." Tears flooded her eyes. "I'm sorry . . . I'm really sorry."

"Weren't you the one who was making fun of Otsū for crying? Look at yourself."

"My tears aren't the same as hers. Oh, life's too much trouble. I might as well be dead."

With that, she stood up and lurched out into the street. The shopkeeper, having had other female customers like this in his time, merely laughed it off, but a rōnin who had until then been sleeping quietly in a corner opened his bleary eyes and stared at her retreating back.

Jōtarō darted after her and grabbed her around the waist, but he lost his hold. She started running down the darkened street, Jōtarō close behind.

"Stop!" he cried with alarm. "You mustn't even think of it. Come back!"

Though she seemed not to care whether she ran into something in the dark or fell into a swamp, she was fully conscious of Jōtarō's pleading. When she had plunged into the sea at Sumiyoshi, she had wanted to kill herself, but she was no longer so lacking in guile. She got a certain thrill from having Jōtarō so worried about her.

"Watch out!" he screamed, seeing that she was

headed straight toward the murky water of a moat. "Stop it! Why do you want to die? It's crazy."

As he caught her around the waist again, she wailed, "Why shouldn't I die? You think I'm wicked. So does Musashi. Everybody does. There's nothing I can do but die, embracing Musashi in my heart. Never will I let him be taken from me by a woman like that!"

"You're pretty mixed up. How did you get this way?"

"It doesn't matter. All you have to do is push me into the moat. Go ahead, Jōtarō, push." Covering her face with her hands, she burst into frenzied tears. This awakened a strange fear in Jōtarō. He, too, felt the urge to cry.

"Come on, Akemi. Let's go back."

"Oh, I yearn so to see him. Find him for me, Jōtarō. Please find Musashi for me."

"Stand still! Don't move; it's dangerous."

"Oh, Musashi!"

"Watch out!"

At that moment the rōnin from the sake shop stepped out of the darkness.

"Go away, boy," he commanded. "I'll take her back to the inn." He put his hands under Jōtarō's arms and roughly lifted him aside.

He was a tall man, thirty-four or -five years old, with deep-set eyes and a heavy beard. A crooked scar, no doubt left by a sword, ran from below his right ear to his chin. It looked like the jagged tear that appears when a peach is broken open.

Swallowing hard to overcome his fear, Jōtarō tried coaxing. "Akemi, please come with me. Everything'll be all right."

Akemi's head was now resting on the samurai's chest.

"Look," the man said, "she's gone to sleep. Off with you! I'll take her home later."

"No! Let go of her!"

When the boy refused to budge, the rōnin slowly reached out with one hand and grabbed his collar.

"Hands off!" screamed Jōtarō, resisting with all his strength.

"You little bastard! How'd you like to get thrown into the moat?"

"Who's going to do it?" He wriggled loose, and as soon as he was free, his hand found the end of his wooden sword. He swung it at the man's side, but his own body did a somersault and landed on a rock by the roadside. He moaned once, then remained still.

Jōtarō had been out for some time before he began hearing voices around him.

"Wake up, there."

"What happened?"

Opening his eyes, he vaguely took in a small crowd of people.

"Are you awake?"

"Are you all right?"

Embarrassed by the attention he was attracting, he picked up his wooden sword and was trying to get away when a clerk from the inn grabbed his arm. "Wait a minute," he barked. "What happened to the woman you were with?"

Looking around, Jōtarō got the impression that the others were also from the inn, guests as well as employees. Some of the men were carrying sticks; others were holding round paper lanterns.

"A man came and said you'd been attacked and a rōnin had carried the woman off. Do you know which way they went?"

Jōtarō, still dazed, shook his head.

"That's impossible. You must have some idea."

Jōtarō pointed in the first direction that came to hand. "Now I remember. It was that way." He was reluctant to say what really happened, fearing a scolding from Daizō for getting involved, but also dreading to admit in front of these people that the rōnin had thrown him.

Despite the vagueness of his reply, the crowd rushed off, and presently a cry went up: "Here she is. Over here."

The lanterns gathered in a circle around Akemi, whose disheveled form lay where she had been abandoned, on a stack of hay in a farmer's shed. Prodded back to reality by the clatter of running feet, she dragged herself to her feet. The front of her kimono was open; her obi lay on the ground. Hay clung to her hair and clothing.

"What happened?"

While the word "rape" was on the tip of everyone's tongue, no one said it. Nor did it even cross their minds to chase the villain. Whatever had happened to Akemi, they felt, she had brought on herself.

"Come on, let's go back," said one of the men, taking her hand.

Akemi pulled away quickly. Resting her face forlornly against the wall, she broke down in bitter tears.

"Seems to be drunk."

"How'd she get that way?"

Jōtarō had been watching the scene from a distance. What had befallen Akemi was not clear to him in detail, but somehow he was reminded of an experience that had nothing to do with her. The titillation of lying in the fodder shed in Koyagyū with Kocha came back to him, along with the strangely exciting fear of approaching footsteps. But his pleasure quickly evaporated. "I better get back," he said decisively.

As his pace quickened, his spirit, back from its trip to the unknown, moved him to break into song.

> "Old metal Buddha, standing in the field,
>   Have you seen a girl of sixteen?
>   Don't you know a girl who's strayed?
>   When asked, you say 'Clang.'
>   When struck, you say 'Bong.' "

5

A Cricket in the Grass

Jōtarō jogged along at a good pace, paying little attention to the road. Suddenly he halted and looked around, wondering if he'd lost his way. "I don't remember passing here before," he thought nervously.

Samurai houses fringed the remains of an old fortress. One section of the compound had been rebuilt to serve as the official residence of the recently appointed Ōkubo Nagayasu, but the rest of the area, rising like a natural mound, was covered with weeds and trees. The stone ramparts were crumbling, having been ravaged many years earlier by an invading army. The fortification looked primitive compared to the castle complexes of the last forty to fifty years. There was no moat, no bridge, nothing that could properly be described as a castle wall. It had probably belonged to one of the local gentry in the days before the great civil war daimyō incorporated their rural domains into larger feudal principalities.

On one side of the road were paddies and marshland; on the other, walls; and beyond, a cliff, atop which the fortress must once have stood.

As he tried to get his bearings, Jōtarō's eyes traveled along the cliff. Then he saw something move, stop, and move again. At first it looked like an animal, but soon the stealthily moving silhouette became the outline of a man. Jōtarō shivered but stood riveted to the spot.

The man lowered a rope with a hook attached to the top. After he had slid down the full length of the rope and found a foothold, he shook the hook loose and repeated the process. When he reached the bottom, he disappeared into a copse.

Jōtarō's curiosity was thoroughly aroused.

A few minutes later, he saw the man walking along the low rises separating the paddies and apparently heading straight for him. He nearly panicked, but relaxed when he could make out the bundle on the man's back. "What a waste of time! Nothing but a farmer stealing kindling." He thought the man must have been crazy to risk scaling the cliff for nothing more than some firewood. He was disappointed too; his mystery had become unbearably humdrum. But then came his second shock. As the man strolled up the road past the tree Jōtarō was hiding behind, the boy had to stifle a gasp. He was sure the dark figure was Daizō.

"It couldn't be," he told himself.

The man had a black cloth around his face and wore peasant's knickers, leggings and light straw sandals.

The mysterious figure turned off onto a path skirting a hill. No one with such sturdy shoulders and buoyant stride could be in his fifties, as Daizō was. Having convinced himself that he was mistaken, Jōtarō followed. He had to get back to the inn, and the man just might, unwittingly, help him find his way.

When the man came to a road marker, he set down his bundle, which appeared to be very heavy. As he leaned over to read the writing on the stone, something about him again struck Jōtarō as familiar.

While the man climbed the path up the hill, Jōtarō examined the marker, on which were carved the words "Pine Tree on Head-burying Mound—Above." This was where the local inhabitants buried the severed skulls of criminals and defeated warriors.

The branches of an immense pine were clearly visible against the night sky. By the time Jōtarō reached the top of the rise, the man had seated himself by the roots of the tree and was smoking a pipe.

Daizō! No question about it now. A peasant would never carry tobacco with him. Some had been successfully grown domestically, but on such a limited scale that it was still very expensive. Even in the relatively well-off Kansai district, it was considered a luxury. And up in Sendai, when Lord Date smoked, his scribe felt constrained to make an entry in his daily journal: "Morning, three smokes; afternoon, four smokes; bedtime, one smoke."

Financial considerations aside, most people who had a chance to try tobacco found it made them dizzy or even nauseated. Though appreciated for its flavor, it was generally regarded as a narcotic.

Jōtarō knew that smokers were few; he also knew that Daizō was one of them, for he had frequently seen him drawing on a handsomely made ceramic pipe. Not that this had ever before struck him as strange. Daizō was wealthy and a man of expensive tastes.

"What's he up to?" he thought impatiently. Accustomed now to the danger of the situation, he gradually crept closer.

Having finished his pipe, the merchant got to his feet, removed his black kerchief and tucked it into his waist. Then slowly he walked around the pine. The next thing Jōtarō knew, he was holding a shovel in his hands. Where had that come from? Leaning on the shovel, Daizō looked around at the night scenery for a moment, apparently fixing the location in his mind.

Seemingly satisfied, Daizō rolled aside a large rock on the north side of the tree and began digging energetically, looking neither right nor left. Jōtarō watched the hole grow nearly deep enough for a man to stand in. Finally, Daizō stopped and wiped the sweat from his face with his kerchief. Jōtarō remained as still as a rock and totally baffled.

"This'll do," the merchant murmured softly, as he finished trampling down the soft dirt at the bottom of the hole. For an instant, Jōtarō had a peculiar impulse to call out and warn him not to bury himself, but he held back.

Jumping up to the surface, Daizō proceeded to drag the heavy bundle from the tree to the edge of the hole and undo the hempen cord around the top. At first Jōtarō thought the sack was made of cloth, but now he could see that it was a heavy leather cloak, of the sort generals wore over their armor. Inside was another sack, made of tenting or some similar fabric. When this was opened, the top of an incredible stack of gold came into view—semi-cylindrical ingots made by pouring the molten metal into half sections of bamboo, split lengthwise.

There was more to come. Loosening his obi, Daizō unburdened himself of several dozen large, newly minted gold pieces, which had been stuffed into his stomach wrapper, the back of his kimono and other parts of his clothing. Having placed these neatly on top of the ingots, he tied both containers securely and dropped the bundle into the pit, as he might have dumped the carcass of a dog. He then shoveled the dirt back in, stamped on it with his feet, and replaced the rock. He finished off by scattering dry grass and twigs around the rock.

Then he set about transforming himself back into the well-known Daizō of Narai, affluent dealer in herbs. The peasant's garb, wrapped around the shovel, went into a thicket not likely to be explored by passersby. He donned his traveling cloak and hung his money pouch around his neck in the manner of itinerant priests. As he slipped his feet into his zōri, he mumbled with satisfaction, "Quite a night's work."

When Daizō was out of hearing range, Jōtarō emerged from his hiding place and went to the rock. Though he scrutinized the spot carefully, he could discern no trace of what he had just witnessed. He stared at the ground as if at a magician's empty palm.

"I'd better get moving," he thought suddenly. "If I'm not there when he gets back to the inn, he'll be suspicious." Since the lights of the town were now visible beneath him, he had no trouble setting his course. Running like the wind, he somehow contrived to stay on back roads and keep well out of Daizō's path.

It was with an expression of perfect innocence that he climbed the stairs at the inn and entered their room. He was in luck; Sukeichi was slumped against the lacquered traveling case, alone and sound asleep. A thin trickle of saliva ran down his chin.

"Hey, Sukeichi, you'll catch cold there." Purposely Jōtarō shook him to wake him up.

"Oh, it's you, is it?" drawled Sukeichi, rubbing his eyes. "What were you doing out this late without telling the master?"

"Are you crazy? I've been back for hours. If you'd been awake, you'd have known that."

"Don't try to fool me. I know you went out with that woman from the Sumiya. If you're running around after a whore now, I hate to think what you'll be acting like when you grow up."

Just then, Daizō open the shoji. "I'm back," was all he said.

An early morning start was necessary in order to make Edo before nightfall. Jinnai had his troupe, Akemi restored to it, on the road well before sunrise. Daizō, Sukeichi and Jōtarō, however, took their time over breakfast and were not ready to leave until the sun was fairly high in the sky.

Daizō led the way, as usual, but Jōtarō trailed behind with Sukeichi, which was unusual.

Finally Daizō stopped, asking, "What's the matter with you this morning?"

"Pardon?" Jōtarō did his best to appear nonchalant.

"Is something wrong?"

"No, nothing at all. Why do you ask?"

"You look glum. Not like you."

"It's nothing, sir. I was just thinking. If I stay with you, I don't know whether I'll ever find my teacher or not. I'd like to go and look for him on my own, if it's all right with you."

Without a moment's hesitation, Daizō replied, "It isn't!"

Jōtarō had sidled up and started to take hold of the man's arm, but now he withdrew his hand and asked nervously, "Why not?"

"Let's rest here awhile," said Daizō, lowering himself onto the grassy plain for which the province of Musashi was famous. Once seated, he gestured to Sukeichi to go on ahead.

"But I have to find my teacher—as soon as possible," pleaded Jōtarō.

"I told you, you're not going off by yourself." Looking very stern. Daizō put his ceramic pipe to his lips and took a puff. "As of today, you're my son."

He sounded serious. Jōtarō swallowed hard, but then Daizō laughed, and the boy, assuming it was all a joke, said, "I couldn't do that. I don't want to be your son."

"What?"

"You're a merchant. I want to be a samurai."

"I'm sure you'll find that Daizō of Narai is no ordinary townsman, without honor or background. Become my adopted son, and I'll make a real samurai out of you."

Jōtarō realized with dismay that he meant what he was saying. "May I ask why you decided this so suddenly?" the boy asked.

In a trice, Daizō seized him and pinioned him to his side. Putting his mouth to the boy's ear, he whispered, "You saw me, didn't you, you little bastard?"

"Saw you?"

"Yes; you were watching, weren't you?"

"I don't know what you're talking about. Watching what?"

"What I did last night."

Jōtarō tried his best to stay calm.

"Why did you do that?"

The boy's defenses were close to collapse.

"Why were you prying into my private affairs?"

"I'm sorry!" blurted Jōtarō. "I'm really sorry. I won't tell a soul."

"Keep your voice down! I'm not going to punish you, but in return, you're going to become my adopted son. If you refuse, you give me no choice but to kill you. Now, don't force me to do that. I think you're a fine boy, very likable."

For the first time in his life, Jōtarō began to feel real fear. "I'm sorry," he repeated fervently. "Don't kill me. I don't want to die!" Like a captured skylark, he wriggled timidly in Daizō's arms, afraid that if he really struggled, the hand of death would descend on him forthwith.

Although the boy felt his grip to be viselike, Daizō was not holding him tightly at all. In fact, when he pulled the boy onto his lap, his touch was almost tender. "Then you'll be my son, won't you?" His stubbly chin scratched Jōtarō's cheek.

Though he couldn't have identified it, what fettered Jōtarō was an adult, masculine scent. He was like an infant on Daizō's knee, unable to resist, unable even to speak.

"It's for you to decide. Will you let me adopt you, or will you die? Answer me, now!"

With a wail, the boy burst into tears. He rubbed his face with dirty fingers until muddy little puddles formed on both sides of his nose.

"Why cry? You're lucky to have such an opportunity. I guarantee you'll be a great samurai when I finish with you."

"But . . ."

"What is it?"

"You're . . . you're . . ."

"Yes?"

"I can't say it."

"Out with it. Speak. A man should state his thoughts simply and clearly."

"You're . . . well, your business is stealing." Had it not been for the hands resting lightly on him, Jōtarō would have been off like a gazelle. But Daizō's lap was a deep pit, the walls of which prevented him from moving.

"Ha, ha," chortled Daizō, giving him a playful slap on the back. "Is that all that's bothering you?"

"Y-y-yes."

The big man's shoulders shook with laughter. "I might be the sort of person who'd steal the whole country, but a common burglar or highwayman I am not. Look at Ieyasu or Hideyoshi or Nobunaga—they're all warriors who stole or tried to steal the whole nation, aren't they? Just stick with me, and one of these days you'll understand."

"Then you're not a thief?"

"I wouldn't bother with a business that's so unprofitable." Lifting the boy off his knee, he said, "Now stop blubbering, and let's be on our way. From this moment on, you're my son. I'll be a good father to you. Your end of the bargain is that you never breathe a word to anyone about what you think you saw last night. If you do, I'll wring your neck."

Jōtarō believed him.

6

The Pioneers

On the day near the end of the fifth month when Osugi arrived in Edo, the air was steamingly sultry, the way it was only when the rainy season failed to bring rain. In the nearly two months since she had left Kyoto, she had traveled at a leisurely pace, taking time to pamper her aches and pains or to visit shrines and temples.

Her first impression of the shōgun's capital was distasteful. "Why build houses in a swamp like this?" she remarked disdainfully. "The weeds and rushes haven't even been cleared away yet."

Because of the unseasonable drought, a pall of dust hung over the Takanawa highroad, with its newly planted trees and recently erected milestones. The stretch from Shioiri to Nihombashi was crowded with oxcarts loaded with rocks or lumber. All along the way, new houses were going up at a furious clip.

"Of all the—!" gasped Osugi, looking up angrily at a half-finished house. A gob of wet clay from a plasterer's trowel had accidentally landed on her kimono.

The workmen exploded with laughter.

"How dare you throw mud on people and then stand there laughing? You should be on your knees, apologizing!"

Back in Miyamoto, a few sharp words from her

would have had her tenants or any of the other villagers cowering. These laborers, among the thousands of new-comers from all over the country, barely looked up from their work.

"What's the old hag babbling about?" a worker asked.

Osugi, incensed, shouted, "Who said that? Why, you . . ."

The more she sputtered, the harder they laughed. Spectators began to gather, asking each other why the old woman wasn't acting her age and taking the matter in stride.

Storming into the house, Osugi seized the end of the plank the plasterers were standing on and yanked it off its supports. Men and buckets full of wet clay clattered to the floor.

"You old bitch!"

Jumping to their feet, they surrounded her threaten-ingly.

Osugi did not flinch. "Come outside!" she com-manded grimly as she placed her hand on her short sword.

The workmen had second thoughts. The way she looked and carried on, she had to be from a samurai family; they might get into trouble if they weren't careful. Their manner softened noticeably.

Observing the change, Osugi declared grandly, "Henceforward, I'll not countenance rudeness from the likes of you." With a look of satisfaction on her face, she went out and started up the road again, leaving the spectators to gape at her stubborn, straight back.

She was hardly on her way again before an appren-tice, his muddy feet grotesquely covered with shavings and sawdust, ran up behind her, carrying a bucket of mucky clay.

Shouting, "How do you like this, you old witch?" he slung the contents of his pail at her back.

"O-w-w-w!" The howl did credit to Osugi's lungs,

but before she could turn around, the apprentice had vanished. When she realized the extent of the damage, she scowled bitterly and tears of sheer vexation filled her eyes.

The merriment was general.

"What're you nincompoops laughing at?" raged Osugi, baring her teeth. "What's so funny about an old woman being splattered with grime? Is this the way you welcome elderly people to Edo? You're not even human! Just remember, you'll all be old one day."

This outburst attracted even more onlookers.

"Edo, indeed!" she snorted. "To hear people talk, you'd think it was the greatest city in the whole country. And what is it? A place full of dirt and filth, where everybody's pulling down hills and filling in swamps and digging ditches and piling up sand from the seaside. Not only that, it's full of riffraff, like you'd never find in Kyoto or anywhere in the west." Having got that off her chest, she turned her back on the sniggering crowd and went rapidly on her way.

To be sure, the city's newness was its most remarkable feature. The wood and plaster of the houses was all bright and fresh, many building sites were only partially filled in, and ox and horse dung assailed the eyes and nostrils.

Not so long ago, this road had been a mere footpath through the rice paddies between the villages of Hibiya and Chiyoda. Had Osugi gone a little to the west, nearer Edo Castle, she would have found an older and more sedate district, where daimyō and vassals of the shōgun had begun building residences soon after Tokugawa Ieyasu occupied Edo in 1590.

As it was, absolutely nothing appealed to her. She felt ancient. Everyone she saw—shopkeepers, officials on horseback, samurai striding by in basket hats—all were young, as were laborers, craftsmen, vendors, soldiers, even generals.

The front of one house, where plasterers were still at

work, bore a shop sign, behind which sat a heavily powdered woman, brushing her eyebrows as she awaited customers. In other half-finished buildings, people were selling sake, setting up displays of dry goods, laying in supplies of dried fish. One man was hanging out a sign advertising medicine.

"If I weren't looking for someone," Osugi mumbled sourly, "I wouldn't stay in this garbage dump a single night."

Coming to a hill of excavated dirt blocking the road, she halted. At the foot of a bridge crossing the as yet waterless moat stood a shanty. Its walls consisted of reed matting held in place by strips of bamboo, but a banner proclaimed that this was a public bath. Osugi handed over a copper coin and went in to wash her kimono. After cleaning it as well as she could, she borrowed a drying pole and hung the garment up by the side of the shanty. Clothed in her underwear, with a light bathrobe draped over her back, she squatted in the shadow of the bathhouse and gazed absently at the road.

Across the street, half a dozen men stood in a circle, haggling in voices loud enough for Osugi to hear what they were saying.

"How many square feet is it? I wouldn't mind considering it if the price is right."

"There's two thirds of an acre. The price is what I mentioned before. I can't come down from that."

"It's too much. You must know that yourself."

"Not at all. It costs a lot of money to fill in land. And don't forget, there's no more available around here."

"Oh, there must be. They're filling in everywhere."

"Already sold. People are snatching it up as it is, swamp and all. You won't find three hundred square feet for sale. Of course, if you're willing to go way over toward the Sumida River, you might be able to get something cheaper."

"Do you guarantee there's two thirds of an acre?"

"You don't have to take my word for it. Get a rope and measure it off yourself."

Osugi was astounded; the figure quoted for a hundred square feet would have been sufficient for tens of acres of good rice land. But essentially the same conversation was taking place all over the city, for many a merchant speculated in land. Osugi was also mystified. "Why would anybody want land here? It's no good for rice, and you can't call this place a city."

By and by the deal across the street was sealed with a ritual hand clapping intended to bring good luck to all concerned.

As she idly watched the departing shadows, Osugi became conscious of a hand on the back of her obi. "Thief!" she shrieked as she made a grab for the pickpocket's wrist. But her coin purse had already been removed, and the thief was already in the street.

"Thief!" Osugi screamed again. Flying after the man, she managed to throw her arms around his waist. "Help! Thief!"

The pickpocket struggled, striking her several times in the face without being able to break her grip. "Let go of me, you cow!" he shouted, kicking her in the ribs. With a loud grunt, Osugi fell down, but she had her short sword out and slashed at the man's ankle.

"Ow!" Blood pouring from the wound, he limped a few steps, then flopped down on the ground.

Startled by the commotion, the land dealers turned around, and one of them exclaimed, "Hey, isn't that that good-for-nothing from Kōshū?" The speaker was Hangawara Yajibei, master of a large gang of construction workers.

"Looks like him," agreed one of his henchmen. "What's that in his hand? Looks like a purse."

"It does, doesn't it? And somebody just yelled thief. Look! There's an old woman sprawled out on the ground. Go see what's the matter with her. I'll take care of him."

The pickpocket was on his feet and running again,

but Yajibei caught up with him and slapped him to the ground as he might have swatted a grasshopper.

Returning to his boss, the henchman reported, "Just as we thought. He stole the old lady's purse."

"I have it here. How is she?"

"Not hurt bad. She fainted, but came to screaming bloody murder."

"She's still sitting there. Can't she stand up?"

"I guess not. He kicked her in the ribs."

"You son of a bitch!" Still glaring at the pickpocket, Yajibei issued a command to his underling. "Ushi, put up a stake."

The words set the thief to trembling as though the point of a knife were being pressed against his throat. "Not that," he pleaded, groveling in the dirt at Yajibei's feet. "Let me off just this once. I promise I won't do it again."

Yajibei shook his head. "No. You'll get what you deserve."

Ushi, who had been named after the zodiac sign under which he was born, a not uncommon practice among farmers, returned with two workmen from the nearby bridge site.

"Over there," he said, pointing toward the middle of a vacant lot.

After the workmen had driven a heavy post into the ground, one of them asked, "This good enough?"

"That's fine," said Yajibei. "Now tie him to it, and nail a board above his head."

When this had been done, Yajibei borrowed a carpenter's ink pot and brush and wrote on the board: "This man is a thief. Until recently, he worked for me, but he has committed a crime for which he must be punished. He is to be tied here, exposed to rain and sun, for seven days and seven nights. By order of Yajibei of Bakurō-chō."

"Thanks," he said, returning the ink pot. "Now, if it's not too much trouble, give him a bit to eat every once in a while. Just enough to keep him from starving. Anything left over from your lunch will do.''

The two workmen, along with others who had congregated in the meantime, signified their assent. Some of the laborers promised that they would see to it that the thief got his share of ridicule. It wasn't just samurai who feared public exposure of their misdeeds or weaknesses. Even for ordinary townspeople in these times, to be laughed at was the worst of all punishments.

Punishing criminals without reference to law was a firmly established practice. In the days when the warriors were too busy with warfare to maintain order, townsmen had, for the sake of their own safety, taken it upon themselves to deal with miscreants. Though Edo now had an official magistrate and a system was developing whereby leading citizens in each district functioned as government representatives, the summary administration of justice still occurred. With conditions still being a bit chaotic, the authorities saw little reason to interfere.

"Ushi," said Yajibei, "take the old lady her purse. Too bad this had to happen to somebody her age. She seems to be all alone. What happened to her kimono?"

"She says she washed it and hung it up to dry."

"Go get it for her, then bring her along. We might as well take her home with us. There's little point in punishing the thief if we're going to leave her here for some other ruffian to prey on."

Moments later, Yajibei strode away. Ushi was close behind, the kimono over his arm and Osugi on his back.

They soon reached Nihombashi, the "Bridge of Japan" from which all distances along the roads leading out of Edo were now measured. Stone parapets supported the wooden arch, and since the bridge had been constructed only about a year before, the railings still preserved a feeling of newness. Boats from Kamakura and Odawara were moored along one riverbank. On the other was the city's fish market.

"Oh, my side hurts," Osugi said with a loud groan.

The fishmongers looked up to see what was going on.

Being gaped at was not to Yajibei's liking. Glancing back at Osugi, he said, "We'll be there soon. Try to hold on. Your life's not in danger."

Osugi laid her head on Ushi's back and became as quiet as a baby.

In the downtown area, tradesmen and artisans had formed their own neighborhoods. There was a black-smiths' district, one for lance-makers, others for dyers, tatami weavers, and so on. Yajibei's house stood out prominently from those of the other carpenters because the front half of the roof was covered with tiles; all the other houses had board roofs. Until a fire a couple of years before, nearly all the roofs had been made of thatch. As it happened, Yajibei had acquired what passed for his surname from his roof, Hangawara meaning "half tiled."

He had come to Edo as a rōnin, but being both clever and warmhearted, he had proved to be a skillful manager of men. Before long he set himself up as a contractor employing a sizable crew of carpenters, roofers and un-skilled workers. From building projects carried out for various daimyō, he acquired enough capital to branch out into the real estate business as well. Too affluent now to have to work with his own hands, he played the role of local boss. Among Edo's numerous self-appointed bosses, Yajibei was one of the best known and most highly respected.

The townspeople looked up to the bosses as well as to the warriors, but of the two, the bosses were the more highly admired, because they usually stood up for the common people. Although those of Edo had a style and spirit of their own, the bosses were not unique to the new capital. Their history went back to the troubled latter days of the Ashikaga shogunate, when gangs of thugs roamed the countryside like prides of lions, pillaging at will and submitting to no restraints.

According to a writer of that era, they wore little more than vermilion loincloths and wide stomach wrappers. Their long swords were very long—nearly four feet—and even their short swords were more than two feet in length. Many used other weapons, of a cruder type, such as battle-axes and "iron rakes." They let their hair grow wild, using thick strips of rope for headbands, and leather leggings often covered their calves.

Having no fixed loyalties, they operated as mercenaries, and after peace was restored, were ostracized by both farmers and samurai alike. By the Edo era, those not content with being bandits or highwaymen often sought their fortunes in the new capital. More than a few succeeded, and this breed of leaders was once described as having "righteousness for bones, love of the people for flesh and gallantry for skin." In short, they were popular heroes par excellence.

7

Slaughter by the Riverside

Life under Yajibei's half-tiled roof agreed so much with
Osugi that a year and a half later she was still there. After
the first few weeks, during which she rested and recovered her health, hardly a day passed without her telling
herself she should be on her way.

Whenever she broached the subject to Yajibei, whom
she didn't see often, he urged her to stay on. "What's
the hurry?" he would ask. "There's no reason for you to
go anywhere. Bide your time until we find Musashi. Then
we can serve as your seconds." Yajibei knew nothing of
Osugi's enemy except what she herself had told him—
that he was, in so many words, the blackest of black-
guards—but since the day of her arrival, all of his men
had been under instructions to report immediately anything they heard or saw of Musashi.

After initially detesting Edo, Osugi had mellowed in
attitude to the point where she was willing to admit that
the people were "friendly, carefree and really very kind
at heart."

The Hangawara household was a particularly easy-
going place and something of a haven for social misfits;
country boys too lazy to farm, displaced rōnin, profli-
gates who had run through their parents' money and
tattooed ex-convicts made up a coarse and motley crew,

whose unifying esprit de corps curiously resembled that of a well-run school for warriors. The ideal here, however, was blustering masculinity rather than spiritual manliness; it was really a "dōjō" for thugs.

As in the martial arts dōjō, there was a rigid class structure. Under the boss, who was the ultimate temporal and spiritual authority, came a group of seniors, usually referred to as the "elder brothers." Below them were the ordinary henchmen—the *kobun*—whose ranking was determined largely by length of service. There was also a special class of "guests"; their status depended on such factors as their ability with weapons. Bolstering the hierarchical organization was a code of etiquette, of uncertain origin but strictly adhered to.

At one point, Yajibei, thinking Osugi might be bored, suggested that she take care of the younger men. Since then, her days had been fully occupied with sewing, mending, washing and straightening up after the *kobun*, whose slovenliness gave her plenty of work.

For all their lack of breeding, the *kobun* recognized quality when they saw it. They admired both Osugi's spartan habits and the efficiency with which she went about her chores. "She's a real samurai lady," they were wont to say. "The House of Hon'iden must have very good blood in it."

Osugi's unlikely host treated her with consideration and had even built her separate living quarters on the vacant lot behind his house. And whenever he was at home, he went to pay his respects each morning and evening. When asked by one of his underlings why he displayed such deference toward a stranger, Yajibei confessed that he had acted very badly toward his own father and mother while they were still alive. "At my age," he said, "I feel I have a filial duty to all older people."

Spring came, and the wild plum blossoms fell, but the city itself had as yet almost no cherry blossoms. Apart from a few trees in the sparsely settled hills to the west, there were only the saplings that Buddhists had planted along the road leading to the Sensōji, in Asakusa. Rumor had it that this year they were sprouting buds and would blossom for the first time.

One day Yajibei came to Osugi's room and said, "I'm going to the Sensōji. Do you feel like coming along?"

"I'd love to. That temple's dedicated to Kanzeon, and I'm a great believer in her powers. She's the same bodhisattva as the Kannon I prayed to at Kiyomizudera in Kyoto."

With Yajibei and Osugi went two of the *kobun*, Jūrō and Koroku. Jūrō bore the nickname "Reed Mat," for reasons no one knew, but it was obvious why Koroku was called the "Acolyte." He was a small, compact man with a distinctly benign face, if one overlooked the three ugly scars on his forehead, evidence of a proclivity for street brawls.

They first made their way to the moat at Kyōbashi, where boats were available for hire. After Koroku had skillfully sculled them out of the moat and into the Sumida River, Yajibei ordered the box lunches opened.

"I'm going to the temple today," he explained, "because it's the anniversary of my mother's death. I really should go back home and visit her grave, but it's too far, so I compromise by going to the Sensōji and making a donation. But that's neither here nor there; just think of it as a picnic." He reached over the side of the boat, rinsed off a sake cup and offered it to Osugi.

"It's very fine of you to remember your mother," she said as she accepted the cup, all the while wondering fretfully if Matahachi would do the same when she was gone. "I wonder, though, is drinking sake on the anniversary of your poor mother's passing the thing to do?"

"Well, I'd rather do that than hold some pompous ceremony. Anyway, I believe in the Buddha; that's all that counts for ignorant louts like me. You know the saying, don't you? 'He who has faith need have no knowledge.' "

Osugi, letting it go at that, proceeded to have several refills. After a time she remarked, "I haven't drunk like this for ages. I feel like I'm floating on air."

"Drink up," urged Yajibei. "It's good sake, isn't it? Don't worry about being out on the water. We're here to take care of you."

The river, flowing south from the town of Sumida, was broad and placid. On the Shimōsa side, the east bank opposite Edo, stood a luxuriant forest. Tree roots jutting into the water formed nests holding limpid pools, which shone like sapphires in the sunlight.

"Oh," said Osugi. "Listen to the nightingales!"

"When the rainy season comes, you can hear cuckoos all day long."

"Let me pour for you. I hope you don't mind my joining in your celebration."

"I like to see you having a good time."

From the stern, Koroku called out lustily, "Say, boss, how about passing the sake around?"

"Just pay attention to your work. If you start now, we'll all drown. On the way back you can have all you want."

"If you say so. But I just want you to know the whole river's beginning to look like sake."

"Stop thinking about it. Here, pull over to that boat next to the bank so we can buy some fresh fish."

Koroku did as he was told. After a bit of haggling, the fisherman, flashing a happy smile, lifted the cover off a tank built into the deck and told them to take anything they wanted. Osugi had never seen anything like it. The tank was full to the brim with wriggling, flapping fish, some from the sea, some from the river. Carp, prawns, catfish, black porgies, gobies. Even trout and sea bass.

Yajibei sprinkled soy sauce on some whitebait and began eating it raw. He offered some to Osugi, but she declined, with a look of dread on her face.

When they drew up on the west side of the river and disembarked, Osugi seemed a little wobbly on her feet.

"Be careful," warned Yajibei. "Here, take my hand."

"No, thank you. I don't need any help." She waved her own hand before her face indignantly.

After Jūrō and Koroku had moored the boat, the four of them crossed a broad expanse of stones and puddles to get to the riverbank proper.

A group of small children were busily turning over stones, but seeing the unusual foursome, they stopped and flocked around, chattering excitedly.

"Buy some, sir. Please."

"Won't you buy some, Granny?"

Yajibei seemed to like children; at least, he showed no signs of annoyance. "What have you got there—crabs?"

"Not crabs; arrowheads," they cried, producing handfuls of them from their kimonos.

"Arrowheads?"

"That's right. A lot of men and horses are buried in a mound by the temple. People coming here buy arrowheads to offer to the dead. You should too."

"I don't think I want any arrowheads, but I'll give you some money. How'll that do?"

That, it appeared, would do admirably, and as soon as Yajibei had passed out a few coins, the children ran off to resume their digging. But even as he watched, a man emerged from a thatched-roof house nearby, took the coins away from them and went back inside. Yajibei clicked his tongue and turned away in disgust.

Osugi was gazing out over the river, fascination in her eyes. "If there are a lot of arrowheads lying around," she observed, "there must have been a big battle."

"I don't really know, but it seems there were quite a few battles here in the days when Edo was only a provincial estate. That was four or five hundred years ago. I've heard that Minamoto no Yoritomo came up here from Izu to organize troops in the twelfth century. When the Imperial Court was divided—when was that, fourteenth century?—Lord Nitta of Musashi was defeated by the Ashikagas somewhere in the neighborhood. Just in the last couple of centuries, Ōta Dōkan and other local generals are said to have fought many battles not far up the river."

While they were talking, Jūrō and Koroku went on ahead to make a place for them to sit on the veranda of the temple.

The Sensōji turned out to be a terrible disappointment to Osugi. In her eyes it was nothing more than a large, run-down house, the priest's residence a mere shack. "Is this it?" she wanted to know, with more than a hint of deprecation. "After all I've heard about the Sensōji . . ."

The setting was a splendidly primeval forest of large, ancient trees, but not only did the Kanzeon hall look shabby; when the river flooded, the water came through the woods right up to the veranda. Even at other times, small tributaries washed over the grounds.

"Welcome. Good to see you again."

Glancing up in surprise, Osugi saw a priest kneeling on the roof.

"Working on the roof?" asked Yajibei amiably.

"Have to, because of the birds. The oftener I mend it, the oftener they steal the thatch to make nests with. There's always a leak somewhere. Make yourselves comfortable. I'll be down shortly."

Yajibei and Osugi picked up votive candles and went into the dim interior. "No wonder it leaks," she thought, looking at the starlike holes above her.

Kneeling beside Yajibei, she took out her prayer beads and with a dreamy look in her eye chanted the Vow of Kanzeon from the Lotus Sutra.

> "You will reside in the air like the sun.
> And if you are pursued by evil men
> And pushed off the Diamond Mountain,
> Reflect on the power of Kanzeon

And you will not lose a hair from your head.
And if bandits surround you
And threaten you with swords,
If you reflect on the power of Kanzeon,
The bandits will take pity on you.
And if the king sentences you to death
And the sword is about to behead you,
Reflect on the power of Kanzeon.
The sword will break into pieces."

She recited softly at first, but as she became oblivious to the presence of Yajibei, Jūrō and Koroku, her voice rose and grew resonant; a rapt expression came to her face.

"The eighty-four thousand sentient beings
    Began to aspire in their hearts
    For *anuttara-samyak-sambodhi,*
    The unsurpassed Wisdom of the Buddhas."

Prayer beads trembling in her fingers, Osugi went without a break from the recitation into a personal supplication of her own.

"Hail to Kanzeon, World-Honored One!
    Hail to the Bodhisattva of Infinite Mercy and
        Infinite Compassion!
    Look favorably on this old woman's one wish.
    Let me strike Musashi down, and very soon!
    Let me strike him down!
    Let me strike him down!"

Abruptly lowering her voice, she bowed to the floor. "And make Matahachi a good boy! Cause the House of Hon'iden to prosper!"

After the long prayer ended, there was a moment's silence before the priest invited them outside to have some tea. Yajibei and the two younger men, who had knelt in proper fashion throughout the invocation, got up rubbing their tingly legs and went out on the veranda.

"I can have some sake now, can't I?" Jūrō asked eagerly. Permission having been granted, he hastened to the priest's house and arranged their lunch on the porch. By the time the others joined him, he was sipping sake with one hand and broiling the fish they had bought with the other. "Who cares if there aren't any cherry blossoms?" he remarked. "Feels just like a flower-viewing picnic anyway."

Yajibei handed the priest an offering, delicately wrapped in paper, and told him to use it for the roof repairs. As he did so, he happened to notice a row of wooden plaques on which were written donors' names, together with the amounts they had contributed. Nearly all were about the same as Yajibei's, some less, but one stood out conspicuously. "Ten gold coins, Daizō of Narai, Province of Shinano."

Turning to the priest, Yajibei remarked, somewhat diffidently, "Perhaps it's crass of me to say so, but ten gold coins is a considerable sum. Is this Daizō of Narai as rich as all that?"

"I really couldn't say. He appeared out of the blue one day toward the end of last year and said it was a disgrace that the most famous temple in the Kanto district was in such bad shape. He told me the money should be added to our fund for buying lumber."

"Sounds like an admirable sort of man."

"He also donated three gold coins to Yushima Shrine and no fewer than twenty to Kanda Myōjin Shrine. He wanted the latter to be kept in good condition because it enshrines the spirit of Taira no Masakado. Daizō insists that Masakado was not a rebel. He thinks he should be revered as the pioneer who opened up the eastern part of the country. You'll find there are some very unusual donors in this world."

Hardly had he finished speaking when a crowd of children came running helter-skelter toward them.

"What're you doing here?" shouted the priest sternly. "If you want to play, go down by the river. You mustn't run wild in the temple grounds."

But the children swept on like a school of minnows until they reached the veranda.

"Come quick," cried one. "It's awful!"

"There's a samurai down there. He's fighting."

"One man against four."

"Real swords!"

"Praise to Buddha, not again!" lamented the priest as he hurriedly slipped on his sandals. Before running off, he took a moment to explain. "Forgive me. I'll have to leave you for a while. The riverbank is a favorite place for fights. Every time I turn around, somebody's down there cutting people to pieces or beating them to a pulp. Then men from the magistrate's office come to me for a written report. I'll have to go see what it is this time."

"A fight?" chorused Yajibei and his men, and off they raced. Osugi followed but was so much slower on her feet that by the time she got there the fight was over. The children and some onlookers from a nearby fishing village all stood around in silence, swallowing hard and looking pale.

At first Osugi thought the silence strange, but then she, too, caught her breath, and her eyes opened wide. Across the ground flitted the shadow of a swallow. Walking toward them was a young, smug-faced samurai clad in a purplish-red warrior's cloak. Whether or not he noticed the spectators, he paid them no heed.

Osugi's gaze shifted to four bodies lying in a tangle some twenty paces behind the samurai.

The victor paused. As he did so, a low gasp went up from several lips, for one of the vanquished had moved. Struggling to his feet, he cried, "Wait! You can't run away."

The samurai assumed a waiting stance while the wounded man ran forward, gasping, "This . . . fight's . . . not over yet."

When he leapt weakly to the attack, the samurai retreated a step, allowing the man to stumble forward. Then he struck. The man's head split in two.

"Now is it over?" he shouted viciously.

No one had even seen the Drying Pole drawn.

Having wiped off his blade, he stooped to wash his hands in the river. Though the villagers were accustomed to fights, they were astonished at the samurai's sangfroid. The last man's death had been not only instantaneous but inhumanly cruel. Not a word was uttered.

The samurai stood up and stretched. "It's just like the Iwakuni River," he said. "Reminds me of home." For a few moments he gazed idly at the wide stream and a flock of white-bellied swallows swooping and skimming the water. Then he turned and walked rapidly downstream.

He made straight for Yajibei's boat, but as he began untying it, Jūrō and Koroku came running out of the forest.

"Wait! What do you think you're doing?" shouted Jūrō, who was now close enough to see the blood on the samurai's *hakama* and sandal thongs but took no notice of it.

Dropping the rope, the samurai grinned and asked, "Can't I use the boat?"

"Of course not," snapped Jūrō.

"Suppose I paid to use it?"

"Don't talk nonsense." The voice brusquely refusing the samurai's request was Jūrō's, but in a sense, it was the whole brash new city of Edo speaking fearlessly through his mouth.

The samurai did not apologize, but neither did he resort to force. He turned and walked off without another word.

"Kojirō! Kojirō! Wait!" Osugi called at the top of her lungs.

When Kojirō saw who it was, the grimness vanished from his face and he broke into a friendly smile. "Why, what are you doing here? I've been wondering what happened to you."

"I'm here to pay my respects to Kanzeon. I came with Hangawara Yajibei and these two young men. Yajibei's letting me stay at his house in Bakurōchō."

"When was it I saw you last? Let's see—Mount Hiei. You said then you were going to Edo, so I thought I might run into you. I hardly expected it to be here." He glanced at Jūrō and Koroku, who were in a state of shock. "You mean those two there?"

"Oh, they're just a couple of ruffians, but their boss is a very fine man."

Yajibei was just as thunderstruck as everybody else to see his guest chatting amiably with the awesome samurai. He was on the spot in no time, bowing to Kojirō and saying, "I'm afraid my boys spoke very rudely to you, sir. I hope you'll forgive them. We're just ready to leave. Perhaps you'd like to ride downstream with us."

8

Shavings

Like most people thrown together by circumstance, who ordinarily have little or nothing in common, the samurai and his host soon found mutual ground. The supply of sake was plentiful, the fish fresh, and Osugi and Kojirō had an odd spiritual kinship that kept the atmosphere from getting stickily formal. It was with genuine concern that she inquired about his career as a *shugyōsha* and he about her progress in achieving her "great ambition."

When she told him she'd had no word of Musashi's whereabouts for a long time, Kojirō offered a ray of hope. "I heard a rumor that he visited two or three prominent warriors last fall and winter. I have a hunch he's still in Edo."

Yajibei wasn't so sure, of course, and told Kojirō that his men had learned absolutely nothing. After they had discussed Osugi's predicament from every angle, Yajibei said, "I hope we can count on your continued friendship."

Kojirō responded in the same vein and made rather a display of rinsing out his cup and offering it not only to Yajibei but to his two minions, for each of whom he poured a drink.

Osugi was positively exhilarated. "They say," she observed gravely, "that good is to be found wherever one looks. Even so, I'm exceptionally lucky! To think that I have two strong men like you on my side! I'm sure the great Kanzeon is looking after me." She made no attempt to conceal her sniffling or the tears that came to her eyes.

Not wanting the conversation to get maudlin, Yajibei said, "Tell me, Kojirō, who were the four men you cut down back there?"

This seemed to be the opportunity Kojirō had been waiting for, for his agile tongue set to work without delay. "Oh, them!" he began with a nonchalant laugh. "Just some rōnin from Obata's school. I went there five or six times to discuss military matters with Obata, and those fellows kept butting in with impertinent remarks. They even had the nerve to spout off on the subject of swordsmanship, so I told them that if they'd come to the banks of the Sumida, I'd give them a lesson in the secrets of the Ganryū Style, along with a demonstration of the Drying Pole's cutting edge. I let them know I didn't care how many of them came.

"When I got there, there were five of them, but the minute I took a stance, one turned tail and ran. I must say, Edo has no shortage of men who talk better than they fight." He laughed again, this time boisterously.

"Obata?"

"You don't know him? Obata Kagenori. He comes from the lineage of Obata Nichijō, who served the Takeda family of Kai. Ieyasu took him on, and now he's a lecturer in military science to the shōgun, Hidetada. He also has his own school."

"Oh, yes, I remember now." Yajibei was surprised and impressed by Kojirō's apparent familiarity with such a celebrated person. "The young man still has his forelock," he marveled to himself, "but he must be somebody if he associates with samurai of that rank." The carpenter boss was, after all, a simple soul, and the quality he most admired in his fellow man was clearly brute strength. His admiration for Kojirō intensified.

Leaning toward the samurai, he said, "Let me make

you a proposition. I've always got forty or fifty young louts lying around my house. How would it be if I built a dōjō for you and asked you to train them?"

"Well, I wouldn't mind giving them lessons, but you must understand that so many daimyō are tugging at my sleeve with offers—two, three thousand bushels—that I don't know what to do. Frankly, I wouldn't seriously consider going into anyone's service for less than five thousand. Also, I'm rather obligated, just for the sake of courtesy, to stay where I'm living now. Still, I've no objection to coming to your place."

With a low bow, Yajibei said, "I'd greatly appreciate that."

Osugi chimed in, "We'll be expecting you."

Jūrō and Koroku, far too naive to recognize the condescension and self-serving propaganda lacing Kojirō's speech, were bowled over by the great man's largesse.

When the boat rounded the turn into the Kyōbashi moat, Kojirō said, "I'll be getting off here." He then leapt onto the bank and in a matter of seconds was lost in the dust hovering over the street.

"Very impressive young man," said Yajibei, still under the spell.

"Yes," Osugi agreed with conviction. "He's a real warrior. I'm sure plenty of daimyō would pay him a handsome stipend." After a moment's pause, she added wistfully, "If only Matahachi were like that."

About five days later, Kojirō breezed into Yajibei's establishment and was ushered into the guest room. There, the forty or fifty henchmen on hand paid their respects, one by one. Kojirō, delighted, remarked to Yajibei that he seemed to lead a very interesting life.

Pursuing his earlier idea, Yajibei said, "As I told you, I'd like to build a dōjō. Would you care to take a look at the property?"

The field in back of the house measured nearly two

acres. Freshly dyed cloth hung in one corner, but Yajibei assured Kojirō the dyer he had rented the plot to could easily be evicted.

"You don't really need a dōjō," observed Kojirō. "The area's not open to the street; no one's likely to intrude."

"Whatever you say, but what about rainy days?"

"I won't come if the weather's bad. I should warn you, though: the practice sessions will be rougher than the ones held by the Yagyū or other schools around town. If your men aren't careful, they might wind up crippled, or worse. You'd better make that clear to them."

"There'll be no misunderstanding about that. Feel free to conduct classes as you see fit."

They agreed on having lessons three times a month, on the third, the thirteenth and the twenty-third, weather permitting.

Kojirō's appearances in Bakurōchō were a source of endless gossip. One neighbor was heard to say, "Now they've got a show-off over there worse than all the others put together." His boyish forelock also came in for considerable comment, the general opinion being that since he must be in his early twenties, it was high time he conformed to the samurai practice of shaving his pate. But only those inside the Hangawara household were treated to the sight of Kojirō's brightly embroidered underrobe, which they got to see every time he bared his shoulder to give his arm free play.

Kojirō's demeanor was quite what might be expected. Though this was practice and many of his students were inexperienced, he gave no quarter. By the third session, the casualties already included one man permanently deformed, plus four or five suffering from lesser injuries. The wounded were not far off; their moans could be heard coming from the back of the house.

"Next!" shouted Kojirō, brandishing a long sword made of loquat wood. At the beginning he had told them that a blow struck with a loquat sword "will rot your flesh to the bone."

"Ready to quit? If you're not, come forward. If you are, I'm going home," he taunted contemptuously.

Out of pure chagrin, one man said, "All right, I'll give it a try." He disengaged himself from the group, walked toward Kojirō, then leaned over to pick up a wooden sword. With a sharp crack, Kojirō flattened him.

"That," he declared, "is a lesson in why not to leave yourself open. It's the worst thing you can do." With obvious self-satisfaction, he looked around at the faces of the others, thirty to forty in number, most of them all but visibly trembling.

The latest victim was carried to the well, where water was poured over him. He did not come to.

"Poor guy's done for."

"You mean . . . he's dead?"

"He's not breathing."

Others ran up to stare at their slain comrade. Some were angry, some resigned, but Kojirō didn't give the corpse a second glance.

"If something like this frightens you," he said menacingly, "you'd better forget about the sword. When I think that any one of you would be itching to fight if somebody on the street called you a thug or a braggart . . ." He didn't finish the sentence, but as he walked across the field in his leather socks, he continued his lecture. "Give the matter some thought, my fine hoodlums. You're ready to draw the minute a stranger steps on your toes or brushes against your scabbard, but you're tied up in knots when the time comes for a real bout. You'll throw your lives away cheerfully over a woman or your own petty pride, but you haven't the guts to sacrifice yourself in a worthy cause. You're emotional, you're moved only by vanity. That's not enough, nowhere near enough."

Throwing his chest out, he concluded, "The truth is simple. The only real bravery, the only genuine self-confidence, comes from training and self-discipline. I dare any one of you: stand up and fight me like a man."

One student, hoping to make him eat his words, attacked from behind. Kojirō bent double, almost touching the ground, and the assailant flew over his head and landed in front of him. The next instant, there was the loud crack of Kojirō's loquat sword against the man's hipbone.

"That'll be all for today," he said, tossing the sword aside and going to the well to wash his hands. The corpse was lying in a flaccid heap beside the sink. Kojirō dipped his hands in the water and splashed some on his face without a word of sympathy.

Slipping his arm back into his sleeve, he said, "I hear a lot of people go to this place called Yoshiwara. You men must know the district pretty well. Wouldn't you like to show me around?" Bluntly announcing that he wanted to have a good time or go drinking was a habit of Kojirō's, but it was a matter of conjecture whether he was being deliberately impudent or disarmingly candid.

Yajibei chose the more charitable interpretation. "Haven't you been to Yoshiwara yet?" he asked with surprise. "We'll have to do something about that. I'd go with you myself, but, well, I have to be here this evening for the wake and so on."

He singled out Jūrō and Koroku and gave them some money. Also a warning, "Remember, you two—I'm not sending you out to play around. You're only going along to take care of your teacher and see that he has a good time."

Kojirō, a few steps in front of the other two, soon found he had trouble staying on the road, for at night most of Edo was pitch black, to an extent unimaginable in cities like Kyoto, Nara and Osaka.

"This road's terrible," he said. "We should have brought a lantern."

"People'd laugh if you went around the licensed

quarter carrying a lantern,'' said Jūrō. "Watch out, sir. That pile of dirt you're on came out of the new moat. You'd better come down before you fall in.''

Presently the water in the moat took on a reddish cast, as did the sky beyond the Sumida River. A late spring moon hung like a flat white cake above the roofs of Yoshiwara.

"That's it over there, across the bridge,'' said Jūrō. "Shall I lend you a hand towel?''

"What for?''

"To hide your face a little—like this.'' Jūrō and Koroku both drew red cloths from their obi and tied them kerchief-fashion over their heads. Kojirō followed suit, using a piece of russet silk crepe.

"That's the way,'' said Jūrō. "Stylish like.''

"Looks very good on you.''

Kojirō and his guides fell in with the bandannaed throng sauntering from house to house. Like Yanagima-chi in Kyoto, Yoshiwara was brightly lit. The entrances to the houses were gaily decorated with curtains of red or pale yellow; some had bells at the bottom to let the girls know when customers entered.

After they had been in and out of two or three houses, Jūrō said leeringly to Kojirō, "There's no use trying to hide it, sir.''

"Hide what?''

"You said you'd never been here before, but a girl in the last house recognized you. The minute we went in, she gave a little cry and hid behind a screen. Your secret's out, sir.''

"I've never been here before. Who're you talking about?''

"Don't play innocent, sir. Let's go back. I'll show you.''

They reentered the house, whose curtain bore a crest shaped like a bitter buckbean leaf, split in three. "Su-miya'' was written in rather small characters to the left.

The house's heavy beams and stately corridors were

reminiscent of Kyoto temple architecture, but the garish newness nullified the attempt to create an aura of tradition and dignity. Kojirō strongly suspected that swamp plants still thrived beneath the floor.

The large parlor they were shown to upstairs had not been straightened up after the last customers. Both table and floor were strewn with bits of food, tissue paper, toothpicks and whatnot. The maid who came to clean up performed her chore with all the finesse of a day laborer.

When Onao arrived to take their orders, she made a point of letting them know how busy she was. She claimed that she hardly had time to sleep and another three years of this hectic pace would put her in her grave. The better houses of Kyoto contrived to maintain the fiction that their raison d'être was to entertain and please their customers. Here the aim was obviously to relieve men of their money as quickly as possible.

"So this is Edo's pleasure quarter," sniffed Kojirō, with a critical glance at the knotholes in the ceiling. "Pretty shoddy, I'd say."

"Oh, this is only temporary," Onao protested. "The building we're putting up now will be finer than anything you'd see in Kyoto or Fushimi." She stared at Kojirō a moment. "You know, sir, I've seen you somewhere before. Ah, yes! It was last year on the Kōshū highroad."

Kojirō had forgotten the chance meeting, but reminded of it, he said with a spark of interest, "Why, yes, I guess our fates must be entwined."

"I should say they are," Jūrō said, laughing, "if there's a girl here who remembers you." While teasing Kojirō about his past, he described the girl's face and clothing and asked Onao to go find her.

"I know the one you mean," said Onao, and went to fetch her.

When some time had passed and she still hadn't come back, Jūrō and Koroku went out in the hall and clapped their hands to summon her. They had to clap several more times before she finally reappeared.

"She's not here, the one you asked for," said Onao.

"She was here only a few minutes ago."

"It's strange, just as I was saying to the master. We were at Kobotoke Pass and that samurai you're with came walking along the road, and she went off by herself that time too."

Behind the Sumiya stood the frame of the new building, roof partly finished, no walls.

"Hanagiri! Hanagiri!"

This was the name they had given Akemi, who was hiding between a stack of lumber and a small mountain of shavings. Several times the searchers had passed so close she had had to hold her breath.

"How disgusting!" she thought. For the first few minutes her wrath had been directed at Kojirō alone. By now it had expanded to embrace every member of the masculine sex—Kojirō, Seijūrō, the samurai at Hachiōji, the customers who manhandled her nightly at the Sumiya. All men were her enemies, all abominable.

Except one. The right one. The one who would be like Musashi. The one she had sought incessantly. Having given up on the real Musashi, she had now persuaded herself that it would be comforting to pretend to be in love with someone similar to him. Much to her chagrin, she found no one remotely like him.

"Ha-na-gi-ri!" It was Shōji Jinnai himself, first shouting from the back of the house, now drawing closer to her hiding place.

He was accompanied by Kojirō and the other two men. They had complained at tiresome length, making Jinnai repeat his apologies over and over, but finally they went off toward the street.

Akemi, seeing them go, breathed a sigh of relief and waited until Jinnai went back inside, then ran straight to the kitchen door.

"Why, Hanagiri, were you out there all the time?" the kitchen maid asked hysterically.

"Shh! Be quiet, and give me some sake."

"Sake? Now?"

"Yes, sake!" Since coming to Edo, the times when Akemi had sought solace in sake had become more and more frequent.

The frightened maid poured her a large cupful. Shutting her eyes, Akemi drained the vessel dry, her powdered face tilted back until it was almost parallel with the white bottom of the cup.

As she turned away from the door, the maid cried in alarm, "Where're you off to now?"

"Shut up. I'll just wash my feet, then go back inside."

Taking her at her word, the maid shut the door and returned to her work.

Akemi slipped her feet into the first pair of zōri she saw and walked somewhat unsteadily to the street. "How good to be out in the open!" was her first reaction, but this was followed very closely by revulsion. She spat in the general direction of the pleasure-seekers strolling along the brightly lit road and took to her heels.

Coming to a place where stars were reflected in a moat, she stopped to look. She heard running feet behind her. "Oh, oh! Lanterns this time. And they're from the Sumiya. Animals! Can't they even let a girl have a few minutes' peace? No. Find her! Put her back to making money! Turning flesh and blood into a little lumber for their new house—that's the only thing that'll satisfy them. Well, they won't get me back!"

The curled wood shavings hanging loosely in her hair bobbed up and down as she ran as fast as her legs would carry her into the darkness. She had no idea where she was going, and couldn't have cared less, so long as it was away, far away.

9

The Owl

When they finally forsook the teahouse, Kojirō was barely able to stand.

"Shoulder . . . shoulder," he gurgled, grabbing onto both Jūrō and Koroku for support.

The three lumbered uncertainly down the dark, deserted street.

Jūrō said, "Sir, I told you we should spend the night."

"In that dive? Not on your life! I'd rather go back to the Sumiya."

"I wouldn't, sir."

"Why not?"

"That girl, she ran away from you. If they find her, she could be forced to go to bed with you, but for what? You wouldn't enjoy it then."

"Umm. Maybe you're right."

"Do you want her?"

"Nah."

"But you can't quite get her out of your mind, can you?"

"I've never fallen in love in my life. I'm not the type. I've got more important things to do."

"What, sir?"

"Obvious, my boy. I'm going to be the best, most

famous swordsman ever, and the quickest way to do that is to be the shōgun's teacher."

"But he already has the House of Yagyū to teach him. And I hear he recently hired Ono Jirōemon."

"Ono Jirōemon! Who gives a fart about him? The Yagyūs don't impress me much either. You watch me. One of these days . . ."

They had reached the stretch of road along which the new moat was being dug, and soft dirt was piled halfway up the willow trees.

"Watch out, sir; it's very slippery," said Jūrō as he and Koroku tried to help their teacher down from the pile of dirt.

"Hold it!" Kojirō shouted, abruptly shoving the two men away. He slid rapidly down the dirt pile. "Who's there?"

The man who had just lunged at Kojirō's back lost his balance and tumbled headfirst into the moat.

"Have you forgotten, Sasaki?"

"You killed four of our comrades!"

Kojirō jumped to the top of the dirt pile, from where he could see that there were at least ten men among the trees, partly hidden by rushes. Swords pointed at him, they slowly began closing in.

"So you're from the Obata School, are you?" he said in a contemptuous tone. The sudden action had sobered him completely. "Last time, you lost four men out of five. How many of you came tonight? How many want to die? Just give me the number, and I'll oblige. Cowards! Attack if you dare!" His hand went deftly over his shoulder to the hilt of the Drying Pole.

Obata Nichijō, before taking the tonsure, had been one of the most celebrated warriors in Kai, a province famous for its heroic samurai. After the defeat of the House of Takeda by Tokugawa Ieyasu, the Obata family had lived in obscurity until Kagenori distinguished himself at the Battle of Sekigahara. He had subsequently been summoned into service by Ieyasu himself and had gained fame as a teacher of military science. He had, however, refused the shogunate's offer of a choice plot of land in central Edo with the plea that a country warrior like himself would feel out of place there. He preferred a wooded lot adjoining Hirakawa Tenjin Shrine, where he had established his school in an ancient thatched farm-house to which had been added a new lecture hall and a rather imposing entrance.

Now advanced in years and suffering from a neural disorder, Kagenori had been confined to his sickroom in recent months, appearing only rarely in the lecture hall. The woods were full of owls, and he had taken to signing his name as "Old Man Owl." Sometimes he'd smile weakly and say, "I'm an owl, like the others."

Not infrequently, the pain from the waist up was agonizing. Tonight had been one of those times.

"Feel a little better? Would you like some water?" The speaker was Hōjō Shinzō, son of Hōjō Ujikatsu, the celebrated military strategist.

"I'm much more comfortable now," said Kagenori. "Why don't you go to bed? It'll soon be light." The invalid's hair was white, his frame as skinny and angular as an aged plum tree.

"Don't worry about me. I get plenty of sleep during the day."

"You can't have much time left for sleeping when you spend your days taking over my lectures. You're the only one who can do that."

"Sleeping too much isn't good discipline."

Noticing that the lamp was about to go out, Shinzō stopped rubbing the old man's back and went to fetch some oil. When he returned, Kagenori, still lying on his stomach, had raised his bony face from the pillow. The light was reflected eerily in his eyes.

"What is it, sir?"

"Don't you hear it? It sounds like splashing water."

"It seems to be coming from the well."

"Who would it be at this hour? Do you suppose some of the men have been out drinking again?"

"That's probably it, but I'll take a look anyhow."

"Give them a good scolding while you're at it."

"Yes, sir. You'd better go to sleep. You must be tired."

When Kagenori's pain had subsided and he had dropped off to sleep, Shinzō carefully tucked the covers up around his shoulders and went to the back door. Two students were leaning over the well bucket, washing blood off their faces and hands.

He ran toward them with a scowl on his face. "You went, didn't you?" he said curtly. "After I pleaded with you not to!" The exasperation in his voice faded when he saw a third man lying in the shadow of the well. From the way he was groaning, it sounded as if he might die from his wounds at any moment.

Like little boys begging for help from an older brother, both men, their faces oddly twisted, sobbed uncontrollably.

"Fools!" Shinzō had to restrain himself from giving them a thrashing. "How many times did I warn you you were no match for him? Why didn't you listen?"

"After he dragged our master's name through the mud? After he killed four of our men? You keep saying we're not being reasonable. Aren't you the one who's lost his reason? Controlling your temper, holding yourself back, bearing insults in silence! Is that what you call reasonable? That's not the Way of the Samurai."

"Isn't it? If confronting Sasaki Kojirō was the thing to do, I'd have challenged him myself. He went out of his way to insult our teacher and commit other outrages against us, but that's no excuse for losing our sense of proportion. I'm not afraid to die, but Kojirō is not worth risking my life or anybody else's over."

"That's not the way most people see it. They think we're afraid of him. Afraid to stand up for our honor. Kojirō's been maligning Kagenori all over Edo."

"If he wants to run off at the mouth, let him. Do you think anybody who knows Kagenori is going to believe he lost an argument to that conceited novice?"

"Do as you please, Shinzō. The rest of us are not going to sit by and do nothing."

"Just exactly what do you have in mind?"

"Only one thing. Kill him!"

"You think you can? I told you not to go to the Sensōji. You wouldn't listen. Four men died. You've just returned after being defeated by him again. Isn't that piling shame on dishonor? It's not Kojirō who's destroying Kagenori's reputation, it's you. I have one question. Did you kill him?"

There was no answer.

"Of course not. I'll bet anything he doesn't have a scratch on him. The trouble with you is you don't have enough sense to avoid meeting him on his own terms. You don't understand his strength. True, he's young, he's of low character, he's coarse, he's arrogant. But he's an outstanding swordsman. How he learned his skill, I don't know, but there's no denying he has it. You underestimate him. That's your first mistake."

One man pressed in on Shinzō as though ready to attack him physically. "You're saying that whatever the bastard does, there's nothing we can do about it."

Shinzō nodded defiantly. "Exactly. There's nothing we can do. We're not swordsmen; we're students of military science. If you think my attitude is cowardly, then I'll just have to put up with being called a coward."

The wounded man at their feet moaned. "Water . . . water . . . please."

His two comrades knelt and propped him into a sitting position.

Seeing they were about to give him some water, Shinzō cried in alarm, "Stop! If he drinks water, it'll kill him!"

As they hesitated, the man put his mouth to the

bucket. One swallow and his head collapsed into it, bringing the night's death toll to five.

While the owls hooted at the morning moon, Shinzō silently returned to the sickroom. Kagenori was still asleep, breathing deeply. Reassured, Shinzō went to his own cubicle.

Works on military science lay open on his desk, books he had begun reading but had had no time to finish. Though well born, as a child he had done his share of splitting firewood, carrying water and studying long hours by candlelight. His father, a great samurai, did not believe that young men of his class should be pampered. Shinzō had entered the Obata School with the ultimate aim of strengthening military skills in his family's fief, and though one of the younger students, he ranked highest in his teacher's estimation.

These days, caring for his ailing master kept him awake most of the night. He sat now with his arms folded and heaved a deep sigh. Who would look after Kagenori if he were not there? All the other students living at the school were of an uncouth type typically attracted to military matters. The men who came to the school only for classes were even worse. They blustered about, voicing opinions on the masculine subjects that samurai habitually discussed; none of them really understood the spirit of the lonely man of reason who was their teacher. The finer points of military science went over their heads. Far more comprehensible was any kind of slur, either real or fancied, against their pride or their ability as samurai. Insulted, they became mindless instruments of vengeance.

Shinzō had been away on a trip when Kojirō arrived at the school. Since Kojirō had claimed that he wanted to ask some questions about military textbooks, his interest seemed genuine and he had been introduced to the master. But then, without asking a single question, he began arguing with Kagenori presumptuously and arrogantly, which suggested that his real purpose was to humiliate the old man. When some students finally got him into another room and demanded an explanation, he reacted with a flood of invective and an offer to fight any of them at any time.

Kojirō had then spread allegations that Obata's military studies were superficial, that they were no more than a rehash of the Kusunoki Style or the ancient Chinese military text known as the *Six Secrets,* and that they were spurious and unreliable. When his malicious pronouncements got back to the ears of the students, they vowed to make him pay with his life.

Shinzō's opposition—the problem was trivial, their master ought not to be disturbed by matters of this sort, Kojirō was not a serious student of military science—had proved futile, though he had also pointed out that before any decisive step was taken, Kagenori's son Yogorō, who was away on a long journey, should be consulted.

"Can't they see how much useless trouble they're causing?" lamented Shinzō. The fading light of the lamp dimly illuminated his troubled face. Still racking his brain for a solution, he laid his arms across the open books and dozed off.

He awoke to the murmur of indistinct voices.

Going first to the lecture hall and finding it empty, he slipped on a pair of zōri and went outside. In a bamboo grove that was part of the sacred compound of the Hirakawa Tenjin Shrine, he saw what he had expected: a large group of students holding an emotion-charged council of war. The two wounded men, their faces ashen, their arms suspended in white slings, stood side by side, describing the night's disaster.

One man asked indignantly, "Are you saying ten of you went and half were killed by this one man?"

"I'm afraid so. We couldn't even get close to him."

"Murata and Ayabe were supposed to be our best swordsmen."

"They were the first to go. Yosobei managed by

sheer guts to get back here, but he made the mistake of drinking some water before we could stop him.''

A grim silence descended over the group. As students of military science, they were concerned with problems of logistics, strategy, communications, intelligence and so on, not with the techniques of hand-to-hand combat. Most of them believed, as they had been taught, that swordsmanship was a matter for ordinary soldiers, not generals. Yet their samurai pride stood in the way of their accepting the logical corollary, which was that they were helpless against an expert swordsman like Sasaki Kojirō.

"What can we do?" asked a mournful voice. For a time the only answer was the hooting of the owls.

Then one student said brightly, "I have a cousin in the House of Yagyū. Maybe through him we could get them to help us."

"Don't be stupid!" shouted several others.

"We can't ask for outside help. It'd only bring more shame on our teacher. It'd be an admission of weakness."

"Well, what can we do?"

"The only way is to confront Kojirō again. But if we do it on a dark road again, it'll only do more damage to the school's reputation. If we die in open battle, we die. At least we won't be thought of as cowards."

"Should we send him a formal challenge?"

"Yes, and we have to keep at it, no matter how many times we lose."

"I think you're right, but Shinzō isn't going to like this."

"He doesn't have to know about it, nor does our master. Remember that, all of you. We can borrow brush and ink from the priest."

They started quietly for the priest's house. Before they had gone ten paces, the man in the lead gasped and stepped back. The others instantly came to a dead halt, their eyes riveted on the back veranda of the timeworn shrine building. There, against a backdrop formed by the shadow of a plum tree laden with green fruit, stood Kojirō, one foot propped on the railing and a malevolent grin on his face. To a man, the students turned pale; some had trouble breathing.

Kojirō's voice was venomous. "I gather from your discussion that you still haven't learned, that you've decided to write a letter of challenge and have it delivered to me. Well, I've saved you the trouble. I'm here, ready to fight.

"Last night, before I'd even washed the blood off my hands, I came to the conclusion there'd be a sequel, so I followed you sniveling cowards home."

He paused to let this sink in, then continued in an ironic tone. "I was wondering how you decide on the time and place to challenge an enemy. Do you consult a horoscope to pick the most propitious day? Or do you consider it wiser not to draw your swords until there comes a dark night when your opponent is drunk and on his way home from the licensed quarter?"

He paused again, as though waiting for an answer.

"Have you nothing to say? Isn't there a single red-blooded man among you? If you're so eager to fight me, come on. One at a time, or all at once—it's all the same to me! I wouldn't run from the likes of you if you were in full armor and marching to the beat of drums!"

No sound came from the cowed men.

"What's the matter with you?" The pauses grew longer. "Have you decided not to challenge me? . . . Isn't there even one among you with some backbone?

"All right, it's time now to open your stupid ears and listen.

"I am Sasaki Kojirō. I learned the art of the sword indirectly from the great Toda Seigen after his death. I know the secrets of unsheathing invented by Katayama Hisayasu, and I have myself created the Ganryū Style. I'm not like those who deal in theory, who read books and listen to lectures on Sun-tzu or the *Six Secrets*. In spirit, in will, you and I have nothing in common.

"I don't know the details of your daily study, but I'm showing you now what the science of fighting is all about in real life. I'm not bragging. Think! When a man is set upon in the dark as I was last night, if he has the good fortune to win, what does he do? If he's an ordinary man, he goes as quickly as he can to a safe place. Once there, he thinks back over the incident and congratulates himself on having survived. Isn't that right? Isn't that what you would do?

"But did I do that? No! Not only did I cut down half of your men, I followed the stragglers home and waited here, right under your noses. I listened while you tried to make up your weak minds, and I took you completely by surprise. If I wanted to, I could attack now and smash you to bits. That's what it means to be a military man! That's the secret of military science!

"Some of you have said Sasaki Kojirō is just a swordsman, that he had no business coming to a military school and shooting off his mouth. How far do I have to go to convince you how wrong you are? Perhaps today I'll also prove to you that I'm not only the greatest swordsman in the country but also a master of tactics!

"Ha, ha! This is turning into quite a little lecture, isn't it? I'm afraid if I continue to pour out my fund of knowledge, poor Obata Kagenori may find himself out of a stipend. That wouldn't do, would it?

"Oh, I'm thirsty, Koroku! Jūrō! Get me some water!"

"Right away, sir!" they replied in unison from beside the shrine, where they had been watching in rapt admiration.

Having brought him a large earthen cup of water, Jūrō asked eagerly, "What are you going to do, sir?"

"Ask them!" Kojirō sneered. "Your answer's in those weaselly, empty faces."

"Did you ever see men look so stupid?" Koroku laughed.

"What a gutless bunch," said Jūrō. "Come on, sir, let's go. They're not going to stand up to you."

While the three of them swaggered through the shrine gate, Shinzō, concealed among the trees, muttered through clenched teeth, "I'll get you for this."

The students were despondent. Kojirō had outwitted and defeated them; then he'd gloated, leaving them frightened and humiliated.

The silence was broken by a student running up and asking in a bewildered tone, "Did we order coffins?" When no one replied, he said, "The coffin-maker's just arrived with five coffins. He's waiting."

Finally, one of the group answered dispiritedly, "The bodies have been sent for. They haven't arrived yet. I'm not sure, but I think we'll need one more coffin. Ask him to make it, and put the ones he brought in the storehouse."

That night a wake was held in the lecture hall. Though everything was done quietly, in the hope that Kagenori would not hear, he was able to guess more or less what had occurred. He refrained from asking questions, nor did Shinzō make any comment.

From that day, the stigma of defeat hung over the school. Only Shinzō, who had urged restraint and been accused of cowardice, kept alive the desire for revenge. His eyes harbored a glint that none of the others could fathom.

In early fall, Kagenori's illness worsened. Visible from his bedside was an owl perched on a limb of a large zelkova tree, staring, never moving, hooting at the moon in the daytime. Shinzō now heard in the owl's hoot the message that his master's end was near.

Then a letter arrived from Yogorō, saying he had heard about Kojirō and was on his way home. For the next few days, Shinzō wondered which would come first, the arrival of the son or the death of the father. In either case, the day for which he was waiting, the day of his release from his obligations, was at hand.

On the evening before Yogorō was expected, Shinzō left a farewell letter on his desk and took his leave of the Obata School. From the woods near the shrine, he faced Kagenori's sickroom and said softly, "Forgive me for leaving without your permission. Rest at ease, good master. Yogorō will be home tomorrow. I don't know if I can present Kojirō's head to you before you die, but I must try. If I should die trying, I shall await you in the land of the dead."

10

A Plate of Loaches

Musashi had been roaming the countryside, devoting himself to ascetic practices, punishing his body to perfect his soul. He was more resolved than ever to go it alone: if that meant being hungry, sleeping out in the open in cold and rain and walking about in filthy rags, then so be it. In his heart was a dream that would never be satisfied by taking a position in Lord Date's employ, even if his lordship were to offer him his entire three-million-bushel fief.

After the long trip up the Nakasendō, he had spent only a few nights in Edo before taking to the road again, this time north to Sendai. The money given him by Ishimoda Geki had been a burden on his conscience; from the moment he'd discovered it, he'd known he'd find no peace until it was returned.

Now, a year and a half later, he found himself on Hōtengahara, a plain in Shimōsa Province, east of Edo, little changed since the rebellious Taira no Masakado and his troops had rampaged through the area in the tenth century. The plain was a dismal place still, sparsely settled and growing nothing of value, only weeds, a few trees and some scrubby bamboo and rushes. The sun, low on the horizon, reddened the pools of stagnant water but left the grass and brush colorless and indistinct.

"What now?" Musashi mumbled, resting his weary legs at a crossroads. His body felt listless and still water-logged from the cloudburst he'd been caught in a few days earlier at Toshigi Pass. The raw evening damp made him eager to find human habitation. For the past two nights he'd slept under the stars, but now he longed for the warmth of a hearth and some real food, even simple peasant fare such as millet boiled with rice.

A touch of saltiness in the breeze suggested that the sea was near. If he headed toward it, he reasoned, he just might find a house, perhaps even a fishing village or small port. If not, then he'd have to resign himself to yet another night in the autumn grasses, under the great autumn moon.

He realized with no small hint of irony that were he a more poetic type, he might savor these moments in a poignantly lonely landscape. As it was, he wanted only to escape it, to be with people, to have some decent food and get some rest. Yet the incessant buzzing of the insects seemed to be reciting a litany to his solitary wandering.

Musashi stopped on a dirt-covered bridge. A definite splashing noise seemed to rise above the peaceful rippling of the narrow river. An otter? In the fading daylight, he strained his eyes until he could just make out a figure kneeling in the hollow by the water's edge. He chuckled to note that the face of the young boy peering up at him was distinctly otter-like.

"What are you up to down there?" Musashi called in a friendly voice.

"Loaches," was the laconic reply. The boy was shaking a wicker basket in the water to clean the mud and sand off his wriggling catch.

"Catch many?" Musashi inquired, loath to sever this newly found bond with another human.

"Aren't many around. It's already fall."

"How about letting me have some?"

"My loaches?"

"Yes, just a handful. I'll pay you for them."

"Sorry. These are for my father." Hugging the basket, he leapt nimbly up the bank and was off like a shot into the darkness.

"Speedy little devil, I must say." Musashi, alone once again, laughed. He was reminded of his own childhood and of Jōtarō. "I wonder what's become of him," he mused. Jōtarō had been fourteen when Musashi had last seen him. Soon he would be sixteen. "Poor boy. He accepted me as his teacher, loved me as his teacher, served me as his teacher, and what did I do for him? Nothing."

Absorbed in his memories, he forgot his fatigue. He stopped and stood still. The moon had risen, bright and full. It was on nights like this that Otsū liked to play the flute. In the insects' voices he heard the sound of laughter, Otsū's and Jōtarō's together.

Turning his head to one side, he spotted a light. He turned the rest of his body in the same direction and made straight for it.

Lespedeza grew all around the isolated shack, almost as high as the lopsided roof. The walls were covered with calabash vines, the blossoms looking from a distance like enormous dewdrops. As he drew nearer, he was startled by the great angry snort of an unsaddled horse tied up beside the hovel.

"Who's there?"

Musashi recognized the voice coming from the shack as that of the boy with the loaches. Smiling, he called, "How about putting me up for the night? I'll leave first thing in the morning."

The boy came to the door and looked Musashi over carefully. After a moment, he said, "All right. Come in."

The house was as rickety as any Musashi had ever seen. Moonlight poured through cracks in the walls and roof. After removing his cloak, he couldn't find even a peg to hang it on. Wind from below made the floor drafty, despite the reed mat covering it.

The boy knelt before his guest in formal fashion and

said, "Back there at the river you said you wanted some loaches, didn't you? Do you like loaches?"

In these surroundings, the boy's formality so surprised Musashi that he merely stared.

"What are you looking at?"

"How old are you?"

"Twelve."

Musashi was impressed by his face. It was as dirty as a lotus root just pulled out of the ground, and his hair looked and smelled like a bird's nest. Yet there was character in his expression. His cheeks were chubby, and his eyes, shining like beads through the encircling grime, were magnificent.

"I have a little millet and rice," said the boy hospitably. "And now that I've given some to my father, you can have the rest of the loaches, if you want them."

"Thanks."

"I suppose you'd like some tea too."

"Yes, if it's not too much trouble."

"Wait here." He pushed open a screechy door and went into the next room.

Musashi heard him breaking firewood, then fanning the flame in an earthen hibachi. Before long, the smoke filling the shack drove a host of insects outdoors.

The boy came back with a tray, which he placed on the floor in front of Musashi. Falling to immediately, Musashi devoured the salty broiled loaches, the millet and rice and the sweetish black bean paste in record time.

"That was good," he said gratefully.

"Was it really?" The boy seemed to take pleasure in another person's happiness.

A well-behaved lad, thought Musashi. "I'd like to express my thanks to the head of the house. Has he gone to bed?"

"No, he's right in front of you." The boy pointed at his own nose.

"Are you here all alone?"

"Yes."

"Oh, I see." There was an awkward pause. "And what do you do for a living?" Musashi asked.

"I rent out the horse and go along as a groom. We used to farm a little too. . . . Oh, we've run out of lamp oil. You must be ready for bed anyway, aren't you?"

Musashi agreed that he was and lay down on a worn straw pallet spread next to the wall. The hum of the insects was soothing. He fell asleep, but perhaps because of his physical exhaustion, he broke into a sweat. Then he dreamed he heard rain falling.

The sound in his dream made him sit up with a start. No mistake about it. What he heard now was a knife or sword being honed. As he reached reflexively for his sword, the boy called in to him, "Can't you sleep?"

How had he known that? Amazed, Musashi said, "What are you doing sharpening a blade at this hour?" The question was uttered so tensely that it sounded more like the counterblow of a sword than an inquiry.

The boy broke into laughter. "Did I scare you? You look too strong and brave to be frightened so easily."

Musashi was silent. He wondered if he had come upon an all-seeing demon in the guise of a peasant boy.

When the scraping of the blade on the whetstone began again, Musashi went to the door. Through a crack, he could see that the other room was a kitchen with a small sleeping space at one end. The boy was kneeling in the moonlight next to the window with a large jug of water at his side. The sword he was sharpening was of a type farmers used.

"What do you intend to do with that?" asked Musashi.

The boy glanced toward the door but continued with his work. After a few more minutes, he wiped the blade, which was about a foot and a half long, and held it up to inspect it. It glistened brightly in the moonlight.

"Look," he said, "do you think I can cut a man in half with this?"

"Depends on whether you know how."

"Oh, I'm sure I do."

"Do you have someone particular in mind?"

"My father."

"Your *father?*" Musashi pushed open the door. "I hope that's not your idea of a joke."

"I'm not joking."

"You can't mean you intend to kill your father. Even the rats and wasps in this forsaken wilderness have better sense than to kill their parents."

"But if I don't cut him in two, I can't carry him."

"Carry him where?"

"I have to take him to the burial ground."

"You mean he's dead?"

"Yes."

Musashi looked again at the far wall. It had not occurred to him that the bulky shape he had seen there might be a body. Now he saw that it was indeed the corpse of an old man, laid out straight, with a pillow under its head and a kimono draped over it. By its side was a bowl of rice, a cup of water and a helping of broiled loaches on a wooden plate.

Recalling how he had unwittingly asked the boy to share the loaches intended as an offering to the dead man's spirit, Musashi felt a twinge of embarrassment. At the same time, he admired the boy for having the coolness to conceive of cutting the body into pieces so as to be able to carry it. His eyes riveted on the boy's face, for a few moments he said nothing.

"When did he die?"

"This morning."

"How far away is the graveyard?"

"It's up in the hills."

"Couldn't you have got somebody to take him there for you?"

"I don't have any money."

"Let me give you some."

The boy shook his head. "No. My father didn't like

to accept gifts. He didn't like to go to the temple either. I can manage, thank you.''

From the boy's spirit and courage, his stoic yet practical manner, Musashi suspected that his father had not been born an ordinary peasant. There had to be something to explain the son's remarkable self-sufficiency.

In deference to the dead man's wishes, Musashi kept his money and instead offered to contribute the strength needed to transport the body in one piece. The boy agreed, and together they loaded the corpse on the horse. When the road got steep, they took it off the horse, and Musashi carried it on his back. The graveyard turned out to be a small clearing under a chestnut tree, where a solitary round stone served as a marker.

After the burial, the boy placed some flowers on the grave and said, ''My grandfather, grandmother and mother are buried here too.'' He folded his hands in prayer. Musashi joined him in silent supplication for the family's repose.

''The gravestone doesn't seem to be very old,'' he remarked. ''When did your family settle here?''

''During my grandfather's time.''

''Where were they before that?''

''My grandfather was a samurai in the Mogami clan, but after his lord's defeat, he burned our genealogy and everything else. There was nothing left.''

''I don't see his name carved on the stone. There's not even a family crest or a date.''

''When he died, he ordered that nothing appear on the stone. He was very strict. One time some men came from the Gamō fief, another time from the Date fief, and offered him a position, but he refused. He said a samurai shouldn't serve more than one master. That was the way he was about the stone too. Since he'd become a farmer, he said putting his name on it would reflect shame on his dead lord.''

"Do you know your grandfather's name?"

"Yes. It was Misawa Iori. My father, since he was only a farmer, dropped the surname and just called himself San'emon."

"And your name?"

"Sannosuke."

"Do you have any relatives?"

"An older sister, but she went away a long time ago. I don't know where she is."

"No one else?"

"No."

"How do you plan to make your living now?"

"Same as before, I guess." But then he added hurriedly, "Look, you're a *shugyōsha,* aren't you? You must travel around just about everywhere. Take me with you. You can ride my horse and I'll be your groom."

As Musashi turned the boy's request over in his mind, he gazed out upon the land below them. Since it was fertile enough to support a plethora of weeds, he could not understand why it was not cultivated. It was certainly not because the people hereabouts were well off; he had seen evidence of poverty everywhere.

Civilization, Musashi was thinking, does not flourish until men have learned to exercise control over the forces of nature. He wondered why the people here in the center of the Kanto Plain were so powerless, why they allowed themselves to be oppressed by nature. As the sun rose, Musashi caught glimpses of small animals and birds reveling in the riches that man had not yet learned to harvest. Or so it seemed.

He was soon reminded that Sannosuke, despite his courage and independence, was still a child. By the time the sunlight made the dewy foliage glisten and they were ready to start back, the boy was no longer sad, seemed in fact to have put all thoughts of his father completely out of mind.

Halfway down the hill, he began badgering Musashi for an answer to his proposal. "I'm ready to start today," he declared. "Just think, anywhere you go, you'll be able to ride the horse, and I'll be there to wait on you."

This elicited a noncommittal grunt. While Sannosuke had much to recommend him, Musashi questioned whether he should again put himself in the position of being responsible for a boy's future. Jōtarō—he had natural ability, but how had he benefited by attaching himself to Musashi? And now that he had disappeared to heaven knew where, Musashi felt his responsibility even more keenly. Still, Musashi thought, if a man dwells only on the dangers ahead, he cannot advance a single step, let alone make his way through life successfully. Furthermore, in the case of a child, no one, not even his parents, can actually guarantee his future. "Is it really possible to decide objectively what's good for a child and what's not?" he asked himself. "If it's a matter of developing Sannosuke's talents and guiding him in the right direction, I can do that. I guess that's about as much as anyone can do."

"Promise, won't you? Please," the boy insisted.

"Sannosuke, do you want to be a groom all your life?"

"Of course not. I want to be a samurai."

"That's what I thought. But if you come with me and become my pupil, you'll be in for a lot of rough times, you know."

The boy threw down the rope and, before Musashi knew what he was up to, knelt on the ground below the horse's head. Bowing deeply, he said, "I beg you, sir, make a samurai of me. That's what my father wanted, but there was no one we could ask for help."

Musashi dismounted, looked around for a moment, then picked up a stick and handed it to Sannosuke. He found another one for himself and said, "I want you to strike me with that stick. After I've seen how you handle it, I can decide whether you have the talent to be a samurai."

"If I hit you, will you say yes?"

"Try it and see." Musashi laughed.

Sannosuke took a firm grip on his weapon and rushed forward as if possessed. Musashi showed no mercy. Time and again the boy was struck—on the shoulders, in the face, on the arms. After each setback, he staggered away but always came back to the attack.

"Pretty soon he'll be in tears," thought Musashi.

But Sannosuke would not give up. When his stick broke in two, he charged empty-handed.

"What do you think you're doing, you runt?" Musashi snapped with deliberate meanness. He seized the boy by his obi and threw him flat on the ground.

"You big bastard!" shouted Sannosuke, already on his feet and attacking again.

Musashi caught him by the waist and held him up in the air. "Had enough?"

"No!" he shouted defiantly, though the sun was in his eyes and he was reduced to uselessly waving his arms and legs.

"I'm going to throw you against that rock over there. It'll kill you. Ready to give up?"

"No!"

"Stubborn, aren't you? Can't you see you're beaten?"

"Not as long as I'm alive I'm not! You'll see. I'll win in the end."

"How do you expect to do that?"

"I'll practice, I'll discipline myself."

"But while you're practicing for ten years, I'll be doing the same thing."

"Yes, but you're a lot older than I am. You'll die first."

"Hmm."

"And when they put you in a coffin, I'll strike the final blow and win!"

"Fool!" shouted Musashi, tossing the boy to the ground.

When Sannosuke stood up, Musashi looked at his face for a moment, laughed and clapped his hands together once. "Good. You can be my pupil."

11

Like Teacher, Like Pupil

On the short journey back to the shack, Sannosuke rattled on and on about his dreams for the future.

But that night, when Musashi told him he should be ready to bid farewell to the only home he had ever known, he became wistful. They sat up late and Sannosuke, misty-eyed and speaking in a soft voice, shared his memories of parents and grandparents.

In the morning, while they were preparing to move out, Musashi announced that henceforth he would call Sannosuke Iori. "If you're going to become a samurai," he explained, "it's only proper that you take your grandfather's name." The boy was not yet old enough for his coming-of-age ceremony, when he would normally have been given his adult name; Musashi thought taking his grandfather's name would give him something to live up to.

Later, when the boy seemed to be lingering inside the house, Musashi said quietly but firmly, "Iori, hurry up. There's nothing in there you need. You don't want reminders of the past."

Iori came flying out in a kimono barely covering his thighs, a groom's straw sandals on his feet and a cloth wrapper containing a box lunch of millet and rice in his hand. He looked like a little frog, but he was ready and eager for a new life.

"Pick a tree away from the house and tie the horse up," Musashi commanded.

"You may as well mount it now."

"Do as I say."

"Yes, sir."

Musashi noted the politeness; it was a small but encouraging sign of the boy's readiness to adopt the ways of the samurai in place of the slovenly speech of peasants.

Iori tied up the horse and came back to where Musashi was standing under the eaves of the old shack, gazing at the surrounding plain. "What's he waiting for?" wondered the boy.

Putting his hand on Iori's head, Musashi said, "This is where you were born and where you acquired your determination to win."

Iori nodded.

"Rather than serve a second lord, your grandfather withdrew from the warrior class. Your father, true to your grandfather's dying wish, contented himself with being a mere farmer. His death left you alone in the world, so the time has come for you to stand on your own feet."

"Yes, sir."

"You must become a great man!"

"I'll try." Tears sprang to his eyes.

"For three generations this house sheltered your family from wind and rain. Say your thanks to it, then say good-bye, once and for all, and have no regrets."

Musashi went inside and set fire to the hovel.

When he came out, Iori was blinking back his tears.

"If we left the house standing," said Musashi, "it'd only become a hideout for highwaymen or common thieves. I'm burning it to keep men like that from desecrating the memory of your father and grandfather."

"I'm grateful."

The shack turned into a small mountain of fire, then collapsed.

"Let's go," said Iori, no longer concerned with relics of the past.

"Not yet."

"There's nothing else to do here, is there?"

Musashi laughed. "We're going to build a new house on that knoll over there."

"New house? What for? You just burned the old one down."

"That belonged to your father and grandfather. The one we build will be for us."

"You mean we're going to stay here?"

"That's right."

"We're not going away somewhere and train and discipline ourselves?"

"We'll do that here."

"What can we train ourselves for here?"

"To be swordsmen, to be samurai. We'll discipline our spirits and work hard to make ourselves into real human beings. Come with me, and bring that ax with you." He pointed to a clump of grass where he had put the farm tools.

Shouldering the ax, Iori followed Musashi to the knoll, where there were a few chestnut trees, pines and cryptomerias.

Musashi, stripping to the waist, took the ax and went to work. Soon he was sending up a veritable shower of white chips of raw wood.

Iori watched, thinking: "Maybe he's going to build a dōjō. Or are we going to practice out in the open?"

One tree fell, then another and another. Sweat poured down Musashi's ruddy cheeks, washing away the lethargy and loneliness of the past few days.

He had conceived of his present plan while standing by the farmer's fresh grave in the tiny burial ground. "I'll lay down my sword for a time," he had decided, "and work with a hoe instead." Zen, calligraphy, the art of tea, painting pictures and carving statues were all useful in perfecting one's swordsmanship. Couldn't tilling a field also contribute to his training? Wasn't this broad tract of earth, waiting for someone to bring it under cultivation, a perfect training hall? By changing inhospitable flatlands into farmlands, he would also be promoting the welfare of future generations.

He'd lived his whole life like a mendicant Zen priest—on the receiving end, so to speak, depending on other people for food, shelter and donations. He wanted to make a change, a radical one, since he'd long suspected that only those who had actually grown their own grain and vegetables really understood how sacred and valuable they were. Those who hadn't were like priests who did not practice what they preached or swordsmen who learned combat techniques but knew nothing of the Way.

As a boy, he had been taken by his mother into the fields and had worked alongside the tenants and villagers. His purpose now, however, was more than just to produce food for his daily meals; he sought nourishment for his soul. He wanted to learn what it meant to work for a living, rather than beg for one. He also wanted to implant his own way of thinking among the people of the district. As he saw it, by surrendering the land to weeds and thistles and giving in to storms and floods, they were passing on their hand-to-mouth existence from generation to generation without ever opening their eyes to their own potentialities and those of the land around them.

"Iori," he called, "get some rope and tie up this timber. Then drag it down to the riverbank."

When that was done, Musashi propped his ax against a tree and wiped the sweat off his forehead with his elbow. He then went down and stripped the bark off the trees with a hatchet. When darkness fell, they built a bonfire with the scraps and found blocks of wood to use as pillows.

"Interesting work, isn't it?" said Musashi.

With perfect honesty, Iori answered, "I don't think it's interesting at all. I didn't have to become your pupil to learn how to do this."

"You'll like it better as time goes on."

As autumn waned, the insect voices faded into silence. Leaves withered and fell. Musashi and Iori finished their cabin and addressed themselves to the task of making the land ready for planting.

One day while he was surveying the land, Musashi suddenly found himself thinking it was like a diagram of the social unrest that lasted for a century after the Ōnin War. Such thoughts aside, it was not an encouraging picture.

Unknown to Musashi, Hōtengahara had over the centuries been buried many times by volcanic ash from Mount Fuji, and the Tone River had repeatedly flooded the flatlands. When the weather was fair, the land became bone dry, but whenever there were heavy rains, the water carved out new channels, carrying great quantities of dirt and rock along with it. There was no principal stream into which the smaller ones flowed naturally, the nearest thing to this being a wide basin that lacked sufficient capacity to either water or drain the area as a whole. The most urgent need was obvious: to bring the water under control.

Still, the more he had looked, the more he had questioned why the area was undeveloped. "It won't be easy," he thought, excited by the challenge it posed. Joining water and earth to create productive fields was not much different from leading men and women in such a way that civilization might bloom. To Musashi it seemed that his goal was in complete agreement with his ideals of swordsmanship.

He had come to see the Way of the Sword in a new light. A year or two earlier, he had wanted only to conquer all rivals, but now the idea that the sword existed for the purpose of giving him power over other people was unsatisfying. To cut people down, to triumph over them, to display the limits of one's strength, seemed increasingly vain. He wanted to conquer himself, to make life itself submit to him, to cause people to live rather than die. The Way of the Sword should not be used merely for his own perfection. It should be a source of strength for governing people and leading them to peace and happiness.

He realized his grand ideals were no more than dreams, and would remain so as long as he lacked the political authority to implement them. But here in this wasteland, he needed neither rank nor power. He plunged into the struggle with joy and enthusiasm.

Day in and day out, stumps were uprooted, gravel sifted, land leveled, soil and rocks made into dikes. Musashi and Iori worked from before dawn until after the stars were shining bright in the sky.

Their relentless toil attracted attention. Villagers passing by often stopped, stared, and commented.

"What do they think they're doing?"

"How can they live in a place like that?"

"Isn't the boy old San'emon's son?"

Everyone laughed, but not all let it go at that. One man came out of genuine kindness and said, "I hate to tell you this, but you're wasting your time. You can break your backs making a field here, but one storm and it'll be gone overnight."

When he saw they were still at it several days later, he seemed a bit offended. "All you're doing here, I tell you, is making a lot of water holes where they won't do any good."

A few days later he concluded that the strange samurai was short on brains. "Fools!" he shouted in disgust.

The next day brought a whole group to heckle.

"If anything could grow here, we wouldn't sweat under the blazing sun working our own fields, poor as they are. We'd sit home and play the flute."

"And there wouldn't be any famines."

"You're digging up the place for nothing."

"Got the sense of a pile of manure."

Still hoeing, Musashi kept his eyes on the ground and grinned.

Iori was less complacent, though Musashi had earlier scolded him for taking the peasants seriously. "Sir"—he pouted—"they all say the same thing."

"Pay no attention."

"I can't help it," he cried, seizing a rock to throw at their tormentors.

An angry glare from Musashi stopped him. "Now, what good do you think that would do? If you don't behave yourself, I'm not going to have you as my pupil."

Iori's ears burned at the rebuke, but instead of dropping the rock, he cursed and hurled it at a boulder. The rock gave off sparks as it cracked in two. Iori tossed his hoe aside and began to weep.

Musashi ignored him, though he wasn't unmoved. "He's all alone, just as I am," he thought.

As though in sympathy with the boy's grief, a twilight breeze swept over the plain, setting everything astir. The sky darkened and raindrops fell.

"Come on, Iori, let's go in," called Musashi. "Looks like we're in for a squall." Hurriedly collecting his tools, he ran for the house. By the time he was inside, the rain was coming down in gray sheets.

"Iori," he shouted, surprised that the boy had not come with him. He went to the window and strained his eyes toward the field. Rain spattered from the sill into his face. A streak of lightning split the air and struck the earth. As he shut his eyes and put his hands over his ears, he felt the force of the thunder.

In the wind and rain, Musashi saw the cryptomeria tree at the Shippōji and heard the stern voice of Takuan. He felt that whatever he had gained since then he owed to them. He wanted to possess the tree's immense strength as well as Takuan's icy, unwavering compassion.

If he could be to Iori what the old cryptomeria had been to him, he would feel he'd succeeded in repaying a part of his debt to the monk.

"Iori! . . . Iori!"

There was no answer, only thunder and the rain pounding on the roof.

"Where could he have gone?" he wondered, still unwilling to venture outside.

When the rain slackened to a drizzle, he did go out. Iori had not moved an inch. With his clothing clinging to his body and his face still screwed up in an angry frown, he looked rather like a scarecrow. How could a child be so stubborn?

"Idiot!" Musashi chided. "Get back into the house. Being drenched like that's not exactly good for you. Hurry up, before rivers start forming. Then you won't be able to get back."

Iori turned, as though trying to locate Musashi's voice, then started laughing. "Something bothering you? This kind of rain doesn't last. See, the clouds are breaking up already."

Musashi, not expecting to receive a lesson from his pupil, was more than a little put out, but Iori didn't give the matter a second thought. "Come on," the boy said, picking up his hoe. "We can still get quite a bit done before the sun's gone."

For the next five days, bulbuls and shrikes conversed hoarsely under a cloudless blue sky, and great cracks grew in the earth as it caked around the roots of the rushes. On the sixth day, a cluster of small black clouds appeared on the horizon and rapidly spread across the heavens until the whole plain seemed to be under an eclipse.

Iori studied the sky briefly and said in a worried tone, "This time it's the real thing." Even as he spoke, an inky wind swirled around them. Leaves shook and little birds dropped to the earth as if felled by a silent and invisible horde of hunters.

"Another shower?" Musashi asked.

"Not with the sky like that. I'd better go to the village. And you'd better gather up the tools and get inside as fast as you can." Before Musashi could ask why, Iori took off across the flatlands and was quickly lost in a sea of high grass.

Again, Iori's weather sense was accurate. The sudden downpour, driven by a raging, gusty wind, that sent Musashi scurrying for shelter developed its own distinctive rhythms. The rain fell in unbelievable quantity for a time, stopped suddenly, then recommenced with even greater fury. Night came, but the storm continued unabated. It began to seem as though the heavens were set on making the entire earth into an ocean. Several times Musashi feared that the wind would rip off the roof; the floor was already littered with shingles torn off its underside.

Morning came, gray and formless and with no sign of Iori. Musashi stood by the window, and his heart sank; he could do nothing. Here and there a tree or a clump of grass was visible; all else was a vast muddy swamp. Luckily, the cabin was still above water level, but in what had been a dry riverbed immediately below it, there was now a rushing torrent, carrying along everything in its path.

Not knowing for sure that Iori hadn't fallen into the water and drowned, Musashi felt time drag on, until finally he thought he heard Iori's voice calling, "*Sensei! Here!*" He was some distance beyond the river, riding a bullock, with a great bundle tied behind him.

Musashi watched in consternation as Iori rode straight into the muddy flow, which seemed about to suck him under at every step.

When he gained the other bank, he was quaking from the cold and wet, but he calmly guided the bullock to the side of the cabin.

"Where have you been?" demanded Musashi, his voice both angry and relieved.

"To the village, of course. I brought back lots of food. It'll rain half a year's worth before this storm's over, and when it is, we'll be trapped by the floodwaters."

After they had taken the straw bundle inside, Iori untied it and removed the items one by one from the inner wrapping of oiled paper. "Here are some chestnuts . . . lentil beans . . . salted fish. . . . We shouldn't run out of food even if it takes a month or two for the water to go down."

Musashi's eyes misted over with gratitude, but he said nothing. He was too abashed at his own lack of common sense. How could he guide humanity if he was careless about his own survival? Were it not for Iori, he would now be facing starvation. And the boy, having been raised in a remote rural area, must have known about laying in supplies since he was two years old.

It struck Musashi as odd that the villagers had agreed to furnish all this food. They couldn't have had very much for themselves. When he recovered his voice and raised the question, Iori replied, "I left my money pouch in hock and borrowed from the Tokuganji."

"And what's the Tokuganji?"

"It's the temple about two miles from here. My father told me there was some powdered gold in the pouch. He said if I got into difficulty, I should use it a little at a time. Yesterday, when the weather turned bad, I remembered what he said." Iori wore a smile of triumph.

"Isn't the pouch a keepsake from your father?"

"Yes. Now that we've burned the old house down, that and the sword are the only things left." He rubbed the hilt of the short weapon in his obi. Though the tang bore no craftsman's signature, Musashi had noted when he'd examined the blade earlier that it was of excellent quality. He also had the feeling that the inherited pouch had some significance beyond that of the powdered gold it contained.

"You shouldn't hand keepsakes over to other people. One of these days, I'll get it back for you, but after that you must promise not to let go of it."

"Yes, sir."

"Where did you spend the night?"

"The priest told me I'd better wait there till morning."

"Have you eaten?"

"No. You haven't either, have you?"

"No, but there's no firewood, is there?"

"Oh, there's plenty." He pointed downward, indicating the space under the cabin, where he'd stored a good supply of sticks and roots and bamboo picked up while he worked in the fields.

Holding a piece of straw matting over his head, Musashi crawled under the cabin and again marveled at the boy's good sense. In an environment like this, survival depended on foresight and a small mistake could spell the difference between life and death.

When they had finished eating, Iori brought out a book. Then, kneeling formally before his teacher, he said, "While we're waiting for the water to go down so we can work, would you teach me some reading and writing?"

Musashi agreed. On such a dismal stormy day, it was a good way to pass the time. The book was a volume of the *Analects of Confucius*. Iori said it had been given to him at the temple.

"Do you really want to study?"

"Yes."

"Have you done much reading?"

"No; only a little."

"Who taught you?"

"My father."

"What have you read?"

"*The Lesser Learning*."

"Did you enjoy it?"

"Yes, very much," he said eagerly, his eyes brightening.

"All right then. I'll teach you all I know. Later on, you can find somebody better educated to teach you what I don't know."

They devoted the rest of the day to a study session, the boy reading aloud, Musashi stopping him to correct him or explain words he did not understand. They sat in utter concentration, oblivious of the storm.

The deluge lasted two more days, by which time there was no land visible anywhere.

On the following day, it was still raining. Iori, delighted, took out the book again and said, "Shall we begin?"

"Not today. You've had enough of reading for a while."

"Why?"

"If you do nothing but read, you'll lose sight of the reality around you. Why don't you take the day off and play? I'm going to relax too."

"But I can't go outside."

"Then just do like me," said Musashi, sprawling on his back and crossing his arms under his head.

"Do I have to lie down?"

"Do what you want. Lie down, stand up, sit—whatever's comfortable."

"Then what?"

"I'll tell you a story."

"I'd like that," said Iori, flopping down on his stomach and wiggling his legs in the air. "What kind of story?"

"Let me see," said Musashi, going over the tales he had liked to hear as a child. He chose the one about the battles between the Genji and the Heike. All boys loved that.

Iori proved to be no exception. When Musashi came to the part about the Genji being defeated and the Heike taking over the country, the boy's face became gloomy.

He had to blink to keep from crying over Lady Tokiwa's sad fate. But his spirits rose as he heard about Minamoto no Yoshitsune learning swordsmanship from the "long-nosed goblins" on Mount Kurama and later making his escape from Kyoto.

"I like Yoshitsune," he said, sitting up. "Are there really goblins on Mount Kurama?"

"Maybe. Anyway, there're people in this world who might as well be goblins. But the ones who taught Yoshitsune weren't real goblins."

"What were they?"

"Loyal vassals of the defeated Genji. They couldn't come out in the open while the Heike were in power, so they stayed hidden in the mountains until their chance came."

"Like my grandfather?"

"Yes, except he waited all his life, and his chance never came. After Yoshitsune grew up, the faithful Genji followers who had looked after him during his childhood got the opportunity they had prayed for."

"I'll have a chance to make up for my grandfather, won't I?"

"Hmm. I think it's possible. Yes, I really think so."

He pulled Iori to him, lifted him up and balanced him on his hands and feet like a ball. "Now try being a great man!" He laughed.

Iori giggled, and stammered, "You . . . you're a gob-goblin too! Stop . . . it. I'll fa-fall." He reached down and pinched Musashi's nose.

On the eleventh day, it finally stopped raining. Musashi chafed to be out in the open, but it was another week before they were able to return to work under a bright sun. The field they had so arduously carved out of the wilderness had disappeared without a trace; in its place were rocks, and a river where none had been before. The water seemed to mock them just as the villagers had.

Iori, seeing no way to reclaim their loss, looked up and said, "This place is beyond hope. Let's look for better land somewhere else."

"No," Musashi said firmly. "With the water drained off, this would make excellent farmland. I examined the location from every angle before I chose it."

"What if we have another heavy rain?"

"We'll fix it so the water doesn't come this way. We'll lay a dam from here all the way to that hill over there."

"That's an awful lot of work."

"You seem to forget that this is our dōjō. I'm not giving up a foot of this land until I see barley growing on it."

Musashi carried on his stubborn struggle throughout the winter, into the second month of the new year. It took several weeks of strenuous labor to dig ditches, drain the water off, pile dirt for a dike and then cover it with heavy rocks.

Three weeks later everything was again washed away.

"Look," Iori said, "we're wasting our energy on something impossible. Is that the Way of the Sword?" The question struck close to the bone, but Musashi would not give in.

Only a month passed before the next disaster, a heavy snowfall followed by a quick thaw. Iori, on his return from trips to the temple for food, inevitably wore a long face, for the people there rode him mercilessly about Musashi's failure. And finally Musashi himself began to lose heart.

For two full days and on into a third, he sat silently brooding and staring at his field.

Then it dawned on him suddenly. Unconsciously, he had been trying to create a neat, square field like those common in other parts of the Kanto Plain, but this was not what the terrain called for. Here, despite the general flatness, there were slight variations in the lay of the land

and the quality of the soil that argued for an irregular shape.

"What a fool I've been," he exclaimed aloud. "I tried to make the water flow where I thought it should and force the dirt to stay where I thought it ought to be. But it didn't work. How could it? Water's water, dirt's dirt. I can't change their nature. What I've got to do is learn to be a servant to the water and a protector of the land."

In his own way, he had submitted to the attitude of the peasants. On that day he became nature's manservant. He ceased trying to impose his will on nature and let nature lead the way, while at the same time seeking out possibilities beyond the grasp of other inhabitants of the plain.

The snow came again, and another thaw; the muddy water oozed slowly over the plain. But Musashi had had time to work out his new approach, and his field remained intact.

"The same rules must apply to governing people," he said to himself. In his notebook, he wrote: "Do not attempt to oppose the way of the universe. But first make sure you know the way of the universe."

12

Mountain Devils

"Let me make myself clear. I don't want you to go to any trouble on my account. Your hospitality, which I appreciate greatly, is quite sufficient."

"Yes, sir. That's very considerate of you, sir," replied the priest.

"I'd just like to relax. That's all."

"By all means."

"Now I hope you'll forgive my rudeness," said the samurai, stretching out casually on his side and propping his graying head on his forearm.

The guest who'd just arrived at the Tokuganji was Nagaoka Sado, a high-ranking vassal of Lord Hosokawa Tadaoki of Buzen. He had little time for personal matters, but he invariably came on such occasions as the anniversary of his father's death, usually staying overnight, since the temple was some twenty miles from Edo. For a man of his rank, he traveled unostentatiously, accompanied this time by only two samurai and one young personal attendant.

To get away from the Hosokawa establishment even for a short time, he had had to trump up an excuse. He rarely had the chance to do as he pleased, and now that he did, he was fully enjoying the local sake while listening to the croaking of frogs. Briefly he could forget about everything—the problems of administration and the constant need to be attuned to the nuances of daily affairs.

After dinner, the priest quickly cleared the dishes and left. Sado was chatting idly with his attendants, who were seated next to the wall, only their faces showing in the light of the lamp.

"I could just lie here forever and enter Nirvana, like the Buddha," Sado said lazily.

"Careful you don't catch cold. The night air is damp."

"Oh, leave me alone. This body's survived a few battles. It can hold its own against a sneeze or two. But just smell those ripe blossoms! Nice fragrance, isn't it?"

"I don't smell anything."

"Don't you? If your sense of smell is that poor . . . you sure you don't have a cold yourself?"

They were engrossed in this kind of seemingly light banter when suddenly the frogs fell silent, and a loud voice shouted, "You devil! What're you doing here, staring into the guest room?"

Sado's bodyguards were on their feet instantly.

"What is it?"

"Who's out there?"

As their cautious eyes scanned the garden, the clatter of small feet receded in the direction of the kitchen.

A priest looked in from the veranda, bowed and said, "Sorry for the disturbance. It's only one of the local children. There's nothing to worry about."

"Are you sure?"

"Yes, of course. He lives a couple of miles from here. His father worked as a groom, until he died recently, but his grandfather is said to have been a samurai, and every time he sees one, he stops and stares—with his finger in his mouth."

Sado sat up. "You mustn't be too hard on him. If he wants to be a samurai, bring him in. We'll have some sweets and talk it over."

By now Iori had reached the kitchen. "Hey,

Granny," he shouted. "I've run out of millet. Fill this up for me, will you?" The sack he thrust out to the wrinkled old woman who worked in the kitchen would have held half a bushel.

She shouted right back. "Watch your tongue, you beggar! You talk as if we owe you something."

"You've got a lot of nerve to begin with!" said a priest who was washing dishes. "The head priest took pity on you, so we're giving you food, but don't be insolent. When you're asking a favor, do it politely."

"I'm not begging. I gave the priest the pouch my father left me. There's money in it, plenty of money."

"And how much could a groom living out in the sticks leave his son?"

"Are you going to give me the millet? Yes or no?"

"There you go again. Just look at yourself. You're crazy, taking orders from that fool rōnin. Where did he come from anyway? Who is he? Why should he be eating your food?"

"None of your business."

"Hmph. Digging around in that barren plain where there's never going to be a field or garden or anything else! The whole village is laughing at you."

"Who asked for your advice?"

"Whatever's wrong with that rōnin's head must be catching. What do you expect to find up there—a pot of gold, like in a fairy tale? You're not even dry behind the ears, and you're already digging your own grave."

"Shut up and give me the millet. The millet! Now."

The priest was still teasing Iori a couple of minutes later when something cold and slimy hit his face. His eyes popped, then he saw what it was—a warty toad. He screamed and lunged for Iori, but just as he collared him, another priest arrived to announce that the boy was wanted in the samurai's room.

The head priest had also heard the commotion, and rushed to the kitchen. "Did he do something to upset our guest?" he asked worriedly.

"No. Sado just said he'd like to talk to him. He'd like to give him some sweets too."

The head priest hurriedly took Iori by the hand and delivered him personally to Sado's room.

As Iori timidly sat down beside the priest, Sado asked, "How old are you?"

"Thirteen."

"And you want to become a samurai?"

"That's right," replied Iori, nodding vigorously.

"Well, well. Why don't you come and live with me, then? You'd have to help with the housework at the beginning, but later I'd make you one of the apprentice samurai."

Iori shook his head silently. Sado, taking this for bashfulness, assured him that the offer was serious.

Iori, flashing an angry look, said, "I heard you wanted to give me some sweets. Where are they?"

Paling, the head priest slapped him on the wrist.

"Don't scold him," Sado said reprovingly. He liked children and tended to indulge them. "He's right. A man should keep his word. Have the sweets brought in."

When they arrived, Iori began stuffing them into his kimono.

Sado, a little taken aback, asked, "Aren't you going to eat them here?"

"No. My teacher's waiting for me at home."

"Oh? You have a teacher?"

Without bothering to explain himself, Iori bolted from the room and disappeared through the garden.

Sado thought his behavior highly amusing. Not so the head priest, who bowed to the floor two or three times before going to the kitchen in pursuit of Iori.

"Where is that insolent brat?"

"He picked up his sack of millet and left."

They listened for a moment but heard only a discordant screeching. Iori had plucked a leaf from a tree and was trying to improvise a tune. None of the few songs he knew seemed to work. The grooms' chantey was too

128

slow, the *Bon* festival songs too complicated. Finally, he settled on a melody resembling the sacred dance music at the local shrine. This suited him well enough, for he liked the dances, which his father had sometimes taken him to see.

About halfway to Hōtengahara, at a point where two streams joined to make a river, he gave a sudden start. The leaf flew from his mouth, along with a spray of saliva, and he leapt into the bamboo beside the road.

Standing on a crude bridge were three or four men, engaged in a furtive conversation. "It's them," Iori exclaimed softly.

A remembered threat rang in his frightened ears. When mothers in this region scolded their children, they were apt to say, "If you're not good, the mountain devils will come down and get you." The last time they had actually come had been in the fall of the year before last.

Twenty miles or so from here, in the mountains of Hitachi, there was a shrine dedicated to a mountain deity. Centuries earlier, the people had so feared this god that the villages had taken turns making annual offerings of grain and women to him. When a community's turn came, the inhabitants had assembled their tribute and gone in a torchlight procession to the shrine. As time went on and it became evident that the god was really only a man, they became lax in making their offerings.

During the period of the civil wars, the so-called mountain god had taken to having his tribute collected by force. Every two or three years, a pack of brigands, armed with halberds, hunting spears, axes—anything to strike terror into the hearts of peaceful citizens—would descend on first one community, then the next, carrying away everything that caught their fancy, including wives and daughters. If their victims put up any resistance, the plundering was accompanied by slaughter.

Their last raid still vivid in his memory, Iori cringed in the underbrush. A group of five shadows came running across the field to the bridge. Then, through the night mist, another small band, and still another, until the bandits numbered between forty and fifty.

Iori held his breath and stared while they debated a course of action. They soon reached a decision. Their leader issued a command and pointed toward the village. The men rushed off like a swarm of locusts.

Before long, the mist was rent by a great cacophony—birds, cattle, horses, the wailing of people young and old.

Iori quickly made up his mind to get help from the samurai at the Tokuganji, but the minute he left the shelter of the bamboo, a shout came from the bridge: "Who's there?" He had not seen the two men left behind to stand guard. Swallowing hard, he ran for all he was worth, but his short legs were no match for those of grown men.

"Where do you think you're going?" shouted the man who got hold of him first.

"Who are you?"

Instead of crying like a baby, which might have thrown the men off guard, Iori scratched and fought against the brawny arms imprisoning him.

"He saw all of us together. He was going to tell somebody."

"Let's beat him up and dump him in a rice field."

"I've got a better idea."

They carred Iori to the river, threw him down the bank and, jumping down after him, tied him to one of the bridge posts.

"There, that takes care of him." The two ruffians climbed back up to their station on the bridge.

The temple bell tolled in the distance. Iori watched horrified as the flames rising from the village dyed the river a bloody red. The sound of babies crying and women wailing came closer and closer. Then wheels rumbled onto the bridge. Half a dozen of the bandits were leading oxcarts and horses loaded with loot.

"Filthy scum!" screamed a masculine voice.

"Give me back my wife!"

The scuffle on the bridge was brief but fierce. Men shouted, metal clanged, a shriek went up, and a bloody corpse landed at Iori's feet. A second body splashed into the river, spraying his face with blood and water. One by one farmers fell from the bridge, six of them in all. The bodies rose to the surface and floated slowly downstream, but one man, not quite dead, grasped at the reeds and clawed the earth until he had pulled himself halfway out of the water.

"You!" cried Iori. "Untie this rope. I'll go for help. I'll see that you get your revenge." Then his voice rose to a bellow. "Come on. Untie me. I've got to save the village."

The man lay motionless.

Straining at his bonds with all his might, Iori finally loosened them enough to squirm down and kick the man in the shoulder.

The face that turned toward his was blotched with mud and gore, the eyes dull and uncomprehending.

The man crawled painfully closer; with his last ounce of strength, he undid the knots. As the rope fell loose, he collapsed and died.

Iori looked cautiously up at the bridge and bit his lip. There were more bodies up there. But luck was with him. A cartwheel had broken through a rotten plank. The thieves, hurrying to pull it out, didn't notice his escape.

Realizing he couldn't make it to the temple, Iori tiptoed along in the shadows until he reached a place shallow enough to cross. When he gained the other bank, he was on the edge of Hōtengahara. He covered the remaining mile to the cabin as though lightning was nipping at his heels.

As he neared the knoll where the cabin stood, he saw that Musashi was standing outside, looking at the sky. "Come quick!" he shouted.

"What happened?"

"We have to go to the village."

"Is that where the fire is?"

"Yes. The mountain devils have come again."

"Devils? . . . Bandits?"

"Yes, at least forty of them. Please hurry. We have to rescue the villagers."

Musashi ducked into the cabin and emerged with his swords. While he was tying his sandals, Iori said, "Follow me. I'll show you the way."

"No. You stay here."

Iori couldn't believe his ears.

"It's too dangerous."

"I'm not scared."

"You'd be in the way."

"You don't even know the shortest way there!"

"The fire's all the guide I need. Now just be a good boy and stay right here."

"Yes, sir." Iori nodded obediently, but with deep misgivings. He turned his head toward the village and watched somberly as Musashi streaked off in the direction of the red glow.

The bandits had tied their female captives, moaning and screaming, in a row and were pulling them mercilessly toward the bridge.

"Stop your squawking!" shouted one bandit.

"You act like you don't know how to walk. Move!"

When the women held back, the ruffians lashed them with whips. One woman fell, dragging down others. Seizing the rope and forcing them back on their feet, one man snarled, "Stubborn bitches! What have you got to groan about? Stay here and you work like slaves the rest of your lives, all for a bit of millet. Look at you, nothing but skin and bones! You'll be a lot better off having fun with us."

Picking one of the healthier-looking animals, which were all heavily loaded with booty, they tied the rope to it and gave it a sharp slap on the rump. The slack in the rope was snapped up suddenly and fresh shrieks rent the air as the women were yanked forward again. Those who fell were dragged along, with their faces scraping the ground.

"Stop!" screamed one. "My arms're coming off!"

A wave of raucous laughter swept through the brigands.

At that moment, horse and women came to a dead halt.

"What's going on? . . . Somebody's up ahead!"

All eyes strained to see.

"Who's there?" roared one bandit.

The silent shadow walking toward them carried a white blade. The bandits, trained to be sensitive to odors, instantly recognized the one they smelled now—blood dripping from the sword.

As the men in front fell back clumsily, Musashi sized up the enemy force. He counted twelve men, all hard-muscled and brutish-looking. Recovering from the initial shock, they readied their weapons and took defensive stances. One ran forward with an ax. Another, carrying a hunter's spear, approached diagonally, keeping his body low and aiming at Musashi's ribs. The man with the ax was the first to go.

"A-w-w-k!" Sounding as though he'd bitten his own tongue off, he weaved crazily and collapsed in a heap.

"Don't you know me?" Musashi's voice rang out sharply. "I am the protector of the people, a messenger from the god who watches over this village." In the same breath, he seized the spear pointed at him, wrested it from its owner's hands and threw it violently to the ground.

Moving swiftly into the band of ruffians, he was kept busy countering thrusts from all sides. But after the first surge, made while they still fought with confidence, he had a good idea of what lay ahead. It was a matter not of numbers but of the opposition's cohesiveness and self-control.

Seeing one man after another turned into a blood-spurting missile, the bandits were soon falling back to ever greater distances, until finally they panicked and lost all semblance of organization.

Musashi was learning even as he fought, acquiring experience that would lead him to specific methods to be used by a smaller force against a larger one. This was a valuable lesson and couldn't be learned in a fight with a single enemy.

His two swords were in their scabbards. For years, he'd practiced to master the art of seizing his opponent's weapon and turning it against him. Now he'd put study into practice, taking the sword away from the first man he'd encountered. His reason wasn't that his own sword, which he thought of as his soul, was too pure to be sullied by the blood of common brigands. He was being practical; against such a motley array of weapons, a blade might get chipped, or even broken.

When the five or six survivors fled toward the village, Musashi took a minute or two to relax and catch his breath, fully expecting them to return with reinforcements. Then he freed the women and ordered those who could stand to take care of the others.

After some words of comfort and encouragement, he told them it was up to them to save their parents and children and husbands.

"You'd be miserable if you survived and they perished, wouldn't you?" he asked.

There was a murmur of agreement.

"You yourselves have the strength to protect yourselves and save the others. But you don't know how to use that strength. That's why you're at the mercy of outlaws. We're going to change that. I'm going to help you by showing you how to use the power you have. The first thing to do is arm yourselves."

He had them collect the weapons lying about and distributed one to each of the women.

"Now follow me and do just as I say. You mustn't

be afraid. Try to believe that the god of this district is on your side.''

As he led the women toward the burning village, other victims emerged from the shadows and joined them. Soon the group had grown into a small army of nearly a hundred people. Women tearfully hugged loved ones: daughters were reunited with parents, wives with husbands, mothers with children.

At first, as the women described how Musashi had dealt with the bandits, the men listened with shocked expressions on their faces, not believing that this could be the idiot rōnin of Hōtengahara. When they did accept it, their gratitude was obvious, despite the barrier imposed by their dialect.

Turning to the men, Musashi told them to find weapons. ''Anything'll do, even a good heavy stick or a length of fresh bamboo.''

No one disobeyed, or even questioned his orders.

Musashi asked, ''How many bandits are there in all?''

''About fifty.''

''How many houses in the village?''

''Seventy.''

Musashi calculated that there was probably a total of seven or eight hundred people. Even allowing for old people and children, the brigands would still be outnumbered by as much as ten to one.

He smiled grimly at the thought that these peaceful villagers had believed they had no recourse but to throw up their hands in despair. He knew that if something was not done, the atrocity would be repeated. Tonight he wanted to accomplish two things: show the villagers how to protect themselves and see that the brigands were banished forever.

''Sir,'' cried a man who had just come from the village. ''They're on their way here.''

Though the villagers were armed now, the news

made them uneasy. They showed signs of breaking and running.

To restore confidence, Musashi said loudly, "There's nothing to be alarmed about. I was expecting this. I want you to hide on both sides of the road, but first listen to my instructions." He talked rapidly but calmly, briefly repeating points of emphasis. "When they get here, I'll let them attack me. Then I'll pretend to run away. They'll follow me. You—all of you—stay where you are. I won't need any help.

"After a time, they'll come back. When they do, attack. Make lots of noise; take them by surprise. Strike at their sides, legs, chests—any area that's unguarded. When you've taken care of the first bunch, hide again and wait for the next one. Keep doing this until they're all dead."

He barely had time to finish and the peasants to disperse before the marauders appeared. From their dress and lack of coordination, Musashi guessed that theirs was a primitive fighting force, of a sort that might have been common long ago, when men hunted and fished for sustenance. The name Tokugawa meant nothing to them, no more than did Toyotomi. The mountains were their tribal home; the villagers existed to provide them with food and supplies.

"Stop!" ordered the man at the head of the pack. There were about twenty of them, some with crude swords, some with lances, one with a battle-ax, another with a rusty spear. Silhouetted against the glow of the fire, their bodies looked like demonic, jet-black shadows.

"Is he the one?"

"Yeah, that's him, all right."

Some sixty feet ahead of them, Musashi stood his ground, blocking the road. Disconcerted, they began to doubt their own strength, and for a short time none of them moved.

But only for a moment. Then Musashi's blazing eyes started to pull them inexorably toward him.

"You the son of a bitch trying to get in our way?"

"Right!" roared Musashi, raising his sword and tearing into them. There was a loud reverberation, followed by a whirlwind fray in which it was impossible to make out individual movements. It was like a spinning swarm of winged ants.

The rice fields on one side of the road and the embankment lined with trees and bushes on the other were ideal for Musashi, since they provided a measure of cover, but after the first skirmish, he executed a strategic withdrawal.

"See that?"

"The bastard's running away!"

"After him!"

They pursued him to a far corner of the nearest field, where he turned and faced them. With nothing behind him, his position seemed worse, but he kept his opponents at bay by moving swiftly to right and left. Then the moment one of them made a false move, Musashi struck.

His dark form seemed to flit from place to place, a geyser of blood rising before him each time he paused. The bandits who were not killed were soon too dazed to fight, while Musashi grew sharper with every strike. It was a different sort of battle from the one at Ichijōji. He did not have the feeling of standing on the border between life and death, but he had reached a plane of selflessness, body and sword performing without the need of conscious thought. His attackers fled in complete disarray.

A whisper went along the line of villagers. "They're coming." Then a group of them jumped out of hiding and fell upon the first two or three bandits, killing them almost effortlessly. The farmers melted into the darkness again, and the process was repeated until all the bandits had been ambushed and slain.

Counting the corpses bolstered the villagers' confidence.

"They're not so strong after all," gloated one man.

"Wait! Here comes another one."

"Get him!"

"No, don't attack. It's the rōnin."

With a minimum of confusion, they lined up along the road like soldiers being reviewed by their general. All eyes were fixed on Musashi's bloody clothing and dripping sword, whose blade was chipped in a dozen places. He threw it away and picked up a lance.

"Our work's not done," he said. "Get yourselves some weapons and follow me. By combining your strength, you can drive the marauders out of the village and rescue your families."

Not one man hesitated. The women and children also found weapons and followed along.

The damage to the village was not as extensive as they had feared, because the dwellings were set well apart. But the terrified farm animals were raising a great ruckus, and somewhere a baby was crying its lungs out. Loud popping noises came from the roadside, where the fire had spread to a grove of green bamboo.

The bandits were nowhere in sight.

"Where are they?" asked Musashi. "I seem to smell sake. Where would there be a lot of sake in one place?"

The villagers were so absorbed in gaping at the fires that nobody had noticed the smell, but one of them said, "Must be the village headman's house. He's got barrels of sake."

"Then that's where we'll find them," said Musashi.

As they advanced, more men came out of hiding and joined their ranks. Musashi was gratified by the growing spirit of unity.

"That's it, there," said one man, pointing out a large house surrounded by an earthen wall.

While the peasants were getting themselves organized, Musashi scaled the wall and invaded the bandits' stronghold. The leader and his chief lieutenants were ensconced in a large dirt-floored room, swilling sake and forcing their attentions on young girls they were holding captive.

"Don't get excited!" the leader shouted angrily in a rough, mountain dialect. "He's only one man. I shouldn't have to do anything myself. The rest of you take care of him." He was upbraiding an underling who had rushed in with the news of the defeat outside the village.

As their chief fell silent, the others became aware of the hum of angry voices beyond the wall and stirred uneasily. Dropping half-eaten chickens and sake cups, they jumped to their feet and instinctively reached for their weapons. Then they stood there, staring at the entrance to the room.

Musashi, using his lance as a pole, vaulted through a high side window, landing directly behind the chief. The man whirled around, only to be impaled on the lance. Letting out a fearsome "A-w-r-g," he grabbed with both hands the lance lodged in his chest. Musashi calmly let go of the lance, and the man toppled face down on the ground, the blade and most of the shaft projecting from his back.

The second man to attack Musashi was relieved of his sword. Musashi sliced him through, brought the blade down on the head of a third man, and thrust it into the chest of a fourth. The others made helter-skelter for the door. Musashi hurled the sword at them and in a continuation of the same motion extricated the lance from the chief's body.

"Don't move!" he bellowed. He charged with the lance held horizontally, parting the bandits like water struck with a pole. This gave him enough room to make effective use of the long weapon, which he now swung with a deftness that tested the very resiliency of its black oak shaft, striking sideways, slicing downward, thrusting viciously forward.

The bandits attempting to get out the gate found their way blocked by the armed villagers. Some climbed the wall. When they hit the ground, most were slaughtered on the spot. Of the few who succeeded in escaping, nearly all received crippling wounds.

For a time the air was filled with shouts of triumph from young and old, male and female, and as the first flush of victory subsided, man and wife, parents and children, hugged each other and shed tears of joy.

In the midst of this ecstatic scene, someone asked, "What if they come back?"

There was a moment of sudden, anxious stillness.

"They won't be back," Musashi said firmly. "Not to this village. But don't be overconfident. Your business is using plows, not swords. If you grow too proud of your fighting ability, the punishment heaven will mete out to you will be worse than any raid by mountain devils."

"Did you find out what happened?" Nagaoka Sado asked his two samurai when they got back to the Toku-ganji. In the distance, across field and swamp, he could see that the light of the fires in the village was fading.

"Everything's quieted down now."

"Did you chase the bandits away? How much damage was done in the village?"

"The villagers killed all but a few of them before we got there. The others got away."

"Well, that's odd." He looked surprised, for if this was true, he had some thinking to do about the way of governing in his own lord's district.

On leaving the temple the following day, he directed his horse toward the village, saying, "It's out of the way, but let's have a look."

A priest came along to show them the way, and while they rode, Sado observed, "Those bodies along the roadside don't look to me as though they were cut down by farmers," and asked his samurai for more details.

The villagers, forgoing sleep, were hard at work, burying corpses and cleaning up debris from the conflagration. But when they saw Sado and the samurai, they ran inside their houses and hid.

"Get one of the villagers to come here, and let's find out exactly what happened," he said to the priest.

The man who came back with the priest gave them a fairly detailed account of the night's events.

"Now it begins to make sense," Sado said, nodding. "What's this rōnin's name?"

The peasant, never having heard Musashi's name, cocked his head to one side. When Sado insisted on knowing it, the priest asked about for a time and came up with the required information.

"Miyamoto Musashi?" Sado said thoughtfully. "Is he the man the boy spoke of as his teacher?"

"That's right. From the way he's been trying to develop a piece of waste land on Hōtengahara, the villagers thought he was a little soft in the head."

"I'd like to meet him," said Sado, but then he remembered the work waiting for him in Edo. "Never mind; I'll talk to him the next time I come out here." He turned his horse around and left the peasant standing by the road.

A few minutes later he reined up in front of the village headman's gate. There, written in shiny ink on a fresh board, hung a sign: "Reminder for the People of the Village: Your plow is your sword. Your sword is your plow. Working in the fields, don't forget the invasion. Thinking of the invasion, don't forget your fields. All things must be balanced and integrated. Most important, do not oppose the Way of successive generations."

"Hmm. Who wrote this?"

The headman had finally come out and was now bowing on the ground before Sado. "Musashi," he answered.

Turning to the priest, Sado said, "Thank you for bringing us here. It's too bad I couldn't meet this Musashi, but just now I don't have the time. I'll be back this way before long."

13

First Planting

The management of the palatial Hosokawa residence in Edo, as well as the performance of the fief's duties to the shōgun, was entrusted to a man still in his early twenties, Tadatoshi, the eldest son of the diamyō, Hosokawa Tadaoki. The father, a celebrated general who also enjoyed a reputation as a poet and master of the tea ceremony, preferred to live at the large Kokura fief in Buzen Province on the island of Kyushu.

Though Nagaoka Sado and a number of other trusted retainers were assigned to assist the young man, this was not because he was in any way incompetent. He was not only accepted as a peer by the powerful vassals closest to the shōgun but had distinguished himself as an energetic and farsighted administrator. In fact, he seemed more in tune with the peace and prosperity of the times than the older lords, who had been nurtured on constant warfare.

At the moment, Sado was walking in the general direction of the riding ground. "Have you seen the Young Lord?" he asked of an apprentice samurai coming toward him.

"I believe he's at the archery range."

As Sado threaded his way down a narrow path, he heard a voice asking, "May I have a word with you?"

Sado stopped, and Iwama Kakubei, a vassal respected for his shrewdness and practicality, came up to him. "You're going to talk with his lordship?" he asked.

"Yes."

"If you're not in a hurry, there's a little matter I'd like to consult with you about. Why don't we sit down over there?" As they walked the few steps to a rustic arbor, Kakubei said, "I have a favor to ask. If you have a chance during your talk, there's a man I'd like to recommend to the Young Lord."

"Someone wanting to serve the House of Hosokawa?"

"Yes. I know all sorts of people come to you with the same request, but this man's very unusual."

"Is he one of those men interested only in security and a stipend?"

"Definitely not. He's related to my wife. He's been living with us since he came up from Iwakuni a couple of years ago, so I know him quite well."

"Iwakuni? The House of Kikkawa held Suō Province before the Battle of Sekigahara. Is he one of their rōnin?"

"No. He's the son of a rural samurai. His name's Sasaki Kojirō. He's still young, but he was trained in the Tomita Style of Kanemaki Jisai, and he learned the techniques of drawing a sword with lightning swiftness from Lord Katayama Hisayasu of Hōki. He's even created a style of his own, which he calls Ganryū." Kakubei went on, listing in detail Kojirō's various exploits and accomplishments.

Sado was not really listening. His mind had gone back to his last visit to the Tokuganji. Though he was sure, even from the little he'd seen and heard, that Musashi was the right sort of man for the House of Hosokawa, he had intended to meet him personally before recommending him to his master. In the meantime, a year and a half had slipped by without his finding an opportunity to visit Hōtengahara.

When Kakubei finished, Sado said, "I'll do what I can for you," and continued on to the archery range.

Tadatoshi was engaged in a contest with some vassals of his own age, none of whom was remotely a match for him. His shots, unerringly on target, were executed with flawless style. A number of retainers had chided him for taking archery so seriously, arguing that in an age of gun and lance, neither sword nor bow was any longer of much use in actual combat. To this he had replied cryptically, "My arrows are aimed at the spirit."

The Hosokawa retainers had the highest respect for Tadatoshi, and would have served under him with enthusiasm even if his father, to whom they were also devoted, had not been a man of substantial accomplishments. At the moment, Sado regretted the promise he'd just made to Kakubei. Tadatoshi was not a man to whom one lightly recommended prospective retainers.

Wiping the sweat off his face, Tadatoshi walked past several young samurai with whom he'd been talking and laughing. Catching sight of Sado, he called, "How about it, Ancient One? Have a shot?"

"I make it a rule to compete only against adults," Sado replied.

"So you still think of us as little boys with our hair tied up on our heads?"

"Have you forgotten the Battle of Yamazaki? Nirayama Castle? I have been commended for my performance on the battlefield, you know. Besides, I go in for real archery, not—"

"Ha, ha. Sorry I mentioned it. I didn't mean to get you started again." The others joined in the laughter. Slipping his arm out of his sleeve, Tadatoshi became serious and asked, "Did you come to discuss something?"

After going over a number of routine matters, Sado said, "Kakubei says he has a samurai to recommend to you."

For a moment there was a faraway look in Tadatoshi's eyes. "I suppose he's talking about Sasaki Kojirō. He's been mentioned several times."

"Why don't you call him in and have a look at him?"

"Is he really good?"

"Shouldn't you see for yourself?"

Tadatoshi put on his glove and accepted an arrow from an attendant. "I'll take a look at Kakubei's man," he said. "I'd also like to see that rōnin you mentioned. Miyamoto Musashi, was it?"

"Oh, you remember?"

"I do. You're the one who seems to have forgotten."

"Not at all. But being so busy, I haven't had a chance to go out to Shimōsa."

"If you think you've found someone, you should take the time. I'm surprised at you, Sado, letting something so important wait until you've got other business to take you out there. It's not like you."

"I'm sorry. There's always too many men looking for positions. I thought you'd forgotten about it. I suppose I should have brought it up again."

"Indeed you should have. I don't necessarily accept other people's recommendations, but I'm eager to see anyone old Sado considers suitable. Understand?"

Sado apologized again before taking his leave. He went directly to his own house and without further ado had a fresh horse saddled and set out for Hōtengahara.

"Isn't this Hōtengahara?"

Satō Genzō, Sado's attendant, said, "That's what I thought, but this is no wilderness. There're rice fields all over. The place they were trying to develop must be nearer the mountains."

They had already gone a good distance beyond the Tokuganji and would soon be on the highroad to Hitachi. It was late afternoon, and the white herons splashing about in the paddies made the water seem like powder. Along the riverbank and in the shadows of hillocks grew patches of hemp and waving stalks of barley.

"Look over there, sir," said Genzō.

"What is it?"

"There's a group of farmers."

"So there is. They seem to be bowing to the ground, one by one, don't they?"

"It looks like some sort of religious ceremony."

With a snap of the reins, Genzō forded the river first, making sure it was safe for Sado to follow.

"You, there!" called Genzō.

The farmers, looking surprised, spread out from their circle to face the visitors. They were standing in front of a small cabin, and Sado could see that the object they'd been bowing before was a tiny wooden shrine, no larger than a birdcage. There were about fifty of them, on their way home from work, it appeared, for their tools had all been washed.

A priest came forward, saying, "Why, it's Nagaoka Sado, isn't it? What a pleasant surprise!"

"And you're from the Tokuganji, aren't you? I believe you're the one who guided me to the village after the bandit raid."

"That's right. Have you come to pay a call at the temple?"

"No, not this time. I'll be going back right away. Could you tell me where I might find that rōnin named Miyamoto Musashi?"

"He's not here anymore. He left very suddenly."

"Left suddenly? Why should he do that?"

"One day last month, the villagers decided to take a day off and celebrate the progress that's been made here. You can see for yourself how green it is now. Well, the morning after that, Musashi and the boy, Iori, were gone." The priest looked around, as though half expecting Musashi to materialize out of the air.

In response to Sado's prompting, the priest filled in the details of his story. After the village had strengthened its defenses under Musashi's leadership, the farmers were so thankful for the prospect of living in peace that they

146

practically deified him. Even the ones who had ridiculed him most cruelly had come forward to help with the development project.

Musashi treated them all fairly and equally, first convincing them that it was pointless to live like animals. He then tried to impress upon them the importance of exerting a little extra effort so as to give their children a chance for a better life. To be real human beings, he told them they must work for the sake of posterity.

With forty or fifty villagers pitching in to help each day, by fall they were able to keep the floodwaters under control. When winter came, they plowed. And in the spring, they drew water from the new irrigation ditches and transplanted the rice seedlings. By early summer the rice was thriving, while in the dry fields, hemp and barley were already a foot high. In another year, the crop would double; the year after that, triple.

Villagers began to drop in at the cabin to pay their respects, thanking Musashi from the bottom of their hearts, the women bearing gifts of vegetables. On the day of the celebration, the men arrived with great jars of sake, and all took part in performing a sacred dance, accompanied by drums and flutes.

With the villagers gathered around him, Musashi had assured them that it was not his strength, but theirs. "All I did was show you how to use the energy you possess."

Then he had taken the priest aside to tell him that he was concerned about their relying on a vagabond like him. "Even without me," he said, "they should have confidence in themselves and maintain solidarity." He had then taken out a statue of Kannon he'd carved and given it to the priest.

The morning after the celebration, the village was in an uproar.

"He's gone!"

"He can't be."

"Yes, he's disappeared. The cabin's empty."

Grief-stricken, none of the farmers went near the fields that day.

When he heard about it, the priest reproached them sharply for their ingratitude, urging them to remember what they'd been taught and subtly coaxing them to carry on the work that had been started.

Later, the villagers had built the tiny shrine and placed the treasured image of Kannon in it. They paid their respects to Musashi morning and evening, on their way to and from the fields.

Sado thanked the priest for the information, concealing the fact that he was disconsolate as only a man of his position could do.

As his horse made its way back through the evening mist of late spring, he thought uneasily: "I shouldn't have put off coming. I was derelict in my duty, and now I've failed my lord."

14

The Flies

On the east bank of the Sumida River where the road from Shimōsa converged with a branch of the Ōshū highroad rose a great barrier with an imposing gate, ample evidence of the firm rule of Aoyama Tadanari, the new magistrate of Edo.

Musashi stood in line, idly waiting his turn, Iori at his side. When he had passed through Edo three years earlier, entering and leaving the city had been a simple matter. Even at this distance, he could see that there were far more houses than before, fewer open spaces.

"You there, rōnin. You're next."

Two officials in leather *hakama* began frisking Musashi with great thoroughness, while a third glared at him and asked questions.

"What business do you have in the capital?"

"Nothing specific."

"No special business, eh?"

"Well, I am a *shugyōsha*. I suppose it could be said that studying to be a samurai is my business."

The man was silent. Musashi grinned.

"Where were you born?"

"In the village of Miyamoto, district of Yoshino, Mimasaka Province."

"Your master?"

"I have none."

"Who furnishes your travel money?"

"No one. I carve statues and draw pictures. Sometimes I can exchange them for food and lodging. Often I stay at temples. Occasionally I give lessons in the sword. One way or another, I manage."

"Where are you coming from?"

"For the past two years, I've been farming in Hōtengahara in Shimōsa. I decided I didn't want to do that for the rest of my life, so I've come here."

"Do you have a place to stay in Edo? No one can enter the city unless he has relatives or a place to live."

"Yes," replied Musashi on the spur of the moment. He saw that if he tried to stick to the truth, there was going to be no end to it.

"Well?"

"Yagyū Munenori, Lord of Tajima."

The official's mouth dropped open.

Musashi, amused at the man's reaction, congratulated himself. The risk of being caught in a lie did not trouble him greatly. He felt that the Yagyūs must have heard about him from Takuan. It seemed unlikely they would deny all acquaintance with him if questioned. It might even be that Takuan was in Edo now. If so, Musashi had his means of introduction. It was too late to have a bout with Sekishūsai, but he longed to have one with Munenori, his father's successor in the Yagyū Style and a personal tutor of the shōgun.

The name acted like magic. "Well, well," said the official amiably. "If you're connected with the House of Yagyū, I'm sorry to have troubled you. As you must realize, there are all sorts of samurai on the road. We have to be particularly careful about anyone who appears to be a rōnin. Orders, you know." After a few more questions for the sake of form or face, he said, "You can go now," and personally escorted Musashi to the gate.

"Sir," Iori asked when they were on the other side, "why are they so careful about rōnin and nobody else?"

"They're on the lookout for enemy spies."

"What spy would be stupid enough to come here looking like a rōnin? The officials are pretty dumb—them and their stupid questions! They made us miss the ferry!"

"Shh. They'll hear you. Don't worry about the ferry. You can look at Mount Fuji while we're waiting for the next one. Did you know you could see it from here?"

"So what? We could see it from Hōtengahara too."

"Yes, but it's different here."

"How?"

"Fuji's never the same. It varies from day to day, hour to hour."

"Looks the same to me."

"It's not, though. It changes—time, weather, season, the place you're looking at it from. It differs, too, according to the person who's looking at it, according to his heart."

Unimpressed, Iori picked up a flat stone and sent it skimming across the water. After amusing himself in this fashion for a few minutes, he came back to Musashi and asked, "Are we really going to Lord Yagyū's house?"

"I'll have to think about that."

"Isn't that what you told the guard?"

"Yes. I intend to go, but it's not all that simple. He's a daimyō, you know."

"He must be awfully important. That's what I want to be when I grow up."

"Important?"

"Umm."

"You shouldn't aim so low."

"What do you mean?"

"Look at Mount Fuji."

"I'll never be like Mount Fuji."

"Instead of wanting to be like this or that, make yourself into a silent, immovable giant. That's what the mountain is. Don't waste your time trying to impress people. If you become the sort of man people can respect, they'll respect you, without your doing anything."

Musashi's words didn't have time to sink in, for just then Iori shouted, "Look, here comes the ferry," and ran ahead to be the first one on board.

The Sumida River was a study in contrasts, wide in places, narrow in others, shallow here and deep there. At high tide, the waves washing the banks took on a muddy hue. Sometimes the estuary swelled to twice its normal width. At the point where the ferry crossed, it was virtually an inlet of the bay.

The sky was clear, the water transparent. Looking over the side, Iori could see schools of countless tiny fish racing about. Among the rocks he also spotted the rusty remains of an old helmet. He had no ears for the conversation going on around him.

"What do you think? Is it going to stay peaceful, the way it is now?"

"I doubt it."

"You're probably right. Sooner or later, there'll be fighting. I hope not, but what else can you expect?"

Other passengers kept their thoughts to themselves and stared dourly at the water, afraid an official, possibly in disguise, might overhear and connect them with the speakers. Those who did take the risk seemed to enjoy flirting with the ubiquitous eyes and ears of the law.

"You can tell from the way they're checking everybody that we're heading for war. It's only very recently they've been clamping down like that. And there're a lot of rumors about spies from Osaka."

"You also hear about burglars breaking into daimyō's houses, though they try to hush it up. It must be embarrassing being robbed when you're supposed to be the enforcers of law and order."

"You'd have to be after more than money to take that kind of risk. It's got to be spies. No ordinary crook would have the nerve."

As he looked around, it occurred to Musashi that the ferry was transporting a fair cross section of Edo society. A lumberman with sawdust clinging to his work clothes, a couple of cheap geisha who might have come from Kyoto, a broad-shouldered roughneck or two, a group of well-diggers, two openly coquettish whores, a priest, a beggar monk, another rōnin like himself.

When the boat reached the Edo side and they all piled out, a short, heavyset man called to Musashi, "Hey, you. The rōnin. You forgot something." He held out a reddish brocade pouch, so old that the dirt seemed to shine more brightly than the few gold threads left in it.

Musashi, shaking his head, said, "It's not mine. It must belong to one of the other passengers."

Iori piped up, "It's mine," snatched the pouch from the man's hand and stuffed it into his kimono.

The man was indignant. "What're you doing, grabbing like that! Give it here! Then you're going to bow three times before you get it back. If you don't, you're going to get thrown in the river!"

Musashi intervened, asking the man to excuse Iori's rudeness because of his age.

"What are you?" the man asked roughly. "Brother? Master? What's your name!"

"Miyamoto Musashi."

"What!" exclaimed the ruffian, staring hard at Musashi's face. After a moment he said to Iori, "You'd better be more careful from now on." Then, as though eager to escape, he turned away.

"Just a moment," said Musashi. The gentleness of his tone took the man completely by surprise.

He whirled around, his hand going to his sword. "What do you want?"

"What's your name?"

"What's it to you?"

"You asked mine. As a matter of courtesy, you should tell me yours."

"I'm one of Hangawara's men. My name's Jūrō."

"All right. You can go," said Musashi, pushing him away.

"I won't forget that!" Jūrō stumbled a few steps before he found his feet and fled.

"Serves him right, the coward," said Iori. Satisfied that he'd been vindicated, he looked up worshipfully at Musashi's face and moved closer to him.

As they walked into the city, Musashi said, "Iori, you have to realize that living here is not like being out in the country. There, we had only foxes and squirrels for neighbors. Here, there're lots of people. You'll have to be more careful about your manners."

"Yes, sir."

"When people live together in harmony, the earth is a paradise," Musashi went on gravely. "But every man has a bad side as well as a good side. There are times when only the bad comes out. Then the world's not paradise, but hell. Do you understand what I'm saying?"

"Yes, I think so," said Iori, more subdued now.

"There's a reason we have manners and etiquette. They keep us from letting the bad side take over. This promotes social order, which is the objective of the government's laws." Musashi paused. "The way you acted . . . It was a trivial matter, but your attitude couldn't help but make the man angry. I'm not at all happy about it."

"Yes, sir."

"I don't know where we'll be going from here. But wherever we are, you'd better follow the rules and act courteously."

The boy bobbed his head a couple of times and made a small, stiff bow. They walked on in silence for a short while.

"Sir, would you carry my pouch for me? I don't want to lose it again."

Accepting the small brocade bag, Musashi inspected it closely before tucking it into his kimono. "Is this the one your father left you?"

"Yes, sir. I got it back from the Tokuganji at the

beginning of the year. The priest didn't take any of the money. You can use some of it if you need to."

"Thanks," Musashi said lightly. "I'll take good care of it."

"He has a talent I don't have," mused Musashi, thinking ruefully of his own indifference to personal finances. The boy's innate prudence had taught Musashi the meaning of economics. He appreciated the boy's trust and was growing fonder of him by the day. He looked forward with enthusiasm to the task of helping him develop his native intelligence.

"Where would you like to stay tonight?" he asked.

Iori, who had been looking at his new surroundings with great curiosity, remarked, "I see lots of horses over there. It looks like a marketplace, right here in town." He spoke as though he had run across a long-lost friend in a strange country.

They had reached Bakurōchō, where there was a large and diverse selection of tea shops and hostelries catering to the equine professions—sellers, buyers, draymen, grooms, a variety of lesser factotums. Men in small groups haggled and babbled in a welter of dialects, the most prominent being the tangy, irate-sounding speech of Edo.

Among the rabble was a well-groomed samurai, searching for good horses. With a disgruntled look, he said, "Let's go home. There's nothing here but nags, nothing worth recommending to his lordship."

Striding briskly between the animals, he came face to face with Musashi, blinked, and stepped back in surprise. "You're Miyamoto Musashi, aren't you?"

Musashi looked at the man for an instant, then broke into a grin. It was Kimura Sukekurō. Although the two men had come within inches of locking swords at Koyagyū Castle, Sukekurō's manner was cordial. He seemed to bear no lingering rancor from that encounter.

"I certainly didn't expect to see you here," he said. "Have you been in Edo long?"

"I've just come from Shimōsa," replied Musashi. "How's your master? Is he still in good health?"

"Yes, thank you, but of course at Sekishūsai's age . . . I'm staying with Lord Munenori. You must come to visit; I'd be glad to introduce you. Oh, there's something else, too." He flashed a meaningful look and smiled. "We have a beautiful treasure that belongs to you. You must come as soon as you can."

Before Musashi could inquire what the "beautiful treasure" might be, Sukekurō made a slight bow and walked rapidly away, his attendant trailing along behind.

The guests staying at the inexpensive inns of Bakurōchō were mostly horse traders in from the provinces. Musashi decided to take a room there rather than in another part of town, where the rates would most likely be higher. Like the other inns, the one he chose had a large stable, so large in fact that the rooms themselves seemed rather like an annex. But after the rigors of Hōtengahara, even this third-rate hostelry seemed luxurious.

Despite his feeling of well-being, Musashi found the horseflies annoying and began grumbling.

The proprietress heard him. "I'll change your room," she offered solicitously. "The flies aren't so bad on the second floor."

Once resettled, Musashi found himself exposed to the full strength of the western sun and felt like grumbling again. Only a few days ago, the afternoon sun would have been a source of cheer, a bright ray of hope shedding nourishing warmth on the rice plants and portending good weather for the morrow. As for the flies, when his sweat had attracted them while he worked in the fields, he had taken the view that they were only going about their chores, just as he was going about his. He had even regarded them as fellow creatures. Now, having crossed one wide river and entered the maze of the city, he found the heat of the sun anything but comforting, the flies only an irritation.

His appetite took his mind off the inconveniences. He glanced at Iori, and saw symptoms of lassitude and gluttony in his face too. Small wonder, for a party in the next room had ordered a great pot of steaming food and was now attacking it ravenously, amid much talk, laughter and drinking.

Buckwheat noodles—*soba*—that's what he wanted! In the country, if a man wanted *soba*, he planted buckwheat in the early spring, watched it flower in the summer, dried the grain in the fall, ground the flour in the winter. Then he could make *soba*. Here it required no more effort than clapping one's hands for service.

"Iori, shall we order some *soba*?"

"Yes," came the eager reply.

The proprietress came and took their order. While they waited, Musashi propped his elbows on the windowsill and shaded his eyes. Diagonally across the way was a signboard reading: "Souls polished here. Zushino Kōsuke, Master in the Hon'ami Style."

Iori had noticed it too. After staring for a moment in bewilderment, he said, "That sign says 'Souls polished.' What sort of business is that?"

"Well, it also says the man works in the Hon'ami Style, so I suppose he's a sword polisher. Come to think of it, I ought to have my sword worked on."

The *soba* was slow to arrive, so Musashi stretched out on the tatami for a nap. But the voices in the next room had risen several decibels and became quarrelsome. "Iori," he said, opening one eye, "will you ask the people next door to be a little quieter?"

Only *shoji* separated the two rooms, but instead of opening them, Iori went out into the hall. The door to the other room was open. "Don't make so much noise," he shouted. "My teacher's trying to sleep."

"Hunh!" The squabble came to an abrupt halt. The men turned and stared angrily at him.

"You say something, shrimp?"

Pouting at the epithet, Iori said, "We came upstairs because of the flies. Now you're yelling so much he can't rest."

"Is this your idea, or did your master send you?"

"He sent me."

"Did he? Well, I'm not wasting my time talking to a little turd like you. Go tell your master Kumagorō of Chichibu will give him his answer later. Now beat it!"

Kumagorō was a great brute of a man, and the two or three others in the room were not much smaller. Cowed by the menace in their eyes, Iori quickly retreated. Musashi had dropped off to sleep; not wanting to disturb him, Iori sat down by the window.

Presently, one of the horse traders opened the shoji a crack and peeked in at Musashi. There followed much laughter, accompanied by loud and insulting remarks.

"Who does he think he is, butting into our party? Dumb rōnin! No telling where he comes from. Just barges in and starts acting like he owns the place."

"We'll have to show him what's what."

"Yeah, we'll make sure he knows what the horse traders of Edo are made of."

"Talking's not going to show him. Let's haul him out back and throw a bucket of horse piss in his face."

Kumagorō spoke up. "Hold on, now. Let me handle this. Either I'll get an apology in writing or we'll wash his face with horse piss. Enjoy your sake. Leave everything to me."

"This should be good," said one man, as Kumagorō, with a confident smirk, tightened his obi.

"I beg your pardon," said Kumagorō, sliding the shoji open. Without standing up, he shuffled into Musashi's room on his knees.

The *soba*, six helpings in a lacquered box, had finally arrived. Musashi was sitting up now, addressing his chopsticks to his first helping.

"Look, they're coming in," said Iori under his breath, moving slightly to get out of the way.

Kumagorō seated himself behind and to Iori's left, legs crossed, elbows resting on his knees. With a fierce scowl, he said, "You can eat later. Don't try to hide the fact that you're scared by sitting there playing with your food."

Though he was grinning, Musashi gave no indication that he was listening. He stirred the *soba* with his chopsticks to separate the strands, lifted a mouthful and swallowed with a joyous slurp.

The veins in Kumagorō's forehead nearly popped. "Put that bowl down," he said angrily.

"And who are you?" Musashi asked mildly, making no move to comply.

"You don't know who I am? The only people in Bakurōchō who haven't heard my name are good-for-nothings and deaf-mutes."

"I'm a little hard of hearing myself. Speak up, tell me who you are and where you come from."

"I'm Kumagorō from Chichibu, the best horse trader in Edo. When children see me coming, they get so scared they can't even cry."

"I see. Then you're in the horse business?"

"You bet I am. I sell to the samurai. You'd better remember that when you're dealing with me."

"In what way am I dealing with you?"

"You sent that runt there to complain about the noise. Where do you think you are? This is no fancy inn for daimyō, nice and quiet and all. We horse traders like noise."

"I gathered that."

"Then why were you trying to bust up our party? I demand an apology."

"Apology?"

"Yes, in writing. You can address it to Kumagorō and his friends. If we don't get one we'll take you outside and teach you a thing or two."

"What you say is interesting."

"Hunh!"

"I mean your way of speaking is interesting."

"Cut out the nonsense! Do we get the apology or don't we? Well?" Kumagorō's voice had gone from a growl to a roar, and the sweat on his crimson forehead glistened in the evening sun. Looking ready to explode, he bared his hairy chest and took a dagger from his stomach wrapper.

"Make up your mind! If I don't hear your answer soon, you're in big trouble." He uncrossed his legs and held the dagger vertically beside the lacquered box, its point touching the floor.

Musashi, restraining his mirth, said, "Well, now how should I respond to that?"

Lowering his bowl, he reached out with his chopsticks, removed a dark speck from the *soba* in the box and threw it out the window. Still silent, he reached out again and picked off another dark speck, then another.

Kumagorō's eyes bugged; his breath halted.

"There's no end to them, is there?" remarked Musashi casually. "Here, Iori, go give these chopsticks a good washing."

As Iori went out, Kumagorō faded silently back into his own room and in a hushed voice told his companions of the incredible sight he had just witnessed. After first mistaking the black spots on the *soba* for dirt, he had realized they were live flies, plucked so deftly they had had no time to escape. Within minutes, he and his fellows transferred their little party to a more remote quarter, and silence reigned.

"That's better, isn't it?" said Musashi to Iori. The two of them grinned at one another.

By the time they'd finished their meal, the sun was down, and the moon was shining wanly above the roof of the "soul polisher's" shop.

Musashi stood up and straightened his kimono. "I

think I'll see about having my sword taken care of," he said.

He picked up the weapon and was about to leave when the proprietress came halfway up the blackened staircase and called, "A letter's come for you."

Puzzled that anyone should know his whereabouts so soon, Musashi went down, accepted the missive and asked, "Is the messenger still here?"

"No, he left immediately."

The outside of the letter bore only the word "Suke," which Musashi took to stand for Kimura Sukekurō. Unfolding it, he read: "I informed Lord Munenori that I saw you this morning. He seemed happy to receive word of you after all this time. He instructed me to write and ask when you will be able to visit us."

Musashi descended the remaining steps and went to the office, where he borrowed ink and brush. Seating himself in a corner, he wrote on the back of Sukekurō's letter: "I shall be happy to visit Lord Munenori whenever he wishes to have a bout with me. As a warrior, I have no other purpose in calling on him." He signed the note "Masana," a formal name he seldom used.

"Iori," he called from the bottom of the stairs. "I want you to run an errand for me."

"Yes, sir."

"I want you to deliver a letter to Lord Yagyū Munenori."

"Yes, sir."

According to the proprietress, everybody knew where Lord Munenori lived, but she offered directions anyway. "Go down the main street until you come to the highroad. Go straight along that as far as Nihombashi. Then bear to the left and go along the river until you get to Kobikichō. That's where it is; you can't miss it."

"Thanks," said Iori, who already had his sandals on. "I'm sure I can find it." He was delighted at the opportunity to go out, particularly since his destination was the home of an important daimyō. Giving no thought to the hour, he walked away quickly, swinging his arms and holding his head up proudly.

As Musashi watched him turn the corner, he thought: "He's a little too self-confident for his own good."

15

The Soul Polisher

"Good evening," called Musashi.

Nothing about Zushino Kōsuke's house suggested it was a place of business. It lacked the grilled front of most shops, and there was no merchandise on display. Musashi stood in the dirt-floored passageway running down the left side of the house. To his right was a raised section, floored with tatami and screened off from the room beyond it.

The man sleeping on the tatami with his arms resting on a strongbox resembled a Taoist sage Musashi had once seen in a painting. The long, thin face was the grayish color of clay. Musashi could detect in it none of the keenness he associated with sword craftsmen.

"Good evening," Musashi repeated, a little louder.

When his voice penetrated Kōsuke's torpor, the craftsman raised his head very slowly; he might have been awakening from centuries of slumber.

Wiping the saliva from his chin and sitting up straight, he asked lackadaisically, "Can I help you?" Musashi's impression was that a man like this might make swords, as well as souls, duller, but he nevertheless held out his own weapon and explained why he was there.

"Let me take a look at it." Kōsuke's shoulders perked up smartly. Placing his left hand on his knee, he reached out with his right to take the sword, simultaneously bowing his head toward it.

"Strange creature," thought Musashi. "He barely acknowledges the presence of a human being but bows politely to a sword."

Holding a piece of paper in his mouth, Kōsuke quietly slid the blade out of the scabbard. He stood it vertically in front of him and examined it from hilt to tip. His eyes took on a bright glitter, reminding Musashi of glass eyes in a wooden Buddhist statue.

Snapping the weapon back into its scabbard, Kōsuke looked up inquiringly at Musashi. "Come, have a seat," he said, moving back to make room and offering Musashi a cushion.

Musashi removed his sandals and stepped up into the room.

"Has the sword been in your family for some generations?"

"Oh, no," said Musashi. "It's not the work of a famous swordsmith, nothing like that."

"Have you used it in battle, or do you carry it for the usual purposes?"

"I haven't used it on the battlefield. There's nothing special about it. The best you could say is that it's better than nothing."

"Mm." Looking directly into Musashi's eyes, Kōsuke then asked, "How do you want it polished?"

"How do I want it polished? What do you mean?"

"Do you want it sharpened so it'll cut well?"

"Well, it is a sword. The cleaner it cuts, the better."

"I suppose so," agreed Kōsuke with a defeated sigh.

"What's wrong with that? Isn't it the business of a craftsman to sharpen swords so they'll cut properly?" As Musashi spoke, he squinted curiously into Kōsuke's face.

The self-proclaimed polisher of souls shoved the weapon toward Musashi and said, "I can't do anything for you. Take it to somebody else."

Strange, indeed, thought Musashi. He could not disguise a certain vexation, but he said nothing. Kōsuke, his lips tightly set, made no attempt to explain.

While they sat silently staring at each other, a man from the neighborhood stuck his head in the door. "Kōsuke, have you got a fishing pole? It's high tide, and the fish are jumping. If you'll lend me a pole, I'll divide my catch with you."

Kōsuke plainly regarded the man as one more burden he ought not to have to bear. "Borrow one somewhere else," he rasped. "I don't believe in killing, and I don't keep instruments for murder in my house."

The man went quickly away, leaving Kōsuke looking grumpier than ever.

Another man might have become discouraged and left, but Musashi's curiosity held him there. There was something appealing about this man—not wit nor intelligence, but a rough natural goodness like that of a Karatsu sake jar or a tea bowl by Nonkō. Just as pottery often has a blemish evocative of its closeness to the earth, Kōsuke had, in a semi-bald spot on his temple, a lesion of some sort, which he'd covered with salve.

While attempting to conceal his growing fascination, Musashi said, "What is there to keep you from polishing my sword? Is it of such poor quality you can't put a good edge on it?"

"Of course not. You're the owner. You know as well as I do it's a perfectly good Bizen sword. I also know you want it sharpened for the purpose of cutting people."

"Is there anything wrong with that?"

"That's what they all say—what's wrong with wanting me to fix a sword so it'll cut better? If the sword cuts, they're happy."

"But a man bringing in a sword to be polished naturally wants—"

"Just a minute." Kōsuke raised his hand. "I'll take some time to explain. First, I'd like you to take another look at the sign on the front of my shop."

"It says 'Souls polished,' or at least I think so. Is there any other way of reading the characters?"

"No. You'll notice it doesn't say a word about polishing swords. My business is polishing the souls of the samurai who come in, not their weapons. People don't understand, but that's what I was taught when I studied sword polishing."

"I see," said Musashi, although he didn't really.

"Since I try to abide by my master's teachings, I refuse to polish the swords of samurai who take pleasure in killing people."

"Well, you have a point there. But tell me, who was this master of yours?"

"That's written on the sign too. I studied in the House of Hon'ami, under Hon'ami Kōetsu himself." Kōsuke squared his shoulders proudly as he uttered his master's name.

"That's interesting. I happen to have made the acquaintance of your master and his excellent mother, Myōshū." Musashi went on to tell how he had met them in the field near the Rendaiji and later spent a few days at their house.

Kōsuke, astonished, scrutinized him closely for a moment. "Are you by any chance the man who caused a great stir in Kyoto some years ago by defeating the Yoshioka School at Ichijōji? Miyamoto Musashi was the name, I believe."

"That is my name." Musashi's face reddened slightly.

Kōsuke moved back a bit and bowed deferentially, saying, "Forgive me. I shouldn't have been lecturing you. I had no idea I was talking to the famous Miyamoto Musashi."

"Don't give it a second thought. Your words were very instructive. Kōetsu's character comes through in the lessons he teaches his disciples."

"As I'm sure you know, the Hon'ami family served the Ashikaga shōguns. From time to time they've also been called upon to polish the Emperor's swords. Kōetsu was always saying that Japanese swords were created not to kill or injure poeple but to maintain the imperial rule and protect the nation, to subdue devils and drive out evil. The sword *is* the samurai's soul; he carries it for no other purpose than to maintain his own integrity. It is an ever-present admonition to the man who rules over other men and seeks in doing so to follow the Way of Life. It's only natural that the craftsman who polishes the sword must also polish the swordsman's spirit.''

"How true,'' agreed Musashi.

"Kōetsu said that to see a good sword is to see the sacred light, the spirit of the nation's peace and tranquillity. He hated touching a bad sword. Even being near one used to nauseate him.''

"I see. Are you saying you sensed something evil in my sword?''

"No, not in the least. I just felt a little depressed. Since coming to Edo, I've worked on any number of weapons, but none of their owners seem to have an inkling of the sword's true meaning. I sometimes doubt they have souls to polish. All they care about is quartering a man or splitting his head open—helmet and all. It got so tiresome. That's why I put up a new sign a few days ago. It doesn't seem to have had much effect, though.''

"And I came in asking for the same thing, didn't I? I understand how you feel.''

"Well, that's a beginning. Things may turn out a little differently with you. But frankly, when I saw that blade of yours, I was shocked. All those nicks and stains, stains made by human flesh. I thought you were just one more senseless rōnin, proud of himself for committing a number of meaningless murders.''

Musashi bowed his head. It was the voice of Kōetsu, coming from Kōsuke's mouth. "I'm grateful for this lesson,'' he said. "I've carried a sword since I was a boy, but I've never really given sufficient thought to the spirit that resides in it. In the future, I'll pay heed to what you've said."

Kōsuke appeared vastly relieved. "In that case, I'll polish the sword for you. Or perhaps I should say I consider it a privilege for one in my profession to be able to polish the soul of a samurai like yourself."

Twilight had faded, and the lights had been lit. Musashi decided it was time to go.

"Wait," said Kōsuke. "Do you have another sword to carry while I'm working on this one?"

"No; I have only the one long sword."

"In that case, why don't you pick out a replacement? None of the swords I have here now are very good, I'm afraid, but come and take a look."

He guided Musashi into the back room, where he took several swords out of a cabinet and lined them up on the tatami. "You can take any one of these," he offered.

Despite the craftsman's modest disavowal, they were all weapons of excellent quality. Musashi had difficulty choosing from the dazzling display, but finally he selected one and immediately fell in love with it. Just holding it in his hands, he sensed its maker's dedication. Drawing the blade from the scabbard confirmed his impression; it was indeed a beautiful piece of workmanship, probably dating from the Yoshino period in the fourteenth century. Nagged by the doubt that it was too elegant for him, once he had brought it close to the light and examined it, he found his hands reluctant to let it go.

"May I take this one?" he asked. He could not bring himself to use the word "borrow."

"You have the eye of an expert," observed Kōsuke, as he put away the other swords.

For once in his life, Musashi was swamped by covetousness. He knew it was futile to mention buying the sword outright; the price would be far beyond his means. But he couldn't help himself.

"I don't suppose you'd consider selling me this sword, would you?" he asked.

"Why not?"

"How much are you asking for it?"

"I'll let you have it for what I paid for it."

"How much was that?"

"Twenty pieces of gold."

An almost inconceivable sum to Musashi. "I'd better give it back," he said hesitantly.

"Why?" asked Kōsuke with a puzzled look. "I'll lend it to you for as long as you wish. Go on, take it."

"No; that'd make me feel even worse. Wanting it the way I do is bad enough. If I wore it for a while, it would be torture to part with it."

"Are you really so attached to it?" Kōsuke looked at the sword, then at Musashi. "All right then, I'll give it to you—in wedlock, as it were. But I expect an appropriate gift in exchange."

Musashi was baffled; he had absolutely nothing to offer.

"I heard from Kōetsu that you carve statues. I'd be honored if you'd make me an image of Kannon. That would be sufficient payment."

The last Kannon Musashi had carved was the one he'd left in Hōtengahara. "I have nothing on hand," he said. "But in the next few days, I can carve something for you. May I have the sword then?"

"Certainly. I didn't mean to imply I expected it this minute. By the way, instead of putting up at that inn, why don't you come and stay with us? We have a room we're not using."

"That would be perfect," said Musashi. "If I moved in tomorrow, I could start on the statue right away."

"Come and take a look at it," urged Kōsuke, who was also happy and excited.

Musashi followed him down the outside passageway, at the end of which was a flight of half a dozen steps. Tucked in between the first and second floors, not quite belonging to either, was an eight-mat room. Through the window Musashi could see the dew-laden leaves of an apricot tree.

Pointing at a roof covered with oyster shells, Kōsuke said, "That's my workshop there."

The craftsman's wife, as if summoned by a secret signal, arrived with sake and some tidbits. When the two men sat down, the distinction between host and guest seemed to evaporate. They relaxed, legs stretched out, and opened their hearts to each other, oblivious of the restraints normally imposed by etiquette. The talk, of course, turned to their favorite subject.

"Everybody pays lip service to the importance of the sword," said Kōsuke. "Anybody'll tell you the sword's the 'soul of the samurai' and that a sword is one of the country's three sacred treasures. But the way people actually treat swords is scandalous. And I include samurai and priests, as well as townsmen. I took it upon myself at one time to go around to shrines and old houses where there were once whole collections of beautiful swords, and I can tell you the situation is shocking."

Kōsuke's pale cheeks were ruddy now. His eyes burned with enthusiasm, and the saliva that gathered at the corners of his mouth occasionally flew in a spray right into his companion's face.

"Almost none of the famous swords from the past are being properly taken care of. At Suwa Shrine in Shinano Province there are more than three hundred swords. They could be classed as heirlooms, but I found only five that weren't rusted. Ōmishima Shrine in Iyo is famous for its collection—three thousand swords dating back many centuries. But after spending a whole month there, I found only ten that were in good condition. It's disgusting!" Kōsuke caught his breath and continued. "The problem seems to be that the older and more famous the sword is, the more the owner is inclined to make sure it's stored in a safe place. But then nobody can get at it to take care of it, and the blade gets rustier and rustier.

"The owners are like parents who protect their children so jealously that the children grow up to be fools. In the case of children, more are being born all the time—doesn't make any difference if a few are stupid. But swords . . ."

Pausing to suck in the spit, he raised his thin shoulders even higher and with a gleam in his eyes declared, "We already have all the good swords there'll ever be. During the civil wars, the swordsmiths got careless—no, downright sloppy! They forgot their techniques, and swords have been deteriorating ever since.

"The only thing to do is to take better care of the swords from the earlier periods. The craftsmen today may try to imitate the older swords, but they'll never turn out anything as good. Doesn't it make you angry to think about it?"

Abruptly he stood up and said, "Just look at this." Bringing out a sword of awesome length, he laid it down for his guest to inspect. "It's a splendid weapon, but it's covered with the worst kind of rust."

Musashi's heart skipped a beat. The sword was without doubt Sasaki Kojirō's Drying Pole. A flood of memories came rushing back.

Controlling his emotions, he said calmly, "That's really a long one, isn't it? Must take quite a samurai to handle it."

"I imagine so," agreed Kōsuke. "There aren't many like it." Taking the blade out, he turned the back toward Musashi and handed it to him by the hilt. "See," he said. "It's rusted badly—here and here and here. But he's used it anyway."

"I see."

"This is a rare piece of workmanship, probably forged in the Kamakura period. It'll take a lot of work, but I can probably fix it up. On these ancient swords, the rust is only a relatively thin film. If this were a new blade,

I'd never be able to get the stains off. On new swords, rust spots are like malignant sores; they eat right into the heart of the metal."

Reversing the sword's position so that the back of the blade was toward Kōsuke, Musashi said, "Tell me, did the owner of this sword bring it in himself?"

"No. I was at Lord Hosokawa's on business, and one of the older retainers, Iwama Kakubei, asked me to drop in at his house on the way back. I did, and he gave it to me to work on. Said it belonged to a guest of his."

"The fittings are good too," remarked Musashi, his eyes still focused on the weapon.

"It's a battle sword. The man's been carrying it on his back up till now, but he wants to carry it at his side, so I've been asked to refit the scabbard. He must be a very large man. Either that or he has a very practiced arm."

Kōsuke had begun to feel his sake. His tongue was becoming a little thick. Musashi concluded it was time to take his leave, which he did with a minimum of ceremony.

It was much later than he thought. There were no lights in the neighborhood.

Once inside the inn, he groped through the darkness to the stairway and up to the second floor. Two pallets had been spread, but both were empty. Iori's absence made him uncomfortable, for he suspected the boy was wandering about lost on the streets of this great unfamiliar city.

Going back downstairs, he shook the night watchman awake. "Isn't he back yet?" asked the man, who seemed more surprised than Musashi. "I thought he was with you."

Knowing he would only stare at the ceiling until Iori came back, Musashi went out into the black-lacquer night again and stood with arms crossed under the eaves.

16

The Fox

"Is this Kobikichō?"

In spite of repeated assurances that it was, Iori still had his doubts. The only lights visible on the broad expanse of land belonged to the makeshift huts of woodworkers and stonemasons, and these were few and far between. Beyond them, in the distance, he could just make out the foaming white waves of the bay.

Near the river were piles of rocks and stacks of lumber, and although Iori knew that buildings were going up at a furious pace all over Edo, it struck him as unlikely that Lord Yagyū would build his residence in an area like this.

"Where to next?" he thought dejectedly as he sat down on some lumber. His feet were tired and burning. To cool them he wiggled his toes in the dewy grass. Soon his tension ebbed away and the sweat dried, but his spirits remained decidedly damp.

"It's all the fault of that old woman at the inn," he muttered to himself. "She didn't know what she was talking about." The time he himself had spent gawking at the sights in the theater district at Sakaichō conveniently slipped his mind.

The hour was late, and there was no one around from whom he could ask directions. Yet the idea of spending the night in these unfamiliar surroundings made him uneasy. He had to complete his errand and return to the inn before daybreak, even if it meant waking up one of the workers.

As he approached the nearest shack where a light showed, he saw a woman with a strip of matting tied over her head like a shawl.

"Good evening, auntie," he said innocently.

Mistaking him for the helper at a nearby sake shop, the woman glared and sniffed, "You, is it? You threw a rock at me and ran away, didn't you, you little brat?"

"Not me," protested Iori. "I've never seen you before!"

The woman came hesitantly toward him, then burst out laughing. "No," she said, "you're not the one. What's a cute little boy like you doing wandering around here at this time of night?"

"I was sent on an errand, but I can't find the house I'm looking for."

"Whose house is it?"

"Lord Yagyū of Tajima's."

"Are you joking?" She laughed. "Lord Yagyū is a diamyō, and a teacher to the shōgun. Do you think he'd open his gate to *you*?" She laughed again. "You know somebody in the servants' quarters perhaps?"

"I've brought a letter."

"Who to?"

"A samurai named Kimura Sukekurō."

"Must be one of his retainers. But you, you're so funny—throwing Lord Yagyū's name around like you knew him."

"I just want to deliver this letter. If you know where the house is, tell me."

"It's on the other side of the moat. If you cross that bridge over there, you'll be in front of Lord Kii's house. The next one is Lord Kyōgoku, then Lord Katō, then Lord Matsudaira of Suō." Holding up her fingers, she counted off the sturdy storehouses on the opposite bank. "I'm sure the one after that is the one you want."

"If I cross the moat, will I still be in Kobikichō?"

"Of course."

"Of all the stupid—"

"Here now, that's no way to talk. Hmm, you seem such a nice boy, I'll come along and show you Lord Yagyū's place."

Walking in front of him with the matting on her head, she looked to Iori rather like a ghost.

They were in the middle of the bridge when a man coming toward them brushed against her sleeve and whistled. He reeked of sake. Before Iori knew what was going on, the woman turned and made for the drunk. "I know you," she warbled. "Don't just pass me by like that. It isn't nice." She grabbed his sleeve and started toward a place from which they could go below the bridge.

"Let go," he said.

"Wouldn't you like to go with me?"

"No money."

"Oh, I don't care." Latching on to him like a leech, she looked back at Iori's startled face and said, "Run along now. I've got business with this gentleman."

Iori watched in bewilderment as the two of them tugged back and forth. After a few moments, the woman appeared to get the upper hand, and they disappeared below the bridge. Still puzzled, Iori went to the railing and looked over at the grassy riverbank.

Glancing up, the woman shouted, "Nitwit!" and picked up a rock.

Swallowing hard, Iori dodged the missile and made for the far end of the bridge. In all his years on the barren plain of Hōtengahara, he had never seen anything so frightening as the woman's angry white face in the dark.

On the other side of the river, he found himself before a storehouse. Next to that was a fence, then another storehouse, then another fence, and so on down the street. "This must be it," he said when he came to the fifth building. On the gleaming white plaster wall was a crest in the form of a two-tiered woman's hat. This, Iori knew from the words of a popular song, was the Yagyū family crest.

"Who's there?" demanded a voice from inside the gate.

Speaking as loudly as he dared, Iori announced, "I'm the pupil of Miyamoto Musashi. I've brought a letter."

The sentry said a few words Iori could not catch. In the gate was a small door, through which people could be let in and out without opening the great gate itself. After a few seconds, the door slowly opened, and the man asked suspiciously, "What are you doing here at this hour?"

Iori thrust the letter at the guard's face. "Please deliver this for me. If there's an answer, I'll take it back."

"Hmm," mused the man, taking the letter. "This is for Kimura Sukekurō, is it?"

"Yes, sir."

"He's not here."

"Where is he?"

"He's at the house in Higakubo."

"Huh? Everybody told me Lord Yagyū's house was in Kobikichō."

"People say that, but there's only storehouses here—rice, lumber and a few other things."

"Lord Yagyū doesn't live here?"

"That's right."

"How far is it to the other place—Higakubo?"

"Pretty far."

"Just where is it?"

"In the hills outside the city, in Azabu Village."

"Never heard of it." Iori sighed disappointedly, but his sense of responsibility prevented him from giving up. "Sir, would you draw me a map?"

"Don't be silly. Even if you knew the way, it'd take you all night to get there."

"I don't mind."

"Lot of foxes in Azabu. You don't want to be bewitched by a fox, do you?"

"No."

"Do you know Sukekurō well?"

"My teacher does."

"I'll tell you what. Since it's so late, why don't you catch some sleep over there in the granary, and go in the morning?"

"Where am I?" exclaimed Iori, rubbing his eyes. He jumped up and ran outside. The afternoon sun made him dizzy. Squinting his eyes against the glare, he went to the gatehouse, where the guard was eating his lunch.

"So you're finally up."

"Yes, sir. Could you draw me that map now?"

"You in a hurry, Sleepyhead? Here, you'd better have something to eat first. There's enough for both of us."

While the boy chewed and gulped, the guard sketched a rough map and explained how to get to Higakubo. They finished simultaneously, and Iori, fired up with the importance of his mission, set off at a run, never thinking that Musashi might be worried about his failure to return to the inn.

He made good time through the busy thoroughfares until he reached the vicinity of Edo Castle, where the imposing houses of the leading daimyō stood on the land built up between the crisscross system of moats. As he looked around, his pace slowed. The waterways were jammed with cargo boats. The stone ramparts of the castle itself were half covered with log scaffolding, which from a distance resembled the bamboo trellises used for growing morning glories.

He dawdled again in a broad, flat area called Hibiya, where the scraping of chisels and the thud of axes raised a dissonant hymn to the power of the new shogunate.

Iori stopped. He was mesmerized by the spectacle of

177

the construction work: the laborers hauling huge rocks, the carpenters with their planes and saws and the samurai, the dashing samurai, who stood proudly supervising it all. How he wanted to grow up and be like them!

A lusty song rose from the throats of the men hauling rocks:

> "We'll pluck the flowers
>   In the fields of Musashi—
>   The gentians, the bellflowers,
>   Wild blossoms splashed
>   In confusing disarray.
>   And that lovely girl,
>   The flower unpluckable,
>   Moistened by the dew—
>   'Twill only dampen your sleeve,
>   like falling tears."

He stood enchanted. Before he realized it, the water in the moats was taking on a reddish cast and the evening voices of crows reached his ears.

"Oh, no, it's nearly sundown," he chastised himself. He sped away and for a time moved along at full speed, paying attention to nothing save the map the guard had drawn for him. Before he knew it, he was climbing the path up Azabu Hill, which was so thickly overhung with trees it might as well have been midnight. Once he reached the top, however, he could see the sun was still in the sky, though low on the horizon.

There were almost no houses on the hill itself, Azabu Village being a mere scattering of fields and farm dwellings in the valley below. Standing in a sea of grass and ancient trees, listening to the brooks gurgling down the hillside, Iori felt his fatigue give way to a strange refreshment. He was vaguely aware that the spot where he was standing was historic, although he didn't know why. In fact it was the very place that had given birth to the great warrior clans of the past, both the Taira and the Minamoto.

He heard the loud booming of a drum being beaten, the kind often used at Shinto festivals. Down the hill, visible in the forest, were the sturdy cross-logs atop the ridgepole of a religious sanctuary. Had Iori but known, it was the Great Shrine of Iigura he'd studied about, the famous edifice sacred to the sun goddess of Ise.

The shrine was a far cry from the enormous castle he had just seen, even from the stately gates of the daimyō. In its simplicity it was almost indistinguishable from the farmhouses around it, and Iori thought it puzzling that people talked more reverently about the Tokugawa family than they did about the most sacred of deities. Did that mean the Tokugawas were greater than the sun goddess? he wondered. "I'll have to ask Musashi about that when I get back."

Taking out his map, he pored over it, looked about him and stared at it again. Still there was no sign of the Yagyū mansion.

The evening mist spreading over the ground gave him an eerie feeling. He'd felt something similar before, when in a room with the shoji shut the setting sun's light played on the rice paper so that the interior seemed to grow lighter as the outside darkened. Of course, such a twilight illusion is just that, but he felt it so strongly, in several flashes, that he rubbed his eyes as if to erase his lightheadedness. He knew he wasn't dreaming and looked around suspiciously.

"Why, you sneaky bastard," he cried, jumping forward and whipping out his sword. In the same motion he cut through a clump of tall grass in front of him.

With a yelp of pain, a fox leapt from its hiding place and streaked off, its tail glistening with blood from a cut on its hindquarters.

"Devilish beast!" Iori set off in hot pursuit, and though the fox was fast, Iori was too. When the limping creature stumbled, Iori lunged, confident of victory. The fox, however, slipped nimbly away, to surge ahead several yards, and no matter how fast Iori attacked, the animal managed to get away each time.

On his mother's knee, Iori had heard countless tales proving beyond a shadow of a doubt that foxes had the power to bewitch and possess human beings. He was fond of most other animals, even wild boar and noisome possums, but foxes he hated. He was also afraid of them. To his way of thinking, coming across this wily creature lurking in the grass could mean only one thing—it was to blame for his not finding his way. He was convinced it was a treacherous and evil being that had been following him since the night before and had, just moments before, cast its malevolent spell over him. If he didn't slay it now, it was sure to hex him again. Iori was prepared to pursue his quarry to the end of the earth, but the fox, bounding over the edge of a drop, was lost to sight in a thicket.

Dew glistened on the flowers of the dog nettle and spiderwort. Exhausted and parched, Iori sank down and licked the moisture from a mint leaf. Shoulders heaving, he finally caught his breath, whereupon sweat poured copiously from his forehead. His heart thumped violently. "Where did it go?" he asked, his voice halfway between a scream and a choke.

If the fox had really gone, so much the better, but Iori didn't know what to believe. Since he had injured the animal, he felt it was certain to take revenge, one way or another. Resigning himself, he sat still and waited.

Just as he was beginning to feel calmer, an eerie sound floated to his ears. Wide-eyed, he looked around. "It's the fox, for sure," he said, steeling himself against being bewitched. Rising quickly, he moistened his eyebrows with saliva—a trick thought to ward off the influence of foxes.

A short distance away, a woman came floating through the evening mist, her face half hidden by a veil of silk gauze. She was riding a horse sidesaddle, the reins lying loosely across the low pommel. The saddle was made of lacquered wood with mother-of-pearl inlay.

"It's changed into a woman," thought Iori. This vision in a veil, playing a flute and silhouetted against the thin rays of the evening sun, could by no stretch of the imagination be a creature of this world.

As he squatted in the grass like a frog, Iori heard an otherworldly voice call, "Otsū!" and was sure it had come from one of the fox's companions.

The rider had nearly reached a turnoff, where a road diverged to the south, and the upper part of her body glowed reddish. The sun, sinking behind the hills of Shibuya, was fringed by clouds.

If he killed her, he could expose her true fox form. Iori tightened his grip on the sword and braced himself, thinking: "Lucky it doesn't know I'm hiding here." Like all those acquainted with the truth about foxes, he knew the animal's spirit would be situated a few feet behind its human form. He swallowed hard in anticipation, while waiting for the vision to proceed and make the turn to the south.

But when the horse reached the turnoff, the woman stopped playing, put her flute in a cloth wrapper and tucked it into her obi. Lifting her veil, she peered about with searching eyes.

"Otsū!" the voice called again.

A pleasant smile came to her face as she called back, "Here I am, Hyōgo. Up here."

Iori watched as a samurai came up the road from the valley. "Oh, oh!" he gasped when he noticed that the man walked with a slight limp. *This* was the fox he had wounded; no doubt about it! Disguised not as a beautiful temptress but as a handsome samurai. The apparition terrified Iori. He shivered violently and wet himself.

After the woman and the samurai had exchanged a few words, the samurai took hold of the horse's bit and led it right past the place where Iori was hiding.

"Now's the time," he decided, but his body would not respond.

The samurai noticed a slight motion and looked around, his gaze falling squarely on Iori's petrified face. The light from the samurai's eyes seemed more brilliant than the edge of the setting sun. Iori prostrated himself and buried his face in the grass. Never in his entire fourteen years had he experienced such terror.

Hyōgo, seeing nothing alarming about the boy, walked on. The slope was steep, and he had to lean back to keep the horse in check. Looking over his shoulder at Otsū, he asked gently, "Why are you so late? You've been gone a long time just to have ridden to the shrine and back. My uncle got worried and sent me to look for you."

Without answering, Otsū jumped down from the horse.

Hyōgo stopped. "Why are you getting off? Something wrong?"

"No, but it's not fitting for a woman to ride when a man's walking. Let's walk together. We can both hold the bit." She took her place on the other side of the horse.

They descended into the darkening valley and passed a sign reading: "Sendan'en Academy for Priests of the Sōdō Zen Sect." The sky was filling with stars, and the Shibuya River could be heard in the distance. The river divided the valley into North Higakubo and South Higakubo. Since the school, established by the monk Rintatsu, lay on the north slope, the priests were casually referred to as the "fellows of the north." The "fellows of the south" were the men studying swordsmanship under Yagyū Munenori, whose establishment was directly across the valley.

As Yagyū Sekishūsai's favorite among his sons and grandsons, Yagyū Hyōgo enjoyed a special status among the "fellows of the south." He had also distinguished himself in his own right. At the age of twenty, he had been summoned by the famous general Katō Kiyomasa and given a position at Kumamoto Castle in Higo Province at a stipend of fifteen thousand bushels. This was unheard of for a man so young, but after the Battle of Sekigahara, Hyōgo began to have second thoughts about his status, because of the danger inherent in having to side with either the Tokugawas or the Osaka faction. Three years earlier, using his grandfather's illness as a pretext, he had taken a leave of absence from Kumamoto and returned to Yamato. After that, saying he needed more training, he had traveled about the countryside for a time.

He and Otsū had been thrown together by chance the previous year, when he had come to stay with his uncle. For more than three years prior to that, Otsū had led a precarious existence, never quite able to escape from Matahachi, who had dragged her along everywhere, glibly telling prospective employers that she was his wife. He had been willing to work as an apprentice to a carpenter or a plasterer or a stonemason, he could have found employment on the day they arrived in Edo, but he preferred to imagine they could work together at softer jobs, she as a domestic servant perhaps, he as a clerk or accountant.

Finding no takers for his services, they had managed to survive by doing odd jobs. And as the months passed, Otsū, hoping to lull her tormentor into complacency, had given in to him in every way short of surrendering her body.

Then one day they had been walking along the street when they encountered a diamyō's procession. Along with everyone else, they moved to the side of the road and assumed a properly respectful attitude.

The palanquins and lacquered strongboxes bore the Yagyū crest. Otsū had raised her eyes enough to see this, and memories of Sekishūsai and the happy days at Koyagyū Castle flooded her heart. If only she were back in that peaceful land of Yamato now! With Matahachi at her side, she could only stare blankly after the passing retinue.

"Otsū, isn't that you?" The conical sedge hat came low over the samurai's face, but as he drew closer, Otsū had seen that it was Kimura Sukekurō, a man she remembered with affection and respect. She couldn't have been more amazed or thankful if he had been the Buddha himself, surrounded by the wondrous light of infinite compassion. Slipping away from Matahachi's side, she had hurried to Sukekurō, who promptly offered to take her home with him.

When Matahachi had opened his mouth to protest, Sukekurō said peremptorily, "If you have anything to say, come to Higakubo and say it there."

Powerless before the prestigious House of Yagyū, Matahachi held his tongue, biting his lower lip in angry frustration as he sullenly watched his precious treasure escape from him.

17

An Urgent Letter

At thirty-eight, Yagyū Munenori was regarded as the best swordsman of them all. This hadn't kept his father from constantly worrying about his fifth son. "If only he can control that little quirk of his," he often said to himself. Or: "Can anybody that self-willed manage to keep a high position?"

It was now fourteen years since Tokugawa Ieyasu had commanded Sekishūsai to provide a tutor for Hidetada. Sekishūsai had passed over his other sons, grandsons and nephews. Munenori was neither particularly brilliant nor heroically masculine, but he was a man of good, solid judgment, a practical man not likely to get lost in the clouds. He possessed neither his father's towering stature nor Hyōgo's genius, but he was reliable, and most important, he understood the cardinal principle of the Yagyū Style, namely that the true value of the Art of War lay in its application to government.

Sekishūsai had not misinterpreted Ieyasu's wishes; the conquering general had no use for a swordsman to teach his heir only technical skills. Some years before Sekigahara, Ieyasu himself had studied under a master swordsman named Okuyama, his objective being, as he himself frequently expressed it, "to acquire the eye needed to oversee the country."

Still, Hidetada was now shōgun, and it would not do for the shōgun's instructor to be a man who lost in actual combat. A samurai in Munenori's position was expected to excel over all challengers and to demonstrate that Yagyū swordsmanship was second to none. Munenori felt he was constantly being scrutinized and tested, and while others might regard him as lucky to have been singled out for this distinguished appointment, he himself often envied Hyōgo and wished he could live the way his nephew did.

Hyōgo, as it happened, was now walking down the outside passageway leading to his uncle's room. The house, though large and sprawling, was neither stately in appearance nor lavish in its appointments. Instead of employing carpenters from Kyoto to create an elegant, graceful dwelling, Munenori had deliberately entrusted the work to local builders, men accustomed to the sturdy, spartan warrior style of Kamakura. Though the trees were relatively sparse, and the hills of no great height, Munenori had chosen the solid rustic style of architecture exemplified by the old Main House at Koyagyū.

"Uncle," called Hyōgo softly and politely, as he knelt on the veranda outside Munenori's room.

"Is that you, Hyōgo?" asked Munenori without removing his eyes from the garden.

"May I come in?"

Having received permission to enter, Hyōgo made his way into the room on his knees. He had taken quite a few liberties with his grandfather, who was inclined to spoil him, but he knew better than to do that with his uncle. Munenori, though no martinet, was a stickler for etiquette. Now, as always, he was seated in strict formal fashion. At times Hyōgo felt sorry for him.

"Otsū?" asked Munenori, as though reminded of her by Hyōgo's arrival.

"She's back. She'd only gone to Hikawa Shrine, the way she often does. On the way back, she let her horse wander around for a while."

"You went looking for her?"

"Yes, sir."

Munenori remained silent for a few moments. The lamplight accented his tight-lipped profile. "It worries me to have a young woman living here indefinitely. You never know what might happen. I've told Sukekurō to look for an opportunity to suggest she go elsewhere."

His tone slightly plaintive, Hyōgo said, "I'm told she has no place to go." His uncle's change of attitude surprised him, for when Sukekurō had brought Otsū home and introduced her as a woman who had served Sekishūsai well, Munenori had welcomed her cordially and said she was free to stay as long as she wished. "Don't you feel sorry for her?" he asked.

"Yes, but there's a limit to what you can do for people."

"I thought you yourself thought well of her."

"It has nothing to do with that. When a young woman comes to live in a house full of young men, tongues are apt to wag. And it's difficult for the men. One of them might do something rash."

This time Hyōgo was silent, but not because he took his uncle's remarks personally. He was thirty and, like the other young samurai, single, but he firmly believed his own feelings toward Otsū were too pure to raise doubts about his intentions. He had been careful to allay his uncle's misgivings by making no secret of his fondness for her, while at the same time not once letting on that his feelings went beyond friendship.

Hyōgo felt that the problem might lie with his uncle. Munenori's wife came from a highly respected and well-placed family, of the sort whose daughters were delivered to their husbands on their wedding day in curtained palanquins lest they be seen by outsiders. Her chambers, together with those of the other women, were well removed from the more public parts of the house, so virtually no one knew whether relations between the master and his wife were harmonious. It was not difficult to imagine that the lady of the house might take a dim view of beautiful and eligible young women in such proximity to her husband.

Hyōgo broke the silence, saying, "Leave the matter to Sukekurō and me. We'll work out some solution that won't be too hard on Otsū."

Munenori nodded, saying, "The sooner the better."

Sukekurō entered the anteroom just then, and placing a letter box on the tatami, knelt and bowed. "Your lordship," he said respectfully.

Turning his eyes toward the anteroom, Munenori asked, "What is it?"

Sukekurō moved forward on his knees.

"A courier from Koyagyū has just arrived by fast horse."

"Fast horse?" said Munenori quickly, but without surprise.

Hyōgo accepted the box from Sukekurō and handed it to his uncle. Munenori opened the letter, which was from Shōda Kizaemon. Written in haste, it said: "The Old Lord has had another spell, worse than any previous. We fear he may not last long. He stoutly insists his illness is not sufficient reason for you to leave your duties. However, after discussing the matter among ourselves, we retainers decided to write and inform you of the situation."

"His condition is critical," said Munenori.

Hyōgo admired his uncle's ability to remain calm. He surmised that Munenori knew exactly what was to be done and had already made the necessary decisions.

After some minutes of silence, Munenori said, "Hyōgo, will you go to Koyagyū in my stead?"

"Of course, sir."

"I want you to assure my father there's nothing to worry about in Edo. And I want you to look after him personally."

"Yes, sir."

"I suppose it's all in the hands of the gods and the

Buddha now. All you can do is hurry and try to get there before it's too late.''

"I'll leave tonight."

From Lord Munenori's room, Hyōgo went immediately to his own. During the short time it took him to lay out the few things he would need, the bad news spread to every corner of the house.

Otsū quietly went to Hyōgo's room, dressed, to his surprise, for traveling. Her eyes were moist. "Please take me with you," she pleaded. "I can never hope to repay Lord Sekishūsai for taking me into his home, but I'd like to be with him and see if I can be of some assistance. I hope you won't refuse."

Hyōgo considered it possible that his uncle might have refused her, but he himself did not have the heart to. Perhaps it was a blessing that this opportunity to take her away from the house in Edo had presented itself.

"All right," he agreed, "but it'll have to be a fast journey."

"I promise I won't slow you down." Drying her tears, she helped him finish packing and then went to pay her respects to Lord Munenori.

"Oh, are you going to accompany Hyōgo?" he said, mildly surprised. "That's very kind of you. I'm sure my father will be pleased to see you." He made a point of giving her ample travel money and a new kimono as a going-away present. Despite his conviction that it was for the best, her departure saddened him.

She bowed herself out of his presence. "Take good care of yourself," he said with feeling, as she reached the anteroom.

The vassals and servants lined up along the path to the gate to see them off, and with a simple "Farewell" from Hyōgo, they were on their way.

Otsū had folded her kimono up under her obi, so the hem reached only five or six inches below her knees. On her head was a broad-brimmed lacquered traveling hat and in her right hand she carried a stick. Had her shoulders been draped with blossoms, she would have been the image of the Wisteria Girl so often seen in woodblock prints.

Since Hyōgo had decided to hire conveyances at the stations along the highroad, their goal tonight was the inn town of Sangen'ya, south of Shibuya. From there, his plan was to proceed along the Ōyama highroad to the Tama River, take the ferry across, and follow the Tōkaidō to Kyoto.

In the night mist, it was not long before Otsū's lacquered hat glistened with moisture. After walking through a grassy river valley, they came to a rather wide road, which since the Kamakura period had been one of the most important in the Kantō district. At night it was lonely and deserted, with trees growing thickly on both sides.

"Gloomy, isn't it?" said Hyōgo with a smile, again slowing down his naturally long strides to let Otsū catch up with him. "This is Dōgen Slope. There used to be bandits around here," he added.

"Bandits?" There was just enough alarm in her voice to make him laugh.

"That was a long time ago, though. A man by the name of Dōgen Tarō, who was related to the rebel Wada Yoshimori, is supposed to have been the head of a band of thieves who lived in the caves around here."

"Let's not talk about things like that."

Hyōgo's laughter echoed through the dark, and hearing it made him feel guilty for acting frivolous. He couldn't help himself, however. Though sad, he looked forward with pleasure to being with Otsū these next few days.

"Oh!" cried Otsū, taking a couple of steps backward.

"What's the matter?" Instinctively, Hyōgo's arm went around her shoulders.

"There's somebody over there."

"Where?"

"It's a child, sitting there by the side of the road, talking to himself and crying. The poor thing!"

When Hyōgo got close enough, he recognized the boy he had seen earlier that evening, hiding in the grass in Azabu.

Iori leaped to his feet with a gasp. An instant later, he uttered an oath and pointed his sword at Hyōgo. "Fox!" he cried. "That's what you are, a fox!"

Otsū caught her breath and stifled a scream. The look on Iori's face was wild, almost demonic, as if he were possessed by an evil spirit. Even Hyōgo drew back cautiously.

"Foxes!" Iori shouted again. "I'll take care of you!" His voice cracked hoarsely, like an old woman's. Hyōgo stared at him in puzzlement but was careful to steer clear of his blade.

"How's this?" shouted Iori, whacking off the top of a tall shrub not far from Hyōgo's side. Then he sank to the ground, exhausted by his effort. Breathing hard, he asked, "What did you think of that, fox?"

Turning to Otsū, Hyōgo said with a grin, "Poor little fellow. He seems to be possessed by a fox."

"Maybe you're right. His eyes are ferocious."

"Just like a fox's."

"Isn't there something we can do to help him?"

"Well, they say there's no cure for either madness or stupidity, but I suspect there's a remedy for his ailment." He walked up to Iori and glared sternly at him.

Glancing up, the boy hastily gripped his sword again. "Still here, are you?" he cried. But before he could get to his feet, his ears were assailed by a fierce roar coming from the pit of Hyōgo's stomach.

"Y-a-a-w-r!"

Iori was scared witless. Hyōgo picked him up by the waist, and holding him horizontally, strode back down the hill to the bridge. He turned the boy upside down, grasped him by the ankles and held him out over the railing.

"Help! Mother! Help, help! *Sensei*! Save me!" The screams gradually changed to a wail.

Otsū hastened to the rescue. "Stop that, Hyōgo. Let him go. You shouldn't be so cruel."

"I guess that's enough," said Hyōgo, setting the boy down gently on the bridge.

Iori was in a terrible state, bawling and choking, convinced there was not a soul on earth who could help him. Otsū went to his side and put her arm affectionately around his drooping shoulders. "Where do you live, child?" she asked softly.

Between sobs, Iori stammered, "O-over th-th-that way," and pointed.

"What do you mean, 'that way'?"

"Ba-ba-bakurōchō."

"Why, that's **miles** away. How did you get all the way out here?"

"I came on an errand. I got lost."

"When was that?"

"I left Bakurōchō yesterday."

"And you've been wandering around all night and all day?" Iori half shook his head, but didn't say anything. "Why, that's terrible. Tell me, where were you supposed to go?"

A little calmer now, he replied promptly, as though he'd been waiting for the question. "To the residence of Lord Yagyū Munenori of Tajima." After feeling around under his obi, he clutched the crumpled letter and waved it proudly in front of his face. Bringing it close to his eyes, he said, "It's for Kimura Sukekurō. I'm to deliver it and wait for an answer."

Otsū saw that Iori took his mission very seriously and was ready to guard the missive with his life. Iori, for his part, was determined to show the letter to no one before he reached his destination. Neither had any inkling of the irony of the situation—a missed chance, a happening rarer than the coming together across the River of Heaven of the Herdboy and the Spinning Maiden.

Turning to Hyōgo, Otsū said, "He seems to have a letter for Sukekurō."

"He's wandered off in the wrong direction, hasn't he? Fortunately, it's not very far." Calling Iori to him, he gave him directions. "Go along this river to the first crossroads, then go left and up the hill. When you get to a place where three roads come together, you'll see a pair of large pine trees off to the right. The house is to the left, across the road."

"And watch out you don't get possessed by a fox again," added Otsū.

Iori had regained his confidence. "Thanks," he called back, already running along the river. When he reached the crossroads, he half turned and shouted, "To the left here?"

"That's it," answered Hyōgo. "The road's dark, so be careful." He and Otsū stood watching from the bridge for a minute or two. "What a strange child," he said.

"Yes, but he seems rather bright." In her mind she was comparing him with Jōtarō, who had been only a little bigger than Iori when she had last seen him. Jōtarō, she reflected, must be seventeen now. She wondered what he was like and felt an inevitable pang of yearning for Musashi. So many years since she'd had any word of him! Though now accustomed to living with the suffering that love entails, she dared hope that leaving Edo might bring her closer to him, that she might even meet him somewhere along the road.

"Let's get on," Hyōgo said brusquely, to himself as much as to Otsū. "There's nothing to be done about tonight, but we'll have to be careful not to waste any more time."

18

Filial Piety

"What're you doing, Granny, practicing your handwriting?" Jūrō the Reed Mat's expression was ambiguous; it might have been admiration, or simply shock.

"Oh, it's you," said Osugi with a trace of annoyance.

Sitting down beside her, Jūrō mumbled, "Copying a Buddhist sutra, are you?" This elicited no reply. "Aren't you old enough so you don't have to practice your writing anymore? Or are you thinking of becoming a calligraphy teacher in the next world?"

"Be quiet. To copy the holy scriptures, one has to achieve a state of selflessness. Solitude is best for that. Why don't you go away?"

"After I hurried home just to tell you what happened to me today?"

"It can wait."

"When will you be finished?"

"I have to put the spirit of the Buddha's enlightenment into each character I write. It takes me three days to make one copy."

"You've got a lot of patience."

"Three days is nothing. This summer I'm going to make dozens of copies. I've made a vow to make a thousand before I die. I'll leave them to people who don't have a proper love for their parents.''

"A thousand copies? That's a lot."

"It's my sacred vow."

"Well, I'm not very proud of it, but I guess I've been disrespectful to my parents, like the rest of these louts around here. They forgot about them a long time ago. The only one who cares for his mother and father is the boss."

"It's a sad world we live in."

"Ha, ha. If it upsets you that much, you must have a good-for-nothing son too."

"I'm sorry to say, mine has caused me a lot of grief. That's why I took the vow. This is the *Sutra on the Great Love of Parents*. Everyone who doesn't treat his mother or father right should be forced to read it."

"You're really giving a copy of whatever-you-call-it to a thousand people?"

"They say that by planting one seed of enlightenment you can convert a hundred people, and if one sprout of enlightenment grows in a hundred hearts, ten million souls can be saved." Laying down her brush, she took a finished copy and handed it to Jūrō. "Here, you can have this. See that you read it when you have time."

She looked so pious Jūrō nearly burst out laughing, but he managed to contain himself. Overcoming his urge to stuff it into his kimono like so much tissue paper, he lifted it respectfully to his forehead and placed it on his lap.

"Say, Granny, you sure you wouldn't like to know what happened today? Maybe your faith in the Buddha gets results. I ran into somebody pretty special."

"Who might that be?"

"Miyamoto Musashi. I saw him down at the Sumida River, getting off the ferry."

"You saw Musashi? Why didn't you say so!" She pushed the writing table away with a grunt. "Are you sure? Where is he now?"

"There, now, take it easy. Your old Jūrō doesn't do things halfway. After I found out who he was, I followed him without him knowing it. He went to an inn in Baku-rōchō."

"He's staying near here?"

"Well, it's not all that close."

"It may not seem that way to you, but it does to me. I've been all over the country looking for him." Springing to her feet, she went to her clothes cabinet and took out the short sword that had been in her family for generations.

"Take me there," she ordered.

"Now?"

"Of course now."

"I thought you had a lot of patience, but . . . Why do you have to go now?"

"I'm always ready to meet Musashi, even on a moment's notice. If I get killed, you can send my body back to my family in Mimasaka."

"Couldn't you wait until the boss comes home? If we go off like this, all I'll get for finding Musashi is a bawling out."

"But there's no telling when Musashi might go somewhere else."

"Don't worry about that. I sent a man to keep an eye on the place."

"Can you guarantee Musashi won't get away?"

"What? I do you a favor, and you want to tie me up with obligations! Oh, all right. I guarantee it. Absolutely. Look, Granny, now's the time when you should be taking it easy, sitting down copying sutras or something like that."

"Where is Yajibei?"

"He's on a trip to Chichibu with his religious group. I don't know exactly when he'll be back."

"I can't afford to wait."

"If that's the way it is, why don't we get Sasaki Kojirō to come over? You can talk to him about it."

* * *

The next morning, after contacting his spy, Jūrō informed Osugi that Musashi had moved from the inn to the house of a sword polisher.

"See? I told you," declared Osugi. "You can't expect him to sit still in one place forever. The next thing you know, he'll be gone again." She was seated at her writing table but hadn't written a word all morning.

"Musashi hasn't got wings," Jūrō assured her. "Just be calm. Koroku's going to see Kojirō today."

"Today? Didn't you send somebody last night? Tell me where he lives. I'll go myself."

She started getting ready to go out, but Jūrō suddenly disappeared and she had to ask a couple of the other henchmen for directions. Having seldom left the house during her more than two years in Edo, she was quite unfamiliar with the city.

"Kojirō's living with Iwama Kakubei," she was told.

"Kakubei's a vassal of the Hosokawas, but his own house is on the Takanawa highroad."

"It's about halfway up Isarago Hill. Anybody can tell you where that is."

"If you have any difficulty, ask for Tsukinomisaki. That's another name for Isarago Hill."

"The house is easy to recognize, because the gate is painted bright red. It's the only place around there with a red gate."

"All right, I understand," said Osugi impatiently, resenting the implication that she was senile, or stupid. "It doesn't sound difficult, so I'll just be on my way. Take care of things while I'm out. Be careful about fire. We don't want the place to burn down while Yajibei's away." Having put on her zōri, she checked to make sure her short sword was at her side, took a firm grip on her staff and marched off.

A few minutes later, Jūrō reappeared and asked where she was.

"She asked us how to get to Kakubei's house and went out by herself."

"Oh, well, what can you do with a pigheaded old woman?" Then he shouted in the direction of the men's quarters, "Koroku!"

The Acolyte abandoned his gambling and answered the summons posthaste.

"You were going to see Kojirō last night, then you put it off. Now look what's happened. The old woman's gone by herself."

"So?"

"When the boss gets back, she'll blab to him."

"You're right. And with that tongue of hers, she'll make us look real bad."

"Yeah. If she could only walk as well as she talks, but she's thin as a grasshopper. If she gets run into by a horse, that'll be the end of her. I hate to ask you, but you better go after her and see she gets there in one piece."

Koroku ran off, and Jūrō, ruminating on the absurdity of it all, appropriated a corner of the young men's room. It was a big room, perhaps thirty by forty feet. The floor was covered with thin, finely woven matting, and a wide variety of swords and other weapons were lying about. Hanging from nails were hand towels, kimono, underwear, fire hats and other items of the sort a band of ne'er-do-wells might require. There were two incongruous articles. One was a woman's kimono, in bright colors with a red silk lining; the other was the gold-lacquered mirror stand over which it was suspended. They had been placed there on the instructions of Kojirō, who explained to Yajibei, somewhat mysteriously, that if a group of men lived together in one room with no feminine touch, they were apt to get out of hand and fight each other, rather than save their energies for meaningful battles.

"You're cheating, you son of a bitch!"

"Who's cheating? You're nuts."

Jūrō cast a disdainful look at the gamblers and lay down with his legs crossed comfortably. With all the rumpus going on, sleep was out of the question, but he wasn't going to demean himself by joining one of the card or dice games. No competition, as he saw it.

As he closed his eyes, he heard a dejected voice say, "It's no good today—no luck at all." The loser, with the sad eyes of the utterly defeated, dropped a pillow on the floor and stretched out beside Jūrō. They were joined by another, then another and another.

"What's this?" asked one of them, reaching out for the sheet of paper that had fallen from Jūrō's kimono. "Well, I'll be—it's a sutra. Now, what would a mean cuss like you be carrying a sutra for?"

"Jūrō opened one sleepy eye and said lazily, "Oh, that? It's something the old woman copied. She said she'd sworn to make a thousand of them."

"Let me see it," said another man, making a grab for it. "What do you know? It's written out nice and clear. Why, anybody could read it."

"Does that mean you think *you* can read it?"

"Of course. It's child's play."

"All right then, let's hear some of it. Put a nice tune to it. Chant it like a priest."

"Are you joking? It's not a popular song."

"What difference does that make? A long time ago they used to sing sutras. That's how Buddhist hymns got started. You know a hymn when you hear one, don't you?"

"You can't chant these words to the tune of a hymn."

"Well, use any tune you like."

"You sing, Jūrō."

Encouraged by the enthusiasm of the others, Jūrō, still lying on his back, opened the sutra above his face and began:

THE BUSHIDO CODE

"The Sutra on the Great Love of Parents.

Thus have I heard.
Once when the Buddha was on the Sacred
    Vulture Peak
In the City of Royal Palaces,
Preaching to bodhisattvas and disciples,
There gathered a multitude of monks and nuns
    and lay believers, both male and female,
All the people of all the heavens, dragon gods
    and demons,
To hear the Sacred Law.
Around the jeweled throne they gathered
And gazed, with unwavering eyes,
At the holy face—"

"What's all that mean?"
"When it says 'nuns,' does it mean the girls we call
nuns? You know, I heard some of the nuns from Yoshiwara have started powdering their faces gray and will
give it to you for less than in the whorehouses—"
"Quiet!"

"At this time the Buddha
Preached the Law as follows:
'All ye good men and good women,
Acknowledge your debt for your father's
    compassion
Acknowledge your debt for your mother's mercy.
For the life of a human being in this world
Has karma as its basic cause,
But parents as its immediate means of origin.' "

"It's just talking about being good to your mama and
daddy. You've already heard it a million times."
"Shh!"
"Sing some more. We'll be quiet."

200

" 'Without a father, the child is not born.
   Without a mother, the child is not nourished.
   The spirit comes from the father's seed;
   The body grows within the mother's womb.' "

Jūrō paused to rearrange himself and pick his nose,
then resumed.

" 'Because of these relationships,
   The concern of a mother for her child
   Is without comparison in this world. . . .' "

Noticing how silent the others were, Jūrō asked,
"Are you listening?"
"Yes. Go on."

" 'From the time when she receives the child in
     her womb,
   During the passage of nine months,
   Going, coming, sitting, sleeping,
   She is visited by suffering.
   She ceases to have her customary love for
     food or drink or clothing
   And worries solely about a safe delivery.' "

"I'm tired," complained Jūrō. "That's enough, isn't
it?"
"No. Keep singing. We're listening."

" 'The months are full, and the days sufficient.
   At the time of birth, the winds of karma
     hasten it on,
   Her bones are racked with pain.
   The father, too, trembles and is afraid.
   Relatives and servants worry and are
     distressed.

When the child is born and dropped upon
  the grass,
The boundless joy of the father and mother
Match that of a penurious woman
Who has found the omnipotent magic jewel.
When the child utters its first sounds,
The mother feels that she herself is born
  anew.
Her chest becomes the child's place of rest;
Her knees, its playground,
Her breasts, its source of food.
Her love, its very life.
Without its mother, the child cannot dress or
  undress.
Though the mother hungers,
She takes the food from her own mouth and
  gives it to her child.
Without the mother, the child cannot be
  nourished . . .' ''

"What's the matter? Why'd you stop?"
"Wait a minute, will you?"
"Will you look at that? He's crying like a baby."
"Aw, shut up!"
It had all begun as an idle way to pass the time,
almost a joke, but the meaning of the words of the sutra
was sinking in. Three or four others besides the reader
had unsmiling faces, their eyes a faraway look.

" 'The mother goes to the neighboring village
  to work.
  She draws water, builds the fire,
  Pounds the grain, makes the flour.
  At night when she returns,
  Before she reaches the house,
  She hears the baby's crying
  And is filled with love.

Her chest heaves, her heart cries out,
The milk flows forth, she cannot bear it.
She runs to the house.
The baby, seeing its mother approach from
    afar,
Works its brain, shakes its head,
And wails for her.
She bends her body,
Takes the child's two hands,
Places her lips upon its lips.
There is no greater love than this.
When the child is two,
He leaves the mother's breast.
But without his father, he would not know
    that fire can burn.
Without his mother, he would not know that
    a knife can cut off fingers.
When he is three, he is weaned and learns to
    eat.
Without his father, he would not know that
    poison can kill.
Without his mother, he would not know that
    medicine cures.
When the parents go to other houses
And are presented with marvelous
    delicacies,
They do not eat but put the food in their
    pockets
And take it home for the child, to make him
    rejoice. . . .' "

"You blubbering again?"
"I can't help it. I just remembered something."
"Cut it out. You'll have me doing it too."
Sentimentality with regard to parents was strictly
taboo among these denizens of society's outer edge, for

to express filial affection was to invite charges of weakness, effeminacy or worse. But it would have done Osugi's aging heart good to see them now. The sutra reading, possibly because of the simplicity of the language, had reached the core of their being.

"Is that all? Isn't there any more?"

"There's lots more."

"Well?"

"Wait a minute, will you?" Jūrō stood up, blew his nose loudly and sat down to intone the rest.

> " 'The child grows.
> The father brings cloth to clothe him.
> The mother combs his locks.
> The parents give every beautiful thing they
>   possess to him,
> Keeping for themselves only that which is
>   old and worn.
> The child takes a bride
> And brings this stranger into the house.
> The parents become more distant.
> The new husband and wife are intimate with
>   each other.
> They stay in their own room, talking happily
>   with each other.' "

"That's the way it works, all right," broke in a voice.

> " 'The parents grow old.
> Their spirits weaken, their strength diminishes.
> They have only the child to depend on,
> Only his wife to do things for them.
> But the child no longer comes to them,
> Neither at night nor in the daytime.
> Their room is cold.
> There is no more pleasant talk.
> They are like lonely guests at an inn.

A crisis arises, and they call their child.
Nine times in ten, he comes not,
Nor does he serve them.
He grows angry and reviles them,
Saying it would be better to die
Than to linger on unwanted in this world.
The parents listen, and their hearts are filled
   with rage.
Weeping, they say, "When you were young,
Without us, you would not have been born,
Without us, you could not have grown.
Ah! How we—" ' "

Juro broke off abruptly and threw the text aside. "I
. . . I can't. Somebody else read it."

But there was no one to take his place. Lying on
their backs, sprawled out on their bellies, sitting with
their legs crossed and their heads drooping between their
knees, they were as tearful as lost children.

Into the middle of this unlikely scene walked Sasaki
Kojirō.

19

Spring Shower in Red

"Isn't Yajibei here?" Kojirō asked loudly.

The gamblers were so absorbed in their play, and the weepers in their memories of childhood, that no one replied.

Going over to Jūrō, who was lying on his back with his arms over his eyes, Kojirō said, "May I ask what's going on?"

"Oh, I didn't know it was you, sir." There was a hasty wiping of eyes and blowing of noses as Jūrō and the others pulled themselves to their feet and bowed sheepishly to their sword instructor.

"Are you crying?" he asked.

"Unh, yes. I mean, no."

"You're an odd one."

While the others drifted off, Jūrō began telling about his chance encounter with Musashi, happy to have a subject that might distract Kojirō's attention from the state of the young men's room. "Since the boss is away," he said, "we didn't know what to do, so Osugi decided to go and talk to you."

Kojirō's eyes flared brightly. "Musashi's putting up at an inn in Bakurōchō?"

"He was, but now he's staying at Zushino Kōsuke's house."

"That's an interesting coincidence."

"Is it?"

"It just happens I sent my Drying Pole to Zushino to work on. As a matter of fact, it should be ready now. I came this way today to pick it up."

"You've been there already?"

"Not yet. I thought I'd drop in here for a few minutes first."

"That's lucky. If you'd showed up suddenly, Musashi might have attacked you."

"I'm not afraid of him. But how can I confer with the old lady when she's not here?"

"I don't imagine she's reached Isarago yet. I'll send a good runner to bring her back."

At the council of war held that evening, Kojirō expressed the opinion that there was no reason to wait for Yajibei's return. He himself would serve as Osugi's second, so that she might, at long last, take her proper revenge. Jūrō and Koroku asked to go along too, more for the honor than to help. Though aware of Musashi's reputation as a fighter, they never imagined he might be a match for their brilliant instructor.

Nothing could be done tonight, however. For all her enthusiasm, Osugi was dead tired and complained of a backache. They decided they would carry out their plan the following night.

The next afternoon, Osugi bathed under cold water, blackened her teeth and dyed her hair. At twilight, she made her preparations for battle, first donning a white underrobe she had bought to be buried in and had carried around with her for years. She had had it stamped for good luck at every shrine and temple she visited—Sumiyoshi Shrine in Osaka, Oyama Hachiman Shrine and Kiyomizudera in Kyoto, the Kannon Temple in Asakusa, and dozens of less prominent religious establishments in various parts of the country. The sacred imprints made the robe resemble a tie-dyed kimono; Osugi felt safer than she would have in a suit of mail.

She carefully tucked a letter to Matahachi into the sash under her obi, together with a copy of the *Sutra on the Great Love of Parents*. There was also a second letter, which she always carried in a small money pouch; this said: "Though I am old, it has become my lot to wander about the country in an effort to realize one great hope. There is no way of knowing but that I may be slain by my sworn enemy or die of illness by the wayside. Should this be my fate, I ask the officials and people of goodwill to use the money in this purse to send my body home. Sugi, widow of Hon'iden, Yoshino Village, Mimasaka Province."

With her sword in place, her shins wrapped in white leggings, fingerless gloves on her hands and a blind-stitched obi snugly holding her sleeveless kimono in place, her preparations were nearly complete. Placing a bowl of water on her writing table, she knelt before it and said, "I'm going now." She then closed her eyes and sat motionless, addressing her thoughts to Uncle Gon.

Jūrō opened the shoji a crack and peeked in. "Are you ready?" he asked. "It's about time we were leaving. Kojirō's waiting."

"I'm ready."

Joining the others, she went to the place of honor they had left open for her before the alcove. The Acolyte took a cup from the table, put it in Osugi's hand and carefully poured her a cupful of sake. Then he did the same for Kojirō and Jūrō. When each of the four had drunk, they extinguished the lamp and set forth.

Quite a few of the Hangawara men clamored to be taken along, but Kojirō refused, since a large group would not only attract attention but encumber them in a fight.

As they were going out the gate, one young man called to them to wait. He then struck sparks from a flint to wish them luck. Outside, under a sky murky with rain clouds, nightingales were singing.

As they made their way through the dark, silent streets, dogs started barking, set off, perhaps, by some instinctive sense that these four human beings were on a sinister mission.

"What's that?" Koroku asked, staring back along a narrow lane.

"Did you see something?"

"Somebody's following us."

"Probably one of the fellows from the house," said Kojirō. "They were all so eager to come with us."

"They'd rather brawl than eat."

They turned a corner, and Kojirō stopped under the eaves of a house, saying, "Kōsuke's shop's around here, isn't it?" Their voices dropped to whispers.

"Down the street, there, on the other side."

"What do we do now?" asked Koroku.

"Proceed according to plan. The three of you hide in the shadows. I'll go to the shop."

"What if Musashi tries to sneak out the back door?"

"Don't worry. He's no more likely to run away from me than I am from him. If he ran away, he'd be finished as a swordsman."

"Maybe we should position ourselves on opposite sides of the house anyway—just in case."

"All right. Now, as we agreed, I'll bring Musashi outside and walk along with him. When we get near Osugi, I'll draw my sword and take him by surprise. That's the time for her to come out and strike."

Osugi was beside herself with gratitude. "Thank you, Kojirō. You're so good to me. You must be an incarnation of the great Hachiman." She clasped her hands and bowed, as if before the god of war himself.

In his heart, Kojirō was thoroughly convinced that he was doing the right thing. Indeed, it is doubtful that ordinary mortals could imagine the vastness of his self-righteousness at the moment he stepped up to Kōsuke's door.

At the beginning, when Musashi and Kojirō had been

very young, full of spirit and eager to demonstrate their superiority, there had existed no deep-seated cause for enmity between them. There had been rivalry, to be sure, but only the friction that normally arose between two strong and almost equally matched fighters. What had subsequently rankled with Kojirō was seeing Musashi gradually gaining fame as a swordsman. Musashi, for his part, respected Kojirō's extraordinary skill, if not his character, and always treated him with a certain amount of caution. As the years passed, however, they found themselves at odds over various matters—the House of Yoshioka, the fate of Akemi, the affair of the Hon'iden dowager. Conciliation was by now out of the question.

And now that Kojirō had taken it upon himself to become Osugi's protector, the trend of events bore the unmistakable seal of fate.

"Kōsuke!" Kojirō rapped lightly on the door. "Are you awake?" Light seeped through a crack, but there was no other sign of life inside.

After a few moments, a voice asked, "Who's there?"

"Iwama Kakubei gave you my sword to work on. I've come for it."

"The great long one—is that the one?"

"Open up and let me in."

"Just a moment."

The door slid open, and the two men eyed each other. Blocking the way, Kōsuke said curtly, "The sword's not ready yet."

"I see." Kojirō brushed past Kōsuke and seated himself on the step leading up to the shop. "When will it be ready?"

"Well, let's see. . . ." Kōsuke rubbed his chin, pulling the corners of his eyes down and making his long face seem even longer.

Kojirō had the feeling he was being made fun of. "Don't you think it's taking an awful long time?"

"I told Kakubei very clearly I couldn't promise when I'd finish."

"I can't do without it much longer."

"In that case, take it back."

"What's this?" Kojirō was taken aback. Artisans didn't talk that way to samurai. But instead of trying to ascertain what might be behind the man's attitude, he jumped to the conclusion that his visit had been anticipated. Thinking it best to act quickly, he said, "By the way, I heard Miyamoto Musashi, from Mimasaka, is staying here with you."

"Where did you hear that?" Kōsuke said, looking anxious. "As it happens, he is staying with us."

"Would you mind calling him? I haven't seen him for a long time, since we were both in Kyoto."

"What's your name?"

"Sasaki Kojirō. He'll know who I am."

"I'll tell him you're here, but I don't know whether he can see you or not."

"Just a moment."

"Yes?"

"Perhaps I'd better explain. I happened to hear at Lord Hosokawa's house that a man of Musashi's description was living here. I came with the idea of inviting Musashi out to drink a little and talk a little."

"I see." Kōsuke turned and went toward the back of the house.

Kojirō mulled over what to do if Musashi smelled a rat and refused to see him. Two or three stratagems came to mind, but before he had come to a decision, he was startled by a horrendous howling scream.

He jumped like a man who had been savagely kicked. He had miscalculated. His strategy had been seen through—not only seen through but turned against him. Musashi must have sneaked out the back door, gone around to the front and attacked. But who had screamed? Osugi? Jūrō? Koroku?

"If that's the way it is . . ." thought Kojirō grimly,

as he ran out into the street. Muscles taut, blood racing, in an instant he was ready for anything. "I have to fight him sooner or later anyway," he thought. He had known this since that day at the pass on Mount Hiei. The time had come! If Osugi had already been struck down, Kojirō swore that Musashi's blood would become an offering for the eternal peace of her soul.

He had covered about ten paces when he heard his name called from the side of the road. The painfully forced voice seemed to clutch at his running footsteps.

"Koroku, is that you?"

"I-I-I've b-been h-h-hit."

"Jūrō! Where's Jūrō?"

"H-him too."

"Where is he?" Before the answer came, Kojirō spotted Jūrō's blood-soaked form about thirty feet away. His entire body bristling with vigilance for his own safety, he thundered, "Koroku! Which way did Musashi go?"

"No . . . not . . . Musashi." Koroku, unable to lift his head, rolled it from side to side.

"What are you saying? Are you telling me it wasn't Musashi who attacked you?"

"Not . . . Not . . . Musa—"

"Who was it?"

It was a question Koroku would never answer.

His thoughts in a turmoil, Kojirō ran to Jūrō and pulled him up by the red sticky collar of his kimono. "Jūrō, tell me. Who did it? Which way did he go?"

But Jūrō, instead of answering, used his last tearful breath to say, "Mother . . . sorry . . . shouldn't have . . ."

"What are you talking about?" snorted Kojirō, letting go of the bloody garment.

"Kojirō! Kojirō, is that you?"

Running in the direction of Osugi's voice, he saw the old woman lying helpless in a ditch, straw and vegetable peelings clinging to her face and hair. "Get me out of here," she pleaded.

"What are you doing in that filthy water?"

Kojirō, sounding more angry than sympathetic, yanked her unceremoniously out onto the road, where she collapsed like a rag.

"Where did the man go?" she asked, taking the words out of his mouth.

"What man? Who attacked you?"

"I don't know exactly what happened, but I'm sure it was the man who was following us."

"Did he attack suddenly?"

"Yes! Out of nowhere, like a gust of wind. There was no time to speak. He jumped out of the shadows and got Jūrō first. By the time Koroku drew his sword, he was wounded too."

"Which way did he go?"

"He shoved me aside, so I didn't even see him, but the footsteps went that way." She pointed toward the river.

Running across a vacant lot where the horse market was held, Kojirō came to the dike at Yanagihara and stopped to look around. Some distance away, he could see piles of lumber, lights and people.

When he got closer, he saw they were palanquin bearers. "My two companions have been struck down in a side street near here," he said. "I want you to pick them up and take them to the house of Hangawara Yajibei in the carpenters' district. You'll find an old woman with them. Take her too."

"Were they attacked by robbers?"

"Are there robbers around here?"

"Packs of them. Even we have to be careful."

"Whoever it was must have come running out from that corner over there. Didn't you see anyone?"

"Just now, you mean?"

"Yes."

"I'm leaving," said the bearer. He and the others picked up three palanquins and prepared to depart.

"What about the fare?" asked one.

"Collect it when you get there."

Kojirō made a quick search of the riverbank and around the stacks of lumber, deciding as he did so that he'd do just as well to go back to Yajibei's house. There was little point in meeting Musashi without Osugi; it also seemed unwise to face the man in his present state of mind.

Starting back, he came to a firebreak, along one side of which grew a row of paulownia trees. He looked at it for a minute, then as he turned away, he saw the glint of a blade among the trees. Before he knew it, half a dozen leaves fell. The sword had been aimed at his head.

"Yellow-livered coward!" he shouted.

"Not me!" came the reply as the sword struck out a second time from the darkness.

Kojirō whirled and jumped back a full seven feet. "If you're Musashi, why don't you use the proper—" Before he could finish, the sword was at him again. "Who are you?" he shouted. "Aren't you making a mistake?"

He dodged a third stroke successfully, and the attacker, badly winded, realized before attempting a fourth that he was wasting his effort. Changing tactics, he began inching forward with his blade extended before him. His eyes were shooting fire. "Silence," he growled. "There's no mistake at all. Perhaps it'll refresh your memory if you know my name. I'm Hōjō Shinzō."

"You're one of Obata's students, aren't you?"

"You insulted my master and killed several of my comrades."

"By the warrior's code, you're free to challenge me openly at any time. Sasaki Kojirō doesn't play hide-and-seek."

"I'll kill you."

"Go ahead and try."

As Kojirō watched him close the distance—twelve feet, eleven, ten—he quietly loosened the upper part of his kimono and placed his right hand on his sword. "Come on!" he cried.

The challenge caused an involuntary hesitation on Shinzō's part, a momentary wavering. Kojirō's body bent forward, his arm snapped like a bow, and there was a metallic ring. The next instant, his sword clicked sharply back into its scabbard. There had been only a thin flashing thread of light.

Shinzō was still standing, his legs spread apart. There was no sign of blood yet, but it was plain that he'd been wounded. Though his sword was still stretched out at eye level, his left hand had gone reflexively to his neck.

"Oh!" Gasps went up on both sides of Shinzō at the same time—from Kojirō and from a man running up behind Shinzō. The sound of footsteps, together with the voice, sent Kojirō off into the darkness.

"What happened?" cried Kōsuke. He reached out to support Shinzō, only to have the full weight of the other man's body fall into his arms. "Oh, this looks bad!" cried Kōsuke. "Help! Help, somebody!"

A piece of flesh no larger than a clamshell fell from Shinzō's neck. The blood gushing out soaked first Shinzō's arm, then the skirts of his kimono all the way to his feet.

20

A Block of Wood

Plunk. Another green plum fell from the tree in the dark garden outside. Musashi ignored it, if he heard it at all. In the bright but unsteady lamplight, his disheveled hair appeared heavy and bristly, lacking in natural oil and reddish in color.

"What a difficult child!" his mother had often complained. The stubborn disposition that had so often reduced her to tears was still with him, as enduring as the scar on his head left by a large carbuncle during childhood.

Memories of his mother now floated through his mind; at times the face he was carving closely resembled hers.

A few minutes earlier Kōsuke had come to the door, hesitated and called in: "Are you still working? A man named Sasaki Kojirō says he'd like to see you. He's waiting downstairs. Do you want to speak to him, or shall I tell him you've already gone to bed?"

Musashi had the vague impression Kōsuke had repeated the message but wasn't sure whether he himself had answered.

The small table, Musashi's knees and the floor immediately around him were littered with wood chips. He was trying to finish the image of Kannon he had promised

Kōsuke in exchange for the sword. His task had been made even more challenging because of a special request by Kōsuke, a man of pronounced likes and dislikes.

When Kōsuke had first taken the ten-inch block out of a cupboard and very gently handed it to him, Musashi saw that it must have been six or seven hundred years old. Kōsuke treated it like an heirloom, for it had come from an eighth-century temple at the tomb of Prince Shōtoku in Shinaga. "I was on a trip there," he explained, "and they were repairing the old buildings. Some stupid priests and carpenters were axing up the old beams for firewood. I couldn't stand seeing the wood wasted that way, so I got them to cut off this block for me."

The grain was good, as was the feel of the wood to the knife, but thinking of how highly Kōsuke valued his treasure made Musashi nervous. If he made a slip, he would ruin an irreplaceable piece of material.

He heard a bang, which sounded like the wind blowing open the gate in the garden hedge. Looking up from his work, for almost the first time since he had begun carving, he thought: "Could that be Iori?" and cocked his head, waiting for confirmation.

"What're you standing there gaping for?" Kōsuke shouted at his wife. "Can't you see the man's badly wounded? It doesn't make any difference which room!"

Behind Kōsuke, the men carrying Shinzō excitedly offered to help.

"Any spirits to wash the wound with? If there aren't, I'll go home for some."

"I'll fetch the doctor."

After the commotion died down a bit, Kōsuke said, "I want to thank all of you. I think we saved his life; no more need to worry." He bowed deeply to each man as he left the house.

Finally it penetrated Musashi's consciousness that something had happened and Kōsuke was involved. Brushing the chips from his knees, he descended the staircase formed by the tops of tiered storage chests and went to the room where Kōsuke and his wife stood staring down at the wounded man.

"Oh, are you still awake?" asked the sword polisher, moving over to make a place for Musashi.

Sitting down near the man's pillow, Musashi looked closely at his face and inquired, "Who is he?"

"I couldn't have been more surprised. I didn't recognize him until we got him back here, but it's Hōjō Shinzō, the son of Lord Hōjō of Awa. He's a very dedicated young man who's been studying under Obata Kagenori for several years."

Musashi carefully lifted the edge of the white bandage around Shinzō's neck and examined the wound, which had been cauterized, then washed with alcohol. The clam-sized piece of flesh had been sliced out cleanly, exposing the pulsating carotid artery. Death had come that close. "Who?" Musashi wondered. From the shape of the wound, it seemed probable the sword had been on the upswing of a swallow-flight stroke.

Swallow-flight stroke? Kojirō's specialty.

"Do you know what happened?" Musashi asked.

"Not yet."

"Neither do I, of course, but I can tell you this much." He nodded his head confidently. "It's the work of Sasaki Kojirō."

Back in his own room, Musashi lay down on the tatami with his hands under his head, ignoring the mess around him. His pallet had been spread, but he ignored that too, despite his fatigue.

He had been working on the statue for nearly forty-eight hours straight. Not being a sculptor, he lacked the technical skills necessary to solve difficult problems, nor could he execute the deft strokes that would cover up a mistake. He had nothing to go on but the image of Kannon he carried in his heart, and his sole technique was to clear his mind of extraneous thoughts and do his best to faithfully transfer this image to the wood.

He would think for a time that the sculpture was

taking form, but then somehow it would go wrong, some slip would occur between the image in his mind and the hand working with the dagger. Just as he felt he was making progress again, the carving would get out of hand again. After many false starts, the ancient piece of wood had shrunk to a length of no more than four inches.

He heard a nightingale call twice, then dropped off to sleep for perhaps an hour. When he awoke, his strong body was surging with energy, his mind perfectly clear. As he arose, he thought: "I'll make it this time." Going to the well behind the house, he washed his face and swilled water through his teeth. Refreshed, he sat down by the lamp again and took up his work with renewed vigor.

The knife had a different feel to it now. In the grain of the wood he sensed the centuries of history contained within the block. He knew that if he did not carve skillfully this time, there would be nothing left but a pile of useless chips. For the next few hours, he concentrated with feverish intensity. Not once did his back unbend, nor did he stop for a drink of water. The sky grew light, the birds began to sing, all the doors in the house save his were thrown open for the morning's cleaning. Still, his attention remained focused on the tip of his knife.

"Musashi, are you all right?" asked his host in a worried tone, as he slid open the shoji and entered the room.

"It's no good," Musashi sighed. He straightened up and tossed his dagger aside. The block of wood was no larger than a man's thumb. The wood around his legs lay like fallen snow.

"No good?"

"No good."

"How about the wood?"

"Gone . . . I couldn't get the bodhisattva's form to emerge." Placing his hands behind his head, he felt himself returning to earth after having been suspended for an indeterminate length of time between delusion and enlightenment. "No good at all. It's time to forget and to meditate."

He lay on his back. When he closed his eyes, distractions seemed to fade away, to be replaced by a blinding mist. Gradually, his mind filled with the single idea of the infinite void.

Most of the guests leaving the inn that morning were horse traders, going home after the four-day market that had ended the day before. For the next few weeks, the inn would see few customers.

Catching sight of Iori going up the stairs, the proprietress called out to him from the office.

"What do you want?" asked Iori. From his vantage point, he could see the woman's artfully disguised bald spot.

"Where do you think you're going?"

"Upstairs, where my teacher is. Something wrong?"

"More than you know," replied the woman with an exasperated glance. "Just when did you leave here?"

Counting on his fingers, Iori answered, "The day before the day before yesterday, I think."

"Three days ago, wasn't it?"

"That's right."

"You certainly took your time, didn't you? What happened? Did a fox bewitch you or something?"

"How'd you know? You must be a fox yourself." Giggling at his own riposte, he started for the top of the stairs again.

"Your teacher's not here anymore."

"I don't believe you." He ran up the stairs, but soon came back with a dismayed look on his face. "Has he changed rooms?"

"What's the matter with you? I told you he left."

"Really gone?" There was alarm in the boy's voice.

"If you don't believe me, look at the account book. See?"

"But why? Why would he leave before I got back?"

"Because you were gone too long."

"But . . . but . . ." Iori burst into tears. "Where did he go? Please tell me."

"He didn't tell me where he was going. I imagine he left you behind because you're so useless."

His color changing, Iori charged out into the street. He looked east, west, then he gazed up at the sky. Tears poured down his cheeks.

Scratching the bald spot with a comb, the woman broke into raucous laughter. "Stop your bawling," she called. "I was only fooling. Your teacher's staying at the sword polisher's, over there." She had barely finished speaking when a straw horseshoe came sailing into the office.

Meekly, Iori sat down in formal fashion at Musashi's feet and in a subdued voice announced, "I'm back."

He'd already noticed the atmosphere of gloom hanging over the house. The wood chips had not been cleaned up, and the burned-out lamp was still sitting where it had been the night before.

"I'm back," Iori repeated, no more loudly than before.

"Who is it?" mumbled Musashi, slowly opening his eyes.

"Iori."

Musashi sat up quickly. Although relieved to see the boy back safe, his only greeting was: "Oh, it's you."

"I'm sorry I took so long." This met with silence. "Forgive me." Neither his apology nor a polite bow elicited a response.

Musashi tightened his obi and said, "Open the windows and tidy up the room."

He was out the door before Iori had time to say, "Yes, sir."

Musashi went to the room downstairs at the back and asked Kōsuke how the invalid was this morning.

"He seems to be resting better."

"You must be tired. Shall I come back after breakfast so you can have a rest?"

Kōsuke answered that there was no need. "There is one thing I would like to see done," he added. "I think we should let the Obata School know about this, but I don't have anybody to send."

Having offered to either go himself or send Iori, Musashi went back to his own room, which was now in good order. As he sat down, he said, "Iori, was there an answer to my letter?"

Relieved at not being scolded, the boy broke into a smile. "Yes, I brought a reply. It's right here." With a look of triumph, he fished the letter from his kimono.

"Let me have it."

Iori advanced on his knees and placed the folded paper in Musashi's outstretched hand. "I am sorry to say," Sukekurō had written, "that Lord Munenori, as tutor to the shōgun, cannot engage in a bout with you, as you requested. If, however, you should visit us for some other purpose, there is a possibility that his lordship may greet you in the dōjō. If you still feel strongly about trying your hand against the Yagyū Style, the best plan, I think, would be for you to confront Yagyū Hyōgo. I regret to say, however, that he left yesterday for Yamato to be at the bedside of Lord Sekishūsai, who is gravely ill. Such being the case, I must ask you to postpone your visit until a later day. I shall be happy to make arrangements at that time."

As he slowly refolded the lengthy scroll, Musashi smiled. Iori, feeling more secure, extended his legs comfortably and said, "The house is not in Kobikichō; it's at a place called Higakubo. It's very large, very splendid, and Kimura Sukekurō gave me lots of good things to eat—"

His eyebrows arching in disapproval at this display of familiarity, Musashi said gravely, "Iori."

The boy's legs quickly shot back to their proper place under him. "Yes, sir."

"Even if you did get lost, don't you think three days is a rather long time? What happened?"

"I was bewitched by a fox."

"A fox?"

"Yes, sir, a fox."

"How could a boy like you, born and raised in the country, be bewitched by a fox?"

"I don't know, but afterward I couldn't remember where I'd been for half a day and half a night."

"Hmm. Very strange."

"Yes, sir. I thought so myself. Maybe foxes in Edo have it in for people more than the ones in the country do."

"I suspect that's true." Taking into account the boy's seriousness, Musashi did not have the heart to scold him, but he did feel it necessary to pursue his point. "I also suspect," he continued, "you were up to something you shouldn't have been up to."

"Well, the fox was following me, and to keep it from bewitching me, I cut it with my sword. Then the fox punished me for that."

"No, it didn't."

"Didn't it?"

"No. It wasn't the fox punishing you; it was your own conscience, which is invisible. Now, you sit there and think about that for a while. When I come back, you can tell me what you think it means."

"Yes, sir. Are you going somewhere?"

"Yes; to a place near the Hirakawa Shrine in Kōjimachi."

"You'll be back by evening, won't you?"

"Ha, ha. I should be, unless a fox gets me."

Musashi departed, leaving Iori to ponder his conscience. Outside, the sky was obscured by the dull, sullen clouds of the summer rainy season.

21

The Deserted Prophet

The forest around the Hirakawa Tenjin Shrine was alive with the hum of cicadas. An owl hooted as Musashi walked from the gate to the entrance hall of the Obata house.

"Good day!" he called, but his greeting echoed back as though from an empty cavern.

After a time, he heard footsteps. The young samurai who emerged wearing his two swords was clearly no mere underling assigned to answer the door.

Without bothering to kneel, he said, "May I ask your name?" Though no more than twenty-four or -five, he gave the impression of being someone to be reckoned with.

My name is Miyamoto Musashi. Am I correct in thinking this is Obata Kagenori's academy of military science?"

"That's right," came the reply, in clipped tones. From the samurai's manner, it was evident he expected Musashi to explain how he was traveling around to perfect his knowledge of the martial arts, and so on.

"One of the students from your school has been wounded in a fight," said Musashi. "He's now being cared for by the sword polisher Zushino Kōsuke, whom I believe you know. I came at Kōsuke's request."

"It must be Shinzō!" There were fleeting signs of severe shock, but the youth recovered immediately. "Forgive me. I'm Kagenori's only son, Yogorō. Thank you for taking the trouble to come and tell us. Is Shinzō's life in danger?"

"He seemed better this morning, but it's still too early for him to be moved. I think it'd be wise to let him stay at Kōsuke's house for the time being."

"I hope you'll convey our thanks to Kōsuke."

"I'd be happy to."

"To tell the truth, since my father is bedridden, Shinzō was lecturing in his stead until last fall when he suddenly left. As you can see, there's almost nobody here now. I regret we're not able to receive you properly."

"Of course; but tell me, is there a feud going on between your school and Sasaki Kojirō?"

"Yes. I was away when it started, so I don't know all the details, but apparently Kojirō insulted my father, which of course incited the students. They took it upon themselves to punish Kojirō, but he killed several of them. As I understand it, Shinzō left because he finally came to the conclusion that he himself should take revenge."

"I see. It's beginning to make sense. I'd like to give you a bit of advice. Don't fight Kojirō. He can't be beaten by ordinary sword techniques, and he's even less vulnerable to clever strategy. As a fighter, as a speaker, as a strategist, he's without rival, even among the greatest masters alive today."

This assessment brought a burst of angry fire from Yogorō's eyes. Observing this, Musashi felt it prudent to repeat his warning. "Let the proud have their day," he added. "It's senseless to risk disaster over a trivial grievance. Don't entertain the idea that Shinzō's defeat makes it necessary for you to settle the score. If you do, you'll simply follow in his footsteps. That would be foolish, very foolish."

After Musashi was out of sight, Yogorō leaned against the wall with his arms folded. Softly, in a faintly tremulous voice, he muttered, "To think it's come to this. Even Shinzō has failed!" Gazing vacantly at the ceiling, he thought of the letter Shinzō had left for him, in which he'd said that his purpose in leaving was to kill Kojirō and that if he did not succeed, Yogorō would probably never see him alive again.

That Shinzō was not dead did not make his defeat any less humiliating. With the school forced to suspend operations, the public in general had concluded that Kojirō was right: the Obata Academy was a school for cowards, or at best for theoreticians devoid of practical ability. This had led to the desertion of some of the students. Others, apprehensive over Kagenori's illness or the apparent decline of the Kōshū Style, had switched to the rival Naganuma Style. Only two or three were still in residence.

Yogorō decided not to tell his father about Shinzō. It seemed that the only course open to him was to nurse the old man as best he could, although the doctor's opinion was that recovery was out of the question.

"Yogorō, where are you?"

It was a source of constant amazement to Yogorō that although Kagenori was at death's door, when an impulse moved him to summon his son, his voice became that of a perfectly healthy man.

"Coming." He ran to the sickroom, fell to his knees and said, "You called?"

As he often did when he was tired of lying flat on his back, Kagenori had propped himself up by the window, using his pillow as an armrest. "Who was the samurai who just went out the gate?" he asked.

"Huh," said Yogorō, somewhat flustered. "Oh, him. Nobody in particular. He was just a messenger."

"Messenger from where?"

"Well, it seems Shinzō has had an accident. The

samurai came to tell us. He gave his name as Miyamoto Musashi.''

"Mm. He wasn't born in Edo, was he?"

"No. I've heard he's from Mimasaka. He's a rōnin. Did you think you recognized him?"

"No." Kagenori replied with a vigorous shake of his thin gray beard. "I don't recall ever having seen or heard of him. But there's something about him. . . . I've met a lot of people during my lifetime, you know, on the battlefield as well as in ordinary life. Some were very good people, people I valued greatly. But the ones I could consider to be genuine samurai, in every sense of the term, were very few. This Man—Musashi, did you say?—appealed to me. I'd like to meet him, talk to him a little. Go bring him back."

"Yes, sir," Yogorō answered obediently, but before getting to his feet, he continued in a slightly puzzled tone: "What was it you noticed about him? You only saw him from a distance."

"You wouldn't understand. When you do, you'll be old and withered like me."

"But there must have been something."

"I admired his alertness. He wasn't taking any chances, even on a sick old man like me. When he came through the gate, he paused and looked around—at the layout of the house, at the windows, whether they were open or closed, at the path to the garden—everything. He took it all in at a single glance. There was nothing unnatural about it. Anyone would have assumed he was simply halting for a moment as a sign of deference. I was amazed."

"Then you believe he's a samurai of real merit?"

"Perhaps. I'm sure he'd be a fascinating man to talk to. Call him back."

"Aren't you afraid it'll be bad for you?" Kagenori had become quite excited, and Yogorō was reminded of the doctor's warning that his father shouldn't talk for any length of time.

"Don't worry your head about my health. I've been waiting for years to meet a man like that. I didn't study military science all this time to teach it to children. I grant that my theories of military science are called the Kōshū Style, but they're not simply an extension of the formulas used by the famous Kōshū warriors. My ideas differ from those of Takeda Shingen, or Uesugi Kenshin, or Oda Nobunaga, or the other generals who were fighting for control of the country. The purpose of military science has changed since then. My theory is directed toward the achievement of peace and stability. You know some of these things, but the question is, whom can I entrust my ideas to?"

Yogorō was silent.

"My son, while there are many things I want to pass on to you, you're still immature, too immature to recognize the remarkable qualities of the man you just met."

Yogorō dropped his eyes but endured the criticism in silence.

"If even I, inclined as I am to look favorably on everything you do, see you as immature, then there's no doubt in my mind. You're not yet the person who can carry on my work, so I must find the right man and entrust your future to him. I've been waiting for the right person to come along. Remember, when the cherry blossom falls, it must rely on the wind to spread its pollen."

"You mustn't fall, Father. You must try to live."

The old man glared and raised his head. "Talk like that proves you're still a child! Now go quickly and find the samurai!"

"Yes, sir!"

"Don't push him. Just tell him roughly what I've told you, and bring him back with you."

"Right away, Father."

Yogorō departed on the run. Once outside, he first tried the direction he'd seen Musashi take. Then he looked all over the shrine grounds, even went out to the main street running through Kōjimachi, but to no avail.

He was not unduly disturbed, for he was not as thoroughly convinced as his father of Musashi's superiority, nor was he grateful for Musashi's warning. The talk about Kojirō's unusual ability, about the folly of "risking disaster over a trivial grievance" had stuck in his craw. It was as though Musashi's visit had been for the express purpose of singing Kojirō's praises.

Even while listening submissively to his father, he had been thinking to himself: "I'm not as young and immature as you say." And the truth was that just then, he really couldn't have cared less what Musashi thought.

They were about the same age. Even if Musashi's talent was exceptional, there were limits to what he could know and what he could do. In the past, Yogorō had gone away for a year, two years, even three, to lead the life of the ascetic *shugyōsha*. He had lived and studied for a while at the school of another military expert, and he had studied Zen under a strict master. Yet his father, after merely catching a glimpse of the man, had not only formed what Yogorō suspected was an exaggerated opinion of the unknown rōnin's worth but had gone so far as to suggest that Yogorō take Musashi as a model.

"May as well go back," he thought sadly. "I suppose there's no way to convince a parent that his son is no longer a child." He longed desperately for the day when Kagenori would look at him and suddenly see that he was both a grown man and a brave samurai. It pained him to think that his father might die before that day arrived.

"Hey, Yogorō! It is Yogorō, isn't it?"

Yogorō turned on his heel and saw that the voice belonged to Nakatogawa Handayū, a samurai from the House of Hosokawa. They had not seen each other recently, but there had been a time when Handayū had attended Kagenori's lectures regularly.

"How's our revered teacher's health? Official duties keep me so busy I haven't had time to call."

"He's about the same, thanks."

"Say, I hear Hōjō Shinzō attacked Sasaki Kojirō and was beaten."

"You've heard that already?"

"Yes; they were talking about it at Lord Hosokawa's this morning."

"It only happened last night."

"Kojirō's a guest of Iwama Kakubei. Kakubei must have passed the word around. Even Lord Tadatoshi knew about it."

Yogorō was too young to listen with detachment, yet he was loath to reveal his anger by some involuntary twitch. Taking leave of Handayū as quickly as possible, he hurried home.

His mind was made up.

22

The Talk of the Town

Kōsuke's wife was in the kitchen making gruel for Shinzō when Iori came in.

"The plums are turning yellow," he said.

"If they're almost ripe, that means the cicadas will be singing soon," she answered absently.

"Don't you pickle the plums?"

"No. There aren't many of us here, and pickling all those plums would take several pounds of salt."

"The salt wouldn't go to waste, but the plums will if you don't pickle them. And if there was a war or a flood, they'd come in handy, wouldn't they? Since you're busy taking care of the wounded man, I'll be happy to pickle them for you."

"My, what a funny child you are, worrying about floods and such. You think like an old man."

Iori was already getting an empty wooden bucket out of the closet. With this in hand, he sauntered out into the garden and looked up at the plum tree. Alas, though sufficiently grown up to worry about the future, he was still young enough to be easily distracted by the sight of a buzzing cicada. Sneaking closer, he captured it and held it in his cupped hands, making it screech like a terrified hag.

Peeking between his thumbs, Iori experienced a

231

strange sensation. Insects were supposed to be bloodless, he thought, but the cicada felt warm. Perhaps even cicadas when faced with the peril of death gave off body heat. Suddenly he was seized by a mixture of fear and pity. Spreading his palms, he tossed the cicada into the air and watched it fly off toward the street.

The plum tree, which was quite large, was the home of a sizable community—fat caterpillars with surprisingly beautiful fur, ladybirds, tiny blue frogs clinging to the underside of leaves, small sleeping butterflies, dancing gadflies. Gazing in fascination at this little corner of the animal kingdom, he thought it would be inhuman to throw these ladies and gentlemen into consternation by shaking a branch. Carefully, he reached out, picked a plum and bit into it. Then he shook the nearest branch gently and was surprised when the fruit did not fall off. Reaching out, he picked a few plums and dropped them into the bucket below.

"Son of a bitch!" shouted Iori, abruptly firing three or four plums into the narrow lane next to the house. The clothes-drying pole between the house and the fence fell to the ground with a clatter, and footsteps hastily retreated from the lane into the street.

Kōsuke's face appeared at the bamboo grille of his workroom window. "What was that noise?" he asked, his eyes wide with astonishment.

Jumping down from the tree, Iori cried, "Another strange man was hiding in the shadows, squatting right there in the lane. I threw some plums at him, and he ran away."

The sword polisher came outside, wiping his hands on a towel. "What sort of man?"

"A thug."

"One of Hangawara's men?"

"I don't know. Why do those men come snooping around here?"

"They're looking for a chance to get back at Shinzō."

MILK

UCLA
to suck
check B

TAPE (ATHLETIC)

PUC - CSI
WOMEN'S defense
getting to NO you

UP - 30 JUST SAY
NO

AMERICAN Health   Sept. 90
smiles / Stretching matches

Iori looked toward the back room, where the injured man was just finishing his gruel. His wound had healed to the extent that the bandage was no longer necessary.

"Kōsuke," called Shinzō.

The craftsman walked to the edge of the veranda and asked, "How are you feeling?"

Pushing his tray aside, Shinzō reseated himself more formally. "I want to apologize for causing you so much trouble."

"Don't mention it. I'm sorry I've been too busy to do more for you."

"I notice that besides worrying about me, you're being annoyed by those Hangawara hoodlums. The longer I stay, the more danger there is that they'll come to regard you as an enemy too. I think I should be leaving."

"Don't give it a thought."

"I'm much better now, as you can see. I'm ready to go home."

"Today?"

"Yes."

"Don't be in such a hurry. At least wait until Musashi comes back."

"I'd rather not, but please thank him for me. He's been very kind to me too. I can walk all right now."

"You don't seem to understand. Hangawara's men are watching this house day and night. They'll pounce on you the minute you step outside. I can't possibly let you leave alone."

"I had a good reason for killing Jūrō and Koroku. Kojirō started all this, not me. But if they want to attack me, let them attack."

Shinzō was on his feet and ready to go. Sensing there was no way of holding him back, Kōsuke and his wife went to the front of the shop to see him off.

Musashi appeared at the door just then, his sun-burned forehead moist with sweat. "Going out?" he asked. "Going home? . . . Well, I'm glad to see you feel well enough, but it'd be dangerous to go alone. I'll go with you.''

Shinzō tried to refuse, but Musashi insisted. Minutes later, they set off together.

"It must be difficult to walk after being in bed so long."

"Somehow the ground seems higher than it really is."

"It's a long way to Hirakawa Tenjin. Why don't we hire a palanquin for you?"

"I suppose I ought to have mentioned it before. I'm not going back to the school."

"Oh? Where then?"

Casting his eyes downward, Shinzō answered, "It's rather humiliating, but I think I'll go to my father's house for a while. It's in Ushigome."

Musashi stopped a palanquin and virtually forced Shinzō into it. Despite the insistence of the bearers, Musashi refused one for himself—to the disappointment of the Hangawara men watching from around the next corner.

"Look, he put Shinzō into a palanquin."

"I saw him glance this way."

"It's too early to do anything yet."

After the palanquin turned right by the outer moat, they hitched up their skirts, pulled back their sleeves, and followed along behind, their glittering eyes seemingly ready to pop out and shoot toward Musashi's back.

Musashi and Shinzō had reached the neighborhood of Ushigafuchi when a small rock glanced off the palanquin pole. At the same time, the gang started shouting and moved in to surround its prey.

"Wait!" called one of them.

"Just stay where you are, you bastard!"

The bearers, terrified, dropped the palanquin and fled. Shinzō crawled out of the palanquin, hand on sword. Pulling himself to his feet, he assumed a stance and cried, "Is it me you're telling to wait?"

Musashi jumped in front of him and shouted, "State your business!"

The hoodlums inched closer, cautiously, as though feeling their way through shallow water.

"You know what we want!" spat one of them. "Turn over that yellowbelly you're protecting. And don't try anything funny, or you'll be dead too."

Encouraged by this bravado, they seethed with bloodthirsty fury, but none advanced to strike with his sword. The fire in Musashi's eyes was sufficient to hold them at bay. They howled and cursed, from a safe distance.

Musashi and Shinzō glared at them in silence. Moments passed before Musashi took them unawares by shouting, "If Hangawara Yajibei is among you, let him come forward."

"The boss isn't here. But if you have anything to say, speak to me, Nembutsu Tazaemon, and I'll do you the favor of listening." The elderly man who stepped forward wore a white hemp kimono and had Buddhist prayer beads hung around his neck.

"What do you have against Hōjō Shinzō?"

Squaring his shoulders, Tazaemon replied, "He slaughtered two of our men."

"According to Shinzō, your two louts helped Kojirō kill a number of Obata's students."

"That was one thing. This is another. If we don't settle our score with Shinzō, we'll be laughed off the streets."

"That may be the way things are done in the world you live in," Musashi said in a conciliatory tone. "But it's different in the world of the samurai. Among warriors, you can't fault a man for seeking and taking his proper revenge. A samurai may take revenge for the sake of justice or to defend his honor, but not to satisfy a personal grudge. It's not manly. And what you're trying to do right now isn't manly."

"Not manly? You're accusing us of being unmanly?"

"If Kojirō came forward and challenged us in his own name, that'd be all right. But we can't get involved in a squabble raised by Kojirō's minions."

"There you go, preaching self-righteously, just like any other samurai. Say what you please. We still have to protect our name."

"If samurai and outlaws fight over whose rules are to prevail, the streets will be filled with blood. The only place to settle this is at the magistrate's office. How about it, Nembutsu?"

"Horse manure. If it was something the magistrate could settle, we wouldn't be here to begin with."

"Listen, how old are you?"

"What business is it of yours?"

"I'd say you look old enough to know you shouldn't be leading a group of young men to a meaningless death."

"Ah, keep your smart talk to yourself. I'm not too old for a fight!" Tazaemon drew his sword, and the hoodlums moved forward, jostling and shouting.

Musashi dodged Tazaemon's thrust and grabbed him by the back of his gray head. Covering the ten paces or so to the moat in great strides, he summarily dumped him over the edge. Then, as the mob closed in, he dashed back, picked Shinzō up by the waist and made off with him.

He ran across a field, toward the middle reaches of a hill. Below them a stream flowed into the moat and a bluish marsh was visible at the bottom of the slope. Halfway up, Musashi stopped and stood Shinzō on his feet. "Now," he said, "let's run." Shinzō hesitated, but Musashi prodded him into motion.

The hoodlums, having recovered from their shock, were giving chase.

"Catch him!"

"No pride!"

"*That's* a samurai?"

"He can't throw Tazaemon in the moat and get away with it!"

Ignoring the taunts and slurs, Musashi said to Shinzō, "Don't even consider getting involved with them. Run! It's the only thing to do in a case like this." With a grin, he added, "It's not so easy to make good time on this terrain, is it?" They were passing through what would someday be known as Ushigafuchi and Kudan Hill, but now the area was heavily wooded.

By the time they lost their pursuers, Shinzō's face was deathly pale.

"Worn out?" Musashi asked solicitously.

"It's . . . It's not so bad."

"I suppose you don't like the idea of letting them insult us like that without fighting back."

"Well . . ."

"Ha, ha! Think about it quietly and calmly, and you'll see why. There're times when it makes you feel better to run away. There's a stream over there. Rinse your mouth out, and then I'll take you to your father's house."

In a few minutes, the forest around the Akagi Myōjin Shrine came into view. Lord Hōjō's house was just below.

"I hope you'll come in and meet my father," Shinzō said when they came to the earthen wall surrounding the house.

"Some other time. Get plenty of rest and take care of yourself." With that, he was off.

After this incident, Musashi's name was heard quite frequently in the streets of Edo, far more frequently than he would have wished. People were calling him "a fake," "the coward to end all cowards," and saying, "shameless . . . a disgrace to the samurai class. If a fraud like that defeated the Yoshiokas in Kyoto, they must have been hopelessly weak. He must have challenged them knowing they couldn't protect themselves. And then he probably ran away before he was in any real danger. All that phony wants to do is sell his name to people who don't know swordsmanship.'' Before long, it was impossible to find anyone who would put in a good word for him.

The crowning insult was signs posted all over Edo: "Here's a word to Miyamoto Musashi, who turned tail and ran. The Hon'iden dowager is eager for revenge. We, too, would like to see your face instead of your back for a change. If you are a samurai, come out and fight. The Hangawara Association.''

23

A Chat with the Men

Before having breakfast, Lord Hosokawa Tadatoshi began his day with the study of the Confucian classics. Official duties, which often required his attendance at Edo Castle, consumed most of his time, but when he could fit it into his schedule, he practiced the martial arts. Evenings, whenever possible, he liked to spend in the company of the young samurai in his service.

The atmosphere was rather like that of a harmonious family seated around its patriarch, not completely informal, to be sure, for the idea that his lordship was just one of the boys was not encouraged, but the usually rigorous etiquette was relaxed a bit. Tadatoshi, lounging in a lightweight hemp kimono, encouraged an exchange of views, which often included the latest gossip.

"Okatani," said his lordship, singling out one of the more robust men.

"Yes, sir."

"I hear you're pretty good with the lance now."

"That's right. Very good, in fact."

"Ha, ha. You certainly don't suffer from false modesty."

"Well, sir, with everybody else saying so, why should I deny it?"

"One of these days I'll find out for myself how advanced your technique really is."

"I've been looking forward to that day, but it never seems to come."

"You're lucky it doesn't."

"Tell me, sir, have you heard the song everybody's singing?"

"What's that?"

"It goes like this:

> "There're lancers and lancers,
> All sorts of lancers,
> But the greatest one of all is
> Okatani Gorōji—"

Tadatoshi laughed. "You can't take me in that easily. That song's about Nagoya Sanzō."

The others joined in the laughter.

"Oh, you knew?"

"You'd be surprised at what I know." He was on the verge of giving further evidence of this but thought better of it. He enjoyed hearing what his men were thinking and talking about and considered it his duty to keep himself well informed, but it would hardly do to reveal just how much he actually knew. Instead he asked, "How many of you are specializing in the lance, how many in the sword?"

Out of seven, five were studying the lance, only two the sword.

"Why do so many of you prefer the lance?" asked Tadatoshi.

The consensus among the lancers was that it was more effective in battle.

"And what do the swordsmen think about that?"

One of the two replied, "The sword is better. Swordsmanship prepares you for peace as well as for war."

This was a perennial subject for discussion and the debate was usually lively.

One of the lancers asserted, "The longer the lance is, the better, provided it's not too long to handle efficiently. The lance can be used for striking, thrusting or slicing, and if you fail with it, you can always fall back on your sword. If you have only a sword and it gets broken, that's it."

"That may be true," rejoined an exponent of sword fighting, "but a samurai's work isn't limited to the battlefield. The sword is his soul. To practice its art is to refine and discipline your spirit. In the broadest sense, the sword is the basis for all military training, whatever drawbacks it may have in battle. If you master the inner meaning of the Way of the Samurai, the discipline can be applied to the use of the lance, or even guns. If you know the sword, you don't make silly mistakes or get taken unawares. Swordsmanship is an art with universal applications."

The argument might have gone on indefinitely, had not Tadatoshi, who had been listening without taking sides, said, "Mainosuke, what you just said sounds to me like something you heard somebody else say."

Matsushita Mainosuke grew defensive. "No, sir. That's my own opinion."

"Come now, be honest."

"Well, to tell the truth, I heard something similar when I was visiting Kakubei recently. Sasaki Kojirō said about the same thing. But it fitted in so well with my own idea . . . I wasn't trying to deceive anyone. Sasaki just put it into words better than I could."

"I thought as much," said Tadatoshi with a knowing smile. The mention of Kojirō's name reminded him that he had not yet made a decision as to whether to accept Kakubei's recommendation.

Kakubei had suggested that since Kojirō was not very old, he might be offered a thousand bushels or so. But much more than the matter of the stipend was involved. Tadatoshi had been told by his father many times that it was of prime importance to first exercise good judgment in hiring samurai and then to treat them well. Before accepting a candidate, it was imperative to assess not only his skills but also his character. No matter how desirable a man might seem to be, if he could not work together with the retainers who had made the House of Hosokawa what it was today, he would be virtually useless.

A fief, the elder Hosokawa had advised, was like a castle wall built of many rocks. A rock that could not be cut to fit in comfortably with the others would weaken the whole structure, even though the rock itself might be of admirable size and quality. The daimyō of the new age left the unsuitable rocks in the mountains and fields, for there was an abundance of them. The great challenge was to find one great rock that would make an outstanding contribution to one's own wall. Thought of in this way, Tadatoshi felt, Kojirō's youth was in his favor. He was still in his formative years and consequently susceptible to a certain amount of molding.

Tadatoshi was also reminded of the other rōnin. Nagaoka Sado had first mentioned Musashi at one of these evening get-togethers. Though Sado had allowed Musashi to slip through his fingers, Tadatoshi had not forgotten him. If Sado's information was accurate, Musashi was both a better fighter than Kojirō and a man of sufficient breadth to be valuable in government.

As he compared the two, he had to admit that most daimyō would prefer Kojirō. He came from a good family and had studied the Art of War thoroughly. Despite his youth, he had developed a formidable style of his own, and he had gained considerable fame as a fighter. The story of his "brilliant" defeat of the men from the Obata Academy on the banks of the Sumida River and again at the dike on the Kanda River was already well known.

Nothing had been heard of Musashi for some time. His victory at Ichijōji had made his reputation. But that had been years ago, and soon afterward word had spread that the story was exaggerated, that Musashi was a seeker after fame who had trumped up the fight, made a flashy attack and then fled to Mount Hiei. Every time Musashi did something praiseworthy, a spate of rumors followed, denigrating his character and ability. It had reached the point where even the mention of his name usually met with critical remarks. Or else people ignored him entirely. As the son of a nameless warrior in the mountains of Mimasaka, his lineage was insignificant. Though other men of humble origin—most notably Toyotomi Hideyoshi, who came from Nakamura in Owari Province—had risen to glory in recent memory, people were on the whole class-conscious and not given to paying much heed to a man of Musashi's background.

As Tadatoshi mulled over the question, he looked around and asked, "Do any of you know of a samurai named Miyamoto Musashi?"

"Musashi?" replied a surprised voice. "It'd be impossible not to hear of him. His name's all over town." It was evident that they were all familiar with the name.

"Why is that?" A look of anticipation came over Tadatoshi's face.

"There are signs up about him," offered one young man, with a slight air of reticence.

Another man, whose name was Mori, chimed in, "People were copying the signs, so I did too. I've got it with me now. Shall I read it?"

"Please do."

"Ah, here it is," said Mori, unfolding a crumpled scrap of paper. " 'Here's a word to Miyamoto Musashi, who turned tail and ran—' "

Eyebrows were raised and smiles began to appear, but Tadatoshi's face was grave. "Is that all?"

"No." He read the rest of it and said, "The signs were put up by a gang from the carpenters' district. People find it amusing because it's a case of street ruffians tweaking the nose of a samurai."

Tadatoshi frowned slightly, feeling that the words maligning Musashi called his own judgment into question. This was a far cry from the image he had formed of Musashi. Still, he was not ready to accept what he had heard at face value. "Hmm," he murmured. "I wonder if Musashi is really that sort of man."

"I gather he's a worthless lout," volunteered Mori, whose opinion was shared by the others. "Or at least a coward. If he wasn't, why would he allow his name to be dragged through the mud?"

The clock struck, and the men departed, but Tadatoshi sat on, thinking: "There's something interesting about this man." Not one to be swayed by the prevailing opinion, he was curious to know Musashi's side of the story.

The next morning, after listening to a lecture on the Chinese classics, he emerged from his study onto the veranda and caught sight of Sado in the garden. "Good morning, my elderly friend," he said.

Sado turned and politely bowed his morning greeting.

"Are you still on the lookout?" asked Tadatoshi.

Puzzled by the question, Sado merely stared back.

"I mean, are you still keeping an eye out for Miyamoto Musashi?"

"Yes, my lord." Sado lowered his eyes.

"If you do find him, bring him here. I want to see what he's like."

Shortly after noon on the same day, Kakubei approached Tadatoshi at the archery range and pressed his recommendation of Kojirō.

As he picked up his bow, the Young Lord said quietly, "Sorry, I'd forgotten. Bring him any time you wish. I'd like to have a look at him. Whether he becomes a retainer or not is another matter, as you well know."

24

Buzzing Insects

Seated in a back room of the small house Kakubei had
lent him, Kojirō was examining the Drying Pole. After
the incident with Hōjō Shinzō, he had requested Kakubei
to press the craftsman for the return of the weapon. It
had come back this morning.

"It won't be polished, of course," Kojirō had predicted, but in fact the sword had been worked on with an
attention and care that were beyond his wildest hopes.
From the blue-black metal, rippling like the current of a
deep-running stream, there now sprang a brilliant white
glow, the light of centuries past. The rust spots, which
had seemed like leprous blemishes, were gone; the wavy
tempering pattern between the blade's edge and the ridge
line, hitherto smudged with bloodstains, was now as
serenely beautiful as a misty moon floating in the sky.

"It's like seeing it for the first time," marveled
Kojirō. Unable to take his eyes from the sword, he didn't
hear the visitor calling from the front of the house: "Are
you here? . . . Kojirō?"

This part of the hill had been given the name Tsukinomisaki because of the magnificent view it afforded of
the rising moon. From his sitting room, Kojirō could see
the stretch of bay from Shiba to Shinagawa. Across the
bay, frothy clouds appeared to be on a level with his

eyes. At this moment, the white of the distant hills and the greenish blue of the water seemed fused with the blade.

"Kojirō! Isn't anybody here?" This time the voice came from the grass-woven side gate.

Coming out of his reverie, he shouted, "Who is it?" and returned the sword to its scabbard. "I'm in the back. If you want to see me, come around to the veranda."

"Oh, here you are," said Osugi, walking around to where she could see into the house.

"Well, this is a surprise," said Kojirō cordially. "What brings you out on a hot day like this?"

"Just a minute. Let me wash my feet. Then we can talk."

"The well's over there. Be careful. It's quite deep. You, boy—go with her and see she doesn't fall in." The man addressed as "boy" was a low-ranking member of Hangawara's gang who had been sent along to guide Osugi.

After washing her sweaty face and rinsing her feet, Osugi entered the house and exchanged a few words of greeting. Noticing the pleasant breeze coming off the bay, she squinted and said, "The house is nice and cool. Aren't you afraid you'll get lazy, staying in a comfortable place like this?"

Kojirō laughed. "I'm not like Matahachi."

The old woman blinked her eyes sadly but ignored the barb. "Sorry I didn't bring you a real gift," she said. "In place of one I'll give you a sutra I copied." As she handed him the *Sutra on the Great Love of Parents*, she added, "Please read it when you have time."

After a perfunctory glance at her handiwork, Kojirō turned to her guide and said, "That reminds me. Did you put up the signs I wrote for you?"

"The ones telling Musashi to come out of hiding?"

"Yes, those."

"It took us two whole days, but we put one up at almost every important intersection."

Osugi said, "We passed some on the way here. Everywhere they're posted, people are standing around gossiping. It made me feel good to hear the things they're saying about Musashi."

"If he doesn't answer the challenge, he's finished as a samurai. The whole country'll be laughing at him. That should be ample revenge for you, Granny."

"Not on your life. Being laughed at isn't going to get through to him. He's shameless. And it won't satisfy me either. I want to see him punished once and for all."

"Ha, ha," laughed Kojirō, amused by her tenacity. "You get older, but you never give up, do you? By the way, did you come about anything in particular?"

The old lady rearranged herself and explained that after more than two years with Hangawara she felt she should be moving on. It was not right for her to live on Yajibei's hospitality indefinitely; besides, she was tired of mothering a houseful of roughnecks. She had seen a nice little place for rent in the vicinity of Yoroi Ferry.

"What do you think?" Her face was serious, questioning. "It doesn't look like I'll find Musashi soon. And I have a feeling Matahachi's somewhere in Edo. I think I should have some money sent from home and stay on for a while. But by myself, as I said."

There being no reason for Kojirō to object, he quickly agreed with her. His own connection with the Hangawara ménage, entertaining and useful at the beginning, was now a little embarrassing. It was certainly no asset to a rōnin looking for a master. He had already decided to discontinue the practice sessions.

Kojirō summoned one of Kakubei's subordinates and had him bring a watermelon from the patch behind the house. They chatted while it was being cut and served, but before long he showed his guest out, his manner rather suggesting he preferred to have her out of the way before sundown.

When they had left, he himself swept his rooms and sprinkled the garden with well water. The morning glory and yam vines growing on the fence had reached the top and returned to the ground again, threatening to ensnare the foot of the stone water basin. Their white flowers waved in the evening breeze.

In his room again, he lay down and wondered idly if his host would be on duty that night at the Hosokawa house. The lamp, which would probably have been blown out by the wind anyway, was unlit. The light of the moon, rising beyond the bay, was already on his face.

At the bottom of the hill, a young samurai was breaking through the cemetery fence.

Kakubei stabled the horse he rode to and from the Hosokawa mansion at a florist's shop at the foot of Isarago Hill.

This evening, curiously enough, there was no sign of the florist, who always came out promptly to take charge of the animal. Not seeing him inside the shop, Kakubei went around to the back and started to tether his horse to a tree. As he did so, the florist came running out from behind the temple.

Taking the reins from Kakubei's hands, he panted, "Sorry, sir. There was a strange man in the cemetery, on his way up the hill. I shouted, told him there was no pathway there. He turned and stared at me—angry he was—then disappeared." He paused for a moment, peered up into the dark trees and added worriedly, "Do you think he could be a burglar? They say a lot of daimyō houses have been broken into recently."

Kakubei had heard the rumors, but he replied with a short laugh, "That's all talk, nothing more. If the man you saw was a burglar, I daresay he was a petty thief or one of the rōnin who waylay people on the streets."

"Well, we're right here at the entrance to the Tō-kaidō, and lots of travelers have been attacked by men fleeing to other provinces. It makes me nervous when I see suspicious-looking men around at night."

"If anything happens, run up the hill and knock at

my gate. The man staying with me is chafing at the bit, always complaining there's never any action around here."

"You mean Sasaki Kojirō? He's got quite a reputation as a swordsman here in the neighborhood."

Hearing this did Kakubei's self-esteem no harm. Apart from liking young people, he knew quite well that it was regarded as both admirable and wise for established samurai like himself to take on promising younger men as protégés. Should an emergency arise, there could be no more persuasive proof of his loyalty than to be able to furnish his lord with good fighters. And if one of them turned out to be outstanding, due credit would be given to the retainer who had recommended him. One of Kakubei's beliefs was that self-interest was an undesirable trait in a vassal; nevertheless, he was realistic. In a large fief, there were few retainers willing to disregard their own interests entirely.

Despite the fact that he held his position through heredity, Kakubei was as loyal to Lord Tadatoshi as the other retainers, without being the sort who would strive to outdo others in demonstrating his fealty. For purposes of routine administration, men of his type were on the whole much more satisfactory than the firebrands who sought to perform spectacular feats.

"I'm back," he called on entering the gate to his house. The hill was quite steep, and he was always a little winded when he reached this point. Since he had left his wife in the country and the house was populated mostly by men, with only a few woman servants, feminine touches tended to be lacking. Yet on evenings when he had no night duty, he invariably found the stone path from the red gate to the entrance inviting, for it had been freshly watered down in anticipation of his return. And no matter how late the hour, someone always came to the front door to greet him.

"Is Kojirō here?" he asked.

"He's been in all day," replied the servant. "He's lying down in his room, enjoying the breeze."

"Good. Get some sake ready and ask him to come in to see me."

While preparations were being made, Kakubei took off his sweaty clothes and relaxed in the bath. Then, donning a light kimono, he entered his sitting room, where Kojirō sat waving a fan.

The sake was brought in. Kakubei poured, saying, "I called you because something encouraging happened today that I wanted to tell you about."

"Good news?"

"Since I mentioned your name to Lord Tadatoshi, he seems to have heard of you from other sources as well. Today he told me to bring you to see him some time soon. As you know, it's not easy to arrange these matters. There are dozens of retainers with someone they want to suggest." His expectation that Kojirō would be immensely pleased showed clearly in his tone and manner.

Kojirō put his cup to his lips and drank. When he did speak, his expression was unchanged and he said only, "Let me pour you one now."

Kakubei, far from being put out, admired the young man for being able to conceal his emotions. "This means I've been successful in carrying out what you requested of me. I think that calls for a celebration. Have another."

Kojirō bowed his head slightly and mumbled, "I'm grateful for your kindness."

"I was only doing my duty, of course," Kakubei replied modestly. "When a man is as capable and talented as you, I owe it to my lord to see that you're given consideration."

"Please don't overestimate me. And let me reemphasize one point. It's not the stipend I'm interested in. I simply think the House of Hosokawa is a very good one for a samurai to serve. It's had three outstanding men in a row." The three men were Tadatoshi and his father and grandfather, Sansai and Yūsai.

"You needn't think I've talked you up to the high heavens. I didn't have to. The name Sasaki Kojirō is known throughout the capital."

"How could I be famous when all I do is loaf around here all day long? I don't see that I'm outstanding in any way. It's just that there are so many fakes around."

"I was told that I could bring you anytime. When would you like to go?"

"Any time suits me too."

"How about tomorrow?"

"That's all right with me." His face revealed no eagerness, no anxiety, only calm self-confidence.

Kakubei, even more impressed at his sangfroid, chose this time to say matter-of-factly, "You understand, of course, his lordship won't be able to make a final decision until he's seen you. You needn't let that worry you. It's only a matter of form. I have no doubt but what the position will be offered."

Kojirō set his cup down on the table and stared straight into Kakubei's face. Then, very coldly and defiantly, he said, "I've changed my mind. Sorry to have put you to so much trouble." Blood seemed about to burst from his earlobes, already bright red from the drink.

"Wh-what?" stammered Kakubei. "You mean you're giving up the chance for a position with the House of Hosokawa?"

"I don't like the idea," answered his guest curtly, offering no further explanation. His pride told him there was no reason for him to submit to an inspection; dozens of other daimyō would snap him up sight unseen for fifteen hundred, even twenty-five hundred, bushels.

Kakubei's puzzled disappointment seemed to make no impression on him whatsoever, nor did it matter that he would be regarded as a willful ingrate. Without the least suggestion of doubt or repentance, he finished off his food in silence and returned to his own quarters.

The moonlight fell softly on the tatami. Stretching out drunkenly on the floor, arms under his head, he began to laugh quietly to himself. "Honest man, that Kakubei. Good, old, honest Kakubei." He knew his host would be at a loss to explain this sudden shift to Tadatoshi, but he knew also that Kakubei would not be angry at him for very long, no matter how outrageously he behaved.

While he had piously denied interest in the stipend, he was in fact consumed with ambition. He wanted a stipend and much more—every ounce of fame and success he could possibly achieve. Otherwise, what would be the purpose of persevering through years of arduous training?

Kojirō's ambition was different from that of other men only by dint of its magnitude. He wanted to be known throughout the country as a great and successful man, to bring glory to his home in Iwakuni, to enjoy every one of the benefits that can possibly derive from being born human. The quickest road to fame and riches was to excel in the martial arts. He was fortunate in having a natural talent for the sword; he knew this and derived no small measure of self-satisfaction from it. He had planned his course intelligently and with remarkable foresight. Every action of his was calculated to put him closer to his goal. To his way of thinking, Kakubei, though his senior, was naive and a little sentimental.

He fell asleep dreaming of his brilliant future.

Later, when the moonlight had edged a foot across the tatami, a voice no louder than the breeze whispering through the bamboo said, "Now." A shadowy form, crouching among the mosquitoes, crept forward like a frog to the eaves of the unlighted house.

The mysterious man seen earlier at the foot of the hill advanced slowly, silently, until he reached the veranda, where he stopped and peered into the room. Stooping in the shadows, out of the moonlight, he might have remained undiscovered indefinitely had he himself made no sound.

Kojirō snored on. The soft hum of insects, briefly interrupted as the man moved into position, came again across the dew-covered grass.

Minutes passed. Then the silence was broken by the clatter the man made as he whipped out his sword and jumped up onto the veranda.

He leapt toward Kojirō and cried, "Arrgh!" an instant before he clenched his teeth and struck.

There was a sharp hissing as a long black object descended heavily on his wrist, but the original force of his strike had been powerful. Instead of falling from his hand, his sword sank into the tatami, where Kojirō's body had been.

Like a fish darting away from a pole striking water, the intended victim had streaked to the wall. He now stood facing the intruder, the Drying Pole in one hand, its scabbard in the other.

"Who are you?" Kojirō's breath was calm. Alert as always to the sounds of nature's creatures, to the falling of a dewdrop, he was unperturbed.

"I-it-it's me!"

" 'Me' doesn't tell my anything. I know you're a coward, attacking a man in his sleep. What's your name?"

"I am Yogorō, the only son of Obata Kagenori. You took advantage of my father when he was sick. And you spread gossip about him all over the city."

"I wasn't the one who spread the gossip. It was the gossipers—the people of Edo."

"Who was it who lured his students into a fight and killed them?"

"I did that, no doubt about it. I, Sasaki Kojirō. How can I help it if I'm better than they? Stronger. Braver. More knowledgeable in the Art of War."

"How can you have the gall to say that when you called on Hangawara's vermin to help you?"

With a snarl of disgust, Kojirō took a step forward. "If you want to hate me, go ahead! But any man who carries a personal grudge into a test of strength in the Art of War isn't even a coward. He's worse than that, more pitiable, more laughable. So once again I have to take the life of an Obata man. Are you resigned to that?"

No answer.

"I said, are you resigned to your fate?" He moved another step forward. As he did so, the light of the moon reflecting off the newly polished blade of his sword blinded Yogorō.

Kojirō stared at his prey as a starving man stares at a feast.

25

The Eagle

Kakubei regretted having allowed himself to be used shabbily and vowed to have nothing more to do with Kojirō. Yet deep down, he liked the man. What he didn't like was being caught between his master and his protégé. Then he began to rethink the matter.

"Maybe Kojirō's reaction proves how exceptional he is. The ordinary samurai would have jumped at the chance to be interviewed." The more he reflected on Kojirō's fit of pique, the more the rōnin's independent spirit appealed to him.

For the next three days Kakubei was on night duty. He did not see Kojirō until the morning of the fourth day, when he walked casually over to the young man's quarters.

After a short but awkward silence, he said, "I want to talk to you for a minute, Kojirō. Yesterday, when I was leaving, Lord Tadatoshi asked me about you. He said he'd see you. Why don't you drop in at the archery range and have a look at the Hosokawa technique?"

When Kojirō grinned without replying, Kakubei added, "I don't know why you insist on thinking it's demeaning. It's usual to interview a man before offering him an official position."

"I know, but supposing he rejects me, then what?

I'd be a castoff, wouldn't I? I'm not so hard up that I have to go around peddling myself to the highest bidder."

"Then the fault is mine. I put it the wrong way. His lordship never meant to imply any such thing."

"Well, what answer did you give him?"

"None yet. But he seems a little impatient."

"Ha, ha. You've been very thoughtful, very helpful. I suppose I shouldn't put you in such a difficult position."

"Wouldn't you reconsider—go and call on him, just once?"

"All right, if it means so much to you," Kojirō said patronizingly, but Kakubei was nonetheless pleased.

"How about today?"

"So soon?"

"Yes."

"What time?"

"How about a little after noon? That's when he practices archery."

"All right, I'll be there."

Kojirō set about making elaborate preparations for the meeting. The kimono he chose was of excellent quality, and the *hakama* was made of imported fabric. Over the kimono he wore a formal vestlike garment of sheer silk, sleeveless but with stiff flaring shoulders. To complement his finery, he had the servants provide him with a new zōri and a new basket hat.

"Is there a horse I can use?" he inquired.

"Yes. The master's spare horse, the white one, is at the shop at the bottom of the hill."

Failing to find the florist, Kojirō glanced toward the temple compound across the way, where a group of people were gathering around a corpse covered with reed matting. He went over to have a look.

They were discussing plans for burial with the local priest. The victim had no identifying possessions on him; no one knew who he was, only that he was young and of the samurai class. The blood around the deep gash extending from the tip of one shoulder to his waist was dried and black.

"I've seen him before. About four days ago, in the evening," said the florist, who went on talking excitedly until he felt a hand on his shoulder.

When he looked to see who it was, Kojirō said, "I'm told Kakubei's horse is kept at your place. Get him ready for me, please."

Bowing hastily, the florist asked perfunctorily, "Are you going out?" and hurried off.

He patted the dappled-gray steed on the neck as he led it out of his stable.

"Quite a good horse," Kojirō remarked.

"Yes, indeed. A fine animal."

Once Kojirō was in the saddle, the florist beamed and said, "It's a good match."

Taking some money from his purse, Kojirō threw it to the man. "Use this for flowers and incense."

"Huh? Who for?"

"The dead man over there."

Beyond the temple gate, Kojirō cleared his throat and spat, as if to eject the bitter taste left by the sight of the corpse. But he was pursued by the feeling that the youth he had cut down with the Drying Pole had thrown aside the reed matting and was following him. "I did nothing he could hate me for," he told himself, and felt better for the thought.

As horse and rider moved along the Takanawa highroad under the boiling sun, townsmen and samurai alike stood aside to make way. Heads turned in admiration. Even on the streets of Edo, Kojirō cut an impressive figure, causing people to wonder who he was and where he came from.

At the Hosokawa residence, he turned the horse over to a servant and entered the house. Kakubei rushed to meet him. "My thanks for coming. It's just the right time too," he said, as though Kojirō were doing him a great personal favor. "Rest awhile. I'll tell his lordship you're here." Before doing so, he made sure the guest was provided with cool water, barley tea and a tobacco tray.

When a retainer came to show him to the archery range, Kojirō handed over his beloved Drying Pole and followed along wearing only his short sword.

Lord Tadatoshi had resolved to shoot a hundred arrows a day during the summer months. A number of close retainers were always there, watching each shot with bated breath and making themselves useful retrieving arrows.

"Give me a towel," his lordship commanded, standing his bow beside him.

Kneeling, Kakubei asked, "May I trouble you, sir?"

"What is it?"

"Sasaki Kojirō is here. I would appreciate your seeing him."

"Sasaki? Oh, yes."

He fitted an arrow to the bowstring, took an open stance, and raised his shooting arm above his eyebrows. Neither he nor any of the others so much as glanced in Kojirō's direction until the hundred shots were finished.

With a sigh Tadatoshi said, "Water. Bring me some water."

An attendant brought some from the well and poured it into a large wooden tub at Tadatoshi's feet. Letting the upper part of his kimono hang loose, he wiped off his chest and washed his feet. His men assisted by holding his sleeves, running to fetch more water and wiping off his back. There was nothing formal in their manner, nothing to suggest to an observer that this was a daimyō and his retinue.

Kojirō had supposed that Tadatoshi, a poet and an aesthete, the son of Lord Sansai and the grandson of Lord Yūsai, would be a man of aristocratic bearing, as refined in his conduct as the elegant courtiers of Kyoto. But his surprise did not show in his eyes as he watched.

Slipping his still damp feet into his zōri, Tadatoshi looked at Kakubei, who was waiting off to one side. With the air of one who has suddenly recalled a promise, he said, "Now, Kakubei, I'll see your man." He had a stool brought and placed in the shade of a tent, where he sat down in front of a banner bearing his crest, a circle surrounded by eight smaller circles, representing the sun, moon and seven planets.

Beckoned by Kakubei, Kojirō came forward and knelt before Lord Tadatoshi. As soon as the formal greeting was completed, Tadatoshi invited Kojirō to sit on a stool, thus signifying that he was an honored guest.

"By your leave," said Kojirō, as he rose and took a seat facing Tadatoshi.

"I've heard about you from Kakubei. I believe you were born in Iwakuni, weren't you?"

"That is correct, sir."

"Lord Kikkawa Hiroie of Iwakuni was well known as a wise and noble ruler. Were your ancestors retainers of his?"

"No, we never served the House of Kikkawa. I've been told we're descended from the Sasakis of Ōmi Province. After the fall of the last Ashikaga shōgun, my father seems to have retired to my mother's village."

After a few more questions concerning family and lineage, Lord Tadatoshi asked, "Will you be going into service for the first time?"

"I do not yet know whether I am going into service."

"I gathered from Kakubei you wish to serve the House of Hosokawa. What are your reasons?"

"I believe it is a house I would be willing to live and die for."

Tadatoshi seemed pleased with this answer. "And your style of fighting?"

"I call it the Ganryū Style."

" 'Ganryū'?"

"It's a style I invented myself."

"Presumably it has antecedents."

"I studied the Tomita Style, and I had the benefit of lessons from Lord Katayama Hisayasu of Hōki, who in his old age retired to Iwakuni. I've also mastered many techniques on my own. I used to practice cutting down swallows on the wing."

"I see. I suppose the name Ganryū comes from the name of that river near where you were born?"

"Yes, sir."

"I'd like to see a demonstration." Tadatoshi looked around at the faces of his samurai. "Which one of you would like to take this man on?"

They had been watching the interview in silence, thinking that Kojirō was remarkably young to have acquired the reputation he had. Now all looked first at each other, then at Kojirō, whose flushed cheeks proclaimed his willingness to face any challenger.

"How about you, Okatani?"

"Yes, sir."

"You're always claiming the lance is superior to the sword. Now's your chance to prove it."

"I shall be glad to, if Sasaki is willing."

"By all means," Kojirō answered with alacrity. In his tone, which was polite but extremely cool, there was a hint of cruelty.

The samurai who had been sweeping the sand on the archery range and putting away the equipment assembled behind their master. Although weapons were as familiar to them as chopsticks, their experience had been primarily in the dōjō. The chance to witness, much less have, a real bout would occur only a few times throughout their lives. They would readily agree that a man-to-man fight was a greater challenge than going out on the battlefield, where it was sometimes possible for a man to pause and get his wind while his comrades fought on. In hand-to-hand combat, he had only himself to rely on, only his own alertness and strength from beginning to end. Either he won, or he was killed or maimed.

They watched Okatani Gorōji solemnly. Even among the lowest-ranking foot soldiers there were quite a few who were adept with the lance; Gorōji was generally

conceded to be the best. He had not only been in battle
but had practiced diligently and devised techniques of his
own.

"Give me a few minutes," said Gorōji, bowing toward Tadatoshi and Kojirō before withdrawing to make
his preparations. It pleased him that today, as on other
days, he had on spotless underwear, in the tradition of
the good samurai, who started each day with a smile and
an uncertainty: by evening he might be a corpse.

After borrowing a three-foot wooden sword, Kojirō
selected the ground for the match. His body seemed
relaxed and open, the more so since he didn't hitch up
his pleated *hakama*. His appearance was formidable;
even his enemies would have had to admit that. There
was an eaglelike air of valor about him, and his handsome
profile was serenely confident.

Worried eyes began to turn toward the canopy behind which Gorōji was adjusting his clothing and equipment.

"What's taking him so long?" someone asked.

Gorōji was calmly wrapping a piece of damp cloth
around the point of his lance, a weapon he had used to
excellent effect on the battlefield. The shaft was nine feet
long, and the tapering blade alone, at eight or nine inches,
was the equivalent of a short sword.

"What are you doing?" called Kojirō. "If you're
worried about hurting me, save yourself the trouble."
Again, though the words were courteous, the implication
was arrogant. "I don't mind if you leave it unwrapped."

Looking sharply at him, Gorōji said, "Are you
sure?"

"Perfectly."

Though neither Lord Tadatoshi nor his men spoke,
their piercing eyes told Gorōji to go ahead. If the stranger
had the gall to ask for it, why not run him through?

"In that case . . ." Gorōji tore off the wrapping and
advanced holding the lance midway along the shaft. "I'm

happy to comply, but if I use a naked blade, I want you to use a real sword.''

"This wooden one's fine."

"No; I can't agree to that."

"Certainly you wouldn't expect me, an outsider, to have the audacity to employ a real sword in the presence of his lordship."

"But—"

With a touch of impatience, Lord Tadatoshi said, "Go ahead, Okatani. Nobody will consider you cowardly for complying with the man's request." It was obvious Kojirō's attitude had affected him.

The two men, faces flushed with determination, exchanged greetings with their eyes. Gorōji made the first move, leaping to the side, but Kojirō, like a bird stuck to a limed fowling pole, slipped under the lance and struck directly at his chest. Lacking time to thrust, the lancer whirled sideways and tried to jab the nape of Kojirō's neck with the butt of his weapon. With a resounding crack, the lance flew back up into the air, as Kojirō's sword bit into Gorōji's ribs, which had been exposed by the momentum of the rising lance. Gorōji slid to one side, then leapt away, but the attack continued without letup. With no time to catch his breath, he jumped aside again, then again and again. The first few dodges were successful, but he was like a peregrine falcon trying to fend off an eagle. Hounded by the raging sword, the lance shaft snapped in two. At the same instant, Gorōji emitted a cry; it sounded as though his soul was being torn from his body.

The brief battle was ended. Kojirō had hoped to take on four or five men, but Tadatoshi said that he had seen enough.

When Kakubei came home that evening, Kojirō asked him, "Did I go a little too far? In front of his lordship, I mean."

"No, it was a magnificent performance." Kakubei

felt rather ill at ease. Now that he could assess the full extent of Kojirō's ability, he felt like a man who had hugged a tiny bird to his chest, only to see it grow up to be an eagle.

"Did Lord Tadatoshi say anything?"

"Nothing in particular."

"Come now, he must have said something."

"No; he left the archery range without a word."

"Hmm." Kojirō looked disappointed but said, "Oh, it doesn't matter. He impressed me as a greater man than he's usually made out to be. I was thinking if I had to serve anyone, it might as well be him. But of course I have no control over how things turn out." He didn't reveal how carefully he had thought about the situation. After the Date, Kuroda, Shimazu and Mōri clans, the Hosokawa was the most prestigious and secure. He felt sure this would continue to be true so long as Lord Sansai held the Buzen fief. And sooner or later, Edo and Osaka would clash once and for all. There was no way of predicting the outcome; a samurai who had chosen the wrong master might easily find himself a rōnin again, his whole life sacrificed for a few months' stipend.

The day after the bout, word came that Gorōji had survived, though his pelvis or left thighbone had been smashed. Kojirō accepted the news calmly, telling himself that even if he did not receive a position, he had given a good enough account of himself.

A few days later he abruptly announced he was going to pay a call on Gorōji. Offering no explanation for this sudden display of kindness, he set out alone and on foot for Gorōji's house near Tokiwa Bridge.

The unexpected visitor was received cordially by the injured man.

"A match is a match," said Gorōji, a smile on his lips and moistness in his eyes. "I may deplore my own lack of skill, but I certainly hold nothing against you. It was good of you to come to see me. Thank you."

After Kojirō left, Gorōji remarked to a friend, "Now,

there's a samurai I can admire. I thought he was an arrogant son of a bitch, but he turns out to be both friendly and polite."

This was precisely the reaction Kojirō had hoped for. It was part of his plan; other visitors would hear him praised by the defeated man himself. Calling once every two or three days, he made three more visits to Gorōji's house. On one occasion he had a live fish delivered from the fish market as a get-well present.

26

Green Persimmons

In the dog days after the summer rainy season, the land crabs crawled sluggishly in the parched street, and the signs taunting Musashi to "come out and fight" were no longer visible. The few that hadn't fallen in the rain-softened earth or been stolen for firewood were obscured by weeds and tall grass.

"There must be something somewhere," thought Kojirō, looking around for a place to eat. But this was Edo, not Kyoto, and the cheap rice-and-tea shops so common in the older city had not yet made their appearance here. The only likely place stood in a vacant lot, screened off with reed blinds. Smoke rose lazily from behind the blinds, and on a vertical banner was the word "Donjiki." The word immediately reminded him of *tonjiki*, which in the distant past had meant the rice balls used as military rations.

As he approached, he heard a masculine voice ask for a cup of tea. Inside, two samurai were energetically gobbling rice, one from an ordinary rice bowl, the other from a sake bowl.

Kojirō seated himself on the edge of a bench across from them and asked the proprietor, "What do you have?"

"Rice dishes. I also have sake."

"On the banner it says 'Donjiki.' What does that mean?"

"As a matter of fact, I don't know."

"Didn't you write it?"

"No. It was written by a retired merchant who stopped in to rest."

"I see. Good calligraphy, I must say."

"He said he was on a religious pilgrimage, said he'd visited Hirakawa Tenjin Shrine, Hikawa Shrine, Kanda Myōjin, all sorts of places, making big contributions to each of them. Very pious and generous, he seemed."

"Do you know his name?"

"He told me it was Daizō of Narai."

"I've heard the name."

"Donjiki—well, I don't understand it. But I figured if a fine man like him wrote it, it might help keep the god of poverty away." He laughed.

After a look into several large china bowls, Kojirō took some rice and fish, poured tea over the rice, brushed a fly away with his chopsticks and began eating.

One of the other customers stood up and peered through a broken slat in the blind. "Take a look out there, Hamada," he said to his companion. "Isn't that the watermelon vendor?"

The other man went quickly to the blind and looked out. "Yeah, that's him all right."

The vendor, shouldering a pole with baskets at either end, was walking languidly past the Donjiki. The two samurai ran out of the shop and caught up with him. Drawing their swords, they cut the ropes supporting the baskets. The vendor stumbled forward, along with the melons.

Hamada yanked him up by the scruff of his neck. "Where did you take her?" he demanded angrily. "Don't lie. You must be hiding her somewhere."

The other samurai thrust the tip of his sword under the captive's nose.

"Out with it! Where is she?"

The sword blade tapped menacingly against the man's cheek. "How could anybody with a face like yours think of going off with somebody else's woman?"

The vendor, cheeks flushed with anger and fear, shook his head, but then, seeing an opening, shoved one of his captors out of the way, picked up his pole and took a swing at the other one.

"So you want to fight, do you? Careful, Hamada, this guy's not just an ordinary melon vendor."

"What can this ass do?" sneered Hamada, snatching the pole and knocking the vendor to the ground. Straddling him, he used the ropes to tie him to the pole.

A cry like that of a stuck pig went up behind him. Hamada turned his face around, right into a spray of fine red mist. Looking totally dumbfounded, he jumped up, screaming, "Who are you? What—"

The adderlike blade moved directly toward him. Kojirō laughed, and as Hamada shrank back, followed him relentlessly. The two moved in a circle through the grass. When Hamada moved back a foot, Kojirō moved forward the same distance. When Hamada leapt to one side, the Drying Pole followed, pointing unwaveringly at his prospective victim.

The melon vendor cried out in astonishment. "Kojirō! It's me. Save me!"

Hamada blanched with terror and gasped, "Ko-ji-rō!" Then he wheeled around and tried to flee.

"Where do you think you're going?" barked Kojirō. The Drying Pole flashed through the sultry stillness, lopping off Hamada's ear and lodging deep in the flesh under the shoulders. He died on the spot.

Kojirō promptly cut the melon vendor's bonds. Rearranging himself into a proper sitting posture, the man bowed, and stayed bowed, too embarrassed to show his face.

Kojirō wiped and resheathed his sword. Amusement playing faintly around his lips, he said, "What's the matter with you, Matahachi? Don't look so miserable. You're still alive."

"Yes, sir."

"None of this 'yes, sir' business. Look at me. It's been a long time, hasn't it?"

"I'm glad you're well."

"Why wouldn't I be? But I must say you've taken to an unusual trade."

"Let's not talk about it."

"All right. Pick up your melons. Then—I know, why don't you leave them at the Donjiki?" With a loud shout, he summoned the proprietor, who helped them stack the melons behind the blinds.

Kojirō took out his brush and ink and wrote on one of the shoji: "To whom it may concern: I certify that the person who killed the two men lying on this vacant lot was myself, Sasaki Kojirō, a rōnin residing at Tsukino-misaki."

To the proprietor, he said, "This should fix it so no one'll bother you about the killings."

"Thank you, sir."

"Think nothing of it. If friends or relatives of the dead men should come around, please deliver this message for me. Tell them I won't run away. If they want to see me, I'm ready to greet them anytime."

Outside again, he said to Matahachi, "Let's go."

Matahachi walked beside him but would not take his eyes off the ground. Not once since coming to Edo had he held a steady job. Whatever his intention—to become a *shugyōsha* or to go into business—when he found the going rough, he changed jobs. And after Otsū slipped away from him, he felt less and less like working. He'd slept in first one place, then another, sometimes at flophouses populated by hoodlums. The past few weeks, he had been making his living as a common peddler, trudging from one part of the castle wall to another, hawking watermelons.

Kojirō wasn't particularly interested in what Matahachi had been doing, but he had written the sign at the Donjiki and he might later be questioned about the incident. "Why did those samurai have it in for you?" he asked.

"To tell the truth, it had to do with a woman. . . . "

Kojirō smiled, thinking wherever Matahachi went, there soon arose some difficulty connected with women. Perhaps this was his karma. "Mm," he mumbled. "The great lover in action again, eh?" Then, more loudly, "Who is the woman, and what exactly happened?"

It took some prodding, but eventually Matahachi gave in and told his tale, or part of it. Near the moat, there were dozens of tiny tea shops catering to construction workers and passersby. In one of these there had been a waitress who caught everybody's eyes, enticing men who did not want tea to step in for a cup and men who were not hungry to order bowls of sweet jelly. One regular customer had been Hamada; Matahachi, too, dropped in occasionally.

One day this waitress whispered to him that she needed his help. "That rōnin," she had said. "I don't like him, but every night after the shop closes, the master orders me to go home with him. Won't you let me come and hide in your house? I won't be a burden. I'll cook for you, and mend your clothes."

Since her plea seemed reasonable, Matahachi had agreed. That was all there was to it, he insisted.

Kojirō was unconvinced. "It sounds fishy to me."

"Why?" Matahachi asked.

Kojirō could not decide whether Matahachi was trying to make himself appear innocent or whether he was bragging about an amorous conquest. Without even smiling, he said, "Never mind. It's hot out here under the sun. Let's go to your house, and you can tell me about it in more detail."

Matahachi stopped in his tracks.

"Is there anything wrong with that?" asked Kojirō.

"Well, my place is—it's not the sort of place I'd want to take you to."

Seeing the distressed look in Matahachi's eyes, Kojirō said lightly, "Never mind. But one of these days soon you must come to see me. I'm staying with Iwama Kakubei, about halfway up Isarago Hill."

"I'd like that."

"By the way, did you see the signs posted around the city recently, the ones addressed to Musashi?"

"Yes."

"They said your mother was looking for him too. Why don't you go to see her?"

"Not the way I am now!"

"Idiot. You don't have to put on a great show for your own mother. There's no way of knowing just when she might find Musashi, and if you're not there at the time, you'll lose the chance of a lifetime. You'd regret that, wouldn't you?"

"Yes, I'll have to do something about that soon," Matahachi said noncommittally, thinking resentfully that other people, including the man who had just saved his life, did not understand the feelings between mothers and their offspring.

They parted, Matahachi ambling down a grassy lane, Kojirō ostensibly setting out in the opposite direction. Kojirō soon doubled back and followed Matahachi, taking care to stay out of sight.

Matahachi arrived presently at a motley collection of "long houses," one-story tenements, each containing three or four small apartments under a single roof. Since Edo had grown rapidly and not everybody could be choosy about where he lived, people cleared land as the necessity arose. Streets came into existence afterward, developing naturally from pathways. Drainage, too, came about by accident, as waste water cut its own path to the nearest stream. Had it not been for these jerry-built slums, the influx of newcomers could not have been absorbed. The majority of the inhabitants of such places were, of course, workmen.

Near his home, Matahachi was greeted by a neighbor named Umpei, the boss of a crew of well diggers. Umpei was seated cross-legged in a large wooden tub, only his face showing above the rain shutter placed sideways in front of the tub for privacy.

"Good evening," said Matahachi, "I see you're having your bath."

"I'm about to get out," replied the boss genially. "Would you like to use it next?"

"Thanks, but I think Akemi's probably heated water for me."

"You two are very fond of each other, aren't you? Nobody around here seems to know whether you're brother and sister or husband and wife. Which is it?"

Matahachi giggled sheepishly. The appearance of Akemi saved him from having to answer.

She placed a tub under a persimmon tree and brought pailfuls of hot water from the house to fill it. When she was done, she said, "Feel it, Matahachi. See if it's hot enough."

"It's a little too hot."

There was a squeaking of the well pulley, and Matahachi, stripped to his loincloth, brought up a bucket of cold water and poured it into the bath before climbing in himself. "Ah-h-h," he sighed contentedly. "This feels good."

Umpei, wearing a cotton summer kimono, placed a bamboo stool under a gourd trellis and sat down. "Did you sell lots of melons?" he inquired.

"Not many. I never sell very many." Noticing dried blood between his fingers, he hastily wiped it off.

"I don't imagine you would. I still think your life would be easier if you went to work on a well-digging gang."

"You're always saying that. Don't think I'm ungrateful, but if I did that, they wouldn't let me off the castle grounds, would they? That's why Akemi doesn't want me to take the job. She says she'd be lonesome without me."

"Happily married couple, eh? Well, well."

"Ouch!"

"What's the matter?"

"Something fell on my head."

A green persimmon landed on the ground just behind Matahachi.

"Ha, ha! Punishment for bragging about your wife's devotion, that's what it is." Still laughing, Umpei rapped his tannin-coated fan on his knee.

Over sixty years old, with a shaggy, hemplike mane of white hair, Umpei was a man who enjoyed the respect of his neighbors and the admiration of the young people, whom he bigheartedly treated as his own children. Each morning he could be heard chanting *Namu Myōhō Rengekyō*, the sacred invocation of the Nichiren sect.

A native of Itō in Izu Province, he had a sign in front of his house saying: "Idohori no Umpei, Well Digger for the Shōgun's Castle." To build the many wells necessary for the castle involved technical skills beyond those of ordinary laborers. Umpei had been hired as a consultant and recruiter of workers because of his long experience in the gold mines of Izu Peninsula. He enjoyed nothing more than sitting under his beloved gourd trellis, spinning yarns and drinking his nightly cup of cheap but potent *shōchū,* the poor man's sake.

After Matahachi emerged from the bath, Akemi surrounded the washtub with rain shutters and had hers. Later the matter of Umpei's proposal came up once again. Besides having to stay on the castle grounds, the workers were watched very closely, and their families were virtually hostages of the bosses of the areas where they lived. On the other hand, the work was easier than on the outside and paid at least twice as much.

Leaning over a tray on which there was a dish of cold bean curd, garnished with fresh, fragrant basil leaf,

Matahachi said, "I don't want to become a prisoner just to earn a little money. I'm not going to sell melons all my life, but bear with me a little longer, Akemi."

"Umm," she replied between mouthfuls of tea-and-rice gruel. "I'd rather you tried just once to do something really worthwhile, something that would make people take notice."

Though nothing was ever said or done to discourage the idea that she was Matahachi's legal wife, she wasn't about to marry anyone who shilly-shallied the way he did. Fleeing the world of play at Sakaimachi with Matahachi had been only an expedient; he was the perch from which she intended, at the first opportunity, to fly once more into the open sky. But it did not suit her purposes for Matahachi to go off to the castle to work. She felt being left alone would be dangerous; specifically, she was afraid Hamada might find her and force her to live with him.

"Oh, I forgot," said Matahachi, as they finished their frugal meal. He then told her about his experiences that day, adjusting the details in a fashion calculated to please her. By the time he had finished, her face was ashen.

Taking a deep breath, she said, "You saw Kojirō? Did you tell him I was here? You didn't, did you?"

Matahachi took her hand and placed it on his knee. "Of course not. Do you think I'd let that bastard know where you are? He's the kind that never gives up. He'd be after you—"

He broke off with an inarticulate shout and pressed his hand to the side of his face. The green persimmon that smashed against his cheek broke and spattered its whitish meat in Akemi's face.

Outside, in the shadows of a moonlit bamboo grove, a form not unlike that of Kojirō could be seen walking nonchalantly away in the direction of town.

27

Eyes

"Sensei!" called Iori, who was not yet tall enough to see over the tall grass. They were on Musashino Plain, which was said to cover ten counties.

"I'm right here," replied Musashi. "What's taking you so long?"

"I guess there's a path, but I keep losing it. How much farther do we have to go?"

"Till we find a good place to live."

"Live? We're going to stay around here?"

"Why shouldn't we?"

Iori gazed up at the sky, thought of its vastness and the emptiness of the land around him and said, "I wonder."

"Think what it'll be like in the fall. Clear, beautiful skies, fresh dew on the grass. Doesn't it make you feel cleaner just thinking about it?"

"Well, maybe, but I'm not against living in the city, like you."

"I'm not, really. In a way, it's nice to be among people, but even with my thick skin I couldn't stand being there when those signs were put up. You saw what they said."

Iori grimaced. "I get mad just thinking about it."

"Why let yourself get angry over that?"

"I couldn't help it. No matter where I went, there wasn't anybody who'd say anything good about you."

"Nothing I could do about that."

"You could have cut down the men spreading the rumors. You could have put up your own signs challenging them."

"There's no point in starting fights you can't win."

"You wouldn't have lost to that scum. You couldn't have."

"No, you're wrong. I would have."

"How?"

"Sheer numbers. If I beat ten, there'd be a hundred more. If I defeated a hundred, there'd be a thousand. There's no possibility of winning in that kind of situation."

"But does that mean you're going to be laughed at for the rest of your life?"

"Of course not. I'm as determined as the next person to have a good name. I owe it to my ancestors. And I intend to become a man who's never laughed at. That's what I came out here to learn."

"We can walk all we want, but I don't think we're going to find any houses. Shouldn't we try to find a temple to stay in again?"

"That's not a bad idea, but what I really want is to find someplace with a lot of trees and build a house of our own."

"It'll be like Hōtengahara again, won't it?"

"No. This time we're not going to farm. I think maybe I'll practice Zen meditation every day. You can read books, and I'll give you some lessons in the sword."

Entering the plain at the village of Kashiwagi, the Kōshū entrance to Edo, they had come down the long slope from Jūnisho Gongen and followed a narrow path that repeatedly threatened to disappear among the waving summer grasses. When they finally reached a pine-covered knoll, Musashi made a quick survey of the terrain and said, "This'll do fine." To him, any place could serve as home—more than that: wherever he happened to be was the universe.

They borrowed tools and hired a laborer at the nearest farmhouse. Musashi's approach to building a house was not at all sophisticated; in fact, he could have learned quite a bit from watching birds build a nest. The result, finished a few days later, was an oddity, less substantial than a hermit's mountain retreat but not so crude as to be described as a shed. The posts were logs with the bark left on, the remainder a rough alliance of boards, bark, bamboo and miscanthus.

Standing back to take a good look, Musashi remarked thoughtfully, "This must be like the houses people lived in back in the age of the gods." The only relief from the primitiveness were scraps of paper lovingly fashioned to make small shoji.

In the days following, the sound of Iori's voice, floating from behind a reed blind as he recited his lessons, rose above the buzz of the cicadas. His training had become very strict in every respect.

With Jōtarō, Musashi had not insisted on discipline, thinking at the time that it was best to let growing boys grow naturally. But with the passage of time, he had observed that, if anything, bad traits tended to develop and good ones to be repressed. Similarly, he had noticed that trees and plants he wanted to grow would not grow, while weed and brush flourished no matter how often he cut them down.

During the hundred years after the Ōnin War, the nation had been like a tangled mass of overgrown hemp plants. Then Nobunaga had cut the plants down, Hideyoshi had bundled them up, and Ieyasu had broken and smoothed the ground to build a new world. As Musashi saw it, warriors who placed a high value only on martial practices and whose most noticeable characteristic was unbounded ambition were no longer the dominant element in society. Sekigahara had put an end to that.

He had come to believe that whether the nation

remained in the hands of the Tokugawas or reverted to the Toyotomis, people in general already knew the direction they wanted to move in: from chaos toward order, from destruction toward construction.

At times, he'd had the feeling that he had been born too late. No sooner had Hideyoshi's glory penetrated into remote rural areas and fired the hearts of boys like Musashi than the possibility of following in Hideyoshi's footsteps evaporated.

So it was his own experience that led to his decision to emphasize discipline in Iori's upbringing. If he was going to create a samurai, he should create one for the coming era, not for the past.

"Iori."

"Yes, sir." The boy was kneeling before Musashi almost before the words were out.

"It's almost sunset. Time for our practice. Bring the swords."

"Yes, sir." When he placed them in front of Musashi, he knelt and formally requested a lesson.

Musashi's sword was long, Iori's short, both wooden practice weapons. Teacher and pupil faced each other in tense silence, swords held at eye level. A rim of sunlight hovered on the horizon. The cryptomeria grove behind the cabin was already sunk in gloom, but if one looked toward the voices of the cicadas, a sliver of moon was visible through the branches.

"Eyes," said Musashi.

Iori opened his eyes wide.

"*My* eyes. Look at them."

Iori did his best, but his eyes seemed to literally bounce away from Musashi's. Instead of glaring, he was being defeated by his opponent's eyes. When he tried again, he was seized by giddiness. His head began to feel as if it were no longer his own. His hands, his feet, his whole body felt wobbly.

"Look at my eyes!" Musashi commanded with great sternness. Iori's look had strayed again. Then, concentrating on his master's eyes, he forgot the sword in his hand. The short length of curved wood seemed to become as heavy as a bar of steel.

"Eyes, eyes!" said Musashi, advancing slightly.

Iori checked the urge to fall back, for which he had been scolded dozens of times. But when he attempted to follow his opponent's lead and move forward, his feet were nailed to the ground. Unable either to advance or to retreat, he could feel his body temperature rise. "What's the matter with me?" The thought exploded like fireworks inside him.

Sensing this burst of mental energy, Musashi yelled, "Charge!" At the same time he lowered his shoulders, dropped back and dodged with the agility of a fish.

With a gasp, Iori sprang forward, spun around—and saw Musashi standing where he himself had been.

Then the confrontation began again, just as before, both teacher and pupil maintaining strict silence.

Before long the grass was soaked with dew, and the eyebrow of a moon hung above the cryptomerias. Each time the wind gusted, the insects stopped singing momentarily. Autumn had come, and the wild flowers, though not spectacular in the daytime, now quivered gracefully, like the feathered robe of a dancing deity.

"Enough," said Musashi, lowering his sword.

As he handed it to Iori, they became conscious of a voice coming from the direction of the grove.

"I wonder who that is," said Musashi.

"Probably a lost traveler wanting to put up for the night."

"Run and see."

As Iori sped around to the other side of the building, Musashi seated himself on the bamboo veranda and gazed out over the plain. The eulalias were tall, their tops fluffy; the light bathing the grass had a peculiar autumn sheen.

When Iori returned, Musashi asked, "A traveler?"

"No, a guest."

"Guest? Here?"

"It's Hōjō Shinzō. He tied his horse up and he's waiting for you in back."

"This house doesn't really have any back or front, but I think it'd be better to receive him here."

Iori ran round the side of the cabin, shouting, "Please come this way."

"This is a pleasure," said Musashi, his eyes expressing his delight at seeing Shinzō completely recovered.

"Sorry to have been out of touch so long. I suppose you live out here to get away from people. I hope you'll forgive me for dropping in unexpectedly like this."

Greetings having been exchanged, Musashi invited Shinzō to join him on the veranda. "How did you find me? I haven't told anyone where I am."

"Zushino Kōsuke. He said you'd finished the Kannon you promised him and sent Iori to deliver it."

"Ha, ha. I suppose Iori let the secret out. It doesn't matter. I'm not old enough to abandon the world and retire. I did think, though, that if I left the scene for a couple of months, the malicious gossip would quiet down. Then there'd be less danger of reprisals against Kōsuke and my other friends."

Shinzō lowered his head. "I owe you an apology— all this trouble because of me."

"Not really. That was a minor thing. The real root of the matter has to do with the relationship between Kojirō and me."

"Did you know he killed Obata Yogorō?"

"No."

"Yogorō, when he heard about me, decided to take revenge himself. He was no match for Kojirō."

"I warned him. . . ." The image of the youthful Yogorō standing in the entrance of his father's house was still vivid in Musashi's mind. "What a pity," he thought to himself.

"I can understand how he felt," continued Shinzō. "The students had all left, and his father had died. He must have thought he was the only one who could do it.

In any case, he appears to have gone to Kojirō's house. Still, no one saw them together; there's no real proof.''

"Mm. Maybe my warning had the opposite effect from what I intended—stirred up his pride so he felt he had to fight. It's a shame."

"It is. Yogorō was *Sensei's* only blood relation. With his death the House of Obata ceased to exist. However, my father discussed the matter with Lord Munenori, who somehow managed to institute adoption proceedings. I'm to become Kagenori's heir and successor and carry on the Obata name. . . . I'm not sure I'm mature enough yet. I'm afraid I may end up bringing further disgrace to the man. After all, he was the greatest proponent of the Kōshū military tradition."

"Your father's the Lord of Awa. Isn't the Hōjō military tradition considered to be on a par with the Kōshū School? And your father as great a master as Kagenori?"

"That's what they say. Our ancestors came from Tōtōmi Province. My grandfather served Hōjō Ujitsuna and Hōjō Ujiyasu of Odawara, and my father was selected by Ieyasu himself to succeed them as head of the family."

"Coming from a famous military family, isn't it unusual for you to have become a disciple of Kagenori's?"

"My father has his disciples, and he's given lectures before the shōgun on military science. But instead of teaching me anything, he told me to go out and learn from somebody else. Find out the hard way! That's the kind of man he is."

Musashi sensed an element of intrinsic decency, even nobility, in Shinzō's demeanor. And it was probably natural, he thought, for his father, Ujikatsu, was an outstanding general, and his mother was the daughter of Hōjō Ujiyasu.

"I'm afraid I've been talking too much," said Shinzō. "Actually, my father sent me out here. Of course, it would have been only proper for him to come and express his gratitude to you in person, but just now he has a guest, who's quite eager to see you. My father told me to bring you back with me. Will you come?'' He peered inquiringly into Musashi's face.

''A guest of your father's wants to see me?''

''That's right.''

''Who could it be? I know almost no one in Edo.''

''A person you've known since you were a boy.''

Musashi couldn't imagine who it might be. Matahachi, perhaps? A samurai from Takeyama Castle? A friend of his father's?

Maybe even Otsū . . . But Shinzō refused to divulge his secret. ''I was instructed not to tell you who it is. The guest said it would be better to surprise you. Will you come?''

Musashi's curiosity was piqued. He told himself it couldn't be Otsū, but in his heart hoped it was.

''Let's go,'' he said, rising to his feet. ''Iori, don't wait up for me.''

Shinzō, pleased that his mission was successful, went behind the house and brought his horse. Saddle and stirrups were dripping with dew. Holding the bit, he offered the horse to Musashi, who proceeded without further ado to mount it.

As they left, Musashi said to Iori, ''Take care of yourself. I may not be back until tomorrow.'' It was not long before he was swallowed up by the evening mist.

Iori sat quietly on the veranda, lost in thought.

''Eyes,'' he thought. ''Eyes.'' Innumerable times he had been ordered to keep his eyes on his opponent's, but as yet he could neither understand the import of the instruction nor get the idea out of his mind. He gazed vacantly up at the River of Heaven.

What was wrong with him? Why was it that when Musashi stared at him, he couldn't stare straight back? More vexed by his failure than an adult would have been, he was trying very hard to find the explanation when he became conscious of a pair of eyes. They were aimed at him from the branches of a wild grapevine, which twined around a tree in front of the cabin.

"What's that?" he thought.

The brightly shining eyes reminded him strongly of Musashi's eyes during practice sessions.

"Must be a possum." He had seen one several times, eating the wild grapes. The eyes were like agate, the eyes of a fierce hobgoblin.

"Beast!" cried Iori. "You think I don't have any courage, think even you can outstare me. Well, I'll show you! I'm not about to lose to you."

With grim determination, he tensed his elbows and glared back. The possum, whether out of stubbornness or curiosity, made no move to flee. Its eyes took on an even more lustrous brilliance.

The effort so absorbed Iori that he forgot to breathe. He swore again not to lose, not to this lowly beast. After what seemed like hours, he realized with a flash that he had triumphed. The leaves of the grapevine shook and the possum vanished.

"That'll show you!" exulted Iori. He was drenched with sweat, but he felt relieved and refreshed. He only hoped he would be able to repeat the performance the next time he confronted Musashi.

Having lowered a reed blind on the window and snuffed out the lamp, he went to bed. A bluish-white light reflected from the grass outside. He dozed off, but inside his head he seemed to see a tiny spot, shining like a jewel. In time, the spot grew into the vague outline of the possum's face.

Tossing and moaning, he was suddenly overwhelmed by the conviction that there were eyes at the foot of his pallet. He roused himself with difficulty. "Bastard," he cried, reaching for his sword. He took a murderous swing but ended up doing a somersault. The shadow of the possum was a moving spot on the blind. He slashed at it wildly, then ran outside and hacked fiercely at the grapevine. His eyes rose skyward in search of the eyes.

There came into focus, slowly, two large, bluish stars.

28

Four Sages with a Single Light

"Here we are," Shinzō said as they reached the foot of Akagi Hill.

From the flute music, which sounded like the accompaniment to a sacred shrine dance, and the bonfire visible through the woods, Musashi thought a night festival must be in progress. The trip to Ushigome had taken two hours.

On one side was the spacious compound of Akagi Shrine; across the sloping street stood the earthen wall of a large private residence and a gate of magnificent proportions. When they reached the gate, Musashi dismounted and handed the reins to Shinzō, thanking him as he did so.

Shinzō led the horse inside and handed the reins to one of a group of samurai waiting near the entrance with paper lanterns in their hands. They all came forward, welcomed him back and led the way through the trees to a clearing in front of the imposing entrance hall. Inside, servants holding lanterns were lined up on both sides of the hallway.

The chief steward greeted them, saying, "Come in. His lordship is expecting you. I'll show you the way."

"Thank you," replied Musashi. He followed the steward up a stairway and into a waiting room.

The design of the house was unusual; one stairway after another led to a series of apartments, which gave the impression of being stacked one above another all the way up Akagi Hill. As he seated himself, Musashi noted that the room was well up the slope. Beyond a drop at the edge of the garden, he could just make out the northern part of the castle moat and the woods framing the escarpment. He found himself thinking that the view from the room in the daytime must be breathtaking.

Noiselessly, the door in an arched doorway slid open. A beautiful serving girl came gracefully in and placed a tray bearing cakes, tea and tobacco in front of him. Then she slipped out as quietly as she had entered. It seemed as if her colorful kimono and obi had emerged from and melted into the wall itself. A faint fragrance lingered after her, and suddenly Musashi was reminded of the existence of women.

The master of the house appeared shortly after that, attended by a young samurai. Dispensing with formalities, he said, "Good of you to come." In good soldierly fashion, he seated himself cross-legged on a cushion spread by the attendant and said, "From what I hear, my son is much indebted to you. I hope you'll pardon my asking you to come here rather than visiting your house to express my thanks." With his hands resting lightly on the fan in his lap, he inclined his prominent forehead ever so slightly.

"I'm honored to be invited to meet you," said Musashi.

It was not easy to estimate Hōjō Ujikatsu's age. Three front teeth were missing, but his smooth, shiny skin testified to a determination never to grow old. The heavy black mustache, streaked with only a few white hairs, had been allowed to grow out on both sides to conceal any wrinkles resulting from the lack of teeth. Musashi's first impression was of a man who had many children and got along well with young people.

Sensing that his host wouldn't object, Musashi went

straight to the point. "Your son tells me that you have a guest who knows me. Who might that be?"

"Not one but two. You'll see them by and by."

"Two people?"

"Yes. They know each other very well, and both are good friends of mine. I happened to meet them at the castle today. They came back with me, and when Shinzō came in to greet them, we started chatting about you. One of them said he hadn't seen you for a long time and would like to. The other, who knows you only by reputation, expressed the desire to be introduced."

Smiling broadly, Musashi said, "I think I know. One is Takuan Sōhō, isn't it?"

"That's right," exclaimed Lord Ujikatsu, slapping his knee in surprise.

"I haven't seen him since I came east several years ago."

Before Musashi had time to make a guess at who the other man was, his lordship said, "Come with me," and went out into the corridor.

They climbed a short stairway and walked down a long, dark corridor. Rain shutters were in place on one side. Suddenly Musashi lost sight of Lord Ujikatsu. He stopped and listened.

After a few moments, Ujikatsu called, "I'm down here." His voice seemed to come from a well-lit room that was situated across an open space from the corridor.

"I understand," Musashi called back. Instead of heading directly for the light, he stood where he was. The space outside the corridor was openly inviting, but something told him danger lurked in that stretch of darkness.

"What are you waiting for, Musashi? We're over here."

"Coming," answered Musashi. He was in no position to reply otherwise, but his sixth sense had warned him to be on the alert. Stealthily, he turned and walked back about ten paces to a small door, which let out onto the garden. Slipping on a pair of sandals, he made his way around the garden to the veranda of Lord Ujikatsu's parlor.

"Oh, you came that way, did you?" said his lordship, looking around from the other end of the room. He sounded disappointed.

"Takuan!" called Musashi as he entered the room, a radiant smile on his face. The priest, seated in front of the alcove, stood up to greet him. To meet again—and under the roof of Lord Hōjō Ujikatsu—seemed almost too fortuitous. Musashi had trouble convincing himself that it was really happening.

"We'll have to bring each other up to date," said Takuan. "Shall I begin?" He was clad in the plain robes he always wore. No finery, not so much as prayer beads. Yet he seemed mellower than before, more soft-spoken. Just as Musashi's rural upbringing had been leached out of him by strenuous attempts at self-discipline, Takuan, too, seemed to have had the sharper corners rounded off and to have become more deeply endowed with the wisdom of Zen. To be sure, he was no longer a youth. Eleven years older than Musashi, he was now approaching forty.

"Let's see. Kyoto, wasn't it? Ah, I remember. It was shortly before I went back to Tajima. After my mother died, I spent a year in mourning. Then I traveled for a while, spent some time at the Nansōji in Izumi, then at the Daitokuji. Later, I saw a good deal of Lord Karasumaru—composed poetry with him, had tea ceremonies, fended off the cares of this world. Before I knew it, I'd spent three years in Kyoto. Recently I became friendly with Lord Koide of Kishiwada Castle and came with him to have a look at Edo."

"Then you've been here only a short time?"

"Yes. Although I've met Hidetada twice at the Daitokuji and been summoned into Ieyasu's presence a number of times, this is my first trip to Edo. And what about you?"

"I've been here only since the beginning of this summer."

"It seems you've made quite a name for yourself in this part of the country."

Musashi didn't try to justify himself. He hung his head and said, "I suppose you've heard about that."

Takuan stared at him for a few moments, seemingly comparing him with the Takezō of old. "Why worry about that? It'd be strange if a man your age had too good a reputation. So long as you haven't done anything disloyal or ignoble or rebellious, what does it matter? I'm more interested in hearing about your training."

Musashi gave a brief account of his recent experiences and ended by saying, "I'm afraid I'm still immature, imprudent—far from being truly enlightened. The more I travel, the longer the road becomes. I have the feeling I'm climbing an endless mountain path."

"That's the way it has to be," said Takuan, clearly pleased with the youth's integrity and humility. "If a man not yet thirty claims to know the least bit about the Way, it's an unmistakable sign his growth has stopped. Even I still shudder with embarrassment when anyone suggests that an uncouth priest like me could know the ultimate meaning of Zen. It's disconcerting, the way people are always asking to tell me about the Buddhist Law or explain the true teachings. People try to look up to a priest as a living Buddha. Be thankful that others don't overestimate you, that you don't have to pay attention to appearances."

While the two men happily renewed their friendship, servants arrived with food and drink. Presently Takuan said, "Forgive me, your lordship. I'm afraid we're forgetting something. Why don't you call your other guest in?"

Musashi was certain now that he knew who the fourth person was, but elected to remain silent.

Hesitating slightly, Ujikatsu said, "Shall I call him?" Then, to Musashi, "I'll have to admit you saw through our little trick. As the one who planned it, I feel rather ashamed.''

Takuan laughed. ''Good for you! I'm glad to see you're up to admitting defeat. But why not? It was only a game to amuse everybody anyway, wasn't it? Certainly nothing for the master of the Hōjō Style to lose face over.''

''Well, no doubt I was defeated,'' murmured Uji-katsu, reluctance still in his voice. ''The truth is that although I've heard what sort of man you are, I had no way of knowing just how well trained and disciplined you are. I thought I'd see for myself, and my other guest agreed to cooperate. When you stopped in the passage-way, he was waiting in ambush, ready to draw his sword.'' His lordship seemed to regret having had to put Musashi to the test. ''But you perceived you were being lured into a trap and came across the garden.'' Looking directly at Musashi, he asked, ''May I ask why you did that?''

Musashi merely grinned.

Takuan spoke up. ''It's the difference, your lordship, between the military strategist and the swordsman.''

''Is it, now?''

''It's a matter of instinctive responses—that of a military scholar, based on intellectual principles, versus that of a man who follows the Way of the Sword, based on the heart. You reasoned that if you led Musashi on, he'd follow. Yet without being able to actually see, or to put his finger on anything definite, Musashi sensed danger and moved to protect himself. His reaction was sponta-neous, instinctive.''

''Instinctive?''

''Like a Zen revelation.''

''Do you have premonitions like that?''

''I can't really say.''

''In any case, I've learned a lesson. The average samurai, sensing danger, might have lost his head, or perhaps seized upon the trap as an excuse to display his prowess with the sword. When I saw Musashi go back, put on the sandals and cross the garden, I was deeply impressed."

Musashi kept his silence, his face revealing no special pleasure at Lord Ujikatsu's words of praise. His thoughts turned to the man still standing outside in the dark, stranded by the victim's failure to fall into the trap.

Addressing his host, he said, "May I request that the Lord of Tajima take his place among us now?"

"What's that?" Ujikatsu was astonished, as was Takuan. "How did you know?"

Moving back to give Yagyū Munenori the place of honor, Musashi said, "Despite the darkness, I felt the presence of peerless swordsmanship. Taking into consideration the other faces present, I don't see how it could be anyone else."

"You've done it again!" Ujikatsu was amazed.

At a nod from him, Takuan said, "The Lord of Tajima. Quite right." Turning to the door, he called, "Your secret is out, Lord Munenori. Won't you join us?"

There was a loud laugh, and Munenori appeared in the doorway. Instead of arranging himself comfortably in front of the alcove, he knelt in front of Musashi and greeted him as an equal, saying, "My name is Mataemon Munenori. I hope you will remember me."

"It is an honor to meet you. I am a rōnin from Mimasaka, Miyamoto Musashi by name. I pray for your guidance in the future."

"Kimura Sukekurō mentioned you to me some months ago, but at the time I was busy because of my father's illness."

"How is Lord Sekishūsai?"

"Well, he's very old. There's no way of knowing . . ." After a brief pause, he continued with warm cordiality: "My father told me about you in a letter, and I've heard Takuan speak of you several times. I must say your reaction a few minutes ago was admirable. If you don't mind, I think we should regard the bout you requested as having taken place.

I hope you're not offended by my unorthodox way of carrying it out.''

Musashi's impression was of intelligence and maturity quite in accordance with the daimyō's reputation.

"I'm embarrassed by your thoughtfulness," he replied, bowing very low. His show of deference was natural, for Lord Munenori's status was so far above Musashi's as to put him virtually in another world. Though his fief amounted to only fifty thousand bushels, his family had been famous as provincial magistrates since the tenth century. To most people, it would have seemed odd to find one of the shōgun's tutors in the same room with Musashi, let alone talking to him in a friendly, informal fashion. It was a relief to Musashi to note that neither Ujikatsu, a scholar and member of the shōgun's banner guard, nor Takuan, a country priest by origin, felt any constraint because of Munenori's rank.

Warm sake was brought, cups were exchanged, talk and laughter ensued. Differences in age and class were forgotten. Musashi knew he was being accepted in this select circle not because of who he was. He was seeking the Way, just as they were. It was the Way that permitted such free camaraderie.

At one point, Takuan set down his cup and asked Musashi, "What's become of Otsū."

Reddening slightly, Musashi said he hadn't seen or heard anything of her for some time.

"Nothing at all?"

"Nothing."

"That's unfortunate. You can't leave her in the lurch forever, you know. It's not good for you, either."

"By Otsū," asked Munenori, "do you mean the girl who once stayed with my father in Koyagyū?"

"Yes," replied Takuan on Musashi's behalf.

"I know where she is. She went to Koyagyū with my nephew Hyōgo to help nurse my father."

With a noted military scientist and Takuan present, thought Musashi, they could be talking about strategy or discussing Zen. With both Munenori and Musashi present, the subject could have been swords.

With a nod of apology to Musashi, Takuan told the others about Otsū and her relationship with Musashi. "Sooner or later," he concluded, "someone will have to bring the two of you together again, but I fear it's no task for a priest. I ask the assistance of you two gentlemen." What he was actually suggesting was that Ujikatsu and Munenori act as Musashi's guardians.

They seemed willing to accept this role, Munenori observing that Musashi was old enough to have a family and Ujikatsu saying that he had reached a satisfactorily high level of training.

Munenori suggested that one of these days Otsū should be summoned back from Koyagyū and given in marriage to Musashi. Then Musashi could set himself up in Edo, where his house, along with those of Ono Tadaaki and Yagyū Munenori, would form a triumvirate of the sword and usher in a golden age of swordsmanship in the new capital. Both Takuan and Ujikatsu concurred.

Specifically, Lord Ujikatsu, eager to reward Musashi for his kindness to Shinzō, wanted to recommend him as a tutor to the shōgun, an idea the three of them had explored before sending Shinzō for Musashi. And having seen how Musashi reacted to their test, Munenori himself was now ready to give his approval to the plan.

There were difficulties to be overcome, one being that a teacher in the shōgun's household also had to be a member of the honor guard. Since many of its members were faithful vassals of the Tokugawas from the days when Ieyasu had held the Mikawa fief, there was a reluctance to appoint new people, and all candidates were investigated with great thoroughness. However, it was felt that with recommendations from Ujikatsu and Munenori, together with a letter of guarantee from Takuan, Musashi would get by.

The sticky point was his ancestry. There was no written record tracing his ancestry back to Hirata Shōgen of the Akamatsu clan, nor even a genealogical chart to prove he was of good samurai stock. He assuredly had no family connections with the Tokugawas. On the contrary, it was an undeniable fact that as a callow youth of seventeen he had fought against the Tokugawa forces at Sekigahara. Still, there was a chance; other rōnin from former enemy clans had joined the House of Tokugawa after Sekigahara. Even Ono Tadaaki, a rōnin from the Kitabatake clan, which was at present in hiding in Ise Matsuzaka, held an appointment as tutor to the shōgun despite his undesirable connections.

After the three men had again gone over the pros and cons, Takuan said, "All right then, let's recommend him. But perhaps we should find out what he himself thinks about it."

The question was put to Musashi, who replied mildly, "It's kind and generous of you to suggest this, but I'm nothing but an immature young man."

"Don't think of it in that way," said Takuan with an air of candor. "What we're advising you to do is become mature. Will you establish a house of your own, or do you plan to make Otsū go on indefinitely living as she is now?"

Musashi felt hemmed in. Otsū had said she was willing to bear any hardship, but this would in no way lessen Musashi's responsibility for any grief that might befall her. While it was acceptable for a woman to act in accordance with her own feelings, if the outcome was not a happy one, the man would be blamed.

Not that Musashi was unwilling to accept the responsibility. On the whole, he yearned to accept. Otsū had been guided by love, and the onus of that love belonged to him as much as to her. Nevertheless, he felt it was still too early to marry and have a family. The long, hard Way of the Sword stretched before him yet; his desire to follow it was undiminished.

It did not simplify matters that his attitude toward the sword had changed. Since Hōtengahara, the sword of the conqueror and the sword of the killer were things of the past, no longer of any use or meaning.

Nor did being a technician, even one who gave instruction to men of the shōgun's retinue, excite his interest. The Way of the Sword, as he had come to see it, must have specific objectives: to establish order, to protect and refine the spirit. The Way had to be one men could cherish as they did their lives, until their dying day. If such a Way existed, could it not be employed to bring peace to the world and happiness to all?

When he had answered Sukekurō's letter with a challenge to Lord Munenori, his motive had not been the shallow urge to score a victory that had led him to challenge Sekishūsai. Now his wish was to be engaged in the business of governing. Not on any grand scale, of course; a small, insignificant fief would suffice for the activities he imagined would promote the cause of good government.

But he lacked the confidence to express these ideas, feeling that other swordsmen would dismiss his youthful ambitions as being absurd. Or, if they took him seriously, they would feel compelled to warn him: politics leads to destruction; by going into government he would sully his beloved sword. They would do this out of genuine concern for his soul.

He even believed that if he spoke his mind truthfully, the two warriors and the priest would react either with laughter or with alarm.

When he did get around to speaking, it was to protest—he was too young, too immature, his training was inadequate . . .

At length, Takuan cut him off, saying, "Leave it to us."

Lord Ujikatsu added, "We'll see that it turns out all right for you."

The matter was decided.

Coming in periodically to trim the lamp, Shinzō had caught the gist of the conversation. He quietly let his father and the guests know that what he had heard pleased him immensely.

LOOK FOR

MUSASHI

BOOK V

THE WAY OF LIFE AND DEATH

The Shōgun is struggling to consolidate his power—and Musashi has been recommended to tutor him in the martial arts. But Japan is torn by new upheavals and deadly internal strife, and when Musashi is denied the appointment he sets off to pursue spiritual enlightenment—only to be slowly and irrevocably drawn into a fatal duel with Sasaki Kojirō, the only man who could possibly defeat him with a sword. The legend of Musashi is spreading across the land and opening the way to a great new age. But while the crowds flock to Musashi, his old friend Matahachi is hired as an assassin—to kill the Shōgun himself!